THE PANDORAN WARS: PRELUDE & EMPIRE

Stephen Parkinson

BY DANTE D'ANTHONY

Illustrated by

Roy Rudder
Stephen Parkinson
Shane Perry
Steve Allman
Eliane CK.

Eliane CK

PRELUDE: EMPIRE
Deneb IV, 2400 CE.

The shift in power from the Sol System to the Deneb System and the conflicts of the era seem inevitable from our long view back. For someone living in the twenty-fifth century, however, the violence and sudden reversals and advances among the worlds must have most certainly seemed a jarring billiards game of worlds. It was an obscure Medical Research facility on one of a hundred bustling boom-worlds that would come to define the age. A dashing young scientist, Lourdes Cassandra appears on the Galactic stage as if at the weightless moment of an apogee...
-Princess Clairissa Maggio, Caldris, "Deneb IV, Empire of Light and Darkness."

Lourdes Charlotte Cassandra watched the construction rigs from her air-taxi over the bustling metropolis of Pink Town, with a curious disdain, as she made her way to the Medical Center. A mysterious government medical research agency had summoned her. The last of Deneb's blinding daylight faded, and she was off.
Bring on the night...
As the world turned away from the light of Deneb (which is far too brilliant for the human eye to bear) she made her course; away from the searing light. Replacing eyes was one of Deneb IV's great skills among the worlds of the galaxy, skills learned out of grim necessity. The world turns away, night falls, and the activity of Humanity on Deneb IV begins. Mankind living there becoming nocturnal, coming out of its caves of steel into the starlight, busying itself in the safe darkness.
The last of the light silvered on the far horizon, frightening in its aspect. Blindness gleamed there. The Medical Center was further out, past Pink town, alone in an area newly developing among the shallow inlands by the Black Sea.

The planet had been building cities without pause as long as Lourdes could remember, back into the misty memories of childhood, as she had peered out of her Grandmother Chen Ping's aircar decades before. Aircars and construction cranes were two constants in her life. It seemed she was always in one, looking out at the other.

Pink Town, Lancelot Station, Clement Gardens, Simmons City: a building juggernaut of three centuries, and with each thirty-year plan the previous estimates of growth are outdone by an order of magnitude. The reality was now a megalopolis stretching along the Southern Shore of the Black Sea across half the planet.

The Medical Center, however, had been founded originally on a large Island as a private concern before being entrusted to the government. It sat alone after a fashion. There were still wide stretches of marshlands, carelessly created with terraforming, and now just as carelessly being eaten up by developers. The pristine ecological care given to some worlds where life was indigenous was less often the case on a terraformed world.

She had been informed suddenly, unexpectedly, that the position she was asked to interview for was classified. She was not to discuss it with anyone. A mild apprehension ran through her at that, breaking her ordinarily serene composure. There was an aspect of sudden adventure-the kinds of things she had seen on the news-clashes of corporations and governments and technologies ending in wars and rumors of wars.

She was a neurologist, an expert in Organic Chemistry. What possible ugly secret use could the government of Deneb System want with her? Her air-taxi broke through a cloud, and she approached the Medical Center in a series of drops through various traffic streams. Her mind drifted through current events that might bode trouble for the government.

Mercury Nearside City had dominated the economic and political life of the Solar system for several bright and beautiful centuries of progress; the rise of Deneb IV had been closely watched and carefully guided at the hands of the Mercurians-always behind the scenes, with a patronizing, somewhat scoffing attitude-less scoffing in the last century, however. Trade routes have always given rise to great cities, and Deneb was in line with the majority of ship routes along the Orion Spiral Arm of the galaxy.

Among the other star systems, there was an inconsistent quality to Humankind's developing cultures, some noble, some corrupt, some downright depraved. At the Deep Frontier, and further-Outspace, profound lawlessness and epic criminal set of warlords came and went.

A warlord would rise, claim a world, begin committing atrocities in the name of glory, or a twisted take on religion and Mercury Nearside City would rally the Solar system to send troops and bring order. The pattern had happened so often it was considered a fifty/fifty chance any longer as a settlement somewhere developed.

Still, it was a stretch to imagine they would call upon a Neurologist in such matters.

Onto the Art deco parapets and landing portals, then she was greeted by a taciturn man, Dr. Scalotta, aged somewhat ungracefully for one with access to the best medical services, she mused.

"Dr. Cassandra, thank you for coming. Right this way." He gestured with a tired, stooped walk and was wearing optical displays-a conceit, she surmised, but kept the question open-why such disregard for his person? His wearing of antiquated optics, apparent aging without youth re-boosting, these smacked of a creep factor.

"Thank you, Dr., Thoughtful of you to come up and greet me personally." She smiled with an earnest glow she knew well had melted many a man's heart, but the old man seemed not to notice and only gave a cursory nod. Instead, Dr. Scalotta peered at the world beyond the landing pad with a curious reverie. Blinding daylight gone now, Deneb IV was a beehive of activity, and all that activity visible in the lights of towers and vehicles.

Higher and bathing the landscape in a form of moon glow, space stations and orbiting solar farms reflected strange geometries in the heavens. At length, he finally responded, "Well, buried in my work as I am, it's a welcome break to be reminded there is a world still out there."

She raised her eyebrows. The old Wizard was poking his head up from his library and incantations. They made their way to a lift and dropped quickly and deeply into the bowels of the tower. It opened onto a brightly lit lab full of researchers, robots, and discordantly-two military police, apparently cyborged scarred battle veterans.

Lourdes glanced at Dr. Scalotta nervously.

"Oh, yes, I'm sorry, they come with the territory. Some of the research we are doing here has been deemed less than popular by certain 'activist' groups"

He shambled, staggering somewhat, "No worries, Miss Cassandra. You'll receive no harm from them," he winked, "they'd take fire before failing by their duty, rest assured, and they must protect us."

"Protect us from whom exactly?" she asked aloud, but he seemed not to hear her, and they were moving along into the research labs directly.

The giant power facilities surprised her. Apparently, they were at ground level now, and a great interior space was busy with the comings and goings of aircars and ground trains and maglevs.

Eventually, he turned his strange visage squarely at her, "The Luddites and Philistines, heh, heh. My research here has not always been warmly received. There have been threats. But I am not deterred. Victorious warriors win first and then go to war, while defeated warriors go to war first and then seek to win. We will win."

"What am I getting myself into?" she smiled nervously as they continued deeper into the cavernous bowels of the complex. "Who are these groups? Will they come after me at my home, should I join the research team here?" The lab bustled with activity and she had a sense of a moment turning as in a river when her last chance to grab the shore was passing.

"They're wingnuts from various worlds who spend too much time on Hypercasts, berating technology all the while living off it. They scream for Humanity's demise and say we are a scourge on the pristine Universe. They want us all dead, as it were."

Finally, Lourdes stopped in her tracks. "Doctor, the rumor is you're creating a better AI, one that goes beyond a Touring test and is truly sentient. Your goal will be an actual Transhuman entity. You want to cheat death."

He smiled beneath his anachronistic optical displays, "Yes, cheating Death…something of an obsession of mine."

"This kind of research has been going on for centuries, with really no way to prove if the AI is self-aware, or not."

"Oh my young Neurologist, I can assure you I'm quite unaware," They approached a figure on a table and she came to the sudden shock and recognition of seeing Dr. Scalotta was quite dead, very dead, and laying on the table. She had been conversing with a hologram AI, "because I'm already dead." The Scalotta hologram said.

The hologram AI of Dr. Scalotta smiled, and seeing her frown, raised a hand.

"Wait, wait, indulge me…the program is quite capable of carrying on as well as I would if I were alive."

Uncertain of how to continue, she raised her chin and waited.

"I anticipated that I may have expired before the objective was met, anticipated our latest developments wouldn't allow for my actual sentience to survive before you arrived, and we are quite on the proper path. You see, it is not our scientific research on the Transhuman system housing I wish you to work on, it is…this."

They came to another wing in the laboratories, and among the giant machines, cavernous spaces, bustling robots, guards, and researchers she saw another table. On the table was a broken, metallic bone. She drew closer. No, not a bone at all, bone-like, seemingly organic-but rather, sculpted to appear organic-the object was mineral; metal, glass- intricate. Technology such as she had never seen.

"This is from preceding our era, my Dear, preceding our civilization, preceding every word ever spoken by the mouths of Humankind; every thought before a single name, from any single place we have known, was spoken, this was first-other words of elder gods, so to speak. Things preceded us."

"This is alien technology! These particular predecessors, Doctor, how long before us in Time?" Her eyes were very wide. She wanted to touch it. Mankind had long assumed now that it was the lone species of higher sentience. Centuries of exploration had not revealed other sentient species capable of technology like this resting before her.

Until recently-she knew there was an artifact rush at the galactic core, but hadn't had a great deal of time to follow it. The molecular computer industry paid highly.

His AI program was unable to replicate Dr. Scalotta's typical reaction, and so he seemed to bounce around excitedly now, "Millions of years, many millions of years."

She was silent for a moment, and then asked, "Why are you showing it to me?"

"Well, we believe it could interface with the organisms that created it, as well as function without them-such that it may have been sentient itself. If that is the case, then all this facility," his hologram arms waived at the buildings around them, "may have finally found a solution to the sentience issue. Genuine Transhumanism may finally be possible."

"So…if it was once sentient, how do you know it wasn't the machine that killed off the creators that made it?"

He sighed, and after a long dreadful pause said, "Well, we don't. That's what the radicals are upset about and why we've had to heighten security. Some feel we are creating a monster, heh-heh; summoning the Demon. Yet, if ignorant both of your enemy and yourself, you are certain to be in peril." He chuckled, oblivious to how truly creepy he was being.

Then she saw his laughter was at the irony of his current state, speaking to her while dead, about monsters.

"Well, I'm sure there is nothing I can help you discover from this fragment of the Predecessor Beings' technology, that you couldn't discover with all this facility at your disposal. I must decline the offer to work on this with you, Doctor. I have a career plan-thank you, but no thank you."

She rather abruptly turned to leave when he called out and pointed to a wall screen, "That is true, Dr. Cassandra, but it is not the fragment we wish you to examine."

The wall screen came alive with the image of a series of structures and a densely packed configuration of stars. "We've discovered an intact base of these Predecessor beings. We want you to go there, to the center of the Galaxy; to an intact alien base."

Lourdes Charlotte Cassandra stood silent and looked for a long moment at the alien structures, perfect and wondrous on the screen. It was a city of dreams to explore, how many millions of years old? Danger or no, she felt wanderlust then, and a burning curiosity to know the minds that had made it. She beamed.

"But of course. When shall we begin?" she said.

One of the young guards approached her, a brutally handsome thing in a fresh camouflage Battle Dress Uniform. She noted the name on his breastplate, Scalotta 2X. "We already have, my Dear." The guard said.

The older, shambling version of Scalotta nodded quietly and moved away. The young guard smiled and gave her a level gaze. "I'll be escorting you from here on out in a Cyborg form, a younger version of me."

Lourdes found herself strangely amused at the AI then-it seemed almost to have a sense of humor and an uncanny sense of what a living person would want to see next. Firstly the grand-fatherly scientist to calm her about the Scientific Assignment, next a stalwart tin soldier to guide her along her journey among the stars.

Sunrider

As Humankind spread out from the Solar system and into the Orion Galactic Spiral Arm of the Milky Way, the great Silk Road of old occurred in a new form; in a myriad of paths traced not by feet and wheels, but by the Star Ships.

Lumbering and slow, they bent space at first crudely and painfully time-consuming by contemporary standards. Colony ships, then trade ships of various rare ores and even rarer pieces of other worlds, the Star Ways crowded as the Silk Road with Interstellar Trade; the Main Orion flight paths pushed centrally along the Orion Arm, and also inward toward the Sagittarius Galactic Spiral Arm, and the Central Galactic Region.

Where the two great conglomerations of flight paths merged sat Ophelia System and Ophelia's World. Rivaling Deneb IV in sheer economic juggernaut, Ophelia's world quickly evolved certain pomp and Baroque Flourish.

The Aristocracy there, keenly aware that they represented the largest aggregation of Human endeavor at the far end of Space, made an extra effort that their cities and developing industries were ever more covered with a patina of artful ornamentation. A hundred and fifty story tower housing state of the art computing and manufacturing center would be clothed in the architectural embellishments of applied ornamental sculptures, and alighting from deep space a traveler might be greeted by angels in the architecture...

-Princess Clairissa Maggio, Caldris-
"Ophelia's World, Gilded Oasis of the Galactic Starways"

Their ship, the Colossus, was a brilliant white Sunrider 2400 gunboat, the pride of the Deneb Space Navy. It was greeted at the system's outskirts with a formal fireworks salute and several dignitaries. Lourdes was a little surprised, but it turned out her appointment was more than mere research, and the good doctor back at Deneb IV had made her Director of the Institute, which now granted her a certain status.

She watched Ophelia's world come in to view from the command deck of the mighty Sunrider and saw the vast solar power array panels in a wide orbit. They gleamed in the star's light-a plethora of stations and service ships buzzing about, like insects around a great hive. She realized the worlds she knew, the great burgeoning civilizations Humankind was creating among the stars, were all but oases in the deep void. Still, the Herculean engineering of the stations and power array dwarfed a mere Human by the gargantuan scale. Still, their complex machine geometries fascinated in their gem-like mirroring of the organic. As the great Sunrider made its slow descent down world, its mighty gravity repulsion in calculated trigonometry of navigational ease now, she glowed with a certain pride and determination to be part of this grand adventure in progress that Humanity was achieving

Dr. Scalotta had chosen her to direct the research and archaeology at the alien base for a reason. He saw something in her-something to stand against the tide of wicked chaos that was also accompanying Humankind's progress in the galaxy...

And by the moon the reaper weary,
Piling sheaves in uplands airy,
Listening, whispers,
"'Tis the fairy Lady of Shalott."

She knows not what the curse may be,
And so she weaveth steadily,
And little other care hath she,
The Lady of Shalott.
-Lord Alfred Tennyson

As a rule, Lance Purusha didn't care about the politics of his marks. He was a professional, and his work was to take them out of this world. The rationale behind his client's desired kills interested him not at all. Something about this target bothered him, however. She was apolitical, a research scientist in medicine, and there was something dirty in the notion of killing her that he quite simply couldn't shake this time. Watching the massive Sunrider make its way down to the luxurious hotels along the shore, he reviewed his info on her, again and again, looking for something she had done that could justify taking her out.

There wasn't anything. She had recently been appointed Director of innocuous research on Artificial Intelligence and Human-computer interfaces. His clients saw all Artificial Intelligence as a threat, he did not. It just made better robots to fix his house chef systems or change the grav units in his aircar. In as many centuries as people had been predicting the doom of mankind from AI menace, nothing had transpired but mundane menial tasks or equally mundane sophisticated data processing made easier.

His molecular disruptor, a top of the line custom job, commonly referred to as a "Disser", included a silencer and a scope, with a tight beam focus and half a kilometer range, if his interface was spot on. The same interface technology his employers railed against, they saw no problem in using to destroy those creating the technologies.

He had seen the likes of his employers on the hypercasts, though he would never actually meet them since he was hired through an intermediary. The anti-technology-anti-AI movement, glowering back at the main thrust of Human civilization from backwater worlds, was always completely comfortable with utilizing the technologies of the current day while lamenting earlier, simpler times. The hypocrisy was so thick you could dance on it.

The atrocities they propagated on lawless worlds abounded with as much variety and imagination as one could create-accept that, truly you couldn't make that stuff up. You just had to dig into the newscasts. Cults abounded where child brides and Human slavery flourished, in the name of ideology, or religion. Basic Human Rights, common for millennia even before the dawn of the Space Ages, were ignored and violated with impunity.

Those were the people who were now paying him to get close enough to kill the dashing, lovely woman, so much better than they in every way-intellectually, socially, ethically. They were the people now paying him to point his weapon at her lovely brain, to fire the molecular disruptor and take that small, beautiful mass of some the most well organized organic matter in the universe and quickly boil it into nothing, and leave her a steaming mass of horror.

It was a job, just a job. He could even make out portholes and command windows on the gallant Sunrider now, as it eased into the water of the inland sea adjacent to the grand hotels. Perhaps she even now looked out in joyous apprehension, anticipating the wonderful future he was about to steal from her.

It was a job. He had run a hundred such hits. Ever and always before however, they were scoundrels every one-mobsters, rival cult leaders, a dealer in illicit substances. This was the first time he was killing a worthwhile person, innocent of any wrongdoing. There was something dirty in the notion of killing her, something ugly and wrong, that even his hardened heart, born fighting; being raised in the random violence of the frontier, something even he couldn't shake.

He didn't like this, didn't like it at all. It was, however, his job. He ran a cloth over his disruptor, Old Painless, and wondered how long this kill would haunt him. The target was so lovely, in every aspect both inside and out. He knew this wasn't supposed to matter. He was a professional and it was his job to kill her.

Scalotta 2X, the younger and strikingly handsome version of the older good Dr. Scalotta eyed the bay and hotels from a variety of security holo-screens with certain inhuman patience. The old Scalotta had graced this clone with Military training programs. He carried with him various skills and experiences he hadn't lived, but which felt second nature. Thus his mind was an amalgamation of Colonial Marines, hard-core Space Navy Rangers, and a variety of seasoned Detectives. He knew this was one of the highest risk points of the journey, for various reasons.

Ophelia's world was a symbol of everything the Independent freebooter colonies despised. They hated its ties to the older economies of Deneb IV and the Sol System. They loathed the Central Federal System's Authority. Ophelia's World, to them, was too Liberal, too technocratic, too corporate, and too godless. Its wealth and flowering prestige stood out in elegant contrast to the hardscrabble frontier's savagery and grim Warlords.

The fabulous Art Nouveau skyscraper hotels along the sea here loomed gracious and delightful. It was a visual fantasia-and a security nightmare. Water ships, starships, aircars, ground cars, maglev trains-what were they thinking having numerous public officials in a time of terrorism at the frontier meet in a place as such easy targets? There was even numerous slow-moving airships pleasure cruising along the shore.

2X's eyes darkened. Here was either a pompous hubris or a setup. Worried about terrorists, he realized they had not considered at all the possibility of internal factions in the Ophelia's World political and business elite.

Lourdes, long and lovely, walked in a Luminism glow at his side as they stepped off the Sunrider and waved to the crowds along the huge pier. A massive robotic giant in the shape of Mercury lifted a torch and brilliant flames shot out to honor her-part of the terraforming, no doubt, but a nice touch. Scalotta 2X adjusted his force field somewhat wider and stronger than might be considered polite. He looked at the flames and giants. Some deep gland in his brain didn't care for either.

Lourdes noted his action as they continued along the pier, the tall lamp standards and palms and glowing Croatans incongruous with this young, death-dealing soldier version of the Good Doctor Scalotta. "Really," she said, "We are among friends!"

The Premier and his entourage were drawing closer.

"Friends are like the jaws and teeth of a beautiful pet. If you are not careful, you will find them chewing you up." He replied taciturnly, but then they were among the entourage, and hugs and kisses and welcoming greetings were spilling out from a dozen voices along with the roar of the crowd.

"Civilization! Reason and order!" The premier boomed, turning back to the crowd after his embrace of Lourdes, "Welcome to the far frontier Director Cassandra!"

He held out a golden key to the star system, smiled, and genuflected artfully.

Lance Purusha ran his scanners of the various defense fields on the pier. The Kingdom of Ophelia's system had made several defensive measures to protect the dignitaries, and Lourdes's bodyguard was included. That, however, was what professionals were hired for. To have the next level of technology that would circumvent such protections, and he did.

Ironically, it was a form of AI included in his travel bags that was now furiously scanning the flux and flow of the protecting fields for a path, using the fields themselves as a means to his target, the lovely Lourdes Charlotte Cassandra who would soon be a boiling, stinking mess of horror on the pier.

Something reflected from one of the other hotels and Lance's instinct quickly steeled him back from the window. He peered slowly as the source of the reflection's movement and increased magnification, closer, closer, closer his vision moved to that source and wonder upon insidious wonder, there was another sniper.

It was the "second bomb" scenario. Either a less expensive backup, in case he missed and bungled the job, or merely some slob to fire wildly at the dignitaries and crowd to mask the importance of the real target.

The other sniper was careless, truly-reflective surfaces among one's equipment? Lance watched the man leaning forward; he saw the reflective surfaces were poorly camouflaged cyborg units-ugh! The careless amateur was now leaning out the window. He would probably not even kill her cleanly, and she would die in a violent, painful, violation. Laying on the pier knowing she was dying in a disgusting mess.

In a violent lifetime of neglect and abuse since his birth, Lance had never backed away from a fight. There was, however a code of his own and the thought of the incredible young research scientist, innocent of any vice and steeled in virtue and discipline, dying at the hands of such a clod, well, that thought violated his codes.

Lance quietly aimed. For a long moment, the two snipers immersed in their separate technologies and weapons took a careful measure and unbeknownst to them, the entire future of the Galaxy and Humanity lay in the quality of their aim.

Two shots fired silently, very nearly simultaneously, and two explosions of human flesh erupted. Lance, whose aim was perfect, took out the other sniper in a clean burst that decorated the interior of the sniper's hotel room with a geometric pattern of blood. The second shot, deflected by Lance, missed Lourdes and took the Premier's hand off.

The crowd and security apparatus erupted, Scalotta 2X grabbing Lourdes and leaping into an open aircar that was cruising along the pier with an on looking couple.

Lance, checking on his handiwork of the other sniper, smiled. Not you, headless dick. He watched Scalotta 2X and Lourdes make away from the pier, and for one brief moment in his life he knew love, he loved the young research scientist like a daughter, and watched her make away into a future he would never be a part of, except that by the strange confluence of circumstances, he determined that her future would happen at all. What she would make of it would now depend on her.

He, of course, was now a dead man walking; but not today, and not without a fight.

The open aircar sped wildly over the tops of the gentle waves in a long arc around the bay. Lourdes eyed the shore angrily, and Scalotta 2X assured the unfortunate couple whose aircar he had just commandeered that everything would be fine. Ophelia's Sun was small, but the terraforming panels in the sky bathed her in heat, and she smelled the perfume of the aircars owner, the spray of the sea, and a copper aroma of Scalotta 2X's military gear. She saw construction cranes of new hotels going up along the shore.

Aircars and construction cranes were always two constants in her life, even now.

They had swung around the bay and there was no evidence they were being followed. Scalotta 2X didn't slow down however and a wall of buildings along the shore loomed as their approach drew closer. Lourdes and the unfortunate couple sat peevishly in the rear of the aircar and watched the massive structures grow larger and larger. Lourdes realized what they were from her readings on the Ophelia's World-grain elevators, more accurately supermassive food production and storage.

Yeast vats, in vitro artificial meats, grain-every manner of human and even pet nutrition. The Breadbasket of Humanity at the far end of civilization. At the moment they were aircar hazards. Scalotta 2X sent the car up, and up, and they dove among bridges between the structures, Head houses and Long houses perched atop a hundred story rises of pure unbroken white. They saw Airships and starships and air trucks and a flurry of robotic activity at the level above the sea suddenly devoid of the swarming humans at the beach and resort hotels. Scalotta 2X was using the industrial and service areas now to weed out would-be suspects that might still trail and seek to harm Lourdes.

Quickly, and with a sudden motion as they rose to the heights of the Silo City, he dropped toward the ground again, around and through the behemoth structures, down and down and then-parallel to a freight maglev he hugged the path along the ground. The huge, red maglev was streamlined like the aircar and they both swept along.

Incongruously Lourdes noticed small residential neighborhoods among the various mega structures-they world had grown haphazard and with unexpected turns of booming-it was worse a conglomeration than Deneb IV she realized, and then they were speeding over another stretch of a different sort of industrial patchwork of hugeness, black and surreal like giant insectoid robots, and then (again incongruously) someone had laid out a series of parks, she saw abruptly a fabulous cascade of epic falls, a kilometer and more across, with giant sculptures of white Lions and hugging the cliff sides nearby, more hotels.

Then more structures again: aqueducts, trestles, and ramparts that supported the industrial complex. More buildings and crowded streets, Lourdes smiled sardonically, what a way to see the frontier. A large stacked art deco transportation center was spun out from a middle tower of a hundred stories of pink stone, a vast seashell design that wound up in splintering geometric fractals. It rose in sharp leaps toward the heavens. Daring, splendid, and bold-it was alive with myriads of Mag-levs and ground cars and air cars and its spires crowded with the slow and casual drift of airships. At its base, a rainforest had been planted and the towers and nature were wound together such that the transportation center might have been a natural outgrowth.

The aircar made its way into an open portal and came to a slow glide to the floor of a parking level. Scalotta 2X made a quick apology, and the owners of the aircar sat gaping quietly: they still had not said a word through the whole strange ride. Lourdes bowed slightly and was pulled away as the young cyborg clone took imperious control.

They stepped through a giant archway, into the immense vaulted halls of the maglev station. Delightful murals of sporty tourists arriving onworld covered a stretch of wall, Tropical scenes and galaxies. This was the central hub for all the cities around the inland seas and three other metropolises along the New Midas Ocean to the East. Many Hundreds of thousands were now moving through the multi-modal transportation hub.

Suddenly the stress of it all seemed to hit Lourdes with a wave of nausea and exhaustion. She fell into the young cyborg's arms and they stepped away from the crowds and maglevs rushing through the station and found a bench. "Officer Scalotta," she rasped, "do you have a first name?"

"Tutu….it was an inside joke. Number two rhymes with Italian "Tu". Dr. Scalotta's grandfather was called "Tu-tu", from an Italian expression of endearment, "You! You!" He loved his grandfather very much…. "And me being 2X, well— "

"May I call you that then?"

"Absolutely, Maam."

"Lourdes. Just Lourdes."

He smiled and the crowds and trains rushed by, oblivious of two small people who a few moments before were being broadcast across the planet in a now-infamous Historic event. Both knew, however, they were sure to be soon recognized-by both the crowd and the security apparatus that had just failed so miserably, and that could mean any number of good or bad things.

"We have to get back to the ship." He said solemnly. He eyed one of the Mag Levs. "We don't know who to trust here. We may have just aircarred out of the frying pan and into the fire, you know. We're all over the live casts; it's amazing no one is noticing us here right now. The ship has been hailing me since we fled the scene of the shooting and the Diplomatic Corps as well, from both worlds."

"We have an Embassy here?"

"Yes, and it's now a toss-up; the ship or the Embassy, but whoever shot the Premier was gunning for you, I think, and there may be more shooters on our trail."

"The Embassy." She said with authority then, taking control for the first time since the blood had spattered her and the hand went flying.

"Roger that." He looked to the hologram screens and something in his eyes flickered: a cybernetic database.

They took the A train and it was an elegant refrain from an otherwise tormenting flight. Service bots brought food and drinks, ladies lounged in gossamer gowns with handsome young suitors in semi-formal garb; no one on the A train seemed aware of anything beyond their own personal dramas and concerns. That was a good thing, she observed, and let the alternating views of tunnels, high cityscapes, and passing stations distract her.

Tutu never let his eyes stop watching, his granite face a mask of determined potential death-dealing. He was always ready to kill, the perfect contradiction inherent in a soldier; protector of some, destroyer of others. He would not hesitate.

Leaving the station, they came up to an open plaza. Various statues to dignitaries and founding settlers ringed a central obelisk of quartz. Tutu eyed the space with bitter darkness.

"Great. Another place we are an easy target." He said, and she sensed he was making adjustments to the defensive fields his suit generated. "Time to go. Come on, move quickly."

She didn't hesitate and they strode purposefully but without the frantic speed that would alert anyone watching that they were fleeing danger. The gates of the embassy gleamed with a metallic sheen of astercrete. She realized they had been imported from the Deneb system by their high-grade molecular kiln signature and felt a quick moment of pride-she was sure there was nothing quite like it this far on the frontier, regardless of how many fabulous structures Ophelia's world had made.

There needed to be order out here; Civilization, her civilization, where assassins and warlords dared not exist openly.

"Director Cassandra!" the ambassador rushed forward. "I, I am at a loss for words. We knew the War Lords of the Frontier would take note of a Deneb Dignitary, but that they would stoop to this…was unexpected." Ambassador Charles Omm was visibly shaken.

Tutu was carefully scanning and recording the Ambassador's vital signals for later analysis.

"They were quite ready, and the Ophelians were not." She replied.

He flushed. "Yes…yes, indeed."

Incongruously, a woman appeared with a baby, a golden-haired infant.

The Ambassador forced a smile, wrapped his arm around the woman and with another reached out to Lourdes. "Director, please meet my wife, Bestla, and our son David."

Bestla dipped her forehead slightly, "Director Cassandra-my deepest apologies for what you have just gone through. I saw the whole terrible event on the holocasts."

"And the Premier?" Tutu wondered aloud.

The Ambassador turned to his wife, "Bestla, this is Officer Scalotta, whose heroic and quick action saved the director today." And then to Tutu, "The entire star system is making awed by your daring action, officer." He turned to one of several holo-screens in the ballroom where Tutu was spiriting Lourdes away into an open aircar, over and over again with talking heads making commentary.

"The premier is fine and scheduled to make an address to the Star system later today," Bestla spoke in a soothing tone, a true ambassadorial wife.

Scalotta 2X brooded, "I require an armored air escort back to the Sunrider Immediately. If the feelings against the Director in this Spiral Arm are this hostile, the gunship ship should make haste."

"Yes," Lourdes agreed, "a lovely world and I would so much like to return at some point and explore it. Discretion next trip will have us come more incognito and with less fanfare."

"Yes. Yes, Right away." Charles seemed deflated, but he bowed and went away to arrange the transport to the Sunrider.

Bestla held David warmly, and gestured to the Embassy halls, "Shall we provide you some privacy until Charles is back? Come, there are drawing rooms this way with refreshments."

Scalotta 2X paced the whole time, scanning, scowling, and otherwise looking dangerous.

"Relax, Tutu. This is our Embassy!" Lourdes pleaded.

"Yes, it is...yes it is. Reports coming back to ship security are indicating there is a talk on the airwaves already-two shooters."

His cyborg implants, she thought. He is never disconnected from the media...

She didn't sense a moment's calm until they were off the armored transport back to the Sunrider and making preparations to leave the system "The press in providing more information and analysis that the Ophelian officials. The big question here appears to be who was the second shooter? As the second took out the first, whose shot was deflected, there would appear to be a conflict of interest. YOU were the target, NOT the premier." He said coldly.

"So...the Ophelian security saved the day? And second shooter?"

Scalotta turned and drilled her with a thousand-yard stare, pausing for effect, then: "No, Maam, it wasn't one of ours or one of theirs. Someone saved your life today-killed for you. But it appears to have been a shot that almost didn't happen.

"Guess I should thank them." She said in a confused tone.

"I don't think you'll ever get the chance. This is starting to add up to an assassination gone sideways, a shooter who went rogue. Either, he took out the other to secure his kill payday, or something else."

"But why not continue firing?"

Tutu looked at the lovely young woman in full flower of beauty and brilliance stretched worn and somewhat languid on the divan. He smiled darkly, the shadows of an idea taking form, and then a sense of connection to the mysterious shooter solidifying in his mind.

"I think he threw this one back, Maam. Too pretty to kill."

She blushed. "Kind of strange for an assassin, one would think." She replied.

"No. Someone who has killed the rotten monsters among mankind, time and again, might very well come to cherish a worthwhile life in ways the ordinary person cannot quite conceive of.

"To redeem themselves perhaps?

He reflected somberly for a long moment, "Probably not redemption. But perhaps, at the end of the day, to define themselves."

She left him them and made for her quarters, lingering by the porthole and looking out to the sea.

The flight path to Tangeonprioc at the galactic core veered above the galactic plane, away from the Sagittarius Galactic Spiral Arm. There were fewer stars as they rose higher and higher above the disc of the galaxy, but the core was taller, and the galactic plume loomed out into the galactic halo. Lourdes watched the reconstruction holograms at the ship bridge with the Command crew, fascinated; the whole massive pool of stars like a toy, filling a full holo-chamber.

She walked the galaxy with a saunter, and its complex form ingrained itself in her memory like a part of her over the coming weeks. She looked at it in different wavelengths and brooded. She looked at political maps and saw the wicked, chaotic, hysterical break from the heart of civilization into warlords. Only Ophelia's World and a string of Arcturian trade routes held a loose order.

The rest of the lines were a grotesque mad man's scribbling.

Then, strangely out of place, one of the systems at the edge of the core reflected a series of worlds and stations in a completely unified order. The Tangeonprioc system was united, organized, and lawful. The good Doctor Scalotta senior had been busy a while there. The Predecessor alien ruins had been known of for a while by the institute, yet even with their methodical searching, they did not expect to find an entire intact base.

As the months passed the crew watched for signs in the hyperstreams of other ships, of possible subterfuge, of hostiles. Tell-tale ripples in the gravity waves, signals on the hyper-casts. Rumors and worries came and went but the speed and ferocity of the Sunrider was something outworlder warlords and anti-technology fanatics would not wish to confront. The farther from the more densely settled spaces the Sunrider went, the less infrastructure existed to build ships that could make a stand against it.

Lourdes was growing convinced the dastardly attempt on her life may have been their only attempt.

The Sunrider rode on, deeper toward the Galactic Center. The high number and density of stars in what is in all reality a single supermassive star cluster drove stellar winds like nowhere else in the galaxy. The wind collisions produced strong x-ray flares; the supermassive black hole enhanced the stellar density around it, further driving the frequency of the storms.

Like all ships venturing into the core region, the Sunrider had acquired additional shielding and upgrades in force fields. Lourdes watched the helium outflow from the storms and an unusual plethora of blue stars among the cluster. Flares in the luminosity of the plumes and accretions disc seemed poetic from the bridge, but she knew they were deadly. Life, even in its most primitive forms, was almost nonexistent among the star systems of the core. The ancient alien predecessors that had built their bases here would have had some other motivation than the discovery of biomes and species which typically flourished in the galactic spiral arms.

Yet the core still teemed with life: Human life, starships, and androids. Like an island on a world, notorious as a trading hub among divergent and sometimes hostile cultures, the core had drawn in a small swarm of riotous Humanity in the "relic rush". She could watch the hypercasts and it wasn't pretty. Today's news on the casts: The Tangeonprioc elections continued in a circus of mudslinging and mean-spirited arguing-what to do with prospector families that run out of resources? "Push them out of the airlocks for a good shake and bake" was the popular slogan of one party. One candidate had even changed the lock codes on a woman returning to base. She was eighty-nine and had fallen behind on booster meds. This, even as finance rates were down.

In other news, several of the domes were threatened by raging fires as a primitive form of moss that covered some of the geographies was prone to periodically flare up.

A serial killer was finally captured who had been haunting prospector camps for a couple of decades. Fifty-eight people had sentences commuted, presumably some who had been previously convicted in what the evidence turned out to be the serial killer. A whole Bank of Communications went missing in the state department of the second largest settlements.

It was going to be a long trip.

Tutu Scalotta found a strange sense of familiarity with the Sunrider that he knew must have come from memory RNA he was created with, memory copied from previous Airmen. He took to the ship with an instinctive enjoyment-a love of sorts-that ran into deep levels of his subconsciousness. So it was with his life. He was three years old and continually finding himself familiar with things military at a level of decades of experience.

His thoughts regarding Lourdes, however, were disconcerting-his training and willingness to sacrifice himself as a soldier he accepted. That she was a lovely woman he accepted as well-he was, clone or no, just a man. He wondered if his original, the good doctor, had put an extra spin in the mix to ensure he go above and beyond the call of duty.

That would piss him off he realized-which was preposterous, in retrospect-he was created, with imperatives. It's what he was.

Making his way onto the command bridge of the Sunrider he sensed the whole mess of disconnected individuals unlinked presented a combat scenario that could be improved. Linking humans had not passed through any Parliamentary or Legislative bodies in known space. It was, in fact, mostly done in research labs and outlaw colonies.

The Captain, Zola Mosey, exuded a bright exuberance that Tutu found at once endearing and sometimes slightly troubling. One sensed that come to the height of the brutal battle, doomed and outnumbered, Mosey would smile all the more and leap into the fray and Death with joy. What was doubly troubling for Tutu, he had an uncomfortable sense that he would cheer and leap in joyously as well.

That smile. Death? Doom? Enemy fleet? *No problem, but let's do this with some gallant dash and élan, aye?*

Zola swung around in his Captain's seat, smiling-an inscrutable Etruscan Kuros grin, "Tutu!" he beamed. He had a full head of jet black hair and aquiline features most women would swoon over. Behind the gleaming ebony eyes, one sensed parallel processing of scenarios. Always watching, assessing, and judging along with criteria of value thoughtfully and personally created through many decades of intense adventures.

"Captain how goes the progress toward Galactic Center?'

"The Core, Tutu. They call it The Core. Sixty-five thousand ships banged into The Core this year. The Hyper tail signatures are fast becoming a permanent mark into the Space-time Continuum on eight-dimensional vortexes now."

"Is that good or bad?" Tutu asked. Tutu was a cyborg and had a running data stream from the ships navigationals. He knew exactly where they were at all times. Mosey did not, so they had to discuss it. He wanted the Captain's take on things in his own words.

The smile deepened as the captain assessed answers to that on several levels, some of which amused, some of which he found ironic, and some of which brought dread concern. He leaned back, looking at some imaginary point. "Depends if you're a navigator or a gunner."

The Hyper trails made for easy navigation. Sixty-five thousand ships would surely account for a whole lot of unseemly lawless characters. "Pirates?"

Captain Mosey rose in his seat, "Fuck them Pirate Pussies. I'll bang them across the dimensional void like the degenerate stepchildren of illegal genetically modified organisms."

Tutu beamed; *beauty.* "Good to know."

"But it might be some work," Mosey added more quietly, easing back in his chair, "This Sunrider would be quite a prize-but to take us down they would have to come in like a wolf pack in a swarm, with the intent of disabling us just enough for a boarding."

Tutu ran through various naval combat scenarios in his memory back up. He said, "Thoughts in this regard?"

"We get as far as Tangeonprioc and hire mercenaries. The Deneb system has money-it's growing at an insane pace. So we put up, and we get some proper backup. This warship is fearsome-but I had a feeling when we set out going it alone was foolhardy-and reading the numbers on the ships in The Core this year, now I'm sure of it."

"How do we know the Mercenaries can be trusted?"

Mosey's grin became a little scary, "I know a few guys we can trust. Long as they know they're going to get paid."

Fischer Shea and Elias Tristan Looked out from the corner offices of level 15 on the domes of Las Olas gardens, Tangeonprioc with somewhat disbelieving amazement at what they had accomplished here in the last several years. It had grown to several hundred miles of interconnected environment domes-each one a small city in itself-swarming with settlers, farmers, traders and prospectors.

The trade in Predecessor Alien Artifacts was driven by corporations and governments across the spread of Human civilization. A piece of garbage tossed thoughtlessly away sixty-five million years ago and left in the right crater shadow or sand drift contained information that was advancing Human technology with ridiculous jumps.

All of those prospectors needed a base to set out. The Core was hard on organic life with radiation and stellar forces at a scale uncommon in the rest of the galaxy. Navigating those dangerous forces one needed knowledge on continually changing space weather. One needed equipment refurbishing regularly, food, sex, and all the complex accouterments of Human life: Diversions.

Welcome to the boomtown.

Fischer was a handsome man. Elias figured he had cosmetic surgery and expensive genetic mods. No one really knew, but he put spells on women and always seemed to be involved with another one. Elias was a giant, bulky, demolition tank of a man and was Gay. He didn't have much to do with women but frequented a corner of one of the domes called "The Grove" where his off hours were spent with a group of gay ex-soldiers; snipers and starship gunners from the Mercury Royal Police.

Elias was one of the few people Fischer trusted, and his somewhat unusual collection of gay soldiers and adventure stories as Mercury had gone about policing the galaxy's settlements only added another layer of colorful characters to Tangeonprioc's endless carnival of Human extravagance.

Bruno Fowler was a client who wanted to build a two hundred story tower over his strip-club dome. He sat fuming and his cologne was stinking up Fischer's office. For a man who had a couple of hundred sexbots working 'around the clock, he was a tiny little troll of thing, and Elias assumed he had muscle handle all the unruly prospectors.

"Mother says I've purchased the best dome and should be able to build whatever I want in it."

He lived with his mother.

Elias's hypercast started blinking. *Saved by the bell.* "Excuse me guys, I gotta take this- "

Fischer scowled and Bruno looked askance, his nose perceptibly rising.

It was Zola Mosey.

"Tristan, you fat fuck how the hell are you!?"

"Doing good, Zola. Real estate development at the Core. Where are you?" They had fought together with the Granger Rangers at Mercury Far-Side station. Zola had a lot of sack and never backed down, even when he should.

"I'm doing a run for a research foundation. Babysitting some smoking hot Science babe. I need a couple back-up ships. You got any guys? You and all them pretty boys from Elite Units- they were good. I know you're all smoking pole out there, so don't tell me you don't have anyone."

"Diplomacy, ever your strong point. Yeah, I got guys. But I'll handle this at home. Look me up at the Core Winds Tavern, it's a skin parlor we're doing some development proposals for and you and your crew can get some comps. Buzz me when you fly in and don't be talking about smoking pole to my gunners or you might get some steel in your ship you don't want."

"Don't be a baby."

Fischer was glad when Elias returned. "What's up, Buck?"

"Friends coming into town-big party. At your place, Bruno. We're going to pack the place tonight!"

Bruno smiled. *Oh good.*

The meetings went down with the usual fanfare of sexbots, second rate booze, and party favors, and Zola had his back up ships. The Mel's Monkey and the Serpentine, with Captain Mel "No-Deal" DePaulo and Captain Roland Dansky. They all set out of Tangeonprioc in the morning with hangovers and didn't encounter any trouble for several weeks on a coded course that made numerous dodges.

Mel noted the course, no matter how twisted, was making its way closer and closer to one of the larger black holes at the very center of the galaxy. He casted over to Zola, "I want more money. You didn't say anything about riding up on a black hole."

Zola piped back, "I thought you Mercury guys were tough? Did I need to tell you there would be searing radiation flares and armed hostiles too? You're a fucking mercenary, not a museum docent. Act like one!"

"I want a bonus for getting this close to that THING."

"What do you want?"

"I want ten percent for me, and the same for Roland."

"Done. Now, can we get on with the mission?"

"Deal. Always happy to do business."

No-Deal and Roland earned their money shortly thereafter. The tail Mosey had been harping *MUST* be there, finally *was there and* they had a dozen nasty little Blade ships too. But No-Deal and Roland were Mercurian veterans, and even Mosey was impressed with speed, accuracy, and relentless prosecution of death without prejudice or hesitation. When it was all over, the marauding outlaws were masses of human gore spread out for several hundred clicks of wreckage. Tutu insisted recon be done, and whatever hard drives and Intel could be gathered on who the hell they were, were being gathered.

When No-Deal found out their objective was an intact alien Predecessor base, the shit hit the fan and he raised holy hell until he got his pay doubled. They were looking at the wealth and technology that a galactic Empire could be built from. Whoever could have this ruled Humankind. And most certainly, would change mankind. Lourdes was here for technologies that could be genuine AI-self-aware and linking with human consciousness.

Eternal life.

Roland was tall and built like a hero from a virtual reality entertainment show, but moving through the doorways of the alien base, he looked like a child.

"What the hell were these things?" he muttered.

"They were big."

"And smart." Roland picked up a gleaming streamlined tool full of jewels."

"Don't touch that" one of the scientists grabbed it away from him, "Are you fucking stupid?"

Roland pointed a disruptor pistol at him casually, "Yeah but I'm armed. *Are you?*"

The scientist held up the alien artifact, "Maybe!"

Roland smirked, "Good answer, little man."

They had pulled her out of her ordinary life and dragged her across the galaxy in a warship, then added some scary mercenaries, firefights, and now a sixty-five-million-year old alien base. It was game time, and she hovered over the research done to date with a mind every scientist on the base came to admire. She had nanoscopes, field records, quantum computers, and the whole damn team and even the mercenaries working at one point, looking at the how, why, and what the aliens had created so long ago.

In a solid month of ceaseless labor and teamwork, she knew she had only scratched the surface of the paint job on Predecessor technology. But her focus was organic interfaces, and the organic chemistry interlinks were discoverable on several levels.

There were immersive VR chambers with Chairs. Really big, sleek, strange chairs, but chairs none the less and control panels with buttons. Not holo screens, but buttons you could press, and alien DNA still on them.

Reptilian, Amphibian maybe, but not second or third wave life forms evolving after several planetary mass extinctions like Humans were, but fresh out of the Evolutionary box reptiles.

"So what did we have here-dinosaurs?" Tutu looked around at the empty halls of the base with a grim thought that he wasn't at the top of the food chain any longer."

Lourdes's lovely eyes beamed back. "Yeah. Probably skipped the mass extinctions of Earth-just kept evolving after they rose up, accumulating knowledge and technology for untold millennia and eons before they ran into something they could never imagine."

"And that was?"

"Something bad. Something worse than them."

"Good thing it's gone"

Lourdes stopped for a long moment. "We know the Predecessors are gone. We don't know what exterminated them is gone."

Evidence suggested the Predecessors represented an earlier sentient species-indeed reptilian-that dominated the galaxy. Evidence on world after world over the centuries had indicated general patterns of mass extinctions in waves across the galaxy, knocking back the evolutionary process. The surviving vermin would rise up, however, after millions of years and become the dominant sentient life. Mice became apes became people: *Variations on that theme.*

The predecessors had taken a big hit 65 million years ago, around the same time of the fall of the dinosaurs on Earth-an eerie coincidence and Lourdes didn't like coincidences. Most of the artifacts found were of that time period. But there were others, a few here and there, which dated later, even until relatively recent times.

So there may have been survivors. A scattered few individuals managing to wander the derelict worlds and avoid whatever stalked them?

She climbed into one of the giant chairs. She looked like a toddler playing in Daddy's comfy chair. The chromium handle was like a Brancusi sculpture. She touched it and watched the holograms sparkle to life. There were whispers in her ear, or was it in her brain directly? A hissing, raspy sound-something primitive and yet strangely there were sophisticated weaves, subtle sounds she knew were language. Most importantly, there was an emotional impact in her soul, something wild and fierce and she felt exultation, a mania.

She withdrew from the chair and looked about with a red-faced guilt-how unprofessional to toy with the damned thing like that. She was a neurologist, for heaven's sake. It seemed to call to her. Several of the techs had mentioned this. One was coming now. He approached, somewhat embarrassed.

"We have kind of made it an unofficial rule not to be close to the chair technology alone, Dr. Cassandra. We're convinced the thing was set up for the aliens like a "hive mind", and that instantaneous communications were running between the machines and the creatures twenty-four-seven when they were in this lab or library, or whatever it is."

"Yes, good practice." She leaned toward him with a certain danger in her eyes, "I felt something."

"There are electromagnetic fields involved that can impact neurons. Wi-Fi for brains."

Months later a data package came into the main research facility at Deneb IV. Lourdes's analysis of the Predecessor organic links to their hardware computer systems. Months after that entire nanosystems and been redeveloped, and the good Doctor Scalotta was taken out of stasis. His first thoughts on experiencing his consciousness linked with the singularity in what would become the great hive Mind of Deneb IV was that for him Lourdes's return would be their first actual meeting. He was now fully Transhuman.

There would be others, and together, armed with the alien technology, they would set about bringing order out of chaos-a brave new galaxy out of the hardscrabble insanity of man's inhumanity to man; "A more perfect day". Utopian schemes and dreams that had failed in the past could now be realized.

One thing remained unsettled, however-there was, among the alien ruins, not a clue to what it was that had driven the predecessors to extinction.

It would be a full Millennium of growth; some even calling is the Deneb Pax. It would be Lourdes who led that epic. It would be Lourdes again who faced the first brutal end of that peace; breakaway independent Colonials from Arcturus, stretching off into the Sagittarius Galactic Spiral Arm in a set of robust systems in a juggernaut of economic and military power. This time it wasn't half-crazed warlords, but an organized Libertarian civilization that rejected the Transhuman order of Deneb IV, whose growth and power remained steady until its entire surface was one megalopolis of Imperial Administration.
-Princess Clairissa Maggio, Caldris,

The Arcturian Colonials defined the aspects of their era more clearly than any of the galaxy's other societies to that point; optimism, technology, and unrestricted freedom of action and trade their ethos. It shone in their architecture, which soared, their economies, which roared, and their sense of life with its easy freedoms.

They achieved it without the all-encompassing grip of the Imperials and their Transhuman Overlords, the continual strife of the Oligarchies and Kingdoms, or the horrific mysticism of the Marauder Cult at the galactic core.

Their business achievements now seem the stuff of mythological greatness, and ironically it is hard to remember they were mere mortals such as us. Looking at the Galaxy today we may ask, "How did we get here?" Again, it is the Arcturian Colonials that step on to the galactic stage...

- Princess Clairissa Maggio "The Arcturian Colonials, Materialists of the abstract."

Flight 107-9 to New Procyon
New Galen, Arcturian Free Colonies, 3197.

Morning dawned lazy, gray, and rainy at the Starport as Dylan tossed himself into a window seat and ran sleepy fingers through his hair. He watched the star liners taxi back and forth along the runway. It was just another flight among hundreds...flight 107-9, to be precise. "The Rip Van Winkle", bound "Out space" for the Sagittarius Arm of the galaxy and the frontier.

All night the big space shuttles had dropped passengers onto New Galen from the orbital Gateway. The passengers moved by the thousands mostly home to the cities and farms of the colony. Dylan's flight plan, however, headed outbound.

He glanced at a couple of stewardesses in pastel, shiny, revealing outfits. They were two beauties animatedly talking politics while floating bots made coffee.

A tall blonde-haired woman with a Slavic look chirped, "Vina, since the Trans human's diplomatic meeting at Arcturus the whole schedule of the airline is turned upside down. My home bot has been feeding my cat all week because I can't get back. Fefe hates the home bot."

20

Her companion, a perfectly formed brunette, replied, "Maybe the cat knows something we don't, aye? Metal-heads! They absolutely will not be happy until they have a star gateway into every system and a database on every economy. They just can't bear the thought of us ordinary humans having any freedom of our own!"

Dylan chuckled to himself; *galactic civilization interferes with cat feedings.* He read the hologram graphics glittering over the terminal in a repeating pattern of faux neon and a glittering starfield: New Galen Starport, Gateway to the Galaxy! He thought to himself, *just another flight.*

He stared out the oblong porthole near his seat. A break in the clouds afforded him a view of the sky. Even at the first gleam of early morn, he could see the glow and ring of the Gateway orbiting New Galen. It was huge, a quarter as large again as the planet it orbited. Dozens of Stations drifted around it; they were smaller rings and sparkling lights. If one looked closely, massive star liners were discernible, appearing as from nothing through the gateway. Having traversed light-years in moments, they reached the borders of one civilization and stepped into another.

He peered at the mighty gateway sardonically, "Stellar Gateways. More control." He grumbled and thumbed a small hologram tape of a lecture from the university. The hologram of his professor appeared, small but stalwart and colorfully robed. "Since the Gateways have been created they have been both a marvel and a curse. They are a marvel of technology, a curse of political contention. A plethora of governments have been established throughout nearly a quarter of the galaxy since the advent of hyperdrives, yet only two truly matter. Firstly, the Cyborgian Central Command Economies-CCCE.

'Mankind's oldest civilization, CCCE is centered around Earth with its capital world at Deneb IV. Secondly, the Arcturian Republics: a few dozen worlds and worldlets, with their Capital at Arcturus Prime.

'The Arcturians have full of control access to further settlement along the Sagittarius arm of the galaxy. They want no more Gateways built there by the CCCE. They believed future Gateways would simply ensure Cyborgian control over trade, which they maintain should remain the prerogative of every people."

Dylan swiped his hand mockingly through the hologram, "Smack, of course it should!"

The hologram professor continued, "The controversy has seen numerous incidents of violence with starfighters taking nips at each other in obscure corners of the star systems."

Dylan clicked the Prof off.

Dylan was simply glad he had not been drafted into the air corps to patrol the lonely orbits of forlorn globes. He looked again at the gateway glimmering in the sky as darker clouds moved in with more rain.

"Gateway to the Galaxy!" He parroted one of their recent holo commercials that had been playing all week on the serials. However, it was the last gateway from which a starship could instantaneously shuttle from system to system. Outward from here, the starships flew on their power, unmonitored and "out of the Cyborgian canal."

Such is how most pilots truly liked to fly-freely.

A fortyish businessman, unusually chipper, bounced down the aisle looking for his seat.

"No God, anyone but chipper man" Dylan grimaced.

The big pudgy face stopped near Dylan and smiled. "Hi, I guess I got the seat next to you here", he said brightly.

"Guess so." Dylan moved his jacket politely and forced a smile. He wanted to feel like a veteran of the skies but these business types flew all the time; so much for his sense of adventure.

"Long haul to Wild Duck, eh?" Chipper man offered.

"You're headed to the Wild Duck nebula? The Frontier-" Dylan's sudden smile bloomed across his face. "I didn't know they were civilized enough for business suits out there yet." He replied, trying to sound unimpressed. However, his eyes were scrutinizing Chipper man with more interest now. The Frontier! Doing business, no less, he snickered to himself at the thought of chipper man moving brightly into a rugged mess of settlers.

"Must have seen some real shenanigans out there?"

The man shook his head affirmatively and replied, "Hey, drop a few cargo tanks down and they start a city. It's only a matter of hours before somebody needs what somebody else has, and business is born."

"Yeah, stands to reason." Dylan nodded his bottom lip pushing up importantly. "Where you headed?"

"New Procyon University. Back to finish the term. Just ending spring vacation, you know, home and hearth. Back to the old discs. Ivy and dusty quantum computers-rah-rah!" Dylan said.

"Yes, I remember. I guess it is ever the same. Tunis Hill, Feininger transportation." he held out his hand with a practiced smoothness.

"Dylan Phalen. Student, Space Engineering" They shook hands.

"Space engineering, you gotta love that," Tunis said.

"Working on auton nanostructures" Dylan ran his fingers over the holo recorder and another hologram appeared where the professor had been: nanobots teemed. "Self-replicating crystalline formations that will form advance settler depots in Oort clouds"

The hologram nanobots swarmed through the cometary bodies, "The advance settlements for humans allow for immediate access to resources." His brow furrowed with delight and power, "Seeding probes hit the Oort clouds sending out millions of 'Nano-ants'. The ants reorganize the raw materials of the rocky ice-balls into the constituent matter, creating rudimentary shelters, easily accessible caches of water and oxygen, even organics in vats for food.

"When the settlers arrive it's like a hotel waiting for them. Then the Nano-ants are shipped off to the next system to repeat the process." Dylan gleamed. Last term he had won honors at the University for developing nanobots that were able to develop at structure five miles long with an interior of wildflowers, streams, and Japanese Gardens.

Tunis's eyes were wide with the intensity of Dylan's presentation. "I've heard about those," he said, his head bobbing solemnly, "Big on the market now aren't they?"

"Yeah, big business, big frontier." He looked at the swarming holo. "And the uncharted sectors, well, they're an even bigger portion of the galaxy. It's going to be like a black hole hitting a fifth-dimensional anomaly."

They were both silent a moment, sharing a male understanding of "big" that drumbeat through the millennia back to the first time a Cro-Magnon hunter spotted a mastodon and thought, "Life is good."

"I got a swarm running in the ice fields right now! I need to turn it off when I get back to New Procyon or the darn things will just keep reorganizing Oort clouds forever, heh-heh."

The passengers were settling in and a steward was doing an age-old puppet dance he had recited a million times about starcraft safety. "And if the hull should be breached at any time in transit, emergency stasis holds will protect you until help can arrive-you won't even notice the passage of time. Help will seem to appear instantaneously." His face shined with delight.

Dylan snickered, "I want some of what he had for breakfast."

Tunis nodded and chuckled, "What they don't tell you is if help doesn't ever arrive, those stasis shields can keep you frozen for a couple of billion years. Rip Van Space-Winkle."

Dylan raised a contemplative brow. "Maybe they would have the big Gateway debate settled by then," he said and eased his chair back adjusting a suspensor field. His eyelids were heavy. It had been a long night of changing space planes. He drifted off to sleep as the Lockheed Martin X-3000 whined into the friendly skies and then slid, turbo-boosters stratocasting, into a widening spiral shot, for deep space.

The X-3000 was a new liner. Five decks high with three hyperdrives. Her alloy hull incorporated millions of nanoscanners, solar and radiation power arrays, as well as magnetic and gravitational scatter fields for shielding. For all the impressive hardware, she took to the stars with the grace of a falcon; swift, smooth, and magnificent. New Galen Starport gleamed in a teeming profusion of activity below. Then it was a landscape of patch quilt weaves of curves and interlaced rectangles quickly receding into a blend of continents hugging a sea. Suddenly then, the horizon curving and falling away into a globe full of brilliant pinwheel clouds. Lastly, Tunis watched out the window past the now sleeping youth as the globe shrank to a point of light and then faded entirely from sight.

Arcturus: New Haven City

Steve Allman

23

Diplomatic envoy David Omm looked out over the sculpted towers and parks forming the capitol city of the Arcturian Democratic Confederation with a strange fascination bordering on wonder.

Beyond his hotel balcony, millions moved, thrived, and lived with only the most minimal of cyborg enhancements. It was terrifying for him to a degree; any madman without mental restraint programs might wield a weapon causing David's destruction. Such primitive organic folly would not be tolerated in the Empire where each citizen was equipped with Hive-Mind interfaces directly in their brains. Yet he beamed, the thought of all those people operating on their compulsions, without the steadying hand of the Hive-Mind! What a brilliant, mad, careening chaos of carnival! That their "Republics" flourished amazed him even more.

The Arcturian Colonial Economies-Capitalism-were matched by no civilization man had created in the galaxy. He found himself ready to guffaw at the thought of their unregulated markets actually working, but of course there was a vicious uncertainty as to when the next economic collapse would come. Nevertheless, amazingly, these economies were working in ways the Imperial command economies were not. Hence David's diplomatic mission.

He represented the oldest of mankind's governments. Earth remained at the Imperial center, although the world of mankind's origin no longer held the honor of capitol world. That belonged to Deneb IV, heir to the longevity of the Transhumans. Earth's sciences had produced a medical tradition, which by the late twenty-second century that was nothing short of miraculous. First, they devised man-machine interfaces. The human nervous system and quantum computers could interact directly.

Over time, genetic enhancements at the cellular level had extended life almost indefinitely for those that could afford it. Nanosystems deftly combined biotechnology with micro-mechanical systems that cleaned and enhanced internal organs, even the epidermis, without the slightest infringement on ordinary human perception.

In the passing centuries Lourdes and the Overlords had refined the technologies and the manipulation of the human genome, the Alien technology, and a Transhuman Hive mind. The resulting class of Overlords, possessing a form of immortality, had Deneb turned into a planet-wide city.

Now Ultra-wealthy, they became a class unto themselves, certain they were an evolutionary step above the common fray of human hordes, the organics; The "Wilds". They were an interface interlocked with sentient programs to a level of complexity as such that where the human ended and the machine began was a moot point. How many angels could dance on the head of a pin?

Should even those extended-wear, heavy-duty bodies, glistening and heroic like Michelangelo sculptures come to life, should even they wear out, there would be a clone ready for them to step into.

David was well over five hundred years old, but his appearance was of a Grecian god. He stood lithe, tall, and eternally young. He almost pitied these "natural" organic humans with their minimal genetic enhancements. If pity could exist with fear and revulsion, then pity would describe his emotions.

Seeing them swarming around him unpredictably, he felt the creeping dread his superiors had warned him about when traveling outside the Imperial realms. Open spaces, unwelded minds, and the relentless danger of personal annihilation. Many of the Transhumans aristocracies had already retreated into secure suspension vats, inhabiting virtual realities, interacting with the material universe only with holograms.

The Arcturian colonies organic societies rejected cyborg enhancements that linked anyone directly to a computer network. They had rejected the Transhumanist Hive mind, the myriad social and sexual patterns of the Empire, and expanding into the Sagittarius arm of the galaxy, they exhibited a reversion to the premodern organic social model of the family. They mated for life, with only one partner, and mostly members of the opposite gender. Like all expanding civilizations, they rejected infanticide in any form, leaned toward agrarian religions and philosophies that stressed abstinence outside of marriage, and personal productivity. Such a culture complex was ignorant and laughable in David's view, and backward in the eyes of the Imperials.

It was a culture war that stretched back to before the dawn of spaceflight. The problem for the Transhumans was the problem all progressive societies had faced over the centuries. Organic societies tended to thrive and progressive to dissolve.

Yet they were too dangerous with their robust economies, unpredictable populations, and independent armed outposts. Most disconcerting, however, was their amazingly disciplined (with no Hive mind!) and dedicated military. Arcturians did not build Star Gates; hence their pilots exhibited a mastery of flight unseen in the empire. Yet quantity had a quality all its own. Ten welded cyborgs in a frigate with an algorithm generating quantum computer could do wonders against even the brightest organic pilot in a dogfight.

"Freedom! Freedom! Freedom!" was the Arcturian mantra, slung out at the universe with the conviction of religious zealots. David chuckled, more like Madness! Disorder! Chaos! Hence their nicknames among the Cyborgian High command- "Wilds" and "Organics".

The contentions which Organics had against Gateway outposts to their civilizations boggled the mind. That they preferred to endlessly rally about the radiation and dangers of deep space in their starships was beyond normal Cyborgian comprehension. When one had the prospect of unending days, danger itself became ever more abhorrent. However, Peace must rule, David mused earnestly. His mission was to create a diplomatic settlement that would define the matter of gateway construction with the Arcturians and allow the two civilizations to cohabit the galaxy.

He considered the Milky Way Galaxy and the spread of humanity across the star systems. Since the dawn of time, mankind had sought out to create an empire that would rule all, and whenever Universal Empire proved imminent, the whole thing would break down. His Diplomatic mission would not establish Universal Empire-merely a trade agreement per shipping; "rules of the sea" so to speak.

David's eyes went grim with the thought of something deeper in the organics than even human culture, some primordial soup of biology no one had ever been able to find in a lab, which set itself against the homogenization of the species under such an artificial construct.

No, the Galaxy was already mucked up with Oligarchies and anarchies, Republics and Kingdoms, Freebooters and Wildcats; simple disorder. He shuddered. The clockwork mathematical beauties of Cyborgian law, the enforced social cohesion of a universal ethical and moral code such as it were, they would not be imposed any time soon.

His droid presented a sleek silk jacket which David swung on with perfect grace. "Then we'll be off sir?" the droid asked with musical tones. Everything in the world of the Transhuman Aristocracy was high Art-even their droids. The Sun-king of ancient France had nothing on David Omm. David looked at his reflection. He smiled a boyish welcoming greeting that would melt hearts.

"Yes Zanti, off it is. Diplomacy! We shall clean their clocks and deliberate the lengths and measure of the star ways!" he snickered. His confidence was voluptuous and rich as a sauce.

"Very Newtonian Sir," Zanti said.

The door opened as they approached and suddenly he there stood before an image of incongruity in place and time; Lisa Sulla, his fiancé from the Pleiades.

"Lisa!" He stammered. "How did you, what are you…doing here?"

He was under Diplomatic security. There should be no way she could be here. Not unless there was more to her, far more than he had suspected. Was she involved with seditious groups? Was she with groups that had infiltrated and compromised the Arcturian governments at the highest levels? An Arcturian spy herself?

"David I don't have time to explain. There is more to this than you think. I need you to trust me. Cancel the delegation. Delay the meeting. Avoid this at all costs. Something is going to happen, something bad." She was lovely, but her beauty was marred now by an ugly intensity-a terror, which wracked her otherwise ethereal features in a gauze of fearful steam.

"How did you get in here? Are you on drugs? This is an outrage, Lisa. I am on a diplomatic mission from the highest levels of my government. What are you mixed up in? Who sent you with this? What are you talking about?"

Zanti leaned forward, "Would you like a beverage Madame?"

She glanced away at a sound of figures approaching, and then glared at him. Her pupils glowed with stim, or worse. "I have to go. Delay this David, somehow! We haven't figured out what is going to happen but it is not what you anticipate."

He began to speak but he saw another figure in the gardens waving for her. The approaching footsteps grew louder-security men in haste. She was a spy, he suddenly felt certain. The sense of betrayal was complete and pervasive; sudden-like a horrible accident witnessed that quickly transforms a loved one irretrievably.

Then she was gone.

Hyperspatial transit, Flight 1079 to New Procyon

They were cruising the hyper streams when Dylan awoke. Outside his window, starlight bent, frazzled, and shook, doing things that made his eyes dizzy. He darkened the window. That was the usual reaction people had to unedited garbage, "light-noise", seeping in from the hyper streams. In the piloting cabin, the captain could put on a MERGE (Mental Environmental Regeneration Graphic Enhancement) helmet where the ships' computer would make sense of it all, and project the stars and universe again as a reasonable simulation in his mind. Dylan could not do so without a MERGE helmet

So he darkened the window with a motion of his hand instead.

"Hyperspace is weird." He grumbled.

The Starliner had bent normal space creating a small bubble around itself, a temporary universe it then pushed "Outside" the normal universe and into the fifth-dimensional hyperspace, the "streams". The normal universe sped "below" them now, as seen through a glass darkly. The forces of the fifth-dimensional quantum hyperstreams were raging chaos. Even the computers of the ship could not make any genuine sense of them. The pilots contented themselves with reconstructions of the universe they had left to cheat the speed of light.

Tunis was engaged in a newscast. He shut it off when he saw Dylan was awake. "Forty winks, good for the constitution aye, Buck?" he smiled.

Buck? Frontiersmen were a singular breed. Dylan smiled.

"Yeah, yeah. I needed it with all this entire star hopping. Any news?" What have the politicos messed up this time?

"Lots! Earth and Cyborgian Central have agreed to the Arcturian Demands for Hegemony. They'll build no more Gateways to our borders." Tunis puffed up a bit involuntarily with a self-satisfied smugness. However, traces of discomfort dogged his features.

26

"They haven't built one in a while anyway. Don't think they want us barbarians storming their precious empire." Dylan smirked.

"Amen and A-men!" Tunis chuckled. "Yes, the mighty Cyborgian Aristocracy is finally giving it a rest. They signed a peace treaty at Arcturus this morning. Peace in our time!" Tunis stretched, grinning, pleased with events.

"Peace in our time?" Dylan frowned. He studied the businessman with a long even look.

"What?" Tunis looked to his clothes for lint.

"You ever study any second-millennium history?" Dylan wondered.

"Not much," Tunis gave him a guilty look that told of numerous hours distracted in scholastic environments. "Pre-space events are all somewhat brutish to me. Short life spans. Small violent territory disputes, deprived economic conditions. Rather depressingly sad lives, you know? To me, history begins with the big mining ventures of the twenty-second century! Now those were great Industrialists. The terra-forming of Venus and Mars. Air cars that do escape velocity. Interstellar convoys. That's history. Third-millennium stuff's what I like."

Dylan nodded agreement, "True enough, a great era. However, back near the end of the second millennium, there was this politician, Lord Chamberlain, who said those exact words-'Peace in our time'-just after negotiating a treaty with an enemy nation-state. Well, the peace treaty was a ruse, and the war that ensued was the most horrible war humanity had ever seen to that point-ever."

Dylan watched Tunis connect the dots.

"Yeah…I saw a holo-tape on that when I was in grade school. You might be right there, kid. It does seem kind of strange for the Cyborgians to loosen up all of the sudden. They have always been so animate about organizing and controlling everything. Now they'll just let the hull spin round? Right, mighty suspicious it is!"

They nodded, sharing a male understanding of "suspicious" that drumbeat through the millennia back to the first time a Cro-Magnon hunter spotted a saber tooth and thought, *"Oh, shit."*

Dylan leaned forward, "They're not human anymore," he whispered. He made a face expressing distaste, "I wouldn't trust them to honor treaties with us. I mean, their bodies are all bottled up in semi-stasis with their brains hooked into a hard drive stretching across twelve star systems. They never die. Yet they're not truly alive. They have got to be looking at us like we're some kind of missing links or living fossils from a bygone era. I don't know what they've become. Zombies if you ask me." Dylan said.

"Zombies," Tunis agreed, "but I think they have gradations of humanity-the lower you are on the totem pole, the more human you are-something like that. But whatever they've become, I'm glad they're not planning any more Gateways into the Arcturian Democracies. Feninger Transportation is based on traditional shipping-starships. The Gateways eat up all the profits with tariffs." Tunis winked. "Before you know it your whole business is just a cash cow they milk and you struggle to support. No deal!"

Vina Yerger was listening to a hyper cast out New Procyon in a kitchen cabin fixing drinks for the passengers when the music went dead. "Rats! Only when it's a good song does the radio die."

Her steward mate, Iyana Polana, snickered "Aint it the truth! Never mind though, no time for that now anyway. We've got service to deliver-with a smile." She tilted her head to the side in a coquettish pose, flashed her pearly whites, and pushed her cart out of the kitchen and into the aisle.

Vina followed and a troupe of small floating bots followed.

In the kitchen cabin, only a roaring static sounded on "NPHC105, the jamming, slamming voice of New Procyon University".

"Awww! Manure piles!" Captain Stanford Izzo cursed as his hyper casts went silent. "What the devil is this?" Switching into a test mode, he tried to reboot the program. There did not seem to be anything wrong with the receiver. His piloting helmet flashed with dozens of icons providing him with the vitals of the ship.

They appeared to float in simulation-the stellar geography of normal space congruent to their hyperstream.

Ed Cooper, his copilot, confirmed. "That's a big ten-four." Checking a wide array of other channels, he found nothing. "I'm not getting anything at all within range. That's FUBAR."

Izzo's chubby, cherubic face was resignation to the impossible, "We'll be coming out of hyper without confirmation, Eddy. Not good. Don't want to fly into somebody's back end."

"Gotcha, Captain. I'm on it. I'll reconfigure an alternate."

Izzo shook his head. "Upgrading the matter detectors now. If you can't get us reception, at least we'll get a better shot at clear space when we come out of hyper."

Vina popped her head into the piloting cabin. "All the radios are dead in the kitchens. Isn't that weird?"

Izzo continued his upgrades with a sudden dread sense of urgency. "They'll all can't go at once. Maybe it's some kind of hyper storm interference."

Of course, hyper casts had nothing to do with radio waves, but the ancient nomenclature had outlived its technology. It irked Izzo that she used civie unscientific terms like "radio" when she knew better. This was a starliner. Why couldn't she simply say "hypercast receiver" instead of "radio"? Cooper saw the building tension and sought to distract him.

"Hyper streams are reading standard Captain." Cooper offered, and then realized that wasn't going to help, only add to the inexplicable silence of the casts.

Vina groaned, "Ooohh! Hey, this is like a holo show! You know the one where the starliner slips into time wormhole dimension and ends up back in the dinosaur age?"

Cooper said dryly, "I missed that one." *Good Lord girl, shut up.*

Izzo eyeballed her from beneath his MERGE helmet, "No Vina, that can't be happening because there were no waves of light or weird sounds. It's gotta be another holo show. The one where the captain writes a bad evaluation of his flight stewardess because she's annoying during a crisis."

Vina scowled and withdrew her head. "Sorry!" she said and left in a huff. Old fat-boy Izzo always taking his job so seriously. Glorified bus driver! Vina thought to herself. She was on a mission to find a man of a certain income. Anyone below that, income liner pilots included, were "little people". The fact that civilization, especially those at the income level she sought to marry into, depended completely on the integrity, decency, and work ethics of those "little people" did not occur to her.

"Well?" Vina craned her head over Iyana's fumbling with a small hyper cast receiver she'd brought up from her cabin.

"Give me a minute!" Iyana replied with a frustrated grimace. It was a TD Daily, a very expensive receiver. It was portable, stylish; and out of the budget of anyone but the Truly Dedicated to hi-fidelity sound. Iyana bought it with her first paycheck when she got her job working the star liners. It was a symbol to her that she'd stepped into another life, leaving her girlhood behind and becoming a real independent woman.

Listening to the TD Daily send static and intermittent silence gave her a creeping sense of foreboding as if the things she measured her world by were somehow profoundly off.

"Nothing." She announced finally.

"That settles it then," Vina's face went pale, "we're in deep doo-doo! Something's wrong with the ship's dimensional stabilizers. We could be blasted into an alternate dimension; never get home."

Iyana clicked off the TD Daily and gave Vina a long poker face blank stare. "Were you sleeping during flight school, Vina, or what? We can't be trapped in another dimension. If we fall out of hyper we reacquire mass instantly. The spatial manipulators unfold space, we light up every molecule or a couple of light weeks, slow down, and coast. We can't exist in the higher dimensions without a space bubble. We're the dimensions they're built on. In a sense, we already are there, but sort of under them. We're not really "in" hyperspace. We're in a bubble universe of our sliding between it and our regular universe. Capeesh? "It's hyper cast interference. That's all. If this TD set can't get a signal, nothing can. It's the best. The best."

Iyana too lived within a world view of Social Darwinism based on income. High minded and high incomes were synonymous to her. If one acquired wealth, one's character was validated. Generations of extortion and murder could be cleaned up with a good country club membership any day. That her expensive receiver had been competitive in the galactic marketplace because of sweatshop labor was an inconvenient factoid.

"If you're so smart, Iyana, maybe you should have been a teacher. Impart your wondrous understanding of all things scientific to future generations of growing minds. But, not. Time to serve coffee, and look for a man with big money! Let's go."

Iyana considered the kaleidoscope holograms on her long fingernails. "Okay!" She brightened. Hyper cast interference slipped from her mind momentarily at the reminder of her real objective in life. Iyana already had several men with big money. She was expecting one of them to have an air limo waiting for her at the station hotel when the starship arrived at the next port. Yet like any good collector, you never can have too many.

"Let me lock my TD up first, Dearie." Iyana tilted her head again to the side, paused for dramatic effect and continued, "I like fine things-and I like to keep them." She swaggered to a cabinet and locked the door.

Turning to the coffee carts into a suspensor field, she felt again a sense of dread creep up. She had never heard of hypercast interference that blocked out all signals.

It was if everything broadcasting within the complete cast range had suddenly just vanished.

As if the world she knew has been a dream, and there was only the liner streaming along in the fifth dimension forever. She would be really glad when this flight was over and her kaleidoscope toenails were on solid ground again.

Cooper had placed his MERGE helmet on, "I've got something, Captain. Amplifying now-" he said solemnly. A noise came up in the cabin-coded short-range transmissions. "It's the flipping air corps!" he grumbled. "I bet this is their doing. They're probably testing some new signal scrambling equipment. Just like them not to notify air traffic control and the airlines first." He activated his com.

Cooper had served in the air corps for many years. He'd been given an honorable discharge, and the division commander had personally swept it under the rug after Cooper beat the living tar out of a recruit who had tormented him for weeks.

"Hey Grandpa!" the recruit had mocked the older man repeatedly while Cooper had gone through the various drills with the cadets.

Such insubordination technically should have been merely written up and punished. The recruit, however, had found Cooper's personal Achilles' Heel-Cooper was an aging Corporal persistently passed over for promotion although he excelled in a wide array of skills. He was passed over because of his temper.

Eventually, the recruit went too far, and Cooper chased him down four flights of stairs screaming in a Berserker rage. Five Hundred men were standing at silent attention in formation in their flight suits as witnesses. It took two four-meter service bots to pull him off the terrified recruit.

His commander had not been a happy flyboy. He chomped on a cigar from New-Cuba and sighed. "Don't kill anybody out there in the civilian world, eh, Cooper?" The commander shook his head, and Cooper watched his military career end with a quick signature.

Years later, running civies on milk jobs to the outer colonies, Cooper still knew those codes. Air Corps encryption. He knew something was happening. Something people weren't going to like. He activated his com, "This is flight 1079 out of New Galen, we're going to be coming out of hyper and need clearance. I've got three hundred civilians on this crate and I need clearance to drop hyper. Does anyone read? We are not receiving. Anyone read us?"

"That's your goofy air-buddies there." Izzo said. He looked to Cooper hoping for a signal that all was well, that something Cooper remembered of his air corps days would set everything back to normalcy. Cooper glared at him as if accusing. He was sweating. There wasn't one in his training for this. Every failsafe and back up communications system eerily dead. But for the enigmas of faint military codes crackling mockingly, there was nada.

Cooper thought of the hundreds and hundreds of civilians behind him. *Don't kill anybody out there.* He thought of the rows and rows of families depending on him.

On the instrument console, Izzo had set a magnetized trophy he'd earned in his youth: a hula dancer. On the hula dancer's pedestal was the inscription:

Blazing Dell Stunt pilot contest
First Place 3163

The '64 contest was Izzo's last run in the annual. He had had a bright yellow and purple flier. The crowds were going wild as he and two other stunt jockeys had banged through the course in record time pulling in an out of various stunts a hairbreadth away from each other with wing burning speeds. Coming around toward the finish, he'd begun a full-throttle push for the gold when one of the other stunt jockeys' turbo went rad. The two craft collided and spun into the sands in a frenzy of noise, smoke, and flame.

Izzo was out of his craft before it had even stopped moving, darting toward the other pilot to help. When he made it out of the stunt flier, it was too late, the damage was done. The other jockey lived but he never flew again.

 Izzo withdrew from the contest thereafter.

The memory of that day suddenly seemed important now.

He pulled up holo data of the stellar neighborhood with diagrams of shipping lanes. There were hundreds of flights, station orbits, asteroids, and cometary data. "Check the flight schedules on everything coming into New Procyon today," he said wearily. "Make sure we're not upending any freighters when we reacquire mass. The matter detectors are clear. The slide fields are maxed. We drop out on our own devices.

 "Wildcat pilots do it every day," he said uncertainly.

"Trillion to one odds we don't hit anything bigger than a grape," Cooper added. "Any unregistered ships will be dropping hyper far out the system to register. System control knows we're coming and they've given us our flight path. Confirmations are formalities." He looked unconvincingly at the Captain.

Izzo was flying dang near blind, deaf, and dumb. For all Cooper's assurances, he knew his copilot well enough to know when he was grandstanding. They were in the shit and he knew it better than anybody.

"We're dropping hyper unconfirmed then for sure?" Cooper hoped the Captain would swing around; search for a break in whatever was blocking the signal. Get out of the shipping lanes. Cooper had pulled up a holo model. "When was the last time you had a flight pattern change on arrival in the system?"

Izzo shook his head. "Last week. At Orion. Thank you very much."

"Sorry." They avoided each other's eyes. Something strange was going on back in normal space, something that froze communications, left spooky military dribble over the casts. If they didn't slam into the back end of a comet hauler, they were still going from the frying pan into an unknown fire.

In the starliner: rows and rows of families unawares, chatting and napping and snacking, playing holo games, listing to music. They were playing virtual reality dramas under headsets, careening through the hyperstreams of the higher dimensions faster than light between the stars.

Izzo placed his MERGE helmet on. It shimmered in the reflected lights of the streamlined cabin.

"Time's up. Take her out of hyper."

Outside the ship, at the edges of a gravity bubble that created an artificial universe, the ship began to withdraw the bubble.

The mini-universe of normal space began to collapse and collapsing, slip back into the normal space streaming along the higher dimensions of hyperspace. The distortion generated by the ship to bend a swath in the hyper streams effectively eliminating the effects of mass faded to zero. As the distortion faded, the ship reacquired mass and sub-light status. The gravity bubble and the ship inside it were now moving at just under light speed and decelerating rapidly.

They were back in the real world, and it was a lot slower. They were still, however, moving at near light speed. If not for the gravity bubble still clinging to the immediate area around the hull of the starship, there would have been serious inertia and G issues to contend with.

Izzo ran through the ship's sensors scanning the star system for abnormalities. It was full of them. Cooper saw it too. Radiation spikes. Clouds of matter streams filled with seared metal and plastics and cooked organic matter. Unsteady light from-burning materials.

"WARZONE!" Cooper roared, "Captain! Whoa, Buddy!" his hands were moving rapidly pulling up data holos. Before them, glowing and radioactive were the remnants of a star system once populated with hundreds of millions of people. Buzzing among the carnage were attack ships like scavengers over a freak mass kill. "Better swing wide and get us powering back up for hyper. Time to go."

"Nuclear First strike." Izzo whispered, a rush of bile filling his innards "The bastards nuked the whole system."

The crackling static of the hypercast unit finally made sense.

"No, Captain. *They've nuked all our systems,*" Cooper snapped, and the wildness in him that had for so long been out of place in the civilized world was suddenly transformed. Survival and fight instincts, the animal response to the true nature of a hostile universe, were instantly reassuring now. Izzo didn't have to worry about his co-pilot wilting under the strain of a fight. Fights were Cooper's elements.

Suddenly the cast unit came to life. An air corps pilot's hologram solidified above the cast screen, "Liner! This is the Arcturian air corps. You had better take evasive maneuvers now. You're going to be under fire! There aren't many of us left and the system is ripe with Cyborgian Central attack ships mopping up. Fix on my codes and defend your people."

Izzo had already begun to swing wide at Cooper's suggestion.

The ships blazed in their streams.

Izzo was surprised the code programming, prepared when the liner was made, powered up suddenly at the air corpsman's signal. Then he remembered his flight training on martial law situations and knew he was now under the command of the dogfighter pilot.

At last, knowing the full scope of his situation, Izzo wasted no time repowering the hyperdrives. He pressed the ship into an evasive pattern and reaccelerating from his cruising. Cooper watched every instrument hologram tach to the max on his MERGE array. Word had it, old boy Izzo had been quite a stunt pilot in his youth. That bit of trivia batted around coffee lounges among the liner pilots for years had just become very, very important.

Cooper was in a cold shock, but he almost smiled as he watched the liner do things he had never seen a liner do before. There were four dogfighters left against three Cyborgian attack ships. Izzo spun the liner in twisting splines, avoiding laser shot that would have sliced the hull open if it hammered well enough. Nevertheless, the attack ships were preoccupied with the dogfighters, their shots were not coming from their big guns.

Drifting and radioactive, an Arcturian battleship would soon plunge to New Procyon World. There was no one left alive there to worry over the collision. Izzo spotted a huge freighter, which had miraculously pulled itself into a low orbit around a gas giant. It seemed to be biding its time or waiting instructions before it made a hopeless break for hyper. If the dogfighters could harry the attack ships long enough, it might run free of the gas giant's gravity well and make a run in hyper. This close to the planet, the hyperstreams would be a deadly riptide that would shatter any field manipulations it could construct.

"Liner 1079, this is Arcturian Air corps. We're on a coded channel. Follow my instructions exactly, and there may a way out of this mess. We figured there'd be civies arriving in the system, so we've stayed as long as we could to help. I've lost all the men I can. Two of us will break the engagement and spin out for the largest gas giant. A friendly ship is hiding there now. On my coordinates, we all break into hyper and run. How you set for fuel?"

Izzo could hear instrument fire as the pilot spoke. "Were good." Izzo looked at Cooper. Were they certain this transmission was from the Arcturians? Cooper understood. He pointed to a holo: all the codes checked. Izzo had a feeling he knew what the dogfighter pilot was planning to do. There were worlds charted deep out space that could sustain human life, but that hadn't been settled in earnest yet, beyond the frontier. Reach one and they might not have all the luxuries of civilization, but they would have a chance. The Imperials weren't going to track down every last Arcturian vessel, were they?

"What's your name Captain?" the dogfighter pilot croaked dryly.

"Izzo. You?"

"Kroug. Percival Kroug. Welcome to my nightmare, Captain Izzo."

Izzo guffawed. He was watching metal fatigue indicators rise.

A large station, blasted out of its L-5 orbit between New Procyon's World and its moon, was spinning slowly toward Izzo's flight path. Izzo realized the station could provide cover. There were bodies and wreckage in a cloud that had poured like a wound from the station side.

Swinging the liner on the dark side of the station, his heart started to ease from its frantic pounding in his chest.

For the first time, he realized there was a noise from the passengers. Without the ship's sensors, they couldn't see the star systems minute detail as he and Cooper could, but they had been aware by the movement of stars that the liner was executing unusual flight patterns. This close to the blasted station, however, they could look out their windows and see mayhem.

Vina darkened the windows out of sheer panic. There had been corpses floating around a station. What the hell were they doing at a station? Why were they doing stunt patterns?

"Omigod-Omigod" Iyana was in a state of panic. "Vina, all those bodies floating around the O'Neil station. What happened?"

Vina tried to remember flight training protocols. Watch the passengers. Prevent unruly behaviors. Keep everyone in his or her seats.

"I don't know. Maybe there was some kind of solar storm. Mess up the hypercasts and blow out the station".

Don't ask Vina-Iyana made a mental note to herself. They both made way into the main cabin where the passengers were growing louder.

"Miss! Miss! If there has been some kind of industrial accident at that station, it's not a good policy for this liner to play the Good Samaritan and try to rescue people. There are trained professionals for that kind of work. Another explosion could rocket that station right as us!" A stern-looking man chided.

"Lighten the windows, that was cool!" from a child.

"Markey!" from his mother. She swatted him and he sunk in his seat pouting.

"I'm not sure why we're stopping here sir, but I can assure you it's not company policy to assist industrial accidents with liners full of passengers. We may have been ordered not to proceed. Perhaps other danger lies in our flight path. The Captain and the first mate are fully aware of what they need to do."

Dylan leaned over to Tunis. "I got a hundred bucks says that captain and the first mate are shitting bricks right now."

"Yeah, I'll second that. That was matter cannon scars on the station. And the holes were blown in. We're in the middle some kind of military incident my friend. And I don't think it's over."

Dylan darkened with foreboding, "But they just signed the peace treaty!" he argued against his own earlier thoughts.

"This would mean war. Total war. That wasn't an industrial station. It was a bedroom community, luxury condos and such." Tunis said quietly so as not to alarm the other passengers.

Total war-citizenry is targeted.

Izzo had seen the hull of a liner among the debris near the wrecked station. He didn't mention it to Coop. No point. If he saw it, he wasn't saying anything. If he didn't, it was all the better for his nerves. As the two men sat waiting in their cold sweat, Iyana appeared in the cabin. She whispered, "Captain?" She needed some kind of explanation. Izzo knew she deserved that.

"We're at war." he tried to hold back the worst of it. She stared silently.

"We're not going to land at New Procyon." *There is no New Procyon.*

"What do I tell the passengers?" Her hands were shaking. She had suspected as much. Flight training protocols-In the case of hostile action passengers are to be informed to remain calm, that their cooperation is vital to survival.

"Tell them everything is under control and they must remain quiet and wait for further instructions. Our landing is being postponed due to a system-wide emergency. They must remain calm and cooperate at all times. There is a state of martial law in New Procyon system due to terrorists, and we've been instructed by the authorities to seek safety elsewhere.

"Iyana, have the crew batten down. I may have to transfer power from gravity at some point."

That one wasn't in the protocols!

"Okay." She answered quietly. "Okay." Beneath the silky sheen of spoiled girlish civilization lurked another woman, an archetype of her distant ancestors-Arcturian colonial women, women who had moved first out to the distant worlds of the solar system and then for generations worlds and stars beyond. It was those women that shown in her face now. Izzo peered at her with stolid respect for the first time since he had known her.

Kroug's only advantage against the CCCE attack ships was Arcturian design superiority. His dogfighter was state of the art for a people that didn't build Gateways. The Cyborgian frigates were still fast though, and heavily armed.

Coming in for another dive, he was able to avoid most of their fire, but his shields took several hits that almost broke his power drives. It was his closest dive yet and he scanned for damage to the frigate.

33

There was none. His group had been pounding them for hours and they looked fresh out of the docks. In his piloting helmet, he bit his lip and longed for rest and a cigar. The Cyborgians must have upgraded their defenses somehow before the attack. They had been planning this first strike for a long time. He glared at the dogfighter's holo display of the array of moving combatants. He muttered a prayer he didn't believe in and ordered decisively, "On my signal disengage," in coded transmission to the other dogfighters. In concert, they all spun out and began making evasive maneuvers toward the gas giant.

Two of the CC attack frigates moved to follow.

Izzo received his codes, and he pressed the liner to high tail it deep out system. The freighter moved less agilely, but it too began to clear the gas giant's gravity well. The dogfighters continued to fire rear guard shots at the attack frigates. With the new destination codes secreted to the liner and the freighter, the last of the Arcturians people left the burning wreckage of New Procyon system. Moving into hyper, Kroug could see his small convoy forming a streaming cluster.

One of the frigates entered the stream also, was almost lost to them as it spun directional data trying to trace their flight vectors, but remained at a distance. There was something else in the stream as well, anomalies trailing. Not big enough to be starships, these anomalies still moved with the convoy and the frigate.

What in the devil now?

The frigate couldn't do any damage to them in the hyper stream-no weapons systems had ever been devised to function in that bizarre other-universe beside and above normal space. Kroug wished one had. He'd have used it on the frigates in ugly pursuit. Why continue after the convoy now? What difference could a few straggling refugees make against an empire that had just wiped out billions in a day?

Billions killed in a day.

A firestorm genocide more dark and evil than all the sordid horrors of man's inhumanity to men across the bloody march of history-but then, the Transhuman Imperials were no longer mankind, where they?

He collapsed into the ergonomically padded mass of his flight cabin. Able to rest for the first time in seventeen hours of straight dogfighting, Kroug felt the reality of the horror he'd just witnessed begin to scorch his mind further. So many Billions murdered in a day, gone. The Cyborgian Central Command had just "one-upped" the complete history of horror in one fell stroke. Why? Being air corps, deep down he knew why.

Admiral Galipo had lobbied the Arcturian Congress at Arcturus for the building of a new fleet. The fleet was nearing completion and it would have capabilities the Cyborgians could not match. Having the use of Gateways had left the Cyborgians falling behind in ship development. Why improve ships if they were merely shuttles from Gateways to planets?

Still, those frigates were better than anything he'd seen the Cyborgians using before. They must have been trying to play catch up, realized it was a losing battle, and decided to preempt being second power in the galaxy. Their command economy, with hundreds of billions of citizens, would collapse if they couldn't dictate trade terms to other governments outside theirs. The outer republics, a huge buffer between Arcturian power and Cyborgians, would no longer be puppets to the Cyborgians. Their power over even their peoples would then have been moot.

Kroug rested in his seat, and with horrible hindsight of a vanquished people, slept through the autopilots careful manipulations of the hyper streams.

"Keen are the arrows of that silver sphere
Whose intense lamp narrows
In the white dawn clear,
Until we hardly see, who feel that it is there."
-Byron Shelly, "Skylark"

Dylan knew enough about star liners to know they were approaching the limits of the ship's range. Passengers were starting to smell bad. For ten long days and nights, they had ridden the hyperstreams at peak capacity. It was a fast liner.

However, the only first-class deck had showers and regular, if small, sleeping cabins. They had spread the utilities as best they could. It was not a cruise liner, with pools and theatres and nightclubs.

It was quick transportation for close system hops. This long in hyperspace and they were beyond the frontier.

There would be nary a mountain man or lone wolf prospector out this far.

The Starliner pilot had pressed the hyperstreams well. Dylan figured the Captain had pushed the liner twice as far as an ordinary hyper trip by edging subtleties out of the chaos. It had given them some extra distance between them and their pursuers, but the Cyborgians persisted.

Disgustingly, bloodthirstily pursuing civilian quarry, only welded cyborgs would pursue such actions. Honorable military men across the millennia would have raised objections against the wanton destruction of defenseless civilians. "Unlawful orders", they would have countered. Such was the root of the Arcturian Colonials objections to such things as the Hive mind. People programmed were capable of any atrocity.

There wasn't much farther the Lockheed Martin could take them however without an overhaul.

Things were coming to a head, Dylan mused. The other passengers sensed it as well. Everyone had become aware that the emergency had bigger implications than they had been informed of.

Tunis and Dylan knew enough between them about space and spaceflight to roughly gauge the goings of the new war.

"Sleep well?" Tunis asked with forced brightness.

"Yeah. I dreamed of spiders, though. Spiders hovering over bubbles on a milky, dark lake. Hungry ones, laughing. Minnows were fighting in a shallow pool, unaware they were all soon to be eaten by the spiders."

Tunis raised an eyebrow. "Quite an imagination their Young man. 'Been watching too many virtual reality dramas. Here, I saved some cookies. The steward came buy a few minutes ago."

"Thanks. How many cookies and sodas you think they'll be able to serve us before the food runs out?" Dylan looked at the cookies with a sense of import.

"I know. We're running, my boy. We're into the edges of the frontier by now and there aren't very big settlements out here. Nary a world was quite suitable for a bunch of soft civies. I tender we're losing the war."

"Not much the optimist is you? You don't think our guys are any good?" Dylan muttered. His hip youthful cynicism had gone and now he longed for good old fashioned propaganda. There was none.

Tunis bowed his head in a dreary reveal from his studied upbeat salesman's chipperness. "I'm a businessman. Too much optimism sends you to the bankruptcy court. I've never been there. Do a cool evaluation of the situation every time, and you stay in the game.

"Right now I say they've got control of every system in the Arcturian Republics, and refugees are fleeing along the Sagittarius arm in liners like this one, tugs, yachts, and freighters-anything that can fly."

"Fleeing to the frontier? Everyone?" Dylan's hands gripped his seat arms tightly. This ship he had so casually taken for granted when he boarded her seemed suddenly now…evidence. Evidence of worlds gone away.

"Afraid so. Can't say how many like us got out. Probably plenty. But they won't be prepared with equipment to handle the frontier. Unless the Arcturians can reach some settlement, we won't be getting any relief supplies for a while."

35

Dylan swallowed, thinking Tunis overly pessimistic. Yet for all of the cynicism, Tunis's assessment of the situation had been light. When the casts had gone out, they had gone out completely. There was no more Arcturian civilization. Its last artifacts and peoples were running ships now reaching frontier worlds, one overworked ship at a time. The rest were radioactive ruins.

Across the chaos and wildness of the hyperstreams, the little convoy of refugee ships and dogfighters soldiered on.

"Captain Izzo, this is Kroug." The hologram of the pilot appearing in front of Izzo now had a beard fresh beneath his visor. Izzo could see system holo indicators just outside the main hologram of Kroug and a number of them were red. Izzo glanced at Cooper and indeed, Cooper's eyes were fixed on the red indicators as well-he knew the dials. Izzo didn't ask.

"Got you loud and clear," Izzo admired their stoic fortitude and sought to match it. If they were to join the majority of their people who had been destroyed in this unprecedented first strike, he would at least do it with his chin up and his middle finger raised, "Are we dropping out of hyperspace?"

Kroug seemed to sense the resolution in the Starliner Captain's voice and amazingly, subtly, derived strength from it himself. "That's affirmative. You'll see the charts I sent over on the system were dropping in to. There's an Earth-size moon orbiting a ringed gas giant in the temperate zone. No settlements, but the air is breathable and there's life. Our files have it listed as an emergency refuge world. You'll put down there. The dogfighters will scramble on the Cyborgian frigate that's tailing us."

"Good luck," Izzo said.

"There are some other anomalies in the stream. Don't know what they are." Kroug wondered awkwardly.

"I've seen them." Bogies. Foo fighters. Mysterious anomalies that have dogged human air and space conflict since the dawn of flight." Cooper chimed in. He remembered an evening at base canteen hearing stories from pilots. Always seemed like something out of a tabloid. Seeing them now on his holoscreens lent another layer of strangeness to events.

"Could be military hostiles of a sort we've never encountered. I don't like it. But there hasn't been a lot I've liked lately. Just gotta deal." Kroug said grimly.

"Ten-four," Izzo replied, and it occurred to him then he was now Air Corps too.

The convoy fell out of hyper high above the system and made for their refuge planet in calculated varying splining vectors. The ringed gas giant which the planet-technically a moon-orbited would provide some cover for the freighter and the liner. The dogfighters would then engage the pursuing Cyborgian frigate. Only one frigate had stayed the whole distance through their flight in hyper. Kroug's belly was an acid bowl digging his heart.

He looked at the system configuration over for some advantage in the lay of gravity wells, the flow of magnetospheres, the radiation spikes. An Oort cloud lay on the periphery, no help there, too far out. A second gas giant hung close to the star- too far in.

The ringed gas giant had a smattering of moons. There were two near-Earth sized planets inward, but they were on the far side of the star now. It was a clear battle then, in the pit of the gravity well of the ringed gas giant. Ion drives again, gravity manipulators and repeller fields. If the freighter and the liner made it down to the world, they'd be harder to find; there were a lot of heavy metals on the planet that could mix up in the scans.

A lot depended on where the Cyborgians dropped out of hyperspace. If one weren't able to hide the civilians on the wrong side of a world, they would be sitting ducks. The freighter captain's name was Zola Mosey. He'd proved level headed so far. Izzo had shown an exceptional flying ability. Perhaps keeping them aloft, and moving, could distract the Cyborgians into an error.

Kroug stared hard into his instruments. He had to make the call now-send them all down or keep the high and moving. Everyone was awaiting his lead. He strangled indecision. "Zola, this is Kroug."

"Got yah."

"Izzo?"

"I'm here."

"Everybody's rad shields up to snuff?" The rings of the gas giant loomed huge before the convoy.

The pilots checked their systems and all reported well.

"We're going to use the rings. I want the two civilian vessels to take orbits on the inside of the rings at the equatorial region. There are two moons relatively close at the sunward side right now. Lay in those regions. When you see us engage the CC frigate, move up or under the rings-whichever places you opposite their line of fire.

Fly evasive patterns keeping the ring between you and the frigate. Then break for a tight polar orbit opposite the engagement and hold dive patterns into the upper atmosphere of the gas giant."

It was a rough maneuver. There was a lot of debris inherent in the rings. Yet it took advantage of the gravity, cover, and magnetic forces. Kroug felt his neurons aching with the strain of continued merging with his fighter's sensory system. The grime on his body felt like an alien slime mold. His feet were swollen and filthy in their boots-not from walking of course, but there was an imbalance in his nutrient stream and it was pushing him to a rapid diabetic reaction.

There was nothing to do, however, but fly on.

The Cyborgians fell out of hyper on the far side of the sun. They came up over its north pole in a daring frenzy firing matter cannon and disruptor beams all at once. They rode the edge of their fire plowing through stellar flares bigger than planets.

The dogfighters engaged, plunging into the line of fire and sweeping above and below it on three vectors. One fell back and around swinging a deep spline path beneath the frigate and hammering it with gravity bombs. The frigate shields took the beating with a purple sparkling flashing of light but held. Kroug could see they had stasis shield defenses blackening around their hull. He had never seen stasis shields flash up and off so quickly. There must have been upgrades.

They had to lure the frigate away from the gas giant. The gravity bombs continued to harass the ship's vectors yet it returned fire with an even, mechanical discipline that only welded Cyborg Transhumans could manage. Kroug and the other dogfighters rode their shields purple frenzy with a screaming, biting pain of overstretched neuron connections. Each second was their last, yet they remained, amazingly, fighting on.

His dogfighter made a spinning corkscrew maneuver. Suddenly there was a sensation like a wet hand sliding over the back of his head in his helmet. He shook hard to break it off.

Something had edged into Kroug's mind; *a hairy spider, hungry to snap his spine*. It crept over his consciousness, transparent through the headlong rush of the dogfighter like a low battery holo.

He was keenly aware that its curiosity sought something else-something that would nuke whole systems of innocent civilians. The spider shadow-being rolled what might be its face over his, and Kroug felt he was looking into a well of deep time, into the primordial soul of energies forged at the reverse side of the event horizon of a black hole. Revolted by the essence of the thing, it appeared to be the squirming collection of a billion souls of vermin, he forced himself to look at it straight on, to prepare a death scream of rage and resistance as it crushed him.

Then it was gone, and he realized he had narrowly escaped a fate far worse than anything the Cyborgians could send him to with their energy weapons.

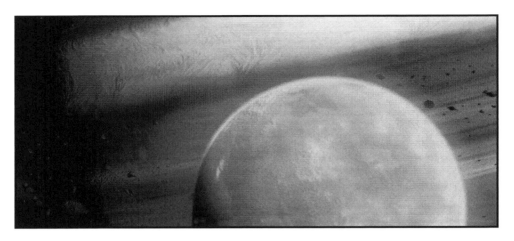

There was screaming over the cast channels then, a god-awful screaming that he would remember until his dying day, not believing what he witnessed, he watched the Cyborgian frigate go into a deep stasis and plunge toward the planet below.

The other Dog Pilots laughed with a sudden burst of triumph. "Did you see that?" One was saying over and over again.

"Did you see that?"

"Straight down!" yelled from another.

They hadn't felt the spider-like Kroug had. Something had forced the Cyborgians down, something dark and ugly. However, it had not done it to save the day for the Arcturians. It was simply assessing another evil, sizing up the competition. Watching the Cyborgian frigate missile down to a huge cloud bank in the black sheen of a stasis shield, Kroug wondered what fate the frigate had. Stasised as it was, it could pommel into the geography and remain buried there for the life of the planet, eon after eon. The Cyborgian crew in a frozen scream at whatever terror had jarred them into insensibility.

His dogfighter pilots were still celebrating over their coms.

"Yeah boys, I saw it. Now let's get these civies downworld so they can start making camp. It might be a long time before we get relief, a long time." Shock and exhaustion stretched his voice to a rasping groan. The hairs on the back of his neck stood up, but there were no more signs of the spider. It didn't like the smell of him then.

He guided the tired refugees down to the planet.

Re-entry was a tedious matter with the field manipulators having worn down for Izzo. Fortunately, the Lockheed Martin maintained the standard aerodynamics of a plane and she rode down with the loss of her fully field manipulators with a steadfast gliding style. It occurred to Izzo as he rode in that he was probably making the last flight of his life. There weren't going to be space line companies where he was going. He took her down with a melancholy half-smile, glad to get his passengers downworld alive, already nostalgic for worlds gone away.

Cooper watched the landscape turn from a mass of mottled colors to an inland sea, "Just like a Hercules Transport."

Cooper laughed. "Airborne daddy gonna take a trip?"

He water ported the liner in a swamp full of dwarf fern trees. The air was breathable, a little thin. The civilians took emergency rafts to shore. Later they managed to get the liner up onto a hammock of scrub and trees. People were glad for water to wash in. They looked at the lonely strange world with both fear and hope. It was, at least, a world again.

Cooper ran his hands over his head; "I christen this camp Hercules" he said and winked at Izzo. One of the passenger's kids ran by, "Camp Herky!" His mother trailed behind, "Marky!"

The shadow of death and loss-unimaginable in its scope hung over the survivors like an unspeakable monster. Yet the exigencies of living pressed them. They were full of the business now of maintaining their existence. The Arcturian Colonies were gone. The efforts and struggles, triumphs and generations of establishing new worlds, wasted.

They were but a remnant of a great people, scrambling among wetlands now on an unknown world facing a future they had never imagined. They had no frame of reference for such loss nor such a challenge.

From Troy through an encyclopedia of Diasporas, the Sagittarius Arm of the Milky Way galaxy was now being flooded with countless such ships.

Zola Mosey brought his freighter, Superior Venture, down and water ported. He took an air bike over to the crowd of people and building fires near the liner, circling twice before he spotted Izzo and Cooper. He brought the bike down with a flourish. "Hey!"

"What's the word?" Cooper smiled.

Mosey strode over with a rolling gait and a grin. "The word is "ALIVE," and you better be glad for that because it's become a rare state of being in this Spiral Arm of late. Which one of you guys is the mighty Izzo?"

"That would be me. Who is asking?" Izzo returned the grin good-naturedly.

"I want to shake your hand, Bucko! That was some pretty sweet aeronautical gymnastics up there."

Izzo reddened, shook his hand, "Couldn't have done it without Coop" he offered.

Cooper laughed and looked away, "Yeah, you could" and tipped his hat back. Zola looked around, "Kroug?"

"Flying recon," Izzo replied. "He says the planet is crawling with life. It was a good call to press the distance. There were a couple of other worlds listed as refuges, but he wanted to put as much distance between us and the Empire as possible."

"That he did." Zola chuckled. His smile, like the others, was forced-pure courage. His eyes betrayed the knowledge of what they would now face; the rebuilding of civilization against all odds.

"This planet had the highest carrying capacity. I figured if we needed to make a new start we'd have a fighting chance here."

Zola nodded, "Life is good. Better than non-life. But let me tell you something, I got a proposition for you. How would you like to have a bonafide Earth livestock to raise?"

"You got cows in that freighter?" Cooper eyed the vessel sizing up the cargo holds and wondered.

"No, I have sheep-sheep fetuses, to be precise, and the machinery to bring them to term. You can birth the little lambs and raise them here. Their original destination is no longer receiving shipment if you know what I mean."

"I gather" Izzo frowned. "But what have we got to trade for them? You want to scavenge the liner?"

"That won't be necessary," he waved dismissively at the suggestion. "I'll take those," he pointed to their caps, "and twenty percent of the livestock's wool and trade earnings upon returning to this world."

Izzo tossed him the cap. "Sounds like a deal."

"Ad infinitum." Mosey finished.

Cooper's eyes widened, "Twenty percent? Forever?"

"That's my deal. I give you the sheep fetuses and birthing equipment, I and my outfit own twenty percent of the herd and its product-forever."

Cooper tossed him the cap. "Guess it will be keeping him coming back, Captain."

Mosey adjusted the cap. "Makes me look official, doesn't it?"

Coop and Izzo looked at each other. "Official what?" Izzo asked.

Mosey lowered the brim a hair, "Yours isn't the only refugee convoy running this Spiral arm, gents. There must be ten thousand convoys. Been getting coded SOS signals off the casts. There are a lot of survivors scrambling around out there. They're going to need traders, and they're going to need a sense of things being official."

Izzo shrugged, "Well, then, it's official. So says the Trade Guild hat with the Mercury insignia."

Cooper looked at the silver emblem emblazing the cap Mosey now flourished, "Mercury? Is that who the little guy on the cap is?"

Izzo looked at him, "You been flying for the airline all this time and you didn't know the emblem was Mercury?"

"Just an emblem." Cooper countered.

Mosey eyed the second cap, "Messenger of the gods!"

Izzo beamed, "God of merchants and travelers!"

Cooper snickered, "and thieves."

Mosey frowned; "Now you wouldn't be implying I've pressed my advantage unfairly would you?"

Cooper shook his head, "Perish the thought."

Zola Mosey climbed onto the air bike and powered it up. "Perish the thought?" he roared, "Cherish that thought! I'll see you with the sheep fetuses in the morning." He reached into the bike's saddlebags and pulled out a bottle, tossed it to Cooper. A bottle of Crown Royal. "Night gentlemen, nice trading with you." The air bike bolted toward his ship.

Dylan and Tunis helped build the first fires on the first night of a new history. "Good, Tunis," Dylan said as the flames started rising, "Got any ideas for business?"

Tunis smiled. "Necessity is the mother of invention. There will be an opportunity. You just keep your eyes open. You'll see." He popped open a briefcase he had brought from the ship. Inside was a lunch container, he unsealed it.

"Your last civilized meal for the duration?" Dylan asked lightly.

"More than that, Buddy. Mushrooms!" Tunis replied and held them up. They were not cooked. It was not lunch, it was contraband.

"You're kidding me, right? Feninger Transportation was smuggling?"

Tunis winked. "Smuggling is such an ugly word. Transportation so much more professional, no?"

Dylan looked at the mushrooms with a devilish grin, "How did you get them through customs?"

Tunis brightened. "Technically they're not illegal in the colonies. These aren't psychedelics. They're just an ordinary species of edible mushrooms. They do have one property that affects the human mind, however.

"They thwart the ability of the Imperial Hive mind to send feedback loops to citizens in the Empire. Eat these as a regular part of your diet and dear old big-brother Hive Mind isn't able to get its compulsions through to your neo-cortex."

"Bet they're illegal in the Empire," Dylan said softly.

Tunis nodded. "Yes indeed, and worth a great deal. Many people, even in the Empire, aren't too keen on feedback from the grid sending them their worldview in digital signals every sixty seconds. MOST people seem to like being told what to do and think in that Byzantine mess. But not everyone. Not everyone."

Tunis snatched a handful of the mushrooms and tossed them at the base of a fern tree. "Our new world's first cash crop" he winked.

Dylan screwed up his face. "That wouldn't go over big with a planetary ecologist. You just contaminated the whole planet with an alien biological agent."

"Now you're sounding like a Nanny State Imperial Transhuman! Every breath you take contaminating this world, and vice versa. Some of these passengers aren't going to be around in six months. Their immune systems won't be able to deal with the foreign microbes. You're familiar with panspermia? Why is it that when blind forces of asteroids blast organics across worlds it's perfectly acceptable but when humans do it the Transhumans get their panties in a bunch? When a bird defecates a seed from one continent to another it's all wonderful and blesses the cosmos, but when a human farmer does the same it's interference with the natural order?

"We are the natural order. Do you think the planetary ecologists of the Empire will raise a hand in objection to the worlds the Transhumans just fried? They might do a study in five hundred years once the rads calm down. The Trannies, they just want CONTROL. Plain and simple. These mushrooms interfere with that, and I like it."

Dylan raised his eyebrows. "Well, you might want to see what that freighter pilot will give you for some, and let him know you'll be raising your cash crop before he takes that freighter back up. Might give him the inclination to come back once in a while and that would probably be a good thing."

Dylan's studied urbanity vanished of a sudden, and he looked for a moment the classic naughty boy. He gave a Tunis a rakish grin. "I just remembered something."

"I figured that, what?"

"My school project, the nanobots. They're still crunching through New Procyon system's Oort cloud making settlement caches."

"Ha! So maybe when the Imperials get around to that study in five hundred years they'll arrive at a completely reorganized and articulated Oort cloud."

Vina assisted the passengers until exhaustion collapsed her and she fell into a well-deserved sleep. Iyana sat talking with one of the fighter pilots who had returned from reconnaissance flights. His name was Blake Nappa. He said the dogfighters were as taxed as the starliner, but they were powered differently and could remain aloft for greater periods. The liner had been intended for frequent reworking and refueling. The dogfighters were more than they first appeared. They were capable of staying up for greater periods than one would imagine from the virtual reality dramas.

"Why haven't they sent more ships? Finished us off?" She asked.

Nappa was a muscular man with a sculpted face. His jaw protruded like a wedge. Hit me if you dare. He grunted, "A better question would be why they bothered pursuing us in the first place.

"This attack on our civilization is going to alienate the rest of the human race from the Imperials-permanently. That was bad enough. Hunting down stragglers, well that will seal them as villains for millennia. If they think they've secured their power, they're grossly out of touch with the true aspects of what power is, and how it is wielded. "

"What do you mean?"

"I mean the other civilizations-the Pleiades Confederation, Paramon, The Caldris League, and the Core Marauder cults-there must be a thousand systems claiming sovereignty in one form or another.

"They're going to do everything they can to avoid Imperial entanglements. Trade, alliances, technological and artistic exchange, all the things that oil the gears of human progress will slow to a crawl. This is going to halt humanity in its tracks. My guess is the Transhuman Overlords got spooked at the Arcturian society's vigor and went way over the top. Probably crawl back into whatever hole they peeked out from and stay there."

"What do you think will happen to the passengers, to us?"

"Kroug is in command here now. If his authority can hold, some manner of an organization can be put in place. There are protocols in the manuals, but how long people will stick to them is anybody's guess. Anarchy would be the worst thing. More refugees will be wandering in over time, then maybe wanderers from the rest of the galaxy. Outcasts and misfits at best-what reason would they have to come here?"

She considered his words with a fatality she hadn't known was in her. Then her resilience surfaced again. She brightened, "When I was a girl, my father took me to Caldris the water world. On the island chains, the cities and the factories spread out over the continental shelf for thousands of miles.

They have a chain of volcanoes that stretches from one pole to another, and around again. Continents forming. The reefs build up on everything. The towers protrude from the shallows and the reefs build up around their base. We took and air truck over one of the reefs and floated there, fishing. Have you ever been fishing?"

He smiled. "Actually, no. I never have."

"Good!" She lowered her gaze conspiratorially, "Tomorrow I will scrounge through the ship until we can acquire something to contrive a line and hooks and I will teach you to fish."

"And I will eat for a lifetime as the saying goes, Iyana?"

She raised her chin regally, "Yes!" and laughed.

The rings of the planet's Jovian companion were rising and the members of the crew still awake watched with murmurs of wonder as the golden crescent grew on the horizon reflecting brilliantly over the waters. It was like a giant gilded rainbow. It occurred to Iyana, as she finally dozed off to sleep, that she was no longer employed with the airline.

Shartharandayaga the bone crusher spun hard, curling back into the higher dimensions. Dark matter and great gravity forces plumed, spewing. She rolled her proboscis, folded the alien souls and energies rippling like sine waves oscillating, coiling them into forces like deep Plutonian bat wings. Below her, the lower dimensions flickered and wavered with the recently finished warring of the new prey species. These lower dimension primates were a good find-intricate minds full of fears. Their brains provided the drug her kind lusted for; dark fears repressed, hologram-like in the deep recesses of their mind. Unknown even to primates, for the repressing they did to protect themselves, those fears could be found and then, shown to them in their entirety all at once.

Their reaction, like most prey species, was an amplification of electric energies-fear-that Shartharandayaga's kind reveled in with an ecstasy of vicious hatred.

Suddenly another of her kind approached her; a dark hurricane. "This prey species has such delicious fears," she croaked fiercely. Bathshardurangayaga glowed and growled in a cascading curl of angst-filled lust.

Spiraling fractals burst along lines of force from Shartharandayaga's mind, a wailing roar from the tortured quantum echo of the millions beings she hoarded in her fetid bellies. Emanations from creatures whose souls she had tortured across countless worlds in the eons of her hunts. They were the mirror shadows of elemental electrical energies and patterns plucked from the lower dimensions, still conscious, still suffering eon after endless eon. Shartharandayaga and her kind consisted of the accumulation of such energies. Energies compiled in blood lust elaborated in torture and gathered in an ugly, dark pride.

Shane Perry

Deneb IV

David Omm stepped out of his small transport as had it ascended casually from the Deneb IV Gateway, down to the Capitol world of Cyborgian Central. He thought on a News channel and information came flooding his mind in a confusing maelstrom of data. *There had been a war!*

Crowds were roaring in plazas below him-cheering him as a brilliant tactician. He felt a sudden swell of pride feedback from the Hive Mind and the desire to wave (his hand found itself raised in a victory signal to the crowd and he beamed with a flush of joy at the victory he still did not quite comprehend). The feedback loops were hitting him hard with emotion, a part of him realized with a bit of concern. Unusual for someone of his rank to be under such strong compulsion

Figures approached him and walked him off the platform in a splendid promenading walk to a victory celebration. Of course, the peace treaty was a ruse before the attack. He wasn't allowed to know because there had to be no way for the Arcturian Intelligence officers to detect him lying. He thought: *Billions have died and I was the instrument of their being deceived. Lisa tried to warn me, but she didn't know what was planned.* Somewhere inside him, beyond even the controls and compulsions of the hive mind, he retched with an agony that knew no description. The cities and the faces he'd spoken with only a short time ago were wiped away irretrievably from all knowledge and existence but in his mind.

All those people. All those lives. Every face, every child, every place-gone. Gone. I am the last witness of the murder of a civilization.

Holograms of his Transhuman Overlord superiors, Lilith Cassas, and Lourdes Cassandra, stood at the end of a long hall. They were bedecked in full Imperial regalia and gowns. David was numb. They had anticipated his confusion and shock. Even now they were flooding his mind with rationalizations of the act from the hive mind.

43

It had to be done to save civilization. The organic wilds seemed peaceful enough on the surface, but their underlying nature was violence. Their birth rates were astronomical. They would have flooded the galaxy and soon outnumbered us.

"You know we couldn't tell you. They would have found you out. The organics cannot have a model such as the Arcturians were providing. The insanity of that unpredictable self-autonomy running rampant in the universe would sooner or later extinguish us under the sheer weight of its seductive vigor." Cassandra said.

David bowed his head, "Of course."

He felt for the news streams and realized much had been shut off from him. The entire Hive was not available for his reference. They were keeping the scale of this assault from him. They knew his profound personal charm would disarm the Arcturians and they used him as a blunt tool.

He looked at them, bewilderedly, "Couldn't you just have infiltrated their civilization? Encouraged them toward debauchery and licentiousness? Encouraged divorce on demand? In three generations they would have burned out their vigor and their birthrates would have plummeted? Instead of butchering them, you could have extinguished them with bad social policy."

Lourdes thought to him rather than spoke: his mind received reports of failed attempts at the very same infiltration. The Arcturians had not bought it. They had seen the collapse of Western civilization in the twenty-first century and wanted no part of supposedly liberating "sexual revolution" that culled their numbers and sent their young off pursuing wasted lives like lemmings obsessing over sex and tawdry affairs.

The clean genocide of social disruption had not worked. So the Imperials had opted for violent genocide as a last resort.

"David. For all we did, it was not a complete victory. Their new fleet was on maneuvers. They're still out there, somewhere, waiting."

David's eyes glared up at Cassandra with a newfound contempt. "For all that we failed?"

Lourdes's face drew a slack blackness. "Oh yes, we failed to exterminate them. Many have fled deep Out Space. Their fleet remains fresh, unmolested, and now probably more motivated than any force in human history. Yet that is not the worst of it. We encountered something new in the battle, something wholly unexpected."

David's anger at the deception cooled a bit seeing the situation was not completely to his deceivers liking.

"And what would that be?" he asked evenly.

Lourdes's dread now became palpable. "Something more horrible than you can imagine."

Billions murdered. A portion of humanity wiped away like so much bug grime on an air car's windshield. What could be more horrible than that? David stared into Lourdes's eyes with the courage of the damned. "Show me. Show me what you discovered while we slew the innocent."

"Yes, David, I intend to. Lest you become self-righteous over what we have used you to accomplish, lest you despise us now and side against us. Not that there would be any place you could go to. You surely will go down in history among the organics as "David the deceitful" or some such thing. I will show you what we found. One of our frigates encountered it in the heat of combat. It came upon them like a curious saber-toothed tiger hearing two monkeys fighting over a melon in the forest.

"Play it for him." She said icily.

From the hive mind came the record of the frigates last transmission pursuing flight 1079 out of New Galen. David heard the CCCE Empires wailing on board the vessel, felt like one of the crew. Then he sensed the presence of something else, something very wrong. David's mind fell back away from the transmission record, reeling in an indescribable horror. His scream echoed along the vast corridor and he fell weeping to the floor.

Lourdes looked in pity at her underling. "Yes, David. Welcome Mr. Omm, to Gehenna." She waved some droids over.

"Take him to rest. When he recovers from the shock of it, bring him to me. We'll need him to help us fight it if we can."

Lourdes watched as they dragged the blubbering mass of David Omm off to rest and to regain his wits. "If we can." She said, "If we can."

Lourdes snapped with urgency, "What of his girlfriend Lisa Sulla, the spy?" She felt the information streaming through the Hive-"Delicious, they've captured her as she fled. Convict her for spying" she closed her eyes and felt through the Hive, "Oh, no, no--she had acquired Imperial Citizenship, delightful. Prosecute her for treason. Her sentence will be full immersion in Cyberspace. Full suppression of her personality and the assumption of an impressed persona on her sentience. That would be justice since she likes to play-act at being someone she's not. Teach these organics a lesson. David is one of ours. What was he thinking, this creature?"

Lourdes shrugged. She ran through some of the records of David and Lisa, standard romantic stuff. "Well, she was an Art dealer and he's always been fond of the Arts"

"Favors the Roman period doesn't he? Well, make her a Roman Patrician-a male, ha! Perfect. Someone who objected to the Empire as she has."

"Senator Cicero. They cut off his head and his hands because he was so eloquent expressing anti-imperial sentiments with them."

Lourdes smiled fiercely, "When he awakes to plant the autosuggestion and compulsion in him to do the same to her in Cyberspace. Her tortures and pains for this betrayal of Empire shall be legendary!" Somewhere, deep in the past, another part of Lourdes had made too many hard decisions; too many compromises in too many battles.

Epilogue to the Arcturian War:

Thus begins the Dark Age, The Age of Pandora:
In a fireball, in a firefight, in dark flight, and terror.
New Galen Before the fireballs, before the maelstrom; Among the Arcturian Republic's;
small scattered worlds of peace, independent and free: Feininger Down, Filla's World, Delauna, Pirch, Galeen City Sprawl, Big Oort Station.
Here the noble towered cities gilded Baroque flourishes glimmer one last time night side, seconds before the fireballs; Two lovers call attention to the stars from Softpark lake (their last words),
A lonely driver feels the shake of his load across New Orion desert's famed maglev highway; he misses his children, only one of which will survive the morning (a biology student classifying bacterium in an Oort cloud, later he'll stand glaring at the unnamed ranges of a frozen world and make a decision that will found a people).
Past the streets and the parks, past the shops and the maglev rails, the canals and the farms-one could spend a lifetime cataloging the ten seconds before the fireballs.
I stand in the New Orion desert and wonder at the ruins of the maglev still stretching away to a city where no one has spoken for a thousand years. Dreaming dreams and sharing moments with the dead as they had lived just yesterday it seems, alive before...
-"Before the fireballs." -Princess Clairissa Maggio, Caldris

45

The refugees of Flight 107-9 named their new world Rip, in honor of the liner that had seen them to their world, The Rip Van Winkle.

For some years thereafter they scrambled about finding food, creating makeshift shelters and discovering unpleasant predators and diseases-of which, fortunately, there were few. In the fifth year (old solar standard year) they weathered their first winter.

Fortunately, the emergency navigational tapes in the starliner had included the information beforehand and they had time to prepare. If not the winter would have surely killed them all. As it was, two decades after their first planetfall a good ten percent of the original group had died. Those had been mostly older individuals dependent on medication no longer available. Mosey returned regularly on his circuit of various worlds, often with more refugees who had the misfortune of landing on less hospitable worlds. They had the sheep fetuses from the freighter which they brought to term and began farming.

A large primitive native animal proved suitable for domestication. Their resemblance to old Earth mammoths earned them the name "mamonths". It was suggested there was more to the combining of the words mammon and mammoth than a mere colloquialism, but in a generation or two such details were lost in a swarm of such imperfect recollections. Yet sometimes, watching the animals who had once been entirely born wild and free laboring at the hands of taskmasters (for money) it wasn't a far leap before one realized in a sense, we too are the mamonths toiling for mammon.

They assembled a great team of mamonths and dragged starliner to higher ground. There, a few crude stone shelters were contrived, articulated, and enhanced. Dylan, unable to pursue his dreams of designing O'Neil stations and supermassive space habitats between the worlds, found his knowledge of engineering still useful for the new community with the draining of Camp Hercules harbor. Herkiestown, as it came to be known, proved to be incessantly busy and exciting camp right from that first day the liner drifted down to the hammock by the inland sea.

The harbor grew into a complex of canals at the main wharf.

An increase in buildings came. With Mosey's new trade guild having been built into a network of ships, Herkiestown became one of their main ports of refuge for the tattered flotsam of humanity which still drifted outward from the war. The buildings spread, growing into a town and with time, an ornamental stone architecture developed.

It was the quintessential "Outworld". After the Arcturian systems were nuked, a large starliner, a couple of dogfighters, and a few transport ships battened down on a forest world. It was the same story all over "Out Space" (literally now the arc of the Sagittarius arm of the galaxy).

General Galipo's fleet, out of port on test runs during the time of the attack, mysteriously never materialized at any of the refugee settlements or the Gateways of the Cyborgian Empire. The mighty fleet, the dread of the Cyborgians, simply vanished as if it had never existed. Some said it never had, others said the Cyborgians must have stormed them, deep out space in an ambush somewhere. Others talked of ghost fleets seen at the edges of Neutron stars and dark nebulae.

That the planet which Izzo had brought his passengers to came to be called "Rip", a shortened version of Rip Van Winkle was not without an ironic touch of unpleasant association for the verb form, as those original Settlers had been "ripped" from the worlds and the lives they had known. They had joined the long list of peoples down through the ages who, having their lives torn apart by the vicissitudes of history, picked up whatever opportunity presented itself and marshaled on.

The refugees from Troy had founded the Etruscans, the Moguls an empire from a routed battle, Cubans a virtual capitol of Latin America at Miami, and Fischer Shea a cosmos of paradises in the Pleiades after the extortion heaped upon him by the Marchand Hayes affair.

Betrayed, starving, alone; middle-aged bankers and college kids stared at worlds they did not make, and so began the slow and tedious work of wrestling from the worlds a way to move forward.

Children were torn from ordinary family life and suddenly beset with Herculean tasks. Artists and construction workers, teachers and clerks, waiters and soldiers-all cast into strange scenarios where they were to begin again under the most daunting of circumstances. It was their defining moment when robbed of their birthrights and dispossessed of their homes; they found they were a right unto themselves and not the confine of a particular space. Their home but anywhere their feet would set. They became as platinum in their dogged will to survive.

Long-distance hunting camps, havens during winter, grew into second and third towns. Likewise, fishing camps grew into ports and towns with names. A generation had grown up that experienced nothing of space travel and interstellar civilization save the rare visits of Mosey's new Mercury hat Trade Guild. Faint paths grew into roads with Mamonths pulling wagons.

Water ships plied the endless lakes and inland seas covering the planet. Combinations of sail and steam were recreated. In 50 years Mosey's Trade Guild was plying among the Sagittarius arm of the galaxy where a plethora of refugee settlements had grown up into bustling communities. Stories had long been passed around "Rip" of the "hyper Bogies" that had spooked the Cyborgians away. The Guild traders confirmed there were similar stories elsewhere. The Cyborgians had retreated after the war and remained inside their Gateways. No further appearance of the "hyperBogies", outside of drunken spacers winded up in old dives occurred and the Bogies fell into space lore along with the planet of gold and the energy beings of pure pleasure.

On Mosey's last visit to Rip, Dylan went off-world with him and it was heard he was finally able to design a habitat for one of the struggling space colonies-a masterpiece it was said-and then no more was heard. No one had ever gone back to New Procyon system where perhaps, it was said his nanobots had transformed an entire Oort cloud.

The traders fostered a search for minerals that were duly found, and a mining rush engendered more settlements in the hills and gullies. By the second century, there were settlements on every continent of Rip, many of them productive mining cities. The traders brought livestock, enhanced genetic fish to stock the seas and increase their output, and life had settled into a primitive industrial level, not unlike early nineteenth century Earth.

Steam Dirigibles and steam trains were not uncommon.

The trading guildsman let some technology pass into the outer worlds- but it remained just enough to keep them buying, but not enough to let them start producing. There was little worry on that point however, as the outer worlds lacked the tools to make the tools to make the technology.

Economies of scale also prevented them even trying-what would take untold fortunes to research, tool up, and produce on their worlds was already being made in mass quantities elsewhere.

The Outworlds, however, offered little that was wanted in the other more advanced societies, and somehow a strange equilibrium evolved. There was little back and forth between the Sagittarius Spiral Arm and the Orion Spiral Arm, save one irony of history that Mosey's Guild grew for a thousand years until it had weaved itself into every corner of human space.

For centuries, the worlds spun around and things remained much the same. After the war, a mysterious group of Marauders came snapping at the galaxy from the galactic core. Originally, a small colony Scientists they became "core cultists", they had mutated. No one knew how or why. Renegades and sheer madmen, they were driven by a bizarre religion they'd dreamed up from relics found of a pre-human civilization that had flourished and faltered eons before the dinosaurs appeared on Earth known across space merely as the "Predecessors".

Disorganized, and schizophrenic, the Marauders were never much more than a nuisance. But the relics they'd discovered proved a boon to technological innovation when they could be understood. Occasionally a new weapons system was developed from them, and the Republics around the Cyborgian Empire (those between the Transhuman Cyborgians and the Sagittarius Spiral Arm of the Galaxy) would shake, rattle, and roll with wars.

The Galactic core settlements, once a ribald series of boomtowns, fell into a strange lawlessness as the remaining Human vied with the Marauders for control.

Boundaries would be reset, the new technology would become common, and the Transhuman Cyborgians, ever untouched and untouchable, would remain their strange, enigmatic selves.

In time even the "Predecessor" technology proved unable to change the basic political, economic, and scientific realities of life for humanity in the galaxy. Slow and steady, life carried on ever the same.

*It would be one of Dylan Halen's descendants, a young smuggler by the name of Vince Phalen, however, who would set in motion a series of events to which an unlikely backwoods dreamer would eventually unravel the mystery of the Evil in the Sunrider which I had seen as a boy at Fort Oort. -**From "Between the Cyborgian Empire and the Core Marauders: A survey of the Outworlds"--Princess Clairissa Maggio, Caldris***

Book One: The Princess of Caldris

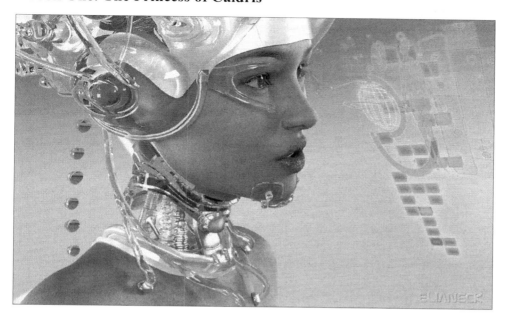

Clairissa Maggio, archaeological log. 3983, New Galen Ruins.

The Arcturian O'Neal station is a testament to that culture's space engineering. Fifty kilometers long, the station had been the largest settlement in the system and directed high energy farming from a solar panel array. The array, of some note in archaeological architectural circles for some time, remains still, in various conditions, a matrix of panels encompassing a full inner orbit of the star, its Herculean scale remains impressive; one more testament to the greatness of the ancients and that era. No modern array equals its size in any of the Republics and Kingdoms save Imperial CCCE of course.

Yet the O'Neal station was not the only find, and from here luck turns to legend; a Sunrider war frigate from the Arcturian War is lodged in the side. It is a timely find as well. The two-artifact menagerie's decaying orbit would reach a soft cloud corona sometime in the near future, and with the hull breach, caused by that long ago Sunrider impact, not even the hard shielded O'Neal Station could shelter the plethora of artifacts inside.

The Sunrider had careened into the hull of the O'Neal. The Sunrider's Stasis Shields had flashed on and off, moving through the O'Neal first like butter, then ragged ultra-steel against ragged ultra-steel. Back and forth, again and again, in a matter of seconds. The interlocked ultra-steel then held like a stinger, while the entire atmospherics on the interior of the O'Neal bled out furiously to space, rushing over the sleek black and silver lines of the frigate.

We're not sure why the other environmental habitat compartments in the O'Neal Station were breached, nor, at the end of the expedition, what was the predication of the welded CCCE Cyborg pilot's plunge into the station. Further examination will surely provide the answers. The breach safeguards should have preserved them. We have found no intact environmental compartments yet.

Conceivably, in a colony station of this size and sophistication, biome environment compartments could still contain living forests. Fauna and ecosystems thriving, unseen by human eyes for centuries, the life support still servicing away soft rains and light.

Now that would be all the stars in a jewel box, aye! Ha! My Archaeological Avarice is showing!

Kunisada has taken a strong dislike to the frigate, an almost obsessive aversion, even for a head of expedition security. "The greatest technologies of an era, mostly unmatched and forgotten," he said grimly with his thousand-yard stare, "all in the service of death. It feels like death still abides here." He said.

Great Space Ghost, what the technological systems on that Sunrider will be worth to the reverse engineering departments of numerous corporate interests..."

Steve Allman

I
Snakes in the Cradle.

My name is Winteroud Sole, and I am twelve standard Caldris years old. The name "Winteroud" was my father's idea, homage to my mother, who was not born on warm and wet Caldris, but on the faraway world of Erial, which is always cold, and mostly grey skies silver shot. He and my Mother met in college, at the University world, Lux, a world of giant arboriforms called forests, where the Neo-Wrightians, the great architects and environmentalists, had settled and built their famous Schools.

I have never been to Erial or Lux, but I have studied them both extensively on the hypercasts, and in the family computer libraries.

Today the Royal Security detectives came led by a giant, stoic man by the name of Odin Hammerstein, and questioned me at length. I could feel their eagerness to know all about me, for I am an empath and that is a very special gift. Mother was furious. Father was somewhat proud actually.

I think Officer Hammerstein is a good egg.

I could feel Officer Hammerstein was deeply troubled over many things. Desperation has formed in his mind, and he believes I may be able to help him sort out his most current sleuthing.

He is probably right, although I fear he doesn't understand that it may kill him if we untangle this particular mystery. Him and many others. In his mind, I perceived a layering, a mentality of his military background that sees everything as a war.

I have always been an empath. Caldris is known for producing an abnormal number of us. Some say it is the massive amount of heavy metals in the planet. Others say it is how the metals interact with the complex fields which stream into the higher dimensions. I don't know. I have always been this way and although my mind swarms with the impressions and feelings of others, I have not yet learned exactly what it means to be a human without empathic powers.

Eliane CK

My Educator at the Empath School says, "You will learn with time how they live their lives in solitary realities. There is sadness about them, alone in their thoughts. But not now. Not yet. Now when you feel their thoughts and emotions across a room it seems you are one with them. It is not so, Winteroud. You share their reality, and they are immune to yours," and so it often is.

Officer Hammerstein is very sad. That much I could tell right away. He is a man with a mission, as they say. His mission has hit a "platinum wall, me boy, a platinum wall with heavy-duty military defense shielding wrapped around an enigma." More accurately, I realized the machinations of very bad and powerful men who wish to keep the Officer on one side of the truth.

I think my mother knows best and rages against the dangers of my involvement in the Hammerstein case. Father is carried away with the pride of his son being treated by the Royal Security Detectives as someone important and worthwhile. Later, I know, he will pass through the sudden pride and begin to mull over dangers to the family and the estate.

We are an old family, long in the business of mining the volcanoes. Danger and opportunity our twin fellows for generations. He will see the danger soon enough.

It's Moonsweek and all four moons are purple in the evening skies. The tides are frothing at the ancient steps of the estate.

Each evening now I have sat on the sea steps and felt the minds of the balloon crabs eager for Silver-darters swarming in the shallows. Hunger and gluttony, simple creatures.

The silver darters have no minds at all. They have the most primitive of neural nets, their existence all stimulus and response. The universe to them is not even a place. Stimulus. Response. That is all. In their swarming, however, wonderful patterns emerge which can be thought of as a hive mind. Although such is a poor analogy; when one thinks of the great and terrible hive mind of the Imperials at far away Deneb IV, with all its billions of humans and millions of Transhumans, I embarrass myself with the analogy.

My android, Edward Gibbon, sits mechanical behind me, ever watchful. Father came around to fear as I knew he would and cautioned the android, "Watch for assassins," he said simply, grim and fingering his disruptor. It is an antique, like so many things at the estate. It was old when our ancestors first plunged onto the world in a fiery ship after crossing the void.

I felt Hammerstein and his men before the bells announced the arrival of the aircars this time. They came in the morning as the moons set and the sun, blue and gleaming, lifted itself with its intense glory among the cumulonimbus clouds, like Marshmallow Mountains in the sky. Six Royal aircars came like they owned the clouds, which in a sense they did.

Father stood defiant at the agents strolled coolly to the gate at the landing pads. "I've considered your offer for my son to work with you on the case, Officer Hammerstein. I think it's best he not."

I could feel Hammerstein's regret like a... *"Heavy-metal core drill"* ...he thought, disappointed that he would have to resort to intimidation. He was an old soldier, long used to obeying orders and giving them. Long-winded pleas were not his forte. I could sense in his memories that it wasn't his size that had earned him respect in his world of constant vigilance, but a personal history of being the first to strike and step into the fray, without long discussions. It was when the enemy began long-winded blustering that Odin Hammerstein liked to strike best, and strike first.

"I'm not at liberty to reveal the crisis surrounding the case, Sir Sole. It is pressing."

Father looked back unmoved. Miners of volcanoes and the heart of a world now for generations, the current scion of the Sole estate wanted to *understand before acting. Measure twice, dig once.*

Hammerstein, however, was an irrepressible force against my father's unmovable object of will. It was like watching the continental plates and their titanic, geologic forces.

"Your family charter, granted by Queen Artemis." Hammerstein said like a sucker punch, like a checkmate: "How many generations now?" Hammerstein said darkly. "A shame if it were withdrawn, having been such a long and fruitful benefit to you, and to yours."

Now, Father's eyes darkened, and blood rose, "You resort to extortion? There are other Empaths! Why does it need to be my only son? Off on a mission so dangerous, you come here in number with heavy-duty air-cars? Do you think I can't see the modifications on those things? Little battle cruisers, and off with the beardless boy you go?"

"We've tried other empaths. Older Empaths are too sensitive. One died, another is in intensive care. It is the boy's very limitations that will make him at once useful to the case, and yet not in danger of damage. Any older and he too would be of no utility.

This case moves into the direct security of our entire stellar system-this world, and all the others under the dominion of the Royal family."

I could feel Father was ready to hand the charter back rather than place me at risk. I could also feel a deep sense of loyalty to the Royals. For many generations, they had stood excellent in the good-government of the worlds under their care. "What is this case that you ask my child to involve himself with? Such that ruins the minds of older Empaths?"

Hammerstein's mind raced with anguish, his orders prevented him from explaining, so I answered for him, "The Princess has been taken."

Everyone at the gate exuded a sickening, palpable shock. My family for the revelation, the detectives that I knew. I tried to hide the wavefront of the pain their shock sent out. My eyes nearly blackened with shame and shock.

Vindication ran deep in Hammerstein now, "The boy is right, and now you see, indeed, his gift is true. I am the only one in this group that was aware of the Princess's abduction."

He glared at me, solemn-yet sympathetic. "Say no more about it, young man, of what you sense lest we are alone." Then, sharply, at his men: "A word from any of you and your rank is gone and you'll find yourselves transferred to the loneliest moon in the belt."

There came a clicking of heels. One of his younger officers, Tokushima, a woman of great beauty and self-discipline, ached with the shock and struggled with all her being to maintain her composure. Tokushima's family had worked long in the service of the Royal family, *security*. It was her brother, Kunisada, lithe and deadly and loyal, that had been the Princess's guard at the time of her disappearance. Tokushima was just realizing this now.

Quite grand, such discipline and depth of feeling. I will never forget her overwhelming pain at the loss of the Princess, and her stolid chin as she held back her tears, I think, as long as I live. Dedication. Devotion.

I determined then I should find the Princess, with Hammerstein, and root out the devils that did this. "Duty, father," I said, of a sudden. I stood, smaller than the fully grown adults, but somehow towering now in the minds of the detectives, "Duty and honor. For the Royal family, for our own."

"Duty and honor," father whispered back and I sensed one of the awkward moments in a parent's mind when the distinctness of their children's character shocks them somewhat how the children are in fact, other than them.

He scowled, proud and annoyed and worried all at once, "Fine, for the Maggios, and their long line of public service and good governance. But the boy takes his android, *and a disser.*"

He tossed me his disser and I caught it easily, knowing before he announced it and felt the generations of my forefathers (and a particularly self-possessed Grand Matron) land in my hands with it.

A half-smile curled up the side of Hammerstein's face, "But of course."

And I gathered with the Royal Security detectives and we took to the clouds in their aircars. The last of the moons had faded and the volcano littered Tangerine Sea glimmered beneath us. Thus began my first great adventure. I knew the ride across the Tangerine Sea well, straight to the Capitol, Cezanne Mons. The tangerine color is from the reefs, thousands of square kilometers of them. I understood the name was from an Earth fruit. I had seen them in a garden once, at the palaces in fact, where we were headed. I had never tasted one. I had eaten oranges though, and they too are an Earth fruit, similar it is said

Odin Hammerstein's angst impinged on my senses like his soapy smell. He had his aircars decked out with some serious weaponry. They were flying in military formation. I picked up bits and pieces of his memories of Navy days. Caldera Squadron, the edge of the system duty. Hard duty, the ships had gone into hyper then orbited the entire system. Over, and over and over again. No communications with command. Silent. Waiting.

Waiting, sometimes years at a clip. The day's we civilians took for granted, the days of our lives playing and working and growing and living-all guarded somewhere by the silent Caldera Squadron, men and women steady at their positions, silent as the grave and just as uncompromising, watching, always watching, that the ones they loved, back in the worlds, would remain free, and safe.

I sensed the man's patience was like a continental plate. Slow, persistent, and capable of volcanism when pressed. I also sensed he cared about what happened to me, didn't want me harmed, and was determined to watch my back even if it cost him his life. That was a good feeling, a rare one I was to learn. Few people are willing to die for their comrades. Hammerstein wouldn't have blinked. He was ready to make the ultimate sacrifice for his duty. *Anytime, anywhere.*

His thoughts that morning, however, were like a hover-tank in a moon battle; not about sacrificing his life for his King and Star System, but about finding the kidnappers and making *them* pay with theirs. It was the first time in my life I had sensed a wave of anger ready to take life. It was frightening. Mother and Father's minds had always been about the family estate. The most anger I had felt from them was when they were ready to fire an errant employee. Hammerstein wanted blood justice.

I hoped it wasn't clouding his judgment. Even my young mind could sense an array of people he suspected, all of them powerful across worlds, all of them deadly-even for a battle-hardened Navy veteran, even for a grisly old detective.

Centuries before, when the great Pleiades settler-developer Fischer Shea, and his colleagues, were confronted by the Imperials from Deneb IV who were demanding hegemony over the Pleiades, Shannon Maggio had been in command of few vessels, the first fledging Caldris Navy. Responding to the Imperials' questioning regarding when the Pleiades would come under the proposed "Trans-Galactic Trade Partnership", and submit to Imperial Authority, Shea had been on Hypercast across several systems live. He looked to his left, Rohr Maggio's eyebrows furrowed, to his right Oglethorpe DePaulo was smoking a cigar from his plantation on Electra VI, "Well, never."

Well, Never.

Never... "Never" had cast itself as a shot through the worlds of Humankind's settlements across the hyperstreams, Shea's handsome face delivering his words with a smile. Like the Imperials should be glad, and maybe, well, buy him a drink and dance.

The Imperials moved on Shannon Maggio's ships then. The Imperial Commander, a somewhat Chauvinistic Alpha-male genetically engineered for combat, had looked at Shannon with a wry superiority, "Come now, little lady. You're not trained for combat, surrender like a good girl and save us the bloody mess." Outnumbered, and with Caldris barely terraformed, the seas still broiling with the recency of the comet showers Shea had sent for them, Shannon Maggio's response to the Imperials was part of her historical collection of music (even then the Maggios historians). She broadcast, "Ladies Night" by *Kool and the Gang* from pre-space Earth over to the imperial commander.

Then she ordered the comet tugs, which were still hauling comets to seed oceans at Caldris, to launch the comets into his fleet. There wasn't much combat training useful when a thousand comets are suddenly banging your war fleet into a supermassive series of shockwaves, as the protective fields of the comet haulers were turned off and, well, I digress. The Imperials never intruded into the Pleiades again. Hammerstein, however, had grown up with that first victory tale from a boy. It was written on every corner of his soul as we moved to the palace.

Navy. Still, his heart and soul, even as he climbed the ladder in the Royal Detectives.

Our aircars moved in unison over the Tangerine Sea. The Detectives were silent, quiet as adults often get when lost in their thoughts. How quickly they forget a boy. A boy who can sense their thoughts even. Thus the quiet was only broken by the hum of our flying machines, but in my mind, their thoughts and feelings were a symphony-sometimes sublime, courageous, and determined. Sometimes dramatic, grim, and portentous.

When Cezanne Mons appeared in this distance, swathed in clouds and smoking that early morn, I felt my usual excitement at visiting the capitol. The city hugged the base of the huge volcano with the casual ease of a people who had learned to ride and manage volcanoes like the pack animals of some semi-primitive world.

The Legislature buildings stood biomorphic, with curving lines, a sweeping and expressionistic architecture. The Palace buildings, smaller and on a higher ridge, echoed the more formal and traditional symmetries of palaces back through the ages, before the dawn of the space ages. They could be any palace perhaps, such as on ancient Earth before mankind took to the planets beyond the world of our race's birth.

The rest of the city, private businesses and such, spread out along the shorelines in various combinations of towers and conglomerations of buildings. Haphazard, come as you are. Sometimes opulent, sometimes tawdry, sometimes respectable. Sometimes-even I knew at twelve standard years-sometimes very naughty.

People, they create new generations, out among the stars, genetic copies of themselves, and ever the same tawdry dramas replay. No wonder. The first families who settled the Pleiades Systems, who became the Royals, put everything they had into terraforming the various young worlds-and then defended them as well. Even in the long centuries since the great Arcturian war, as civilization has remained somewhat the same and the leaps of technologies of earlier eras have halted, the Pleiades are synonymous with good government.

The palace was not an indulgence; it was the love of the people made manifest. One only had to look at the state of many other systems to see why.

The Detective's aircar's windshields were graced with special displays-many of which not visible to the ordinary aircar mind you-and I could see the force field domes over the palace. The general public is not privy to such things.

"Odin Hammerstein, six cars. Royal Security. Arriving with Empath to review crime scene."

We hovered for a moment and holes appeared in the force domes. I could sense the hidden guns in various parapets of the palace engaging on us. They trusted naught. I hadn't noticed them on visits to the palace before, field trips with my teacher. Mr. Gibbon sat mechanically and glistening behind me, "Such a disappointment to finally get back to the Palace, and have it be under these dire circumstances!" he whispered to me, and I nodded.

My father's disser stuck out of a pocket on my vest like an old Earth cowman. This was no frontier shack, however. The Royal Palace at Cezanne Mons was storied and fabulous and built with the finest refined metals mined from the very volcano poised behind it. Platinum mostly.

Some said it backed the currency. I felt that was hyperbole.

We followed a flight path illustrated in a hologram on the windshields. Hammerstein was looking grimmer than ever. I sensed he was hoping against hope the Royal family would be away today, and he would not have to look into their eyes having no news for them, but another Empath and a boy at that.

I steeled my resolve.

We traversed the holes in the force domes and they resealed behind us. The tension I read from the gunners at the parapets remained high until all six of the aircars were down and we stepped into the courtyard.

55

It was full of tangerine trees, and I felt the echoes of many long evenings which others had spent there pleasantly. A good portent, I thought, but it didn't last. There was a shadow of dread hanging over the palace, and a few steps forward the tangerine dreams faded and sadness prevailed.

Caldris is, of course, a slightly higher gravity world than old Earth standard, and as such most Caldrisians are more muscular and shorter than say, a typical Earth person. Hammerstein, his fellows, and now the Palace Guards, however, I noted, were tall. Even for Earth and worlds of comparable gravity. The guard that approached us in the courtyard was exceptionally tall. He must have towered over the King and Queen.

Impressions assailed me; the guard didn't think much of Hammerstein and the Royal Security team in general. The guard felt it was their fault, to begin with, and their investigation was a bumbling farce.

Hammerstein's methods were circumspect however, so I rejected the guard's opinion as self-important judgmentalism by a person unqualified to assess Hammerstein's efforts.

"Agent Hammerstein." The guard said coolly.

Hammerstein bowed, "Captain Venkatesan." He turned to me then, "May I introduce Master Winteroud, heir of the Sole estate, certified empathic. He will review the scene with us, slowly, and in phases."

Captain Venkatesan's immediate emotion was a concern that I would be harmed. This surprised me. He didn't strike one as a soft-hearted man with maternal instincts toward young people. One of the things one learns as an empath early; people's exterior appearance is entirely meaningless more often than not than as a reflection of their deeper selves. Captain Venkatesan looked as cold an uncompromising as the business end of a disser. His essential nature was to protect the weaker around him.

"I don't like it, Hammerstein. Any harm comes to the boy and I'll have the Kings ear that you face negligent homicide charges."

Hammerstein had been expecting that. "I've conferred with the top planetary experts regarding Empaths. Firstly, the boy's sensitivity to the quantum echoes hasn't fully developed. Secondly, we move toward the scene slowly; the first sign of discomfort we withdraw him."

"On your authority then and with my stated reservations." The Captain's face was flushed, but he stepped aside and we moved through the gardens past a series of low, long fountains with holograms of sea creatures leaping. We came at length to a tall pointed-arched doorway to an exterior antechamber. A stainless steel door of immense size was carved with geometric triangular motifs and inlaid with mother of pearl and brilliant blue lapis lazuli.

"This is the Library and the Princess had been doing research-she was profoundly concerned that an aspect of the Arcturian Wars had completely been misunderstood by the public. She would return to the archaeological site soon after and then she was taken." I sensed things then. Doorways are like that, capturing the passing thoughts of people busy with tasks. This was the Royal libraries and private schools of the Royal children, and some of the more esteemed nobles, but there was something else.

I could sense the Princess, though I had never actually been close enough to sense her before. A muddled compilation of self-images came through-as she thought the world saw her, as she saw herself, and a grave concern regarding a task-she had been researching something... "The Arcturian Wars," I said aloud.

Hammerstein's female officer spoke then, "Brilliant!" At which Hammerstein felt obligated to introduce her at last, "Winteroud this is officer Tokushima."

I already knew that, of course. I bowed and wished I was older. I could sense she thought I was a "cute little boy", which was infuriating to no end. She was in the full flower of womanhood; every tiny corner of her body and soul was Epic Beauty. All I could do was wait, grow, and dream. I also sensed she was in love with Hammerstein, which was funny because he didn't have a clue and thought of her as far too young for him, and more or less a distraction with all her beauty moving through criminal investigations like a fine art piece at a demolition site.

"Maam," I said, which I immediately regretted.

"She was indeed researching the Arcturian Wars. Specifically, New Galen. Had even funded a small expedition there, a couple of bots," Hammerstein looked at Mr. Gibbon who had been dutifully following, "No offense."

"None taken." Gibbon lifted his chin.

"A couple of bots, nothing Major. Maybe a dozen in the team total. An analysis of the remains of shipbuilding facilities on an outer moon had her convinced the Arcturian Fleet was far smaller than the Transhuman Imperials at Deneb IV have long asserted. Much of her research, however, has been deleted from the Royal Archive." he said.

The doors opened and I felt the well of time like a vortex. I stepped back a moment and Captain Venkatesan held my shoulder. Hammerstein's chin went forward like a fist, he stepped in ahead of me like a prizefighter, like he would protect me from the quantum streams. He still didn't get it, I managed to muse with a smirk, that this wasn't something he could find and wrestle to the ground.

It was a vast circular room, many levels high. A multicolored skylight crowned its dome. In the center of the floor was a holomap of the galaxy. Built even before colonies had spread to the globular clusters. "Something dark, she found," I said. "A hatred and hunger!" I stepped back from the room.

"Away, boy!" Hammerstein snapped. "You rescue no Princess if your wits fail you."

So I retreated towards the fountains with their hologram sculptures, away from the geometric doors. Away from the room where the hologram of the galaxy glittered across the floor like a toy, *like a pond full of fish*, I thought strangely to myself.

Tokushima, for all her martial arts and weapons training, exuded nothing less than the same emotions my mother glowed with when I was sick or bruised. Men frame it in terms of "motherly love", but there is something fierce and feral in it for all of that. Men would do better to think of Artemis; the ancient Greeks had it right with that. If one seeks to understand humanity, go to the Age of Bronze.

Of course, even at twelve, I was compelled, in the presence of such a female archetype, to find my center; my archetype. Courage and duty and honor in the face of danger.

So I looked back toward the room. Toward the darkness that had eaten the Princess in her search for truth. Caution sometimes the better part of valor, I was slow in my probing. A great lie had been foisted upon mankind. The Princess had discovered pieces of it, revealed like a beast too large for its camouflage. A wicked talon here, a fang there.

"Hammerstein!" the captain of the guard snapped. "No more today! Get this child home or I will summon the King."

Hammerstein, for all his unbending determination of will, sought hard within himself to grasp and understand my weakness. Hammerstein would have walked into the dark, with not a thought to his comfort or safety. It is what he was. The warrior archetype; there was no retreat for him. It took him time, only moments really, too undue his lifetime of training and instinct to move into battle. When he was able to detach long enough, he pulled me away from the room. It seemed like an eternity. The detective's ethos, "death before dishonor", almost undid us both. There was a place and time for his code; *this was not that day*. He struggled with the concept of retreat, found it, and retreated for my sake.

We judge such men harshly, I think, in the realms of civility and safety. In their world, such pauses more often than not cost life rather than save it. We must give them that much; born fighting, it is not the charge into the fray that gives them pause, but the hesitation that garners an enemy time to reconnoiter.

I had learned enough that day. Firstly, the Princess had found evidence that the official histories of the Arcturian Wars were, in fact, incomplete, which alone put her at odds with great powers in the far away Imperia. Secondly, a darker secret lay even behind that; vile, inhuman, and something not even considered. I slept in Hammerstein's aircar, all the way back towards the Sole estate I was beyond tired, beyond rest, and reach. Only Mr. Gibbon's chromium assurances reached my consciousness, and with a joke at that. Gibbon's jokes were not very good. I remember forcing a smile and then fading.

We were high over the Tangerine Sea when I woke suddenly. Something was coming. Something bad. My impressions were of waspy things, cloaked things with bad intent. Dead things, then-no, not dead. Mechanical.

"Assassin bots," I said.

Hammerstein was like a well-oiled matter cannon. His attention snapped to his screen. "Defensive maneuvers, scan for cloaked bots."

The other Security aircars broke formation in a floral geometry, spiraling and splining in different directions. High energy defensive shielding was glimmering in the night, and I felt my seat come alive with emergency protocols; personal shielding. *This was not your grand papa's aircar.*

The world moved like a giant toy, first below us, then besides, then above; round and around Hammerstein dipped and dove. A gravity bubble saved us from hi-gee pulls in the dives. Over and over again he dodged, still unsure where the bots might be. The other Security aircars were doing the same.

The bots finally revealed themselves in a sudden and impossible volley of disser fire. Had I not warned the Security team, we would have surely been killed. As it was I could see cuts and slashes of heat ripping at the body of our aircar.

Sizzling, steaming. Wicked.

Firing, however, they revealed their positions, and now Hammerstein and his team paid back. The rapid click of modified guns sung like electronic dance music, a cool mechanical cursing, and vengeance served up cold.

Hammerstein's eyes gleamed and I sensed the thrill of a grown man in combat. Violent death winged about us with clockwork impunity such are bots-and there was no fear in him, only an even, amazing sense of "now' and "act" that precluded any of his life before or after.

Now. Act. Respond. Win. Survive.

Existence reduced to a sport, a contest, a ballet of destroying a menace. In the end, he and his team made short work of the bots. I had provided an unexpected ace in the hole for them; the warning they needed to act, to respond, to win-and they did what they were trained to do, flawlessly, *beautifully in fact.*

I knew then, at twelve standard Caldris years, something most civilized humans never truly understand; the place a warrior goes in combat, a timeless place where they are one with all their ancestors, outside the well of time-with all their descendants hanging in the balance.

Now. Act. Respond. Win. Survive.

"Hammerstein, this is Palace security. We've just recorded the attack and will have a CSI team on it stat!" a small holo-face spoke from Hammerstein's screen.

Suspicion ran dark and wild in Hammerstein's mind, "Sure, you do that. I'll have our unit expect the results as soon as they come in."

He wasn't counting on any of the information being helpful. Whoever had sent the bots were professionals. Their trails would be curled and Byzantine. He glanced at me and I sensed his gratitude and passing curiosity if maybe I could find something even the CSI team missed.

"Thanks, kid, you saved our-err, well…you know. Hope you had that disser ready, aye, Buck? Hit 'em back, hit 'em hard, and hit 'em hot."

I placed my small hand on the disser. "Yeah!" For I am a Sole, and we are from a long line of those who go first, into the unknown; beyond the charted worlds, to settle and build, and fight if need be. That was the first time in my life a warrior had acknowledged me. I held the moment clear and bright, the thick of the fight, glory. My ancestors were with me that day.

"Let's get the kid home, people. Tokushima, staff that estate with a platoon of combat duty guards with tech support. Police orders."

He held back a very ugly and profane expletive, for my sake. I chuckled a little. The ribald words people invent to snap back at the madness of the universe. In a way, they're an art form unto themselves.

Mother was furious when informed of the attack, of course. Father's growing pride in his son, his strange and inscrutable boy, well, it was something new and pleasant for me. No longer merely the child with "special needs" who couldn't fit into the ordinary world, I was instrumental in the search for the Princess. I had just preserved the lives of several Royal Detectives.

He had discovered something he hadn't sensed in me before, call it courage. I realized then too something I hadn't sensed in him before, his mind so full of business and tasks, errands, responsibilities as it were. How profoundly he valued this thing. Courage. The essential virtue on which all others depend.

I sensed then too how fragile that virtue-how years of it could be broken with a single moment of weakness, and how often it was so for otherwise brave and worthwhile people. Should that day ever come, should I succumb to fear and fail him, I hope he could find it within himself to forgive me.

For even at twelve I was not fool enough to think the courageous were always so. Fear and doubt; on the edge of our universe always, ready to pull us into shambling other-worlds of surreal nightmares. At the end of the day, we have no weapon but our courage, our faith. Woe the one that reaches such a state without a friend. Without a mighty Hammerstein ready to stand in the fire with you.

Mother had a few expletives of her own withheld when she saw the disser marks on the aircars.

I have no clue where Gibbon had gotten this bit of programming, but when we alighted from the aircars he surveyed the damage and amazingly, whistled. A long one too. Then he quipped, "Ayie, caramba!"

Tokushima gave him a look of surprise. "Okay!" she said, "I'll escort the boy to the kitchens?" she looked to my parents.

"Crab cakes." Father said, "He likes crab cakes."

I wore the disser in the kitchen while the Chef made the cakes. It made him uncomfortable, and I felt my first guilty pleasure of swaggering machismo. The Chef, an artist to his hypersensitive core, was thoroughly nonplussed.

"Dissers in my kitchen? Nyet!" He swatted at me with a spatula.

Tokushima leaned forward, "He saved us from assassins today." She said softly. "Nasty assassins. Probably from the Transhuman Imperials out of Deneb IV. Auto-bots with cloaking technology. Only he knew they were coming."

His eyes widened. "I see." He turned the crab cakes. "It is, after all, a stylish disser of great antiquity and value. Perhaps worthy of my kitchen after all."

I beamed; glory.

59

"Should they come again, please kill them cleanly, and do not mess up my kitchen," he added.

II
All the stars in a jewel box.

"Not the fountains and holograms of the palace and its parapets. No, not them.

Not the staid Royal Guard with pomp and ceremony deftly done, nay, not the silks and cashmere hauled through hyperspace by stalwart brave star trading guildsmen.

NO!

These are not my treasures.

Not elegant floating divans crafted in the minds of brilliant architects and engineers-nay, these are not the treasures as Princess of the realm I value most.

Nay, but the library and art gallery-there are my greatest treasures. Histories upon histories; all the songs of divas tragic and triumphant, the orchestras of countless kingdoms, the fire lit bongos of hardscrabble settlers in steaming jungles, their ships still warm from the hyper-streams, the gallant calls of doomed officers singing their final charge on lonely strange last stands. The collected tales connecting all of humanity across time, their moments of dash and beauty and even their ignominious wretchedness when all was lost and stand they still did.

These are my treasures. I never cross the threshold of the palace library without a moment's pause to wonder: what soul shall share their insights and brave fortitude against the fading of their light with me that day?

Creature comforts and possession? They are but a room at the Inn, at best, then gone with the fading of the light. Our stories as such, all that remains for us to forever whispering in the ears of our posterity, 'Shine, delight, and rise-you are what you do this day.'"

–Princess Clairissa Maggio, "All the stars a jewel box; come look." Caldris.

As fitting for a scholarly Princess, her name's roots went back to ancient Earth Latin. Clairissa meant "brilliant", and "Maggio" May, a month of Spring. Like the pure light of an impressionistic painting of flowering trees in the South of France, captured forever, her essays had been food to my young soul. I never told my father, or my mother, only Mr. Gibbon knew how eagerly I had awaited the posting of her journals. Now she was gone, my muse and light-absconded with by whatever short-sighted fools, or worse-scoundrels.

Hammerstein secured a small detail of agents around the Sole estate with combat droids. The palace put security satellites on alert and a station in geosynchronous orbit added another layer of surveillance. The estate secure, we gathered in my father's study. It was time for me to reveal what I had sensed in the palace library. Night had long since fallen. An eventful day, to say the least.

My father sat at his desk. Hammerstein and Tokushima took chairs on either side. I sat opposite them all. I could sense apprehension, eagerness, and dread. Beyond the large windows, volcanoes glowed in the distance; father and mother's massive company machinery working the lava.

I remembered the library and the impressions that had struck me. "Her research regarding the Arcturian wars had been all-consuming." I began, "I could feel her paths to and fro; her mind's echoes like a perfume lingering. Her first concern was, of course, the question of the war's justification which the official Cyborgian Central Command Economies-the Transhumans-had given for the first strike they had made upon the Arcturian Colonies."

Recognition filled their minds. Memories of school days and history lessons regarding those wars. The official justification had been the Arcturians building a fleet of their own with intentions of a massive attack against the Deneb IV. The Cyborgian Central Command Economies-CCCE had been mastering control of trade in the civilized portions of the galaxy through the building of interstellar gateways.

The Arcturians stopped granting star gateway rights along the Sagittarius Spiral Arm. Claiming the settlements in the Arm, their frontier, as Arcturian territory, CCCE would not be allowed to extend its tariffs and hegemony. So CCCE leapfrogged ahead into the Spiral Arm and began establishing "settlements" of their own. Gateways began construction. The Arcturians defied them, fighting broke out.

"The Arcturians had long established that CCCE in the Arm was not building legal settlements at all, which would have required settlers, but military outposts. Intergalactic law regarding settlements required civilian settlers."

Hammerstein's emotions shot across to me, a cynical, grim understanding that indeed the CCCE settlements were a farce. CCCE's command economies controlled all aspects of their citizen's lives from the cradle to the grave. In such a culture, frontiersmen could not be created. There were no clamoring masses yearning to breathe free. I smiled back. He understood.

Father looked apprehensively at the large windows. I felt he regretted their ostentatious openness now. He wished they were smaller. Menace lurked in his mind now at every large window. Would there be more cloaked assassin bots?

I sensed none. I continued, "The Galaxy had long taken the official CCCE justifications of the war with guarded cynicism. No one wanted to be next. Clairissa felt a real answer to the history that could be found among the ruins in the various Arcturian worlds. She requested the funding of some small archaeological expeditions and followed their research diligently."

I felt her excitement lingering at the palace. "Calculations of the ruined shipyards sizes and capacities didn't match the official story. She was growing convinced the attack was unjustified."

"Motive," Hammerstein interjected. "CCCE didn't want their history soiled."

Father's eyes darkened, "Motive enough to kidnap a Princess of a sovereign star system?" Hammerstein shrugged. "Perhaps."

"There is more," I said. "One of the expeditions had discovered a CCCE frigate."

"The invincible armada," Tokushima said bitterly. "This inexplicably, by the end of the war, was largely absent."

"Yes. The armada of Cyborg warriors which after the war was replaced with a new cast of non-hive mind warriors, the new Spartans of CCCE. The irony being that civilization-from their Transhuman ruling caste and the population of citizens more or less under the influence of the hive has long now been defended by a separate caste. Ordinary humans such as ourselves."

That strange combination and order now filled the room with perplexity. It was what it was, the CCCE Samurai defending an empire unlike themselves in every way. The galaxy's civilizations and worlds taking it, as a matter of fact, its oddness, however, striking all, far and near, as a queer sort of arrangement.

"And the ship the Princess's expedition discovered?" I asked aloud.

Now my eyes darkened for sure. "That is what I stepped back from. That is what killed your first empath and left the second in intensive care. The ship's logs possessed a recording. In the recording is evil."

"You mean something evil?" Tokushima corrected my phrase.

"No. I mean Evil. *Evil itself.*"

They all smiled apologetically at what they perceived as my hyperbole. "Evil is not a thing, Winteroud." My father said gently. It is an adjective, describing an action."

I remembered the impression that had assailed me. "No father, they had discovered Evil. As in a thing. A noun."

The discomfort continued among the adults. "Can you describe the nature of this Evil more?"

"When you pulled me back, Officer Hammerstein, so I could not sense more of it, you were wise. As you noted when you gave me this assignment, my empathic powers have not progressed to the sensitivity of an older empath. But it has progressed enough to know when something is dangerous."

I could feel his frustration. So close to more clues, so delicate the search.

"People describe predatory animals as evil. This is because of the destruction they wreak when humans accidentally fall prey to such things. However, I often feel the minds of such animals in zoological gardens or the wild. They are not evil. They are merely meat machines going about their business of preying. They have no hatred of their prey, merely hunger. Sometimes a thrill of a hunt. No malice, no diabolical viciousness."

"And you felt that…there?" Tokushima asked with an impending sense of dread.

"Yes."

"Where did it come from?" from Father, sharply. Hammerstein gave a cold thousand-yard stare.

I looked at him directly, "Officer Hammerstein knows, in more detail than I can sense from a threshold darkly." I said. "Princess Clairissa."

"Her archaeological expedition," Hammerstein answered with steeled emotion. "…at the ruins of an Arcturian Neely station, which was in a decaying orbit around a red giant star."

That was the first time I had heard anyone use the expression "Neely" to describe an O'Neal station. I knew what he meant though, a very long cylinder with high-grade environments on the inside. An Arcturian O'Neal station would have been a thousand years old.

"An attack frigate from the CCCE Armada had crashed into the Neely," he said.

"Kamikaze?" Farther hissed.

Hammerstein's bottom lip rose stoutly, "Valid question, but no. There's evidence it was a combat accident. However, the archaeologists opened two files on the ship. A black box log and a transmission the ship had received.

"A Sunrider 3000 attack ship." I suddenly knew. Hammerstein's jaw tightened. "Yes. Then the expedition went dark. Whatever was on that transmission completely disorganized the neural nets of the entire Cyborgian CCCE crew. And when the archaeologists opened the file, a millennium later, it did it to them too. Strangely, it seems the file was sent from the archaeological site to the hypercaster at the palace by automated systems."

He let the implications run through my mind a moment before he continued.

"*It sent itself,*" I said, and let him consider the implication; a sentient program.

"Why didn't it hurt the Princess?" Tokushima wondered aloud.

"The Palace hypercast receiver runs automatic screens on all incoming transmissions. This file was coded so unusually, it tripped the screens. The Princess never saw the files. The data on the files was incredibly dense, and a cursory scan reveals a hologram with…numerous geometries in three-dimensional patterns and fractals."

"Where is the original hardware?" A worried look shot across father's face.

"In the Sunrider. We brought the ship back; it's at Fort Oort Station. In the Kuiper belt." Hammerstein said at last.

Something was turning in the back of my mind. I didn't know what yet, but it was not good. "Don't bring it any closer in this star system. Keep it out in the Oort clouds. I should go there as well. I need to know if the transmission in the Library is fundamentally different than the transmission on the derelict frigate. I think they get weaker with each iteration. The one in the Frigate will be more toxic."

Father rose, "Hammerstein"-he cut himself off, his thought unfinished. Only his emotion conveyed to me across his den: dread, desperation, and a chillingly morose sense of imminent doom.

"What choice do we have, Sir Sole? The boy himself insists with a warning. He hasn't missed yet. We can't ignore him. He needs to go. He needs to go now. I can have a Hammerhead make an in-system hyperjump. With normal space-time on both ends of the jump, he'll be at Fort Oort in the morning. He can sleep on the journey."

I gathered my resolve. A Hammerhead jump ship. The jumps Hammerheads were designed for were to large star carriers to planet jumps and back. I had never heard of one with hyperjump capabilities. The Royal Security Police had made some modifications. In-system jumps were not that unusual, but neither were they very common either. There is a lot of stuff to hit in an Oort cloud at the edge of a star system. Hammerheads were manufactured in CCCE space.

The irony of going to meet the galactic derelict, an ancient CCCE frigate, on a contemporary CCCE manufactured vessel struck me then. However, even their fearsome Hammerheads are incomparable to the technologies of CCCE's first armada.

The Great Arcturian war, devastating the Arcturian Colonials, had left an economic and technological chill in the Galaxy for centuries. When they say they 'don't make them like they used too," rest assured they mean the likes of a Sunrider.

One of the greatest starships ever built, military class or civilian; and I was going to see one.

III Flyboys and Archaeologist girls.

Time to go.

I remember vaguely, for even Empaths tire, Tokushima helping me into the aircar that morning. There came a strange, maternal sense which she conveyed, mixed with the warrior aspects of her police training. The two worldviews, like a yin and a yang, were curled up comfortably in her being. I could feel my mother's fears as the estate seemed to diminish with distance like a toy. A dark winter had of her own had come now. I knew she would not feel the light and warmth of Caldris again until she held me safe again in her arms. That day would come, I pledged. This was not that day, but I am an Empath and I know: there are greater things in Cosmos and Worlds than men imagine. That day would come.

Tokushima's family had long served security details for the Royals. The first of their ancestors to play that role had been a drinking buddy of Rohr Maggio, and through thick and thin, he always had his back-more often, first in the front of the fray. Back at home now, Kunisada, her brother, was in a state of constant meltdown. Their mother had died, or disappeared-the stories from her childhood were often contradictory, but Kunisada and Tokushima had always been there for one another. Seeing him carry the weight of a failing of the Royals and his own family, and especially, it seems, the loss of his friend Clairissa, she was motivated on many levels to resolve the case.

We came to her headquarters, and she took comfort at the familiar sight; the Royal Police Headquarters on the tangerine sea exuded a strong sense of "home" for her when we arrived, but to me it's Brutalist style architecture, a combination of form follows function and mechanical exigencies, looked none the less like giant robots, vanguards watching over the waters.

The sun was rising before the Hammerhead was fully prepped. Hammerstein fumed, walking around the service bay like a caged Ripjackle from some primitive Outworld one sees in the holo-dramas. He kept thinking of how back in the Navy, if such delays were taking place he would have had the joy of dressing down the techs at the top of his lungs calling them, "Pinhead-dung-birds-pencil-necked-booty-grabbing-clowns-without-a-pair", but this was the Royal Police and their protocols were different than the Navy, so he merely whispered it under his breath as he walked around and around the service bay, eyeing them with murder in his eyes.

Finally, one of the techs gathered the courage to stand their ground and face the leering Detective, "Sir," he said, "It's a modified troop shuttle. The in-system hyper-jumps she'll be making are the stuff of stunt pilots and professional racers. I don't know what your emergency is, because it's above my pay grade, but whatever it is, it will get a whole lot worse if you start popping in and out of normal space deep in the complex gravity wells of a star system and one of the field manipulators fails. Even a little failure and g-forces will turn you, the lovely police lady, and the kid over there into a crushed pulp in a microsecond. This bird isn't going up until she's five-five-five, good-to-go and secured. Okay?"

Steve Allman

Hammerstein made a low growl at the tech but I felt a grudging respect forming. He just raised his hands in defeat and found a place on a stainless steel bench where Tokushima and I had been half sleeping, half watching.

At length, my rest restored me enough to grasp the excitement and strangeness of what I was experiencing again. This was no pleasure cruise with oversized cushions, buffets, and family chattering. The plexisteel and astercrete world of the police base mimicked the military Spartan furnishings from which most of this police force had come up through in their careers.

65

Comfort was for civies; contemptible. We were headed to Fort Oort, and already I could feel the sensibilities of the Space Navy. As had often been the case through Human kind's long and twisted histories, the military's main source of recruitment was from men and women in the worker-bee classes; farm boys no longer needed on the farm, daughters of forklift operators from corners of the worlds where economies dragged-children from situations and scenarios proper society moved away from.

Through the ages, they had come, to the brutal and uncompromising training bases. Mastering the arts of war, ready to give that last full measure of devotion–their very lives, everything they had and would ever have, for the very nations and peoples who more often than not watched the wars comfortably from home, sometimes even profiting, and morosely, fashionably, protesting indignation. Through the ages the soldiers had come, duty, honor, and sacrifice. To stand in the horror for their fellows. No matter what world or before the worlds' nations; their uniforms earned in struggle and often deprivation spoke the same words: "I will die that you may live."

So when the pilot arrived I wasn't surprised he was Navy. Justin "Coco-butter" Parsons. Son of an avocado farmer from the Southern archipelagoes, he assumed any number of pilot clichés easily; devil-may-care daring-do, live for today because tomorrow your hyperdrives must miss a cog, find all the pretty ladies and give 'em a big wet kiss before you fly away.

The funny thing about clichés, I realized then. Clichés or no, the pretty ladies are still beautiful when they're getting a big wet kiss, and the flight is still dangerous as you order the engage command. Beauty and danger. They are what they are, and those that have the mettle to pursue them, well, they are what they are too.

Even swaggering, live for today, Coco-butter Parsons got a big fat dose of "Uh-oh" when he walked into the service hangar and felt the vibes oozing off Hammerstein. Parson's pay grade didn't make him privy to the abduction of the Princess, the details of the salvaged Sunrider at Fort Oort, or the fact that the government had commandeered the son of an aristocratic family as psychic to root out an unsolvable crime, but a lifetime of living by his wits and landing on his feet gave him the sense to know this was a…. well, he had some very artful expletives in his mind when he summed up the situation.

As a young gentleman whose Grandmatron had always told him, "Remember who you are, Winteroud! Chin up and white tie for dinner", I'll, of course, leave the ribald Navy expletives out of my recounting of the tale, but they are, as I said before, rather an art form unto themselves; a proper response, at some level, to the absurdity the universe so often persists at presenting mankind.

Parsons whispered to the head tech, not knowing I could read him across the service bay, "You got any idea what's going on here with this little fly by night run?"

The tech gave him a sidelong glance, "Nope. The Detective is top brass, the kid is rich, and the female captain is smoking hotter than a volcano. They all have to be at Fort Oort yesterday. Any questions?"

Parson looked at the Hammerhead. "Yeah, how's my Honey?" He ran his gloved hand along the hull with a loving caress.

"Well, Officer Hammerstein over there wasn't too happy with the time we've been eating up prepping your Hammerhead, but I've kept it by the numbers."

"Thanks. I like coming home with my heart still beating. Any word on the winds?"

"Solar wind at a minimum. One more diagnostic and you're good to go."

"Roger, Roger, Kazi, kitty! Thanks Buck!" Parsons quipped and climbed into the Hammerhead and began his flight deliberations and lockdowns.

The tech nodded to Hammerstein and we climbed aboard. There wasn't a thing on that airship that didn't need to be there except a small plastic Hula dancer someone had glued over a structural reinforcement over the door and painted, "Aloha baby let's dance!" below. Dancing, of course, a metaphor for combat flight. If you're going to die in combat, in a Hammerhead, best to do it with a Cavalier attitude. You've either got, or you haven't got style.

Welcome to the dance.

The Hammerhead hummed to life and all I could think of was "The Little Engine that could." Not much bigger than a standard city airbus, the vehicle was mostly intended for air support of ground troops securing areas in conflict. Their simplicity, reliability, and sheer versatility had made them beloved of any military or police forces that acquired them.

One of the airmen buckled us in, "Each of your seats has an emergency force field and life support back up pending a hull breach. If you get knocked out into the void, you'll have twenty-four standard hours of protection. Then the seat trips into a stasis mode to preserve you. Time will stop within the stasis field. If someone one homes in on your beacon before it goes stasis, you may be picked up. Otherwise, you're under stasis indefinitely-alive, but unable to call for help.

"Thank you for that, Airman." Tokushima eyed him dryly.

"Just doing my job, Maam."

"Woolly Bully!" Parsons snapped from the cockpit and I could feel the craft alight itself, aloft quickly into the airstreams and high lights of dawn, rushing like a puppy to the cumulonimbus and the high places in the stratosphere. Parsons delight was palpable to me; behind us a shimmering white line, purposeful action made tangible arcing up and across the sky. Below us marshmallow clouds now, subdued and silent in their perfect patterns and spiral motions over the seas and the volcanoes of Caldris.

Far and away…. Below us, my world, spinning, turning, its geographies like abstract speckled studies of color and light; above us the planets of Caldris System. The sky becomes black and the sun a star and still; from Parsons, wonder and joy; ever and always the miracle of flight for primates such ourselves, the staid gleaming of dreams ineffable since our dawn of self-awareness when our distant ancestors, worlds away, looked out upon the hummingbirds and eagles with envy and impossible aspiration; to fly.

And thus we set upon the worlds, to fly, in search of our Princess.

Parsons' calls to his co-pilot were less poetic than his joy, but they too were a form of phonetic poetry of flight: *"Apogee reached, increasing thrust, apparent solar wind five, radiation shields five, current velocity at target, orbit traffic control clear, flight path gravity assist off Electra, gravity assist off Maia to jump point EMC5."*

And thus we jump skipped among moons to a point where we could shoot deep through the wall of space-time and cheat the laws of physics for a fast forward to the distant corners of the star system in a day instead of months or years.

Sleep came again with Tokushima's radiant glow (with echoes to another floating world, Japan, Edo period) on one side of me, and Hammerstein's sharp-shooter dead-eye-dick focus (with echoes of John Henry and a heavy metal sledge) on the other. They, my surrogate parents now, with badges and high energy particle weapons as big as my arms.

I was twelve, and that was as magnificent as it gets. Gonna be missing school for a while. Sorry (not really).

Sleep, dream, sail away, beyond the tangerine seas and volcanoes, dream, the moons of Caldris, the daughter of Atlas, sail away.

Somewhere in the dream, Parsons gives the command, "Swirl the Mesons, Buck! We're breaking for Hyper!"

Shane Perry

And all the stars in a jewel box, darkly.

Standing in the ruins at the great starport at New Galen I came for the first time to that nihilistic place whereas Ecclesiastes said, all is vanity. Among the crumbled stones I picked up a broken brick. In the still radioactive ruins lie the ultimate futility of life and reason, so many people-come and gone-and where to go from there, and what should I respond to this inevitable wall of dark and unknowable fate? Yet Einstein claims time is a continuum; the past in all its beauty, struggle, folly, and grandeur somehow remains. Perhaps it is good there comes a rest from this existence, and dipping into the well of quanta we become again?

Foolish musing! Still-philosophers and Priest kings debate upon the epochs these eternal questions-one must answer this present darkness. I didn't have an answer, so told my droid to play Gershwin's Rhapsody in Blue as loud as his speakers would, back into the ruins. Music came again to the long era of devastation, a small revolt against man's fate. I imagined the ghosts of New Galen danced that day, grateful that I slapped back at despair. Perhaps they did. –Princess Clairissa Maggio.

Parsons woke me with a yell from the cockpit, "Ba-boomah! Thank you Great Space Ghost we are home and dry, normal space again, Oort Cloud below us, above us only sky! "His co-pilot (I forget his name, perhaps intentionally, he was quite the irritant) was lamenting loudly, "I really, hate, hate, hate the Oort Cloud. What a dump."

"Don't be a Baby. Man up a little, will you? This is a walk in the park if you've got a pair that is."

"I've got a pair, and they both say it's a royal pain."

"Baby. Just for that, I'm not giving you any phone numbers from my little black book when we get to Fort Oort. I don't want you embarrassing me at the base canteen."

"You've got numbers from Fort Oort?"

"Silly boy, I have ALL the numbers from Fort Oort. Watch your vectors, you big baby."

The Oort cloud was looking a lot better to the co-pilot, I sensed. I also sensed Parsons was going to hook him up the ugliest beast on his list just for laughs.

I felt sorry for the poor beast. Ugly is an accident of birth, rock-head annoying is a failure of basic common sense.

Tokushima noticed I was awake and once again I was struck by her yin and yang duality as she pushed her particle beam disser off to the side and said, "There, there, little fellow! Did you sleep well?" and brushed her lovely hand through my hair. Every single officer in her Unit would have bought dinner for the crew to have that hand caressing them, I thought, and cursed my diminutive size and few feeble years again. What a goddess!

"Yes, Maam," I said, keeping all my goddess thoughts to my humble boy self but thinking, *someday, you will be mine.*

"Oh good!" She smiled down like a Da Vinci Madonna, angelic, unaware of my boy plans to grow up and propose marriage.

Well, sometimes you just got a take it as it comes. Eat your heart out Unit. I smiled coyly back into those huge Asian eyes. I sensed my cuteness was making her want to find a husband and have babies. Foiled by my cuteness, she would surely set about and complete that mission before I had time to come of age.

I sighed and glanced at her big disser. Oh well, at least the babies will learn to shoot well. I had an impression of her putting a smiley face on a target at 300 yards unassisted, and knew that it was true. She had changed her hair color to a darker shade of black during the flight, some sort of ready-for-death symbolism I sensed.

She didn't worry about death, however. She worried that her brother was going to slide completely off the maglev rails and into a slovenly drunken end, blaming himself for the whole missing princess scenario. Dead in a bar fight at some Island beach tavern. She worried that drinking he wouldn't fight well, and it wouldn't even be an honorable death but a sloppy disgrace.

She worried if he was eating enough. Her impending death on the high spaces, in a modified Hammerhead, yawn, just another day at work.

Hammerstein tossed me an MRE. "Eat up Kid, you'll need your strength. This CCCE ship at Fort Oort is so loaded with quanta we're going to have to work at it slowly."

Hammerstein's duty in the Navy patrolling the cloud had been decades before, but for him, the place held a strange familiarity. "The sticks. Snowball Ocean, The Ninth Circle (Dante's frozen Hell for the treacherous), Outer Darkness-the place had a hundred nick-names for the unfortunate military stationed out there.

Vectors, weight, momentum, and the clockwork stillness of a million ice kingdoms. Time, deep time, it creeps in the quanta, very nearly empty of the Human race, here and there the faintest echo of thought riding the belt. Oddly enough, prospectors-and Hammerstein, liked the celestial quietude, the glacial slowness, and the epic sense of geologic deep time.

Once, Hammerstein had been given orders to watch a mining camp suspected of smuggling weapons. He sat watching for so long, his communications gear froze. No way to call for help, and the next expected pass by the Navy weeks away, he decided to find the contraband ammo himself. He did, in a cargo tank. He ignited it, blinding the smugglers, temporarily-long enough to get a bead on them, round them up and lock 'em down.

When the Navy finally got around to checking on Hammerstein again, he was grilling lobster tails for himself, feeding the smugglers oatmeal and water, and dipping into their spiced rum. They found him with his feet up, drinking the rum through an emergency tube, watching the tumbling close passes of giant purple ice balls that portion of the cloud was famous for.

"Took you long enough, these wannabees were gonna be running out of lobsters and rum soon!" was all he said when the NCO's and a platoon of Rangers piled out of their transport.

Today, however, he pushed that memory back into his mind forcefully and realized this wasn't any old two-bit, six or eight asteroid stalking yahoos peddling bootleg matter cannon ammo to wannabe mobsters on the moons.

Whoever was behind the kidnapping, well, there were a lot more of them than eight, and they wouldn't be taken down with mischievous ammo-reindeer-games. No Soirée at the harbor bar this time. Moreover, there still wasn't a definitive direction regarding motive and suspect.

Hammerstein and the crew couldn't know things were about to get a lot worse. Fort Oort was still a haul away when I got the impression of someone. Vague at first, just that sense of being watched that doesn't come from giant snowballs in deep space, but from eyes. Sentient eyes, self-aware, and busy.

But whom, and busy at what?

Busy looking. Looking for...a Hammerhead.

"Get out!" I yelled. "Pilot, get out! Something's coming!" I howled, screaming, frantic-*they were coming.*

"Detective, do you need to sedate the child?" Annoying-man barked from the piloting cabin. Parsons, however, had better instincts, and changed his flight pattern hard and fast, bringing us up nimbly in a rush above the stellar plain.

The Hammerhead rose like a balloon released from the bottom of the Tangerine sea, and I knew Parsons had taken it to maximum vertical thrust, inertial dampers straining to keep us from crushing Gees.

Just in time. A warp ripple slammed the space where we had been just moments before, and I knew not even the inertial dampers of the massive Hammerhead would have preserved our skins through that shockwave.

"What the devil was that?" Annoying-man croaked, and even my twelve-year-old mind knew he needed a slap in the head big time.

"Watch your dials, Ensign, or I'll let the kid co-pilot." Parsons shot at him.

"Wormhole Generator," Hammerstein said evenly. They're trying to knock us out with a shock wave. Get ready for a snowstorm."

Comet Storm, to be precise. Six light weeks of super dense Oort cloud shaken with the force of a wormhole, suddenly bending the very fabric of time and space with the full force of a gravity bomb whose implosion diameter probably spanned a full hundred kilometers, suddenly sucked away to who knows where. Like a snowstorm, it came on us with hurricane force, in the darkest, coldest part of the system.

"Find its center, Pilot," Hammerstein howled over the squealing engines banging into the red to maneuver the storm.

Find its center-

The Hammerhead swerved in the raging onslaught of primordial ice and rock. I got a big jolt of fear from Annoying-man as the field shielding too slipped into the red. "Shoot us a path through that snow, Buck, or we're gonna buy it right here, right now," Parsons said coolly, eyeing his readouts looking for the center as Hammerstein said.

Annoying-man turned out to be a good shot when his hide was on the line, and the particle beam weapon atop the hammerhead wailed into the dark, creating a shockwave of its own which gave the shields on the Hammerhead a respite from the pounding.

Hammerstein didn't feel a moment's fear, merely an overwhelming frustration that he Tokushima's warrior soul finally broke through, yet somehow merged, and not indistinct, from her maternal soul, as she still managed a worried glance in my direction.

I reached out in my mind, deep through the raging proto-comets rushing at us through the long wave cycle. Unlike the shockwave, the quanta in the debris had followed eons of predictable, Newtonian orbits, a complexity like a sponge dragged through a five-dimensional squeegee. I looked for an anomaly in the quanta, through the storm, what I had felt before watching us.

The gunner and the pilot rode the storm, the gunner spewing expletives, the pilot, still-*such control*-hunting the eye of the storm.

I found it in the quanta-*yes-a ship with bad intent.*

Hammerstein was wrong-finding the center of the storm would only lead to the wormhole's exit point. The assassins were at its origin, but wide, low, then around- "They're on a spiral course on the outside," I said, "three o'clock"

"Well, Hello Kitty!" Parson's hissed as the assassin's vessel gleamed on his holo-screen.

"Who is that kid?" Annoying-man whispered from his guns, and dead-eye-dick squeezed his tracer center mass. He said "kid" with a kind of awe. I reveled, we were in a gunfight-our second now!

It was a hit, but the other vessel wasn't finished yet.

"Let's dance!" Parson rolled the Hammerhead forward and the combat was engaged into a dog-fight.

Hammerstein's only thought was, should we live, they better leave him some evidence.

I pressed my mind again into the spaces of the dog-fight, hurling with the combatants, searching for a stray thought, a reveal that would help us define who, and why.

The ships danced in the darkness, but there was no love between them. Tokushima longed for a gunner's controls. Her face was not so lovely then, and the red emergency lights cast her fearsome and transformed.

I felt the inertial dampers strain, the G forces begin to pull on myself and then the others. Parsons rolled the Hammerhead, then splined it erratically so the enemy couldn't get a clear bead on him. He watched his fields and plasma shots ahead of the vessel, set on an encrypted random pattern of flux to avoid enemy targeting computers.

Then I felt it. A bloodlust from the other side. They were powering up- "Wormhole! "They're powering up another wormhole and we're flying right into it! Dive!" I screamed in a voice too high for a boy my age.

"Gravity Bombs Parsons!" Hammerstein barked coolly, "Put one up their hind end right now and see what happens to their little wormhole"

This time it was Annoying-Man whose instincts were good. His thumbs were all over that button before Hammerstein even had the sentence out and there came a FOOSH-CLANG! Loud from somewhere in the bottom of the vessel, I could sense the wicked tool careening toward its target.

Its onboard computer was even semi-sentient, rather cruel that-like an insect hatched with a very short life and one hideous objective. The gravity bomb's inner workings were already unlocked in a clockwork nightmare of force fields. At the microscopic level first. Miniature particle colliders racing, then a very small black hole, and somehow its engineers had devised that the systems of the device remain functioning up to nanoseconds before implosion.

Suddenly the gravity bomb met the enemy's wormhole, shot through with an aspect of psychotic horror. A gruesome sheen and sudden skew, all things in our universe bent and twisted, ragged and broken. Time and space scuffled in a nightmare of there, and here, then and now, all raging in sickening chaos of NO!

Parsons rode those psychotic shockwaves like a mad surfer in a volcanic whirlpool, "Well, Hello Kitty!" The Hammerhead groaned and the metal fatigue tested its designers' best intent. Still, the pilot was flush with joy that the enemy was down and all that he had to contend with was tidal forces sheering at his stabilizer fields.

Tokushima gave me an unlikely Edo era geisha smile, like a woodblock print ephemeral across the ages; "Welcome to the Navy Air, kid. Glad to have you flying with us." she said. She knew the only reason we were still alive was I kept giving us a small jump on the assassins. I hoped my prescience held up.

Hammerstein's mind was already past the combat, past the whirlpool ride, and into the wreckage of the enemy vessel. "What have we got?" he boomed.

"The G-bomb sucked the front and the bottom of their hull apart just as they fired the wormhole shot. Looks like you have evidence to scour, Sir," Annoying-man said in a too cool tone. He was grandstanding. The sweat was still drying on his face and his heartbeat returning too normal.

"Good. Get a team on it from Fort Oort. And get us warm and dry, NOW." Hammerstein eased back in his seat with miserable indignation. On the ride home, he thought, he was bringing a bigger ship. I had Gibbon tapping the black box of the Hammerhead the whole while. No one suspects a kid. I had no intention of relying only on my impressions of what was out there-I wanted to examine the ship camera records later.

IV Fort Oort

I was too overwhelmed with the sheer number of minds reaching for disciplined self-control to realize the formation wasn't for us, it was just five hundred airmen waiting for breakfast and their NCOs to give them a hard time, fresh out of bed, just because. It was, however, grand, and dashing, in a very powerful way. Formation. Five hundred airmen; every chin, every toe, every knee, every hand, every eye holding themselves just right, steady, steady.

Roy Rudder

Stepping out of the Hammerhead I wanted to wave. I could sense their sudden curiosity like a wave of realization: *a kid was climbing out of the gunship.*

The scoured and seared hull bore witness to how close death had raked its bony fingers across our beings and missed. It would be back, of course, it always is. I would dodge it as long as I could. The airmen, unmoving, watched from their peripheral vision-an acquired skill I realized. I looked bizarre to them, like a baby Buddha. A baby Buddha wearing an antique disser.

A wave of ironic familiarity hit me as one of the officers approached us, "Captain Hammerstein, welcome back. Officer Tokushima." He nodded to the female officer respectfully and gave a sort of cavalier grin at Odin.

"Admiral Kemp." Hammerstein didn't have to salute since he was now officially civilian. This pleased him to no end. Long ago and not so far away (this very hangar in fact) he had once been under Kemp's command. Kemp hadn't been an Admiral then, however.

"Is this necessary, Hammer? I mean," Kemp looked at me, "No offense kid, but really? Did you bring an empath? Really?"

Hammerstein shrugged, looked at me, "What-dah-yah-say, Sole?"

"Well," I looked back at Kemp, enjoying where this was going because it brought Hammerstein a moments respite, "Admiral Kemp," I touched my forehead for effect, " you've got six months left to retirement and you're just hoping the CO back in the world doesn't putz it upon you, because your wife has been coddling your grandson, who should be in graduate school by now, and you can't wait to get in his face and tell him "what for" and how you have 'seen ten thousand better men doing hard duty out here on the ice, while he finds his silly self-pondering volcanoes and the meaning lava flow.' Your CO, Burke Sherwood, 'Analwood' as you and the other officers call him…"

"Okay, okay! Okay! That will be enough of that young man, you're in." Kemp eyed Hammerstein. "Good to go. Officer's quarters. You know the way, Hammer. Report to Quartermaster and make yourself at home, but uh-no more of THAT, aye?"

"Understood, Sir," Hammerstein said and looked at me with a smirk. He put his finger to his lips, "Shhh," and the Fort was ours, just like a holo-show. The big toys, the big boys. Only, when all that armor and hardware is sitting out in front of you, for real, it's not just cool. It's deadly, and its true grim purpose and function-to break things and kill people, well, it's rather sinister and menacing actually. Your mind wanders to what it would be like to be on the business end of it all. "Don't touch any of the bombs or anything kid. These grab-ass clowns are mussing up stuff all the time."

Especially since we just were at the business ends of destructive devices. Walking to quarters, I could sense strange respect from the airmen still waiting in formation for breakfast. They saw the scars on the hammerhead and knew we had just been in the "doo-doo." They had another word in their minds for it, but I am a gentleman, after all.

Combat veterans, I realized. I was now a combat veteran. Half the unit was envious. Most of them hadn't seen combat yet. I rested my hands on my disser and gave them a look. Dead Eye Dick, yeah, that's right. We were just in the doo-doo. Walking by their ranks I basked in the glory.

Coco-butter Parsons stepped up from behind in a rush, "Come on let's eat before these chow hounds get released and the mess hall is swarmed."

"Officers lounge, flyboy. First-class on this run. You certainly earned it."

Annoying-man chuckled. "Breakfast at Tiffany's," he said.

Tiffany's? Ugh, that guy could take the sheen off a convertible Corvette making a one-point landing at a beach bash. Mr. Gibbon gave me a small tilt of the head. One of our private signals: *"Chuckle-head."*

We moved along toward the officer's quarters and I tried to savor the moment. Fort Oort! Caldera Squadron! Yet a troubling realization had begun to form in my mind and its implications shot a cast of foul refuse and menace. Menace over myself, my small cadre of new companions, and even over the five hundred stalwart airmen waiting for breakfast. I remembered then my impressions of the assassins with the worm-hole device. I hadn't felt the same organization was behind them. There were distinct and different culture complexes, syntax, motivations. Thus more than one powerful enemy was seeking our destruction, capturing royal persons, and making acts of war across the worlds. I glanced up at my Detective friend, Hammerstein, steamrolling across the astercrete of the hangar floor.

I remembered my fears when he first approached my family at the Sole estate regarding this case, that it would be the end of him and many others should he find the answers he sought.

Foreboding whispered in my ear, stroking my head with bony fingers.

The Officer's mess had a bit more privacy than the main cafeteria but currently it was populated with pilots who were still glued to flight reports, and having at their food and beverages with the indifferent stoicism of fueling a machine. They were trained men-the objective was everything, food was a tool to sustain their quest. They took no joy in it like the grunts-it was just something they had to do to continue flying. Eat, bathe, sleep; simple maintenance work. There was only the flight that mattered; the high spaces, the void, the patrolling of the deep Plutonian Oort cloud.

Obsessive-compulsive, to a virtue. I looked at them and felt their impressive, single-minded absorption in their tasks. No foolish boys here, but men and women-veterans with decades of duty on their stripes. Careworn souls who could do eighteen hours at a sitting before they realized they'd done an hour.

I, however, was still twelve-and hungry. We took heaping portions of various foodstuffs-synthetic mostly. Hearty, I realized-but then Hammerstein's mind was back on task, like a deep space run, plowing through a glacier on a Plutoid, shaking loose from a "snowball." He wanted to know, "So what did you sense kid?"

"More devils," I said. "But devils we don't know, meaning another faction. Two distinct echoes and cultures lie behind the attacks. We're in deep, and everything and everyone," I looked about the mess hall, "is in danger."

Coco-butter Parsons' eyes went dark. "Come on, I'm you're dancing' dolphin. Come on!"

An Autobot came out from the kitchen with more something-something in a dish. It looked surprised at Parsons for a moment and fled away.

Hammerstein shot him an icy look, but the underlying emotion under his granite face was pity. Coco-butter, he knew, would die valiantly-but still die. Hammerstein was beginning to grasp the layers of menace. The Imperials wouldn't want evidence that their genocide in the Arcturian War had been a premeditated horror on a bunch of disorganized Ranchero colonials. Who knew how far, even now, they would go to maintain the fiction otherwise? The corporations, tapping the old technologies the Imperials had let slip for a millennium or had secreted in the first place, they would not want word toxic sentient programs were loose in the technologies frying brains for sport.

Princess Maggio had uncovered an eel's nest at the edge of an undersea lava flow, and we were her dive buddies.

He sensed my fear, and he responded with camaraderie. Not that I was in any less danger, rather, he was letting me in on a secret-the tools of the trade, as it was, facing dangers, "Look, Kid, it's like this. If the entire Caldris system, it's Navy, and worlds and industries and culture, be overwhelmed-take heart, little man. Neither the Imperial Transhuman Overlords nor the Multi-Star-system mega corporations are truly united within themselves. There is their weakness-within each Colossus are various competing sub-interests-iron vs. copper, copper vs. tin, tin vs. clay-and thus a small dedicated force with subterfuge may divide and conquer the giant idol."

His stone features creaked, a visage that spoke of eons, patience, and geological deep time. "We will find them out, root them out, and then set them upon one another."

Now it was I with an icy look covering pity. No, I thought. Like Coco-butter Parsons, you will make a valiant stand then die-unless I used my powers to tip the balance.

Perhaps my young mind was too deep in gloom. Parsons had just slammed the ship that hit us with the wormhole shock-wave. Hammerstein was producing leads with my assistance. Yet the time for me to view the Sunrider relic was close at hand, and even from the mess hall, I could feel its grim presence, emanating hopelessness. My body seemed caught in thickening cement, an astercrete mined from the loneliest asteroid in the darkest corner of the cosmos.

Something wrong, something that ate human ambition and dreams, something that whispered, "All is lost; look now upon the wreckage of your species' aspirations, and weep."

Gloom indeed.

Ecclesiastes, vanity, vanity, all is vanity. It drummed upon my mind. Early in my obsession with history and its repetitions I went into a virtual reality play, commonly known as a virtreel, and found myself at the fall of Troy. It was a splendid virtreel, carefully crafted by its makers with the most accurate details of the period recreated in all their Bronze Age glories. After the commonly known drama unfolded, I found myself as one of the refugees making haste away on a water ship. The land shrunk with distance and as the last light of day ebbed, there was only the water, the ships, and the sky. Ominously, even from that distance in the fading light one could see the smoke of Troy's burning like a funeral pyre.

Today we made more scans of the Sunrider lodged into the side of the O'Neil station at the Arcturian colonies and found myself wondering what the refugees from that war might have seen and felt looking back. –Princess Clairissa Maggio.

V Hangar 3

In the morning, station time, we made for Hangar 3 and the relic Sunrider. My sense of foreboding increased with every step. I could sense with the beefed up security who knew it was there, and who merely knew something was amiss in the hangar. Few knew. Very few. Even the guards at the outer locks didn't know.

Inside, we'd been given wide berth. No techs were poking and prodding at the thing, and it sat in all its streamlined glory as one era's ultimate killing machine. Hammerstein watched me like the proverbial hawk waiting for a sign when too much became too much.

Yet for all my foreboding, curiosity was having its way with me now. Like any boy of twelve seeing a great and mysterious warship, my mind raced with a ridiculous excitement. It was a frigate, large indeed but no more so than some of the great space planes which it resembled after a fashion. My first impressions were the quantum echoes of its lost crew-they had been proud. They had been convinced they were serving their Imperial defense from the menace of the Colonials.

Then I sensed their shock, still echoing-sheer confusion like a firestorm-something wrong. Wrong, it had fractured their sanity in a wild snap, and there was only chaos in its wake. The chaos still lingered, somehow, I knew, like a spider fallen into a hot pan, squirming.

The chaos that hated mankind.

It had hated the Imperials, hated the Colonials, hated us all-no, hated all living things with outrage, a disgust, a lust for destruction. "You will do well to keep your techs from the vessel's neural net and computers," I said. I had spoken involuntarily. "I suggest rudimentary bots only-nothing approaching even a modicum of an AI should even touch it. Toxic is too mild a word."

"An Imperial trap?" Hammerstein asked dryly, wishing it were so.

I gave him a look beyond my years, "No. Something is here which demolished the minds of strong, brave, hardened Imperial Cyborgs. It was not of their making. Nothing could have broken those men, no ordinary tribulation. Here is a poison which perhaps the very, very fewest of men could have endured."

"And the Princess and her archaeological team were exploring it unawares. Perhaps our nemeses are after it as a weapon?"

The smile on my face, at that, set poor Hammerstein aback. I looked like a Devil myself then. "Fools beyond measure if they do."

Fools beyond measure...

"*The ship itself is a Sunrider 3062 Frigate. It's equipped with five drive systems and backups for various flight conditions. The center of the system is the antigravitational, or gravitational antipolar response field- a helicon magnetic plasma sail system for emergency fuel efficiency and movement in and out of heliopauses-a hyperstring enabling system to negate mass through five-dimensional wormhole hyper streams-a super ion drive Buzzard ramjet array for normal space bursts through complex field distortion areas-and emergency use limited standard rocket backup fail safes. Navigation systems are collated through eighty quasar emissions and the galactic plume...*"

I stopped and stepped back-I had inadvertently begun reading from the ship's data core.

"Easy boy!" Hammerstein stepped forward and instinctively placed himself between me and the relic.

"Rather well engineered, weren't they?" I quipped sardonically, seeking to add a note of levity. "Must have been a nasty surprise to the poor Arcturian Air corps when these monsters showed up."

"Yes, yes indeed," Hammerstein smiled, "although nasty, I think, was probably not the expletive the poor buggers must have lipped when they engaged."

"And now we have one, nearly intact, and still packing the poison that brought her down." My voice shook. A sense of otherness, a frightening aspect of bad intent and somehow, a doorway to a bad place-it all simmered behind the hull of the relic.

Hammerstein looked to me icily, and I did not read his feeling, "After the war, the Imperials stopped using Cyborged crews. They raised an entire new caste of soldiers, ones not linked to their Hive mind at all." Hammerstein said quietly. "This was the last Great War of multiple systems. Since then, there have only been small inter-system wars. No one dared challenge the Imperials again."

"I think Princess Clairissa Maggio may have found that the Arcturians were not threatening the Imperials," Odin mused. He was, however, already out of feeling out of his depth.

"Whatever echo still lingers in the neural net of that ship's computer systems, well, I think that is something more menacing than a galaxy full of feisty Colonials. Both factors provide your motive-and it falls doubly on the Cyborgian Central Command Economies-the Empire. As for the other as yet unknown suspects, we'll have to wait for them to strike again." I offered coolly.

There simply weren't words I could dredge out of my experience to match what echoes I felt behind the hull of the ancient Sunrider. A centipede came to mind, black, dragging a portal to Hell, like a sack of tortured victims, and through the sack-

Hammerstein glowered impatience and looked at the relic. "We've got a crew picking the remains of Parsons' kill in the Oort now. There will be something. There always is."

We made back to the Officer's mess for a breakfast of cakes and coffees. At least that's what they called it. I ate silently, knowing Hammerstein had already requisitioned the bots I suggested from a com. By lunch, the bots would be scouring the relic.

The wreckage salvaged from the wormhole attack had arrived at the Hangar as well, and the techs were happily after that for clues. I could sense Hammerstein was pushing back an idea that had validity, so I drilled him with my little kid eyes and he knew that I knew.

"So what is it, detective? What is it about the wormhole attack that you don't want to face?'

He chortled, a grumbling laugh that bordered on a burp and looked at me with a bittersweet half-smile. "No hiding anything from you, aye?" His eyes darkened and I felt a rush of emotion he'd walled up for decades suddenly opening up, and its impact was palpable to me.

His sense of self from that long ago decade was profoundly different-he had been young, a handful of years older than I. His self-image from that time impacted me like a strange reflection of the man in front of me-leaner, with swift hair, a reckless step, and unquenchable awe and thirst for adventure. Youth. Caldris had been in a territorial dispute with the Paramon Republic near the Pleiades.

Paramon was always disputing some silly rock, and this time it was one of our Kingdom's trade stations near Baal One, a horrid seared rock of soullessness-but our trade station orbited it and operated important business with Chrysalis Isla, deep in the Pleiades Confederation.

Hammerstein's memories came at me then-the flight deck of his first assignment, glorying in the sight of the Kingdom's ships of the line at the ready. Anticipation, joy, a thrill of imminent combat-and then the impossible, the unheard of-a wormhole deep in the gravity well of Baal One sweeping at them like a cobra, hard and fast and the young Hammerstein watched as the ships of the line (and all of his friends were on those ships) disintegrated in the irresistible shock wave.

He was nineteen and alone. The only real family he had ever known had been those fellows on the other ships. He had been transferred from one of those very ships that morning.

There was an awkward moment as the face of the young Hammerstein morphed into the older iron man in front of me, more muscled, more scarred, more resolute. Suddenly, I knew, he was still carrying his nineteen-year-old self around, standing forever on that flight deck watching his friends die, and indescribable loneliness taking their place for the rest of his life.

"Paramon and wormhole shock waves," I said, breaching the subject like pulling a patch from a wound-quickly so as not to drag out the inevitable.

Most people would have barely perceived the slightest flicker in his eye. For me, however, it was as if the line of ships once again ruptured in violent sequence across his soul.

He smiled, and I realized the old iron Detective had been forcing that smile for a very long, painful time.

"Yes. No one uses wormholes in combat except pirates, madmen, and Paramon. Too dangerous. I was at the Baal One Station disaster. In a lifetime of military and police service, I've never seen anyone use them since, until now. I'd stake what's left of my career on it-we follow the bread crumbs and there will be a Paramon agent at the end of the trail."

I glowered, sick with the sudden knowledge of how a nineteen-year-old cadet feels after watching his comrades perish, and Fifty Years of loneliness after that, always stepping back from that personal bond that would leave the soul wretched come to the loss. Fifty years of heavy metal shielding for the soul and underneath it all, a brutalized nineteen-year-old boy on the flight deck.

"Don't let your desire to settle accounts with Paramon prejudice your judgment, Detective," I offered from the strange place of his memory.

A tech came in with a report; efficient, cool, and detached-he handed the data to Hammerstein. The detective's eyes widened and a name came loud to me as if the old block had spoken it aloud.

"Colonel Herb Lahman, Black Devils," I said.

Hammerstein looked about the room, "Cut that out. Come on. We need a bigger boat."

Coco-butter looked up at the mention of "bigger boat." Hammerstein saw the eager eyes.

"Pick out the best ship at the Fort, pilot, and tell them we're requisitioning it, King's orders. You can fly a bigger boat right?"

"I can fly any ship in this Navy, Detective. I was born in flight, my mother at the helm, single-handed, strato-caster."

Hammerstein chuckled back and winked. "Good! Then pick out a good one."

We stepped out of the Officer's mess and I was struck with the realization that Coco-butter's description wasn't hyperbole. He had been born in a flight dive with his mother at the helm. She'd lost his twin in the struggle, but had managed to save Justin "Coco-butter." She was an amazing woman. But that is another story. I looked back at Coco-butter as we left with a newly found respect.

The wheels of his mind at that moment were running through a mental inventory of ships he had seen at the Base. Somehow I already knew he was going to pick the--"Eberhardt?!" Kemp was steaming. "That's my flagship Hammerstein! I want to see a letter of a requisition signed by the King himself before you fly out of here with the pride of this base!"

Fifty years of heavy metal shielding over one's soul can be a particularly painful defense mechanism to build. However, when he chose to use it, Hammerstein could crush groups of trained men with it.

That smile. In your face. "Really? Admiral Kemp? Because I have a hypercaster right in the Hammerhead and I can get the Royal family on the line right now, and you can explain how you need the ship more than they need their daughter?"

Kemp folded like a kitten, "No, no, no!" He showed both palms, "Take it. Take it-and take a platoon of Airborne. I don't want to see you or that ship back at this base again without a very attractive Royal personage by the name of Clarissa on board. Alive, viewing historical tapes, and driving the ship's cook crazy with peculiar dinner requests."

Hammerstein shrugged. "It's a big Galaxy. Have those bots pick that Sunrider apart for clues and I'll cast you on a coded line."

The old granite detective looked weary.

Now Kemp smiled, "Go find her Hammer. Bring her back. The Royals-they picked the right man. I know you. You'll be having lobster and feeding them oatmeal before it's done."

For a moment the memory of the long-ago smugglers lifted Hammerstein's gloom.

But my mind was on the ship Coco-butter had picked. The Eberhardt.

What a ride.

VI The Eberhardt

It was a beast; built for speed, blood, and fury. Two massive warp cores and two smaller crossed the back end of the ship could ride the hyperstreams like a surfer on the Tangerine sea, or bend space in normal space like taffy at a high-winter fair. She was a charger, like a knight's stallion of old, well armored, well-muscled, and meant to break the enemy lines in one savage, dashing berserker bolt.

"Come on kid, let's go find out what our techs have dug up from the wormhole wreckage." Hammerstein was working on an idea, I sensed it.

Past the serpentine tunnels deeper and deeper into the older core of the base we careened as Hammerstein's idea turned and turned in his mind.

I sought to grasp it but it wasn't fully formed. At length we came to one of the labs and a small group of techs were immersed in scanning equipment over various bits of wreckage. One of them, an older woman, sported a cigar and produced one from a pocket and gave it to the stodgy detective with a flourish, "Hammer, old boy, so good to pick through the blasted bits of your targets again."

Hammerstein lit the cigar, "Glad to oblige, Candy, my dear. What's the word?"

She puffed and blew smoke in his direction playfully. I sensed her fondness of the "old boy" ran deep. "The word? The…words are 'Langley Stay'."

Hammerstein's face turned into a grinning death mask. "Herbivore…?"

Now she smiled and I sensed they had been thinking alike. "Yes, Herbivore. Colonel Herb Lahman. The Lord God King of the wormhole counter maneuvers back at… the Pleiades incident."

"The only one who saw it coming in time to pull his ships out… The only one capable enough to countermeasure."

"There is no smoking gun here, Hammer. But the last word is Colonel Lahman was operating a large hardware operation on Langley Stay. Ships, military equipment, all sorts of goodies-black market. The trace navigationals in the computer systems in this wreckage all indicate a flight plan out of Langley Stay."

"Put that together with the wormhole attacks and one gets…"

"Herbivore. He's the only one who would keep that kind of equipment flight worthy-just because he could. I just had to confirm the ship was out of Langley to confirm my suspicions."

Finally, Candy acknowledged my presence, "You going to introduce me or am I already read like a book?"

"Both. Lieutenant Candy Parker, forensic Science. Please meet Master Winteroud, of the Sole estate at the edge of the Tangerine Sea. A bonafide, genuine, empath. Historian archaeologist adventurer in training."

I beamed. It was the first time anyone had called me a "Historian-archaeologist-adventurer" but it was not to be the last. I felt an immediate affinity with Lieutenant Parker; forensic science is not so different from archaeology in so many of its methodologies. There was an intelligence and good humor about her. Sensing deeper, of course, one often finds various sadness. I found the sadness shadowed in the back of her mind. I left it alone, tried to keep my focus on what she had discovered in the wreckage of the ship.

I sensed it had taken her some time to dig through layers of encryption, but like Hammerstein, she had instinctively sensed the involvement of the "Lord-god-king of wormhole counter maneuvers" from the onset, and had set about reverse engineering lines of code meant to cover up the attack ships origins until indeed she uncovered it.

"Pleased to meet you, son! Welcome to Fort Oort!"

I took her hand and gave her an aristocratic bow. She smiled, and long-ago memories of other aristocratic bows she had once been given came to mind. At the estates near the Military Academy Specialist Candy Parker had won the hearts of many cadets; at first sight. Athletic, statuesque, and ever a gleam of laughter in her eye-then the memory passed and her thoughts moved her back to the encryption codes she had unraveled, and the older, more storied woman looked back at me again.

Several bots moved through the wreckage, scanning. My mind shifted between decades and the deep emotions and perceptions of Candy's life back to the present crisis. Such was my lot in life as an empath, even at twelve standard Caldris years.

"So, you two both sense the hand of "Herbivore" behind this-and yet, Herbivore I gather is also an asset for our side?"

Candy's eyes darkened with slightly wicked intent.

Hammerstein glowered, "Wormhole strikes were a chaotically unpredictable affair. Herb's uncanny skill with them was about to get him dissected and analyzed by Intelligence Science Division, I figure, but the war ended and Herb went off the grid. Not just off the planetary grid, but off the Galactic grid as well."

Candy interjected and more shadows moved behind her, deep recollections, implications of intrigue, "Herb and his covert-ops teams could get behind enemy lines, wreak havoc, and then be back before Command knew they had left. Herb had lost faith in the government's rationale for the war, this one and others. He was, in all reality, on his own."

On his own…with wormholes.

"He liked Hammer, though. Like a son."

Somehow this had embarrassed Hammerstein, his ancient granite façade pulled down and his bushy-haired cadet revealed underneath.

"Yeah, I was assigned to escort him from the flight deck after he struck back after the Baal incident. They had drawn blood; Herb hit back-and hit back hard. Laid waste to a portion of Baal's Northern hemisphere with a nasty comet dump. Ba-Booma: the sky opened above an enemy division and suddenly a rain of cometary material wormholed down, going from below zero to high temperature in a sudden furious explosion with such relentless and persistent mass most of the personnel shields were fractured and collapsed."

There was a grim satisfaction behind the story for Him-Herb had delivered payback to the enemy. At the same time, that "enemy" who paid was in all reality just a bunch of grunts and guys and gals like himself-people who didn't want to be there, no matter how much machismo they mustered, and who had no say either in the orders to attack in the first place.

Candy took Hammerstein's pause as an invitation to finish, "The shields that did hold, well, that did them no good either. Suddenly buried under tons of molten cometary rock, shielded or not they weren't going anywhere.

Surely it was a more merciful fate to go quickly.

Herb and his covert team rode down in the debris hidden in faux boulders that passed any air and space-born defense scans. They assumed control of the region, planting themselves atop the cooling cometary debris and making sure no rescue arrived for any buried enemy units.

He pushed the rules of war right to the line between battle and atrocity, to that ugly grey area nobody likes to think of."

The two of them dropped silent and I realized then the bond they shared-the Baal incident had been their first combat experience. The mass and sudden death, the dislocation from the romantic notions of youth directly to the reality and banality of war with its ugly evils; they had lost their innocence together. Not in some romantic fairy tale love story set in opulent gardens and universities, but in the sights and sounds of the war.

"And you think Herb masterminded these attacks and the kidnapping of the Princess?" I asked, sorting through their emotions. Candy, curiously dark, Hammerstein suddenly revolted.

"Herb is an arms dealer. A used starship salesman. Expensive curious-contraband. He is no longer a mercenary or master assassin. He would, however, know many such men. I believe Herb can point us in the right direction," Hammer said crisply.

Candy filled with dark humor, "The trick will be finding Herb. Langley Stay is an Outspace world, its cities carved out of solid stone in endless canyons, and interlaced with labyrinths of canals. A lynchpin between the refugee worlds of the Sagittarius Arm of the galaxy and the Orion Arm, any Imperial order is purely pastiche-it is a smugglers' and mercenaries' world. They will not hand over their own to some Royal request from Caldris."

"If I can find him, he'll talk to me."

Herbivore had pushed the rules of war to their limits. "Rules of war" --such as they are, the protocols of mass murder.

Hammerstein's faith in his long-ago friendship with the old "black devil Herbivore" was a ghost of a ghost. Strangely, I felt in many ways these ghosts were made of things more real than much of the universe mankind concocted…

The monument to the lost ships of the line in the Baal incident is not at the capitol as one would expect, but at Cooper River Valley where the main city fades away to the highlands. The planet's greatest city, Cooper Trans, built on trade and shipping rather than governing, dissolves into patterns of less dense and dense buildings on bluffs overlooks the shipyards where the ships of the line had been built. The shipyards can be seen spilling out and out into the sea where the underwater and floating habitations predominate.

On the bluff, an artist had been commissioned whose answer to the design problem was a series of symbolic vanes resembling the command and communications towers of the battleships. They are striking obelisks, smoothed in places like a Henry Moore work from the 20th century, and laced with holograms like a Sanj Moghul from the 29th.

It was the greatest loss of life ever experienced by the Caldris Royal Space Naval Forces. At the end of the sculpted obelisks, many human-scale figures are looking back. The first group represents the bridge crews of the surviving ships who witnessed the tragedy. They stare back forever in shocked disbelief. The second group represents the commandos who raided back. It is a strange yin and yang, this duality of man-the first group idealistic and traumatic, the second-grim justice personified.

-Princess Clairissa Maggio.

Shane Perry

VII

Eberhardt to Langley Stay

There was room enough in the Eberhardt hold for Coco-butter Parsons' Hammerhead which delighted him to no end. He took command of piloting with a flourish and the lot of us made for deep space. Fort Oort fell away and Parsons brought the flight plan vertical to the stellar plane negotiating the easier clear of the cloud.

On the holo screens and main piloting cabin, I watched a holo model of the Caldris system. It shrank and the stellar configuration of fifty light-years appeared with the Caldris system highlighted. Then that configuration shrank, and three times was replaced with various magnitudes of scale until at last the gap between the Orion and Sagittarius arm of the galaxy appeared.

A system was highlighted, there in the gap. Langley Stay, Void's End

Coco-butter was MERGED with his new toy, happily playing music, when he broke into hyper. A platoon of Rangers was milling about the quarters and playing cards and eating on the ship's cruise. The Detective and his assistant were conferring and reviewing forensic data in the officer's mess.

A droid was serving co-pilot to Parsons. Mr. Gibbon's by my side, it occurred to me were smaller mirrors of the two. We watched the Caldris system fall away in a simulation on one of the screens. We were moving at incomprehensible speeds, but the simulations mastered those speeds and recreated them with accurate models.

Eberhardt was a charger. Faster than any ship I'd ever been on. Even my father's racing yachts were no match.

I reached into the hyperstreams and felt for bad intent. There was, however, nothing but the epochal spaces expanding with their radiant energies since the bang of our universe. Forces, vectors, molecules in the deep streams, beyond the edge now since we rode the hyperstreams.

No more assassins. For now.

Days came and went aboard the ship. The routine of hyperspace. Since Star systems were full of gravity wells, the best courses avoided them until one arrived at the destination system. We made for the space between the galactic arms-the void. Very few systems in the voids.

It was my first venture outside the five or six star systems around Caldris, beyond the Royal Hegemony.

My head ached and my body was wracked with sudden pains after a time. Thoughts of the missing Princess had taken a toll. There was, however, a small solace or retreat.

The warmth old Hammerstein granted was a comfort-but the continual hustle and bustle in strange environs, the attacks as well, battered me. The Eberhardt streamed through the hyper dimensions and I tried to gather my strength in my bunk.

Who to trust-and who were sharpening their knives to plant them deep in our backs?

It would only get worse, I knew, at Langley Stay. Light years away I could sense that system like a tangled web of intrigues looming in the void. I glanced at Mr. Gibbon, always watching, and was glad for him-a faithful friend in a universe of treacherous rogues.

The ruins of New Haven City were particularly disturbing. Here the bold colonists had dared reclaim the best in mankind's dreams only to have it come to this. Here they had carried their cherished ideals and set out upon the uncharted with dash and brilliance, and here too the meaner aspects of human vice had ground those hopes once again to nothing. The genius of their architecture-once soaring, deft and Dexter-sad relics.

My team and I negotiated the strange landscape of horrors with a curious confusion; unsure at all times the realities that lay behind the war. CCCE claimed always the Colonials had built an armada planning attack-but such was not the character of the colonists to take by force that which they earned by creativity and dogged work. The macabre landscape told of ultimate betrayal. Betrayal of an ideal, nay-a betrayal of all that was ideal in mankind.

My eyes must have been a frightful sight.

Later, underneath the Capitol, I chanced upon a disk in the transportation hub and wondered. It contained the transportation logs of the entire city the week before the war. I could recreate that week in its ordinary prelude to the tragedy. How strange that would be.

-Princess Maggio, Caldris.

Langley Stay, Void's End

Tokushima was at the helm when the Eberhardt signaled Langley Stay system. The edge of the Sagittarius Spiral Arm of the galaxy, the world was an anomaly among the Outworlds in several ways. It had been a spearhead settlement at a time when the ancient nation-state of "America" had still existed before Earth itself became just one more world in the Imperium. From there, the Americans and various affiliated nations had settled the Arcturian Colonies, and then Langley had too fallen into Imperial hands, and in a final twist won a sort of de facto independence after the war when the Imperials abandoned it. In the thousands of years since, with the rise of the refugee Outworlds, now it was important again but its culture was entirely untamed.

We were being hailed. Systems were responding to auto-scans when holos of Security officers from their system police appeared. "Processing registrations," one of the holos said, with a sudden widening of the eyes when he realized it was a Royal Warship from Caldris.

"Caldris Royal Envoy," Tokushima informed him.

"Officer Tokushima on official business." "Yes, we see. Rather a large warship, officer. What is the nature of your business in the system, and what is your anticipated stay?"

"Two criminal acts of extreme violence against law officers-one at Caldris, and one near Fort Oort. We traced the vessel to a possible source and wish to confer with the same in the system" she replied coolly. "A week perhaps."

I smiled. Police, they stick together no matter what star system they were from. An unwritten code-police were attacked; you have to let us hunt down the buggers.

"Registration confirmed, keep us updated weekly. The warship is to port at system security station main hangar. You have shuttles down-world we presume?"

She hesitated, "One Hammerhead."

Now they hesitated. The holos looked back and forth at each other, finally, one shrugged-the cop code prevailed- "Yeah, well, alright, please confer any suspects before engaging fire."

"Absolutely." She smiled.

Now she owed them one, but we were in. In for a long docking protocol at the security station and finally after red tape, tiddlywinks, dirty looks, and berthing fees, they let us take the Hammerhead downworld with a bit of finger-wagging and "if there is any untoward activity please...no interplanetary incidents!" Don't kill any bad guys, leave that for us. Hammerstein nodded and nodded and nodded and sighed and finally Coco-butter got his music playing and we were airborne over the bright arc of the planet, "Going down, baby!" Coco-butter informed us as if the whole brilliant planet in front of us was invisible.

"So we are...." Hammerstein smiled.

Coco-butter looked at him expectantly, "Any place in particular...Sir?"

The Hammerhead was heating up and I sensed Coco-butter Parson's flight instincts easing the gravity repulsion field to counter the pull of the planet. He played with the controls a bit and the craft turned into a huge spiraling corkscrew slowly down. From Hammerstein came a flood of memories. Herb arriving at the fleet after the enemy wormhole massacre. Herb's glassy-eyed orders for the counter strike. Herb's surprising declaration after the counter strike's success, "All those men and women on both sides, dead. For what?

Some piss-ant real estate? Look around, kid. The universe is overflowing with worlds and resources. At the end of the day, when people go about killing each other, it's because someone somewhere simply WANTS to. I didn't sign up to be a butcher for fools and monsters. I'm out, after this tour, I'm out...you can take the King's Navy and--"

Hammerstein's thoughts raced back across the decades to the present, "There, where the Yellow Seas meet the delta. Take the flight pattern over there. You'll find a city." They hovered over a vast spread of warehouse blocks serviced by canals, the fjords shouldering the sea. The city was built into the rock of the cliff sides, canals carved through solid stone bluffs. On the pinnacles of stone buttes, spires and domes proliferated. Air transports buzzed about, some in streams, others freely. A metropolis carved into and piled on the limestone crags.

We put down in an open fish market at the delta which included some flats with water ships dry-docked, a busy wharf and a number of small transports such as ourselves.

I reached out to the ether, as it were. I sensed no malice or subterfuge. We were barely raising notice. We were just another transport at a busy port. I felt a couple of the fishermen's thoughts take small ire at a military vehicle taking up space in their work areas, but that was a mere annoyance. It seems we had arrived on the world and none of the police at the station forewarned any criminals-a good sign they were an honest bunch. Peering from a window I got my first look at Langley Stay for myself. It was as the stories said; everyone was wearing masks....

We made do with flight helmets. I felt quite ridiculous, Tokushima, Hammerstein and myself making our way casually onto the wharf and open spaces...with flight helmets on. Not even the possibly stylish MERGE helmets, but second rate crash helmets.

"We need to buy masks." Hammerstein declared the obvious.

"Shopping! On assignment. At the edge of the Outworlds. This promises to be...different." Tokushima snarked.

Hammerstein's flight helmet turned and I didn't need to be a psychic to feel that vibe.

"Sorry, Sir," she retreated.

We did look ridiculous.

As it turned out, not for long. Hammerstein quickly rooted out a shop of masks and what a shop it was-much to Tokushima's chagrin, the place was a wonder of fabulous items. I chose a Ripjackle mask-a a particularly fierce beast from Opa-locka's world. Hammerstein selected one of Mercury, the Roman god of travelers, merchants, and thieves. Tokushima found one bearing a stylistic feel for Japan, and we made a quick return to the Hammerhead to lose the flight helmets and bore the weary look of Parsons.

He was wise enough, however, not to say anything.

Then we were off along the canals again, masked and ready. No one spoke, Hammerstein trolling on sorting his distant memories against the realities of the present. Things are always smaller or bigger in our memories.

He was heading for a waterfront nightclub. The masks didn't cover one's mouth, so if we wished we could even eat and drink with them on, such was the custom of the place.

It wasn't long before the sight of a bare face would have been shock-when in Rome, as they say.

It was daytime so the club was virtually empty. There was all manner of arched and carved ways and rooms, decorative plants, hologram art. A bunch of screens with games from the Empire. Various hypercasts. It was a small galaxy, it seems. I knew some of the channels.

We sat and were promptly approached by a bejeweled and masked waitress. Supple-beautiful, and centuries-old I realized-a cloner, this was her third clone incarnation. Somewhere behind her mask, and behind the frivolously attractive clone lay a personality of a woman from worlds away, and generations before.

I was, in my way, suddenly awed. Behind an ordinary façade, an extraordinary history.

"Welcome," she offered brightly, placing chilled water glasses and bread before us, "I'm Sasha."

The table glowed presently with images of food for us to choose from.

Fish, fish, and more fish.

Tokushima selected a bread soup.

"I'll have the fish," I said, "Caldrisian Salmon. With garlic butter, and crab cakes on the side."

Hammerstein selected a steak.

We ate quietly. Waiting for something to happen.

When it happened, it was a balding slight of a man, dark-skinned and masked with a strange golden happy Buddha face.

"Travelers from afar?" he hovered and swayed in a faux attempt at grace and light-heartedness he did not feel. He was a trader, eager to overcharge tourists.

"Indeed. Indeed. Very far." Hammerstein was always like a well-oiled trap ready to snap.

"My name is Hugo," he smiled behind the Buddha, "if there is anything I can do to assist while you stay here at…Langley Stay?"

He said it like a question even though it was an incomplete sentence that wasn't a question.

Now Hammerstein smiled beneath the Mask of Mercury, "Indeed. Indeed. We need an aircar. But not just any aircar, no, no. We require an exquisite ride of early model, retrofitted with the most contemporary appointments and technologies, with the security, of course, being no small issue for my wife and son."

Tokushima blushed, but with a distinct pleasure at that. Sensing it, and all it implied, I too blushed, thankful for the mask of a sudden.

"Ahhh, yes, of course! Nothing but best!"

An impression was coming across then from the Buddha man. An older version of Herbivore. Hammerstein knew this gig like a well-practiced drill. I was in awe.

"You know then where we may find such an aircar?" Tokushima asked coyly.

"Yes. I do." He replied smugly. "And I shall be delighted to take you there immediately after lunch!" He bowed.

Hammerstein showed his teeth in a forced smile. But only dashing Mercury looked back at the trader.

"Thank you."

Now hit the road 'till we're done eating.

It was a delicious lunch. Then Buddha was back, sporting a long brocaded coat and an effected casual saunter.

He gave a momentary pause and Hammerstein didn't miss a beat, "Five percent?"

"Done."

An open aircab drifted down and we all piled in. Buddha leaned over to the driver, "Herb." was all he said and all that was needed to be said.

We were aloft, below us the boat-filled canals and shops suddenly falling away, above us security fields glimmering transparent. The sky was abuzz with all manner of vehicles. I traced very few traffic control guide beams but there didn't appear any urgency or concern from Buddha or the driver.

We careened about the city and then finally there was a large stone warehouse with numerous roof levels. Rows of vehicles and servicemen and bots tending them gleamed in the sun. A wonderland of styles, aircars from all corners and ages of the galaxy.

My eyes widened beneath my mask, "Whoa…" I said stupidly and Tokushima chuckled a little at that.

We landed and Buddha took Mercury about the rooftop of a collection of aircars the like of which I had never imagined.

I began to wander when Tokushima took my hand, "SON!" she said, "Remember, Daddy is on business!"

She was so awesome, even when chiding me I took little notice of the chide. So were the aircars, however, and I was getting my first taste of decadent luxuries in an exotic place. With a sporty female officer, and there was not even a peer on the planet with whom I could flaunt it.

There was, however, a serious matter of a kidnapped Princess-my Princess, and I sought to pull my delight over the delicious design excesses of centuries of artistry back into some manner of perspective relative to the scenario.

I managed.

Herb had arrived. Older. I synchronized the images Hammerstein's memories had Conveyed-Herb the mighty Navy officer, bane of star legions, with an ordinary appearing aircar salesman.

Herb leaned forward toward Hammer. They recognized each other's jawlines across the decades, even masked.

Soldiers forever.

"Hammer!"

"Herbivore."

Herb chuckled, "Herbivore…yeah. Long-time ago. I'm assuming you'll need the best and all the special extras."

"Of course."

"The Hermes. It comes with a droid. Seats seven. It can make escape velocity and will go a full parsec before you need to…refuel, dock, or die."

"Prefer to dock than die."

"Me too. You'll want the Hermes."

"Done."

"No haggling, you always did have a certain class. But it tells me you're either rich as the Royals or working for them."

"The latter. Yes, I'm here on official business. Let's go inside."

Herb signaled one of his men, "Get the Hermes done up, it's sold."

We moved into the warehouse-proper and I saw Herb's collection was not limited to the aircars on the rooftops. There were star yachts, dog-fighters, freighters-on and on. The quantum echoes of all these vehicles slammed at me with their histories and I found myself dizzy from the impressions.

I tried to follow the conversations. Hammerstein was asking Herb about wormhole equipment. Had he sold any recently?

Herb was resigned, not out of fear, but out of some strange moral code he operated by. He and Hammerstein were of a kind, they shared an experience that made Hammerstein…unique. When he needed information, Herb would provide it.

"Don't get much call' for it. Not many that can handle wormholing. Mostly they try, and mostly they die. Takes a special breed to ride that storm. This group-they looked kind of tawdry. Wannabees. But they could pay, and who am I to keep a fool and his money together longer than the fates would conspire?"

Hammerstein barely held back a grim snort.

Herb continued, "I'd heard the name before-No-Deal DePaulo. Supposed to be a bit of a player at the Core. He didn't look like much to me. Said he had a client, Imperial. Needed a wormhole capable frigate. We went over the equipment, he gave me the money, and he and the ship were gone before the suns set."

"The Core? He's a core smuggler?"

"Galactic core-Tangeonprioc to be specific. Hangs out at the Corewinds Tavern."

"He told you that?"

Herb's grizzled visage smiled, "He didn't have to-he was wearing the T-shirt, "Corewinds Tavern. Best Damn Bar in Tangeonprioc."

It occurred to me then, our entire investigation could have run into a dead-end at Langley Stay if it weren't for a slimeball smuggler's choice of bad sentimentality of attire one day. Yet there it was.

"And his ship…a rather creepy name, "'Mel's Monkey'…nasty looking mutant monkey as the ship's emblem. Has a bayonet in its mouth and 'Central Galactic' underneath as if there was any sort of civil authorities out there, which there ain't."

"Thanks, Herb. The Hermes, she ready?"

"She was ready before you left the Caldris system, Buck. Don't forget who you're buying from-my hardware works."

"Yeah, well, I got that. Almost took us out-they hit us with the wormhole."

That brought a frown to Herb. "Sorry to hear that. You spank 'em?"

"Yeah, hard, A little dodgy, but we got lucky."

"Are you taking the kid and the lady on a payback run? To the Core? To Tangeonprioc?"

Hammerstein paused, I sensed he thought for a moment to explain, but didn't see any good would come of it.

"Yeah, that's the plan."

"Lot of Marauders in the core. Make sure that Hermes is battened down good before you start shooting Marauders, aye Buck?"

"Will do, Herb. We'll make sure the Hermes is safe and sound before the firing starts."

"Good. Good. Don't want to see any scratches on her when you come back and tell me how the story plays out."

"Herb, if I can fly that Hermes back to this…warehouse, I'm going to make sure there's not a scratch on it."

So went our visit to Langley Stay at voids end where we acquired a particularly well-appointed luxury aircar of Classic Make from the Pleiades. We had a suspect-the notorious No-deal-DePaulo, and a destination. Tangeonprioc. Sin city of the galactic core, smack dab in Marauder territory. Marauders, worse than the smugglers and the core syndicates, harbingers of a strange cult-rumored to be entirely mad and without ordinary human remorse, fear, or reason.

I was, however, distracted. One of the techs had brought up the Hermes and it was one sweet ride.

Shane Perry, Steve Moore

Book Two: No-Deal DePaulo and the Core Pirates

Prelude

...They were waiting for us when we dropped out of hyperspace, I could sense them then, a dirty little swarm, and sickeningly the most frightening thing was they had once been human.

CCCE Empires hammered my ears and my empathic senses were then overwhelmed—the strange Marauders' minds, with their ugly snake eye stares hammering my mind, then the sudden tussle of twenty hardcore airmen their adrenaline and training kicking in with a slam.

"This is not a drill!" Coco-butter Parsons howled but the airmen's boots were already banging steel, half of them at their guns.

We were sitting ducks and there were a dozen Marauder ships, easy. Particle beam fire slashed away at our ship, the Eberhardt. The Marauders doubtless had never seen a Caldris Royal Navy warship here at the Galactic Core, even through their snake infected minds I could sense a huge wave of surprise come back as we took their fire and the mighty Eberhardt rose through the maelstrom of ionized particles and maligned atomic clouds her guns announcing payback.

Nobody missed and the Marauder shielding, magnetized ore layered over their giant ramjets began to strip away in a fireworks show such that the demonic, snaky victimizers were revealed for the devils they were, squealing and riding fire with the hellish super-massive black hole and its light-years of swirling accretion disk as their background.

Still, no one stopped firing on either side and we rode the streams in a twirling death volley of destruction. Hammerstein, impossibly, was cursing and longing for a gun port...

Three weeks earlier…

Destination: Tangeonprioc

We had a suspect—the notorious No-Deal-DePaulo. Destination: Tangeonprioc. Sin city of the galactic core, smack dab in Marauder territory. Marauders, worse than the smugglers and the core syndicates, harbingers of a strange cult—rumored to be entirely mad and without ordinary human remorse, fear, or reason.

I was, however, distracted. One of the techs had brought up the Hermes and it was one sweet ride. We hovered over the fishing port where Coco-butter waited. I could feel his surprise, and a bit of boyish excitement—and yes, as a twelve-year-old I DO recognize that it often lingers well into manhood—over the Hermes.

"Nice ride, Sir." He quipped across the com.

Hammerstein contained a small glow of pride; then made a guilty glance at Tokushima. She realized the two gentlemen were having an "OH YEAH!" moment amid a serious investigation and she looked away embarrassed for them both.

"Uhhh, yeah, well, yes, it is. A necessary part of the game though—Herb had his price for the information and it was…"

"The most expensive class A-luxury aircar in an entire warehouse the size of a small city." Tokushima finished slyly.

Hammerstein gave her a dry look, "Anyway, the intel was priceless—we have a suspect's name and location, so we need to get back to the Eberhardt."

"Yes, Sir."

The Hammerhead was already powering up. We hovered a bit more until it was airborne and the two craft made for the station.

The Hermes's gravity bubble was a luxury unit—you could have set a crystal wine glass full of red on a white silk napkin on its console and it wasn't so much as going to ripple—no matter how hard the gees or tight the banks. I watched Langley Stay become a world again, the station a place (with annoying customs agents) all without the slightest sense of movement—although the world and station banked about me at the most amazing angles as Hammerstein ruminated at the wheel over his lost years and his honor and his career and his princess all at risk in the same unimaginable contest he now faced.

The old granite beast had two families from two marriages, I realized for the first time—so focused his thoughts were on his mission, so compartmentalized his mind—he had not revealed them. I took a frightful note then; even with my psychic abilities, there were important and central aspects of some people that could be put out of their minds. I realized why, too, at that moment he did this—if the full weight of his concerns pressed in on him at any given time he would simply become catatonic. He managed his survival by stripping away from his thoughts whole aspects of his life and living in watertight time compartments.

We docked with the Eberhardt, parked and locked down the Hermes in its massive hold. Beside it, Coco-butter spun the Hammerhead down with the natural flourish of daring-do. They pressurized the hold and we also spilled out of the vehicles with a sense of "home" as it were for spacers—and how quickly that sense fills one up—like seawater into a spongy reef. The Eberhardt was home.

THE PANDORAN WARS

"Forrr-maation! Droids at the helm. All human personnel in the hold!" Hammerstein's command voice was different from his detective's voice. War and Reason two realities that intersected, and yet War with its special creeping edge of Chaos ever at the perimeter. Hammerstein was now about to break protocol with the Royal police confidentiality. This was one of those moments when one understood command included risks and couldn't all be pulled out of the manual.

At length, the platoon of Rangers took up a nervous formation in the hold. Coco, Tokushima, and I stood to his side none of us any more informed than the platoon at that moment. Something in Hammerstein's bearing changed; memories were flooding his mind and body now. Stances: attention, at ease, parade rest. His mind swept back through the years to a sunburnt lot and he was a ridiculously young recruit keeping his fingers and thumbs—just so— his heels and toes—just so—his knees bent in the slightest.

He walked up to the platoon, getting right in their faces, "Are you ASHAMED to be under the command of an old fart retiree like me who isn't even Navy anymore? I'll give you a shot, right now, every last one of you city sissies, one after the other, and I'll injure your sorry selves before we go on the mission. Go ahead. The cameras are off."

There were no takers. He couldn't know, but I could. They all somehow knew he could take them, by force of personality, if not by sheer strength.

"Okay, good. You're smarter than you look. Now, since the cameras are off—and yes, I learned that trick in basic training, or I wouldn't have gotten my blue cord, I'm going to fill you in on the mission: In full, for real, and no cards in my pocket. You break faith with me, and you break faith with your platoon because what you are about to hear is not supposed to be told to you, according to my superiors. However, I am not about to fly into harm's way with my superiors, but with you.

We are going to the Core. There are no recognized governments in the Core, only Warlords, Marauders, ghosts, and bones. We are The Law, the arm of the Royal family, Justice and Honor, and we now ride into the belly of The Devil."

The rush of pride that swept the platoon was like a wave of metallic hydrogen deep in a gas giant's dark seas, lit with a million square miles of lightning; death before dishonor. Duty. Joy. Purpose.

"Now, I'm going to tell you why."

They barely breathed.

"The Princess has been stolen."

I don't have words for what came from the platoon then—it was too confusing a mass of emotion—rage, disbelief, despair. At the same time, their muscles strained to remain at attention. Watching Hammerstein from their peripheral vision—a blurry, grizzled detective outrageously placed in command of them, and now informing them on the far side of the void they were going to the Galactic Core on a suicide mission and the Royal family had been violated.

"My recommendation, if we make it back alive if a full grade promotion for all of you. In the meantime, there is more. We believe the princess was kidnapped to prevent her from revealing two aspects of her archaeological work on a Sunrider battle Frigate she and her academics had discovered in Arcturian Space. First, there were no weapons of mass destruction in the Arcturian Colonies, and second, the Sunrider fleet was taken down by some kind of THING—we haven't figured out what it is yet, but it destroys the minds of any person who interacts with it."

I bit my lip and looked to Tokushima. She didn't think we were going to make it out of the Core and was feeling an enormous sense of dread. Sadness for the Princess, AND sadness... sadness that I would not live. That was disturbing, but I smiled anyway. I was determined to prove her wrong in this assessment.

91

"We were attacked twice. Once near the palace, and once near Fort Oort in the Oort clouds. The first attack has shed no clues—we suspect any number of Multi-Stellar Corporations in the armament industry. It's a big list. The second attack we were able to trace at least the origins of the attacking ship's last place of sale—and I just met with him and he provided us a lead."

"We're flying a Royal frigate. Flying the law's colors into the heart of darkness. Our quarry is a man who goes by the name of No-Deal. Mell "No-Deal" DePaulo". When the pirates of the Core give you the name, "No-Deal", chances are you've earned it. His ship is emblazoned with the logo of an evil mutant monkey with a bayonet in is sharpened teeth.

If you're captured, don't expect mercy—they won't be taking any prisoners and they will probably stick you in a pain simulator—possibly for years, in some ungodly humiliating position like a coffee table."

Simultaneously everyone in the room had an ugly feeling that Hammerstein had seen that little horror before. No one wanted to know.

"So be sure and do not allow yourself to be captured. You're all going to be issued a gravity bomb. If the time comes, take out whatever vermin-infested radioactive dome we find ourselves on, but do NOT allow them to take you alive."

The Core Marauders

The ship broke into the hyper-streams a few hours later. She bolted hard, straight up it seemed, though it was an arc trajectory, Galactic North into the Galactic Halo: Quieter up there, better for a long jump. Hammerstein had Coco-butter running full throttle. We hadn't wasted any time so far in this investigation—barely taking time to "wash your hides, your city sissies, and move, move, move…" as the dear old detective would bellow at the men.

They loved that stuff. I think the platoon would have died of boredom before duress. One of them lived at his bunk, polishing his weapons and combat EVA suit over and over. A couple of them went through gunner simulations more often than not. When they weren't watching the ship, it was like they were daring something to be wrong. They checked the systems. Then they checked them again.

Underneath it all however, I sensed their former selves, the civilian selves, like lost loved ones; always there, in the background. Forever younger, back in the world, back at Caldris—memories of their former lives that refused to be forgotten. Bringing lunch out to the over-eager local cop who had been stalking his house, "Well—I figured since you were going to be out here, you might as well have a decent meal..." The sweethearts left behind (one guy had two, always on his mind like the proverbial angel and devil on the shoulders) the mothers and fathers and brothers and sisters and families, now perfect with distance in their memories.

In a little over a week, we were far and away past the last recognized government, past the Sagittarius Galactic Spiral Arm. The crew was nervous about the pace. Even Coco-butter wasn't happy about the strain on the Eberhardt's mighty drive systems—he was quite desperate, though he refused to show it outwardly, being a pilot of some dash.

I heard with Tokushima in a corridor near the piloting cabin, "Can you talk to him? We aren't going to save any princesses if the ship collapses in on itself. We'll make a great light show blasting back into normal space atomized—but no one will probably see it for a couple of million years this far out, and they'll never know who it was."

Tokushima raised an eyebrow. "Don't be a baby. You run it till it breaks the seventh dimension if he says" she snapped, but she was posing too—she knew he was right, and she was scared, sweating in her flight suit. He saw it in her eye, felt badly for her, and put on a face as if wounded to mask that he saw her fear. Games within games between the two of them in a moment's comment and they both walked away grim, death before dishonor.

Blowfish brains and dancing dolphins—I was a kid and hadn't sworn any oaths to die for anything.

"Detective," I said when I next had his ear, "Are you planning to run this ship into the seventh dimension and make us a light show for some arcane astronomer a couple of millennia from now when the light of our collapse and exploding matter slamming back into normal space, or are you going to do the right thing and not test the engineering specs on this vessel with all our lives?"

I smiled my cutest little-boy smile, but my eyes were cold. I liked the detective, but I didn't feel like dying that week.

He almost looked relieved, an excuse to move the dials a couple of notches to the left, swirl the mesons in the colliders a little slower. Mess with the quantum physics of the universe a tad lighter. However, he was Hammerstein and would just as soon die in a blaze of glory as arrive a moment later, even though all logic and reason warranted otherwise. He grunted and went to command. A short while later the whining and humming and vibrating of the ship eased a small but measurable amount.

When we reached perihelion I went up to the bridge. They had the windows unshielded and running a simulation (what the view would look like from where we theoretically were if we were in normal space). So I got to see the Galactic plume and the Core from above as the Eberhardt heaved imperceptibly then down in its flight path.

"Take a look kid," Coco-butter pointed as if I could somehow miss it, "better than anything back in your astronomy classes on Caldris, aye Buck?"

It was one of those moments, when you realize you may never be in that particular astrographic locale again, and something spectacular—in every sense of the word spectacle—is in front of you, and you wish it was more like the holo shows—you know, music, heroic stance, etc. Nonetheless, it was frighteningly beautiful.

The plume is many light-years long, streaming out more energy than the human mind can comprehend, blasted from a black hole larger than most star systems, and surrounded with more stars, fury, and light than all the rest of the galaxy combined.

The kind of things religions are born of; mind-bending awe. The knowledge that you could take all your years, and all the years of everyone you know, stand them end to end and it would be a scratch on the surface of the deep time the object in front of you existed in.

As such, as a spectacle of awe, deep time, and wonder, one would expect religions born. Here too, existed a religion; it was, however, born of no human sense of wonder. The Core was plagued by the Marauder cult. A mysterious, violent, and insane population of sociopaths lost to the rest of humanity: Beyond reason, diplomacy, or compromise. Enough was known about them to know they merited the definition of a culture, not enough to how they had left the realms of ordinary humanity and become worshipers of death, theft, and rampage.

They were waiting for us when we dropped out of hyper at the edges of the Tangeonprioc system. Hammerstein had the men set about the ship at guns, back engines, and gravity bomb ports; we were expecting the run in the system wouldn't be pretty.

They were hard to identify at first, Marauder ships aren't like most ships in the worlds. They pack raw ore around their superstructures to the point they look like nothing less than an asteroid.

Effective disguise in an Oort cloud and most systems are surrounded by Oort clouds. Moreover, the radiation is higher here at the core (one of the techs whistled in surprise when we came out of hyper and he saw the readouts). The raw ore around the Marauder ships provides good protection from the rads.

The Eberhardt streamed through the asteroid and proto-comet fields of rubble out-system with graceful, perfect ease. Here and there flares of energy brightened momentarily among the rubble and we took fire.

Eberhardt was a Royal frigate, and her defense fields diverted the fire with ease.

At first.

More flares and they were moving. In number, and along different vectors, I could feel them in the distance. They didn't feel like human minds, as such as I was used too. They reminded me of snakes, roosters—any number of primitive life forms at Caldris native or imported. There was something "off" about them.

Yet they were still human.

I traced the vectors in my mind and realized they inscribed a long series circling our vector. However, "off" these people were, their stalking strategies remained intact.

"They're hunting us," I said quietly on the command bridge.

This is one creepy little kid, a thought came loud and clear from one of the platoon members.

Coco-butter thought differently.

He's right. "We dropped out of hyperspace into a really bad spot. They must lay here in waiting for less seasoned shipping in from the Sagittarius Arm." Even without the sensitive instruments of the starship MERGE helmets; I sensed the snake-minded-Marauders moving in the dark, hiding among the proto-comets and dust: Streaming along in the strange alternate cold and radiant spaces of the core.

The Galactic Plume here defined the spaces—the mightily assembled myriads of stars, star clusters, huge swirling mega spaces of exploding nebula, jammed together, turning like seas—all this huge roaring menagerie, orders of magnitude scaling up and up—a pile of bulb ornaments at the base of a Yule holiday tree.

Somehow the Druid and Celtic roots of that same Yule tree came back to me then; human sacrifice to dark gods of unknowable realms of starlight and aurora.

Thus we careened through the Tangeonprioc system. Around us, invisible snake-minded people rode in asteroids blasting along on hellfire, hungry for our blood and souls. Justin Coco-butter Parsons, our little crew of stalwart Rangers, the grisly old granite detective and the Geisha-doll Tokushima seemed suddenly silly children who wandered into Hell.

Then came the Marauders, what had appeared as mere asteroids suddenly alive.

"This is not a drill!" Coco-butter Parsons howled but the air men's boots were already banging steel, half of them at their guns.

We were sitting ducks and there were a dozen Marauder ships, easy. Particle beam fire slashed away at our ship, the Eberhardt.

The Marauders doubtless had never seen a Caldris Royal Navy warship here at the Galactic Core, even through their snake infected minds I could sense a huge wave of surprise come back as we took their fire and the mighty Eberhardt rose through the maelstrom of ionized particles and maligned atomic clouds her guns announcing payback.

Nobody missed and the Marauder shielding, magnetized-ore layered over their giant ramjets, began to strip away in a fireworks show such that the demonic, snaky victimizers were revealed for the devils they were, squealing and riding fire with the hellish super-massive black hole and its light-years of swirling accretion disk as their background.

Still, no one stopped firing on either side and we rode the streams in a twirling death volley of destruction. Hammerstein, impossibly, was cursing and longing for a gun port...

Velocities. Vectors. Magnetic and Gravitational field generators. Plasma and Particle beams. I was glad I was strapped in, glad for the personnel emergency grav bubbles because the micro-adjustments of the larger warship, no matter how finely tuned, could never be perfect, and with the gymnastics Coco was putting us through even a micro imperfection could send rip your DNA apart at a molecular scale.

The Eberhardt was ripping and whirling space-time in a sickening swirl of some psychotic juggler clown in a shooting gallery of a carnival nightmare of living rocks, snake minded half men, and ever and always the dark, evil primitive godlike black hole, and plume as the background.

Empathically I shuffled through the noise of the whole crew's thoughts and zeroed in on Coco. Here then was a pilot's mind in combat. He had imaged in every one of the Marauders' ships, visualizing where they were, where they would be on each vector, and the tracers of their fire.

Microseconds, the man's mind never stopped calculating the visual dynamics, motion; parry, riposte, spline. The specific energy of the craft weighed in his thoughts like—like a dancing partner, yes—he flew us through the combat fire at the foot of the great core black hole and his dancing partner was death.

He never broke a sweat, and for the second time in my young life, I was given a window to a grown man's mind in combat. Two primal motivations walled his consciousness—the enemy fire and his responsibility to the crew. Even as the snake minds and the bustling crews' thoughts impinged on my empathic young mind in the chaos of weapons fire and the unpredictable evasive maneuvers, Justin "Coco-butter" Parsons' mind came back in my perceptions with a platinum clockwork and atomic precision.

Duty trumped danger, and his focus was complete.

I pulled my mind away from the pilot's then—one of the Marauder ship's magnetized ore shielding had finally surrendered to the persistent electroplated jackhammering of a determined gunner and there came a wild wail from the deepest levels of searing hell as a crew of snake minds witnessed their violent deaths and a brutal yet cool satisfaction from the gunner.

"Bird down!" he snapped, his MERGE controls already joining his fire on another target.

The explosion of the Marauder's vessel blinded Coco for a split second and too late I sensed the Marauder Captains calculated advantage as he targeted a fold in the defensive fields of the Eberhardt. Before I could yell warning we were hot aft, near the main warp collider.

The particle beams ran through conduit ducts in an ugly parody of the duct's intent. The energy stream cascaded, twisted, convoluting and slammed hard into one of our gunners killing him instantly.

Coco-butter's soul then shifted like a hyper phase change than to a condition I will ever dread to recall. That one death had equated somehow to the death of us all and in wicked sneering spin, already dead in his mind, we became Death and vengeance.

His gunners' emotions echoed his, and dead already in their minds and hearts, all concern for survival was secondary to reeking as much death and payback as possible before our fiery demise.

Horribly, in a surreal nocturnal realm, there came a kind of music from their souls and they too took on an aspect of reptiles themselves in a savaging blood lust and fury.

It was a maneuver that took the Marauders entirely by surprise and as they overshot their marks the Eberhardt's gunners suddenly calmed, their wild-eyed aspect freezing in a "five-five-five-lead-FIRE!"

Three more of the Marauders ate their demise in a limb rending and atomizing waves of obliteration.

The remaining demons then fired ramjets and shifted away, and away, and away.

Sanity returned from the berserker fury of Coco-butter's mind and he eased the mighty Eberhardt around, returning the warship to its original flight plan.

The domes of Tangeonprioc.

Palace log entry a.c. 236904.b Clairissa Maggio. Prewar and postwar—this pattern has been repeated in its various forms through the many centuries, the prewar conditions of the various societies generally peace and prosperity and postwar; hellish dystopian ruins of their worlds: Dispossession, death, loss. Come the Dark Age.

And so it has been with the Core worlds. Before the Arcturian Wars, the Core worlds were the Gallant Frontier and strange shining achievement of all frontiers mankind had ever reached. The Galactic Core was a singular sort of exclamation and affirmation of all hyperbolic dreams of Heaven and celestial ambition.

Everything at the Core…larger than life and the settlers as such heroic archetypes, explorers, settlers, builders of cities and worlds in a manner exemplified and edified by the scale of the Core. The giant Black Hole and its super streaming accretion disc, the density of the stars, like an epic choral of angels; the metals, the crystals, the energy streams and then finally, the discovery of Predecessor base ruins.

Then, came the deluge. Strangely the Arcturian war's first surprise attacks didn't come announced over the hypercasts, they came at archaeological sites as the Predecessor ruins lit up—equipment many, many millions of years in the dust coming to life in a kaleidoscope of holograms, colors, and lights.

The archaeological crew, over a hundred academics, and staff disappeared. They were, however, little noted except for one more strange and suddenly supernatural tale among the abounding horrors of the war, the war whose death toll single-handedly trumped the entire history of man's inhumanity to man.

The core worlds…once proud archetypes of heroic courage suddenly found themselves cut off from the comings and goings of mankind. The Arcturian civilization had been their bridge to mankind, and the Arcturian Colonials were no more. What had been the bright new frontier was now merely a lawless desperate mass of ill-equipped cities. Then, as the legend goes, the Marauder Cults appeared. Something had changed these people, profoundly and mysteriously. Preying on the remnant civilizations left in the Core and the meager trade still dribbling back and forth, the Marauders still LOOKED somewhat human but the few taken prisoner behaved so bizarrely as to deem them de-facto aliens after a fashion.

There was nothing left of their mammalian natures and they were, it seemed, very intelligent dragons in their minds.

At Tangeonprioc, the former Capitol world of the core Colonies, what has followed since has been a thousand years of brutal criminal culture. This morning I chanced upon some star charts in the palace library. They were of the core, and hadn't been updated since…

"Haven't been updated since antebellum times." Hammerstein tossed the charts on an instrument dash. Justin "Coco-butter" Parsons looked back darkly.

"We're lucky to have them at all, Sir. The Caldris system hasn't had many dealings with the Core. We're going to war, as it were, with the Army we have."

Hammerstein smiled and it wasn't a happy smile. "Yeah, well, I might have worked through some…unofficial channels to get us better charts had I known. What other wonderful insights do you have for me this morning? Why did we have to drop out of hyper so far out from Tangeonprioc?"

"System protocols. That's what the hyper beacons dictate."

Hammerstein glowered.

"The psychic kid says the Marauders are still on our backend. He can 'feel them, like evil lizards' moving through the void, through the wastelands of this system's battered Oort cloud."

"Not surprised at that."

"Perhaps, but they're outside our scan range. So if the kid is right, it means although they've never seen a Caldris Royal War Ship, they're chalking up crucial system data on us, very quick. Bim, Bam, Boom—and that's creepy."

"They were pretty spooky from the get-go, aye? Just knew where we'd come out of hyper; good pilots riding the stream to Tangeonprioc make for point 'A'. So we did, and they were waiting."

"The kid says they got minds like lizard-birds!"

"We bring the Princess back, and I want a big retirement bonus and a houseboat on the Tangerine Sea."

At the mention of the Tangerine Sea both of their rugged and fierce aspects faded and there came over them a quality of teenage boys with a crush.

"Living off the fat of the Sea!"

They were quiet a moment, and there came a hailing on the com.

"I'll get the kid, you answer and stall them, I want his empathic powers sniffing for trouble."

I was already at the door.

"Good timing!" Hammerstein brightened.

"Timing has nothing to do with it, Detective." I winked. I was getting cocky.

"Prescience," Parsons whispered.

The com still hailed.

Hammerstein gave a nod. Parsons flipped a toggle.

"Royal Caldris War vessel, please respond."

I smiled up at Hammer. The Core! The glorious, corrupt, storied and criminal Core. They were hailing us.

"This is Royal Inspector Hammerstein. We are here on peaceful official business."

Hissing interference.

"Glad to hear that, inspector. This is Carleton Spriggs. Now, we don't have much in the way of official titles out here at the Core. Guess I'm kind of a …enforcer of Common-Law protocols.

"Now that's a lot of dead Marauders you left in your wake. Not to say I don't personally celebrate such an artful performance of death-dealing among the Rooster heads, but they'll be back. So, please, what is your business at Tangeonprioc?"

"We're here to discuss Royal Family business with an individual by the name of 'No-Deal DePaulo."

There came a long pause, and then a laugh from somewhere behind Spriggs. Ha. Ha-ha. Then a staccato burst of laughter and it seemed the whole room of people with Spriggs was laughing.

"You flew a Royal Caldris War ship through a convoy of Marauders, Thirty Thousand Light-Years from home to meet with 'No-Deal'?"

Another pause, then even more raucous laughter let go.

'We're recording this Mr. Spriggs, if you and your people would refrain from mocking the Royal Family, please."

Spriggs must have waved down his comrades because the laughter subsided. He returned, "Officer Hammerstein, no offense to the Royal Family. It is the thought of the Royal family's stature and credibility associated with the likes of 'No-Deal' that seems quite preposterous."

"I assure you it is not. And I assure you, the Royal Family is quite serious about me meeting with Mr. No-Deal DePaulo. We have plenty of more warships besides this. The matter that concerns us is serious enough for us to come in a warship, and mention we have many more.

"I would suggest your cause for amusement is misplaced, and the whereabouts of Mr. No-Deal DePaulo be ascertained."

I didn't need empathic senses to know the voice from Tangeonprioc just got a lot cooler and less amused.

"We'll have to discuss this when you arrive. Our security bots have determined you took a serious hit in that engagement and you're leaking plasma; your warp colliders will need to be serviced. We don't hand over our citizens to foreign governments without an explanation or a criminal act and tons of expedition paperwork. An escort will meet you deeper in the system."

Behind us, I sensed the Marauders had begun to move again—closer. Already I sensed the system, and extrapolating thus all the systems of the Core, was in a perpetual state of siege. At the wide peripheries of their systems, like Fort Oort, hardscrabble embattlements ever ready for the claxon call of wailing horror and the Marauder ramjets.

This we had just passed.

The worlds of the Tangeonprioc system had two gas giants relatively close to its star, inside the Goldilocks zone. There were three more rocky planets outside the zone. The star was a small thing, not much bigger than Sol. Tangeonprioc was the first of the rocky worlds: Small, yet still large enough to get classified M-class. Its atmosphere wasn't anything one could breathe, the original settlers had planned terraforming and their cities were domed.

The domes of Tangeonprioc thus ubiquitous, boom towns which had mushroomed up with the metals trade of the antebellum era. With its massive black hole, the cosmic forces unique to the core produced its massive supply of ores. With the discovery of a plethora of Predecessor ruins in the region, even the Great Arcturian War had not crushed the trade of the region.

The Galaxy remained eternally hungry for Predecessor relics.

The Eberhardt passed a dozen stations on asteroids. They were covered over with ugly, sloppy metropolises of surreal construction, mechanized settlements with no grace or pattern. Then down to the Domes of Tangeonprioc

The Domes of legendary reputation; peopled with the lawless, byzantine, corrupt. The Royal Caldris warship was given berth in a mechanic's bay where our combat damages could be repaired.

"Keep your teams on the ready." Hammerstein glowered at Parsons. "Tokushima, take the kid, his android, and a sniper. Meet me at the Hermes."

Down in the Hold, we clambered into the aircar, waited for the big doors to open. The car lifted and drifted into the city proper. The service bays were buzzing with the activity of dozens of ships. Everyone was armed to the teeth.

Hammerstein looked at me grimly. He knew my mind would now be impinged upon with the crude thoughts of rough men and women. It was already a chorus in my head, and it wasn't pretty.

An officer on an air bike met us. We followed. There were numerous other spies I realized and not just official ones either. Five families seemed to hold sway over the city, and numerous gangs. It was a spy party as we pulsed along in the Hermes, nearly all of them engaged in some sort of work so unless I was there no one would have been the wiser.

We crossed through force fields between divergent sectors. If a dome was breached damaged would be limited to the immediate area of the breach. Overhead the plexisteel of the domes glowed with an eerie translucent light from the crowded stars of the Core.

Each of the open areas of the domes was surrounded by steeply rising walls and terraces of buildings. The pattern was repeated in variations.

The substructures consisted of complex radial and concentric corridors, astercrete vaults running multiple layers deep into the bedrock of the planet.

The main areas of the domes featured gardens. Elaborate decorative detailing of Core metals and glass, resplendent with large mirrors, polished moon's marble, mosaics of glass from inner worlds battered by supermassive stellar flares, and borders of designs faced over on all sides in difficult patterns arranged in many colors like paintings.

Pools of water overflowed, irrigated, and flashed up in the muted light of the plexisteel monumental hemispherical interiors. These were ancient spaces from another era, before the Arcturian war. Original colony cities as such trying to create a natural environment of park-like spaces for their inhabitants who expected someday the planet would be terraformed.

It was to the actual first of the terraforming towers the Hermes streamed. We crossed a field barrier, came at length to a particularly vast space whose dome was a clear plexisteel revealing four pylon bases of thirty of forty stories', with only one of the pylon towers finished. A few lights near the top indicated the offices of Mr. Spriggs I realized.

Our sniper contingent was a Sergeant Roszak. Besides having eyes for Tokushima, he was persistently calculating distances of individuals the aircar passed. Only the female officer distracted him from his mental targeting, and even then only briefly and against his will. He fought down the distraction of her beauty, persistently.

It was, of course, a bit of a task; two million years of female evolution had designed her specifically to be noticed. Noticed, and captivating. I laughed inside.

The poor fellow was focusing so hard on being ready to defend us to the death. Then she would turn, or the light catch her cheek, and his bayonet—sharp concentration was knocked off balance again.

There had appeared several airbikes and police cruisers by the time the Hermes came to rest on a cantilevered terrace near the top of the tower. Apparently, no one had informed the other police regarding our identity; I could only sense annoyance from them. The gangsters and pirates spying and mulling about in the domes as we passed had been better informed. They knew we were Royal Caldris Navy and we were looking for No-Deal DePaulo.

DePaulo, I sensed, was either loved or hated: Strangely enough, seeming sometimes both at the same time. "The British Bull Dog', he hailed originally from Merry Old Earth, Londinium, and Angeland. Then Duty with the Mercury Marines. He famously wore a sleeveless shirt with a Union Jack flag printed on it. The impressions were strong enough, and he was well known enough, that I was able to garnish this while drifting by in the Hermes.

This was all to be confirmed at Sprigg's office.

"Well, No-Deal," Spriggs began, "He's had a few run-ins with the Law but nothing serious. Subsidized his professional licensing growing and selling controlled substances for a few years. When the shipping is slow, they do that sometimes. We mostly look the other way. We need the Pirates to prey on the Snakeheads' shipping, and to get trade goods back and forth across the Dead Arcturian Systems, into Imperial Space."

Tokushima raised an eyebrow, "Snakeheads?"

Spriggs rose one back, "That's what we call the Marauders that attacked your vessel out there. They may still LOOK like humans, but every other aspect about them screams 'reptilian'."

I was staring at Sprigg's picture of No-Deal he had provided, but Spriggs was staring at me.

"May I ask why you have a boy on your Royal Navy Warship, Sir?"

Hammerstein didn't miss a beat, "That's no ordinary boy, dear fellow. This is Count Von Berklin El Marna the III. We are training him to be a great General."

Von Berklin?

Tokushima almost lost it, but at the last second managed to transmute an imminent outburst of laughter into one of her beaming and beautiful, inscrutable Edo-Geisha smiles, and hold a pose.

I realized amid this sudden absurdity Hammerstein had hidden the subterfuge—he and we were too busy repressing our natural response to his comical naming to reveal ourselves hiding the important secret of my Empathic abilities.

Since there was no one else on Tangeonprioc who knew I was an Empath, I was of particularly high value to our mission. Nothing opens people's mouths and minds like an overblown sense of superiority.

Spriggs smiled and looked down at me, "Welcome, little man!"

I wanted to puke but managed merely to smile instead. Not that he was a bad guy; he was actually trying to do his job. My mother had called me her "Little Man" for a long time when I was a toddler, everyone had agreed I looked nothing less than a scaled-down "little man".

Twice in combat, a felled comrade at arms, halfway across the Galaxy in a legendary Pirate realm and I was still the "little man."

"Von Berklin," I sneered, "Count Von Berklin."

Hey, sometimes you just gotta run with it.

"Yes, yes, no offense, Count."

My nose rose in the air.

"Well, as you can see, DePaulo is an ugly fellow. Sleeveless shirt, Union Jack—that's an Old Earth symbol, ancient nation-state," he stammered.

We all knew of Britannia, frighteningly I realized many of the denizens of Tangeonprioc might not. Pre-space history to most was merely a matter of note; ugly, brutish, and short lives best not thought about. As a historian, I did not hold that specious illusion of the superiority of the Modern.

"Ugly as sin" Hammerstein Said.

"Kind of a big head," I added.

Tokushima threw in, "Big head on a little body…. not very impressive for a pirate who harries Snake-men Marauders. Looks rather dowdy and decidedly unimpressive I think," and I loved her even more.

"Yes," now Spriggs was oddly miffed we were dissing his pirate, "enough DePaulo bashing! He is I assure you, quite dangerous, treacherous, and clever. He has also been known to be a bit of a cave bear when pressed in a fight, so never underestimate his criminal mind."

I looked again. Still ugly. If this was the guy that had kidnapped the Princess of Caldris, I would personally ask the King to legislate new fashion crimes and punishments, for such an artless man was truly an affront to all things noble and aristocratic.

"So, what are you charging him with?" Spriggs asked.

The moments of levity we had somehow managed to squeeze into this horrific time faded then and we were merely three vulnerable, desperate pilgrims on a hopeless mission seeking a lost soul.

Hammerstein was the first to find the steel of mind again. "We're not charging him with anything. We just want to talk to him."

"I can't just track down a citizen and bring him in because you want to talk to him. We're Law enforcement. Unless he's breaking a law or planning to, his whereabouts on the world are his business, and not ours—or yours, for that matter. I can help you, but you have to tell me more than just, 'you want to talk to him.' You didn't haul that warship across the Galaxy, through a storm of Snakeheads, and lose an airman's life to have a glass of rum with No-Deal down at the Corewinds Tavern.

What did the weasel get himself into this time? If it could affect this Star System, and it already has, I have an obligation to know."

"Well, let's start with involvement in wormhole weapons."

"Where in the great Space Ghost's name would anyone find wormhole weapons in this day and age?"

Hammerstein's eyes darkened, "There are places."

"No one's used wormhole weaponry since— "Spriggs caught himself in midsentence. Caldris Royal Navy…he mentally calculated Hammerstein's age and made the connection to the great Baal incident where the Navy had experienced a tragic loss of ships due to a wormhole attack. "I see the reason for your concern. Unless there is actual evidence, however, we can't help you bring him in. Hearsay doesn't muster legal standing, even out here."

"I see."

"No, Detective, you don't see. The flip side of this is since you're not going to actually bring charges and we're not involved in an investigation you're perfectly within your rights to look the man up."

"But you won't help us find him?"

"How much help do you need? Ships port registries are public information. Mel 'No-Deal' DePaulo captains a small transport called the 'Mel's Monkey'. The ship docks at the Corewinds Marina and Resort."

All we had accomplished then was to notify the whole damned pirate's lair we were after the guy and give him ample time to escape…

Then we were back in the Hermes making for the Corewinds. The city was seething with menace and spies: everyone armed everyone dangerous. I sensed a sudden hostility in the crowd, too late I realized. The vehicle swerved with the force of a shot, a blast hard against the side of the aircar. The emergency sequence popped a door open and Tokushima dropped out, breaking into a run for cover. Hammerstein's face set in a grim smile; Herbivore has selected a heavy-duty armor and field shielded the classic.

"Seven O'clock." Our sniper snapped and his gun turret rose from the aircars hood, swept around and returned bright blasts at the shooter. We careened toward the fallen enemy and Tokushima was on him as he hit the ground, pulling him in the vehicle.

"You're under arrest." She said and I searched the assassin's mind quietly probing. Quickly the impressions assailed me; No-Deal DePaulo had sent him. A cheap hitman, no real skill or training, not aligned to No-Deal or any of the major gangs.

"He's just a thug sent by DePaulo. He doesn't know anything." I said.

"Where is No-Deal?" Hammerstein leaned hard into the rogue's grimy face.

"Corewinds. He's always at the Corewinds when he's not surfing the hyper-streams." He suddenly understood he had just assaulted officials from another star system. He didn't like it.

We'd passed through several more domes and were approaching the resort.

"What is the sentence when they convict you for the attempted murder of a Diplomatic Envoy?" Tokushima sneered.

"I have no idea. And it wasn't attempted murder, or you'd be dead. I was just supposed to scare you out system."

"No-Deal doesn't know why we are here," I offered, "they're all clueless and just wanted us to LEAVE."

Hammerstein held out his hand. "Give me your credit jack."

The man obliged with forlorn despair. Hammerstein took it and plugged it into the Hermes's dashboard. An ID came up: Hadrian Aurelius' Kelly. "Okay Mr. Kelly, here's the deal. You're working for me now, and the Royal House of Caldris. I see your last jack was three-hundred Credits from Mell's Monkey for… 'Deck cleaning'. Ugly euphemism and underpaid at that. I'm crediting you six-hundred now and you're going to be our guide and no criminal charges for the assault will be filed."

I sensed Kelly was relieved and pleased, anticipating the extra pay and status this new turn of events would confer on him even after we had departed. Hammerstein glanced at me and I gave him a slight nod.

We parked the Hermes outside the Corewinds and made our way into the clubhouse. The place was packed, but what was turning heads wasn't anyone but us; specifically, me. Probably no one had seen a kid in the Corewinds tavern, and my entourage of Hammerstein, Tokushima, and Kelly took the cake.

No-Deal DePaulo was at a corner table with an entourage of his own. He didn't look happy to see us, and through the wave of surprise hammering me, his was distinctly loud.

"Mr. Kelly, what a surprise." He snickered. Against my better judgment, I found myself liking No-Deal—his rouse of frightening us off-world having failed, he was almost amused at the fact we were now showing up with his muscle man.

There wasn't a trace of the Princess in his mind and my inclination was that he had no clue. Were we all the way out here on a wild ripjackle chase?

Hammerstein couldn't know what I was sensing, and he stepped right up. The biggest of DePaulo's goons stood up and Hammerstein quickly hammered him to the floor with a right hook that snapped out silent and connected with a bone-crunching ugly thud.

The goon folded and comically fell back to his seat.

Hammerstein stuck his scraped hand out for DePaulo, "Officer Hammerstein, Mr. DePaulo, nice to make your acquaintance."

DePaulo was in the doo-doo now. So he ran with it. "And what brings you and your compliment, and a kid no less, all the way here to the Core for little old me?"

"Wormhole riders." Hammerstein fired back coolly.

DePaulo's cocky devil-may-care dropped a few parsecs, but he recovered.

"I see."

"Slightly problematic trade goods, Mr. DePaulo."

"Hey, they had the juice, they wanted the tool, and I arranged the transaction. What are we discussing this for? Sit. Please."

He waved away his crew and we all sat down. His goon still passed out squeezed between.

"To avoid an interstellar war, and to avoid you slapped in a pain simulator for the rest of your natural life, extended indefinitely too."

DePaulo's heart sank at that as he realized something bad had happened: Something really bad, with his wormhole transaction.

Hammerstein was no amateur. He didn't answer right away. He sat cold as the Oort cloud, letting it sink in.

Like the hard rock bottom of a black hole.

It was a very long moment.

"What did they do?" DePaulo glared, wishing he was never born.

Hammerstein waved him closer. He whispered in his ear, "They kidnapped the Princess of Caldris."

No one heard but No-Deal, but from the expression on his face its rush to white horror, a wave still ran through the club of observers pretending not to notice.

"I see."

Hammerstein drummed his huge fingers slowly.

"Well, Mr. Hammerstein, this is unexpected. We'll have to rectify this, must rectify this with all due expediency. I place my ships, the Mell's Monkey and the Serpentine, at your disposal."

"Our destination?"

DePaulo was, if nothing else, not a coward. "Deneb IV, Pink District."

The Imperial capitol's underworld.

This kaa-kaa just got real. The Royal House of Caldris would be storming the Empire's darkest corners with a warship and two Pirate sloops.

Some drunk in the mix couldn't help himself and stood up raising a glass, "No-Deal's riding wingman to Deneb IV!"

They all started singing and buying rounds.

Win or lose, No-Deal DePaulo had just made himself a legend. Kelly was livid. This was just getting better and better. Strangely enough, these madmen all seemed to relish the thought of dying as legends.

The big guy Hammerstein had slammed got back up. His name was Roland Dansky. Forgetting he'd just been pummeled into his seat, awakened by the singing and the celebration, he looked around, found his drink still cold on the table, lifted his glass and gave a howl like a Viking, "Let's party!"

Space Pirates. Go figure.

So now we were a convoy. We bolted into hyper straight up, away from the realms of the Marauders and men, up and around the stream of the plume in a wicked spiral dash, a careening wild apogee stretching beyond the limits of known dimensional theories.

High, until the galactic disk lay serene and silent below, soft and supple like a longed-for love; Three desperate ships, unlikely allies, madmen and soldiers, brilliant and beautiful in their way. Three desperate ships: Two seeking redemption, and one seeking the heart and soul of a world stolen and missing. A mission to rescue an ideal none of them were worthy of, and in a way that's why it mattered most.

DePaulo, it seemed, was an educated man. Missing opportunities by a hair, too often, he had found his compromises compiled and the face in the mirror was one he didn't recognize. Someday perhaps his compromises would drive him down. Today was not that day.

Roland was tall, long blonde rakish hair, strikingly handsome and cursed with a love of battle, an inescapable thirst for challenges and drawn through his looks above and beyond the things most men crave—love and adoration always at his feet, he longed for humor, combat, and danger like others might crave a kiss.

He always found it. Now, on a wild ride into the mighty, singular, and mysterious ancient capitol of the CCCE Empire, his mood was glorious either at the guns of the Serpentine or at the helm. Having been bested by Hammerstein at the bar, he was often sending little barbs across the com, "Hammy? Hammy?"

"What do you want, you big goofy girlie man?"

"You know this is a hopeless ride to our doom don't you?"

"Shoot straight, Blondie, and we'll live."

"You're such a butch old thing aren't you?"

Hammerstein tried to stay mad but he couldn't. Roland was just too funny.

"You overdressed, prima-donna wanna-be pirate."

Sometimes I could tell he was looking forward to Dansky's goofy remarks. I would have never called him on it, but the old butch bear eventually came to appreciate the Pirate's taunts as a release from the pressure having to rescue the Princess.

Justin Coco-butter Parsons stood aghast that the giant Viking pirate of endless jokes was first slammed into his seat mercilessly by the old Detective at the Corewinds tavern; then had formed the most unusual sort of "brothers in brawls" bond. A full platoon of professional Rangers (Yer jo-ob is to break things and kill people!) well, they wouldn't mess with the old detective.

I knew though. Empath or not, I knew. The old Detective saw himself in the pirate. If it wasn't for the Royal Caldris Navy, he too might have had a pirate sloop.

A spiral apogee and on to Empire

Before the disappearance of the archaeologists studying the Predecessor relics at the Galactic Core, and the subsequent appearance of the strange Marauder cult peoples, the archaeologists had constructed various computer models of proposed celestial histories regarding the giant black hole at the central galactic region.

They figured ten million years past a smaller galaxy merged with ours, its central black hole nearing ours in a long slow orbit until the two merged together in a collision producing a massive bubble of material thrown up into the plume, ejecting upwards thousands of stars from the central region, out into intergalactic space at super high velocities.

Along with this ripple and among this wave of expelled materials are some of the densest and most unusual mineral and crystalline materials in the galaxy, their properties unique, coveted, and cause for the initial settlement rush at the Core...

-Princess Clairissa Maggio, Caldris

The snake-minds in the stream compressed on my thoughts and body like a weight of water at depth while skin diving on a Levi-Boca infested reef at the Tangerine Sea in volcano season. Even as the three ships careened in formation through the hyper-streams, the shadows haunted me. First as strange hallucinogenic beings—an Evil I had felt among the derelict Sunrider fighter the archaeologists had found in Arcturian Space, that I had sensed in the palace— and then the Snakeheads. Somehow later when I was awake I distinguished between the two a very different sense.

They were not the same. Although the Sunrider derelict and the Predecessor ruins were tied together in the same history of the Arcturian war, the Predecessor ruins were much older. They could not, however, have remained inert for untold millennia and then come to flashing glorious life just as the Arcturian wars occurred.

How did they know the Humans in a distant set of star systems, way out in the Spiral Galactic arms, were engaged in genocide? Why had all the previous Human wars failed to light them up before? Or was it not our species at all that lit the Predecessor base? The evil thing in the Sunrider?

What had Princess Maggio found? Certainly, her computer systems must have alerted her to the danger. Certainly, she would have hyper-cast to the archaeological expedition at the Arcturian ruins. Certainly...Her casts must have been being spied on.

The question, of course, is why anyone would want to hide the thing I felt in the Sunrider? They had not gotten a firsthand taste of it. Twice now the memory of it had haunted my dreams in flight. Here in the hyper-streams, I could sense trails, those times there would be nightmares.

We had pressed the Eberhardt hard, making for the Imperial space. Two days into the rabid run alerts went off in the piloting cabin. I made my way up and in a holo sphere, there was a visual construct of the space which we were traversing. A massive bubble of super-heated plasma, light-years across, filled the screens.

Tokushima was at the helm. Hammerstein glared, "This is what we get for following the navigationals provided by outlaws and dirt-bag pirates."

He slammed the comm.

"DePaulo!"

Moments later DePaulo's sleazy visage appeared in the holo. "Yeah, yeah, yeah, I know, it's a little nasty. Don't be a baby."

Don't be a baby?

Tokushima smiled and shook her head. "Unbelievable."

"We're going get fried here. You may not value the lives of your crew, but I value the lives of mine. Is this some sort of macho pirate rite of passage or something?"

Roland appeared in another Holo. "Hammy!"

"Stay out of this, girlie man."

"Well, the gangs all here." I found myself saying.

DePaulo snickered.

"Have you got a pirate song for this one, Roland, because if we're going to die out here in the Core, we can all just break open some rum and cheer to our demise?" Tokushima shot out drolly.

"Don't give them ideas." Hammerstein replied coolly, "How long in this stream, before we can bank back into the main galactic halo, you know and point our crates in the direction of the star systems we are flying to?"

DePaulo's mug seemed to consider. "Well, no on the songs, officer Tokushima. Shortly regarding the navigation though, actually banking outward from this stream soon. You're going to like the rush we get out to the spiral arms. We'll make the Big void like we're skipping stones across a stream in Tangeonprioc park."

"We smugglers know all the tricks," Roland said earnestly.

Parsons was floating around in the main engine room with the gravity turned off. It was hot from strain, filled with steam making fog something terrible.

"We should hold, Officer Hammerstein. You tell those pirates the Eberhardt has the ultra-steel to ride with their tugs."

Starship machismo. STEAMING starship machismo.

"Right!" Tokushima shook her head again.

In spite of his better judgment, Hammerstein was caught up in the space peeing contest, and I knew if it wasn't for my doe-eyed little-boy eyes looking up at him he would have cursed the pirates and told them, "You're on chowderheads!" Instead, he just growled a bit and puffed on a cigar.

The pirates smiled from the separate ships. DePaulo chided, "As I said, don't be a big baby. Next time you guys come rescuing Princesses out here in the mighty Core, where the real Spacers soar, bring a bigger ship!"

Then he broke com and it was only me, Tokushima, Hammerstein and the giant plasma bubble. Hammerstein wanted to be concerned, for my sake. I could feel his guilt though, he loved this stuff and the old bear never felt quite so alive and in the game as when all was in an ugly, desperate, brutal edge.

DePaulo was right though regarding the stream beyond the plasma bubble. I recorded it for Caldris University, and it should keep them quite busy drooling over their quantum computers trying to figure out exactly what happens to the hyper-streams there. Parsons didn't know, neither did any of the Rangers.

I caught them beaming over the holo-dials a couple of times.

"Whoa."

"That's pretty fast."

"Not possible."

Yet there we were.

CCCE. Cyborgian Central Command Economies grew out of Humanity's most ancient of origins, our homeworld Earth. Transhumanism had long been predicted, back to the dawn of the Space Ages. The Transhumans became a caste born of the richest and most powerful of that early age. Immortal, they remain even today, secretive, inscrutable, and behind much of that which transpires in the galaxy.

As the first colonies were established in nearby star systems, faster than light drives eventually and suddenly would open up a further wave of expansion birthing the civilizations farther out, our own among them. It was then the original colonies came under the sway and eventual engulfment into the empire.

It seemed for an ugly, dangerous time all of humanity would merely settle and then fall under the Imperial grip. It was the Terraforming Industrialist Shea Fisher who eventually stopped them in the Pleiades Confederation. Building a small fleet of warships, he blew their intrusions out of the skies.

When confronted in a conference on when he would relent and submit to their rule, he stared back quietly for a long moment and replied famously, "Uhh...Never."

Never.

The Pleiades have remained to this day forever free. Not without a thorn in their side, however. A number of the systems in that star cluster had already gone over to the Imperials— the Paramon Republic. Paramon and the Pleiades Confederation have had intermittent war ever since, thus it was with a grim resolve when Caldris came to arms against Paramon at the Baal System that our Royal Family too, resolved to never relent.

-Princess Maggio, Caldris.

CCCE.

Roy Rudder

Imperial Space, mighty, and with the oldest running government in all of the galaxy. Dropping out of the stream we were immediately barraged with incoming hypercasts and registration protocols. Why are you here? What are you carrying? What is your destination?

Tokushima took the com and began the arduous protocols and procedures.

We were investigating a missing person. We have no cargo. We are not expecting to remain long. Amazingly, to me at least, for an empire dreaded and feared across time and space, the whole process was rather painless. DePaulo and Dansky came there often and were chock full of any number of fake ship IDs. A Royal Caldris warship, however, took a little more doing. We had to give notice to the Caldris Embassy there, they verified and we made for our first port deep on the edge of the Deneb system.

They had no intention of letting out warships on Deneb IV, the Capitol. There were very large ring stations orbiting Deneb VII. We docked our ships there. For the Ranger Platoon, we rented an Airbus. Parsons, Tokushima, Hammerstein and I climbed into the Hermes.

DePaulo and Dansky had their own aircars, appropriately enough rather menacing rides at that. We all loaded onto an interplanetary ferry and made deeper in the system. The scale of the space architecture was already daunting, and ancient. Older than anything on our worlds, these mega constructions had been accreting for millennia.

Tyrants, megalomaniacs, and savvy Pharaohs had long known the intimidating power of mega structures. Seeing these structures in a virtual reality "virtreel" show is one thing. It is somehow different when they're there, in all their trillions of tons of mighty astercrete and plastisteel: spinning in the deep vacuum's radioactive stellar wind, buzzing with the teeming traffic of empire: The swarming billions going about their intrigues, their mendacities, and their daily pleasures.

When I sensed everyone was settled in for the ride through normal space to Deneb IV I gathered myself out of the Hermes and looked for windows. There were some.

The interior of the Ferry had not escaped graffiti and I looked at some of the dates and my budding "archaeologist adventurer aristocrat" beamed. The Ferry had escaped an interior wash down it seemed, at least from some of the deeper inscribed graffiti.

I found one that was five hundred years old. At that point, I was getting queasy from my empathic feedback and Gibbon came over and adjusted a field that protected me somewhat from the echoes.

I became aware then that several of those I thought "passengers" milling about were quantum echoes, "ghosts" as they were once called. I decided things were complicated enough for this young empath right now without long conversations with the imperial ghosts so I headed back to the Hermes where Hammerstein was snoring and Tokushima rolling her eyes.

She gave me a frustrated look. What does one do when one's commanding officer snores?

Babylon. Rome. New York. Aitken Basin City Luna. The legends of every great city were rolled into one at Deneb IV, but it is more than a city. An entire M-class planet mercilessly first terraformed into the likeness of a world mankind would want.

Then, ruthlessly built upon to become the stuff of every architect's ultimate fantasy.

Then, through the centuries, a world still built upon more. Built past perfection, past glory; past all imaginings sheer wonder upon wonder upon impossibility; the ultimate materialism of the abstract.

The windows in the ferry darkened as we approached. Deneb's brilliance would have blinded us. The world they say never sleeps, but when they do, and of course they do, they mostly sleep in the day while the buildings suck up the solar power. Deneb's luminosity is two-hundred thousand times that of Sol, where our eyes evolved to see.

As the planet neared, through the darkened window, I could see the patterns of cities on the night side streaming deep into the seas and across them. There were cities where space elevators had evolved and grown, century upon century, into cities themselves. Linear cities were streaming up, and down, beyond the atmosphere and into space where the traffic of untold billions pour continuously, up and down.

At the top of the space-elevators were giant stations, great counterweights eternally pulling the nano-fibers of the elevator's material taut. We embarked the ferry there with our various aircars and the airbus and plunged headlong downward where hundreds of millions of spires impaled the sky.

The skies were cities, cities that seemed to know no boundaries either vertical or horizontal. I knew they plunged also deep into the ground. The universe I had known seemed gone, the universe of skies and worlds, seas and space. There was only the city.

A small holo of DePaulo appeared in the Hermes. "Hammerstein, we go in, I'll need you to follow my lead. This isn't going to go well with my clients."

107

Hammerstein's eyes darkened. "Your 'clients' will remain, forever after this, on an ugly list. This little group of Rangers are merely soldiers. There are other levels of the military, worse than Rangers, much worse. Should your clients come out of this alive, they will be watching their backs the rest of their natural lives."

Even in a hologram, I could see DePaulo's grim certainty of that truth.

The aircars and the airbus sped at terrible speed across the endless cityscape and eventually, we seemed to be following a group of hovercycles on a maglev highway.

"So who are they?" Hammerstein grunted.

Roland appeared. "We sold them those hoverbikes. Generally, we like to include some tracking devices as insurance with these deals. One never knows when one might want to meet again. Like now," he chuckled.

The city impinged on my empathic senses like the weight of an ocean. Gibbon was good, however, and set the protective fields high. I would lose most of my empathic abilities thusly. Experiencing the cacophony of structures and people as a regular person was strange and the sixth sense blindness unnerving. We were nearing the kidnapper's lair in the Pink district, and my whole reason to join this op was now very much moot.

No-Deal had given everyone some special mushrooms to eat before we entered the imperial capital. They interfered with various subliminal transmissions CCCE broadcasted continually at the population. They too were now affecting my empathic abilities. I was essentially no longer a gifted aristocrat. I was an adolescent from a backwater world in the company of warriors and pirates at odds with the mightiest city in human history.

Turns out the mushrooms were one of the main trade goods smugglers brought into imperial space. Originating in the Sagittarius Galactic Spiral Arm, in the refugee-Outworlds settled after the Arcturian War, I had the ugly suspicion they may have been one of the underlying real rationales for the Imperial attack on the Arcturians in the first place. A natural and untraceable antidote to the Imperial Subliminal Compulsion broadcasts…

Our aircars made their way still across great expanses of Deneb IV. The hovercycles must have crossed several hundred kilometers. From the looks of this society, energy supplies were no issue and travel an endless and ongoing aspect of their lives. This little group, whatever their business that day, made no thought to distance—they lived as much with their vehicles as with their residences it seemed.

The city teemed, a hive. Here, as it were, the physical manifestations of their famous hive mind. As chaotic a storm of activity as their physical cities was, the hive mind was, even more, the carnival of activity. Billions of minds in perpetual communication—song, story, political discourse, mercantilism, and casual social discourse—creating a ceaseless roar of information.

The hovercycle riders were tireless. Riding was no journey to them. It was merely another stage in their destinations. We switched out the lead tail, fist the Hermes, then DePaulo's aircar, then the Airbus, finally Roland's long red open aircar—a conceit actually, since the top was merely replaced with a force field and he had donned his MERGE helmet from the Serpentine.

We shuffled the tail.

It seemed to go on forever. The behemoth structures and spaces of the planetary megalopolis, the tailing. DePaulo appeared now and again in a hologram, muttering to Hammerstein details of his previous interactions with his clients.

He was telling him things, I realized even without my sixth sense, which he had been uncomfortable revealing before. Out of time, the grimy specifics were now coming out.

"Well, they're a strange lot. I get into Paramon sometimes, mostly after vacationing at the Capitol of the Pleiades, Chrysalis Isla." DePaulo's hologram in the Hermes seemed to sweat. He was hiding something—his "vacationing" at Chrysalis Isla obviously involved something he'd rather not reveal to a Law Officer from the Pleiades. "Yeah, Paramon is so close. Well, so I'm at a club I throw some bones, some dice."

He smiled a long moment and I realized he too was watching a hologram—of Hammerstein.

"Well I'm rolling the bones and I'm on a winning streak and this Voodoo looking character—really scary guy, you know—he comes over to my table and he's watching me more than the dice so I knew this was not an accidental situation.

"So Voodoo boy, representing Izzy Gould, offers to buy me a drink and we go and sit in a more private area of the Casino. He says he heard I could get some collectibles out past void's end—Langley Stay. Says he wants some classic aircars, rare models, a high penetration military-grade sloop, and if at all possible, a Feynman Quantum Falcon."

Hammerstein's eyes darkened and I knew this was the moment DePaulo had been dreading. This went beyond smuggling collector aircars past customs to avoid luxury taxes. The Feynman Quantum Falcons were the wormholing equipped frigate which Herbivore had used, one of which we had shot out of the sky with a gravity bomb in the Oort clouds at Caldris system.

These were then most certainly the very people who had tried to kill us. We moved lower into the towers.

"And you got all this at Langley Stay Voids End?" Hammerstein glowered.

"Yeah," DePaulo replied, "they appeared to be ordinary collectors. They have a Gallery—I checked it. Very old. Millennia Fine Art. That appears to be where we are headed now."

"A Gallery in the Pink district?"

DePaulo's hologram shrugged, "Not a nice neighborhood now. When the gallery originally opened, who knows? That Gallery has been in existence over a thousand years. The story is it was originally owned as a front for an Arcturian spy convicted of treason, Lisa Sulla."

"If the CCCE Transhumans convicted Sulla for spying that long ago, conceivably they have had a stake in the gallery ever since?" Hammerstein's expression went cold.

"Perhaps. Everybody knows Paramon has long been little more than CCCE's ankle-biter lap dog since Fisher Shea's famous 'Uhh…never' stand. I didn't see any signs this particular group had any Transhuman affiliations."

We had arrived. Ground level, I realized—there were very old stone structures that looked to be early Deneb IV settlement buildings. The Airbus set down with the Rangers, all in their civies, and looking nothing more than a football team on holiday. Hammerstein had them disperse to the streets in their tourist roles, ready as back up. DePaulo and Dansky remained in their aircars.

Tokushima departed silently as well. She was carrying an ominous case. The Hermes made for the Gallery's parking area. The hovercycles had disappeared into the main structure.

The gallery showroom was a gorgeous affair of collectible aircars either in mint condition or with frame-up restorations.

Hammerstein, Parsons, Gibbon and I made our way past them I had Gibbon turn down the protective fields a bit so I could use my senses. I felt for echoes of Princess Maggio and instead received a mind full of the echoes of salesmen spinning deals.

A man in black formals, with several sales ladies and some rather large robots, approached us all teeth and warm fuzzies, "Welcome to Millennia, Fine Art and collectibles for the ages!"

"Thank you." Hammerstein eyed him up and down and didn't return the smile.

"Anything special you would like?"

"A Feynman Quantum Falcon. Have one in your inventory?"

The man froze, and I sensed a sudden desperation pique in him. Hammerstein had pulled a disser.

Coco-butter had his out and fired; one, two, three and the Robots were scrap metal steaming on the floor. None of the sales ladies screamed but they all stepped further away.

"Stay," Hammerstein ordered.

The man was terrified, but he forced and indignant impression. "What is this? If it is money you want, we can oblige, and a first-class vehicle or two as well."

He was lying. Recognition came too late, but he recognized Hammerstein now and had just made a desperate bluff.

"He knows who we are," I said softly.

Hammerstein winked. "You heard the young man. Skip the pretense, save it for your customers. What this is, is an arrest for the kidnapping of Princess Maggio of Caldris. For your sake, and Paramon's, I hope she is unharmed."

The man, of course, was Izzy Gould, and his awareness that Hammerstein knew his origins in Paramon came as a surprise.

Suddenly then, two of the aircars alighted on the showroom floor and heavy-duty guns trained on the three of us.

"Your weapons, please. No one is going to be arrested today. You may discover though, not only do you not have any authority on this world, but a CCCE conviction and sentencing can involve rather unusually long and unpleasant conditions." Gould laughed then.

One of the "salesladies" approached us. More robots appeared.

"Yelena, take a robot and get the biker boys down here. Have someone do some recon around the galleries and on the street. Officer Hammerstein isn't likely to walk into an enemy stronghold without back-up."

He walked over to me, "This one's an empath. Winteroud Sole, heir to the legendary Sole Industries and estate. That should bring us some coin and collectibles as ransom, though we'll have to wipe his memory before we send him back drooling to his mansion."

"You're in deep Gould. If you join us, tell us who is behind all this and help us return the Princess you can maybe walk away with some sort of immunity. A stipend. Head over to Chrysalis Isla in the Pleiades, hide at a little resort island and live out your life in comfort." Hammerstein gambled an offer, but I sensed he knew it was a long shot.

"Take them in the warehouse," Gould said icily. "I would probably jump on that, Officer Hammerstein, if the people behind the kidnapping were not, well, a lot scarier than you."

"Well, now you're just being stupid, Gould. I'm a very scary guy. Just ask my ex-wives. I snore, fart like a factory, and am totally out of touch with my feelings."

Gould raised his eyebrows and was honestly amused.

"Ex-wives don't count. They're biased witnesses with a longstanding pattern of exaggerating their spouse's abominableness."

We were shuffled into the back warehouse but even Hammerstein had caught Gould's tone when he referred to his "people". A dead giveaway there was CCCE Transhumans involved and most likely behind the kidnapping. Paramon and CCCE then—as we long suspected.

The warehouse was overflowing with all manner of items from across the Imperium and beyond. The quantum echoes were a storm. I had Gibbon tone down their winds and I watched the woman and her robots carefully for any signs as to their intentions with what sixth senses remained.

Hammerstein and Parsons being the combat soldiers they were; Gould didn't leave the woman alone with us but a moment before one of the biker boy showed up with a particularly large combat bot.

"Your boss isn't thinking very clearly." Hammerstein began. "Whatever he's paying you, it won't be worth the Royal Family at Caldris perpetually after revenge. You should consider influencing him to stand down, and reach a truce."

The man with the big combat bot oozed discomfort.

"What is he talking about?" he barked to the woman.

"I don't know, and I don't want to know." She replied.

"Oh but you do, you very much want to know." Hammerstein's tone was full of dread and implications. "Right now you are taking a side in an issue that will forever determine your fate."

The woman lashed back, "Forever is a very long time, Copper. The only people with that kind of time are the Transhuman Overlords. I think we're on the right side."

"Well, they're not here in this building, are they? I am, and although the benevolence of the Transhumans in protecting you from the vengeance of the Royal family at Caldris is a maybe, their seeking vengeance is a certainty."

"Why would the Royal Family at Caldris seek vengeance against us?"

"Izzy is involved in a kidnapping. He and whoever he is working with took the Princess of Caldris." I said.

A wave of discomfort swelled up from the man and the woman.

Nervously, the woman replied, "Izzy takes his orders directly from the Overlords. Lourdes Cassandra 20X, in fact. You're going to have a hard case making that one of the Overlord High council absconded with a minor dignitary from a distant star system."

The man turned his helmeted face toward her, "What did you tell him that for?"

"Because it's true. And he's not going to be able to tell anyone very shortly"

"What if what he is saying is true? Is Cassandra aware of what Izzy had done? If she's not, and she finds out—we all could end up in a virtual prison for a thousand years of whatever horrors they dole out there."

Hammerstein had them. As he figured, Izzy was playing his cards close to his vest. They didn't know about the princess. She was elsewhere.

There came a sound of a holocaster signaling and one of the machines in the room lit up.

Izzy stormed in, "get them in another room, I have to take this call."

A woman appeared in the holocaster and I was able to see her fiery red hair and perfect looks—I had seen the same woman on giant screens on buildings in the aircar flight in. A Transhuman Overlord, the very Lourdes Cassandra the woman had mentioned, no doubt. We were shuffled away.

I could make out Izzy's desperate tones through the cheap walls, however. He was covering. I had Gibbon let the fields down and was able once more to use my gift. Now I could not only make out his speech, but I could also feel his intentions. He was struggling with pure terror.

"Nothing I can't handle. A mere anomaly in the hyperstream as they say. Some nosy Parkers. I can handle this."

"Oh, you will handle it, Mr. Gould. Wipe them all. Wipe their minds, and drop them on Caldris for their people to get the message."

Then she was gone… something new though, I could feel it, a new presence someone…female and feral, in their natural habitat. Tokushima was coming. Having set the Rangers to create a diversion at the front, the whole loitering mass of them posing poorly as tourists and drawing out Izzy's entire crew of biker muscle men, combat bots, and even some of the women, she had entered the rear service ducts and was quietly making her way toward us.

My Edo Geisha angel Tokushima now moved like a quantum echo, a ghost, silently and smoothly through the interior, closer. She had her katana—apparently what was in the case.

She came through a panel in the wall.

She was in the corridor beyond this room, approaching the frustrated and panicking Izzy Gould. Quietly—she had donned silk slippers, she drew the katana.

Step. The Katana was drawn. Step.

I rose, turning to our captors and their bot.

I pointed my father's disser. They forgot to check the kid.

The man with the combat bot pulled off his helmet, "What is that? Hey, what is the kid pointing?"

I fired, disabling his bot, and he began to draw on me.

"Don't shoot! He's a kid, you idiot!" The woman scowled.

"He's got a disser!"

Hammerstein took three steps and disarmed the man. Parsons was thinking, "He took his helmet off to look at the disser? What an idiot."

When we stepped outside Tokushima had Izzy against a wall with her Katana at his throat. He was bleeding a little, it was very sharp. "Now, you Paramon puke, where is my Princess?"

"Paramon Republic," I replied, reading him now like a neon hologram since Gibbon had lessened the protective fields.

DePaulo, Dansky, and the Rangers had swarmed the warehouse now.

"Paramon Republic?" DePaulo sneered, "Voodoo Man!"

There were suddenly Sirens outside. DePaulo hadn't waited for a signal and had jumped the bikers. Dansky and the Rangers had only too gladly also jumped in it seems.

Hammerstein looked at them all with dread, "What the Oort happened out there?"

Sergeant Roszak pointed at DePaulo. "The Pirate Sir. Went over jumped all the bikers and their combat droids."

"I am NOT a pirate." DePaulo fumed.

Roland looked at him menacingly, "What? Of course we're Pirates. Dashing, daring, and dangerous!"

Hammerstein raised his hands, "What happened out there and why are there sirens?"

"Like I said Sir, the uhh...' Not-A-Pirate' jumped them. Wasn't going to let him have all the fun."

The other Rangers nodded in agreement.

"Somebody must have called the cops," Roland said, wide-eyed and muscle-bound.

Hammerstein wheeled around now, four square all fists and boots, towering over DePaulo. "You attacked the bikers alone, and didn't tell the Rangers?"

DePaulo snickered, "It ain't the size of the dog in the fight, it's the size of the fight in the dog. Besides, if I had warned anyone, it would have tipped off the bikers and we would have lost the all-important element of surprise."

The sirens were furious now, and there came an unpleasant voice on a loudspeaker, "THIS IS THE POLICE. COME OUT OF THE GALLERY NOW!"

Outside the street was lit like an amateur dance party with sirens and lights. A couple of dozen uniformed officers were standing behind their aircars with force fields and high-intensity combat disser and I couldn't count the number of droids.

One figure stood in the center. A hologram, he wasn't truly "there" at all. A Transhuman Overlord! He was wearing a trench coat and a Fedora.

He seemed amused.

"Ahh, the legendary Millennia Fine Art Galleries, the Florentine room, too. The ballroom. Very historical you know."

He approached us sorting out quickly it seemed who was rank and, who was file.

The street was full of beat-up bikers and sizzling combat bots.

"Do you have a license for those combat bots?"

Hammerstein looked at Izzy.

Izzy gave a furious snarl. "What? They're antiques!"

The Transhuman hologram smiled, "I see. Properly disarmed?"

"We were working on that. They just came in."

"Looks more like they just went out."

"Officer, we are here on official business," Hammerstein said evenly.

"Overlord."

"Pardon me?"

"Overlord. You called me 'Officer'. My title is 'Overlord'.

"Sorry, Overlord. Let me explain— ".

"Overlord David Omm, Six X."

"Yes, Mr. X, I can explain."

Hammerstein was losing his patience with the Overlord and I feared that might go badly so I interjected, "Winteroud Sole, Overlord Omm 6X." I bowed. "We are here on official business. Mr. Gould here is helping us resolve a missing-persons case that would be highly embarrassing for a number of distinguished persons when some of our elite guard and some of his bodyguards got into a little manly game of 'who's better in the ring', only none of them were actually willing to wait for a ring so— "

"Here we are!" Izzy smiled and showed his palms and gave an ugly look at his men strewn about the street.

Sergeant Roszak shook his finger at the other Rangers, "You guys are going to be doing KP till the Oort turns!"

David Omm looked at Tokushima and his eyebrows lifted the hologram Fedora. "Nice outfit"

She kind of blushed and fidgeted with her katana, saw some of Gould's blood on it and made a face. "Thank you. You too."

Steve Allman

Omm 6X shook his head, "You're all full of old beans. Gould, your neck is bleeding. Get these people OFF my planet, and that Maggio girl better find her way back to that palace in one piece, or there won't be a nightclub in the Pleiades for you to hide in."

We all looked at each other. I couldn't read a hologram, so I will never know exactly what this Overlord knew or how he found out. I only know what he said next.

"I've covered this whole incident from the hive mind, so I'm giving you three weeks. You bust hyper and get your fanny to wherever it is she is. Then, I will let THIS mess slip to Lourdes."

He turned, and then he changed, no longer dashing and handsome he became pitch dark, with snakes suddenly writhing Medusa-like out of his head and hat, his eyes glowing red, his smile becoming sinister, "Then, Izzy Gould, YOU will know what a kidnapping is like, and you will despair upon endless ages!"

Needless to say, Izzy was cooperative henceforth.

Roszak looked to Gould, "That wasn't Voodoo Man?"

"No. Voodoo Man is at the Paramon Republic."

"Another one like this?"

"Not quite." Izzy sighed.

Tokushima came over to Roszak, 'Get your Rangers on the airbus and let's get the flock out of here before that thing changes its mind."

"Yes, I'll get the Hermes as well." Hammerstein waved to me, "Come on Kid; bring your robot. We got a Voodoo man near the Pleiades in Paramon to contend with."

...Nations as pawns, the galaxy as a board game, civilizations in relative decline—some say we are in a dark age—it seems the pieces are long left on the table from an old game now. The Arcturian Wars opened Pandora's jar for mankind. In the Pleiades Fisher Shea's dozens of ultramodern and meticulously planned worlds still serve as something of a tourist draw, but even their great wealth has not been the same.

Paramon, a much smaller "Republic" (it truly has none of the attributes of the rule of law and is a Republic in name only) is the only other Government in the Pleiades, still sits in that corner of the galactic board game. Ever ready to harass and harry the King of the Pleiades who descended from Shea's family line.

Mostly the two Governments fight an unofficial war of privateers menacing each other's shipping. Occasionally full-scale small wars break out. Paramon's last folly at war was with Caldris, however, a horrid affair at the Baal System. I fear there will be more, and that Paramon will soon strike again at Baal, this time at Shea's interests there.

There came an ugly visit recently to our expeditions work on the Sunrider. A Paramon Art dealer by the name of Izzy Gould. He claimed to have galleries at Deneb IV and asserted since CCCE had won the war with the Arcturians, we needed CCCE permission to explore the Arcturian ruins.

He possessed no official documents from CCCE, and I indicated there was no International Law regarding the Arcturian colonies. Radioactive as long as they had been, until a century or so ago the point would have been moot.

He left, but I don't think I have seen the last of him.

-Princess Clairissa Maggio.

"Directly from the palace via hypercasts, Mr. Gould. It places you squarely at the Arcturian ruins in the New Galen system. Should you ever attempt to circumvent us, in any way —at Paramon, or in the future, should you manage an escape or betrayal of us there, an official warrant will be issued via the Royal family at Caldris and even CCCE will not shelter you; they don't need every government in the galaxy sharpening their swords and looking at CCCE as a kidnapper of dignitaries." Hammerstein laid a hardcopy printout on a conference table and stared hard into Gould's eyes with menace.

Gould, however, needed no more persuasion.

"When we drop out of hyper in the Pleiades, make for the top of the star cluster. Adjacent to the Baal system is a piddling star with its second world in the habitable zone. Fisher Shea had been terraforming it when Paramon had started its first war with him. Shea had dropped a couple of dozen comets and there is a small ocean that remains to this day from those efforts. There is a base there that Paramon is quietly ignoring and the King of the Pleiades is unaware of. The Princess is there."

"What kind of base?" Hammerstein's nickel-plated soul seemed to gleam with sheen.

"A Marauder base…"

114

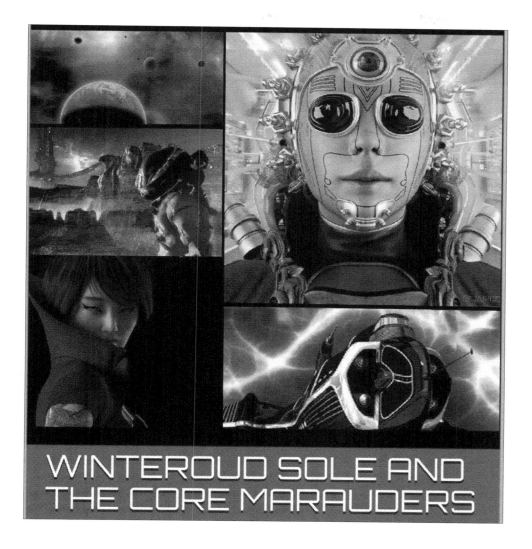

Book Three: Winteroud Sole and the Core Marauders

Kyllini Prime, Pleiades Cluster

Snake eyes.

Below us a world, a half-finished dream deferred of a man long gone. A world-first forgotten in the exigencies of the moment; a war, a stand, victory-then time delays, and some plans are not resumed. Oceans half-filled, disputes among the worlds and still the half-finished dream spun around its star, days upon years at the top of the Pleiades.

Snakes eyes, here on this unfinished, neglected world, snake minds-Marauders far from the Galactic Core where no one suspected. Devious doings, here among the star systems of ordinary mankind which they, the mysterious half men of the Core seemed to have abandoned and preyed upon at the Galactic Center.

Snake eyes in the Pleiades, below us, hiding in plain sight the worlds unawares. Our three ships, The Eberhardt, The Serpentine, and The Mel's Monkey took orbit armed and ready but the snake eyes, assured of the derelict and unheralded nature of their hideout seemed not to be watching. Something in the strange nature of the inhuman condition they had assumed gave us that much an edge; we had come to high orbit unrecognized and unchallenged.

"Gould is right." I said, "They're only watching the spaces above them. As long as our orbits remain geosynchronous, and we don't appear above their base, the snake eyes won't see us."

Gould felt he had to explain. "I noticed it on another occasion with a surprise. They think of themselves as the predator and ordinary Humans as prey. Overconfidence. One should always be aware of overconfidence in a potential foe. It is a profound weakness.

DePaulo's holo chimed in, "I've fought these dung bird Marauders all my life. Gould's right-they have lapses sometimes, and you just stare at your wingman, smile, and press, 'fire'. But whatever pretzel logic is running through the Marauders' brains, we're still on the edge of two governments here-The Pleiades Confederation and the Paramon Republic. Paramon will have at least one base down there. Keep looking."

It was Dansky who reported almost immediately, his big, ridiculously handsome, muscle-bound visage appearing in the holos, "Let's Party! Yeah, Buddy. Equatorial region. Paramon base. Right there, Buck!"

So they had that settled, but this was the Pleiades, not the core, and my sixth sense wasn't just picking up a few stray Marauders.

There was fleet down there, and the quantum echoes were latched hard into deep time, and wrapped in a complexity signature that only meant one thing. Predecessor technology.

My eyes grew leaden, "The Marauders, they're swarming down there, and they've brought things with them." I said.

"What kinds of things?" Hammerstein barked.

Dansky stuck a big custom disser in the holo field, "Nothing Roland's 'Meet your Maker' can't handle." He laughed.

Gibbon, who had rarely interjected in the human discussions regarding combat scenarios, raised a brass hand and spoke, "Well, Captain Dansky, might I suggest a proper complement of ammunition with your 'Meet your Maker" weapon then, and a very good heavy duty personnel shield?"

Even the robot wasn't giving us long odds on this op.

Across the com from Mel's Monkey a hologram Mel held up his hands. "I got this one, Dansky. The Paramon base is going to engage us sooner or later. Sun Tzu says, always control the time of your battles. I'll go down there with the Monkey and stir up that little hornets' nest so they won't interfere with your approach to our little Marauder mess."

Hammerstein's mind traced a moment of suspicion, but I felt nothing from Mel except a sheer delight at the thought of his Monkey picking off second rate Paramon pilots like a kid in a video virtreel.

I winked and nodded at Hammerstein and he understood.

"Alright. Roland, you approach the Marauder base from the North. Parsons, Tokushima, and I will come at them from the South with a few Rangers and I'll have the remaining Rangers crew the Eberhardt and engage any air support the Marauders might have."

"So we're going to provide diversions, and then spank 'em!" Roland said gleefully.

Even Hammerstein smiled.

"Baffle them with Mastodon poo, and then slam them with a wicked sucker punch!" DePaulo chortled in a low evil delight, which quite frankly was kind of creepy.

Then, the plan outlined, the joy of imminent combat welled up among the crews of the ships. Hammerstein spun on his heels eyed the NCOs on the bridge, "That's correct. Let slip the dogs of war! You tell those Rangers it's time to earn their gruel. Your job is to break things, and kill people! No prisoners, no mercy. This is a rescue and the only target I need coming out of this skirmish alive is the Princess. Those dung birds look at you cross-eyed, shoot them."

The Officers saluted, spun on their heels, and made down the main gangway of the Eberhardt barking orders to the Rangers. The Rangers' joy couldn't have been sweeter. This is what they trained for, what they lived for, and these were the moments of glory, should they survive, they would long to know again the rest of their days. There wasn't a one of them afraid to die that day, their only concern was to fight, fight well, and complete the mission.

We went down in Parson's Hammerhead. He had been tooling her systems over and over again with an obsessive fascination for all her parts-it bordered on a love affair-but the ship was prepped and ready, and we dropped.

Kind of an ugly planet when one considered it was a Fisher Shea world, but it was an unfinished Fisher Shea world. A really big construction site abandoned centuries ago.

I could sense things around that world, things that didn't belong. The Marauders had brought all manner of Predecessor technology, and there were life forms as well-things I had never encountered. The planet had no indigenous life forms-nothing in the Pleiades did before Fisher Shea showed up terraforming. Whatever was down there was imported. Such ecologies of vermin and circumstance were generally frowned on. With the Marauders in the mix, all bets were off.

Some of the things struck me as quite large, and that was unusual for a vermin ecology.

Captain Roland Dansky and Captain Mel DePaulo were keeping in constant communication with us on coded channels. On several screens in the Hammerhead now their ships cameras reported their descent and maneuvering into the ugly landscape of Kyllini Prime. Roland swept by the cold outer settlements of the Marauder base and drew out the attentions of a few Marauder ships.

The Artifact

There were no raw ore pilings and one could see the ships were ancient, confirming the myths that the Marauder origins were from the time of the Arcturian Wars when a group of archaeologists had suddenly found Predecessor tech come to life and...did something to them.

"What is that?" Hammerstein pointed to the screen at a large construction.

"A giant half a circle made out of heavy metal." Roland offered.

His ship banked away then and began a retreat. The three Marauder vessels were in pursuit.

"Looks like Predecessor technology," Tokushima added.

"Yeah, it's old. Really old. The Quantum echoes-they go back into time. The thing is full of traces." I said, sick with the sudden wave of them. Gibbon motioned to indicate he would activate protective fields for me, I waved him down. I wanted to feel more, but we were at a huge distance, and I was only seeing it on a screen.

Hammerstein's mind raced. "A predecessor hyper-gate, they're planning an invasion of the Pleiades, he said "and should the lose they won't have to hold this world, they'll just retreat through the gate and shut it. Or, more likely, they'll simply blow it up so the King of the Pleiades can't pursue them in force."

"Do you think they sent the Princess through it, to the Core?" Tokushima wondered aloud, her face turning a couple of shades paler.

There were stories that the Marauders sacrificed captives to some strange god they worshipped at the Core, on worlds in sight of the plasma plume emanating from the great black hole. Sacrificed or transformed people into snake men like themselves.

Hammerstein's eyes grew cold, "If they harmed a hair on her head…"

I felt for the traces of the personality I had sensed at the Palace that day. There was none.

"I don't know," I whispered, and it sounded like a desperate confession and I guess it was.

Roland rescued me then with a sound of laughter coming across the com, "Hahaha! Come to Rolly!"

There was a volley of fire. His shields were holding well. This wasn't his first rodeo with the Marauders.

"BABOOMAHHHH!" he howled like one of his shots came true and a Marauder scout went spinning to the ground. His ship was making time at Mach IV.

"Sergeant Roszak, you have the bridge. Get a couple of droids on Gould. Watch him closely."

Roszak saluted.

Then we made to Parson's Hammerhead in the hold. It was prepped and ready, in less than a Deneb IV minute we were out and streaming toward Kyllini Prime. The Pleiades gleamed all about us and we rushed to the planet.

DePaulo's ship was buzzing the Paramon base by then. He was in an evening lightning storm. As he predicted, he was soon pursued by Paramon Air. The Monkey's cameras revealed a major facility, with jump ships as fighter support for a battle frigate.

Whatever Paramon was up to with the Marauders, they were backing it up with the military. Mel's Monkey began to lead them on a wild chase, and I was honestly surprised how easily the pirate managed to stay just far enough ahead of them to lead them away.

In the lightning storm, he began picking off the fighter support. His little crew of pilots and gunners were calm, deliberate, and good. Mel's voice came on a coded channel, yet he could not resist a bit of bragging. "Paramon, ha! Meet the real Core Pilots!"

Tokushima set up several holoscreen feedback units in the Hammerhead center to receive recon data from the two pirate ships, and between their feedback, and the empathic impressions I could sense from the minds I was awash in the blow by blow of the raid on Kyllini Prime. The lightning storm confused my impressions from DePaulo. I could also feel the confusion and anxiety of the Paramon pilots.

Paramon knew who DePaulo was from him delivering the Wormhole tech to Gould. They wanted him dead now, he and his whole crew, and would sort out the details later.

DePaulo, however, was a better pilot than the whole base combined and was making an easy pudding of them. Another of their fighters fell.

"Let's Party, you snake-headed degenerates!" Now Dansky's howling came across the com along with the sound of his favorite weapon of choice-matter cannon. Naked Marauder fighters continued to swarm out of their strange base. Flocking behavior and the reptile-bird-lizard impressions superimposed over the remnants of their human minds assailed me.

Dansky's Serpentine was as heavily laden with field shielding as one could imagine, such was his life at the Core. His trade-off with diverting so much energy to his shields was less generating power for energy weapons-his answer to that; matter cannon and gravity bombs.

The Serpentine's matter cannon and gravity bombs fired at the trailing Marauder ships were unlike any he had ever seen before. He suspected there was more to this than finally seeing them without their usual ore shielding. Their technology was unfamiliar, entirely unfamiliar. I could hear Roland barking orders to his crew and the staccato rapid-fire response of the guns and bombs.

It was at that point Roland did something that was to become legendary, even among the Core Pirates.

The Serpentine dipped into a valley, mere meters above the rugged rocks and trees, and he opened the Serpentine's hold, jumped on an airbike, and flew out the rear of the craft. It was a gamble that the Marauder ships wouldn't notice, at those speeds, a single person on an airbike.

They didn't. They continued their single-minded pursuit of the Serpentine with the relentlessness typical of their kind. Attuned now to Roland, and with the input from his helmet cam now signaling us, I felt his wild glee.

DePaulo now had the Paramon fighter support backing off. The Frigate, however, was moving in for a kill. Mel's Monkey raged red and violet with a savage barrage of fire from the frigate's big guns. Her shields were barely holding.

I sensed worrying from Mel's crew as their evasive flight patterns and return fire seemed to naught in the ship's defense. DePaulo's only advantage now, ironically, was the lighting storm. They were high over a sea created by Shea with a comet centuries before.

DePaulo appeared on the hologram and sneered at Hammerstein, "I hope this grants us a full pardon with the Royals at Caldris. If we don't buy it here, Paramon will certainly be after my head."

The hologram turned to his crew, "Fire it all!"

There came a hard metallic clanging among the other noises. I could see from one of the other feeds now a swarm of missiles break from the Monkey. The frigate's gunners were targeting them-one, two, three, and more never made it near the pursuing beast, but that wasn't Mel's intent.

They were gravity bombs, and once within a certain range, they all began to implode in a series of savage sucking whirlwinds and light. The frigate spun like a toy, parts of it breaking away, then her running lights went dark and backup systems fought to service.

For a moment, the frigate hung suspended above the sea lit ominously by the lightning storms. Then she began a careening descent to the sea.

The hologram DePaulo beamed, "That's what I'm saying. Can you hear me, aye? No Deal! Yeah!"

Hammerstein offered a small gratuitous smile, then his old soldier's senses came to the fore, "Don't get cocky, that was a lucky maneuver. Watch your backs DePaulo, there are still enemy ships out there. Lucky. Just lucky."

DePaulo laughed back.

With the ships feeds reporting the image of the downed frigate slamming into the sea and with lighting dancing wickedly, DePaulo looked quite triumphant, grand, and archetypal; an indefatigable rogue among space pirate legends.

Surely when the tapes of the engagement leaked into Tangeonprioc, his reputation would be further boosted.

Roland was making back toward the Marauder base now on his airbike. "Who's been monitoring this planet anyway?" he said from his feed.

Our hammerhead cruised low; I hadn't glanced out the window in some time since I had been watching the holos and feeds. There was an unfamiliar aspect to the flora and fauna.

"This is some creepy stuff." Roland quipped.

DePaulo was still in the loop, "Don't be a baby."

"Roland, Creepy how?" Hammerstein demanded. "Shut up DePaulo, he's reporting." Hammerstein growled, "That's called reconnaissance."

"Yeah Mel, shut up. I'm reconnaissancing!" Roland chuckled.

"Just a dead reptilian thingy, nothing I can't handle."

Suddenly the Eberhardt chimed in, "Officer Hammerstein?"

The old granite detective turned red, "What now, more creepy thingies?"

"Pardon me, Sir?"

"What is it!?"

119

"That was some serious fighting from the Monkey, Sir, but they're not out of the weeds yet. There are still fighters from the Paramon base aloft, Sir. Looks like they've reconnoitered and they've changed vectors again. They are heading back to the Monkey

"You get that DePaulo?"

Interference fuzzed on the holocaster.

"Serpentine?'

Suddenly both ships responded then, but the casts were weak. I felt a grudging concern from Hammerstein. DePaulo had redeemed himself by drawing out and taking on an entire flight group of Paramon's Air Corps and the last thing the old detective wanted now was the grubby bugger to "buy it after that performance…'

"I see them." Mel's holos flickered in the cabin.

"They have a ways to get back now. Serpentine, keep my coordinates updated from the Eberhardt. Meet on my heading and surprise them from behind."

That would leave the Serpentine out as back up when we stormed the Marauder base, and it would introduce all the Marauder ships still on Serpentine's tail into the melee.

They would, however, be on the other side of the world when we went in for the princess.

Coco-butter was watching his dials. He was keeping us low, we didn't know what kind of scans we might be under. I didn't sense awareness from the Marauder base regarding us. I could sense activity, their urgency to get the Serpentine and some sense that their Paramon allies were also engaged. I could sense they had become aware of the Eberhardt and they were making the connection…

Making a connection with the princess!

I found myself blurting out, "They have her, I can sense her now clearly-oh my, *what a mind!*"

Tokushima put her hand on my shoulder, "Stay with her, young man. Is she alright?"

She was aware of the distress signals and the Marauders launching ships. She was hoping it was a rescue. I beamed. In the years since I could first read I had followed her writings. It had never occurred to me to use my empathic powers to sense her as a person.

She was magnificent. The nightmare of being kidnapped and then held by the strange Marauders had not broken her at all. She had found a stoic place in her heart to endure the physical menace, left an aspect of herself there, and managed another part of her mind to observe and in a detached and calculating manner, the things that were going on around her.

I realized then, however, this particular strategy of hers placed her in very real danger of psychological "splitting", where her mind could fracture into actual separate personalities. She was not there yet, but if we wanted "one" functioning and whole princess, we would be arriving none too soon.

"Stay with her, kid. We don't have floor plans for this place when we get there." Hammerstein said coolly.

Tokushima eyed her disser with vehemence and I moved away from her with the shock of her intensity.

The Hammerhead continued over the strange unfinished construction-site landscape with its biome of weeds and happenstance life forms. I could sense from Roland a growing frustration with staying low in with the airbike. His video feed revealed the starkness of a half terraformed world run wild for centuries, this was not the manicured garden paradise Shea's other finished worlds had become. It was an obstacle course where vermin crawling off the occasional freighter resupplying its hydro system had come to dominate.

There was, however, more.

I could sense them-more than the marauders, more than the sentience of vermin; strange things, unfamiliar things. Then, with a lull in the combat and our ships moving to or away from the base as per the strategy, one of the things I had sensed lunged from a swamp in a savage bolt at Roland's airbike.

He howled and was thrown from the airbike.

There came a visual of him scrambling through the water, then out of the water. Then we could see what he saw as he looked back. Dinosaur dragon creatures of immense size wallowed in the shallows. His airbike was nowhere to be seen, presumably sank.

"Remember that little creepy reptilian thing I saw a while back?" he said, breathing heavily.

121

"We see them. Looks like you found its parents." Tokushima offered quietly.

"Hey, Hammie?"

Hammerstein looked grim, "Yeah, you big wanna-be. What's the matter, you don't have a hair on your hind end? You can take them."

"Not so sure, Hammie. There are a lot of them."

"Look, if I don't make it to the base, and you rescue the princess, can you get my crew some kind of recognition? Medals or something. They're a good lot...for pirates."

"Will do, soldier. One for you too."

The cameras went blank and I sensed nothing from Roland except dark oblivion.

Hammerstein and Tokushima and the Rangers in the cabin all looked to me.

I looked away.

Even DePaulo was quiet for a long dreary moment, "All right then, Captain Dansky is missing in action. Let's not buy him yet, this ain't a funeral, it's a combat engagement, you sissies, so as captain Dansky would say, 'Let's Party!'" DePaulo growled with a cadence and a fury.

Hammerstein approved, and once again I felt his grudging respect for old Mel "No-Deal" DePaulo.

"That's correct!" Hammerstein added, looking sternly to the Rangers in the cabin. "We don't know he's dead, and if he is, he died amongst us, our friend and brother. Carry on, don't dishonor his memory with a bunch of downcast looks."

There came some grunts from the Rangers as a response. Dansky, whatever else you want to say about him, could light up a room with laughter and courage and charge into the melee with style.

Neither DePaulo nor Hammerstein tried to engage the crews regarding Captain Dansky the rest of the flight.

They would be facing both the Paramon and Marauder fighters.

Our Hammerhead made for the ground. We were half a click away from the Marauder base now and would make for the rest of it on foot. We spilled out of the Hammerhead and the strange landscape enfolded us with its hodgepodge collection of life forms.

The Rangers communicated amongst themselves coordinating geo-positioning equipment. They ran a final check on their gear. Caldris Rangers, they looked at the landscape with deep disdain. We made our way at first through a forest of giant land sponges and sand lice the size of our feet. Amongst the drifting sand, I recognized the typical meteorites leftover from a cometary drop terraforming process.

Sand lice lumbered toward us. Tokushima kicked one away, "That's disgusting." She said. Fortunately, they didn't bite and they were slow. They crawled in and out of the sponges and peered at us, twirling antennae, sniffing their air. Their minds were like the silver sea darters on my world-stimulus, response. Very little that could be considered sentience, merely hunger, and mating impulse.

The sun was fading, twilight time upon us. This high above the Pleiades there was not the great plethora and show of huge stars that drove away "night" and "day" distinctions the Pleiades Confederation is famous for, at least not at this latitude. Near the South Polar Regions, it would be different, but we were in the Northern Hemisphere.

Above us, there was a gas giant, however, a ringed beauty of considerable size and grace and it lent some poetry and light.

"Any sense of the princess, Winteroud?" Hammerstein asked quietly, his disser drawn and his distance eating stride never seeming to slow in its even loping gait.

I felt towards the Marauder base; snake eyes and her splitting soul. She was there among the demented and twisted things the Marauders had made of their humanity. The activity had quieted a bit, and she was fighting her sense of dread and hopelessness.

122

"She is there, she is alive, and her mind aches with despair. She had hoped the noise was the coming of her Royal Space Navy."

I was amazed at a sudden then; a wave of pride and determination among the whole group with me when I said the princess awaited us. Their hearts were platinum sheen, resolute, fierce, and hungry for a fight. Their paces quickened and E Gibbon and I pressed on harder to stay with them.

We came to a series of clefts in a rock wall, it was darker between them and we had to pass their narrow passages. We moved ahead single file. The stone was damp, and pools of water had collected at the ground.

I could sense something again-a life form, mindless hunger, excitement at its sense of motion near it. It was readying itself.

"Something ahead," I said in a low ominous voice.

The Rangers steeled their nerves and kept their dissers up and before them as we moved through the rocks like ghosts, furtively, crouching and eyeing our way in the dim light. The rocks were a labyrinth of twisting alleys as if the planet was mocking Shea's long ago intentions with a dark pantomime surreal ghost city.

I kept feeling for the neural nets of the unknown life form. I could feel their dusky excitement at the prospect of food. Tokushima adjusted a motion sensor on the arm of her suit. "Things growing on the rocks, they are squirming."

I could see nothing at first and then, yes, a slight variation in the texture.

Then: Woosh! Suddenly the growths exploded and expanded into jack-in-the-box hands, slimily, dripping and sticky, reaching for us in the enclosed spaces. One of the Rangers fired at them, then the rest followed suit in an ugly barrage of fire, slimes, and squealing as the things died.

Their death throes slammed my empathic senses, yet I was saved by the resolute and quick action of E Gibbon who adjusted the muting fields to protect me. Coming to my senses, it was not a complete improvement as our group still struggled to work through the long trap.

We pushed on through the horrid tendrils and their arms lunging and probing. For the Rangers suited up it was slightly less a stomach-turning event and by the end of it we had cut a gory path through to the other side.

"Well, they didn't just drop off the exhaust port of a star freighter!" One of the Rangers observed.

Tokushima agreed, "Exactly-I have a sneaking suspicion they and the dragons that attacked Roland Dansky were brought here by the Marauders."

E Gibbon spoke out then, "Sirs, if I may?"

The whole group of Rangers stopped, E Gibbon had been somewhat silent along the adventure, and everyone was quite surprised at his sudden vocalization. The Rangers took the opportunity to pull rags from their suit compartments. I realized it was a very advanced sterilization and cleaning cloth with numerous nano-systems then.

"My digital library is quite extensive. Most of the species we've seen on this world are famous invasive species-typical vermin. The arboriforms we first encountered, however, are from a previously thought extinct subfamily of the species. So are the water dragons Captain Dansky encountered, and the Anemone among the rocks we just passed.

"Those are interesting factoids, Mr. Gibbon. I'm sure the Princess will relish this data-once we save her from the Marauders and the Paramon."

"I believe what Mr. Gibbon has indicated, what he's trying to say," I interjected, "is he sees a connection to the Marauders. This fits another aspect of the Marauder anomaly. We know the Marauders appeared after a group of Archaeologists reported Predecessor technology coming to life. We've seen unfamiliar Predecessor technology here today, probably more of it than even the Core Pirates have encountered in their dealings with the Marauders. We know the Predecessor civilization existed many for many tens of millions of years ago. These species were preserved somehow by the Predecessors."

"He said all that?" Tokushima raised an eyebrow.

I smiled, there in dim light with the Rangers, the old detective, this glorious Edo Geisha Angel, and the planet of Lost Species. Fischer Shea's unfinished terraforming project just took a much unexpected weird turn.

"Well, that was what he was leading up to," I said.

E Gibbon bowed slightly

"Still, just interesting factoids." Hammerstein said, then, for my benefit in front of the Rangers, "Keep it in mind though, Rangers, who knows how it might come in handy? Who knows?"

Somehow, it did matter, mattered vitally for us to understand the connections. The sequences seemed to transcend time-like these strange animals. Millions of years ago the predecessor race disappears from the galaxy-along with all higher life forms in a still-unexplained galaxy wide mass extinction.

Millions of years later, during a war among humans, the Predecessor technology suddenly comes to life, and there appear out of nowhere the mutant Marauders. Then, centuries after that, the Princess of Caldris is on an archaeological expedition to an artifact of that very war when she is deemed dangerous and kidnapped.

The greatest enigma of all, however, the Evil I sensed in the derelict Sunrider she was excavating. One mystery, after another, upon another, tied across many millions of years and two human epochs. The Evil, I sensed, went deeper still. Dark dimensions, deep time and quanta, formless voids of which mankind is not aware, there, Evil fiends, lurking just outside our perception.

Worse than Paramon, worse than Deneb IV Imperials, worse than the lawless Tangeonprioc or the enigma of the Marauder cult, a shape-shifting timeless Evil I had sensed. How was it all connected?

"Drink water," Hammerstein commanded the Rangers who hadn't used the pause to hydrate. Then it was marching again.

Soon, we were in sight of the portion of the Marauder base where I sensed the Princess was being held. There were some patrol bots, but no sign of guards yet.

"Those are not Marauder bots," Tokushima observed.

"Paramon must be in pretty deep with them to be providing them tech from the Orion Arm."

I reached out to the bot's quantum echoes; sensed what I could from their trail in the time continuum, "The Marauders have agreed only to raid the Pleiades Confederation. This base and the predecessor Gateway we saw on the video feeds-they're a staging area to raid and torment the King of the Pleiades."

"And the Imperials at Deneb IV? Are they supporting this?" Hammerstein's gaze was desperate, but that I couldn't know for sure from these bots-only the echoes of the Paramon techs that had worked on them before sending them to the Marauders.

"I don't know. There was a Transhuman communicating with Gould back at Deneb IV via a caster."

A call came over com, it was the Serpentine. They had caught up with DePaulo and laid into the Paramon ships at his back in a deadly pummeling series of rear action cannon fire, "Let's Party!" someone on their bridge howled in homage to their lost Captain, and four Paramon fighters that had been harrying the Monkey were burst apart in a spray of molten metal, nano-circuitry, and guts.

A remainder broke away to the East and West, but a small swarm of the unfamiliar Marauder Predecessor fighters was behind the Serpentine, so it seemed a Pyrrhic victory. Of course, that's how we wanted it to seem. The entire hoopla was merely to draw their piloted air support away while we made for the base.

That left only the bots.

"Sniper," Hammerstein called out. Two of the Rangers and Tokushima signaled back. Hammerstein signaled with his fingers at the sky, one, two, and three. The three of them took up positions in the dirt.

One.

Two.

And Three.

The bots fell from the sky. There came no reaction from the Marauder base, it remained inscrutable on the horizon. A broad sweep of ring and world hugged the horizon, a scattering of lesser Pleiades beyond. I gathered from Hammerstein's post sniper observations of the base he had been making a calculated risk.

He had gambled that the Paramon bots and the Marauder base would be poorly coordinated. His gamble had played true, and he had eliminated the bots and the base was none the wiser.

The buzzing of the feeds from the Serpentine and the Monkey again began disturbing Hammerstein's focus on the base. Among the Marauder fighters now were several larger ships. Relics of that much Predecessor technology would have surely caught the interest of the Transhumans. With each revelation, the ties were thicker, yet still, there was no definitive answer to what it all meant.

The Marauder ships were coming from a height, diving at the two fleeing pirate vessels with a roaring and screeching of power drives. One of the Rangers muttered an expletive at the sight of the holo, 'What are those things?"

Tokushima's eyes darkened, "Reasons among many to kidnap a young Archaeologist Princess that was finding out too much...?"

Particle beam weapons fire emerged from the Marauder ships in waves slamming down on the Monkey and the Serpentine who took the onslaught, rolled this way and that, and returned fire.

Tokushima's comment delineated my conundrum, however. She was wrong, it wouldn't be the Predecessor Technology Princess Maggio had been kidnapped for. Paramon was already working with the Transhuman's-at least one of them.

We had seen that with Gould's communications on Deneb IV. It had to be related to her work on the Sunrider excavation; that and the Evil I had sensed in the derelict vessel.

We left two of the Rangers behind to keep in communication with the Serpentine and the Monkey and made then directly for the base. Furtively, silently, we stole across to last open spread of rock to the pylons and buildings.

I reached out to the quanta for her, sensed which portion of the base they had her in. There were doors, they were not locked.

We moved into the barren facility with the precision Rangers were noted for, the detectives and I slightly to the rear and the Rangers moving in a series of patterns, ever forward along our objective.

There were strange runes written all over the walls-no language I had ever seen, nor any intelligible quanta coming back, just incoherent nightmarish impressions-I fought them back, I needed to stay focused on the Princess.

Her sadness was epic. Even though I knew she may soon be rescued, I felt a terrible incapacity regarding being able to allay that sadness. We would see. The Rangers took another corner. More hallways and still no interference from the Marauders.

Then we saw the guards.

They became aware of us at the same time, and the shooting began. It was an ugly volley of back and forth. One of the Rangers hit home and the first Marauder fell.

The others continued firing in our direction and moved steadily toward us.

One of the Rangers screamed as his shoulder was hit with disser fire and he fell back. Another took his place and stepped away from cover for what seemed an eternity but was only a second or two. A Marauder aimed but the Ranger was quicker, hitting him center mass.

The two others continued without pause moving toward us. We had them outnumbered, it was only a matter now of how many of us they could get before we got them.

Without a word the whole of the rescue team rushed them then, each placing himself in the line of fire and each returning fire in a continuous forward motion.

One of the Rangers took it hard and fell to the ground, but the Marauder Guards were dead.

Tokushima reached the door first, blasted away the lock and opened it.

Princess Maggio was there, alive and well. She looked back, worn but triumphant. I could feel her sense of faith in the universe make a small step forward, again and then a huge relief that she was no longer alone with the mutant Marauders.

"Tokushima!" the Princess recognized the sister of her Security chief and the well of joy both women felt then was profound.

Hammerstein called in the Hammerhead then he and Tokushima fell on one knee, "Your Highness. Royal Police and Royal Rangers. We must leave here now."

The Rangers remained outside the door weapons drawn and aimed in every direction.

"Yes." Was all the Princess said and we began moving back to the exit.

Coco-butter had made an easy time of the distance it had taken us hours to go over on foot. He and the Hammerhead were at the door even as we exited. Everyone clambered into the main cabin and Tokushima began administering a light sedative and checking the Princess's vitals. The Rangers tended their wounded as well.

One of the Rangers we had left to communicate with the Serpentine and the Monkey looked up from his communications gear, "It ain't over. The Monkey and the Serpentine are still under heavy fire.

Hammerstein glared, "Get us to the Eberhardt. Push this thing as hard as you can."

"Aye, Aye."

We were fighting back at the heavens.

It was me the Princess spoke of first, "You brought a boy?"

I bowed my head.

"An Empath Ma'am, we couldn't have found you without him," Hammerstein replied.

Glory.

I fell to one knee and bowed my head, "Winteroud Sole, you Highness, your loyal servant, and greatest fan. I've read every one of your journal publications; brilliant work!"

Tired beyond description, in all reality in a state of shock, she still managed a humble blush. "Thank you," she whispered.

We rode out the rest of the several minutes of the flight in silence. Then Coco-butter docked in the Eberhardt.

"Take us out of this system, NOW!" Hammerstein roared and began a stride toward the command bridge.

He was stilled in his steps, however, by what came next. The Princess, weary, in shock, and still disbelieving she was at last rescued said, "You still have ships engaged with the enemy?"

Hammerstein lifted his chin, "Yes, Your Highness. There are two Core Pirate vessels, smugglers really, whom we implicated in this affair. They came over to our side when they learned you were kidnapped with the weapons they sold."

Her eyes darkened, and I felt her weigh her duties.

"Then they are our men. Is this not a Royal Warship, and are they not engaged in combat for our King and Country?"

"Indeed, your highness."

"Then we go to their aid now and make war beside them!"

A cheer went up in the hold. Hammerstein saluted, grabbed a cigar and strode away to the command bridge.

"Let's party." I heard him say under his breath.

The Serpentine and the Mel's Monkey had been performing an orchestrated retreat in a series of bounces away from the fighters' immediate range, then up and back in attack passes, and away again. Using a Beam Defense position, they Thach Weaved, drawing in one of the enemy fighters at a time, crossing each other's path and then away, and back again.

A difficult strategy to hold together when they were outnumbered, the two ships' history together was holding up. For being severely outnumbered, it was they, and not the Marauders, who were dictating the terms of the engagement. The Paramon pilots seemed to be skirting the edge of the engagement altogether.

The flight arcs changed with each pass, but even I could see their strategy remained the same.

"Target the largest two vessels in sequence," Hammerstein ordered and the Eberhardt began its dive.

We hit the atmosphere and began a fireball descent, a magnetic wave of super-heated plasma shot blasted out in front of us.

Coco-butter spun a wild splining vector down around, up, and then down as such when their particle beams and ordinance came we were already on a different vector. They made evasive maneuvers too, but the two largest lacked the maneuverability of the Eberhardt.

We straddled the first again and again with rapid-fire passes. Using a lag pursuit strategy, we maneuvered the ship just outside the enemy's turning radius and then ripped into what were their main drive units.

The first went down into the shallow sea and lay there like a huge wounded sea monster on a beach. The Princess's chin rose somewhat then and she looked over to me with a triumphant smile. The honor of Caldris was being defined with each slashing blast of weapons fire.

"Welcome to the party, Hammie. You got your package?" DePaulo barked.

"Yes, and she insisted we join the dance with you."

"The Belle of the Ball!" DePaulo laughed.

The Monkey banked and strafed the enemy again in a primordial light show. The enemy fighters kept heading back toward their fallen mother ship. We were shooting fish in a barrel now.

Hammerstein, looked to the Princess, "My Lady, do you wish the honors?"

Victory. Her heart was leaden but triumphant. She rose on the bridge.

"Paramon and Associated fighters, this is Princess Clairissa Maggio, heir of the Royal Family of Caldris. I ask you, for the lives of your men, to stand down and surrender."

There came a long moment, then, "Your terms?"

"We will be leaving. Further discussions on the matter will be dealt with by our Ambassador."

At last, "We will cease hostilities and surrender. The victory is yours. Please reconnoiter with all your people on world."

The Princess looked to Hammerstein, "We have more people on world?"

"One Casualty Ma'am. One of the Pirate Captains had gone out on an airbike. He was to meet us at the base and help rescue you. He never made it."

Her eyes darkened, "I see. We must retrieve his body then, and be sure he is buried with honors and a proper memorial." She said softly.

It was quiet on the bridge.

"Mr. Parsons?" Hammerstein said crisply.

"What was Captain Dansky's last position before we lost communications?"

"He was on route to the base as we planned. I'll set a heading down there now and we'll begin a search pattern, Sir."

"Thank you."

"Sir...?"

"Yes?"

"He was alone...and the dragon things they..."

Hammerstein's eyes went kind of glassy then...Hey Hammie! You Butch old Bear, you!

"We all die alone, Parsons. The important thing was how he lived. Find whatever we can. Do what we can.'

The three ships made their way to the area of Dansky's last reported position. A scan of the rocky pools showed indeed the airbike was at the bottom of one of the pools. His combat helmet was there too in the water as well. No trace of the big Captain's body.

We were about to give up when one of the Rangers called in.

"Officer Hammerstein. Please confirm!"

"Hammerstein."

"I think you should see this, Sir."

"What is it?"

"A man on a dragon, Sir. He's riding a dragon."

"What?"

There came a third voice, "Ohhhh, Shoot, I said I want confirmation from none other than Officer Hammerstein! Is that you Hammie?!"

Captain Dansky was alive; alive and riding one of the dragons we had assumed ate him.

"Yeah, this is Officer Hammerstein. Please leave the dragon now and get in the Hammerhead so we can get you over to the Serpentine, aye?'

"Yeah, yeah, yeah. First I want to show you something. I think your archaeologist Princess will find it very interesting."

"Well, naturally Captain. Paramon has surrendered. Everything on this rock is Royal property now. We all thought you were dead. Glad to hear you made it through."

"Well, it was a little touch and go with the dragons, you know...but I offered it some Rum I had in a flask. Very low Rum tolerance these dragons."

"You got the dragons drunk?"

"Uhhh, yeah. Plastered actually, clocked. Totaled, wasted. Drunk as a skunk. But your Princess needs to see this artifact thing I found, her and the psychic boy."

"Captain Dansky, this is Princess Maggio."

"Your Highness!"

"So glad to see you're alive."

"Thank you, your Highness!"

"What is it you've found, besides Rum loving dragons?'

"Something Predecessor."

"I see. Delightful. Well, we are on our way!"

Hammerstein looked to his navigator and waved him on, "Go. Get the coordinates from the Ranger and let's get on with it."

Tokushima smiled, "Dragons are good luck in many cultures."

The artifact

Dansky left his dragon at the jungle with a pat on the snout and we brought the Eberhardt to his location with apprehension. The Marauders had stood down, apparently following suit from Paramon-whatever raiding and pillaging they had planned to unloose on the Pleiades was now moot-they were fleeing through the gateway and taking huge portions of their base with them.

Dansky's artifact was probably on their list as well, so us getting a look before we left was a wise move. The Princess recognized it at once.

"There were similar constructs at the ill-fated archaeological expedition at the Core, before the Arcturian War. They activated during the war and the entire expedition went missing." She said, striding along the rocky slope.

"Maybe a good idea to stand back away, Ma'am. I think it's a pretty good bet the Expedition didn't just go 'missing', they went 'Mutant Marauder'." Tokushima had stepped between the Princess and the artifact, automatically trying to shield her.

The Princess made a disgusted face, "Yes..."

"Which begs the questions-why were they activated then, why are they active now-after so many millions of years? How can they affect Humans, who didn't even exist when these devices were originally fabricated?' I wondered.

"Did the expedition ever actually date the things? There has been a broad and ongoing dispute among archaeologists as per the dates of the Predecessor relics found. They seem to stretch across an unreasonably long time." The Princess countered.

Great point. She was amazing, barely out of her tribulation, and then combat, she had bounced back and her mind was keenly thinking through this new riddle.

Hammerstein wasn't a scientist, but he was a detective, and his next observation would ring true, "It has a similar structure to a hypercasting device-the plan is radial and directional."

The Princess's adrenaline ticked up a bit at that.

"Broadcasting to whom?"

"They're relics of the Predecessor network, we could presume firstly." I offered.

"Why?" She wondered, and her face glowed.

Hammerstein interjected, "Perhaps it has something to do with what you found on the Sunrider that predicated your kidnapping?"

Now her eyes went cold, "Yes. We must get the Eberhardt and our new Core Allies away from this planet and system now. The Marauders are fleeing through their gateway now; there is no telling they won't just as soon swarm back here with reinforcements."

She looked to Hammerstein, "The Sunrider relic I found?"

"We moved it to Fort Oort, your Highness. It is under heavy guard and Winteroud has sensed an alien entity there he feels we should not make any contact with."

At the mention of the Sunrider, dread filled my mind.

"My Empathic impressions were unlike those I have sensed from Predecessor relics. There is, or was, something else in the Sunrider. There is a connection-the Sunrider, the Arcturian war, the Predecessors, the Imperials and the Marauders-but I am unable to ascertain what that connection is.

"A Transhuman Imperial was backing your kidnapper Ma'am, we discovered as much on Deneb IV while searching for you. Strangely enough, there was another Transhuman that seemed to run interference for us."

Her eyes widened, "A Transhuman Ally?"

"David Omm 6x," I said.

She recognized the name immediately. David Omm, before going into the Transhuman singularity, was the CCCE Imperial Ambassador to the Arcturian Colonies before the Arcturian War.

We made haste then to leave that world for home, for Caldris, at last, with our Princess. I took a last look at Kyllini Prime and its glorious sky of gas giant and moons. I felt a pang of sadness that Fischer Shea's visions for this world were never realized-it would have surely been a fine planet. And what happens to a dream deferred? Lilies left to fester…

I thought of all the dispossessed peoples in Human history, from the Fall of Troy to the Fall of the Arcturians; great nations and people's cut short at first flower from their dreams.

What dreams had the Predecessors before their fall, and how did it fit in with the same patterns now repeating along with Human history?

> *They that have the power to hurt and do none,*
> *They that have the power to hurt and do none*
> *That do not do the thing they most do a show,*
> *Who, moving others, are themselves as stone,*
> *Unmoved, cold, and to temptation slow,*
> *They rightly do inherit heaven's graces*
> *And husband nature's riches from expense;*
> *They are the lords and owners of their faces,*
> *Others but stewards of their excellence.*
> *The summer's flower is to the summer sweet,*
> *Though to itself it only live and die,*
> *But if that flower with base infection meet,*
> *The basest weed outbraves his dignity:*
> *For sweetest things turn sourest by their deeds;*
> *Lilies that fester smell far worse than weeds.*
> *-William Shakespeare*

Return of the Princess

That was seven standard Caldris years ago. I was rewarded my effort and contributions in the great rescue mission with a fabulous star yacht, which I was too young at the time to use, and a signed copy of "Sometimes a Great Notion". I adored the book, and decided to name my star yacht the "Lord Kesey" and thus she has remained ever since, upgraded and modified as I can find authentic period parts.

Seven years. Of course I followed her journals with faithful tenderness, pined for her and Tokushima alternately, enjoyed a large degree of celebrity which has helped in my own writing of Galactic Histories being given some fair consideration in an impatient and often unfair Galactic literary community where everyone, even in our lesser era, everyone is so, well, busy.

The King of the Pleiades and the King of Caldris, of course, strengthened their relationship considerably after the whole Kyllini Prime affair.

DePaulo made his way back to the Core with his Monkey; enjoying the fame, well, famously. Dansky lost the Serpentine in a card game at the Zamoran O'Neil Station, and was last heard trying to get it back looking for a piloting gig and hanging around the notorious pilot tavern, "Mac's Club Deuce".

Hammerstein Retired with special honors, his replacement, of course, Tokushima, whom he had been grooming for the role forever. I saw them at his retirement party and again at her ceremony of assuming her new command. He still didn't know she loved him; she still couldn't bring herself to reveal it. She collected a series of dashing beaux, one after another, never willing to admit to herself, much less confess to Hammerstein, none of them could ever be anything close to the old granite detective.

Coco-butter Parsons made full Captain on the Kings Royal Escort. "Babe Magnet, kid. Babe. Magnet." He winked, pretending it was just a tool to attract women, and not important to him. He lied, it was his most cherished personal honor, and he was only still single because he hadn't met the right one. It was good bravado, however, and I'm sure it served his reputation well with others. Not so much with an empath.

The year my father let me pilot the Lord Kesey I took her on a grand tour of the star system, solo piloting from Key's landing and the sand reef fort ruins, all along the great island chains, through the purple moons, past the central O'Neil habitats, all the way to the Oort cloud and finally to Fort Oort where I was told, 'Due respect, Sir Sole, we're on orders to discourage civilians from visiting."

I wondered if the Sunrider was still in hangar three, still a menace?

I had published another of my Histories of the Outworlds without having been to one unless you consider Langley Stay Voids End an Outworld (and I am NOT getting into that argument) when a call came in from the palace.

It was Princess Clairissa Maggio.

"Your Highness." I bowed before her hologram.

She was hypercasting with a video feed from some moon on an expedition, and there was a celestial phenomenon beyond her in the sky-it looked like a quasar.

"Sir Sole." She smiled, "Now, thank you for the honors, they are worthwhile and important in their time and place. I deem it more important now you dispense with them for a time and call me Clairissa."

Clairissa!

She had never done that before.

"Clairissa," I said and the word was like a sacred tome.

"Yes. Good," She pointed to the quasar, "you see that?'

"Variable star, quasar?"

"No. One would think, but it is not so." she replied, "it is, in fact, a predecessor base in old Arcturian space. It and three other relic bases lit up this week, all of them on a vector to the Silurian nebula. The Diablo Nebula!"

Ghost ships and Hyper-Bogie demons! The Diablo nebula.

"We may have trouble getting the scientific community to take any theories regarding the Diablo nebula and Siluria Seriously," I suggested, warned actually. Where was she going with this?

"I am the Princess. They will have to take it seriously or I will cut their funding."

Girl power.

"Well, are you planning an expedition to the Silurian Nebula? All the stories are merely- "

"Merely a reflection of the fact that our drive systems cannot be counted on to function properly there, causing a significant series of starfaring disasters in the anomaly. Are you going to quote me more of your first book or are you going to listen?"

"You read my first book?"

She read my first book. She quoted it. *No way.*

"Shhh! Please, listen! Men, you're all the same, even the smart ones. I can't get into the theory on the darn caster, now. Bring E Gibbon and the Lord Kesey to the Capitol this evening and land at the observation park at Cezanne Mons. Have your star yacht provisioned for a long trip."

"You have the King's approval, Clairissa?"

"Yes, we have to bring Officer Tokushima and some very scary combat droids and some gravity bombs and things, everything will be ready at the observation park in an old aitruck-you'll love it, classic."

She blew me a kiss, "Mwah!"

My heart stopped for a long moment and then I remembered for it to beat again.

"Don't be late, my little hero!"

Then she was offline.

There aren't enough superlatives for this scenario so, I won't bother.

I wanted to sit down at the estate beach and look out over the ocean for a bit and CRY because I knew life could never get any better than this.

I was on time for my arrival at the capitol. Well, I was a little early, actually, two hours early.

Tokushima arrived first. She had a couple of officers with her, several combat droids and the same aircars (laser blasts observable if you were a classic paint job connoisseur as I was) we had when I took my first run to the palace with her and Hammerstein seven years before.

"Oh, you're so tall!" she said and hugged me and I felt the discomfort she went through coordinating her image of me then with me now. "You grew."

I smiled, "That happens."

Her officers and their droids buzzed about us incessantly and I was plagued with their technical readouts of various signal searches, sniffers, and scans. She and I made small talk as best we could, with gaps as it were of years between the occasional invitations and communications.

My boyish adoration of her had been supplanted now with a fuller understanding of her as a person struggling with daily routines, deadlines, and career objectives. Somewhere though, beneath the bureaucracy, the disappointments, missed life markers (she had long expected to have a family by now) there was stirring a great relief to be on this assignment.

The rescue of the Princess had been, at the end of the day, an adventure and a triumph. This promised to be also an adventure, hopefully, one without the perils and loss of life for the first. The Ranger who was killed in the mission had received a special burial and memorial, and the thanks of the star system-the only consolation such men and women get. Yet, that is who they are. Selfless; heroic.

The memorial was here at the park, on Cezanne Mons, and when the Princess arrived she went to it first. She laid a special wreath of frangipani flowers and bowed her head for a long moment.

I had never read of, nor discussed with the Princess, anything about her religious beliefs, or if she prayed, some of her writings had indicated certain agnosticism.

She was, however, determined to show her respect and pay tribute to his memory.

She approached us then and we went to one knee and made a slight bowing of heads as was customary.

"Winteroud!" She laughed, embraced me, "Look how tall! You grew!"

"Yes, Your Highness. Hopefully no more."

"Officer Tokushima! Thank you for coming on the assignment on such short notice."

"My Honor and Duty and greatest desire," Tokushima replied, and I knew it was true.

Tokushima's security people had finished with the Lord Kesey. The hold was open and the Princess signaled her classic air truck to the hold. Some other crates of provisions were loaded and she graced us with another of her lovely smiles.

"We will be weeks in transit, let us forgo any further greetings and pleasantries as there will be time enough in space." She said.

And so we departed Caldris and began the long journey to the Arcturian ruins.

I believe, should long I live, I will remember those long weeks of flight as some of the best days of my life. Officer Tokushima's first name was Jingu, and although I had known this, we had never before been on a first-name basis. Jingu, Clairissa, and I spent many hours on the long journey discussing aspects of History, Art, and Military Strategy. Sun Tzu, of course, came up now and then.

Mostly, however, the conversations inevitably came back to the Arcturian War-we were, after all on route to the ruined derelict worlds crushed in that war. It was, after all, Clairissa's excavations of a CCCE Sunrider frigate from the war that had predicated her kidnapping.

"Yes, it is still at Fort Oort," she informed me, "but we haven't detected the Evil again. There are various theories regarding what you sensed. Two seem to hold sway with my people now. One, that what was sensed was an echo of an entity, or that it was a 'piece' of an entity that was left inside the Sunrider when it went into stasis.

"At Deneb IV," Jingo added, Gould was receiving orders from a woman. She never appeared to him in person, always in a holo. Gould was convinced she was the Transhuman Overlord Lourdes Cassandra."

"So that would rule out Paramon being after the Sunrider for its ancient war era Imperial Technology-Lourdes could have provided that from the CCCE Imperial archives," I said.

"Yes." Clarissa's eyes gleamed, "So the only factor that connects my kidnapping to the Transhumans is the Sunrider, and only the anomalous sentience you described as Evil makes that Sunrider anything more than a glorious relic. Overlord Lourdes Cassandra then wanted me out of the way because I had discovered the Evil. She knew of it, and wanted it to remain unrevealed."

"Birds of a feather." Jingo smiled wickedly then, "having gone over to the great digital singularity, the Transhuman Lourdes Cassandra recognized the disembodied sentience of the Evil."

"When would she have first encountered it?" Clairissa wondered aloud.

"The original CCCE Sunrider fleet of the great Arcturian war was manned by welded Cyborgs. Part of the Hive mind, they were all interconnected." I said, not liking where it was going.

"After the war, CCCE introduced a new caste of Air Corps. They're not connected to the Hive mind. They are the only portion of CCCE society which is not connected to the Hive, except for criminals." Jingo took a sip of wine and seemed to taste it as if looking for clues.

"That Evil, or a mere remnant piece of it, killed the older Empath the Royal detectives had sent in before you, Winteroud," Clairissa added.

"Perhaps it was an AI? Some form of weapon the Transhumans had loaded onto the Sunriders with the intent of poisoning the Arcturian minds? But it got loose in their ships…" I was reaching, but it was plausible except that—

"The Arcturians didn't use a Hive mind, neither in their Military or Civil Society. They despised all forms of collectivism as tyranny." Clairissa said ominously.

"Good thing, from the looks of it the whole CCCE Cyborg crew had their minds fried in seconds when they encountered that Evil," Jingo's eyes widened, "imagine if it hit the great Hive mind at Deneb IV."

We had arrived shortly after that conversation to the New Galen System with its ruined settlements and worlds stretching from its farthest world to its former main population center the M-class planet New Galen itself. I wondered had the Arcturians brought the destruction down on themselves with the creation of a weapon the CCCE feared above all weapons?

If CCCE, still fearing such a thing, suspected Princess Clairissa Maggio had discovered it, why had they only had her kidnapped and left the relic at Fort Oort undisturbed?

New Galen.

If Kyllini Prime was the confused conflagration of a dream deferred, then New Galen was the bitter shock of pride stolen and betrayed. The full weight of my empathic powers was now in play, and here was a world where the ghosts of billions cried out injustice.

Injustice! Injustice! Day upon ruined day, a decade into a century, it seemed to ooze in the curling sand-devils and linger among violet shadows. The ninth circle of Hell in Inferno was for the treacherous, and the Arcturians had been betrayed and destroyed in a manner and on a scale never before or since. Yet CCCE had not received any sentence to a ninth circle, they had remained the dominant power in the galaxy, and the ghosts cried out.

There was an interstellar gateway built by CCCE before the war, such had been the open nature of Arcturian Society. It still spun around slowly at a wide orbit. We made out, way past it and downworld without having to register title.

We were the only living people on that world, but I was beginning to have the first of many powerful visions-the last days of the Arcturian Colonies.

They would become the most haunting aspect of my sixth sense. We traversed over landscapes where once great farms had produced the foodstuffs of nations. Mutant weeds and radioactive dust whispered on the wind.

Sentient life affects the quanta in ways our science is still in infancy regarding. Millennia of prejudice against "superstition" has closed the minds of researchers, and thus "ghosts" and "gods", "demons" and "dark spirits" have remained increasingly the province of astrologers and soothsayers, witchdoctors and charlatans.

Yet even the scientists will admit we change the universe when we observe it. Little do they know? We Empaths, sometimes we see things. Are they an echo of what was, or something else? I still do not know.

We approached the cities and the ruined megalopolises stood dark and brutal, some molten into surreal sculptures of death, others with bits and pieces of neighborhoods still semi-intact, decaying slowly to the elements.

I had E Gibbon increase my empathy baffles.

It was the only way I could endure the echoes.

The Princess was filled with gloom and Jingo Tokushima with a dread fascination.

"What happened here?" Jingo whispered and her words should have been, "What happened here?"

The official stories and histories, we knew, were incomplete propaganda. Such is war. Yet this was the lynchpin of the Galaxy's past, and somehow, I knew, its future too depended on the answers.

We came to the ruins of a great starport and spent a couple of days among its ruins. On the runways, star liners were still lined up to take off for flights they would never make. I could hear the echoes of that final day; I had E Gibbon set the baffle higher.

Strangely, I could even see the echoes of the last flights out, their quanta slightly different hues. I had no answer for this and logged it in my mind as something to pursue further.

Jingo asked if there were mutant survivors perhaps to menace us. I assured her no unless one counted dogs.

There were various packs of mutant dogs and livestock that had survived, I sensed. In their dawning consciousness, they somehow knew the great constructions were made by others now gone, and I wondered if their first mythologies would be of the lost gods who built the ruins then died in a tragic war from heaven.

Then after several days, we made our way to the Predecessor relic. Similar to the one Roland Dansky had found, it was farther North in a cold region of the planet. A silvery behemoth glimmering in the bright sun it was alive with whatever strange forces the Predecessors had harness those many millions of years before. Were we, like the dogs prowling the ruins of New Galen, a lesser species seeking answers regarding a war long ago?

Was this part of the reason CCCE had attacked the Arcturians, and if so why had they not destroyed it in their attack?

So that first expedition finished us with more questions arisen from the voyage than answered. We took our measurements and surveys like proper scientists. We wrote up this hypothesis and that, and the Princess requested upon our return to Caldris a mission to the Silurian Nebula and was denied.

I determined I would go back, something still troubled me regarding the star liners I had seen in my visions. The ones that had made it off-world and not been destroyed.

The difference in their hue, it had to mean something...

Book Four: The Taloned Sire

The Crash Trail
Rip, Sagittarius Arm, 4110.

Screaming Ghost Lake.

Violet and crystalline, stone stacks spread from horizon to horizon, jutting out from the slopes of the hillsides and the waters of Screaming Ghost Lake like ancient sentinels. Two small green evening moons accented the reflective surface, confusing the mirror-smooth sheen of the loch, making it seem the very sky itself. It appeared to Vince Phalen his speedboat ran across a mirror of the heavens. He could see mossy objects beneath the surface; they made the waters particularly treacherous if one did not know where the shallows hid the submerged stacks. Lumbering mega-koi fish twirled slowly beneath the perfect surface of the water, swimming in the reflections of the stars. From an ornate leather case, he pulled brass binoculars and ran a search over the waters and hillside.

No sign of the coast guard.

Vince set his binoculars down on the speedboat's elaborate fern-wood and bronze dash and wiped sweat from his eyes. It wasn't that hot. "Nerves," he said. That was all. Maybe merely the heat from the idling engine? He bit his lip and cursed himself for letting Andrew talk him into these "deliveries". He wiped sweat and a stray strand of his long red hair from his face. Yet Charon and he had recently wed and winter was coming; he needed the money. If the coast guard caught him, he would be a decade in the stasis block.

The Tunis mushrooms in the hold were illegal.

He picked up the binoculars again and scanned the horizon. It was then that he saw what everyone else had missed since the first fall. A long straight streak on the side of a distant hill.

"The crash trail of a starship?" he whispered to himself. It was slashing the landscape, overgrown, but there. He changed the binoculars to infrared, clicked to high contrast. Something was there. If a ship had gone down hard with stasis shields at max, it could have torn up the side of the hill and left just such a feature. She would have banked and dug, leaving a mound. Stasis fields were notorious for the unpredictable way they interacted with unstasised matter-each element and molecule reacting differently than similar combinations might when impacting ordinary matter. At this distance and among the trees it could not be determined. However, he would come back. Momentary considerations were to get the mushrooms delivered. He recorded his position and moved the ornate drive lever forward to a steady cruise across the water.

The oversize sweeping lines of the speedboat roared across the lake. He had an appointment at the docks of Herkiestown.

There was no sign of the coastguard; even they avoided these stretches of lakes and inlets. Legends abounded about the "Screaming ghosts" of these lakes for centuries. Vince, however, had been through them all his life and hadn't seen so much as a newt much less a screaming ghost. He pressed onward. The sun was getting lower. "Screaming-ghost Lake my butt."

A wail came up slowly then and for an instant, his mind hovered in a zone of unreality thinking the sound was the screaming ghost leering back at his comment. Then, small in the distance on the lake, he saw a boat and realized it was the coastguard. He was plunging straight toward them. Instantly, he responded with a savage turn of the speedboat to hard left and then, letting the boat heave to in the wake, made a determined throttle to the max.

The speedboat now was lunging into its wake from only a second before. It careened headlong back, and then off to the right a bit of the wake. He turned around and they were gaining. Still, they certainly could not make him out yet to identify him. He would have to chance the shallows and the hollows.

The coastguard boats were larger; they would draw deeper into the water. He swung his boat past a shoal and stack of violet and mauve quartz. Massive schools of fan rays reacted, and for a moment even the clear waters of the loch were a fog of them and he could not see the depths. The boat careened onward in its lunge past them. He narrowly missed a hulking arc of stone just beneath the surface and cursed aloud.

A passage up ahead, a hollow. He knew it led through one of the frequent escarpments and fjords that cleft The Thousand Lakes and their gloomy hills. If he remembered correctly, there were so many. He chanced it and slowed, eyeing the rocks, straddling the throttle with the whole of his body ready to pull back in an instant. He pressed his speed as fast he dared, not chancing a look back. Low branches of the ferns hung down.

He zigged and zagged through the twisting cleft. The coastguard would not be much longer entering it themselves, but he doubted they would pursue in such a shallow rock-filled stretch. As it were, he was surprised to see them. Reaching the end of the cleft, he chanced back a look, and at that very moment, the prow of the coastguard's boat poked into view. Slamming the speedboat forward now was a gamble he had to take and he broke for the deeper waters and swerved to the right behind the sheltering walls of the cliffside.

He had evaded them. They would not pursue through the rocky hollow in their larger boat. He made for his appointment in Herkiestown.

Cold night shot an eerie blue fog across the harbor by the time Vince approached the docks at Herkiestown. Khitaman's Lantern, a tall white shaft of a lighthouse, flashed a warning of the shoals. Beyond the lantern, a thousand water ships crammed and docked. Muffled conversations snapped in the creeping cold; nobody's business, better not to hear some of the things being said. Rip was a world of villages and church bells peeling in the vineyards, but the cities of the inland seas, Herkiestown, Khita, Blakeston, and Kroug-these were massive, hulking labyrinths of Lakers and shanks.

The lantern's light swept a few starships water ported, glistening in the night-the Star Trading Guildsmen. They were given wide berth. Herkiestown took a measure of pride that Zola Mosey had originated the idea of the Guild at Herkiestown, but the denizens of that city had no illusions about the traders being sentimental. The Space Trade Guild's power now rivaled even the Imperials. In the intervening centuries, it had become the trade guild that first sustained civilization in the refugee "Outworlds", and then, in an irony of history not lost on the trade guildsmen, the guild that controlled the flow of raw materials into the empire via the black market.

The Imperials command economy could not function without illegally supplied raw materials. Totalitarian governments expanded to the point where to function one had to break their law.

Vince's speedboat plied the oily blackness of the chilly waters, past the warehouses looming in the dark silhouetted by the brilliant blue star field poking through the wisps of fog. He was young; the vicissitudes of the galactic economy were mere abstractions in his mind. He focused on the dark water immediately in front of him. Flotsam and litter from a dozen continents floated in the inky blackness. Vince had seen corpses hauled out of the harbor in the bright light of early morning on past visits to Herkiestown. He wondered what unfortunates might lay there now.

He came to a large open brick boathouse with elaborate corbelling and intricate weaves of interlaced brickwork. A lean old figure in coveralls and a pointed cap stood stoking on an elaborate pipe. A scent floated down. It was Smitty.

"Hey do wharf rat. Staying long?" He asked amicably, knowing full good Vince never stayed long.

"No, Smitty, just paying a visit to a sick friend. Any news?" Vince asked.

"Hear tell there are two for one well-drinks down at Raygun's Backstreet Bar. Hear too Andrew Deck was wondering when his speedboat was going to be returned. You take Screaming-Ghost Lake back?"

"Sounds like a plan. Yeah, I took the lake."

"One of these days you're going to regret that path. 'Telling you Vince, something is wrong about that lake. Gave me a bad feeling ever since I was a kid."

"Power of suggestion," Vince replied. "They tell you it's spooky, and so you feel spooky when you go there." Vince thought of the crash trail he believed he saw beneath the tree line and smiled. No wonder no one had found it before.

"That place is haunted I'm telling you. Take your boat through Fredonia bay, Silver Creek, Sunset Harbor. Been a trail of suicides and missing people around that lake since people fell onto this planet. I'm telling you."

Vince and Smitty had attempted to hop one of the new fusion steamer trains out of Kroug city once, and watched all their carefully chosen souvenirs acquired in the night before go riding off without them when the train acquired speed much faster than they anticipated, and Vince had to jump back as Smitty could not get a handhold. "Smitty caution" was ever after deemed disreputable in Vince's mind.

139

"I'll give it some thought." He paid a rental fee and secured the speedboat, added a friendly gratuity-more than he could afford-and broke off into a hearty swaggering stride to Central wharf and Raygun's Backstreet bar.

Central Wharf was a series of three-story stone and brick buildings with walkways such that each level could be accessed. It ran the full length of the harbor and its side branches wound similarly up various canals into the city.

One of the canals stretched beyond the city limits and giant grain elevators, then off a couple of hundred miles to Chester's falls. Central Wharf was a city within a city. Lakers and canal men supplied a steady stream of customers to music emporiums, dance halls, houses of ill repute, gambling halls, and smoking dens.

Phantasmagorical carnivalesque paintings and signs lined the buildings, some with holograms and occasional electrical and neon brought in from deep space, but mostly with gaslight and lanterns.

Further, into the city, the buildings were rising higher with more elaborate terracotta tracery, brass trolleys, theatres, and grand hotels. Here at the Central wharf, however, a backwoods boy like Vince could stomp along the icy wrought iron walkways with no silk tie required. A discordant array of music drifted across the wharf from half a dozen establishments. Closer to Raygun's he could hear The Voodoo Sailor's, the house band, metallic and pipe rhythms hammering at a high tempo. They were playing "Famous blue raincoat" one of their headliners.

Yusuf Greenberg was at the door. His boyish face smirked knowingly from beneath a tight mop of red curls, "Hey do, wharf rat. Five shillings." He was dressed entirely in green with a double-breasted coat and tails, a smokestack silk hat with silver filigree and a bulge in his vest that Vince was sure was loaded. His teeth were completely gold. He showed them conspicuously with a tight muscled jaw. Vince had seen him grab a man's wrist like lightning one time, quickly, even before Vince had seen the bloody knife the fellow had been sporting in his hand.

Vince could see the band at the back under the stage lights, through the door panes. The giant Drew Iko was belting out his lyrics with a mighty baritone while his strong massive hands caressed his holosynth strapped across his belly with a deft intelligent grace, *"Star-rr-light ladies-"*

"Hey, Yusuf, good crowd tonight?"

"Just another night of trolls and lost sailors. Welcome aboard."

Vince paid the cover and stepped into the warmth and noise of the crowded Raygun's. Smells of perfume and food assaulted him with a mixture of jasmine and cinnamon, pepper, crab grease, alcohol, and fern-rose petals.

"Don't mess with no backwoods dreamer-"

"Hey, Phalen! You ever finish that course on, what'd ya' say it was, hyper stream piloting?" One of the Lakers at the bar called over to Vince when he came in. The man was just off the water from a long ore ship and reveling in the idiosyncrasies of Herkiestown characters of whom Vince figured prominently. "I'll give you this kid; you got a big set of kahunas for that. Me, I'll take a water ship any day." He handed Vince a tall golden glass of fern mead.

Several of the patrons laughed.

"You can take 'dem hyper streams, I like my space normal, thank you very much!" Someone else chimed in.

"Finished a couple of seasons back now, maybe six. Good course." Vince answered and took a seat by his partner Andrew Deck. Andrew rolled his eyes. The Laker turned back to his fern mead.

"Well, it's old Vinny-always a tale or two, eh? Nothing like a low profile. And you're late." Andrew said and pushed him another drink of fern mead. "Any trouble?"

"One patrol, I dodged them through a cleft. We're good. It's in my boots."

The door opened and four Coast guards came in. One of them looked right at Andrew. Another went over to the bartender asking questions. How long had Andrew been here? All day?

He walked over, "Nice boat Deck," he said smiling. He let a silence weigh down with implications. "First class ride, it is. Must have run a few pennies. Saw one similar out at Screaming Ghost Lake today. Wasn't in much of a mood to say hello. The bartender says you been here all day or I would have sworn it was your boat. I'm watching you, Deck."

"Thanks. I try." Andrew smiled back, staring innocently, perfectly believable.

The guardsman looked at Vince. "Ahh, the illustrious Vincent Phalen. Any luck finding a job on a star yacht?"

"Nothing yet. Seems pretty wrapped up."

"Well, there are so few starships coming to Rip as is. It could be a long time before you get a spot; it's pretty rare they need a crew. Good luck though. The Rip Winter's coming."

Winter...five standard Earth years.

"Times they are a-changing, Officer Meyer. A hundred years ago we were virtually isolated out here in Sagittarius. The galactic economy is expanding again. There will be ships. A hundred years from now, you won't recognize this city," Vince replied.

The guardsman was already busy eyeing other patrons, "Yeah well, maybe a hundred years before all that coursework you took does you any good at the rate, kid. In the meantime, stay away from spoiled rich youth with fancy boats," he said and moved along.

Andrew scowled. "I am NOT rich."

"Your family has done well, Andrew. From that Copper's view, you guys are rolling in it. "Deck dough" they used to call it back at the Hamlet school when we were little."

Andrew smirked in spite of himself. His long coat was a fine sheepskin patchwork with an oversize collar. His wide-brimmed hat hung slung casually on a hook by their table and that too was sheepskin, with an expensive Offworld sash for a band.

His shirt was a thick fern weave and his loose wide tie glimmered. Vince never did figure what it was made of and did not want to be seen as too much the hick to ask. More and more Offworld products were finding their way to Rip these past years. The governments were even discussing the possible purchase of orbiting satellites.

Vince took a tug on his ale and thought of the crash trail he had seen out on the lakes. An intact engine would be worth a king's ransom. He remembered the mushrooms in his boots. The Coastguards were so close. Andrew chimed in on some banality, and they finished a few more drafts before stepping out into the cold night and the dark streets.

They walked quietly eyeing the alleys for jumpers. Faint snow was in the air but it melted when it hit the cobbles. The sky was tinged now with a yellow light-ever so faintly as the rings of Tyhrin rose. Tyhrin was the name given to the enormous gas giant Rip orbited. When it rose, the night would come alive with a glow, and the hulking lake stone buildings would glimmer with the ornate etched patterns of centuries of craftsman in a bewitched golden sheen.

Andrew looked over at Vince and laughed, "Only you." He said.

"What?"

"Trudging along with that bouncing walk like you was off to Sunday meeting and pumpkin cakes after. They never know what hits them till you pull that left hook."

He did have a good left hook.

141

ince never knew why he amused Andrew so much but he accepted it with a laugh. As out of place the woodsman was in the city, Andrew never knew him to lie, or back down from a fight. Still, for a smuggling partner, he had picked one that stood out like a sore thumb anywhere, and everywhere. Probably so at Sunday meeting and pumpkin cakes after, as well. One of a kind.

His lanky backwoods demeanor did turn an occasional head. Nevertheless, he came through. When it was time to fight, he stepped right in like each battle his last stand, and each friend by his side his only friend. When the journey was long and arduous, he tied up his bootstraps and set about it.

They stopped at a big lake stone Inn with a glowing neon sign; The Yellow Jaguar. Simple blocks of tan sandstone. Vince banged on the door and a small viewport popped open. There came a grunt of recognition.

The door opened. Inside they were met by two enormous blue tattooed doormen-Obscurofrioians. Noted for their strength and obstinate nature, they came from an ice world where the original settlers-refugees like Rips-had genetically altered themselves to survive the cold. The tattoos were ice worm blood. As a rite of passage, a boy went out on to the ice alone to lure an ice worm. Killing it, he would then cut out its spiny teeth and use them to tattoo paisley-like patterns of whorls on their face and upper body. The process began with mortal danger and ended with searing pain. The more intricate the pattern the more danger and pain one had endured. These were very intricate patterns.

"She's upstairs," one of them growled. He had a short-gun strapped casually over his back. Imperial disser, it could disassemble molecules in seconds. Leave a boiling mass of radioactive goo. Someone had retrofitted it in local polished beach-wood with silver inlay. Customizing death-dealing with a personal, homegrown style.

Vince and Andrew clambered up a winding stair of fern runners, worn smooth with indentations. They went up, and then through a series of locked chambers. Jane was waiting. An ancient prune of humble origins, she had amassed some wealth through patience and stealth but hungered always for something more. She looked at Vince as if he brought fond memories of some studly beaux she had toyed with in her younger days.

Jane's mouth creaked a sideways slant. Her ancient hair matted into a comical cap that clung to her head like a pasted thing. Her features were gnomish, wrinkled, peasant-like. But something in her eyes hinted at other things, a sense of mastery and determination.

142

They were beady blue marbles that once possessed an ethereal, oriental beauty of curve and angle that could, if traced by a knowing geneticist, be determined to originate with the Mongol warriors sweeping through Eastern Europe, worlds and millennia away.

"Ahh, dashing Andrew, and the handsome Vincent, welcome. Sit down. Come. Brave travelers, I trust you've brought me my goodies?" Her accents fell loud and high on the ends of words.

Her bulbous nose rose with a snobbish gesture that was comical considering her humble background but told of the character that drove her to amass her wealth.

Vince and Andrew sat on the large overstuffed Ottomans. Vince reached into his boots and pulled out the packets of mushrooms from sewn compartments. The boots were hand-tooled with fine designs by his new wife, Charon. They were mamonth leather, they would last two lifetimes. He set the mushrooms on a small coral table imported from one of the island worlds in the Pleiades.

"Ohhh nice." She said. "Yesss, a fine picking this time. Tunis Shrooms. Bring a good price in the Empire these will." She eyed one of her men coldly, "Pay them!" she snapped.

Two silk purses were handed over, one to Vince, one to Andrew. Jane never haggled over money. Haggling would have been beneath her. The two smugglers stayed with their old cohort for a time having tea and fern rum, making small talk over inane political events in the provinces. Vince's mind could think of nothing but his discovered crash trail.

"Well then," Jane finally said with a flourish, "You heroes' best be off while Tyhrin's high and the light is good. Winter's coming." She waved an ancient hand toward the door and one of her blue machos appeared to see them out. From a window, she peered at the street and watched them walk away.

When she was young, she had a love that Vince reminded her of. He was a musician; they lived in a garret with a small fern garden on a balcony. She dropped him like a bad habit when she discovered the joys of fat old businessmen and easy money, long black carriages stocked with fine liquors. Handsome top-coated drivers with braided leather whips snapping at the mamonths, off through the ice and snow to fine restaurants and luxury, ease, splendor.

The musician had gone mad when he found this out. He languished for a couple of years, drinking himself to oblivion and eventually dying one drunken night-kicked to death by the coastguard.

143

He was weak; Jane thought and found the destiny of the weak.

She smiled her half-smile at watching Vince and Andrew make their way up the street. Weakness was not one of those two's vices for certain. Word had it the two of them had taken on a small crowd at Squeezer Floyd's harbor bar, with Andrew knocking numbers out with single jabs, Vince straight-arming the original attacker back against a carriage and banging his head into it repeatedly until Andrew finally grabbed him, and they both made off in the speedboat bleeding from broken bottles that had been slammed against them.

Jane snickered. The stories that had come back regarding these two never seemed to end. Even the coast guard was taking bets on their next appearances in town. No weakness there. Foolhardy perhaps, weak no. She looked at the mushrooms. Wilderness, icy waters, Coast Guards, and street gangs stood between her and the Tunis Shrooms. Nevertheless, Vince and Andrew delivered.

Along the shores of the ten-thousand lakes, jutting peaks of quartz-like igneous rock cradled inlets and fjords where occasional settlements could be seen. Bright white clusters of stout buildings, spires, and silos propping up above the greenery.

Up from the shores into the lowland plains, the settlements grew into hamlets and towns, with vineyards and orchards from seeds brought long ago by the Star Trading Guild. The settlements faded off as the plains rose to highlands, and hills full of hollows, and gullies where miners mixed shepherding on freshly cleared land which looked back again, down to the plains and the sea where the settlements were spread like toy villages, as seen from the high distance.

Vincent's place was only nominally cleared and worked. Where he had cut back the fern trees there broke a view of the sea stretching across the horizon like the end of the world in a crisp golden blue-green line.

"Damn it, Vincent!" Charon held the purse accusingly at him, "Tunis-Shroom money! They catch you with those mushrooms and you'll be straight to the stasis block." She handled the money with disgust as well as fascination.

Her small mouth drew firm in stern resolution, framed by a broad face, mildly tanned from this last of summer work. Her sleek brown hair swept a swift line diagonally across her forehead and back around her ear. She wore a woolen sweater with intense indigo, spotted with iridescent designs of fruit.

One of these adventures he's not coming back, she mused, and I'll sit here by these windows until the fern trees grow back in the spaces he's cleared and the view of the sea turns to woods again.

There was a plague of snails that year chewing at crops across the northlands. It was a bitter year for many. Vince set his gaze away. He took a long weary breath and said, "We've gone around this before. It's too late in the season to get work in the mines, even if there was any. The new lasers the star traders have brought in have cut the need for miners in half. My father was lucky to keep work with that, handy with a beam they said. What do you want; I should end up like the old man and his father before him-subsistence and barter? Slave wages and a spit of dirt?" He sealed his lips tight; it was an old refrain.

Sheep and potatoes, nutrient still-vats.

Only the winter promised the demise of the snails, a winter of want at that.

Fern oil burned a dewy spice to the room. Geometric patterns on wool coverlets. Patterns hand-carved on the fern-wood furniture second-hand from shops in Herkiestown, hauled up with family on mamonths, patterns on a pattern, patterns in patterns. Holo-tapes Vince had collected since boyhood-stellar geography of the galaxy's far-flung states, worlds and places far removed from this spiral arm of the galaxy. They seemed mythical.

144

Imbued with fantastical larger than life powers. Pictures and holograms of family and friends, and from Vincent-ancestors. Always for him, distant times and people, places, and principalities loomed in his imagination important just for the knowing though no useful thing could come of it. A breadless embellishment of life. "Give me the luxuries in life, and I will do without the necessities," he once told her. So it was coming to be.

Her eyes looked around desperately as if the house could provide a referee.

Charon's miniature boat collection sat lined up proudly above the hearth, her one indulgence and the reason she met him. Andrews's boat out at Sunset bay had caught her eye, Vince then at the wheel.

She lowered her eyes to the carpets, then up at him again: so tall, so daringly mad, so like one of his holotape characters. So out of place in the quiet countryside of Rip, she thought.

There came silence and the purse between them. Their enemy, their survival. They looked at it for a long moment. Vince's lips bent upward forming a grim, sardonic smile. The snails had driven the price of mushrooms very high on the black market.

Charon covered the glow tubes. "Never mind now. Come here," she said softly then. *Come love me.*

Instead, he walked to the doorway and opened it to the star-filled night. Tyhrin had long since set. The Eagle nebula glimmered in the west and faintly, beyond that, the Orion Arm. Empires and glorious civilizations ancient since the dawn of mankind. Far and away, gilded cities and space stations, the star lanes jammed with hyper yachts and lumbering star freighters.

"If we could get off this backwater tumble of rubble and ferns-up there. Cherry-I just want something else for us besides these people and this place," he said coolly as if it were not a plea, but a destiny.

Charon's face grew leaden.

That's what I'm afraid of, Charon thought. Stars and worlds away again. It was an aspect of his character that frightened her deeply. She didn't want to go live among the stars, she loved Rip and the fern forests. The endless hamlets twisting through the gullies and the lakes. She didn't know what he thought he saw among those points of light. She only knew it could take them from the only world she'd known. "Oh enough starlight!" she said, "Come here!" She patted their tall, high-backed bed. Its cushions and pillows lay orderly and inviting.

The wind turned in a sudden icy curl before the house, thick with fern spores and the scent of snails. Thick with the patterns of ages before mankind had come.

Relentless blind ages which known previously only the savage impulse of the animals, eat, run. Watch. The biomechanical clockwork aspects of the plants, shooting roots and tendrils into the soil, spores into the moon's light.

"Listen," he answered, "we'll be splashing at the beaches of Chrysalis Isla with all the Pleiades sparkling bluely above us. No winter there. Fly over to Deneb Four and look at a city that spans a globe, and rules the oldest empire known to man! Imagine-tens of billions of people on a single world,"

"Yes Vince, the same Empire that nuked our ancestors in Arcturus and drove the rest as refugees to the Outworlds," she said quietly.

He gave her a look. "Charon, that was a thousand years ago." Vince thought it a virtue to embrace mankind as a whole; of course, mankind did not.

"You're too open-minded for your own good. You'll always be an Outworlder in the Empire. What makes you think they'll ever bear you any goodwill? They say, in the inner Empire, the people receive impulses right into their minds. How to feel, what to think-everything is top-down. What do you think they'd do with a free spirit like you? You're too good, Vince. But you're being naive. You think because they have advanced technologies they will have advanced moralities. Do you think it was a fluke what happened it in past? It was not. It's the nature of humanity-evil, as well as good."

145

"Charon, it's a galactic economy now. The peoples of the galaxy are more fluid now than before. Borders are soon to be things of the past." Even as he said it, he felt unease. Somehow, the underlying aspects of the premise seemed unworkable.

"Noble aspirations; one galaxy, freedom of movement. It's an illusion, Vince, fed you by people who profit from the flow of labor. Rest assured, humans are territorial. They'll always be holding cards you don't see.

"If you go there, you'll be used by them merely to drive down the wages of their fellow citizens, who will hate you for it. Or you'll end up in the underground economy. You have a world. You have a place here."

A yellow snail clung to a window. Its yellow underside ringed with violet. In truth it was not a snail at all, but when the refugees had come centuries before it looked like a snail, and so it was named. Vince drew a circle around it on the opposite side of the glass, dew made a drip at the base of his circle. He smiled and kissed her. Evil empires…it all sounded so preposterous. Wars had always happened. "I'm sure they're more sophisticated than that, my love. Enough politics."

The wind came up again through the fern trees and blew against the house. It made a whistling sound. "Listen," he said, but said no more, only then he came to her silently, falling into the white softness of her arms. He imagined he could see the gold specs that sparkled in the blue of her eyes, but it was too dark. He pulled their goose down quilt over them and she cooed in delight.

They touched each other tenderly, pressing in the elation of first love, rolling luxuriantly in its oblivions and ecstasies, until yesterday and tomorrow were no more, and there was only that moment, and each other.

The snail perceived them as a turning mass of bright pink heat that tussled. It did not, however, perceive time or timelessness.

That night he dreamt of the crash trail. He walked along the scattered rocks of the trail until he came to its end. There he swept away a growth of Tunis mushrooms and lifted stones looking for the buried starship. He spoke to himself, "It's here, it's here, and it's here!" Tyhrin's rings glistened goldenly through the canopy of fern trees until the rocks too were golden. All around him gold, gold, piles of it he thrust to one side digging deeper ever deeper into gold looking for the golden ship. "It's here!'

Charon was pulling his shoulder, "Vince! Vince!"

He turned and saw walls, windows, furniture; their home. "You were dreaming, talking aloud. What were you dreaming of?" she asked.

"Gold, a world of gold, and a starship," he mumbled and stretched. She had tea and biscuits ready. "A starship?" She forced a smile.

He told her of his sighting of the crash trail from the lake the evening before. "Probably a pursuit frigate from the Arcturian war. It might have been shielded under stasis when it hit. Good chance there is salvage there."

"That's an old spook tale, Vincent. It's not real. Screaming ghosts. Lost frigate's." Charon looked pale.

"You alright?" Vince asked.

"The Arcturian war was a long time ago, Vince. What do you think would be left of a ship that crash-landed?" she bit her biscuits nervously; afraid of what was coming next. So many of his schemes went unrewarded. Hyper yacht piloting courses, etc. Long hours, big dreams, empty pockets.

"If the shields held until the rubble settled on the frigate, the structural integrity of the ship itself would hold together under the mere weight of a few tons of ordinary matter." He looked to her for confirmation she understood, but she was a loathing of the conversation.

"Ships like that are designed to withstand incredible forces even without force field shielding being activated. There could be any number of serviceable systems still in there. One drive unit would be worth a fortune out here in the Sagittarius Arm."

So this is what that hyper yacht course brings us, Charon thought.

"We could trade it for a small star boat good enough to get us to the Orion Arm. I could find a real job there. You could live a hundred stories in the air in a golden deco tower and watch the deep-space liners drift up to the stars.

"When you get tired of that we'll buy a cottage on a floating fishing cooperative, with the ring nebula shimmering over the water world Thanjavur." he enveloped his hands over hers with a kiss. He wanted to go on and on, his imagination, it seemed, was only limited by his need to breathe.

"And if pigs had wings." she snapped dryly. "Aren't we in enough danger with you smuggling contraband into Herkiestown? Now you're digging for buried starships?"

"I can get some mining lasers from my father. I'll follow the crash trail to its end. If there is something there I'll know in a day or two. I'll find it." he said.

After breakfast and a bath, he put on a fern-silk tunic and a wool vest with a colorful pattern trim, sheep leather pants, and mamonth boots. He made for the door lest she confront him more, or more likely coo him into submission. Then he was gone.

She looked with dread upon the meager provisions they had made for winter. Then her eyes fell upon the ceramic jar he had brought from Kroug City. It was packed with mushroom profits. Still, her dread did not abate.

Even from the makeshift barn across the still stump-ridden clearing, Vince's large mamonth could sense his presence. It moaned a hoarse cry of approval at the coming of its' master. Vince rode his possessions as hard as he rode himself; mamonths had a taste for hard work. The animal took delight in tasks other beasts would find onerous. Neither the man nor the beast took thought for comfort or safety.

They were quite a pair.

Mamonths were evolved well for heavy labor and even heavier yokes. Their snouts were short and trunk-like, their necks long and shoulders broad. Their even-length legs were sturdy and their three-toed feet spread wide and firm.

They had a resolute nature and domesticity rare in the toss of worlds which humankind found in the early spread through the galaxy. They had proved indispensable after the Arcturian wars when the refugees fell to Rip.

Just as the care and breeding of horses and fostered a horse culture on Earth millennia before, so too mamonth care and breeding was on Rip a subculture. Vince, however, was ever cavalier with the animal.

Rather than adjust to the reality of it being a mamonth, Vince had always related to it as if it were just another person. A big, speechless, powerful person, who needed an extra bit of direction and occasionally a rider to provide it.

"Morning to you Budzinski." Vince ran his hands over the big snout. "Once more, good friend, into the fray of work and sweat. Perhaps the last we'll share old Boy-I got me a line a salvage job the like of which this ball of fern trees and slate never saw."

Budzinski's eyes widened and his head bobbed up and down excitedly.

"That's right, me bruddah from anuddah species, we're riding!" Vince said with pat and jumped into the saddle. He rode it easily out of the barn, the heavy mamonth feet crushing tiny fossils of shells in the crumbling slate. He borrowed his father's mining lasers and from there went forward headlong into the woods.

By early evening with Rip's fat, pale sun lingering above and shining down through the trees, Vince had reached the crash trail.

It occurred to him, once his excitement passed, that he was in fact camping alone at Screaming Ghost Lake.

In the last light of day, he sat on his mamonth staring down at the giant gouge that stretched along the hillside. He pitched a simple camp and set to rest. Sleep came and swirled in his eyes; it became a spin of rolling surf along a beach full of leaping dolphins and Boca-fish. Mer-people twirled in the water and the starlight singing. Then his dreams reeled on as dreams do, into other and other things. Dark things that crept up and peered at him, that ran back into the shadows should he turn and look toward them.

Nevertheless, there came no screaming.

Morning broke the darkness, silent and bright, and he looked out upon dying ferns and frost, rolling hills of rock and shale. Winter's coming. Somehow, he still remembered a warm sea. He was at the crash trail. Inspecting the giant gash further proved he was on to something. Excitement built slowly up in him as his mind careened with the potentialities of success. Finally, he was right! Although the weather had worn away the blue-grey shale, it was apparent something unnatural had happened here in the distant past. How long?

The Arcturian wars.

Vince could imagine the jet-black surface of the time stasis shields throwing off a red light as the starship careened down through the atmosphere. *Something had gone wrong*, and the shields must have remained locked. A stray shot and the shields would have gone up automatically, freezing the ship in an impenetrable time bubble, utterly impervious to matter and energy.

At the moment of impact tons of rubble could have been ejected into the sky and the ship ricocheted back into the air only to repeat its fall now with less force, leaving the giant furrow of the crash trail. The angle of inclination must have been such that the rebound was but a short, wild apogee; and then the trail. At the end of the trail a mound of stone. Budzinski snorted uneasily as Vince stared ahead blankly-the sudden rise of stone at the end trail, exactly as Vince imagined.

"Easy Buds, you're reading my mind."

Vince was projecting. It was not excitement the animal had intoned with its moaning, but dread.

The mound seemed to speak to Vince. It was a promise and a threat; *you could be so right this time, or not. Which is it, boy?* Budzinski stepped back a little, snorting. It considered the mound. Tall and leafy ferns grew there. To Vince, the mound had shown evidence enough, as if a fresh crash cloud of dust floated over a tail vane sticking out.

Gleefully he tied the mamonth, who eagerly grazed at the ferns. Vince set about building his mine at the foot of the mound. He worked frantically, steadily hour after hour, and the day sped by. He started up a small fusion generator and rigged lamps above the designated dig spot.

He plugged in his diggers and placed his father's clockwork silver lasers over his hands. Clumsily, as he had avoided mining with a distaste bordering on foreboding all his life, he took to the stones now with relish.

He worked through the middle of the night, sweating in the cold, oblivious to his body's cries for rest. Tyhrin's yellow orb and rings dashed the fern-forest in spectacular light, a solemn, tarnished, golden luminosity double light bathing the landscape. Tyhrin was of singular beauty in Rips star system, Vincent's favorite aspect of Rip's night sky. He came up from his digging to smile once at the familiar rings, and then he feverishly bent back to his labors.

He had become oblivious to his pains or the exhaustion that lingered in his sweat and alternate cold. At the end of each curved and bucketed digger was a short burst laser. The intensity, variation, and length adjusted to the type and quality of the rock dug through.

Hours slipped away.

He pounded rock. He blasted rock.

Vince moved a substantial amount of stone when he finally decided to sleep. The golden-ringed gas giant had gone. The sun was rising among a toss of diamond stars. Charon tracked his mamonth from his father's that morning and found him sleeping against the side of his beast.

She thought: a boy and his dog. And their mining claim for buried starship engines. She laughed aloud.

He woke with a start grabbing a pistol and pointed it at her. "Don't shoot!" She yelled, her eyes widening.

He let the gun fall and dropped his back against Budzinski. The beast was unperturbed; it opened an eye, snorted once and fell back to sleep.

"How did you find me?" He rasped, running his hands through his thick locks of burnished red hair. "Shit, Charon, don't sneak up on me like that!"

She pointed to the ground and he saw his mamonth tracks among the ferns. "Your Dad pointed the way and Budzinski's clompers showed me the rest." She said. "What'd ya' think I was, the Coast Guard?"

His hands were shaking. His mother's father had been a Postmaster in Kroug City; the pistol was an heirloom Vince had inherited. He brought it along "just in case".

There was an uncomfortable silence.

"Sorry." She said dryly. "Next time I'll call first." She kicked him hard. "You could have killed me!"

He looked at the gun. Suddenly it was hideous. "My grandfather on my mother's side..."

"I know. I know...Postmaster to the Rip system, Kroug City."

She looked at his miserable condition. He was covered with welts and dirt. "Dang pistol probably wouldn't fire anyway. Here, I brought you some food. A real breakfast." She went to her mamonth and dug into the saddle packs. The pack's inlay twisted and spiraled with designs reminiscent of originals lost when the Arcturian worlds were nuked, but lovingly reproduced by an art student from the original starliner.

The student had spent the rest of her life painstakingly recreating the lost patterns; they lived on across that world now, echoed and varied endlessly in the handiwork of future generations.

Vince looked at their elaborate care. They matched his boots-Charon's clan symbols.

She came over and kissed his forehead, set the food beside him and waited for him to eat. After a while, he noticed her watching him silently, forlornly. With his mouth full he suddenly said, "Wha-at?"

She stared for a long moment, unsure of how to say what she was thinking. Finally, she said flatly, "It's Andrew."

They looked at each other. Vince chewed and wondered what had happened, he feared the worse the longer she delayed.

"What happened to Andrew?"

Her blue and gold eyes drilled at him accusingly.

"He was killed," she whispered.

The Coast Guard...

"Well...how?" Vince's eyes darkened and his thoughts ran wild with a vengeance, then cooled.

She was delaying her responses for effect. She wanted this to sink deep in his mind and stay there. She looked away, angrily now, trying not to accuse him. "He drove his boat into the docks at Herkiestown."

"Border patrols?" Vince rasped.

"Of course. They chased him and he eluded them among the boat traffic in the harbor for a while, then he bolted for the docks but he got too close- he was trying to shake them among the piers. Lee Anne came up the hill this morning and told me, she figured you'd want to know, how you and Andrew have been friends and all for so long."

Nice boat, Deck.

I try.

Vince shuddered and took a wary glance into the forest. If the Patrols found anything linking him to Andrew and the Tunis mushrooms, they would bring charges of conspiracy and smuggling. "They connect him to me?"

Her look was feral, "No! The boat exploded. He was incinerated. Nobody knows why he ran, they're calling it an inexplicable suicide but they're very suspicious obviously. They think he might have been drunk and panicked. They figure he just wanted to beat a long sentence in the stasis house. He was coming in from Screaming Ghost Lake and they said he was driving the boat erratically"

Andrew never panicked. He had nerves of ice.

"Straight down! You bring anything to drink in that sack?" He and Andrew had faced death in a continuing array of unlikely and preposterous situations. It had stood next to them like a third wheel, always there, smiling. They knew it. They came to relish it. Eventually, the smiling third wheel would take one of them or both. Now it had taken Andrew. Somehow, there was no surprise, no sadness, and no shock. The two of them had been riding the tiger for years.

"Uh-huh. I figured as much." She felt into the saddle pack and drew out a jug of hard cider. Vince took it gratefully and swung back a long hard belt of five gulps only stopping to come up for air.

Her eyebrows shot up.

He passed her the jug, "To Andrew."

Andrew and his famous coats. His flamboyant bravado which he could somehow make slip away chameleon style and blend into a crowd like magic.

She drank slowly. "Yeah, Andrew." Budzinski howled then, an unexpected commentator on the death of poor Andrew Deck. Charon's throat was tight with fear. Somehow, the animals groaning wail seemed to come from elsewhere than the quiet forest, somewhere deep and dark, and ever wrong. Her sense of dread crept up her toes and feet spreading gloom into her soul.

This is madness, she thought bitterly to herself. Vince is acting like a maniac digging in the forest for starship salvage. Andy is dead. When winter is over, I will be stepping from the stasis house shamed as a fool who chose a fool. Have I loved a loon?

"Something you want to say?" Vince asked through a strange grin. He could see despair wrangling through her features like a fern fire.

"What could I say?" she drawled flatly.

"Don't lose faith just yet. Deck lost his nerve. That's why I did most of the running; he was never quite steely enough. He was good. Tough, bold. But he couldn't keep it up forever.

"Last night I reached a layer of stone that had been compacted vertically and at a great temperature. It can't be much further 'till I reach the wall of the starship. The salvage rights will put you in a new house on the big hills of the first fall before winter. After that, the stars."

He kissed her with a flourish.

Suddenly he did not seem so mad. The daring in his voice and the swagger in his eyes enthralled her. She chuckled a little; the chuckle bloomed into a small smile that held all the hope of youth and imminent victory. As for Andrew, her sadness was without blame. Surely he could have handled things differently? A stasis sentence for running Tunis shrooms wasn't worth dying over. He should have surrendered instead of going out in a blaze of glory.

Two days came and went. Days of cutting and hauling stone. Inside, the mine was growing rooms and shafts. The central room seemed as big as a house. Vince began taking stimulants. He hadn't slept in twenty-six hours when Charon came next upon him.

He was covered with scratches and welts. His face was drawn back, pale, a skeleton's head. His hair was matted and filthy.

His arms moved frantically, digging, pounding at the stone with a savage flail of lasers and elbows.

He was breathing hard and talking to himself. He didn't see her watching him.

She bit her fist and quietly began to cry, pushing herself to try and remember why she had ever loved him. How could she have loved this idiot who was digging in the middle of a forest for a starship?

His ranting carried around the walls of stone to her.

"Gotta be here!" he was saying, "Where is it? Gotta be here! Stone! Stone! The compact layer-here-gotta be right here.

"The trail! Only a ship makes a crash trail like that! This is Andrew putting some kind of jinx on me, I swear. Shit! I couldn't bear to put her in the stasis house this winter, oh God, not that. Oh please."

He stopped. He seemed to come to some realization. He squatted on his parted knees in a swelter of heated mud and stone, his clothing tattered.

"Or worse, the border patrol will find the rest of the Tunis mushrooms."

The last bit was too much for Charon. The irony of the border patrol coming upon this fool digging was outrageous. Disgusted, a fury rose up in her. Her eyes grew dark, face reddened and she yelled out at him, "Border patrol! You have got to be-"

He turned, wildly then, delirious, lifting the cutting lasers around in a broad arc. They clicked on, reeling in an atomic power that sheered through the columns. She stared at him a moment realizing how close they had come to her. Then there came the sound of rocks slipping in an ugly grinding cascade.

She folded like a rag doll, crushed as the rock ceiling collapsed.

He screamed in jagged desperation, "Nooo!" and the howl reached from the bottom of deep time, growling in primitive rage, and all human regret followed after. A mass of stone slammed him; he saw a flash, fell crushed to the ground near her. He struggled shortly, dizzy, and then lunged at her in a bloody dive, tearing stone away from her. He felt for her pulse and it was not there. He pressed down on her chest in an attempt to resuscitate her, a useless effort as her skull lay smashed. Eventually, he stopped. He stood. From over her, he stared at all his dreams remembered. She was crushed dead instantly. She would never know the shame of the stasis house. She would never hear the scornful words that she was the fool's wife or face the grim prospect of unending want. She was gone forever.

He loomed monstrous, shaking. Too late, he had snapped the lasers off. He fell to his knees, and hands still in the diggers, stroked her bloodied corpse in agony, longing, and confusion.

Then he saw it.

Just below her twisted flesh where the lasers had cut away a few more centimeters of stone. There lay the prefect jet black of a stasis shield, barely discernable and glimmering beneath. The hull of a starship lay in the stone. He had been right all along. "Charon..." he said tenderly. Morosely, like an automaton, he gently carried her aside. His expression was blank, stunned, ruined. He blasted away more stone, on and on until he had the better part of a panel cleared. The ship was not only intact; it was still functioning, aging ever so imperceptibly as its malfunctioning stasis shield faded.

It might have rested, sealed in the stone, until the end of time if he had not seen the crash trail. Somewhere inside that ship, a whole crew of Cyborgian Central Air Corps was time-frozen in a moment of a war long since history.

151

They had inadvertently just taken the last civilian casualty in the war. He found the emergency hatch after a matter of mere hours. It protruded from the stasis field, surprisingly only slightly corroded. He ran his hands along its mechanism, felt it turn, press out, turn again. The stasis shield went down. He could hear the mighty rumble of the ship's engines. They had not missed a beat in all the intervening centuries.

He slipped into the hatch and made his way into the ship. The crew had been hunting down and killing his ancestors, in a string of cause and effect they had taken the life of Charon. He showed them no mercy. They were still the enemy. He wondered idly what he must have looked like to them, suddenly and inexplicably appearing on the deck garbed in the strangest of gear, slashing madly, covered with blood and mud.

He became Fury. He was the unimaginably perfect blackness of space, as the last star is extinguished, a digit in a countdown to the other side of an event horizon. Amazingly, the welded cyborg aviators made no contest with him. They were all in some bizarre state of shock. Some were crying, some were shaking. A few just stared like scared rabbits. He slashed away, again and again. In the midst of it, one of them stared coldly into his eyes.

There were legends of the ship that had gone down; straight down…

"Kill me! Please," the Cyborgian air corpsman pleaded. Vincent's answer was a primitive visceral grunt and a lunge with his lasers. The Cyborgian's head spun away from his body with an expression of relief. They longed for death here, and it had not found them until now. Had they been conscious in some fashion during the intervening millennium since the war?

What would it mean to sit frozen and insane, alive in the dark with one's horror spinning around you?

When they were all dead, he gathered the remains of Charon and put her in a freezer hold. He stripped the Cyborgian corpses of their helmets and gear and shoved their bodies in a recycling unit. He loaded his father's mining gear on Budzinski and slapped the beast, "Home!" he said. The mamonth snorted, it knew what to do.

The beast took a last longing gaze through massive eyes and snorted. It was aware tumultuous events had transpired. Some primitive corner of its emotional constructs lamented for the human: the human who, even among such unsatisfied beings as humans were, was one to press ever deeper into the fern wood.

Alone in the huge frigate, entombed in the impacted shale, he walked the halls, marveling. The technology was the High Imperial era, much of it no longer commonly produced. The Empire, it turned out, had purchased much of its hardware in the years before the war from other societies, many of whom promptly collapsed after the Arcturian economies were blasted out of existence. He found the Captain's quarters. No surprise, they were little different from the rest of the crew. One thing the great Transhuman overlords had been was egalitarian in their treatment of the masses beneath them, soldiers included.

He showered. He put on a red jumpsuit and realized they were a tad smaller than he was. He adjusted it best he could and walked the bloody halls of his new ship. He remembered his star yacht piloting and went to the bridge. It was an elegant sweep of streamlining, candy-apple red, burgundy, and salmon, edged with poly color chrome, alive with holograms and lights. It seethed and beckoned like a beautiful sea goddess. On the other hand, was it the space fiend himself crooning?

He was no iconoclast, or worker rebel misled by some profiteering anarchist who despised machines. The machines could be used for evil or good, as the men who used them saw fit. Yet he hesitated, knowing these machines were often sentient themselves. He held the MERGE helmet shortly in his hands uncertain of his ability to master it. Another man would have run tests. Gone back to Herkiestown and gathered allies. Vince found he cared not whether the ship fried his brain, or obeyed his commands. Charon was dead. His life here was over. There were either the stars or death.

He smiled strangely then, a strangled empty gesture.

Snapping the MERGE helmet on, he braced himself for his mind to meld with the ship's sensory system. There came a soft, imperceptible shift, and he became aware of other things around the ship. He could feel tons of debris on the ship's hull-it was a soft blanket of the stone matter he could shake with a shrug. The knowledge was elating. Connected to the frigate ship, his mind rushed with manic enthusiasm. His consciousness soared and spun into the navigational star yacht training memory.

He found the original approach to Rip. Replaying it, he saw the legends were true. The transport vessel-Arcturian star liner Rip Van Winkle-had been evading the frigate desperately. The starliner dodged with dashing rolls and a sophisticated twisting of fields. Watching the ancient replay, Vince was astounded at the skill of Izzo. Everyone had seen the recordings from the liner's black box. Some had even made reconstructions of what he was seeing. However, he was the only human in centuries to witness the actual scene as viewed from the frigate. A sudden shot had appeared then-one of the dogfighters had hidden it among the twisting fields so the frigate could not detect it until too late. The shot slashed into the frigate's sensory array.

Nevertheless, there had been something else too; something that shocked the ship's recording system into complete failure before one massive transcription into the hypercast codes to Deneb. Then the recorded memory stopped. Vince sat alone in the piloting cabin in wonder at the strangeness and the mingling of events far separated in time. He pulled his mind to the present. He had the ship.

It was a good frigate, built for the pressures and speeds of warfare. It lifted swiftly from the bottom of the mound as if it were brushing off a stack of dried ferns. Vince was wild with delirium, compelled with bright fascination as the starship lifted with a whine above the lakes and Herkiestown in the far distance to the bewilderment of the people below.

Somehow, his father knew, all at once, the connection with the strange starship when Budzinski rode into his spread loaded with the bloody mining gear. He could not know the whole story. Legend would have it later that Vincent and Charon flew off together after seizing a long stasised ship, which only he had discovered leftover from the Arcturian wars.

The real story, however, was Vince alone that day, riding with a crew of ghosts. Many months later in the void between the galactic arms, it would occur to him to call up the name of the stolen frigate. It was a Sunrider 3062, long ago christened out of the Deneb industrial rings as "Lady Luck". Vince stared at the glowing name in a long ironic silence. "Lady Luck," he whispered to the ghosts laughing all around him. The frigate leaped through the darkness for the better part of a light-year as Vincent's mad, loathsome laughter cackled with his tears and rage. However, just as the Cyborgian Air Corps' private war had held still, unseen and unnoted within the walls of the frigate, sealed from the universe beyond, so the desperate laughter of the mad young pilot held within the hull, penetrating not at all to the hyperstreams of bent and twisted space. -Princess Clairissa Maggio, Caldris. Rise of the Taloned Sire

All the King's men

Deep void off Pleiades Cluster, 4110.

It was a long nasty haul across the void...

The resurrected ship was ancient, designed before the Arcturian wars. Most of Vince's flight training didn't apply.

He figured things out by trial and error while moving through Zero Space, fine-tuning a MERGE piloting helmet as he went. There were the CC corpses he'd dispatched- they'd have been able to explain everything, but he couldn't have risked even a questioning before he killed them.

In his fury, he had murdered them all, slashing riotously with his father's mining lasers, spilling guts and entrails mixed with plastics and software from another era, another era when they had committed genocide against the ancestors of his people, against the Arcturian colonials. They had sent them back to the Stone Age, the refugees dispossessed of their birthrights, their civilization, their heritage. For one who had spent his entire life rather contemptuous of those who clung to the ancient animosities, he found himself suddenly thrust into the heat of that battle again. Charon had been killed and the cyborg astronauts were all about him, carried across time in the stasis field of the frigate, living proof of Charon's admonitions against the Imperials.

He taught himself to fly the ship alone, building on rudimentary knowledge he possessed. He dare not run any instructional RNA programs, not yet anyway. Not until he was master of the ship. No matter, the void was big and empty, with plenty of room for error. Nothing to hit, even his exploratory dips into the hyper gamma spaces lunged through the void between the spiral arms with a sort of careless abandon. The comets, asteroids, and systems in the void sparse enough to give him his playground, his school, and there he taught himself. He careened alone through the darkness. Just him, the ship, and space that matched geologic time with an uncompromising perfection. Here he learned the intricacies of his frigate. He learned its ways, and he waited.

Vince had his ship, and when the bitter, vicious, irony of what it had cost him wore off, his twisted, mad laughter sated, he found quiet sanity again.

There were the hypercasts; he listened to the garble of a hundred civilizations. The inane claptrap of lonely freighter pilots, virtreal stations that offered to fry your brains with ugly pleasures, and occasionally a fresh cast off some glistening new outpost light months away. Along the Sagittarius Spiral Arm, the Outworlds for centuries soldiered on, struggling to build. In the Orion Spiral Arm, however, civilizations had carried along much as before the Great Arcturian Wars. Many had faded with the loss of trade and technologies from the robust Arcturians.

The Empire, however, seemed eternal; corrupt, Byzantine, huge. Nevertheless, even the Empire had stalled after the Arcturian Wars. One could find the same aircars still produced there in some places as before the wars. If examined, the current warships were no match even for the very frigate Vince now possessed.

He pieced miscellaneous items of news together from the hypercasts. It seemed the king of the Pleiades star cluster was at war, and the Pleiades were his destination. A good place to show up with a warhorse star frigate in mint condition, therefore, he would begin his career as a mercenary. Certainly, he could pack this ship with rouges ready for an opportunity to set about the war zone looking for Merc gigs and glory.

The Pleiades were an independent kingdom, with an interesting history. The star cluster was only fifty million years old. When humanity's first settlement ships had reached there, they found no worlds old enough for life arisen yet beyond the stage of microbes. Fisher Shea, an enterprising visionary, had come up with a plan to terraform dozens of worlds.

He met opposition from every narrow-minded organization extant at that time. Environmentalists who insisted the microbes had rights, neo-religionists who insisted the star cluster was sacred and inviolate, and corporations who wanted centuries of piecemeal looting and discordant development that better to orchestrate for graft and fraud.

Shea had remained undeterred-a human dynamo. He armed a fleet of privateers, and any of the interests from Earth that tried to scuttle and sabotage his efforts found themselves dealing with the business end of an energy cannon.

Fisher Shea built his kingdoms and they became the luxury playground of the galaxy. Eventually, they built hundreds of terraformed worlds of islands, canals, balmy shallow seas, and brilliant, ultramodern towers. Those worlds gloried among a star cluster so crowded with suns that there was in all no night, only day, and a slightly less bright night of lesser suns. Empires and civilizations ever after turned, rose up, fell, and transformed; the Kingdom of the Pleiades endured. Elegantly enduring at that, with a tan, a rum drink, and if need be a call to arms.

Vince's ship plummeted on, yet even the void between the spiral arms had an end. Vince came in high from his trajectory that had taken his above the galactic plane. He dived into the Orion Spiral Arm from the hyperstreams. Approaching close to the Pleiades, the gravity tides and hyperstreams were magnificent. Too much for him, his mind raced trying to balance flow systems, meson fields, Feynman drives. The star cluster roared more hugely with each millisecond. He could see thousands of hypercasts like speckled static, countless warp trails-the traces of a starfaring civilization, mere footprints in galactic surf.

Suddenly then the ship came alive with matter indicators and distress signals, CCCE Empires, and wailing alerts. Who could hail him? No one in the Pleiades cluster knew he existed. However, distress signals had not changed in millennia. S.O.S. protocols outlive civilizations.

His ship was recognizing a distress signal. He brought his fields down gently from hyperspace, reacquiring mass in a graceful arc. Still, he was too rough in reentry. He found himself blasted into normal space just under light speed.

Two nearly vertical stasis fields ignited every ion in his path so that his dimensional reentry broadcasted with a flash of light that stretched, glowed, and trumpeted his appearance.

For a split second, he marveled at the Pleiades beneath him, and then a shot crossed his bow.

He came out of hyperspace from the spiral void into a firefight.

Several attack ships were menacing a small freighter in a volley of fiery vectors. It was costing them dearly. As Vince watched, two of the attackers ruptured, falling away from the fight in a brilliant burn. Seeing Vince, the other attack ships broke formation veering off in divergent tangents, giving their quarry sudden relief.

The small freighter dodged fire with a nimble grace; he seemed to know where their shots would be before they arrived. He used the break Vince gave him well, ducking, dodging, and rolling through a maelstrom of particle-beam cannon fire. The desperate attack ships twisted at phenomenal velocities, bending space into points of fiery light. Vince knew there were people in those dots on his holoscreen, people who regarded him now as a mortal enemy. He had moments to take a side. He could not know who was who. They were a pinwheel of lights now, a pack of Ripjackles circling. Even the freighter had a chance at him, an open shot.

He ran through their transmission codes in a split second waiting for the shot to come. The freighter's codes had been slower, noncombatant. An innocent being ambushed?

Like Ripjackles circling their prey...

Vince's frigate had already armed the cannon. He let loose the heavy guns on the attackers in a savage barrage of fire, powering his flight plan in vertical rise off the galactic plane. His ship lifted above their shots with the blue diamonds of the Pleiades all around him in a panorama of forces and light as he had never seen or imagined. His stasis shields crackled in a twister of energies.

His ordinance struck home on one of the Marauders' vessels in a flash of a lightning-filled explosion of antimatter and streaming diffusion, and again the freighter made a roll and escaped. The forces faded and the ripjackle marauders were fewer in number and making a quick retreat towards some nameless moon to lick their wounds.

It was a real lucky turn of events in a generally unlucky life. Every dog has his day. Vince bit his lower lip inside the MERGE helmet and swept the frigate hard in a spline. There was a long dreary minute while the freighter's crew debated what had just transpired.

Certainly, Vincent's ship configuration was unusual, something out of a historical drama. It had been centuries buried. Nonetheless, he had gone to task for them. Vince had killed again. Numbly, he sat listening to the hum and whine of his ship.

The freighter hailed him

His holoscreen glowed green. Merged with his ship's senses, he swung his piloting chair around, searched the merge codes for communications and opened a line. The holoscreen became a room with a large man on a golden chair regarding him with piercing eyes.

Carved sea creatures leaped from aquatic carvings on the golden chair. Vince noted the man was slightly obese, with a persona of great mental and physical powers held in check. He seemed of an authority honed and practiced in realms where intelligent assessment continually meant life or death.

"Well done," he said.

He was making a pun.

Vince let out a short cackle of surprise. He liked the man's cavalier voice, no treachery in it. Amusement, at a time like this. Here was one that looked at life's mad scenarios and snickered. Not be outdone, Vince smiled and said, "Any time. The pleasure was mine. Perhaps you have news of the war with King Victor of the Pleiades?"

The heavy man's eyebrows rose as if Vince had just asked to sleep with his wife. "Information? From me? To be purchased at the mere price of a few foundling marauder suicide ramjet hides? No, no, I think not-blast away!" He laughed.

That was unexpected.

Things must be worse in the Pleiades than Vincent first surmised. Better for him, mercenary's prices would be all the higher. Moreover, he had just begun to build his reputation. Yet he was bartering for an unknown element in an unknown scenario. No choice. He could go no further without knowledge. The next time he stepped out of hyper he might be met by the Kings Air core shooting first and asking questions later.

Information? From me? To be Purchased-He was a trader.

"I see." Vince said, "Perhaps a courtesy then, your word on what rates a mercenary might hire under. I have provided some service at a loss of life to your enemies and a benefit to you. They'll have records of my ship now-and comrades to avenge. Fairness now would make us allies after the fact."

For a long moment, the fat man stared and Vince wondered if he had gone too far. He sighed then, "Fairness," The man finally said, "will do much more than that. You have just saved the life of a trade guildsman. What I have to offer you will be a life of equal value. We have much to discuss. But first, tell me. Where did you get that vintage vessel?"

At the foot of the Pleiades with their two starships running parallel courses, Vince remembered the marketplace at First fall. The decades and the light-years fell away, and he was a tiny child again looking up at the Star Trading Guildsman so tall and unlike the people of Rip. "Take the player, pay me when he can. It'll give him something to work for". He held up the holo-player and the Pleiades glimmered in the marketplace.

Outside the hull, decades later, Vince watched those same Pleiades filling his vision field now from horizon to horizon. They were in King Victor's realms now, most certainly. The heavy guildsman staring at him now was Elias Tristan. He still held his inscrutable smile, more broadly at the moment. "Mercenary rates? Very good now, certainly. But whose flag would you fly under?"

A test? Choose quickly, choose well.

"King Victors." Vince offered.

"Ahh, yes. The Royal police," In the hologram, he rose from the big golden chair and moved about what appeared to be a library of sorts. "And before I recommend you to the good king, how do I know Cyborgian Central Air Command won't come looking for that frigate? You're still booting their codes and very old codes they are. You can get in many places, no questions asked, with codes that old.

"People will think you're a Cyborgian Overlord with that ship. People who know such things. But you'll need more, more codes. Most will think it merely a restoration, that you are perhaps an eccentric and wealthy trader. But not everyone-and for them you'll need another pass.

"How you came into possession of that ship I can only guess-I won't wallow in conjecture. The question begs too many other questions. But it shows a certain level of resourcefulness that I admire.

"You're from the Sagittarius Arm, I see-an Outworlder. Well, you saved my life today and asked nothing in return but information. But what I'm going to offer you now comes only by invitation, and then, only rarely. I'm going to offer you a Guild initiate."

Vince felt his stomach drop; he had no protocol in mind for such an offer. "I humbly accept." He said quietly.

Good answer, Elias smiled less enigmatically, more humanely. Good answer. So it was that Vince came into possession of the silver insignia of the Mercury-head helmet, and wings of the Trading Guild which he wore with a black captain's jacket and cap.

"Your first job as a guildsman will be to provide escort for my ship and her company to the Zamoran O'Neil Station at the edge of the Oort clouds of Electra. That battlewagon you're Captaining will do. But first, there is the matter of salvage-a good guildsman never misses an opportunity for salvage."

He and Elias went EVA to examine the wreckage of the Marauder's vessel. Vince had never been EVA. He sealed his ship and swam out to the depths of deep space and zero-gee with a mind-bending terror he had never known possible. Such complete and awful knowledge assailed him like a sudden slap once he was outside the ship. Only emptiness extending in every direction. It threatened to plunge him into complete insanity. He shivered, wanting to scream. Instead, he focused on the ships glimmering in the starlight, and then, like a thousand blue jewels, the Pleiades.

Slowly his sanity returned and he concentrated on maneuvering his thrusters. He saw the big, burly Elias moving toward him with that cavalier grin and he thought, if I die, I die. Fear of EVA, like any other form of death he had faced down, could be mastered with a will.

"Big universe, huh?" Elias quipped. Then he broke out laughing and did a spin. Watch your dials. A lot of radiation out here."

They floated over together and Vince saw immediately that the construction methods of the Marauder's vessels were unlike anything he'd ever seen water ported at Herkiestown. Instead of the smooth metal hulls manufactured with sophisticated layers of alloys, reinforcements, and field nets of interlaced molecular insulation sheets, they had simply magnetized and cemented huge panels or raw ore and propelled them from giant blast shields and antenna that manipulated anti-mass rip shots.

An alloy as such would be extremely effective if you were flying near massive radiation plumes and spatial distortions. A disadvantage this far from the galactic core where it would be clumsier mass. "What were they doing out here? I thought they only raided near the core." Vince asked aloud.

He and Elias plumbed the edge of the ripped hull.

"Woah! Lotta radiation there!" Elias waved him away from the outer hull, scanning with an odd-looking instrument the likes of which Vince had never seen. "Yeah, well, they don't come this far, usually. Rarely. Sometimes. When there's a war on they know system governments will be too busy to watch traffic, won't have the manpower to guard the edges of things. More irregular shipping, more opportunities for piracy."

Though Elias played at a certain Wildman demeanor, Vincent could see the man's nimble hands manipulating scanners with an intelligence that was steely, sure, and steady. It was the intelligence of an intensity that Vince had not encountered before. As he watched the man, he sensed layers and layers of meaning and experience moving behind a facade that offered only gleanings of what was there.

A trade guildsman-how old? Centuries perhaps. Certainly knowledge of ages gone by and myriad worlds lived behind the fierce blue eyes. Always wild and amazed, yet knowing the folly of mankind and concurrently it's missed potentials. They were in the Marauder ship now. The interior splattered with bizarre graffiti, languages, and runes. There were hieroglyphics and obscene pictures. *Vince had the distinct impression the runes were a desperate magical attempt to keep things out.* Things even the murderous marauders could not live with and sleep.

Everything had heavy bolt locks attached.

"Watch for booby traps. If anything is locked down, leave it alone! They do that even to one another. No honor among thieves." Elias said. "If they've got any Predecessor hardware it will be at the command quarters. It's part and parcel with the blackhole thing. Somehow, they got the Predecessors, the black hole, and extra normal dimensional space all tied together into some kind of sacrifice cult, I don't know, nobody does but them, I guess. But you knew that, right?"

Vince had heard rumors. "No, I didn't. Go ahead."

Just what Elias hoped to hear. In another life, he would have made a good teacher.

"They live at the core and worship the black hole at the center of the galaxy. That," he pointed in the direction of the galactic center and Vince's faceplate ran through several imaging programs, "massive antimatter plume that shoots up from the center, that's their god, of sorts. Nobody knows, they don't make converts, they make sacrifices. Me, I think the Predecessors traveled through the event horizon at the center to some other universe. But I'll never follow to find out. Ha. Ha! Ha!"

Vince had seen the plume when he first went into the Taloned Sire's sensory array. It was beautiful, a simple jet stream stretching for light-years. It was the first thing he learned about in the piloting tapes. The plume; it functioned as the great navigational beacon of the galaxy.

Such piloting courses leave out the details of Marauders, however. There should be an addendum: *Sociopathic Raider Cultures presenting travel risks.*

They moved through the gloomy ship searching for Predecessor Booty. Predecessors. Those who preceded mankind in the Milky Way Galaxy. Untold ages before the human race crawled down from the trees and stood upright, the Predecessors had built a galactic civilization. All that remained of them were dusty ruins and pieces of technology found on forlorn globes. They indicated a great galaxy-wide war, but whether it was a civil war between members of one species or if there had been a second species was unknown; only one style of technology was discovered. These relics gave humanity quantum leaps in knowledge when they were examined and their riddles solved. There were no Predecessor bodies ever found but certain reptilian images discovered in their hieroglyphs, and it was generally believed they represented an apex of a reptilian branch of life.

Elias was right about the command quarters. When they reached what appeared to be the center, they pulled several corpses away from their cyber seats. They were wearing Predecessor jewelry. There was no other evidence of Predecessor technology anywhere connected in the ship that they could find. Elias gently lifted the ornamented metal.

"Thank you very much, psycho-killer."

The jewelry was astonishing, streamlined and biomorphic bejeweled sculptures. Elias split it with Vince. "Henry Moore had nothing on the Predecessors. A billion years old, think of it!" Elias said, holding one shimmering necklace to his helmet light, the curved lines unscratched by millennia upon passing millennia. Vince was not familiar with Henry Moore sculptures, so he merely nodded.

The pair moved deeper into the disemboweled Marauder vessel. Elias was nimble, deft and easy. Cautious. A combination of EVA thrusters and hand pulls. Vince was not experienced enough to match the heavier man's grace. Their suit lights sent beams arching back and forth into the darkness of the nightmarish crypt-like ship, revealing more runes and graffiti and symbol covered walls.

"Like stepping into a bad nonobjective art piece." Elias mused.

Vince began to speak when Elias's EVA field crackled with aurora, "Disruptor!" he howled and shoved himself into an alcove. Vince saw his suit shield flash into life. He pushed hard behind an air processing duct and fumbled for the unfamiliar weapon in the CCCE air corps suit.

"Use 'em if you got 'em!" Tristan barked and the interior brightened with a laser shot. Holo diagrams on the inside of Vince's helmet brightened automatically indicating the vectors and origins of the enemy line of fire. He switched the safety off on his weapon and fired.

A projectile blasted forward and slammed into a wall, reverberating with a shockwave that spun the entire Marauder vessel in a savage lurching scream of metal fatigue. There came a sudden pulling and Vince wrapped his arms hard around the air duct for dear life.

"Awwww Shit!" Elias roared and threw a strap onto a metal bulkhead like lightning. The huge man swung around on the strap and planted his boot hard against the hull. There came a rush of objects swarming past them and then a slowing reverberation.

159

"Gravity pistol?" Elias snapped. "Dang, boy. Easy with that thing."

The Marauder who had been hiding was now compressed with a pile of rubbish into an incredibly dense ball of mashed flesh and rubbish.

Elias marveled. "Got to get me one of those! Standard issue on your boat?"

Vince hadn't been aware of exactly what sort of pistol it was. "Guess so. I'll, uh, get you one from the ship when we get to the station."

"How much?" Elias asked.

"Haven't priced them," Vince said earnestly.

"I'll be fair," Elias added.

"Okay," Vince said flatly, looking at the ball of slime and rubbish that a few moments before had been a Marauder seeking his death. He and Elias moved cautiously over to the slimeball. There was still evidence of tattoos on the remnant skin.

"Skinsuit." Elias pointed out. "These sick devils sacrifice one another and make suits out of the victim's skin. If death by Marauder ever becomes imminent, make sure you have a nice grenade to say goodbye or you'll be your killer's next outfit. Blow yourself up, deprive the psychos of a new set of evening wear."

"Okay," Vince said flatly, again.

Elias just shrugged. Evening wear for psycho killers he was not going to be.

They made their way back in EVA to their respective vessels.

Vince escorted Elias's vessel a few more light-years inward and downward to the Pleiades cluster. Elias, Vince found out later, was transporting civilians through the war zone.

"I'm taking them to Zamoran Station, a high outpost near the northern 'pole' of the Pleiades Cluster. Some of them are traveling incognito and do not want attention. Go to a bar there, Max's Club Deuce. You'll find a crew there. It's a gunner bar."

"O'Neil station" was the formal term for a can job, an enormous cylinder spinning to create gravity, usually with an artificial habitat environment on the inside. O'Neil was the scientist who first conceptualized the ancient design; they were common as housecats in the galaxy for some time. Often they bore the nickname "Neelys". Elias said this Zamoran Neely even had a beach. It was gargantuan, a silver oblong of a world spinning like a lighthouse in the middle of the void with seeming no rhyme or reason for its existence.

The Zamoran O'Neil station huddled hugely in a particularly heavy Oort cloud left over from the formation of the star cluster. The edge of the edge so to speak, the high ground of the cluster. It was a busy industrial area, not very fancy as that star cluster goes, but on a scale of space architecture and economies that dwarfed Vince's previous experience. Tristan let him know the place was crawling with Imperial spies, syndicate counterspies, Royal Military Police, and Space Trade Guild agents in a perpetual dance of intrigue and disguise.

Around the station thousands of ships moved about, buying, selling, and resting before moving on. The semi-permanent residents of asteroids and cometoids were uncountable.

Some ships would never take hyper again, remaining merely to process water, service other ships drive units or harbor those who did not wish to make legal registration with the station.

With the codes Elias illustrated, (memorize them Vincent-you are the instrument of your survival) Vince was able to make full registration. He used some of the credits he had earned by fighting the Marauders to post pay for a potential crew.

His antique frigate caused a lot of commotion among the mechanics and techs in the service bay. They thought it was a frame-up restoration. Such a restoration would have indicated great wealth and an inhuman amount of patience. No one did a credit check. Therefore, Vince did it himself. Elias had paid him well.

"When the trade guild was founded," Elias had told him, "It initially served only the refugee planets of the Arcturian Genocide. Then it forayed into trade with those out of the way Republics that grew up between the Cyborgian Empire in the power vacuum left by the Arcturian Colonies.

"Finally, even the Empire itself needed to trade with us to survive. But you must always remember, in the Empire you're like a beneficent microbe in a large organism. The Empire is nothing more than a technologically perfect financial, political, and oligarchy of Transhuman tyranny. If that organism, for the slightest microsecond, perceives you as hostile, you will be swept away like so much sputum and manure.

"Unless some freak of circumstances forces them to, there will be no hearings, no trial. Only the unanswered hyper casts to your last locale. We might guess, we might even surmise your fate. But there would be nothing the Guild could do formally for justice."

"Informally?" Vince had queried.

Tristan's beard took on the likeness of an ancient Gilgamesh statue; grinning a hard and unflinching stare at a cruel universe. "Vengeance is mine, sayeth the Lord. But justice remains a matter of perspective."

Vince had pressed no further, but an ambiguity echoed in Tristan's words that haunted him.

He had a creeping feeling the Guild and the Transhuman Overlords had taken each other's blood more often than anyone would admit. From history's perspective, the Cyborgians did not like people getting one up on them. If they needed the Guildsmen for trade, that was a big one up.

Vince's frigate made its spin approach, matching the turn of the station. It edged slowly in.

When the vacuum seals and the scatter fields wheezed and whined down, Vince stepped out the door of his ship. The service deck flowed over with staring faces. His reputation now preceded him. The young guildsman with the antique frigate. The one who solo piloted into a Marauder array and glided out with the dust clouds and ashes and not a scratch him.

"He saved the refugees." "Say he was backing up Elias the whole time. Yes, the Guildsmen take care of their own, you know."

"Ships name?" One of the service techs asked with forced nonchalance. "What?" Vince asked.

"You haven't logged your vessel's name, sir." The tech made a face as if to say, "you know". "Yesss...she's the Sire," he said softly. He remembered the mining lasers strapped to his hands like awful talons, "The...Taloned Sire".

It was an odd sensation suddenly being respected in the eyes of men. He'd spent the better part of his life suffering the contempt of fools for his ambitions. Now they were playing out. It was pleasant, but also a hollow thing. Yet, it could be used to his advantage if he was not a fool enough to start believing it all himself.

He had found the frigate by mere chance. He had saved the refugees by mere necessity. Nevertheless, the techs stepped out of his way. They saw a hero; they saw the ship, a tall young guildsman who defied the odds. Vince thought, from dreamer to hero in one go.

He needed a drink.

Shane Perry

Baal One, Central craters, combat zone

Sweating and breathing heavily, the beefy soldier stared ahead, challenging all, and challenging nothing. The first sonic booms of the assault which battered the crater side all morning quieted suddenly. There would be more. Baal's unrelenting suns scorched the rubble and sand. The night was a chronological observation since the binary star was the center of a mini-cluster of closely packed new suns. Sleep and rest escaped him.

Occasional violent smacks of small weapons fire shocked the silence, barely noticed. Brilliant red tracers sparkled in the searing light. Of the six or seven men in his platoon with any native combat intelligence, Sagamore Salvatore was the best. He had spent the formative years of his childhood in an industrial ghetto before Engineering College on a scholarship. He was an educated thug, a wharf bull with brains.

His education told him, and his guts agreed, that the war was a meaningless political trump. It promised him nothing but an ignominious death. The Kingdom, perhaps even the King, was corrupt. Sagamore grumbled in the sand, cursing the day he was born.

Somewhere a shield popped and another poor soul shrieked in agony.

Madness, Sagamore thought grimly. He lowered his gaze, like all his class, he had cherished the Shea monarchy as the champion of the small. Yet there was no justification for this carnage. None. Baal was a useless hunk of rock spinning around an unimportant star. No one had spent the time or money to make things otherwise for centuries. Suddenly it was worth this?

Crack! Crack! Dust, sonic booms, and more tracers slapped around him.

"Damn it!" He bellowed and rolled forward feeling bits of gravel penetrate his EVA field.

He found a large boulder and ruined ship that shaded him and rested his weapon on the ground. His faceplate sights came on. He looked out over the blistering fields of mica and igneous rubble. His pals from the base lay among the dead out there in cooked heaps. Some colandered by claymores into bloody bags full of holes, others boiled to exploding by disruptor fire. Their stench drifted back to him.

They had died to blow open an enemy drop bunker that had landed the previous "day". Sagamore could see several of their corpses caught exposed on jutting rebar and busted astercrete. A wind caught them and limbs waved in the air. Hello, we are in Hell now. Come join us, old friend, great fun. Always room for one more...

"One...more!" The big blonde haired spacer at the bar howled. "Let's party!" He smiled and looked around for takers. The bartenders at Mac's Club Duce chuckled and an odd assortment broke from conversations long enough to pony up another drink to the King. Then he saw Vince staring at him. He walked over beaming. "One more for the king!" the big blonde spacer bellowed.

"Hey do," Vince replied peevishly and took the drink.

"Roland Dansky." The man offered and shot his hand out. "At your service."

The man was huge and powerfully built. Youngish, sculpted like a virtreel actor, his chest puffed up brightly, and his face a wash of smiling contentment. One liked him instantly when one realized-*this is he, plain and simple.* A slap-happy gunner.

Vince shook his hand and they drank to the King.

"Vincent...Vincent Leavel." Vince lied. He would never say, "Phalen" again.

Roland smiled from behind his drink induced joy, "Are you sure?" Then he roared laughing, "Works for me! Where'd you get that accent? You're from the inner arm, aren't you? Tough birds out there."

"Different kind of life," Vince said. "The edge of the rim, by the big void, 'place called Rip."

"Sure, born in the Sagittarius Spiral myself. Further than you, 'last world out before the dark matter ripples', Electra, near Fort Oort. But I've been here in the Pleiades so long I think I'm growing fins. What tank are you crewing on?"

"The Taloned Sire," Vince said casually.

Roland paused, looked at the Guild jacket. "Oh. You're the guy. Nice ride!"

"A lot of questions. How 'bout you?"

"Me, I'm shopping. Looking for the right assignment, you know something with style. Something like that frigate you've got sitting down in the docking bay. Now that's it, that's something old Rolly could sit comfy in, in zero space. With big guns strapped on. In the solar storm, in the rage!" He snickered. "I'll send you a resume in the morning, Captain Leavel. In the morning as the station turns. Now it's drinking time. To the King!"

They drank to the King until station bells chimed four. After that, they dashed in and out of "pad parties" closer and closer to the interior of the Neely.

Waiting by a maglev station where a horde of darkened shops crowded closed and forlorn, Roland suddenly said, "Well then, you can drink with the best of them. We're mates then. So what's the story? Am I crewing?"

"I wouldn't be drinking with you if you weren't."

"Good, because we're the only ones on this can without a bug up our arse, I think. Us and your other guildsmen perhaps. Well, the syndicate boys too I imagine."

"What do you mean, 'bug up our arse'?"

"What I mean is you and me, we're Outworlders. We don't have any implants in us so the authorities can track our every move. Less, of course, they slipped one in-but that'd be easy enough to scan before we board the ship. We'll do a thorough internal check later."

"You saying these people are tagged?"

"But of course! The Zamoran station is an Imperial Outpost-it's not Pleiadian. It has alliances with the Cyborgian Imperials. Anyone covered by Universal Peace Medical Assurance...any number of "Imperial Citizen" protections. They're tagged. Tagged, clocked, conditioned and molded into the image of a thing so ugly that nature's god never made it. It made itself out of bad ideas and good intentions, delusions of grandeur so pointless, well-it's something you can't fathom, mate. Something dark and grimy and indifferent. Something smelly in the heart of the oldest confederation of stars in human civilization. The Transhuman devils"

"All that from a medical tag?" Vince slugged back a bottle of synth. He pulled one out for Roland.

"Worse! Those Cyborgian overlords, bad as they are, they're nothing. 'Least they're remnant human, somewhere, somehow. But the HyperBogies, the word is they're altogether nonhuman."

"HyperBogies?" Vince laughed," Time to head back to the Sire, pal."

"Listen, Outworlder Captain, just you listen!" Roland waved a wild finger in Vince's direction. "I may be a little tipsy here, but this true as your back up drives out of emergency cast range, see? Listen!" Along the darkened row of shops, a small animal skittered. Machinery rumbled inanely. Vince rinsed some synth between his teeth, swallowed.

"Ever wonder why the Cyborgian Empire doesn't extend itself any further?" Roland leered and Vince saw something in his eyes he'd missed before, beneath the beaming smiling robust "tomorrow-we-may-die".

"They're extended to the limits of their military capacities," Vince said, venturing the pat response of barstool philosophers everywhere.

"Nonsense!" Roland snapped. "Their real space military is only the outer shell of their capacities. Inside the CCCE Empire, their citizens are controlled by Cyborg implants with direct ties to the really big mainframes on Deneb 4, every registered soul. Of course, the Underworld has ways around it, heh. Yet the relays and the hard-drives stationed among the star systems of the Empire are interconnected with radio links via the Gateways-no hyper casts!"

Vince did not see the implication. "Why don't they use the casts?"

"Nobody knows! However, the casts are quicker, with the casts they could set up relay mainframes and control everybody, everywhere, all the time, but they don't. What are they afraid of? It's like the overlords don't like hyperspace.

"HyperBogies! Something scares them bad. Look at a holo of the galaxy and you'll see the Republics spread around Imperial space like a wall in the Perseus arm. Beyond the wall, the Outworlds in the Sagittarius-like a moat. Beyond that and you're at the galactic core and things REALLY get weird. You've got the Marauders; you've got the big hole and the jet stream. Don't fly there. Spent a lot of time there myself, very rough spaces."

"The Marauders pretty much keep away from the Outworlds," Vince added drunkenly. "Cause we're just as sick as them."

"Perhaps. Perhaps. But you ran into some Marauders here in the Republics didn't you?" Roland didn't know where his conversation was wandering.

"Maybe the Overlords are scared of the Marauders." Vince offered.

Roland made a face, "Pugh!" He took a swig, "They'd pick their brains for shits and giggles. I'm telling you, it's something doing with hyperspace. It just doesn't make sense."

Hypercasts had been around for centuries. Why did the Overlords not use them more?

They made their way along the grimy underbelly of the station, deeper into strangeness and darkness. Along a wall someone had scrawled in day-glow crayon: *Dirty feet is the best on floor '84.*

A group of figures suddenly floated along in the semi-darkness enclosed in small metallic and glass bubbles. They were chanting to themselves, gesturing. Some did elaborate pantomimes. Vince watched them for a long moment. "What's with the bubble people?" he asked.

Roland snickered. "You'd think they were communicating, right? They're receiving programs. They ride around the station like that. Musicals, poetry, literature, all transmitted to them while they're traveling. Their bubble aircars drive. They get programmed. The transmissions tell them everything they're supposed to think, feel, and understand. It's common here in the empire. Not so much in the Pleiades but in the fringe Neelys, yeah. Huge portions of the populace derive their total understanding from the transmissions."

Vince gave him a disconcerted look: "Something isn't right with that."

Roland nodded. "You just said a mouthful."

They came to another club, the Zarath Vlasti Max. The club wound up a series of pilasters at the end of the station. People were dancing on cantilevered platforms, and Vince found the whole architectural arrangement somewhat confusing. You could see a half a mile into the Neely. Although Vince understood the centrifugal forces were holding everything in place with the massive station's spin, he couldn't help but feel everything above the club was going to come tumbling down or that the whole collection of cantilevered terraces was going to plunge into the huge interior spaces of the Neely.

Roland, buying rounds, began to ramble about the difference between the Outworlders and the rest of humanity.

"Us? We were all born of the shakedowns of Empires. We're the living proof of the dusty dreams of people who lived in lost cities on near-forgotten worlds long wasted. We know them from books, from tapes, from holos. From our very name-Outworlder."

Up another flight of wide glowing stairs. Strange flowers and huge caterpillar-like things under glass in foggy cases. Women in outfits that seemed painted on. Closer inspection showed the must have been sprayed on. Looking too long engendered a haughty response which they seemed to at once enjoy and despise. Vince practiced not looking to long.

Roland was still pontificating on the deeper meaning of being an Outworlder and the conspiracies of the Imperial Transhuman Cyber beings who he asserted ran the galaxy from behind the cover of their computer networks yet were scared willy-nilly over hyper Bogies.

165

"Yeah, our ancestors were the ones in the air and space when the Cyborgian Central Air Corps gave a little surprise attack, single-handedly eliminating any future threats to its autonomy over human endeavor. Heralding in the long era of Central Cyborgian Peace, they did. That and all that's come with it."

Vince stood up straight trying to balance himself, dizzy with synth. He felt if he leaped into the great space of the Neely he could fly without an aircar. Roland grabbed him by the shoulder and pulled him back from the edge. A flock of bubble people swooshed by.

"But not for us, my boy." Roland continued and slapped him on the back directing him away from the glass railings and the edge. Vince staggered fell forward then righted himself again.

Roland looked at him wide-eyed, wavered himself, and then continued, "We're the spawn of that confused populace on star liners and transports forced to flee until the fuel ran out. Forced to put down on any uncharted rock they could find. Far and away from the Cyborgian Empire, or its affiliated republics. Alone and defeated, our ancestors learned how to survive in Stone Age conditions on half a thousand worlds and moons and asteroids.

"That's why we're different and don't you ever forget it! Because you are different. Left alone during the long piece of the Cyborgian era, we've grown into a medley of new cultures on our own. Independence, self-reliance; you'll need them now. The Cyborgian era's calm, well let me just say that age is over. The new age?

"More like the age of Pandora! Something halted the Cyborgian air core, something that scared them. We're the proof of that, or they've had never let our ancestors survived. It's the truth."

"Something halted the Cyborgian air core, something that scared them!"

Vince remembered the air core men he'd killed when he took their ship. They'd been in shock. Insane. *Please, kill me!*

"You might be on to something there, Buck."

So the evening rolled on with drunk-talk of space demons menacing the mighty Transhuman Imperials from behind the mask of other dimensions.

In the morning Vince was hungover.

"Tripe, Captain. Boiled tripe is the magic cure, that and a little tabasco sauce. I learned that from a real live Pampas Caballero on the planet Rubio. We drank for a week." Roland said and left the ship to get some tripe. Vince wondered idly if they had herds of cattle on the station. Most likely, it would be tripe produced in vats of bacteria-creating meat. Vat meat for sure, he reasoned, unless Roland knew where to get real meat imports.

Those too probably existed on the station, if one knew where to look. Vince had the feeling if anyone would know; it was his new cosmopolitan drinking mate Outworlder gunner Roland Dansky.

Vince dragged his beleaguered messy self to the piloting cabin and signaled the holoscreen to a station news channel. There were many commercials. The war was still raging, and the King's enemies had tightened their blockade around Baal One. The price for blockade runners had gone up while they slept. It had gone up a lot. Elias was chiming on a secure channel. Aching, Vince turned on the holo com.

"Wanna' see something?" Elias asked his huge bearded head a sculpted Gilgamesh era king again, smiling at the absurdity of the universe and all mankind's folly. In his hands was a screen full of fluctuating numbers. They kept going up. "Big dough, if you got the sack. Don't forget who told you. I want a percentage. Blockade-runners are banking fortunes. I see you and the famous Roland have connected. I knew he would be at the Deuce. Best gunner on the station, 'cept 'fer maybe you. You got a gift, kid. Make the most of it." He snickered, "Taloned Sire aye? Good name. Sire."

166

The smell had become like a sentient presence. It was putrid, familiar; at once ancient and surreally new, a dark horrific scent of rotting corpses. Sagamore had remained dug in now for twenty-six hours straight, drifting in and out of sleep.

Companions long dead would speak to him occasionally, suddenly there and then not. "Hey Sag, watch your back." Sometimes they would walk up from their shattered bodies to tell him something, but whenever Sagamore looked over they were still dead.

"You're dead." He would say, but they'd already be gone again.

Something ugly was happening at the front. Something new to man, perhaps, but Sagamore knew it was a primordial ugliness. Someone had figured a new take on Predecessor technology. Found some "tricknology" in a ruin or a derelict newly discovered. The new take had a military application which gave them an advantage. Hence the war. The balance of power had been tipped enough.

Whatever it was, it was wreaking havoc at the front. Strange bulbous shapes rose and dropped on the horizon. "Hey Sagamore! This is it, bro. You're coming down. What you got in your pocket now? No aces today, friend.

Hahahahaha!"

Sagamore turned to glare at the dead things face but the air was empty.

"She's a beauty! Never seen anything like it in all my life." Roland slid his hand along the curving metal and plasticene lines of the Sire's interior. Here the stylization was even more evident than the exterior. "Didn't know the old Cyborgians had it in them."

"Watch your flying or you're going to drop us in gravity well!" Vince laughed at the big blonde flyer's boldness. He too had been bedazzled by the elegance of the ship's sweeping lines, salmon-colored ultra-steel. The intricate shimmering chromium instruments and their mother of pearl. The quartz and halogen displays, ever alive with holographs and diagrams.

Outside, the Pleiades roared away in the strings and streams of hyperspatial forces. They were a big, noisy cacophony of myriad rainbows laced with a billion blues. The Zamoran O'Neil station disappeared behind them with Elias, his first friend in a new and uncertain life. "The guild will contact you." was all he said as he ran in his finder's fee on Vince's new job.

Don't forget who told you.

The Sire ripped and danced toward darker space as if to make up for the lost time.

They were in the heart of the blockade in a matter of days. One of them or both was on the main deck at all times. Several unknown ships had begun to approach them at far depths; Vince could barely make them out with his sensors. They skittered back like crabs at the unfamiliarity of his hyper trail. Vince was unaware if there were any other Sunriders still aloft. The odds were there were still some, though very few had seen them, if so.

"The ships scaring them off," Roland whispered in awe as another blockader turned tail. "You think they could be setting us up.?"

"Could be, stay on a deep scan. They're warships. Why would they run so easily?"

"We're an older Cyborgian vessel. Occasionally an Overlord, older than the hills, will venture out of the Denebian labyrinths. People steer clear of them. They fly old ships like this one. Maybe they think we're an observer from the Empire." Roland said knowingly.

Observers. Watching to see if all are playing fairly.

The Baal system hung suspended against the bright strings of hyperspace. A black and violet pinwheel pitched amongst the other pinwheels of the stars at the forgotten heights of the Pleiades edge. For twenty straight hours now, under suspension but dipped in stim, Vince had watched the convoluted gravity well grow in size and fearsome strength. Ships and battles flashed here and there like army ants warring around a very big hole.

"Dropping into normal space now," Vince said.

The ship arced clean into the system. There weren't any warp mines or even a drone scanning them. "Pretty quiet for a war zone," Roland observed nervously.

"Yeah. Maybe all the actions happening somewhere else."

Baal One's orange and pewter visage rose before them, first came a shimmer of color, then a map, then a world huge and full. The King's stations were afoot with convoys and shuttles, battle cruisers, and strange freelance runners.

They were hailed. "Codes now, or take fire. This is a Royal Pleiades station." A voice came crisp and quick.

"This is convoy escort Taloned Sire Hailing Colonel Galeotta. Codes coming now. We have a delivery of goods." Vince responded coolly, too coolly for one so young.

A dogfight raged silently in the distance. Figures in desperate struggles for their lives riding the technology of millennia of effort for the same effect a stone would have had ten thousand years before the destruction of an opposing human force.

The King's station remained ominously quiet then. Were the codes bad?

Roland sweated at the heavy cannon. Vince gave him a reassuring look.

Finally: "This is Galeotta. Codes are clear, Guildsman. Come on in. Where'd you get that antique frigate boys?" On the Sire, a long sigh of relief went out.

"I dug it up Outspace," Vince answered.

The Sire's gravity bubble threw off the effects of entering Baal One's atmosphere with ease, keeping the ship cool. Yet the ambient heat of the system was pervasive. The stars and the system's binary were a rad sink. The cratered surface belied the influence of an atmosphere. They were at 30,000 feet when Vince received the escort signals.

Battles raged in the skies to the West and far to the North. On the ground, light shows gave evidence of more. Roland was silent at his guns. The frigate followed the escort dogfighters. They were so close Vince could see one of the pilots give a wave through his cockpit window. The base lay below them spread out for miles and miles. An amalgamation of dropships, thousands of astercrete structures, force domes, and enormous energy cannon aligned in rows blasting arced fire to the horizon where fields of smoke billowed and mingled with return tracers and more indications of fire.

At length, the Sire landed and soldiers scrambled with hover loaders.

Roland stayed at his guns. He didn't trust anyone. For all his booming smiles and chatter the night before, on the ground in a war zone he was silent death waiting to strike at a moment's notice.

Vince set his MERGE helmet down. "Going to supervise the last of this and make sure they sign the manifests." He said.

"Aye Captain." Roland forced a smile and winked.

Vince lingered in the cargo bay watching the soldiers. Baal One's light and heat assailed him. He pulled a visor out of a locker and put it on.

A Sergeant approached the bay doors. "Sergeant Mercurio," he said, his eyes looking through the manifests. "Nice frigate you boys got there. Rare item. Good shape." He was a bald stocky fellow with an air of self-possession. Stubborn resolution. Vince could see healing wounds on his head, flash burns. He was just back from the front.

Vince compared the manifests. "That she is. Rare." He ran down the last of the list assuring everything was checked off as delivered. "Everything seems complete."

The last of the hover loaders was pulling away from the now empty cargo hold. Everything was quiet when they had finished. The war seemed to have taken a coffee break. "You're good to go, trader," Mercurio said, glancing up at the dark lines of the Sire. "Good luck."

"You as well." Vince offered and took a last look at the brilliant and awful landscape of Baal One as he sealed the cargo bay doors. On his manifests payment numbers were flashing.

Having made delivery and taken payment, they began power ascent and running checks on defensives. With this and the money he'd earned rescuing Elias from the Ripjackle marauders, Vince was now very well off. His black and silver guildsman's jacket hung on his shoulders as if it had always been there.

They left the King's base and began for the high places over the galactic plane. Once out of the war zone they would drop back into the Pleiades.

"Chrysalis Isla, baby!" Roland was laughing with glee. "Been too long a time since I stuck these feet in some pink sand and chased a sea horse or two."

"Chrysalis Isla." Vince beamed with abandon. All these years since first seeing a hologram of Chrysalis Isla as a boy he had yearned to see it. Crown jewel of that storied kingdom.

"Playground of the Pleiades. Suns, surf, and reef gardens! More synthopiate rum than you can drink in ten lifetimes. I have been wanting to get back there with a few silver dollars for some time, Captain Leavel."

"Never been." Vince smiled.

The frigate watched the war and the worlds of the Baal system fade away.

Vince lifted his MERGE helmet. The gunnery cabin was cramped and artificial but it was comforting at the moment. Good to get the fireworks and the voices out of his mind.

He yawned, "Hey doo!"

Then came the claxons and the sirens. "Incoming! Captain, let's go!"

He dove back hard into the seat, shoving his sweaty head into MERGE. Space came into view. "I repeat, Incoming." Roland spat out again.

Vince could see them now. Particle beams slashed through the darkness around them. A transport was being harried by a clutch of dogfighters-four of them. Who was who? Anybody's guess at this point.

Roland powered up the alnico rings steadily. Collider fields sprang into action. Mesons swarmed below. "Who's who?" Vince asked, quickly scanning for registration marks.

"They're all reading Pleiades Royal Air Corps. They're all the King's men!"

The small transport was riding the Sire's wake, hoping the dogfighters wouldn't fire for fear of hitting a noncombatant. Warp charges dropped, shattering the continuity of normal space like glass. A huge bubble of quark particles flashed into existence heating the ether.

"Gotta do something now Captain or our weenies are roasted!" Roland howled. MERGED, Vince barely heard him over the roar of forces.

Particle beams scanned their shields. Stasis anomalies came up in defense. Vince remembered the last time those stasis shields had gone up. Please don't freeze on me now. They worked without a flaw.

The transport wasn't firing at them.

"Take out the dogfighters!" Vince bellowed.

Roland and Vince engaged them with the Sire's big cannons. "Let's Party!" Roland squealed as the firefight came alive in full.

"Evasive-" Vince slammed the navigationals straight down, then madly to port in a wild spin. The transport managed to avoid the crossfire and stay with the Sire.

"Shit." Vince snapped.

Roland fired again and the dogfighters were shrinking smoke. The transport behind them rolled in anticipation of more fire.

"Whoever he is, he's a better pilot than those dogfighters were," Roland observed.

"Yeah, maybe. Or maybe they just didn't figure we'd fire on them." Vince tried to push the creeping dread that was forming in his mind away. He couldn't. He couldn't escape the feeling that he'd fired on the wrong side in this little conflict.

"That transport is running hot, Captain. She's not an intersystem ship. She's a jumper. Quick bolts through hot spots to bigger amour for safety, that's all."

Roland showed a thermal scan. It wasn't pretty. There was metal fatigue throughout the transport's hull. Weakness spelled death.

"Well, let's come up on him. Hail him loudly. If he doesn't respond, push him down, there." Vince isolated a gaseous proto-planet left over from the Pleiades formation.

Stubborn to the end, the transport didn't respond, but it didn't fire either.

Vince had picked up local navigationals back at the Zamoran O'Neil station. They gave him an accurate picture of the proto-planet the Sire forced the overheated transport down on. Even uglier than Baal One from a distance, its lumpy mottled surface improved not with the landing.

"We've landed on Shit World," Roland said dryly.

"What's he doing?" Vince asked.

"Cooling fast." Roland quipped.

"Powers off, cooling at this rate their ship could crack like an iron skillet thrown in water." Vince peered anxiously at the transport. "Hope they got their suits on."

"That puppies throwing off a lot of radiation. If they're not already suited, they're dead."

One of the blast shields on the side of the transport opened suddenly. A solitary figure was backlit from pale emergency lighting. The figure staggered forward in a heavy-duty military-grade EVA suit. He appeared unarmed. But then, where would he go if he fired? There was only one ride off this frozen piece of dung.

"Here he comes," Vince said quietly.

Roland had a particle beam trace aimed at him the whole time, but the figure was, as he seemed, unarmed. He paused for a moment near the Sire, came to a stop. He leaned back taking a long look at the Sire from the front, then to back.

"He likes your ship," Roland smirked.

At the airlock, amazingly, the figure knocked at the door.

"Well if that don't beat all," Vince said.

Roland looked over for confirmation. Vince raised his hands, "Let him in." and shook his head in disbelief. Roland opened the outer lock. The inner lock cabin pressurized. They watched him on a small camera Vince had rigged back at the Zamoran O'Neil (amazed the Cyborgian Air corps hadn't one there already).

He unlatched his helmet. For a moment Vince hoped it was a woman. Gorgeous and exotic, with lots of fiery spirit and long, flowing, red hair.

It was, however, a man. A beefy grunt of a soldier with a long dash of a scar across the side of his head and a scorpion tattoo. The tattoo was emblazoned with the motto, "Eat this" in Gaelic script.

"Thanks," He said raspingly. "I'd have answered your hailing, but you never know who's listening out here in the zone, do you?"

He watched the Camera but it made no response.

"Sagamore's the name, Sagamore Salvatore. Ex-special forces with the "mad-dog" unit of the King's rearguard. I stress the "ex" part a whole lot. I've just resigned. Thanks for pulling me out of that little spot of trouble there. "

Vince shuddered. The dread he'd been trying to ignore just rose up sure and confirmed, solid as the deserter standing before the camera. Vince had fired on the King's Air Corps killing six pilots to save the life of a runagate.

Roland whistled, "Uh-oh." Vince stared. "Perhaps they didn't relay our I.D. in," Roland said.

"I didn't see any transmissions. If they did they'll make us outlaws for sure. Let him in, power us out of here."

"We going to turn him in? We could leave him in the airlock, deliver him to the authorities and plead self-defense." Roland grasped at straws.

"You trust the cops?" Vince asked.

"Yeah, right."

Vince put on a speaker, "Okay, Mr. Salvatore. That was some good flying there. You looking for a new job?"

"Absolutely!"

The airlock opened and Sagamore Salvatore stepped into the Sire directly. "Nice ride you boys got here, where'd you find her?"

Steve Allman

.... And so it was that the Taloned Sire's first recorded registration at a station was under the protection and authority of the Sagittarian Trade Guild. Here legendary appearance rescuing Tristan's ship was followed up by the questionable involvement with a certain deserter, Sagamore Salvatore.

She remained for many years on and off the grid, building a reputation as shipping and sometimes fearsome mercenary vessel, one of the few Sunriders known to exist in mint condition.

The Taloned Sire again became famous when arriving at Chrysler city…

--Princess Clairissa Maggio, Caldris. Rise of the Taloned Sire

Book Five: Renegades of Ophelia's World

The Kith Blade

ObscuroFrio, Sagittarius Arm.

"Obscuro! Frio!"

So it is said, "Obscuro…. Frio," were the first words muttered by a Spanish speaking Arcturian as he stepped from a ruined starship and looked out at serrated glacial peaks stretching dark and magnificent in all directions. Refugees from the Arcturian genocidal wars, it was their last planet of call.

There was no more fuel.

Literally, Obscuro Frio means, "Darkness and Cold". It was an apt nomenclature. The planet's dying sun cast an ugly light over jagged teeth of mountain ranges. The biome on that frozen world consisted of pumped-up vermin. Bottom feeders that had managed to evolve when grander and higher life forms died away.

A world's vermin, the lowest and most despicable of creation, had stepped into the eco-niches of giants. Orbiting a fading Red-giant star at the end of its life-cycle which had passed Red-giant status and was now fading to cool, it was the last chapter of the planet's existence. Eons had ebbed away in the sputtering twilight of that world when mankind stumbled off the refugee ships.

Amazingly, the indigenous life forms had been evolving right along with the slow and dreary death.

How the planet's life forms had survived the star's expansion was a matter of conjecture. A barely temperate zone at the poles? The crushing depths of dark seas? The stars retreating heat, then, had been slow enough for the vermin to conquer again the now freezing globe.

Snow spiders mimicked rubble to avoid ice worms that hid in the glacial rivers fearing sudden clouds of stoneflies that smelled them in search of a place to lay larva. It was a looter's struggle for the last energies left of better days.

Someday the star would nova, but there was still an eon or two to play out.

The refugees fought a vicious battle for survival. Their solution to stay alive is a legendary testament to their will. Among the Outworlds, a story of overcoming unnatural odds is the first story of each place. But the ObscuroFrioians' story is the most arduous.

One can still see the ship's logs at the Brady library and witness what happened there in 3197.

Louis Silvera of the transport vessel La Sirena was awakened early on his shift by an emergency com from the bridge. All around his cabin were posters of various daring-do resort hotels across the colonies. Jump from Space at New Procyon. Swim the whales at Thunder's down. Dance in New Cuba!

172

He made his way out the cabin ignoring the collection of a bachelor's life.

Holograms of New Cuban dancing girls reached out from the walls as he made his way down the halls of the ship, "Buenas Capitano!" each said and blew him a kiss.

"Turn off the holograms Artie or there is going to be trouble!" he bellowed, but the kisses followed him to the bridge where a whole troop of them were dancing around Artie who had his feet up on the command console."

Silvera slapped a toggle on the wall and the girls disappeared. Artie, however, remained, slightly perturbed.

"What?" Silvera growled.

Artie said nothing but touched some screens and diagrams came up all flat.

"This is a full spread of the hypercasts we are receiving" he finally quipped. "De nada."

Silvera tilted his head sarcastically and made a face, "Soooo-fix it. Don't wake me up for this shit and turn off the holo-girls in the hallways it doesn't cheer me up anymore. I'm going back to bed" he said and turned to leave.

"Not broken," Artie said quickly before Louis could escape.

"Uhh, hello-it has to be broken or there would be some chatter on that screen. You know, a whole bunch of yapping lonely freighter pilots, advertisements for cheap resort hotels on obscure little asteroids, droning bullfeathers cast about the universe aye? Fix it."

"Not broken," Artie repeated. His eyes left the floor where they had been examining his boots which he had removed from the console. They met his Captain's face waiting for the implications to finally sink in.

"So nobody is broadcasting from the other side?" Silvera's eyes went dark.

They were hauling twelve tons of frozen fish and three hundred colonists to Rearden, a boomtown on an asteroid of the same name at the frontier. The fish were illegal-the La Sirena didn't have the proper facilities to haul them.

Artie had rigged up a bunch of liquid nitrogen tanks and handed the inspector a 500 credit note. The inspector got a case of "gotta go" really quick. Silvera had asked him if the fish would keep till they got to Rearden and Artie had replied with a shrug.

Rearden's meat processing vats had gone bad when they had been running twenty-four seven trying to accommodate the boom. The price of meat sub and fish had gone through the roof. Silvera was looking to clean up.

The colonists were your usual bunch of green civies that imagined themselves more rugged and adventurous than they usually ended up being. Whole families eager to get a claim on a world or worldlet and were ready to risk all.

Artie and Louis often ran bets on how many would run home and then checked the transport manifests on future visits.

Sometimes they stayed, sometimes they fell out. Louis was figuring this particular crop looked like the grand collection of wimps-extraordinaire.

"I'll take you up on that assessment, sir. Two to one, that over half are still on Rearden next time we drop shipment."

So now Louis was facing dead casts from the Rearden side of hyper and a ship full of melting frozen fish and soft civilians.

"Marauders?" Louis looked expectantly an Artie, but Artie was too cynical to even throw him that bone.

"No S.O.S. signals? None of their usual psycho howling and strutting? If somebody hit Rearden, they did it with military precision. Fast. Take out communications, then mop up at leisure.

"The targets run around in confusion unable to organize a response." Artie returned a sardonic smile.

"Yeah, well...those targets would have been our friends and colleagues this go-round." Louis conceded grimly.

"We come out of hyper for three seconds. Auto scan a wide field, then punch the hole again and go right back into zero space. We can go through the auto scans from hyper. If everything is five-five-five, we turn around and come back."

"If it isn't?" Artie asked, certain in his mind the auto scans were going to be scenes of carnage on Rearden.

"Thank the great Space Ghost we put those extra drives in the ship to outrun the inspectors aye?"

There was no one left at Rearden.

They made a quick burst out of hyper in a daring sweep of the colony and found it a radioactive wasteland. Artie had been right.

Captain Silvera pressed the ship deep into the Sagittarius Spiral Arm. They watched for pursuit and were relieved when none followed. However, La Sirena was an old ship.

Silvera had managed to buy it from the Air Corps surplus. He was planning major retrofitting at Rearden-he had pushed her as far as was reasonable and they were now blasting through the universe with chewing gum and duct tape holding together systems in dire need of care.

There were no more colonies on their current vector. Even the charts were scant on information. It was then when the two bachelors felt the old boat was flying blind into a great unknown that a strange passenger appeared at the bridge doorway like someone out of a mystery holo.

The Arcturian colonies weren't warm to cyborgs, yet the passenger was brazenly wearing headgear the screamed of enhancements.

Mental enhancements.

Artie remembered him then. Born with congenital brain damage, the passenger had been licensed certain hardware that allowed him to function in regular society.

Ian Brady, born with a brutal disability and having spent a lifetime of social ostracism, had now become a lifeline for their survival. He had databases in his head which included information from university probes and research stations on a world they could reach.

An unnamed globe orbiting a red giant. M6103. There was a breathable atmosphere. Indigenous life forms. Lakes located near several geothermal vents. The rest of the planet was largely an ice ball of wicked mountain ranges.

La Sirena would have to make it to one of the geothermal vents. They could survive there because of the lakes.

In a heroic attempt, the ship crash-landed a thousand miles short of their destination. In the weeks that followed it became apparent they crew and passengers would freeze to death. Again, it was Ian that provided a solution. His enhancements had enabled him to pursue a career in biological sciences. Desperate to survive, he offered the crew and passengers of the castaway's genetic enhancements by recombinant DNA from some of the indigenous life forms. They had been freezing, now they could endure the cold. They had been facing starvation, now they could metabolize the local fauna. So began a new people.

--Princess Clairissa Maggio, Caldris. ObscuroFrio, Iceworld of the Outworlds

Atlas Mountains, ObscuroFrio
Sagittarius Galactic Spiral Arm.
4120

Aggregate ice lay in furrows along the edges of the New Aiguilles Expupery range. Black stoneflies, long and waspish, flew in a maddening frenzy when the boy appeared. Hovering over a corpse, they were a cloud of sudden, surprising motion.

The boy recognized the corpse immediately, it was his father.

Just like that, a glance, a moment, his life irretrievably diminished.

Swallowing hard, young Millin Quinoa pulled out his Kith blade from his long white boot and swung a full circle scanning for the murderers. They had gone, leaving the body exposed to the wildlife as food-an ultimate sign of contempt.

He stood among the flies, approached the body. The flies came at him to sting and lay larva but Millin swung his blade wide side, and the crack of hard fly bodies smashing sent the whole buzzing mass away.

He took his father's tools and small belongings as mementos, but it would be the flies that he would remember. Their buzzing calls like words from the dead.

ZZZZZZ Remember this! Remember and be spared it.

A giant half-circle of sun spanned the horizon, resting enormous over the marching stretch of jagged mountain peaks. Millin's wet eyes scanned the escarpments and drifts about him again. His father's betrayers might leap at him any moment.

ZZZZZZZ.

He buried his father's corpse and sat sentry by the grave, watching stoneflies land on the icy rocks, returning now to search for their hidden meal. When he could sit no more, he stepped away and clambered down the ice with expert steps.

His father had always been a wide smile and a booming greeting, a determined step into action-they had made him a helpless patch of fly-covered shame.

Millin glanced warily across the stretch of jagged peaks, seeing for miles and miles. There was no end of them on this world. Any one of the villages tucked among the rocks and valleys might harbor the murderous betrayers who'd made a quick end of his father.

He would become caution; it was Millin they were after, Millin and the kith blade.

Angered that his father had chosen Millin instead of them as the next holder of the blade, the killers had to be among his kith.

He had to go where they would not find him, at least for a time, until he was ready to extract justice in blood. Still holding the blade wide and ever deadly, he slid down the ice of the mountain and made it away.

Lake Potter sat atop the world collecting ice and snow for millennia before the first refugees had arrived. Centuries later it still looked much the same, but for the now old and storied city of Potter's falls. That city and Sullivan's landing clung to the lake with massive granite buildings like a herd of fat beasts resting, implacable and bulky. Millin had found the city's mirth always a thin cover for more devious doings.

His father had taken him there often on trading ventures with the handiwork of his smithy; silver necklaces, silver cups, ornamental silver blades. Their kith was famous for them. Always on those trips, there had been stops at huge stone taverns full of singing, manna beer (he'd sneak a drink when his father wasn't looking), and comradeship.

The streets never looked as dangerous as they did this day. Anyone might be a kidnapper ready to abscond away with him for ransom. He passed the familiar taverns and heard familiar songs drifting through to the alleys and passageways. Perhaps the betrayers even now celebrated their evil act among those fellows. Millin climbed among some forlorn bell towers and slept.

Alone, hungry and afraid, he watched the lake.

Sooner or later a starship would port there. He would stow away on it. Days came and went. He went down to the streets when closing hours came and traded a few coins for manna bread and crab juice.

175

He tried to be unobtrusive among the bustling crowds but the shopkeeper's brows raised when Millin produced even his smallest coin. "Small boy for such a big piece of silver." The shopkeeper observed.

"My mother gave it to me, sir. She's impatient for her snack. Please hurry."

"Bold too." The shopkeeper handed him his package and change. As Millin scurried away the man leaned out the doorway watching. Millin followed after a woman, hoping she wouldn't notice him. He thought the shopkeeper believed the ruse.

Back in the hulking bell towers Millin ate eagerly and watched the sky above the lake.

A few nights later, his patience was rewarded. The bells in the tower roused him suddenly-arrival bells! He rolled out of his corner and went to a window. Stone ice spiders were carved in the ornament, they shimmered red in the moonlight. Once, ObscuroFrio had a single moon. With the expanding of its star, sometime in the distant past, it had broken up into a near ring of rubble that now cast its light over the lake and city.

Millin searched the sky. Dawn lay on the horizon. Suddenly he saw the starship, drifting down in its gravity field, alighting in a bubble-like transparent sphere, a giant beetle floating in from a realm of unknown beings. As it neared the lake to waterport, brilliant purple lights emanated from the bubble and took strange curving geometries, flashing, changing, and dancing.

Millin knew the star people came in a variety of colors, mostly variations of pink and brown, rarely blue.

Once his people had been like them. Long, long ago. He would stand out among them, but at least he would be safe from his kith. *He was the carrier of the kith blade.* His father had chosen him not out of favoritism, but out of an unerring observation of Millin's great courage and even greater intelligence. Millin had taught himself to read by six and was tutoring other children in the kith by nine.

He had slain an ice worm that winter, saving the lives of half a shelter. It was now his boots. The future of the kith depended on a leader with these qualities.

Someday he would find his father's betrayers and bury the kith blade deep in their bellies. Today was not that day.

For a time, he must remain fugitive.

The starship had ported, steaming the lake with its great heat.

Light ebbed over the city and a great noise went up at the arrival of the starship. Merchants and buyers appeared from the town like a mysterious flock of pilgrims. Millin lost himself in the throng, ever wary of an approaching hand or suspicious glance.

On the docks now were all manner of goods from simple silver blades to lasers and holograms. It was mostly the silver the star men wanted. The technology goods had originated in the stars; rarely did they go back. Somehow though, whenever the starships returned, the new technologies were improved upon in some small fashion.

Just enough to make them enviable.

Millin stepped into the hold of the starship with a merchant, pretending to carry goods for a few coins. When his work was done he hid in the shadows.

The merchant, now having to pay the boy, made no noise of his disappearance. He looked around for a bit with a confused expression, rumbled the coins he could now keep in his pocket, and finished his business.

Millin watched him go from behind a noisy rattle of giant sea crab boxes, huge crates of worked silver goods, leopard-seal hats, and ice-tortoise bandoliers. He watched the crowd from that vantage for the whole day without moving. He saw several of his kith eyeing about with no business. They had anticipated his plan but they were too late.

Ludivoccio, Shadrik-and Polana! Polana, among the betrayers. Millin's heart sank. She had been his most beloved after his mother's death. Her dashing red hair had been the swiftest among the kith, her beauty like the promise of all good and courage. He'd adored her, and she'd sold him out in envy. Davron and Shadrik's simple-minded lack of loyalty; he'd suspected them from the start. They took no joy in others' gain, even their kith members. Polana, he'd misjudged her all along.

The hold doors were shut on Millin, and he sat alone in the dark crying for his lost father, and Polana's betrayal. Deep in the metal bowels of the hyperspatial transport, hearing the rumble of foreign machinery, feeling an alternate heat and cold of the workings of the ship jarring him out of a state of half awareness, he remembered better days and a life he was to leave behind.

Ludivoccio Quinoa was the cousin of Millin Quinoa and by rights, he felt he should have been the keeper of the kith blade. From his apartment in Potters falls he had led a life of sublime achievement, earning accolades in any endeavor he had chosen. He'd even become the star of several men's holos going about in certain circles and was adored by many. Adored by all except but Millin's father. Millin's father who clung to the past and its pathetic mores with an idiocy that Ludivoccio couldn't bear to be as much as seen with.

Fud. They called the old man Fud. Short for fuddy-duddy.

Well, no matter. The old man was dead. Bye, bye Fud! All that remained was to eliminate the little favorite-Millin.

Just like his father, the boy had exhibited a conservative bent that Ludivoccio feared. Ludivoccio viewed all of the past-its mores, culture, and history as a repressive strangle on the human soul. A new era of progressive change was to come, and he would lead.

He would hold the kith blade and sway over the clan. Tolerance and freedom would grace ObscuroFrio, but first, he had to squash the life out of the boy's dreams and aspirations.

He glared out at the city below. The little savage was out there somewhere. Well, where could he go? One small boy with no allies and no resources. Sorry! You're leading nothing, going nowhere-very fast!

"Ludy! Let's go to the club!" His roommate Nando called from the kitchen. Yes, Ludivoccio thought. Dance, dance, dance!

Tonight they will adore me! A victory dance!

Day came again and Millin found a viewport in the giant hold door. He listened as the behemoth ship powered up. Without warning then, he watched the city drop away from view and then the luster of Lake Potter and finally the Atlas Mountains. At first grand, a white veil spread over a thousand peaks of brown shot with grey, they shrunk to porridge with sugar. The city was a web of boxes then a smudge in the porridge. The world became a ruddy snowball, then a star.

Just like that, a snap really, and he was gone.

He thought of them still searching for him on the streets of Sullivan's landing. For the first time since the buzzing stoneflies, he smiled.

Millin was two worlds away before the traders finally found him. They weren't about to take him back, so they hired him on. They weren't Guildsmen, he spotted that right away.

They were a hardscrabble lot, sleazy and cheap. Millin proved a quick study and learned as much as he was able about the ship, but they never taught him navigation.

He was a year on the high merchant star routes in the systems adjacent to ObscuroFrio before he asked for the balance of his pay. He was hoping to find work on another ship.

They sold him into slavery at the next port.

Opa Locka's World
4121
A good slave, he was not.

177

Angering his master, Millin was thrown into a betting pit and chained to a giant slab of rusting iron. Behind a small gate at the other end of the pit, a noise of baying Ripjackles could be heard. They'd been starved for days readying them for the contest. A crowd of vulgar men and women waged their bets, howling with glee and bloodlust.

Lightning crackled in the distance. It had rained off and on since Millin arrived on this hothouse of a planet. He would be fighting in mud.

They were betting on how long he would last before the Ripjackles disemboweled him.

"And to the closest better on the lad's time in the pit will go this fine Kith blade." The bet master held up Millin's finely jeweled blade. "But first, of course, he'll need it!" He laughed and tossed the blade down to Millin.

The crowd roared with laughter.

Millin picked up the muddy blade. "Morons. Am I to die for the entertainment of morons?" The bet master raised his hand for silence. "And time!" he shouted.

The gate dropped and the Ripjackles shot out. Foolishly they charged right in. Millin took the heads of the first two, then a third.

"Yeah! Come on, little doggies!" Millin shot back.

Newly aware that their prey wasn't defenseless, the remaining Ripjackles circled in their way, darting in and out, snapping.

Millin slashed and twisted.

They took blood.

He took blood.

Still, it was only a matter of time. He was lasting much longer than any before him, so the crowd was losing money and placing second bets hoping to win it back. There was a roar of calls and waving arms as the jackals nipped at the boy. Time and again the jackals came in only to be fought back.

Each time, however, with slightly less fervor.

Millin faded the circumference of his chain- a little at a time with each blade swing. Thus the jackals were tricked into misjudging his reach.

On one of their lunges then he leaped out three steps farther than they anticipated and took another head.

Now the crowd was furious, amazed, and delighted all at once.

Millin was standing among the headless Ripjackles when he ventured to kick one of their heavy bodies out to the other animals. They sniffed it. Cannibals they were not.

Worth a try. Millin thought.

His body ran with adrenaline, but his strength was still diminishing fast. It would be moments now, surely, and he would fall, ripped to pieces. His blue skin was covered with blood already. The crowd was in a frenzy. The lead Ripjackle circled back, Millin lunged taking a piece of its throat. It came again driven by hunger, excited by the noise of the crowd.

Suddenly, the noise quieted.

Millin saw a man in black and silver approaching the ring of the pit riding a large animal. The man's face was scarred, and one sensed some immense sadness about him.

The crowd seemed to know him. No one said a word when he rode his beast smoothly into the pit. He looked at the jackals; they growled but did not charge.

He looked at Millin, then at the crowd.

There was a long, dreadful silence. Only the Ripjackles bobbing heads and low baying broke the perfect stillness. The man lifted a strange silvery pistol and the air flashed with a dazzling light.

Millin looked down and the chain was severed. Everyone just stared.

Then Millin rushed the jackals in a furious sprint through the mud, his blade swinging a death song through the air, separating each beast's head from its body until there was only he standing before the unbelieving crowd who now backed away at the armed and unchained boy.

"All bets are off!" the bet master howled and Millin leaped out from the area with a shifty run, shadowing the man on the strange beast. He came closer upon the man further down the road. He moved up behind him. Then, at his side, Millin asked, "Why'd you do that?

A breath. A sigh. A memory of chains?

"Hop up, kid. Why is it always the gentle ones that pay the price for everyone else's ambition?"

They rode all night. A thunderstorm threatened in the distance but never appeared. Morning found them far from the towns, riding right into the yellow sea where a strange starship rested waterported and idling. In the distance supermassive cetaceans arced the horizon with glimmering silvery bodies and made huge splashes of foam.

"The Taloned Sire." the man announced. "And I, young man, am its Captain. Captain Leavel. Welcome home."

Resting idly in the emerald waters, the Sire struck a grand figure. She stretched easily, languid, telling of powers at rest, but ready. The leaping black, red, gold, and chromium lines shimmered with spots of bright accents. Millin tried to assess the hull, the colliders, and the field generator vanes. It was all bright and beautiful, of a kind of reason and science dipped in objectivity without superstitious darkness.

"Yeah, she's a beauty. But she's deadly too. A world wrecker if misused. A carrier of hope if handled well. It's all on the captain, me boy. Remember that."

Cassiopeia Supernova remnant
4124

Sagamore watched the lines of force shift suddenly on his faceplate knowing there wasn't a rational explanation within his realm of knowledge, and more grimly that Vince and Roland were now cut off from him, and he from the ship.

Below him lay a shattered spread of a planetoid, and the glistening sparkle of rich heavy metals and jewels, glimmering in the nebulae of Cassiopeia. A tiny mass of forces and light were mining equipment manned by Vince and Roland.

"Sag, what the hell's up with that neutron star?" Vince howled.

"Saggy! We're getting a lot of shifts in gravity, magnetic fields, rads-oh shit, oh shit!" Roland's usual nonchalant voice was full of panic.

"I know, I know. It's off the scale. I can't move, or I'll be crushed in the sweep of forces. Just hold steady. Maybe it'll pass."

"Maybe it won't! Can you remote the ship?" Vince looked over the mining equipment with dread; none of it was designed for use in forces shifting as suddenly as this. It was some kind of freak storm on the neutron star. Something he'd never seen or heard of before. There was a lot of work and wealth in the cache at hand. Yet he'd die with it if they didn't think of something quick.

"Sag, we're shifting too far. Much closer and our whole damned EVA systems are going to collapse, bro. You gotta remote this ship now."

"I can't. My readings are burned. I'm floating blind."

Roland barked into his com, "The kid! The kid's on the ship! Have him remote it in!"

"In this gravitational nightmare?"

"Call the kid Sag. Call the kid!" Vince could feel his Eva systems failing. The air and fields around them were shaking. The last thing he would feel would be their rushing collapse, the icy cold of space, and his blood begin to boil.

Inside the Taloned Sire, Millin was listening. "I'm right here Captain. What should I do?"

Sag sighed in relief. But he couldn't imagine the boy handling the huge frigate in the supernova remnant's massive wasteland of space debris.

Millin waited and ran his hand along his kith blade. *I am the keeper of the kith blade. Though I am a boy, I must now be a man.*

"Kid. I need you to plug into the ship. You're going to download some flight training programs into your nervous system. Just enough so you can steer the big boat over to us, okay?" Vince offered desperately.

Millin's small blue hands were shaking. He could see the crew as tiny points of light on the main screen among the blasted and twisted clouds, asteroids, and glowing dust. They weren't close. He climbed into the piloting chair and the Sire Merged with his nervous system.

Sag's voice was strained.

"You in the MERGE kid?"

"Yeah. Everything looks so real. It's like I'm a bird in space!"

"I know kid, I know. It's great, ain't it? Now I want you to talk to the ship."

"What should I say?"

"Say, 'Instructional RNA sequences'."

Millin said it, and a row of objects appeared in space before him.

"Now say, 'Flight protocols and navigational background.' "

Millin said that, and several of the objects got bigger, the rest disappeared. "Okay!"

Sagamore's voice faded in a burst of static.

"Vince! Sag! Roland?"

Silence. Static. ZZZZZZ. There came a memory of stoneflies on a mountainside and profound loneliness.

Millin began to cry.

"Oh Dad, oh Dad, help me!"

Silence. But there was no time to cry. He reached out and touched the first object. Suddenly his mind was full of voices and pictures rushing by-

An historical outline of the Space Ages to modern times- The Acquisition of the Solar system- 1961-mid twentieth-century Earth's first ventures into space- the establishment of the L5 station 2045- Lunar mining 2050- mining of the asteroid belts and the first great upgration 2100- the sleeper ships- terraforming and settlement of Venus and Mars 2130-2300- the rise of the outer moon colonials and gas giant siphon mining 2300-2450

Millin reached for another object, scrambling afraid, and suddenly aware of a whole era of mankind's endeavor that he hadn't an inkling of before-

Mercury nearside city dominates solar systems economic and political structure throughout the twenty-sixth and seventh Centuries-Luna Farside station 2700 bans immigration- Neptune's Oceans mined through the great scoop shuttles - the spread of the O'Neil city rings systems off Mercury-

Millin pulled away, "Sag, which one?" He grabbed another-

Faster than light drives-bubbles of space warped into inestimably curled dimensions negating the effects of mass and allowing the transport of large amounts of matter in apparently small strings of space-time-report of the galactic structure Infrared line observations of the nuclear region show a rich structure of clouds and arched filaments-OB stars associated with a small tilted disc- the antimatter plume typical of large black holes at the center of spiral galaxies- the magnetic field orientation has been mapped in great detail-

Millin couldn't stop the tears now. He knew this wasn't the information he needed. Sobbing, he grabbed another- and howled for Vince.

"Millin!" It was Vince's voice scratching through another channel.

Polarized dust emissions and the fractal structure of local molecular clouds -

"Drive systems, Millin, drive systems!"

Millin saw an object looking like the guts of some engines piled together. It said "Drive Systems". He grabbed it.

The Sunrider 3062 Frigate is equipped with five drive systems and backups for various flight conditions. The center of the system is the Anti-gravitational, or gravitational antipolar response field-a helicon magnetic plasma sail system for emergency fuel efficiency and movement in and out of heliopauses-a hyperstring enabling system to negate mass through five-dimensional wormhole hyper streams-a super ion drive Buzzard ramjet array for normal space bursts through complex field distortion areas-and emergency use limited standard rocket backup fail safes. Navigation systems are collated through eighty quasar emissions and the galactic plume...

Vince woke in a med lab tank, staring at a mass of hair that turned out to be the back of Sag's head. Roland was a couple of fluid tanks away. Millin was busily operating equipment, his hands flashing over keyboards and grabbing hologram icons in the air.

"Nice to see you, Captain! You took a lot of forces out there. A miracle your EVA's held up as well as they did. Haven't figured what sent that Neutron star haywire, but we've got the whole event on the disc, and there'll probably be a couple of universities pay a pretty penny to see it."

How much did the boy download?

"I managed to salvage your cargo too. I eased the whole lot of you into a containment field and scooped you, me, and the frigate out of the system with a broad flash of the Buzzard Ramjets until we could squeeze enough momentum off the heliopause remnants near the first shockwave ionizations a couple of light hours out."

Vince stared quietly a moment. Finally, he said, "Okay." and gave thumbs up from the med tank, noticing the boy had the Kith blade hanging from a belt at his side.

What else could he say?

In the coming years, Millin would get to know his Captain well. Many things he would come to know, from the educational programs, and from growing up aboard ship. Yet when it came to Vince, it would always be a flash of light smashing a chain in a slave pit that Millin would remember.

Captain Leavel was the one who busted chains...

181

Shane Perry

Riptide

Central Galactic Region: Tangeonprioc, 4185

Someone was asking a lot of questions down at the Corewinds Tavern.

Too many questions for Mel "No-Deal" DePaulo. He took a long toke on a crystal water bong and watched the questioning figures in a mirror behind the long aluminum bar.

"Time to lift off this little corner of the Multiverse," he said quietly to Roland Dansky, sitting beside him.

Their ships, the Serpentine and Mel's Monkey, were sent an emergency departure signal-directly from Mel.

"Nobody asks a lot of questions this close to the galactic core, Roland me boy. Too many highly prized minerals passing about. Too many Predecessor relics to be gotten."

Too little law.

If someone was snooping around it was personal. That meant a hit or a raid was coming. No chance for negotiations and no opportunities to cut a deal.

Better to cut anchor instead. He and Roland made separate paths through the gardens and domes toward the station docks where their ships were bayed. Clambering into the airlock of the Mel's Monkey, Mel fumed, "Get the rest of the crews in here. We're leaving. Now!"

When he reached his piloting seat he dropped in it like a shot of lead. He was raging as he began ship deliberations for departure. The crews were pissed.

The last Pilot was scrambling with keyboards and lockdown fields when the two ships paid port duty and swung hard out to space.

Tangeonprioc's domes and craters fell away with unreasonable speed. Half the crews hadn't time to go cyber.

On the main hologram, the globe seemed to fall away like a toy, a mirage.

Now the crews were *really* pissed. Yet Mel's attention never wavered from his MERGE helmet. Banging the warp drive that close to the galactic core was painful on your neurons. When you got used to the pain, and you remembered you were running, then you were angry. When the anger passed, then there was fear. A creeping awful dread when you begin to wonder: What's behind us?

Most of the time Mel was a mellow leader, a taciturn man-almost foolish in appearance. Yet underneath that gangling neurotic facade was a fiercely competent fighter, a shrewd soft sell. A battle-hardened Captain. The crews knew it. If Mel was silent, in a hurry, and running, something bad was coming.

The two ships wailed in the fuming plasma streams, funneling on a billion string courses through the hugeness that spread out and up from the galactic plume.

Roland Dansky commanded the Serpentine. After a few grim hours of silence, he cast over in code, "Ugh-Mel? Everybody's kind of curious. You got any idea what's this all about?"

"Nothing! Nothing big." Mel snapped. "We got a coded message from the Taloned Sire and the Loose Cannon. Says they want us downwind pronto in the rift void. No questions. Just watch our asses, and drop all the gravity bombs we got if anybody tails us. See? Now, no more transmissions for a while. Just burn those engines for what they're worth. The Sire will recompense us later.

"Now, out for now! Till we're in sight of the big guns on the Sire, fly hard! Out!"

Roland shut off his com and stared for a grimy moment at the bulwark sides of the companion ship streaming in the redshift. Mel had just secretly told him several things, none of them good. Firstly, no other ships were waiting. The Taloned Sire and the Loose Cannon hadn't sent any messages. Secondly, neither ship had any gravity bombs in stock. It was a bad hand of poker Mel had just played.

Roland didn't believe that bluff would have fooled a dockhand. The two ships broke through a veil nebula. The full brightness of the central region's gaseous, crowded mass of stars came up in view above them.

It was like some primitive god raging with x-rays, spewing accretion matter streams, and spattering shattered stars with tidal forces too rapid and complex for even the strongest onboard navigational computer to configure and visualize.

They rode the hyper storms. They trusted their intuition in spaces where there was nothing else. Days came and went.

Silence from behind. The crews took shifts; Mel stayed on stimulants and never left his seat, refusing to come out of MERGE.

Simone Borges tried to stay with him. She watched matter indicators till her hands shook. There was no keeping up with an old huffer like Mel. He could live on the stim. He'd replaced a couple of livers already.

Borges found nothing outside but normal heavy freighters and metallic planetoids, seared and bare.

Tangeonprioc had been the only semblance of normalcy Borges had known in months. It was the closest thing to real civilization this close to the galactic core. Back in the Perseus Arm, the civilized world would pay well for their cargoes. Out here, it was station law. You kept what you got with your guns and your wits. She'd been negotiating a leading part in a virtreal synth holo. It would have left her some nice royalties at the big drop city and a bit of prestige to boot.

Boada had been bidding on a piece of Predecessor artwork. But when Mel radioed everyone back to the ships, all that was over. Marauders sometimes took down whole stations; then they disappeared, plunging toward the massive black hole at the very center of the galactic core. They lived there along the event horizon. Some say they came out transformed and demonic, having ventured into some other realm.

183

Some said that was how even the great Predecessors had become corrupted and lost. Lost in the spirit as well as the flesh. Boada came over with a cigar of Pleiadian red. "To be home on the islands of Chrysalis Isla."

"To be anywhere but here," Simone replied, thinking of the domes and gardens at Tangeonprioc. They seemed ominous to her now, as if she was leaving them forever.

Perhaps, she thought, the real universe was a nightmare of radiation factors, menacing gravity wells, and icy bits of rock floating somehow wrong in glowing distances. Ever more darkly with distance and ever more wrong. Perhaps that was reality, and all of mankind's cities and days were but a fleet-footed dream.

She shuddered.

"You're brooding Simone. Think happy thoughts." Boada said with a smirk.

The cigar tasted good. The stars took on a more familiar aspect. She remembered the thrill of flight school days. The rush and power of heavy-metal, space bending, gravity squeezing, field shielded, cannon laden hyper yacht at her fingertips.

Enough to make you squirm.

The two ships careened through the hyper gamma spaces. The galactic core overloaded their crew's sensory input with vast swarms of gravitational data. The crews doggedly maintained their flight pace.

Days and nights onboard went by. Now even the hugeness of the plume was edging toward its more typical perspective.

Finally, even Mel went off stim and withdrew from MERGE. He crawled into a sleep inducer and had his arteries bathed with recombinants. He looked fresh as a day at the beach when he came up to the bridge again.

He had put on a newly pressed dress uniform with a big Union Jack on the right breast. Then, shaved and pretty, he cast himself over to the Serpentine's big holoscreen.

"Hello, hello, hello, boys and girls!" Mel said brightly. His teeth were white and his skin clear with micro lifts.

Roland slid his MERGE helmet off with the sweat and stench of days.

"Ohhh, Mel. Is it over?"

Mel was delighted. "Roland, me boy, I can smell you across the vacuum. Go take a bath. Whatever was tailing us back at Tangeonprioc didn't have the steel to run with the big boys. I'd venture to say we're clear. Dig out your favorite virtreal and go have some good, safe…cyber fun!"

Roland stared unbelieving at the hologram of Mel.

"Heck with you Mel! When we hit Imperial space I want a bonus."

Mel was gleeful; "Mercenaries. You gotta love them."

Then the claxons and sirens burst into full volume.

Gravity simulators went wild on both ships. Every object not battened down went flying off in different directions.

Borges was MERGED, "Spatial distortions! List to port hard; we've got anomalies out of smooth space! Jagged edged, moving, linear event horizons! Radiation flares, temperature contrasts, moving out full ahead!" For all the urgency in her voice, she was steady.

The crew watched as the universe ripped open.

Boada groaned, "Tu Madre!" and plunged himself into a cannon cockpit.

Amazingly, like two canyons of darkness and lightning springing out of a sea of normal space, a sputtering of white dwarfs and neutron stars the size of moonlets came rising like an eighteenth-century balloon show. Comets and bits of asteroids, Predecessor station ruins, busted planets; a hurricane menagerie spilled before them.

Twisting in the storm, their ships fought to maintain equilibrium. "What the devil is this?" Mel roared across the com.

Tidal forces battered the crews of the two ships. Wild variations of sensory input burned and confused their minds. Only the most primitive parts of their brains were of any use to them now as reptilian and mammalian instincts scrambled for survival.

Borges saw them first. They were riding on columns of twisting lightning.

Rising out of the distortion canyons as if on the edge pole of a singularity. They were fifteen silhouettes of battlewagons dressed out of luxury yachts the size of small liners.

Roland's voice came across the com among the noise of CCCE Empires, "Should have kept the pedal down a bit longer eh Mel?"

A moment's pause among the noise, then: "Guess so. Give 'em what you got Roland, this ain't a trade negotiation. Fire at will."

Dansky needed no further instructions. He'd been making matter cannon since he was a kid. "Let's party!"

The big guns sang into the distortion canyons.

Perseus Arm: Luxus
University World, 4185

The candy-apple-red yacht darted out of hyper at the edge of the Luxus system flawlessly, almost recklessly. Its navigational coordinates had to be recent, fresh out of Deneb 4. It negotiated satellites and stations like there had been trial runs.

There hadn't. The pilots were simply good, very good.

System police barely had time to raise eyebrows and alerts. Then priorities and override codes cast in. The yacht was permitted to continue toward the second planet without even having to register title. It broke atmosphere without hesitation, slowing only a little then, coasting toward the mirror seas.

There wasn't a scratch on it.

Obscenely expensive, seductively luxurious, the yacht was embossed with the name RIPTIDE in letters two meters high on either side. It looked frighteningly out of place when it water ported on the placid inland sea of Lake Lux.

Yet there it was among a cache of small, white, in-system shuttles, tugs, transports and water ships.

Vincent Leavel noticed the red yacht early that same morning from an elevated maglev train that ran along the waterfront.

He smiled when he saw the Riptide's oversize hyperdrives. The lines of the yacht were sleek, sexy, bent forward as if ready for action.

"Hot, quick, and easy." He whispered to himself, straining his neck to get a better look at it. The lure of interstellar travel hadn't left him when he took to studying Architecture at Luxus.

The yacht made the topic of several conversations at the university canteen, mostly of older students who had flight experience like Vince.

By evening, however, most had forgotten it, but not Vince. He spent the day reminiscing over the high and deep spaces he'd known while active as a Guildsman. The life of starships, and those who go where they want to, because they want to.

The yacht was on his mind when he saw the man in white. It was a couple of nights later at club Twenty-Five-Twenty-five, and he knew the man in white had to be the owner of the red yacht. The white suit of an officer, Pleiades Confederation. On Chrysalis Isla, capitol of the Pleiades, such wealth as the yacht was not uncommon.

The man in white had silver roses clipped to oversize cuffs; the silver rose of the King of the Pleiades. Only given to those who had shown incomparable valor in battle.

So, an honored officer, perhaps retired, touring Luxus of all places. Who was this man, and what was he doing onworld?

Vince took a long swig of apple wine and watched dancer's meringue among the orchids and layer cake fountains of the club. He watched the man in white mingling with the crowd. To the sides of the man, always in the shadows, there were two others. They were not wearing white if fact their clothing seemed purposefully dark. The first was a very tall one with a handlebar mustache and a large brimmed hat typical of the Pampas on the planet Rubio. The other was stocky. He had a Mohawk haircut and a golden horn where his left ear should have been.

Expensive jewelry adorned them both.

Vince knew it wasn't mere jewelry. He recognized the crystalline cyber equipment of the finest make when he saw it. The man in white and his two companions were pilots-very rich pilots. Higher grade crystalline cyber equipment could only be afforded by wealthy governments and the underworld. There was nothing on this planet of old books and educational tapes to attract such men.

Yet there they were.

Slender wolves come hungrily into the forest.

They were losing the battle. The merciless double sun of Baal One seared down on the landscape as blood and bodies hit the stones in a hurricane of violent death. Seconds seemed slowed to hours as Harry kept the armored ground tank plowing forward into the beams of red and blue.

Infantry shields popped with sickening thunder as organs and limbs exploded. Over and over his comrades were dying in a storm of blood as the enemy came on.

The air was pink with it. Among the intolerable screaming, a vortex of motion and carnage swept encompassing a path around his unit.

Miraculously, he lived.

His mouth vomited bile as his shields failed under the pressure of enemy fire. The heat of the unshielded atmosphere came up in a burning, radioactive stench-filled wave. He gripped his cyber helmet reflexively and his hover tank lunged forward...

Waking with a scream, Harry shot forward in the bed. Flailing in the lonely dark at shadows and battles worlds away, he despaired.

It was always the same dream; that day when he embraced the rushing torrents of Hell and he had become something else. Something he had never thought of. Someone he had never known. Inescapable. Inevitable. Indomitable.

The hover tanks, the heat, the exploding men, the dying...their dying-and he holding his ground, remaining in place. First through the shock, then the disbelief, the wonder-he was still alive-disbelief again-but how?

Sitting back, he oriented himself. He was sweating.

The war was over he thought; we won that battle. Calming himself, steeling his emotions; I am on Luxus and my quarry will soon have its wages for the deeds of that day. Soon, soon, soon.

There were treatments. Doctors could prescribe things to make the nightmares go away, but Harry would have none of that. Never forgive, never forget. The horror and the pain were a part of him now. They defined an element of his strength and perceptions. With each friend he remembered killed before him, his resolve grew like a rancid beast.

It was a dragon curled around his heart.

Leyla Veronica lived with Vincent in a terraced apartment that hung, with thousands of others, afforded shelter and shade, among sequoia-like arboriforms whose roots were twisted down and down into the soil since before the dawn of human flight. The towers and their hanging apartments had been magnificently commingled with the ancient trees with a minimum of environmental intrusion. One of the tenets of the Neo-Wrightians who'd settled the University world. They managed to slip humanity on that fair world gently; with a velvet glove onto a soft hand. Like surgeons, do as little damage as possible when intruding; look for the natural order of things. Patterns and balances.

Each quiet morning on that placid university world, Vince and Leyla would take a casual breakfast of pita bread and sushi before merging with their educational programs. In the holograms realms of the university files, AI personalities of professors long since physically dead interacted with students born on worlds undiscovered in the professors' eras. Leyla was studying Interstellar Trade Law. Vince had given up flying to study Space Engineering and Terraforming.

The sense of purpose which Vince had discovered in Architecture and Engineering was complete and saturating. His mind was filled with the possibilities of settlements on the various worlds he'd seen.

Monastic villages set on ruddy stacks, floating cities held safe in gravitational bubbles, aqueducts housing millions across desert-scapes. Mankind had taken a vicious and violent smackdown on its progress since the Arcturian wars. He would be part of a new Renaissance in the Sagittarius Arm. Progress. Restoration of things as it were. Project after project, the strange young man from an unknown backwater world had managed to earn the grudging respect of his professors.

Only Leyla thrilled him more than his studies. They would lay awake at night and dream of the life they would make together. They would have three children. Alexandra, Leah, and Victor. They hadn't decided who would come first. Sometimes Vince would catch Leyla going cyber and toying with gene combinations.

It was a good life they were building. It was Vince's third, he often thought. His days on Rip would come to mind occasionally and a quiet longing for Charon and the life they never had. Then he would remember flying the Taloned Sire, punching into a wormhole and finding a hyperstring to a corner of the galaxy where humanity was unknown. The galactic halo. That was his second life.

He closed his mind to them: If I am to live it is to be in the present. Anything else is a death of shadows. He lived for the present, then, and deepened his love for Leyla. For their future.

He looked at his sushi. "Any tea on, Babe?"

"Right here." Leyla set it before him.

"Thanks," He thought, incongruously; *big slender wolves come into the forest.*

She held up a house com, "Hypercast!" She smiled excitedly.

"What is it?"

"Fashion show from Chrysalis Isla!"

Another one, Vince forced a smile.

They watched the show for a while. In the holoviewer, they were "right there." Vince tried his best to enjoy it for her.

Elegant models strutted along a catwalk with the Kings Royal gardens in the background. The crowd was huge. Vince wondered how many, like them, actually sat on other worlds.

A messenger in a formal dress approached them.

"A most urgent call." He said. "You must leave."

"Rats." Leyla glared at Vincent. The holo shut off.

The fashion show, the crowd, and the royal gardens disappeared. They were back in their breakfast porch overlooking the forest.

187

Vince answered the "urgent call" and the hologram changed. They were in the piloting cabin of the Taloned Sire. Millin Quinoa, six-foot-two and blue as a parrotfish, stood smiling at them. Sagamore Salvatore's churlish, stocky visage sat curled and watching.

Leyla scowled, "Oh great, it's your friends from your life in transportation."

Sagamore raised a disapproving eyebrow.

"Transportation?"

Millin shut her out completely.

"Captain!" Millin howled with joy. The giant man would ever and always see Vince the chain breaking hero. Even after the micro lifts and nano rejuvenation that made Vince seem younger now than when Millin had first met him years before.

Vince beamed. Leyla stepped out of the holo and was gone.

"Rogues!" she snapped tightly and gave him a sidelong glance.

Vince sobered. "Sorry guys. You know she's...kind of funny about my old days."

Sagamore sat up indignantly. "Transportation? That's how she sees us? We're Galactic star merchants, baby!"

"Well, she's afraid I'll fly off and not come back."

"Sure Vinny, she looks terrified." Sagamore chortled.

Vincent sighed, "Yeah, well. What's the occasion?" he asked.

A look of apprehension passed between the two pilots. Millin finally spoke "Got a strange one here, Cappy. Old Mel "No deal", DePaulo says he's got a job for the Sire. But he won't take us on without you. Says it's really dangerous. Says he's been tailed through three star systems.

"Says somebody's setting him up. He needs you, says you're the only one with the 'magic'."

Sagamore growled, "Which I take offense to! I'll show him some magic of my own." He pointed his thumb at his chest, "I have magic."

Millin shot him a look, rolled his eyes, "Yeah, but that's the way it is. That's the situation."

Vince looked sadly at the interior of his old ship. "No way boys. I'm out of the mercenary trade. I've got another life now. Nothing against Mel, but if he wants he Sire it's without me. Tell him the answer is no."

Sagamore dropped his eyes. Millin showed mixed emotions. Happy to see Vince stand on principle, he was still disappointed they wouldn't be sharing a good gig.

Sagamore stood up, "Twenty G's." He rolled his fingers. "Come on Capt'n." He placed an imaginary MERGE helmet on and spread his arms as if he were merged and flying. "The stars are calling. Twenty G's-for each of us."

Vince looked at the hologram Sag. "The Stars are calling? Did you see that blonde that just stepped out of the holo?"

Millin's blue face just stared. He took a puff on a stogie and shrugged as if to say twenty G's was twenty G's.

Vince swallowed hard. What did Mel get into this time? He wasn't smuggling protected antiquities off Luna this time, for certain. Unless he'd acquired the Mona Lisa.

"That is a lot of Coin." Vince said. The temptation of easy money seemed to ooze through him like molasses. Leyla was listening outside the holo.

"Won't buy you a cup of coffee in Hell," she said.

She placed some roses on an old psalm book, but Vince couldn't see.

Vince considered her with a sidelong glance.

"Right. Not this time. Tell Mel I'm out."

Sagamore's larking attitude fell like a heavy-metal field accelerator through balsawood. He shook his head, waved, and stepped out of the holo.

Millin looked at his old friend.

"Look, there are a couple of stations just out system I wanted to check out. We'll stall Mel. I got half a month's pay says you change your mind. Besides, you could open a first-class office on Khita with this kind of capital. See yah!" He ended the transmission before Vince could respond.

Leyla was adamant.

"I want to go too, but I can't," Leyla said. "I want to go too, but I shouldn't. Sheesh, at least when you were a smuggler you could make a decision."

"I'm not going!" Vince snapped.

But Vince was alone when Mel called the next day. Mel said there were things he hadn't told Millin and Sagamore, things Vince should know. Things about Roland Dansky.

Vince didn't like the sound of that. He agreed to a meeting.

Galapagos Not
Uninhabited moon, Luxus system

There were forty-two moons in the Luxus system. Eighteen of them were littered with typical nasty service stations and drop cities that somehow appeared and became permanent without anyone ever really knowing when, or even why. The rest were frigid wastelands of ice and rock scoured by lonely prospectors, weirdo loners, or no one at all. Mel arranged for a meeting on one that was virtually uninhabitable because of a nasty ice sheet that had a bad habit of caving in. Ammonia oceans underneath the ice sheet had vanished eons ago leaving an unstable surface.

Two ships, The Taloned Sire and Mel's Monkey, came to rest in shallow pools of ammonia beneath that ice sheet. Jutting broken cliffs of ancient shoreline glowed in the distance. Mel and Vince walked casually through puddles of ammonia that would have been killed them if their EVA fields ever failed. They tromped along, Vince grim as a corpse.

Mel was nervous, shaky.

"Damn it Mel, was this really necessary?" Vince waved at the geography. "How many light years did you push that tub just for me?"

Mel looked like he'd spent his last hundred credits in a cheap virtreal and synth den. He had suitcases under his eyes. His usually fit figure seemed burdened by freshly remembered sin and culpability.

"Yeah, Vinny. Yeah. You can pull this off. You got some kind of dumb luck."

Vince lowered his gaze. *He's in something real raunchy. If I had a brain in my head or a hair on my bottom, I'd get the flock out of here right now.* "And what about Roland?" he asked.

"I came a long way, Vinny. I pushed it through a hundred or two. We were at the core. Tangeonprioc. I need you, man." He was dissipated, on stim for far too long. Vince figured he smelled bad beneath the EVA field.

"Somebody's on my back. They hit us in the rift void and took down the Serpentine. I tried to fight but there were fifteen ships.

"They're professionals. They're still on me somehow.

"Who knows what information they got from the Serpentine? I need somebody that can take on a fight when it comes along."

"Don't stroke me, Mel." Vince shot back. Yet even as he said it he enjoyed the stroke. Vince the invincible. His reputation was fooling even himself. His legend. He missed it. Missed the glory of battle. He knew it was a bad deal. If he pulled this off they'd be drawing yarns about it from the Outworlds to the black-market on Deneb 4. *Yeah, they killed his friends and he came out of retirement. Fifteen ships didn't deter him.*

The odds were the murderers were still in the picture.

Slender wolves come hungrily into the forest.

Vince remembered Roland playing his guitar and reciting poetry on Chrysalis Isla. Telling tall tales of exotic worlds and manicured castles.

Let's Party!

"Who else was on the Serpentine besides Roland?" He asked.

"Dahl, Laureano, Willis, Hornidge. They showed them no mercy. They were savages. Worse sort of mutant ice-monkey pirates spawned in faulty drive sections. Filth. Real killers."

"Borges?"

"Yeah. But she's alive. They were taunting us. They wanted me to go back a die trying to save them."

"You should have." Vince sneered.

"Screw you."

Vince turned and walked away. "I'll do it. I want to find these pukes and cut them into subordinate units on a stasis loop."

"I knew I could count on you, Leavel. Everybody knows your loyalty to your crews. Don't you want to know what we're hauling?"

Vince started climbing onto the Sire. "Just pay me when we're done. And get more firepower on that tub next time you port out."

Mel stared at the closing airlock and remembered the screams of the Serpentine's crew.

"I already have," he said.

The Sire's integral anti-gravity wailed, the ship banked and made its way from underneath the treacherous ice sheet. Vince smiled a narrow, diminished smirk when he saw the cool arm of the Milky Way appear on the navigational visuals as Mel's coded block came up. Destination: Chrysler City. Right in the heart of Cyborgian Central Space. Old money; gilded skyscrapers half a millennia-old. Two thousand square miles of sweeping, smooth, cultivated lines of megacity pointing up with an unembarrassed phallic macho glitter.

An old pimp with a title.

Chrysler City, grand and ancient!

Chrysler City, the Big Bull.

Yet beneath the perfectly ordered commerce was something else. Under the manicured gardens hanging cantilevered a hundred stories up, huddled a people fed but empty. Below the spindly aqueducts and maglevs, trellises spun like gossamer webs, lay down a soulless population bent on the next sensation. The next idol to hit the virtreal channels, the next synthetic opiates to be pumped into their tanned and perfect bodies, the blood of saints if they could find it.

Babylon would have blushed. Ancient legends had given various names to the anteroom of Hades, but they hadn't known Chrysler City. Perfect and pretty as the nineteen-year-old clone the five-hundred-year-old millionaire just transplanted his brain into.

Marvels!

The sight of its miles-high skyscrapers could still stop a well-traveled pilot with awe. Even as one sensed the slime under the jutting towers, one heard the roar of the big bull. Vince, merged with the winds of hyper streams cool against his cheeks, and his arms stretching the ships spatial fields into the arched filaments of the radio continuum structures of the high galactic halo, and shot away.

Away from Luxus (it dropped into nothing), he sensed the old familiar power of the frigate. His spirit soared with the ship. His old life came back to him like a familiar glove. He let the academic world slip away, jumping back into the conflux of acid intensities and ribald shattering paths

Sixty-eight light-years to the Big Bull, Chrysler City.

Surprisingly, Leyla hadn't cursed or even made much of a fuss when he finally told her he was going. At the harbor where the starships water ported, Vince had taken a perverse sort of pride at the sight of his old frigate The Taloned Sire. Match it against the Riptide any day. Leyla looked it over coolly, surveying the hull that had been Vince's true realm for so many years. She'd kissed him quietly, seeming as if a part of her felt he would fly away and never come back.

The hyper streams shimmered as the high spaces carried him away.

Sagamore smiled at the sight of his old captain back at the MERGE.

"Not what you expected?" Millin asked accusingly.

"He belongs here." Sagamore countered.

Millin tossed his MERGE helmet quietly into his seat.

"I need a beer. Maybe a little neuron-restore? I'm going to my cabin to get my system retreaded and a night of long sleep on the autodoc."

He belongs here, Sagamore thought again stubbornly.

Here, at the helm of the Sire with a billion stars at his breath. Any which way to go he chooses-and nobody daring to say different.

Here... here!

Steve Allman

Chrysler's World, Cyborgian Central Space, Orion Galactic Spiral Arm 4185.

Morton Definity's office sat perched atop the Customs and Imports building like the small oblong on a bishop's headpiece. High and wide, he could see a huge stretch of the planet. What he couldn't see out his gargantuan windows, a model provided; a holo of the planet spinning over his roundtable. The turning continents of Chrysler's World glimmered continually, night into the day-a display for his constant reminder that it was he in charge to serve and protect.

"Insidious infestations of errant life forms, innumerable violations of contraband, addicting virtreels, economic chaos..." He would announce, "You've met your match."

He was the antibody of loose scum. Nothing was to come on the world without his permission. Not a bug, not a shipment of software, not an illegal looking to sell her smile in the virtreels and fly off later lusted after and rich.

Yet, things did get in. That's when "Sportin' Morton" played a little stamping game on the bugs, on the software, and occasionally on some illegal butt too. Rarely, however, did a prize ever deliver itself so neatly as the stoolie that walked into the vast and ostentatious office that bright morning as Morton stood gazing at the model of the world he watched over.

191

It was an eerie little puppet of an android armed with top clearance codes and a perfectly disguised payoff jack as a bribe.

"I have come a long way," the android said, and Morton doubted it not one bit.

The make of the thing was ancient. Scars and numerous burn marks decorated it like medals from the fray of battle. Along one side someone had welded a couple of hundred military I.D. tags, the kind encoded with holo messages solders make up in case they are killed in combat.

If one was to play them, Morton realized, the loving last words of many young men could be heard. They were dust now.

The effect was unsettling, even for Morton. The droid seemed to have dragged itself across some time barrier to carry the words of the lost into the present.

"I see," Morton said. "Yes, make yourself comfortable. Any upgrades or system overhauls I can offer? You must be exhausted!"

"Oh no, Mr. Definity. Only my outer shell has remained unworked. My innards, I assure you, are pristine."

The droid staggered and jerked occasionally, it looked like a glorious madness had come over it. A madness that had come to delight in something.

"I am but a messenger." The thing went on. "I've come to deliver a criminal into your capable hands. A master thief, rouge. An expert at slipping through planetary customs barriers such as yours."

"Really?" Morton smiled. This was either going to be a very low skid-row hitter or worse. "What part of our star system have they violated so far? I assume they have a ship, a crew?"

A go-cart?

The head of the android shook then, like the little dogs one sees on the dashboards of air cars. It squeaked.

Pristine innards my arse. Someone had gone lengths to make this thing as weird as possible.

"Yes, a crew. A good crew and a good ship. Gangsters, thieves, and smugglers. The ship is not only in the system, but it's also on the world right now."

Morton's ire rose in disbelief.

"No way!"

"Way!"

The android hand shot up as if invisible cords yanked it. "No hurry! Wait, I must finish. My people, who which to remain anonymous, will pay you highly if-" He looked around comically and gestured for Morton's ear.

Morton leaned forward.

The Android whispered in his ear.

Morton opened his mouth to respond but the droid suddenly began folding itself into a defensive dimensional vortex.

It seemed to be stepping backward, hastily returning from whence it came. Morton had seen that particular move once in an old war holo.

Finely tuned wormholing!

It was like seeing a ghost.

Smoke and mirrors!

Morton went to his desk to replay the whole conversation. It showed only him speaking to the empty air. The credit jack appeared in his hand as if out of thin air. He looked at the jack. It was the only evidence the conversation took place at all.

That and the transport data on a ship just in from the Perseus Arm. An odd, old warhorse called The Taloned Sire.

When the orders came in from Definity's office, Unit 1088 felt the sudden adrenaline rush of the hunt. It was strong this time, more strong than he had ever experienced in the hive mind. Definity had sent out a high priority then. In the faceted visions of his collective patrol, images of a multitude of faces moving through the city shown in his mind.

Faces blandly pursuing pleasures or goods took on a new intrigue and menace. One of the wild humans and his crew were fallen now into a trap. With that thought, 1088 felt a rush of pride in his superiority as part of the Cyborgian collective. Of course, even Definity wasn't collective. Individuals, self-interest, freedom-illusions. Yet Definity had proven a fine caliber.

His patrolmen scanned, scanned, scanned. There! A sleek looking man with pre-imperial genome-an Outworlder for sure. Common enough, but the description fit.

Vincent Leavel. Beside him, Pleiadian but feral-Sagamore Salvatore, bright blonde hair, and a muscular build.

Another facet; a large ObscuroFrioian with facial tattoos. Millin Quinoa. 1070 floated above the galleries and shops of the Galleria Canyon. It stretched for miles, but the suspects' positions had been established with pinpoint accuracy. Alerts went out to proceed with extreme caution, suspects are armed and dangerous.

Whoever had butchered Roland and the crew of the Serpentine hadn't surfaced. Everything had the look of a simple under-the-codes smuggling job to avoid tariff charges. At every inch of the run Sagamore drew deep scans for hyper tidal movements. Nothing came up. No-deal DePaulo didn't appear to be being tailed by anyone.

No deal.

No tail.

Vince didn't like the symmetry of this whole thing. If it hadn't been for his murdered friends and the possibility of retribution, Vince would be back at the university working on the design of a Ring World for one of his classes. Even more than the money, it had been his chance to avenge Roland that had brought him here.

He stopped in his tracks.

Quinoa almost fell over him. "What's going on?" He looked around uneasily, first at Vince then at the crowd. "Something's not right. This is a setup. They're not after the goods or we'd have been hit already. They're not after Mel, or they'd certainly have acted by now. Somebody wants something to happen but I just can't seem to figure it out."

They paused by a fountain of broken tiles artistically decorated with sea horses and Rigellian water spiders shaped from the mosaics.

"Somebody got a reason?" Millin wondered and opened a can of ale. He sat down by the fountains.

"You guys cross anybody lately?" Vince asked.

"Square deals Vinny, everybody gets paid, and everybody goes home. You know me. Besides, Mel was looking for you.

"He said it had to be you."

I knew I could count on you, Leavel. Everybody knows your loyalty to your crews.

"That's it! They want me. They killed Roland to bait me. Then they broke Mel, sent him with that patsy story to lure me here."

"Why not just kill you?" Millin asked.

"I don't know. You get back to the Sire. Try to get her out of here. I'll stay here and bait them."

"Captain?"

"Just do it, Millin, get my ship out of this trap, and I'll catch up with you later."

Millin hadn't been gone but a few minutes when Vinny heard a woman's voice calling out in the crowd.

"Vinny! Vinny!" She was calling him.

It was Leyla on a luxurious new airbike.

She smiled. "Come on, you! Private limo, first-class cabin on the starliner! Airbike!

"You're a dear. How could I have thought you'd run off and leave me?"

Vince watched another piece of this strange puzzle fall into place.

"Oh, no. Oh, no! Leyla, you have to get out of here. Go back to the starport and take another liner home." He said.

Time seemed to slow down then, as if in some dream of a stasis. The Galleria Canyon went mad, and in the confusion, Vince felt one part of his life slip forever from his grasp. Cops were coming out of the Galleria Canyon walls past glistening elevator shafts from an upper air car ramp. Most of them were on air bikes, but there were floor patrols too.

The main halls were packed with civilians that would slow down police fire, Vince thought. Give him time to find a way out.

"Sagamore, it's a freezer! It's a freezer!" Vince said into his comlink. Hopefully, Millin had already warned him.

Vince pulled his disruptor. Too late, he was suddenly grabbed. Two figures from the crowd-plainclothesmen?

No. The man in white's bodyguards Vince had seen at club "Twenty-Five-Twenty-five".

"Easy there." The golden horned one said, chuckling.

They slipped something onto his head. Leyla was screaming. They shoved him against a wall hard. When he swung around, they were gone. He tried to pull the thing from his head but it wouldn't come off.

The crowd was livid, everyone pointing and talking at once. The men had placed a perceptual recorder on his head. On one of the screens advertising in the galleria Canyon, Vince could see a live-action cast.

They were casting his perceptions.

Frantically he glanced around the mall. It was on every screen. He saw the cops coming for him-so everyone was seeing his arrest. He looked at Leyla, then away. She was broken down and sobbing. He didn't want the cast to show her. He thought of running or fighting but it was futile. They were all around him now, yelling in synchronicity and pointing their weapons.

A huge noise came up and Vince realized it was the Sire. He raised his head and watched the ship banking away above the geodesic skylight vault of the mall. Millin was making a break for it. The cops were still yelling and Leyla was shaking, hiding her head under her arms. Vince let his weapon drop and stared them blankly in the face as they came to cuff him.

Millin fought his way out of the system that day alone. The cops had taken Sagamore too. It was all over the galactic hypercasts. All over. Whoever set Vinny up had the whole arrest cast through relays from one end of known space to the next.

Vinny was already pretty well known in certain circles. Ever since he'd rescued Elias Tristan and Tristan's passengers back in the Pleiades, he was some sort of folk hero.

Now he was the talk of the galaxy. If they had intended to humiliate him, they did. But it backfired. With a little time, his folk-hero status returned, now with the special edge of being arrested in front of the entire galaxy. They sold his perceptions of the arrest as a virtreal tape and it was a trillion seller. Untold numbers of people felt his cool nerves, his quick wits, his impending sense of the trap. They felt his will to sacrifice himself for his men and his ship, his agony at the realization that Leyla had been lured into the trap also.

It was Art. Pure, real, and perfectly tragic. People loved it. But it didn't stop Transhuman Cyborgian Central from sentencing him to seventy years' ground labor on the coldest penal colony in their prison system. Vincent Leavel, Sagamore Salvatore, and the unlikely Leyla Veronica all went down together to Ophelia's World penal colony, armpit of the galaxy.

"The Chrysler City Take Down"
-Winteroud Sole, Caldris

194

Ossa

Steve Allman

In the constructs of Deneb Four's cybernetic realms there existed places and beings only the human imagination had known before. Pure spiritual realities where only thought was needed to make it so. The Cyborgian overlords romped in a virtual universe of their fashioning. Yet, like Nebuchadnezzar before them, they would find their idol had feet of clay.
-Princess Clairissa Maggio, Caldris, "Deneb IV, Empire of Light and Darkness."

Frigate class attack ship First Strike moved through the Denebian high command's Hyper Gateway coolly on impulse power, requiting controls to deep Cyborgian O'Neil monoliths and orbit net holos. Onboard, the ship's officers were grimly silent; avoiding general Ossa's gaze in what had become an ugly ritual.

Only the general knew what took place on these visits to the capitol world. However, the whole staff knew the fierce and diamond-hard general dreaded these meetings with a distaste that bordered on revulsion.

For general Vega Ossa, trips to the private realms of Omm 6X were unpleasant and incomprehensible. He knew the overlords were ancient, but their origins were privileged information. Anybody's guess. Omm, however was known-in his original Human form he had been Ambassador to the Arcturians before the war.

He only knew that the being he would observe, the halls he would traverse, and all Omm's attendants were not physically real.

Yet their realities would be as consistent-and possibly fatal-as if their physical selves could be dragged away and weighed in real space. This was no harmless dream.

For Ossa, it was a nightmare. David Omm 6X was his direct superior, had been for several centuries. There appeared no end in sight for their association. It seemed to Ossa that Omm enjoyed the irony of their positions.

Ossa had directed fleets into battle with pirates, he had engaged small packs of Marauders in uncharted space, and he'd watched attack ships burning in the Crab Nebula a mere hundred meters from his own. But in the Transhuman cyber world, Omm was a demigod and Ossa a flea. Omm would never let him forget it.

Flea, underling, peon.

Ossa registered in the main reception area of Fleet command and was called forward. The transition in the Transhuman cyber hologram world would be imperceptible. He took a solemn glance out a magnificent portal at the capitol's towers, perhaps his last? The shimmering plastisteel and plexiturqouise ornamented structures loomed endlessly up and down, lost in the grey distances of the sky and distant ground.

They were vertical aqueducts and roads. Linear cities traversing planet to orbit without missing a beat. Ancient gardens hung from their sides, cultivated since the dawn of the Space Ages. The real world. His world.

"Walk this way, please! Welcome to the Halls of Omm." A naked android styled female with long butterfly wings guided him. Someone's idea of public art.

Sometimes the Halls of Omm would be familiar, but as many times as not they would shift to strange caverns, unnerving walks on uncharted moons without atmospheres. One time he walked onto the surface of a balloon being on some Jovian world. Omm had looked over smiling. Ossa knew if he'd slipped off the balloon creature Omm would have let him fall through the icy eight-hundred kilometer an hour methane winds until he reached the deep layers of the atmosphere and the gravity crushed him into the dark liquid metallic helium.

Anything was possible in Omm's game. Riding bareback with a stampeding herd of giant spiders, Omm had snickered, "It's a tribute to my ex-fiancé. I call it 'shopping with the Art collectors'".

Today it was, fortunately, the familiar hall Omm favored most-the luxurious baths of Caracalla, faithfully reproduced, Roman's and all. The Romans were sentient programs, Omm's companions. As Omm moved in and out of their virtual world, he was perceived by them as a god.

Omm had once asked him, "General, how do you know this world isn't real, and yours the phantasm?"

Ossa had felt a strange brew of doubt turn in his stomach. Had Omm been sending him back after their meetings not into the real world, but merely a facsimile? Ossa pulled out the only defense he'd known in real war and Omm's virtual nightmares; his ability to face uncertainty and possible death with calmness, even curiosity, and sense of adventure. He gave the demigod a rueful, smile. He knew, at the bottom of things, Omm could never take the same dreadful defense that was, in the final analysis, no defense at all.

Omm had screwed up his face a moment then, seeing Ossa's answer in the attitude (Que Serra, Serra); Ossa's ability to stand on that precipice where Omm would have raged back in terror.

What this time, mighty Overlord?

Ossa felt the familiar ridiculousness of his forty-third century CC uniform and equipment walking through the gallery of naked Romans. In the center of the frigidarium, a bizarre golden figure of enormous size lounged. Omm 6X. Snakes writhed medusa-like eerily on his head.

"Ossa! Warrior, General, Star Farer!" Omm bellowed mockingly.

There came a second voice, "What news you bring from the frontier?" Ossa noted then Cicero standing in the water near Omm.

He held his head and hands cradled the stubs of his arms. The head had spoken.

"No news, Cicero. I come at Omm's beckoning." Ossa had traveled from the far end of Imperial Space, no small task.

Ossa leveled his gaze at them coolly. He struggled to maintain his dignity, to remember who he was. Who he was, however, was an ordinary soldier in a hellish universe where Omm's every thought was a harsh reality. Here he was not the commander of a fleet.

"Go away, Cicero!" Omm said, and the tortured creature shuffled angrily away. Whether Cicero was a construct of Omm's or an old general who'd failed an assignment was never explained to Ossa. He'd often wondered, knowing he'd die in the field before he let himself return to such a fate.

Cicero gone, Omm 6X leaned forward menacingly, his golden head huge, snakes writhing blackly. "Sixty-five hundred assassins and mercenaries have swarmed Ocho's World, raiding, pillaging, and leaving. CC resistance was a trifling embarrassment. The Governor of that planet has disappeared, fearing for his life perhaps, his indolence surely his culpability. He should have died defending his Capitol World. He is surely lost to CC, but I should take some comfort knowing he will play out the rest of his life hiding in Outworlder Suburra slums."

Ossa said nothing, he had heard the rumors. It was as if the Republics and CC were in an undeclared war. Fifteen hundred years of minor incidents were nothing to the trouble he sensed brewing now. Still, there was more. Hidden things, secret codes on the hyper casts. Things even fleet generals weren't privy to.

He was haunted by the sense that if men like him didn't learn the bigger picture soon, overlords like Omm would succumb to whatever trouble lay hidden-and take the rest of the human race with them.

"I want you to form a small force," Omm continued, "and linger in the region. Break up into Gaurdacostas if you would, subterfuge if you must. Do as you will. But I want some information on this lot of runaway criminals and old madmen that attacked the planet. They were effective, trained, well-led.

"Acquainted with the military Arts, someone of stature was behind them. A mind for you to measure yourself against. We suspect the syndicates in the republics are massing armies in toto now. Our concern is that they may make a run on the gateways in an attempt to control Cyborgian space."

That much, Ossa had gathered. The gateways were being beefed up with huge armies of deep-cyborg conscripts on auto flight programming. Where the conscripts were coming from was anybody's guess. Thousands of them had been assigned from the gateways to the Oort clouds at the edge of every gateway system. They were manning single person spheroid ships.

Kamikaze gravity bombs, every single one. It all must have been costing CC big money, but then again, dead men don't collect paychecks. And chances are life insurance was not in the contract. Mercenaries.

"Go then, you're dismissed. Remember, trouble's afoot!" Snake eyes glittered from a dozen tossing heads. Ossa saluted,

"Sir," he said tersely, turned and began walking. Departing, he could hear Omm's laughter following him back into real space.

Ossa never knew when he re-entered reality, but he was glad when he was certain he was there.

The whole exchange had taken but a few minutes.

His aircar was waiting on the car porch. Ossa could see an endless stretch of metal towers gleaming in the night of Deneb. Further down toward the ground, the buildings still were of the ornate stone the first terraformers had built of centuries before. At that level it was dark. They were minuscule compared to Deneb's Stratoscrapers; symbols of man's ingenuity and reason for an empire built on logic.

Ossa smiled grimly. Reason and order. What a farce.

If the trillions of inhabitants, the technocrats, the economists, the solders-if they could see what was at the top of their perfectly machined Empire-Ossa shuddered. He knew it was the generals that held the Cyborgian Empire together. The Government is Force. He looked at the night sky full of aircars.

The starships easing down from the heavens, the billions of citizens teeming at the center of human endeavor.

They all had him, and men and women like him, to thank for their secure existence.

Not, of course, that they would be grateful. More often than not they would take a fashionable anti-military political stance. Out of humanitarianism? No. No one wanted peace more than the men and women who had to stand in the line of fire. The inconsistencies of the public position toward the military defined pretzel logic.

During the Arcturian war, the air corps destroyed a whole civilization of innocent civilians and the public had been made to see it as a victory. Unbeknownst to the public however was the mass failure of the Cyborgian corps as a mental virus spread through their hive mind collapsing tens of thousands of ships and corpsmen at once. Since then the military had bred its autonomous soldiers-as had the Spartans. Ossa and his fleet were not subject to the Hive collective-he could access data streams, but only at will and for limited periods.

He stepped into the waiting aircar. Moreover, he knew, in truth CC was of two minds, the populace, and the overlords.

The aircar dipped into a stream of traffic and then higher into a government air path less crowded. He peered into the distance, some of the towers rose into space itself. His car rose into higher and higher streams, the view now becoming not unlike that of attack ships on a near approach, with the exception that it was a rare world that was built to such density.

Such pride he'd felt when was commissioned here. So long ago. Such a younger one, sure in himself.

Sure in the virtues of the Cyborgian Central Command: Reason and order.

One learns, however, one learns; there are no clean hands-only victors whitewashing their sins as they live well on stolen lives and murdered peoples. Rumor had it that Omm hadn't knowledge of the ruse that had taken down the Arcturians so long ago. Rumor had it. Either way...the Overlord seemed to have gone mad with the guilt.

He leaned back in a small comfort field, indicating food. Some fruit and drink slid out of a panel and Ossa took quiet sustenance.

He scanned the hive minds police files looking for bits that might provide a link to the Ocho's World fiasco. Several Sheriffs had taken up after bounty in the region. That was to be expected.

Accessing more priority codes on the region, he noticed bits and pieces of data streams trimmed and edited. A report from a deep space intergalactic probe had been stifled. Why? Such probes were the numerous stuff of universities who wondered whether Lepton spins in the deep void went left or right. What could such a mundane drone have found at that distance to warrant editing? He queried further under restricted access codes.

His air car bent to a more vertical angle but his gravity well didn't even ripple his drink. It was then he found an unedited file. The void drones had increased speed capabilities in the deep intergalactic black. Computer-generated dark matter calculations allowed them to run the void with little or no fuel cells, scooping the dark matter through a hyper shield that rested on the edge of dimensional boundaries. An unpredicted dark matter indicator had swelled in the void-something big, unnatural was indicated. Then the port went blank. Someone had edited out the drone's report.

Ossa was furious now with the editing. He queried the hive. The Hive knew nothing. Perhaps the probe had come out of hyper too quick? An unexpected matter indicator went off, and slashed its nerve endings? The anomalous matter that deep in the void might be unchanged since the big bang? Lepton frenzy. Something ugly?

Some kind of ship?

The hive was incredulous.

Ossa ran through field tracers for ship signatures. There were thousands, but the matter signature was huge, sudden, steep, still climbing when the report had been edited. He calculated the size of a ship at the point of editing-too big. Big as an O'Neil station. He kept searching through the signature files going back centuries, still, he found nothing. If humans built it, it should have been there in the records.

Predecessor?

Or had they edited even the record of the behemoth ship? How did they expect him to do his job if they never let him know what was going on? He had to be privy to the data! Deneb, far below him now, shown as a full globe with tendrils reaching out to numerous O'Neil's. It reminded him of nothing more untoward as Omm 6X's snake-infested head.

His ship the First Strike came into view-lean, mean, and gray as a ghost. She opened her docking bays and the military airlimo touched down without a sound. He let none of his frustration show as he strode onto his fleet leader's deck. A perceptible air of relief could be felt through the ship as he said, "Out system to Ocho's World, swirl the mesons!"

They made for the gate.

Deneb IV, Halls of Omm

Omm fondled a nymph for a few moments watching Cicero's greedy eyes follow him. He sneered at the construct- "Longing for what you cannot know?"

Cicero averted his gaze. "Humanity is stretched across half the galaxy. Life spans of even the moderately wealthy are averaging seven hundred years. The economy is generating wealth at an increasing weight. Such good tidings." His voice oozed sarcasm.

Omm let the snakes on his head draw toward Cicero. "Annnnd?"

"And it is all the Devils orchard soon. Why do we waste time with provincial pirates when more pressing matters howl at the gates? What of Bandor's research?"

"Away!" He bellowed, and the baths were gone. He thought of the galaxy and it appeared. Floating above the hologram stars he looked at the edge of the imperial domain and shuddered. A panic grabbed him, one that had haunted him for a thousand years with a terror more gripping than he or any of the other Overlords could fathom.

Among those terrors was another creeping ambiguity: Bandor base in the Diablo nebula, Siluria. They'd chosen the nebula for its inhospitableness. A good place to hide things, a good place to test the mettle of new weapons and systems.

But now the place seemed to have some association with the very terror they sought to abate.

He could access the complete store of human knowledge at a whim. He could possess any world his imagination could dream of, here in the hive mind. Yet the hive mind was not truly sentient-only the individuals that comprised it could possess that. There was no hive AI.

The coveted "Singularity" which mankind had at once feared and longed for like a savior had never appeared as intended. Intelligence remained the prerogative of the individual thing. Sentience had eluded the mass mind.

Only trends and megatrends remained its special province. Statistical realities. Omm's body, somewhere enclosed and sustained by technology, was still human.

Human, not human? Sentient, not sentient-subjective realities. Terror, however, that was still very human, handed down through sixty million years or so from smelly little burrowing mammals that ran and hid from Tyrannosauruses.

It was that part of him-the human part, that knew the terror and groveled madly now for hope. Hope that men like Ossa, standing in a hulk of metal careening about exploding nebulae and neutron stars, skirting death at every step, would fight the terror he felt gripping him like blackness on the edge of an event horizon.

Terror creeping and inevitable.

He despised men like Ossa for the very courage they possessed. To preserve that courage, to keep them from the madness that had gripped and incapacitated many of the overlords, they must be kept ignorant of what was coming. Ignorant until a weapon could be devised. Omm looked to Cicero, "Bandor's research is promising. But the element, or combination of elements, eludes us. There is still time. You fear?"

"Yes. Yes. I fear."

Harry's Tale
Chrysalis Isla: Capitol World, Pleiades Confederation
4210

Harry swung the net with ferocious ease. Dodging in a flurry of color, the Ahura-Mazda bird evaded the net for the third time, diving to lose the man. Again the net was flung with superhuman strength, the man stepping easily along with a steady unrelenting gait.

The dragon bird squealed with anger and confusion, turning a moment to face his pursuer knowing it would be a futile gesture.

If he engaged combat and managed to hack the man to bloody shreds, the man would continue fighting until victorious.

Caged, humiliated, beaten, the bird would then see the man appear the next day, without a scratch, at the front of cage bellowing with laughter at the whole affair. "It ain't over." he would say, and another time a hunt would begin. Futility ran vicious through the bird's small mind until it simply lay its dragonhead down and succumbed to its fate.

"Harry, you broke its spirit! Ha! What a luxury. Kick it around a bit, see if it will fight some more." Maximus Mercurio hovered about like a rogue comet, his gleeful face red with anticipation of pain. Maximus had one gear-war. Since returning from Baal One, his rage had been a weapon. A weapon Harry had directed into various nefarious activities. For Max, there was only war. Everything else was just waiting. Harry let the net drop. "The fun is out of it if there's no fight left in the thing. Besides, come on. I got something else to show you."

They strode together toward the docks where Harry's fleet lay being retooled. The Ahura Mazda's and most of the other birdlife of Chrysalis Isla weren't true birds. No, that famous world's abundance of darting, posing, singing, kaleidoscope profusion of feathers and wings weren't even native to the Pleiades. They'd been collected from a hundred planets, reengineered genetically over a thousand years. Only a tiny fraction were true birds with Earth lineage. People, however, still thought of them as birds.

A couple of workmen were running nano crew on the Riptide's red hull.

"Open the cargo bay! Let me see my new toy!" Harry waved his muscled arms like a conductor.

"You know Max, nothing's native in this cluster but steaming rocks. Rocks now buried under palms and ferns and flowers.

Those blue and white diamonds in the sky-they're much too young to have sprung all this. No, this is man's doing, and it's done like this-"

In the back of the bay was a large cage. Another Ahura-Mazda fluttered and turned in paces. They were fabulous creatures, dragon-like, possessing an elongated colored scale instead of feathers. It had been the emblem of Harry's Wife's family for generations. The Ahura Mazda estate, once known and famous on the planet, sat now hidden behind huge security domes. One could see out but one could not see in.

The emblem had emblazoned all of the businesses for centuries. Harry waved his arm at the cage "Another flyer to my collection."

Maximus Mercurio, ever the joiner, ready to die in a heartbeat for the beloved hero Harry Stark, said, "Magnificent, truly, Magnificent!" Harry could ask Max or any of his men to walk naked into a burning building and they would, with a salute. Harry had done more than that for them when he had turned around the retreat on Baal One. He had saved their lives, saved their honor, and organized them again after the war when society sought to cast the away as rubbage.

From the parapets of the estate, Harry could see the glimmer of the force domes that kept his flyers in and snooping eyes out.

Although they didn't obstruct his view of the cliffs and gentle waters beyond, from the outside his domes looked for the entire planet to see as immense chromium bubbles, which pleased Harry to no end. He would steal even the image of the estate from the planet. Looking down he could see his wife, Sanitaria, moving through the gardens forlornly, tending white roses.

At one time she peered down from the same parapets at a much younger Harry Stark when he wooed her. He was stunning in a white officer's uniform with a long sword. Her family's rejection of him was complete and humiliating. She loved him, thought of him constantly for a short period-then the weight of her family and friend's disapproval came down on her. He was not of the Aristocracy, and no number of sensual kisses, heroic stature, or gallant uniforms would change that in their eyes. He pleaded with her to see him before he went to the war, but she would not.

Her brothers had laughed at him standing outside the gates of the estate.

He glared at them, "It ain't over." he said, spun on his heel, and strode off to meet his unit.

BAAL ONE, PLEIADES CLUSTER 4210

The King of the Pleiades was well prepared for the last war. This, however, was not it. Harry was in charge of Five hundred young men assigned ground armor defense of a continent-sized mass of craters along with thousands of others. Month after month Harry fought bravely and watched his friends die.

Their retreat was a heavily guarded group of jump ships dug into escarpments at the far south of their front lines. No one could use the ships without jump codes, and a special "Mad Dog" platoon held those.

Enemy forces came in for days butchering the King's men. Rumor had it Predecessor technology had allowed them to breach the individual soldier's armor and force-field shields. The merciless double sun of Baal One cooked the corpses that couldn't reached. Busted EVA suits spattered men in "blood fireworks". The retreat threatened to become chaotic as discipline broke down.

"Coral sky Unit is folding in the west. They've reported half their number dead. Jump ships are not responding, Sir. "The Corporal's face was desperate.

"Tell them to hold their position. We move back in an orderly fashion." Harry snapped. He'd been following orders for a dignified retreat when what was in order was a wholesale run to the Jump-ships. Outside, the whine of tracers and cry of ripping force-shields battered on.

Suddenly, the air was red, this time a smacking explosion coming together in a wave of searing air. The came swirling massive dust cloud, the men piled in heaps among settling hot ash. Moments passed as he checked the integrity of his EVA fields. They were holding, barely. He cursed and looked about him again.

"On your feet!" He howled, "Coral sky, can you hear me?

Voices came over the communications channels by the thousands. It was like opening a hatch on the torments of Hell.

Harry returned to his communicator, Coral sky came through. The soldier's voice sounded as if he was gargling. Harry realized the man was drowning in his blood.

"Heavy losses, Sir. Men gone, gone-".

Silence. Shuffling.

Another voice came. "I've never seen anything like it, Sir. Armor defenses washed through like nothing. Tanks glowing purple. Some kind of radiation flares coming from the bodies of the men. Units are breaking all over. Do you have orders, Sir?"

"Can you return fire?" Harry asked.

Shuffling. "Uhh, yes Sir! Batteries are intact. Several of the men are dead at the guns though. They've turned into some kind of flares, the rest of us were shielded by the crater walls. We're alright."

Dizzy from struggling for air, his head spun. "Throw up an alternating arc of fire to cover the retreating armor and men. I'll send out fire commands to the other artillery units. Stand your ground until further orders. Over and out." He said and lay down the com without knowing it.

Then he saw his armor crew, they hadn't been shielded by the crater. There was a strange fluorescent flaring rising from their corpses. The tank appeared unharmed, almost pristine. He climbed into it with the flaring men.

Across the plains and among the craters, thousands of soldiers were fleeing now in a chaotic maddened rush. They died by the dozens each horrible minute, screaming for their mothers if they lived long enough to speak. They were mostly boys. Most of them had never been in a street fight.

Into and through this wave Harry drove his tank toward the enemy lines.

His forward motion wavered in the maniac rush of blood and men. Looking back, he could see the whole group of battalions scrambling. Looking forward; a sea of men came retreating toward him. Their faces were wild where helmets had fallen. Where they had not they looked like strange automatons loping away from the enemy fire.

The sky was a psychotic maelstrom of warping fields and laser blasts; dust, rocks, and blood shimmered in the full light of the Pleiades. Baal One had no artificial atmospherics to soften the star clusters relentless dazzle.

His Hover tank rode in a frenzy over his broken comrades.

203

Time weighed down, and there was only the sweep of armies, his aching muscles, his lungs pulling hard for air. He screamed at the retreating men but his voice was swallowed in the artillery fire. He dropped into the tank and went into its computer. Among his personal effects was a holo-projector he brought from Chrysalis Isla. He connected it to the computer and went back to the turret's hatch.

Then he projected himself fifty feet high.

To the retreating men, it was as if some mythical hero had come to rescue them from Hell. There, suddenly on the battlefield, a giant.

He screamed, raising his sword, "NEVER!"

It was as if a ripple of stopping went out through the battalions, wider, then wider until the whole mass of men had stopped and turned. Some died soon as they changed direction, the force of the enemy's new secret weapons still slaughtering.

Yet a call went up among the troops and the retreat stopped. They went forward again, reorganizing around the armor then, taking cover where they could.

Fischer Shea, the founder of the cluster, had famously simply said, "Never" to the Imperials centuries before.

It was all Harry had needed to say to remind them who they were.

That moment they had found their courage again. Alone, Harry had turned them back. Many would die anyway-but their last moments would be bravery instead of cowardice. Honor had swept through the tide of fear, and fear had lost its power.

In hours the whole battalion had become an effective force once more. The Coral Sky artillery unit had held to the last man, Corporal Alonzo firing matter cannons with his guts ripped out. The retreat became dignified in that the men held their positions to the death. Around ten thousand men made it back to the jump ships days later. Beaten, half-starved and running out of life support, they made it to the cliffs.

But a deserter had stolen the jump codes.

Only thirty-five hundred miraculously survived the enemy's final onslaught, it was a roll of the dice where searing matter cannon swept through armor, where one might be protected by corpses piling on you or even the hull of a burning jump-ship.

In the most bitter irony that echoed a Sun Tzu principle, having nowhere to retreat, the thirty-five hundred became berserkers in one of the great unmatched charges of military history. Harry this time sent them forward.

They slipped through and past the enemy's frontal assault, and took the enemy command center, slaughtering the officers there with their bare hands and bayonets.

It was Harry himself, caked in mud and the blood of his fallen comrades, who had given the order, "No prisoners".

They left the butchered officers who had shown no mercy in their advance as grim testament.

The soldiers came home to their various worlds to find the noble families rearranging the government though a series of judicial fiats that extended the powers of the Imperials to influence trade and commerce within the cluster. Civil liberties were being gutted in legislation purportedly masked in patriotic terms under the guise of "protecting the star cluster from terrorism".

Thus the King had been victorious in war, he soon lost the peace. Harry went back to his holo-painting and attended parties in a small circle of artists called "Nada" frequenting the penthouses a hundred stories up along Bicycle Bay.

There were Eighteenth-century paintings on the walls along with Thirty-fifth-century holos. Retro droids of famous personages through history mingled in the crowd, and pretense was so thick and mannered it had become an art form itself. The art form, Harry realized as he glared disdainfully about him.

As the party swirled, Barry Printzlau let his voice rise so that all might hear him, "They say the king is on Earth in Cordoba with a lover. He's the last of the line and he won't come back and lead against the domination of the noble families.

The balance of power on Chrysalis Isla has tipped forever; no one will stand against the nobles now. The Monarchy has fallen for a piece of touche."

Harry spun toward the man with a platinum menace of an automaton. He grabbed the back of the man's tunic and slammed him hard against the wall. Then he swung him to the edge of the balcony. "Speak against the King again in my presence. Do it now!"

Barry said nothing.

Everyone at the party was silent. None of them had ever seen a man struck in anger. Until now the brooding ex-soldier and his tortured sweeps of action painting and flitting holo scenes, where bits and pieces of men seemed to appear and disappear, had all seemed fascinating. No longer. There was rabid wildness in his eyes and hate in his white knuckles that filled the room with primeval dread.

A man who had been continually trying to organize a band, "Phoenix", wasn't larger than Harry; he was dressed in a martial arts outfit with tattoos and leather. It was his party. Leaping with impish swiftness, moments after the fact, he reached Harry and placed a hold he'd learned in martial arts class on Harry's arms.

Phoenix, of course, hadn't attended more than a couple of the martial arts classes, but he sensed the moment's actual danger had passed and never missed an opportunity to seize the stage. "Don't do it, man, it ain't worth it. Come on, LET HIM GO!!"

Harry thought about slamming them both, then felt the anger pass. He let go of Barry who ducked back into the party.

Harry wanted nothing more to do with "Nada".

Harry's current girlfriend walked up to him horrified. Her name was "Starpeace". Evermore Harry would refer to her as "That Piece".

She looked at him a long moment silently for effect.

"You're really sick, you need help." She said. The next week she ended their tenuous relationship and started seeing that man without a band who called himself "Phoenix".

Harry started running hazardous waste disposal into Chrysalis Isla's Sun. The money was good because the work was dangerous, but it gave Harry a long missed sense of excitement he hadn't felt since the ground wars. It wasn't long before the profits from his work allowed him to buy his own ship. He would fly the hazardous waste right up to the coronal riptides where the heat and the gravitational forces might sheer his fusion drives into a million slices if he wasn't careful, then he would let the material drop into the star and feel his ship lunge outward with the loss of weight until space was cool.

He met his first love Sanitaria again at a benefit. She hadn't changed a bit. Her wealth had kept her perfect in the way only perfect wealth can. There were traces of worry on her face that evening which even beauty could not mask. Harry kissed her and reintroduced himself.

"Harry! Yes, of course, I remember you, a-long time now, how have you been faring?" she asked as he took her arm and walked along toward the outer decks of the water ship that hosted the benefit.

"Oh, that's wonderful, Sanitaria, wonderful. Work has been so busy and I do love my work," he answered smiling.

Money had kept him looking good too, but there were shreds of evidence of age that the early years of his rise to power had left him, a line here, and a faint scar there. He was wearing white again, with an Ahura-Mazda scale, pure scarlet, and gold, poking up from his pocket.

"I love the Mazda scale," she said coyly, "did you think of me when you placed it there?"

"But of course, yes I did." He grinned hugely. She didn't believe him, but it was true. He had never forgotten the hurt her family's rejection caused him. He had never forgiven them either for the part the played in the alliance against the king. His innocence and joy of life had died with so many of his comrades' ludicrously defending Baal One and the king. He had thought of her, of all of them, every day of his life since the war.

Her class had made a personal and social war against his.

"Oh now, Harry, you're too good!" she laughed, "You haven't thought of me in ages." she laughed again, "Oh-too funny.

Come; come by the railing with me. I'm very depressed as of late, my family is having a terrible row with the business and all.

"I need a diversion from it all and here you are, handsome, successful, and dashing as ever." she sighed.

Yes, be a diversion again for me Harry, my disposable play toy, Harry thought coolly. He had loved her so deeply and she had cast him away so easily.

They looked out over the sea and she remembered how he had stood so gallant in his uniform calling after her time and again from the rose garden. She remembered how it had seemed she could be free of her family and roam about the universe at will like an ordinary woman.

"But I have thought of you, Sanitaria." He said fingering the Mazda scale, peering at the waters. It was night, and that meant only half the light of day in this part of the star cluster with the Pleiades glittering over the fluttering waves. She didn't know he was the cause of her family's business troubles and neither did they. He was an aggressive trader and he had them cornered on the markets.

He was squeezing them slowly and he loved it. The feather scale in his pocket was a sort of trophy, an inside joke to himself.

"I've never stopped wanting such a one as you, Sanitaria-what sort of man could?" he said, and that too was true. However, he had stopped loving her a long time ago.

They would be married just after the New Year.

The hologram brass seems to trumpet from the stars, and then:
"Run away with me!" She whispers, leaning forward exposing the perfection of her cleavage. The percussion throbs into a march, her arms moving to the beat and the synthetic sounds pouring forward, silver-blue textures forming walls, a house of cards, all singing.
"Come on you, I know a place where the suns never set, a tiny little island on Chrysalis Isla, the Pleiades shining down on us, run away!"
An emerald bird alights to her hand, an Ahura-Mazda dragon slithers around her feet, you look again and now she's wearing the blue and green of the Royal officer's air core, with a vermillion cape and an olive cap, "Run away where they'll never find us!"
From the popular holodisk, "Fornicarrion" -Star Peace,
Starky Barky Holos unlimited.

The aircar kept signaling that a slower speed would be preferable, but the couple ignored it as if the lightning bolt flashing of towers and the slipping of other cars to their rear could somehow assuage the tensions they were feeling. It was the deal of their lifetimes and they both knew it.

Star Peace, whose real name was Betty, and Phoenix, whose real name was Gilberto, should have brought a lawyer–but at this point, things were too strange for sensible thinking.

"Why now? And worse, why would he want to help us? You dumped him like a bad habit, Star." Phoenix had been ranting for days.

He only used the short form of her stage name in private, when he wanted something. She resented that. He was trying to weasel himself closer to her in fear of Harry buying him out.

Phoenix's management of her career had gone nowhere until an anonymous donor had backer her last two hits.

They'd squandered that money quickly. The donor who'd backed them turned out to be Harry.

"Oh please, 'Why now? Starrrrr!'" She mimicked him rolling her eyes. She gave him a sidelong glance full of contempt.

"One thing about Stark, Gilberto, he's strictly business and no bull.

"He doesn't care about my relationship with him a million years ago. He knows I'm good and he wants to make "MON-NEY, get it? MON-NEY. While you've been going to openings trying to find yourself and your inner child, he's been working his fanny off purchasing the best holo recording equipment in the galaxy. So he could make more MON-NEY."

Phoenix said naught.

She was right. Harry was the quintessential man's man.

Their air car alighted to a private trajectory higher above the traffic stream as they were approaching the Ambrosino building. It had been rumored to have been sold by the Ahura-Mazda company to an unnamed trading conglomerate from Baal One. The planet had seen much growth after the war, someone was terra-forming it. Already a thousand comets had been seeded over its poles and small oceans were forming.

The Ambrosino building was an old and magnificent structure whose massing reminded one of a mountain turning itself into a towering star yacht, spires rising in dozens of points and culminating in a fabulous crown of woven lights and terraces.

Their air car slowed and came to rest on one of the terraces.

Harry was there, staring out over Bicycle Bay like he owned it, sipping a martini, and tended to by three female chromium-skinned androids.

Phoenix, stepping out of the aircar, found them delightful.

Harry smiled and held up his arms, "Star Piece and Flagstaff!" he said.

"That's Phoenix," Gilberto said dryly, "As in the mythical bird that rose from its ashes." His planetary geography was minimal so he missed the dig.

They all kissed, and continued their greetings for some time, exchanging pleasantries none of them felt. Business is business. Harry and the chromium machines took them inside the crown of the building where they went into a large holo-viewing room. Star Peace beamed, "I never knew this was here!" she exclaimed.

Harry's chin lifted, "It wasn't." he replied and let her consider the implications. Phoenix let out an audible gurgle of surprise. Redoing the Ambrosino crown! He was sure the building was on the register of historic places. There had been offices here where great families had held dominion over ancient businesses for centuries. *Not anymore.*

"I am forming a new company," Harry began, "one that has already begun with distribution," One of the chromium nymphs chirped a laugh then and fluttered away, Harry raised an eyebrow and continued, "Yes, well, the new company has already begun with distribution of holo-discs. I wish the company to produce, promote, and finance new artists struggling to break into the market."

"Sort of like us." Phoenix offered.

"Sort of like Betty." Harry returned coolly, "Whatever she pays you will be her business and will concern me not a bit."

He smiled. The law had been laid down.

Her business, Phoenix thought. Enough said.

Star was hardly flattered, hardly amused, but slightly aroused. It had been Harry's boldness that attracted her to him in the first place.

207

She had been walking past a bunch of empty cafes one night when he'd looked at her and said, "Pretty athletic."

Years later, here in his office, he was still the same, only richer. He owed no respect to Gilberto, who for all his endless artistic posing had never known a moment of creative genius in his life.

Her business, she thought. "Harry, I'm no emergent vocalist. I've had a couple of hits now and-" She paused and thought; *Go ahead you Levi Boca.* She said, "After you."

"My offer stands, three million to purchase your rights to the three hits that you've made, plus full backing on all your next thirty holo collections and fifty-five percent of the rights to those too."

He had just doubled his offer.

She felt it hit her like a sweet, forbidden fondling.

Full backing. No conditions. She'd have access to the best production facilities in the star cluster. When Harry was through with her, she'd be the Pleiades. The siren of Chrysalis Isla. The galaxy would know her name, love her face.

Her music would be hyper cast to the edge of time and space. Maybe into the multiverse! Immortality on a scale she never dared to dream.

"Gilberto," she said, "get the auto reader out and let's review the contracts."

"Star Peace." Harry tilted his head as if begging her indulgence like a sweet harmless puppy. So they did.

Somewhere in Sagittarius
On an industrial moon
there lies a tepid salt flat
orange against a shot black night
You done left me in a stasis field
but Darlin', it's incomplete
cause everybody knows
you can't feel a thing deep in stasis
and I feel the drag
and a slow pull of time.
-Star Peace "Meat machines"
Starky Barky Holos unlimited.

Harry scowled at his mistress and ordered her away from him as if she were less than a dog. She quietly complied. She had heard Sanitaria singing in the rose garden and knew how it irritated Harry. She didn't want to remain in his presence knowing the mood he would be in after his dallying had been interrupted from its completeness.

Sanitaria was singing lines from Star Peace's, "Meatmachines". Lust and loneliness howled through the tune. Harry knew she wailed the brassy tunes mourning her lost love for him, or perhaps his of her. No matter.

Half his drive had been revenge against her and the noble families. When he served it up cold to them it was like a little gazpacho before lunch.

When Star Peace's manager Phoenix had burned up in the upper atmosphere-apparently pushing an aircar to its maximum height until it overloaded and then dropping like a stone, the whole planet mourned with "Star". Months later she disappeared, the cluster went mad with rage and fear. Harry was visibly unmoved, whistling her tunes about his mansion.

She sold far more presumed dead than ever alive. In time her music became the star clusters unofficial anthems, crooning in the marketplaces, seaside clubs, even the workplaces. Harry never tired of it, "That Piece," he would say, "was a good piece."

Standing unfulfilled in his office he watched his little trollop run off and thought of Betty and Sanitaria. Luxuries, he thought. It's the little things in life that matter. "Hyper cast, now!" he bellowed and the windows of the room darkened, a huge wall at the back of the room unfolded a secret hyper casting unit.

"Give me that metal head Bandor." He ordered and his house computer obeyed. In seconds the hyper casts "spooky action at a distance" bridged light-years, and the office of an Imperial Cyborgian research facility appeared as if in the other half of the room.

The Cyborgian Overlords wouldn't extend their consciousness through the hyper casts, a mystery and weakness lost on no one but the masses. The research facility was well outside Cyborgian Imperial space-a fact that could protect them from public opinion in the Republics' case, should the illegal research ever became known. A fact that would also keep anything that happened there outside of their hive mind.

The Diablo Nebula. They'd chosen the most wretched piece of space outside the core itself for their slimy illegal research. More lost ships and ugly myths about that space than-yes, than even the core. That was part of their strategy too. Keep away the riff-raff. Unmanageable field distortions, huge black holes, impenetrable dust clouds, and proto-star forming regions. Smack in the middle of the entire mess and mystery one world sitting pretty with prehistoric oceans and jungles and more nasty creatures than a drunkard's phantasm-Siluria.

Bandor had been an obscure shipping clerk CC pulled out of deep hive manipulation to run the distant base. They pumped him full of memory RNA, nano programs, and directives, but the poor boy just wasn't getting the hang of personal autonomy. Harry had moved in and found him easily led.

"Harry." He said in a wooden greeting. He thought Harry was casting from a nearby yacht, but Harry was too wily to let anyone know his whereabouts or even his appearance. What Bandor saw was a construct of Harry's predetermination.

"Bandor, my friend, we've got to talk. Several of my ships have been attacked near Ocho's World."

"General Ossa. The overlords have assigned a fleet to sweep the fringe systems in search of pirates." Bandor answered.

"Pirates? Please."

"Privateers?"

"Alternative taxation" Harry mused, "But go on."

"That's all I know. Anyone could surmise that. Ossa leads that fleet and the fleets there. The Overlords dictate fleet movements. Your people must have considerable firepower for the overlords to move the fleet. Such action is rare, usually reserved for political situations."

"Well, we try." Harry smiled, "And I am a political situation." Harry snickered at the face of the poor devil. Bandor thought he was going to make it out of the realm of CC altogether and join the ranks of the wild humans. But there would be no way back for old Bandor. CC would probably have him operating a surveillance satellite after this with so much of his humanity circumvented he wouldn't remember his name much less the concept of personal autonomy.

Serve the little wicked bastard right, the way he ruthlessly altered the cells and hormones and introduced nano-circuitry into the Out pilots there on Siluria experimenting. Not much room for empathy me boy, not that I've any of that capacity left myself...

"Our research is moving along nicely; we've got a new protein that can function as a bridge in the dendrites-"

"Bandor," Harry interrupted, "I don't care about protein unless it's wearing a dress."

Bandor's eyes widened. He hadn't had time to explore the world of women yet, but he was looking forward to it. In the Hive, they had suppressed that whole aspect of his humanity on a whim. Some people in the Empire seemed to be having a wild time, others they just shut down. The Wilds, they did as they pleased.

"So we've brought on their dogs? What about this blockade Paramon's setting up around your system?

"Why hasn't Ossa just slammed the government there into dust and expanded the Overlords hegemony out a little further?"

Harry watched for a reaction and it came, involuntarily as a slight twitching from Bandor's eyelids-deeply repressed memories of something frightening. Something he knew when he was in the Hive mind.

"Expansion further at this time would compromise the integrity of Cyborgian population's property and welfare."

Horseshit. Something out there scares the balls off them and it ain't Paramon.

"I'm losing millions, see, millions. I have a lot of accounts with those French worlds for my luxury food business. The pretense is lost to the starving. How are you enjoying those foodstuffs we've shipped?"

"Delightful. I've never known such sensations before."

"I know; I know...great ain't it? And I want to sell more of it without having to engage the blockade with my ships.

"Might hurt my contracts if they find out I was scuttling their air core to sell them coffee. When is Ossa going to get the fleet back over there and straighten this out?"

"That's far beyond my status to learn such information. It may take as long as our research here is done before they normalize relations with the Paramon Republics again.

That way they can make it look like they yielded to Paramon and withdrew the base in a retreat.

Satisfies the overblown political ideations of the Republics, limits their losses and time in warships."

They're saving their firepower for something bigger. Bigger conflicts mean bigger prizes. Fresh forces coming in after the combatants have exhausted themselves can dictate terms to both. Such forces coming in late can rewrite the whole history and paint themselves as avenging angels, heroes.

"I don't care if it's beyond your space-time, get me information, fleet positions, anything they got, so I can get a few freighters of coffee down there and make an honest coin, okay?"

Bandor was taken aback. The audacity of the wild humans never failed to amaze him. How CC had held these peoples at bay for so long was a mystery he couldn't fathom. Surely so many independent variables presented equations of infinite complexity. Growing in his consciousness was a sense that terror, the terror of CC's surprise nuking of the Arcturian worlds so long ago, had left the wild humans long underestimating their strengths.

"I'll come up with some excuse to send a light craft on through the blockade and get you more information from this end," Bandor said evenly, surprising himself. He had learned another wild habit; he had learned to lie.

Harry smiled, "I like it. I like it."

Bandor frowned, "These codes...they're your best, right? They can't be broken?"

"I've permission for my yachts anywhere in Paramon, remember, I'm a big player out here-or was till your CC boys muddied the waters. As far as codes go, you want a three-way line into their presidential palace? They're secure. Rest easy and do what I ask you to, and when this is all over you'll be drifting in your yacht off some Republican world so far from Imperial entanglements it will be rare news when you hear about them."

Then Harry was gone.

Bandor was alone in the office, alone on a world in a nebula he'd never heard of, on the edge of a system-wide blockade.

His was a mind that had never known solitude, never know his humanity. Now he committed research crimes against others whose humanity he was only now beginning to understand. His only tie in the galaxy to another human mind was this strange trader Harry, who had befriended him at the beginning of this assignment.

Fighting back the fear and confusion, he clung to the visions of a better life that Harry had so adeptly painted in his mind. Yet with each passing day the implications of his research, and what it was doing to the experimental subjects, became more nightmarishly profound in his unfolding persona.

He had become, as the wild humans described it, evil.

Harry walked to the parapet and looked down on Sanitaria tending to a fallen Ahura-Mazda. Darn things never get used to the force shields. Sometimes he thought they flew against it on purpose. They'd have to be a lot smarter and meaner if they were going to get those shields down. They'd have to figure the source, and kill the guards, and damage the machinery.

They were bright animals, true enough. But surely that was beyond them. It would be something to see though, tearing up the guards, attacking the field generators. Could that be staged as an evening's recreation? No, the emblems of Sanatoria's clan would stay just where he'd put them, contained and constrained at his will.

"Sanitaria," He bellowed, "Let the stubborn thing die in its vomit! I'll buy more."

He whistled. One of his flyers, an iridescent parrot of old Earth stock, came over and rested on his shoulder rubbing its beak on Harry's cheek. Harold Stark had done much in his life. He'd laid out a city this month on the newly terra-formed Baal. A city to commemorate where he'd been decorated for valor in the face carnage and overwhelming odds, again and again, in that war.

His holograms art pieces were shown in many Galleries on Chrysalis Isla.

His business ventures would have been legendary if anyone could have traced them. His piracies in deep space lent a new definition to the duality of man in spite of all this.

He had not, however, solved the mystery of exactly why the Transhuman Cyborgians were experimenting illegally on Siluria. Even Bandor didn't know that. All of Harry's accomplishments and all his depravities might prove to be a child's play in the light of something that terrified the Cyborgian Overlords. The Overlords had nuked a civilization into the dust. What could scare them?

Then there was the potential for a missed opportunity.

If the Cyborgians were scared, they probably had a good reason. Something was threatening to take them down. If someone could step in after the Cyborgians and their mystery foes had expended a bunch of energy in a fight, perhaps that someone could then take all. It was a classic military tactic the Ancient Americans had used not once, but twice in one century to set up their hegemony over Europe. Albeit had they pressed their advantage better the first time, they wouldn't have needed the second.

Harry looked over to the Riptide. She was the pride of his fleet, but it was a fleet. From the Baal Wars, he knew the fighting ability of hundreds of men. Those were the leaders in his army of private assassins. By 4210 half of the noble families on Chrysalis Isla had lost key members inexplicably. There was some talk of the Dark Corps, a mysterious legion that took vengeance on the Nobles for their betrayal of the King.

Harry smiled.

They said the King had died an ignominious death touring Old Earth, heartbroken over the loss of his Pleiades. Perhaps, but he was not the only one to die.

Have you ever really looked; the depth of night?
Between the stars falling away forever?

When the stellar winds catch your fancy
You feel the lunging starship step on the hyper streams
The winds of the universe
And still, the physicist knows not whence
They come or they go
Like the courage of the damned?
Star peace, "Never had a chance".
-Starky barky holos unlimited.

4

The Derelict
Hercules Cluster, 4211

Millin Quinoa, Memoirs entry 1017.

I fought my way out of the Chrysler system by hook and crook. Blasted into hyperspace solo for the first time in my life.

They arrested Sagamore, Vince, and later, I learned, Leyla. The arrest was cast from a headpiece someone stuck on Vinny.

Seems they rigged the whole thing so all the cast stations carried it live. Galactic wide. No one knew how they did it. The largest single cast in Chrysler City history. Vinny was already well known for rescuing Tristan and several other stunts. Now he, Sagamore and Leyla were bonafide celebrities.

I don't think it was the intended effect. Intending to humiliate Vince, they made him into some kind of folk hero. That didn't, however, help them him with Cyborgian Central criminal sentencing. They were all convicted of smuggling and shipped off to Ophelia's World-a frozen penal colony that had once been a teeming place of some repute.

I came out of the zero wave cycle up under the Hercules cluster with my alnico rings spanked out. Good time for a reset.

A lot of talk on the casts about Vince and Sagamore-enigmatic myths. Rumors. I just laugh. I think of the real men I know and the plasticene characterizations on the casts, funny that. Funny too that the real men did what the plasticene heroes would have done. So what makes a hero?

Looked up Simone, she was bartending on an industrial Neely. She was bored behind the bar, felt like getting back on the steel wings. I got people to crew with Simone and myself. Drifters mostly. They come and go when they sense the legend's boots.

I've run some good runs with some big players, got the Sire. Yet even I sense the boots. I miss that can-do smile, that walk that's always weightless, no matter what the G's.

I can still see him sitting up the big stack in a snowstorm working the steel. Like he was playing cards, easy, steady. Like you could throw the end of the multiverse at him, and he'd snicker and start looking for loopholes. Crack open a can of synth, down it, and smack it up against some big mouths head.

All that, those days, those guys, good times compared to what was coming.

When I rounded the last of the shattered unformed webs of nebula and neutron star derelicts that skirted the darkness at the edge of the galaxy, I came up upon the big Hercules cluster. I could see the final void of intergalactic space just past the Echo City mines and the alloy camps of Phlegra station. Into that labyrinth of red and black smelters and dark skeletal forms looming against the void, I shot. The casts then were nearly silent, but for a maddening background of static and wailing signals like the ghosts of the Predecessors warning doom.

Empty casts, I knew what that would mean.

Raiders and marauders taking out the cast relays with neutron cannon! Corpses and busted shields, empty silver starships drifting in the charcoal wastes, in the cold and radiation.

I booted some stim, but my chemical plant was low. I had been manufacturing life-support for a long while without reconditioning. The station was near. I wasn't going to sweat it until the air got bad, if I still had light-years, then I'd worry.

Thought about looking through the wreckage and corpses to salvage, but I think that was just self-abuse. At that time, I'd been crewing alone for over a year, I needed company. Besides, the raiders surely picked through it all.

Past the wreckage, on to the station.

I lay awake in the stim glow when Phlegra's deep purple crescent finally loomed in my path, and I could see the lights of the station spread across the dark side. I ported and locked it down in the mechanic's bay, registered, and slept in my cabin when the stim faded. A few days later when I awoke, my life support had been scrubbed, and the ship's air was sweet as an alpine meadow on a big Alp O'Neill station.

I drifted down the alleys of the station, over to "Bongo Joe's down the hatch" for a few drinks and news of the Marauders.

There was no news, which doesn't mean good news. Believe me, this far off the edge, every word for the Milky Way seems like a connection to a more solid reality. The most interesting thing at Bongo's that day was the condition of one of the pilots. He was sledgehammer drunk and hotwired to the neurons. He stared, straight ahead, as if his merge helmet had malfunctioned and left him permanently trained on a quasar beacon.

"They'll be back," he said flatly, taking a long oblivious sip of his gin. "They'll be back." He was talking to no one in particular, but I felt like it was me he wanted to hear him. I was the choice of an audience for the insane. The harbinger of madness that evening had chosen me as his disciple of doom.

I cursed at him under my breath. "Whacko pinhead drunks in every bar from the Tarantula Nebula to the Big Streak run."

"Whazat?" he chortled and raised his swollen head.

"Nothing, nothing at all. Just you pipe down bonehead, or I'll contact Cyborg Central about your expired pilot's licenses." I replied with a tone of belittlement.

"Frac you too, woody lips. And your sister! My licenses are up to date in every respectable government in the galaxy.

"Some unrespectable ones too. And my credit jack has maxed the station bank. So who the flock are you?" he snapped back from his worn face. "CC doesn't give me no how-to anyway. More chip than dip."

He waited for expected abuse, but I have more pride than to banter with the likes of him. Usually, I wouldn't be caught dead in a popped gravity bubble with him.

Suddenly the geezer pulls out a disruptor, an expensive silver job with an inlaid mother of pearl handle. That was worth big bucks. It made me wonder about him.

"Sit down and listen to Me," he said. I didn't recognize his accent from anywhere. After a while, pilots kind of lose touch with their roots and become, well, just themselves. Too convoluted by time and various perspectives of experience to genuinely fit in anywhere but the stations.

That disser he's waving looks pretty well charged, too.

"Yeah, sure old-timer. Just put that piece away, okay?"

The pearl-handled disser was too much. The derelict, wherever his origin, was Outworlder now. Must have made a fortune smuggling controlled substances into the command economies of the Cyborgian Empire. Or so I assumed. There were big scars on either side of his eyes, more on his forehead.

Bugger's been in a few scrapes.

His jacket, I noted, like his disser, was top of the line. He needed a shave. On the jacket was an emblem; Turquoise Line.

Earth-based luxury ships. My assumptions are wrong again, a liner captain? At one time. Now I'm downright curious.

"I was taking a Merc Sixty-two-thousand off the Tarantula Nebula to go over the galactic plane" he began, "I could see the big jet stream shooting out of the nuclear regions of the core. I'm up above the galactic clouds, the arched filaments are shining, and I see the tilt of the disc. There are all the bright UV sources, the OB stars. Submillimeter emissions from the cooler dust- you know? You know.

"The hyper stream is easier up there, fainter. Better for the old boats. Must have made that plunge, shee-it, fifty times if I made it once. It's quiet up there. If you have got a mind to, you can look out over the arc of the stream and out to the fade between.

"That's the run I was making, ten years ago now.

215

"The Silurian Nebula was right in my flight path, but me, hey I'm a rational man. I don't buy-in for old myths of ghost ships and lost star systems. I'm not about to recalibrate a half a million hyper stream calculations to avoid a grim spot on my galactic travels now, eh?"

He wiped at his sweaty face as if to clear away the present and peer into the spaces of the reported journey once more. He tugged on his gin.

"Well, it's just me and the old Merc and the stream for weeks. I'd been riding high for eighteen hours one shift, and needed some sleep. I pulled down to a minimum and set the autopilot on a deep scan. I'm ready to get on off to sleep when I hear this nasty howl of cackling lightning coming over the aud.

"I think, shee-it, some damn systems going to fail and I'm going to spend months coasting in the Merc till one of the hyper relays picks up my distress, and Central comes out and pulls me.

"No Sir-ee. Uh-uh. No buddy.

"No buddy. Well, it sounds like the Devil and damned if it wasn't!"

He wiped the sweat from his brow nervously again and I notice for the first time he's wearing a very large silver cross. From ObscuroFrio, the Parrish range. I knew that place well. The cross looks worn from being held. Worn from rubbing and desperate prayers. He's stopped talking, he's staring, thinking. So I waited.

Then he drills me with that smacked-out stare, all of the sudden, and he says, "The goddamned thing was crawling around my normal space bubble! On the hyper side of the bubble! Riding my friccin' bubble, man. Riding the fractals. Just like that. It couldn't be, but it was there."

Now I knew that was madness. Nothing could live in hyper; much less crawl around on an energy field like it was solid glass. It was an energy field to prevent the matter inside from deatomizing. Such thoughts were the stuff of metaphors. There was nothing metaphorical in his gaze though.

"I saw it." he insisted.

"Sure, old-timer. I hear stuff like this all the time in the taverns between the stars. Hyper Bogies they call them. I'm sure you saw it." I got ready to get up and leave when he waved that pearl-handled disser at me again.

"I ain't finished," he said.

I sat back down.

"It talked to me." He rasped. He pointed the disser; oblivious to its threatening me. I looked down the muzzle at an uncomfortable sudden death. He might as well have been waving a cigarette.

I don't know if it was his weapon or the story, but I didn't want to hear any more. I suddenly had a picture of me sitting at a table drinking gin and talking to myself. I didn't like where this was going. I especially didn't like the dreary disjointing sense oozing in the back of my head that his story had some validity.

"Aint no friccin hyper Bogie I'm telling you, it talked to me. Changed faces. Made faces of people I know. Even looked like an old girlfriend of mine, but I wasn't fooled she's been dead a long while."

I'd never heard of hyper-Bogies changing faces.

"Look, friend," I said, "everything you see while you're piloting is a computer construct, see? All those views of hyper, the galaxy, everything is synthesized from raw data your ship receives on its sensors. Then it's translated into images intelligible to human senses. Somebody dropped a virus into your computer-somebody you knew, by the sounds of it.

"And even if something could live in hyperspace, it wouldn't resemble anything from normal space, certainly not humans."

He wasn't moved by my voicing reason.

"It didn't resemble us. It looked like a gargoyle. But it could change form. Shapeshifting! It had a face like a demon made of lightning, hair made of golden hyper fire. It had a dozen appearances, changing them like it was playing with me to see which one scared me the most. It spoke in Cyborgian Central Standard English. It called us pig monkeys. "Called me by my name and said, 'Hey Pizzaro, you stinking pig monkey. I'm going to rip your guts out and play with them.' "

He gurgled and laughed hideously, sucking his gin again to drive away his fear. His head sunk low between his shoulders and his grin was like a Cheshire cat nightmare. He smelled like stale smoke from a dozen illicit substances, and sweat, unnatural sweat for the cool air of a station such as this.

He looked so very afraid. I thought of my patronizing threat to call Cyborgian Central. This guy's just laughed at that. I knew if a platoon of CC drones came in here armed to the teeth, he'd take them on without raising his pulse, I could see that. But whatever he thought he'd seen out there in hyper had him choking on his gin. A gargoyle on the bubble had him shaking like a kid?

Roland Dansky used to talk like that. Cyborgian Overlords don't do hyper casts, see. How come? They're scared of connecting with hyper. Sure, they come out of Deneb once in a while. Not often though. *HyperBogies, Millin, HyperBogies. So it's all going to come down someday. In the meantime, let's party!*

"Gin? Come over, here you big blue baby, have a drink."

Well, it was good gin and the old boy shouldn't be so alone and fearful.

"Another glass bartender," I said.

We drank for a while. I tried to move the conversation into other streams, other subjects. But always, like the great attractor is tugging at him, he goes back to the Bogie.

"It gets worse, see? That thing crawling around like a spider on a bottle ain't bad enough, being where it couldn't be, I know. Out beyond the bubble where you usually see just the flow and ripples of the stream, there were more of them. Hundreds more, each uglier than the last. They were flying, damned things had bat wings. Horns, scales, like a medieval menagerie of devils, like a twelfth-century etching.

"It knows me. It'll be back. They'll be back."

Then, as if to say, "But I won't be here for it", he pulled out his disser and opened his mouth placing the weapon's muzzle inside. Very calmly he fired and the back of his head exploded and collapsed at once. Then he was atomized, completely gone.

That's how it happened. The few sad patrons of the bar stood up. Someone started repeating, "What the? What the--?"

The bartender hollered for station security. A crowd formed by the door before a couple of beefy Guards finally arrived, clambering over themselves.

I was questioned for a couple of hours, and let go. I heard one of the officers in security whistle when they saw how much money the derelict had squirreled away in his credit jack. The hyper rat's codes were in order like he'd said. He was a top-flight pilot flying, counter to the galactic spin for ten years, always away from the Tarantula Nebula and always away from the Silurian clouds as well.

Pizzaro was there one moment, gone the next.

Me, I did what business I could there, and moved on, back toward the more crowded parts of the galaxy. I've stayed away from the high galactic spaces.

Strangely, since the station, I haven't been able to escape the feeling I'm being watched.

Shane Perry

Leon's Last Stand

Ophelia's World was terra-formed at the dawn at the space age. A mere fifty systems were settled then. She'd been a glorious achievement of planned cities and ornate white towers. Promenades stretched along with semi-tropical gardens when the terra-formers finished. In the right place at the right time, industries piled on her continents one after the other, until for a time she rivaled even Deneb 4 as one of the galaxy's finest worlds.

Her glimmering platinum spires flanked golden clockwork maglevs that spun silently past ladies in billowing gossamer gowns. Her name was tantamount in the settled worlds of humankind with reason and virtue, industry and progress. After 3127 the Arcturian wars cut off much of her trade and so began her slow and aching decline.

With time the Cyborgian Empire's only use of her was to house dissidents. Of course, the terra-forming monoliths installed centuries before were shut down then. The planets natural coldness returned. Ice formed on the multicolored Croatans and Frangipani, which shattered and lay still, frozen like lilies left to fester without even the dignity of raising a stink.
-Princess Clairissa Maggio, Caldris, Ophelia's World."

Ophelia's World, Orion Arm 4212

The ship was coming.

Yes, right on schedule. Leon was going to stow away or die trying. From somewhere beyond the god-forsaken dirty grey of Ophelia's pallid atmosphere, past that, yes, beyond the junkyards of satellites and dreary stations...the ship was even now heaving into normal space. Lunging, blasting away from the hyper streams, coming to the prison world...coming to Ophelia.

Coming to Leon. Leon Percival Po Tsai-"wild dog extraordinaire". He snickered at that, "Ha! Come to papa!" cackling to himself with a roaring madness born of glee at the prospect of freedom. He'd labored over his plans with devilish patience through endless bitter hours of lonely humiliation and regret. The ship was coming, yes, and when it came he was going to stow away.

Fifty-thousand tons of interstellar freighter.

Drifting slowly down to the prison world, safe in a gravity bubble, yielding, descending like a dandelion seed cast out by a terra-forming bot. Down and down, unknowing of the eager little convict glaring back into the night waiting, hoping, longing desperately for the lights. Still hot from the ambient pressures which hyper streams leaked as it strung through the void.

"Swirl the mesons boys, Leon's coming." The night was frigid and stinging.

Fifty thousand tons drifting, spinning, turning down.

Down to the prison world.

The night side planet loomed. An ancient world, all but abandoned by the Cyborgian Empire that had spawned it millennia before.

Time had covered it over from pole to pole with cities, towers, and factories. Kilometers high, kilometers deep, cities empty now but for a few ragged convicts interred here and there. They were Pirates, losers, loners; misfits not having earned a death sentence or a stasis block, just cast out of the way to go gracelessly in cold derelict cities.

They were Wildcat Out pilots, smugglers...

"Ophelia's world!" Mothers would curse at misbehaving children across half of the civilized space. "Behave or they'll send you to Ophelia's world!"

To live out your natural life among the ice and weeping ghosts.

The wind turned in on a frigid hopeless night, as Leon watched for the lights. The wind hooted its indifference. Fifty thousand tons of interstellar freighter sank beneath the clouds and continued its easy silent descent toward the icy seas where it would make waterport.

"Right on time" Leon snapped excitedly as he saw the lights appear in the gloomy clouds above.

"Tell me, tell me do-how lame can they think we are?" he asked aloud to the night, "a coherent landing schedule on a prison planet? Might as well send invitations. Blowfish brains and dancing dolphins!" he shivered and adjusted his wetsuit, endlessly fitting and refitting the seams, peering out a window of an abandoned hotel toward the dark waters and the sky.

Bergs of ice moved about in the slushy blackness. He could see them now reflected by the light of distant power panels in orbit.

Their soft light cast a weird glow to Leon's face.

Leon had been popular in the labyrinth grotto nightclubs on the coral shores of Chrysalis Isla. Warm, lovely Chrysalis Isla.

Yet here even the power panels had been abandoned centuries before by the Imperials and with them the terra-forming that had once made Ophelia's World a semi-tropical paradise. Once like Chrysalis Isla.

The power panels here now merely reflected the light, rather than generating power with it. A strange sort of irony existed there that escaped Leon's rather sequential mind.

"Damn frozen hell!" Leon ranted to himself.

Cold menace skulked in the inky waters. Regretfully, he waved down his glow tubes and sat in complete darkness but for the power panel light reflecting over the ghostly cityscape. A large station was rising over the horizon, and that too added a little light.

A blow of snow whistled by like a dust devil, obscuring the freighter, the station, the power panels. Then it passed, and the freighter shone clear. He could even hear its mighty drive units humming and whining. He could make out the familiar superstructure above the smooth lines of the hull, and the massive rings of the field accelerators.

219

Now, like aurora gentle and angelic, a purple and phosphorescent sparkle and cackle came up. Field manipulators in action, glimmering. They reflected in the cold sea like a resplendent announcement.

He moved away from the window and clambered over to a huge opening in the wall. Lifetimes before, a giant robotic arm had moved goods along a conveyer through the opening into warehouses. Now it was merely a corroding gash of metal.

Leon leaned out looking down. Five stories down to the glacial waters below. The freighter wouldn't dock here; it would water-port on the sea before unloading. Like a rat jumping ship, Leon dropped into the darkness.

He watched the surface of the water rush up to meet him like a giant wall of uniform death. He felt a smack and then was plunged into a noisy blackness of rushing bubbles. Frantic with primordial fear of the complete darkness that had enveloped him, he swam to the surface in a mad flailing of arms and legs, struggling against his handmade wetsuit. Finally, he broke the surface and his dread. Sucking cold air hard he treaded water for a moment reorienting himself. He scanned for ice chunks but there were none close by.

Lucky for that, there would be more ice ahead for sure.

He steadied himself and began his long swim out to the star freighter. He could hear a hiss of steam now, as the smooth, hot hull eased into the inland sea. The sound brought a wicked smile to his square jaw. But characteristically, his eyes remained steely. He kept his hands to the front, careful of ice chunks. He wondered suddenly if there were unknown predators in the seas of this horrid prison world, but it was an idle fear. Perhaps the Cyborgians had brought some in just for spite.

Leon moved gracefully. He was an excellent swimmer. In his homeworld in the Pleiades children learned to swim before they walked. Back in the turquoise waters of Thanjavur, in a houseboat working a fishing collective, he'd grown up in the water. He was not, however, in the Pleiades.

In the oily jet black sea, he was shivering and inestimably small. Among the gargantuan derelict factories, stretching from horizon to horizon, lining the endless forgotten harbors, he remembered the brilliant light of the Pleiades like a lost love. They turned brightly in the skies of his imagination, luminously beguiling the senses with a radiant spectrum of splashed color.

Fat flowers, speckled Croatans, million blossomed Poinciana trees running with honey sap, parrots, macaws, and dragon birds peeling calls into the light. A secret, sandy, sunlit cove where one could pull up a boat and drink synthopiate rum, till you slept for days and woke feeling decades younger and fresh, raw with the joy of life. In a moment he'd called it all back to his mind, more real than icy imprisoning blackness in front of him.

Dark menace stretched beneath him. If he swam into a rusted piling or a razor-sharp chunk of ice, he'd bleed to death before he could make it back to shore. He'd empty his blood into this foul violation of the notion of water, helplessly draining every ounce of life that God had so graciously given him charge over, in an irresistible relentless passing darkness, unknown and forgotten.

Between him and the star freighter there stretched a couple hundred meters of ice and water. From where he was swimming he could see the purple phosphorescence of the ship's gravity fields winding down. The freighter hummed and chirped, its surface cooling rapidly. He pressed on with his careful breaststroke.

Dip, stroke, push.

Something jabbed his armpit. Panicking, he swung his arm around to meet it-ice! It only managed to bash his elbow. Cursing, he looked at the idle intruder bobbing innocently in the water. A stupid breadbox size chunk of ice. He felt around his armpit and found a tiny puncture is his suit. He had to be careful not to further tear it. Death's first tickles were chilling along his left flank with each stroke now. Cold, cold, he hated the coldness.

It was something one never experienced in the Pleiades, on Chrysalis Isla.

No. Not unless you wanted to.

His lungs seemed to wail for a rest. The suit was losing a battle with the icy water. Not like skin diving at Bicycle Bay.

Stroke, push. Keep going.

Coldness...no.

Push.

It was the colorlessness of Ophelia that finally drove him to his madcap plan where death even now tickled and teased him in the frigid sea. The odorless air of a frozen bone yard planet where nothing lived save the other pallid hulks of humanity, removed from the wildcat freedom they cherished most.

Gray abandoned factories loaded with toxins, crumbling ugly monuments to the futility of man's labors hugging the shorelines of plutonian seas dirty and neglected for time untold.

Stroke push. Must get to the freighter.

Push, stroke.

Something poked at his leg. He gasped, flailing around and going under. He was shocked; he took a gulp full of acrid water and spit it out. He coughed and swam wildly backward, fear rising like a feral beast in his chest.

Just more ice, nothing more. There's nothing there.

His cough had been loud. Twisting back around in the icy water he looked to the freighter. Had they heard him? What manner of sound sensors was operating on that thing? No, no one was expecting a madman to try these waters. The noise of the freighter's drive units surely covered him. Its Cyborgian pilots were still probably running internal scans of the tachyon props, collating systems and reviewing manifests.

Cyborgian Central was comatose when it came to internal security. Everyone and everything in their worlds obeyed their rules. What else could one do in a surveillance society? What could one do when a bio-chip was planted smack in your liver and monitored your every move? When relentless mind programming was broadcast on every holoscreen in every shop and every corner?

Leon had gone in with a red-hot needle and removed the chip. The needle's heat cauterized any bleeding immediately. The chip was dropped in a bio simulator he'd rigged up from a tape he ran of his vitals for a month.

Thusly, according to Cyborgian Central, he was sitting in an old factory loft right now sleeping. However, he didn't know what other security measures they might have taken.

Surely they couldn't expect him to swim the icy harbor. His mind drifted with the slow rhythms of his breaststroke. Dip, pull. *Keep moving, keep moving.*

Keep moving. Shiver in the icy water and long for the shiny warmth and light of the Pleiades. The Pleiades! A brilliant swarm of glimmering blue diamonds shining on a distant water world's tropical turquoise sea. Coral seas and Spanish dancing. Hologram festivals and tourists dropping in from the sky by the millions to throw money around from a thousand distant worlds. Rum, Ahura-Mazda dragon rum to slide over your tongue and run down your throat with a promise.

His leg was suddenly numbed where the ice had bashed him. Perhaps it had bled out the warmth? If he could only see in this cursed darkness.

Push, stroke, push.

Waves came splashing at his facemask. The water grew choppier.

Got to get to the freighter. Hide. Soon it'll be running back up to the stars. Gotta be on it. Last week another prisoner removed. Another to their death lab-Leyla Veronica, a virtual innocent dragged along with Leavel and Salvatore. What would they do to her? Carve up her brain looking for Out pilot flying skills she didn't have.

221

Oops, well, she's not even a pilot-sorry!

The ice water was taking its toll. He felt strange disorientation and the realization that his suit and its thermal limits were breaching his warmth. If he could just get out of the water, get on the freighter. On his facemask were numbers. Estimated countdown to the gravity fields complete drop to nil. Then the barrier shields would go up to protect just such an intrusion as he sought. He'd have a split second then to get inside the perimeter of the barrier. If he made that split second, he could sit on the outside of the ship. Take cover under some insulated equipment. The normal space bubble would carry enough atmosphere through the freighter's next voyage for him to ride stow away to the next port.

He knew her next port was the Pleiades. This ship carried luxury foodstuffs for the officers and the planet's guards.

Amazingly, he drew up to the perimeter of the fields. The numbers on his facemask were drawing down; just moments now.

He watched the numbers for what seemed an eternity. They reached zero and yet the fields remained. He miscalculated!

There would be no swimming back, and no treading water. He would surely die now and sink to the bottom of this forgotten sea unknown forever to mankind.

Then the fields dropped.

Savagely he plunged forward, sinking into the blackness for long blind seconds, caring not that he couldn't see. Wildly his arms and legs lunged, moving his body in the direction of the ship. When he finally broke for air again, he saw the hull. He pulled his tired flesh onto the metal-it was still warm from the hyper streams. He dragged himself exhausted over the huge collider pipes. He heard the click and rattle of the security barrier go up.

Too late now boneheads, I'm free.

He rested on the shimmering ultra-steel of a late model star freighter unbelieving, even then, that he had pulled it off.

What could go wrong now? He looked back at the dark shoreline and its jagged riot of silhouetted dead factories, and knew in his heart he would never return there-not alive anyway. The taste of freedom already in his blood was like a wellspring of will. Only death could drag him back to that arcane little Hell.

Chrysalis Isla-her memories began filling up his being with immanent, insistent desire. Lovers and friends. Gardens and parks. Islands and beaches and mansions and happy crowds. Art galleries and rum laced with synthopiate. The Pleiades sitting in the sky like fiery legends of mythical beings born for pleasure and promising more.

The ship hummed suddenly. Leon felt a nervous rush of dread. Had they discovered him? Was the freighter equipped with sensors that searched for a stowaway? Did they have sensors locked on him now with particle beams ready to shatter his organic molecules into mush? Were there implants inside him he missed, even now giving him away?

The humming stopped. He sat quiet and unmolested. He thought of his leg, a small gash was all. A memento of his most important swim. They'd not get him again. He smiled, and in his mind ran a little prayer:

This is my creed
Out, out-out!
Away from the imperial devils
Into the arms of God.

A wind of Ophelia's storms came up and buffeted the barrier fields; useless whimpering. He tightened his grip on the ship needlessly. The cold wind could no longer touch him. He continued his silent prayer.

Out to thee, oh Lord
Asking mercy for my trespasses
Asking safety to the uncharted stars
This is my creed
Ever running up
Out to the uncharted stars

Later, the monitors reported when he missed a duty assignment. Blood was found on the ice at the harbor and a small scandal avoided when a guard simply shrugged the whole incident off and filed him as dead, killed in an escape attempt-Leon's last stand. As for Leon, I last saw him drinking rum in a little cove we know at Bicycle Bay. There a club there by the water with dancing girls. He was singing El Manisero. He had a hangover and sunburn, and a lot of tales to tell. I listened and enjoyed the rum.

Mohanga River
Ophelia's World, Perseus Arm, 4212

Leon was supposedly dead. CC sent a bunch of guards out searching for him. There was no trace of his body. They did a light-duty search and wrote him off. That evening Vince, Sagamore, and a woman Outpilot named Moss walked out on the ice and stared at the blood. They'd found his trace chip in a stasis loop with a timed signal back at his lair. Vince laughed so hard he almost fell down. CC would never look for Leon again, anywhere. In a matter of days, Leon would be cruising the beaches at Chrysalis Isla, drinking rum and synthopiates, gambling, and nursing his sunburn. It was a beautiful ruse he'd pulled.

He was officially dead. In reality, however, he had a sunburn and hangover.

"Little bugger buggered the buggerers," Sagamore said smiling.

"Let's get off this ice before it collapses. The planet's warming a bit." Moss said.

They turned and started moving back toward the giant grain elevators at the edge of the sea.

"If we had some good software I could run a field mockup of a landing. See how he pulled this off. I never tried to board freighter water ported without a gangway, and odds are it is virtual suicide. But the power of the fields down might preclude defensive shield initiation. Even by a few seconds, and that's all he'd need to get inside the shield perimeter." Vince offered.

A whistling wind curled in from the bay.

Sagamore grumbled. "Yeah and if you're off by a nanosecond you'd be sliced clean in half."

"Mr. Salvatore," Moss Chided. "You don't want to spend the next seventy years on this ice ball do you?"

"No. Can't do that. Guess I'd rather be sliced in half."

A CC aircar was prowling between towers in an abandoned city center across an inlet. Its glistening metal and lights were a bright contrast to the pale and faded grimy towers.

"Let's hurry. Company's patrolling the friendly skies." Vince said. They quickened their pace across the ice.

"There's a major transportation hub a few kilometers into the restricted zone," Moss explained, running her hands through a holo map. It runs the power and working systems for some maglev transportation systems still functioning. Cc wouldn't have gutted the center because they wouldn't have been able to anticipate future needs. They'd have wanted to set it back up at will, without costs, at any time. The software there would be able to handle gravity simulations, vector and field manipulations, and hypothetical landing constructions-anything about moving an object through gravity bubbles and repulsion fields."

"And all I'll need to do is walk out with it?" Vince was not hopeful.

"There will be floors, buildings, acres of abandoned equipment. Find one they're not using, and bring back the software.

Sandbox simple. Reach in; pull it out, walk away." Moss smiled.

"In a restricted zone!" Sagamore laughed as if to say, "not so easy".

"Admittedly, we've lost some convicts in there before. CC can be unpredictable in the restricted zones. I think they're just bored. Stay under viaducts as much as you can. Wear a heat sink." Moss said, pulling out some gear. "This will muffle your chip for a while." She held up a garment. "We've tested them before. CC usually doesn't get around to responding to the muffle for about six hours. We think the guards don't report it until the end of their shift, passing the work on to the next crew. Good for us, stupid of them."

"Six hours?" Vince looked unhopeful but relished the chance to do mischief.

Moss looked at him evenly. "That's pushing it. Don't linger looking at the architectural relics, okay Vince?"

"Sure. Get the software, get back." He smiled and made his way through the door, into the steel and ice.

High, high above the airways
In the darkness alone with the silvery stars
Long ago my heart moves back
To your soft face asleep in the clouds
High in the night above the airways
My love too late recalled
The deep azure night
Where my spirit raged free
Too late recalled the passing of our time
Too late, my love, recalled.
Starpeace, "Never know what you got till it's gone"
Starky Barky holos unlimited.

Vince hitched a ride on a repair crew's maglev. It was an old red vehicle with dirty rounded streamlined forms that rode over the frozen rails with a noisy shaking uncertainty that the crew took for granted like everything else on this running down world. When Vince called to be dropped off, they slowed the hulking noisy monster to a crawl. One of the crew smiled and winked from behind a tattered work hat that covered most of his face, 'Hey do-Outy! Run up, run free."

Vince jumped off, "Hey, do!" and made his way along another line toward the restricted zone. It was just another pallid, frozen, grey twilight on Ophelia. He trudged along stoically. A blizzard was threatening in the distance. It was to be a grueling walk, but moving along the aqueducts, trestles, and ramparts that supported the ancient industrial complex was a good way to shirk any obvious monitoring from CC patrols.

They always watched, they never watched. One never really knew.

Leyla. You're gone and I'm to blame. Absconded offworld without due process. I never meant to love you, to wrap you up so with my life and being. How I've dragged you into this awful mess of horror.

He moved through abandoned buildings, empty streets, making for the software. The storm on the horizon moved ever closer. But with each step, he lived in two worlds; the prison of his present, and the prison of his past.

224

Leyla. Standing in a backstreet bar the night they met. Tall, Nordic, with big smiling cheeks and a white jacket. In time she had gotten under his skin, and before he realized it the carefree glamour girl with the happy-go-lucky attitude was a much a part of him as himself. Opposites, her obsession with fashion and wealth as obtuse as his with philosophy, art, and history.

Yet she laughed, and he loved her laughter. Loud, raucous, sometimes even vulgar, she smiled at life and refused defeat.

His conscience dug into his belly with bile he could taste welling over his whole being with culpability.

I've done this, sent you down a path you'd have never chosen. If I was a better man, more patient, more clear, we'd be resting now somewhere safe in each other's arms.

Vince peered into the sky. The present prison compelled attention. Maybe a drone, maybe an aircar; lights in the distance threatened. Occasionally a satellite lasered a prisoner in half. No explanations-just pop. Gone. Intrusion into a restricted zone would qualify that. Moss needed the software to perform an analysis. Send Vince. Mad Vince. Always the Avant guard. Over the rainbow Vince, always looking beyond the farthest star. Send him.

That's that.

He trudged on. Vince was sensitive to a sense of the life left behind in the cold structures. The echoes of ambitious and industrious people. It seemed very wrong CC had abandoned such a wealth of history. Their ghosts must rage at this indignity, Vince thought. He was sad for them. They had achieved great things here. It had come to neglect when it should have been heralded.

The wind curled in at his feet. The last of the pale day had long faded. The transportation center was spun out from a middle tower of a hundred stories of pink stone. It rose in sharp leaps toward the heavens. Still daring, splendid, and bold in abandonment. A station of ghosts changing trains in the land of the dead. He shivered, the cold seeped into his bones, and he thought he too would freeze, small and extinguished.

He adjusted the night vision on his faceplate and stepped through a giant archway, into the immense vaulted halls of the maglev station. Delightful murals of sporty tourists arriving onworld covered a stretch of wall. Tropical scenes before the silenced terraforming. This had been the central hub for all the cities around the inland seas, and three other metropolises along the New Midas Ocean to the East.

Many Hundreds of thousands had moved through here once easily each day. Now frost and dust ruled the halls. The artists who made the murals, the people they depicted-dust.

Suddenly there came the whine of an aircar. Vince turned and ducked down a glide ramp, its suspensions fields amazingly still in service. He was swept down a couple of floors. He stepped off the ramp and stopped. The aircar had moved on. He felt the muffle Moss had given him nervously. Surely they couldn't know here was here. Did the glide ramp have a traffic counter? Maybe even now a signal swept into CC indicating the presence in the old Station.

The glide ramp did seem to have tripped several systems into service, however. Vince followed their trail of lights-it was serviceable systems he was after. In an elevator, he saw there were a hundred and seventeen floors in the tower. A time capsule of the week before CC shut the planet down. Long, long, ago. Long enough for this world to become a legend of fear across the galaxy.

Night vision cast a weird blue hue over everything. He moved into the elevator and keyed the only floor still lit-the ninety-ninth floor. It was risky, taking the lift like that-who knows what systems might fail and leave him trapped there. But following the lights had logic too. They seemed a natural trail to follow.

Stepping onto the ninety-ninth floor, he saw it was undisturbed from its last days of operation. A workman's shirt lay casually tossed aside and forgotten; it had been warm that day. Perhaps later he'd looked for it, or had they all been gone when the cold came? There was a cyber access desk with an oblong jewel-like screen for virtual visualizations. Standard technology for over a millennium.

It had a blinking light on the top-*the end of the trail.*

"Okay, I'll bite," Vince said. He took a seat in front of the Virtual screen. The room disappeared and was replaced with another. It took him a moment to realize it was the same room-only bright an alive. The place was full of office workers in casual clothing. They were noisily going about their business. The sky was intense and blue and littered with colorful air cars. He looked at himself in his ragged prisoner's clothing.

"Well aren't you quite the ragamuffin." A female voice quipped.

Vince turned and saw a rather slight woman with green eyes and an upturned chin. She was wearing thirty-fifth-century office clothing, a light green sundress with a white frill which matched her eyes perfectly. A secretary?

"Yes… Guess I am now." Vince responded quietly.

"Caught you on the glide ramp down below." She confided conspiratorially, "I set it a while back so as I'd get a call when someone came around. Couldn't leave the place totally without a welcome. Where you from? I don't recognize your accent."

"The Sagittarius Arm. A little world called Rip."

Her eyes rose at that. "Come now, there's naught out there but scattered refugees, and hardly a ship scratching around the worlds to the worlds since the war."

"Well, things have changed." Vince offered, still unsure what he was dealing with.

"How long since they shut the world down?" She asked.

He hesitated.

"How long?"

"About five centuries now."

"For heaven's sake!" She quipped. "I'm long gone then. Long gone."

"Who are you?" Vince asked.

The slight woman in green looked him squarely in the eye. Not one to flinch from things as they were. "Who *was* I. Hazel Mary Butler. Born in 3512 on the bustling world of Ophelia, which I daresay has wound down a bit since then apparently."

She smiled. "I worked in this office for years and years. I logged in every morning before anyone. Saved my logs for every day-"

"And couldn't bear to erase them when they closed the company." Vince finished.

"Yes. I….well, she couldn't bear to erase them, and I couldn't bear to tell her she'd left a full psychic mirror in the programs because-heavens-that would have meant she'd have erased me!"

"You're a sentient program created inadvertently who have hidden away here for five centuries?" Vince chuckled. "You're illegal, you know."

She guffawed. "I'm me. What nit-wit can make me illegal?"

"Don't worry Hazel; I'm not one for enforcing CC laws. I'm here for breaking them. Your secret's safe with me."

"Hmm. The rainforests and the beaches must be frozen now. The ladies with the billowing dresses and the lovely parasols gone? The silvery maglevs with the velvet interiors. Gone. Are they sitting empty? The fairs and music festivals? You don't know what this place was like in its day do you?"

Vince looked around the bright and bustling office. Through a window, he could see a glimmering world of color, and wonder, and life. The towers were clean and proud.

"I've only imagined."

"Goodness," she said. "I fear what it's become. What did you come here for?"

"I need software that can handle creating a visualization of a field landing when a star freighter waterports."

The office chattered and bustled and flashed the excitement of the day, and she gazed steadily at him. "Whatever for?" she asked.

"Because I'm illegal too. And I want to leave."

"The nerve!" she said.

Vince smiled and showed her his palms.

She turned to a keyboard and fussed over it for a time. Then she pointed to a bank of panels along a wall. One of the panels lit up and eased out of the wall.

"There you go. It has everything you need." She looked as if he'd asked her for a big favor.

"Thank you," Vince said and walked to the panel. When he pulled it out the room went dark and quiet again. The woman in the green dress, the office full of light and people, all of it was gone. There was only he, standing there holding the panel, it the dreary dark and cold. He slipped it into his pocket and sealed it tight.

With the pilfered software in hand, Vince made his way through the vast and empty vaulted halls of the maglev station.

Here the station opened into the Transportation building. The stonework above danced in white leaping pinwheels of lace terra-cotta patterns; abstracted galaxies. Beneath the repeated galaxies, figures strode through a history of transportation with an important purpose. Watching the Ages reach their dull conclusion of abandonment and decay, Vince was gripped with a desolate sense of nihilism.

Vince peered outside. In the grim dark rattled a loose piece of metal, caught in a sudden wind. The wind passed, and silence once again ruled the empty yards. Hulking maglevs sat undignified on the ground, their levitation equipment deactivated even before the final closing of the world.

There was no sign of the Cyborgian patrols as he first stepped under the starlight, dashing over the rows of barren maglev rails. He began his jaunt in earnest, scanning the skies for the tell-tale glimmer of silent lights. There were none. No rhyme or reason to the Cyborgians enforcement of the restricted zones. He suspected the lower level Cyborgs of keeping the Hive mind at minimum input while they ate doughnuts or slept on duty.

If he could make it across the Mohanga River he'd be clear. If not, there'd be hell to pay, and they might even begin fitting him with programming chips. It'd take some trumping, clearly unconstitutional even in Cyborgian space.

But while the mass of the population was diverted with their sensorama plays, their athletic contests, non-objective art, and their alternative lifestyle trivia fashions, the government had been disassembling their liberties for centuries like a slow irresistible tide. More importantly, it had shaped society in such a way that any real economic or personal freedoms would be unacceptable to the populace because they would introduce a level of uncertainty that would necessitate them living in the real world.

Vince passed out of the maglev yards, spindly ground car roads spun off in graceful arcs of bridges. The bridges still held their form after ages of ice storms; a testament to their engineers. He followed one of them, taking a different route back to the sea than the one he had come. The snow was melting-Ophelia's brief summer would be upon them soon. Some of the snow never did melt, and it was in those places, where year after year layers of ice formed, that it was most dangerous to walk. Honeycombed beneath the ice could be other levels of the megalopolis. Not everything held up as well as the ground car bridges.

So he tried to follow the roads, trudging back along a slightly different route in case they followed his trail coming in. Now certainly paranoia was creeping into his brain. The Mohanga River marked the edge of the restricted zone along his new route. He need only make it to the river.

He had two hours left when the blizzard hit.

He watched the storm come, a darker patch of sky in an already miserably ruddy night. It crept along like some evil being intent on his soul. He took shelter under a maglev trellis-one of a group of trellises affording reach over a wide abandoned rail yard that edge the Mohanga. A few hundred yards more and he'd be out of the restricted zone and clear of CC patrols. But the wind and the sleet would have easily killed him before he could make it across. Instead, he sat cowering under concrete and plastisteel.

Vince Phalen who'd captured a CC frigate changed his name to Leavel and pirated the star lanes smuggling goods into imperial space, Vince Leavel, who made it to Luxus University World studying Space Architecture with a lovely fiancé; there he sat alone under a bridge huddling from the weather.

The muffle Moss gave him was running out. Ironically, only the storm protected him now from prying CC. Surely they'd have registered his signal missing. No one, however, was going to sport around in aircars in this weather.

They'd need huge gravity manipulators, and even with the patrol cars that had them, no one would bother.

Let the nasty little convict die in the snow. The storm wouldn't last forever. Haul his corpse in later-register it a suicide.

Shane Perry

Suicide at Mohanga River.

Suicide! Never. Of all the indignities piled on my reputation. Never that. Not that!

Vince cursed the whole of CC under his breath and trudged again into the storm. The wind buffeted him in careening whirls. The ice slammed into the crevices of his clothing. Each step was maddening. Worse, he was soon to the trellises over the river. Once he found himself flailing for balance over the trellis. Looking back, he realized he would have fallen to an escarpment of rocks in the channel, crushed to his death. Star pilot falls off a bridge. He cursed the absurdity of his life and stepped on.

He was in the middle of the bridge, buffeted by sleet and wind when he looked up to see a CC air car steady and in front of him, its lights barely pierced the storm.

Why the lazy turds had come out after all. Their aircar was holding up admirably. Now, however, his goose was cooked.

"Leavel." Came a voice over a loudspeaker, "You're standing pretty close to a restricted zone. What are you doing out in this storm?" a voice boomed metallically over a speaker. It carried strangely in the air and wind. Was he dreaming?

If they found the software they would trace it to Moss and Sag. He looked at the lights of the aircar and then the rushing waters below. Oh well. He jumped.

The CC guards in the aircar poked their heads forward and watched him fall into the water.

"Not another one!" the patrolman blurted as he watched the con fall to the water.

His partner adjusted the aircar so they had a better view of the descending prisoner. "And...splash!" he said.

"Register it a suicide, let the next shift fish him out if they can. I'm not dealing anymore with this storm. They got a new shipment of Coffee from the Pleiades the other day. What do you say, early break?"

"Yeah, sure. Just let's fly around a bit so we can log in that we looked for this con, eh? That was the guy in the big arrest tape you know?"

"No shit? That's the guy? Ain't so hot no more. Eh-heh. Eh-heh!"

"Yeah. Now he's cold toast. That river isn't going to cough him up easy. Let's get out of here. Feel like a doughnut?"

"Yeah. Java time."

The aircar spun away.

The Boiler

Vince hit the water like it was a slab of plexisteel. The noise of the storm was instantly quieted with the strangle rush of bubbles, and then the silence of the huge river. He was under. The cold felt like a million daggers shot into his body at once-the only relief was that he'd already started to go numb from the sleet. He fought for a moment and then went black.

Above the waters, an angry wind shook the world, searching to vent hostility. Below, he rolls in the blackness and cold, spinning faster and ever more disingenuously unaware of the cold and dark.

Oh for my comrades, my crew-we've delivered a large shipment of diamonds to Caldris on a run this morning. The mighty Sire is in wet dock off the shore. Simone, Millin, Sag, Roland-we've all rented a light blue saucer-shaped aircar and flown over to the shallow oceans where the sculpted red pylons of Caldris's metal processing plants jut out of the waters. They are rows of identical towers. The sun is setting over the warm water which is so clear you can see straight down-four meters easy.

Half a dozen air cars are perched on one of the pylons and people are diving into the soft warm water. Millin has a tank of Margaritas; he's just back from the store.

Millin is saying "The tides of history have ebbed, still and unmoved for centuries, Vinny. It's all creep and rot. CC hasn't constructed a gateway in over a millennium, no new technologies have been constructed albeit those that are rediscovered from Predecessor relics. Something scared CC back in the days of the war. Something's coming Vince, something horrible and frightening and inconceivable up until now."

I remember the CC crewmembers on Rip, screaming and bloody and wild as Cyborgs should never be. I say nothing, but I know he's right.

I look out over the turquoise waters.

229

"You've been listening to Roland and his fairy tales, Millin."
Leyla swims over to the pylon. "Come back in boys, the waters lovely."
Leyla can't be here. I wasn't to meet her for years-
"Pull!" Moss says through gritted teeth. "Damn! It's cold!"
"He's a goner." Sagamore's mighty thews lift the wet Captain from the icy side of the river. Like a piston engine with a mono program, he carries the other man steady and unwavering. At the maglev line, a huge old red machine sits waiting.
"They got him!" One of the men says, opening the doors.
"Yeah, same we guy we gave a lift to earlier."
"He's alive. Gimme that medkit. Holy stars what a lucky muck!"
Moss felt the side of his jacket. After they tended to Vince, she looked in and saw the software panel. *He got it!*

Moss's place was in the head of a twenty-meter-high loading robot along the shore by the grain elevators. She holed Vince up there and nursed back to health. The colossus head had an apartment-sized engineer's room with some amenities and a lot of hardware that used to operate the loading equipment. The giant body of the robot had long since been deactivated, but much of the head's brains were still good. Moss slipped Vince's pilfered software into the main computer and had been constructing elaborate field studies for several days.
She was biting her lip and fussing over one of them when Sag pounded on the door and sauntered in.
"Leon got out because they're shipping us offworld without due process." She said.
"Yeah, I know." Sagamore slapped a stimulant on his arm and his countenance brightened. "Unconstitutional. I can't figure why CC would bother to mess with their own laws. None of it makes sense."
"Something's got them desperate. The whole mess reeks of desperation. Hell, this is their space. They don't bend the rules here. Cloak and dagger stuff-shipping pilots deep out space to secret bases." Moss sneered.
Vince was still comatose with meds. But his eyes were sharp.
Something's got them desperate. Cloak and dagger stuff.
Moss continued, "What could frighten the largest and most powerful government in the galaxy? After the Arcturian wars, they've never had a full-scale war in a millennium. No one can stand against them."
"Not for real anyway," Sag said.
"CC plays by the rules generally because they can afford to. Bread and circuses, virtreels and synthetics-a populace numb on namby-pamby pabulum. There's an unknown factor here. They're using us for lab rats out there at that lab-everybody suspects it."
"Perhaps Paramon?" Sag offered.
"No." Vince finally spoke. "Paramon is the egg, not the chicken-they built the research base first, then Paramon threw up the blockade. If anything, it's more convenient for them. Less traffic in and around the star systems out there. It's something else."
Moss and Sag stared waiting for what he would say next.
"There a story on my homeworld about the last battle before the refugees fell to the ground," he said, "The CC frigate that was chasing them suddenly went mad and disengaged the battle. Some psychic being crept into their minds and drove them insane." Vince looked at them through his frostbitten and salved face like he was a psychic being.
"Vince." Sag looked amazed. "I can't believe you're toting out that old campfire story now. Leyla's up there. This is big trouble."
"I know. There's more. Where do you think I got my antique frigate?"
Sagamore looked like he'd been hit with an obvious brick. "Of course-"

"Yes. It was the frigate that went down in the last battle. Under stasis, under some rock-a lot of rock. But I found it, dug down to it. Found the stasis controls and eased off the stasis. I went into the ship and the crew was there, just come out of stasis and still in the middle of a horror that was a millennia-old to us and a moment ago to them.

"They were maddened creatures. Animals really, more bizarre and awful than any men I've seen in conflict, before or since. I've traversed the galaxy since that hellish day, and not seen the likes of these despicable things. Whatever they experienced left them-I don't have the words. I killed them all myself and I swear to you these pricks were so gone it was damn near mercy killing."

The room was silent. Moss looked at Sagamore. The expression on his face was one of explanation, like pieces of a mystery were falling in to place. Something dark and inexplicable had always haunted the Captain, made him fearless where other men would cower, moody and solemn when other men would cheer. Sag saw a part of it then.

"Spooky stuff," Moss said. "Fitting for a spooky nebula. The Diablo nebula." She set the field manipulations away and called up another program. It was the Diablo nebula.

Sags eyes widened. "I didn't know you had galactic charts in there-"

She gave him a wicked smile. "I didn't. That software Vince brought back-it's a virtual encyclopedia of knowledge. Most of it about five centuries old, but a huge resource nonetheless. You won't find half this stuff on standard CC data output today. Very clever Vince. You brought a universe in a box when you brought that back."

Vince guffawed. "I had no idea. I just asked for some visualizing software."

"Asked?" Sag queried. "Who'd you ask?"

Vince sighed. "I'll tell you later."

Moss called up the hologram of the Diablo Nebula. "The Devil's Clouds," she said. "An anomaly. Moving counter to the turn of the galaxy, unknown origin. Many black holes surrounding a rather large star-forming region. A play of gravitational forces that mysteriously counter and repel each other-without any appreciable antimatter plumes-a shuddering, shifting the mass of dark and un-navigable meson nightmare. Ships go in and often don't come out. Sometimes they come out years later thinking only days have passed. Often there are tales of lost Arcturian fleets. Relics, Predecessor ships.

Then, of course, there are the insane ones, the ones found rambling nonsense on the casts. Perhaps their navigational constructs fried their brains trying to create holos of all them interacting black holes at once."

Vince stared grimly ahead. Lab rats, they're using us as lab rats to push the realm of science where it shouldn't be pushed.

Roy Rudder

Siluria

Bandor had never seen furious rage before. The figure in the holoscreen of Harry now was livid. He moved about the room like an experimental subject having a bad reaction to a new protein complex in his cerebrum.

"He's dead! He's alive! He's dead! He's alive! What the hell is going on at that penal colony at Ophelia anyway? What it is a health club? They're roaming around the planet freely, making new friends!

"Look Bandor, I set those smugglers up for public humiliation and incarceration. What happens? They become even more famous as rouge folk heroes than before. Now what's supposed to be a torturous penal colony becomes a place for them to regroup and build new alliances. This is not working according to my plan. You contact your people at CC and have them little pricks placed in the nastiest hard duty conceivable, see? I mean carcinogenic fibers, dirty black dust in the air to breathe, machinery so old there aren't replacement parts. Temperature extremes-danger, poison, and ugliness! Every day of their rotten lives!"

"Yes, yes. I'm sure that's workable." Bandor didn't understand the motivation of revenge yet, but he knew it was important to Harry that the convicts he'd set up suffer.

"I'll take care of the rest." Harry smiled.

"What do you mean?" Bandor was confused now.

"What I mean is enough games; I'm going to have the little pricks killed. Killed, killed, killed, killed, and killed some more until they're fracking D-E-A-D dead! Dead for good-bye, bye!!"

Then the holo was gone. Bandor walked out of the holo room and stood at his director's desk. An ultra-steel wall in front of him opened over the research laboratories and he could look down on the workings there. Screens in his office showed details of various operations taking place. Regret welled up in him with each turn of the micro knife. Surely this was wrong. He remembered his days a simple clerk in the hive mind and the happily organized illusions CC had sent out about its nature as a government; benevolent, purposeful, humane. A lie. The truth was this: people mattered not at all. They were things to be used, butchered, spent and forgotten.

Bandor almost longed for the ignorance of the lie again. It was such a lovely deception. Regret filtered into fear. Something was driving CC to this butchery, something they wouldn't even speak of. Wild humans believed in a higher being a God thing. Of course, they believed in the opposite of God, a Devil thing. They had named this bizarre nebula after the Devil thing- Diablo. Bandor began to wonder at such notions. He began to know fear in new ways each day. Outside the base, slithering primitive creatures slashed in primordial forests and seas. They were enormous monstrosities with claws and scales. Devil things.

He shuddered.

Harry walked to his parapets and watched his flyers moving about the skies of the gardens. White roses wafted up sweet scents. He called Maximus Mercurio on his com. Momentarily, Maximus's short and muscled self was striding arrogantly along the terraces, confident and proud as ever.

Mercurio the great. Harry snickered to himself. Without self-absorbed egomaniacs such as this, the buffalos would still be roaming en-mass in North America.

"Max." Harry said, "Time to clean the toilet."

Maximus smiled. "Sir?"

"I want you to knock off those Outpilots we set up, you remember the one-the Taloned Sire's Captain and his mate?"

"But of course. The Butcher of Baal One. Thought you would never ask."

"Yes. They're getting too comfortable in that icy cage, and I daresay showing muscle again. That Leavel creature managed to survive a tumble into a nearly frozen river."

When Harry had gotten word his favorite pet convict had been killed in the river, he'd experienced an awful sense of missed opportunity that seared him. Why had he not been the taker of that foul life? When later word had come that Vincent had survived, he nearly wet himself with glee when it occurred to him this go around he could off him.

Maximus grunted. "Got the lives of a cat, eh sir?"

Harry nodded. "Damned cat. I want you to show up there as an observer-I'll provide the codes and equipment. Bomb them, burn them, whatever. Just make it clean, and don't leave a trail should anyone start sniffing around."

Maximus rubbed his golden horn in hungry anticipation. "Sweet mystery of life!" he chuckled.

Somewhere deep in Harry's soul, there stood a young soldier dressed in white. All the goodness a man could aspire to live in that soul. Next to him, covered in the blood of horrors and betrayals and idiocy, stood the slightly older self, eyes widened and hungry for revenge. Of the two, the second was by far the stronger.

By duty assignment time Vince was back to reasonable health. CC had dragged him in for questioning and medical review when his chips started feeding in normal bio information. They gave him a warning but nobody took the incident seriously. Moss was able to work on her simulations unmolested, and Vince found himself assigned to repairing boilers in a particularly unpleasant section of a nearby city.

In the darkness of the dirty factory, Vince remembered all he had lost. The elegant parties, the spontaneous trips to crystal cities full of art, music, and dance. Leyla's swift hair and bright eyes.

Leyla. How could I have let our wonderful dreams slip through my fingers? What is to become of you know?

233

The boiler he had to repair that shift was seven stories high. There were four of them in a row in this section of the plant, and several more in an adjacent section. From the dirty catwalks and metal railings where he stood, he could see whole maglev trains parked in gargantuan rooms like toys.

Dirty fat pipes and crusty computer units hummed with the growling workings of mindless programs. His welding unit flashed brilliantly and the ancient wall of the boiler was revealed. Scribbled notes left by other workers, who knows when. Dust and rust.

Leyla's memory was always next to him. Her laughter hung a bitter clarity in his mind. Where was she now? Did she live-had they moved her on? Did she lay broken and dead on a CC research table?

One of the insectoid computers, a pressure pump Vince figured, lifted an ancient robotic head.

"Greetings good worker." It said.

Protocols from another era.

Vince winked and kept welding. The Cyborg attachments he threw on that morning were scanning for microscopic fissures and resetting the metals. It was a good six stories to the bottom-the most important thing to remember was footing.

There came a banging of corrugated metal loosed somewhere in the unforgiving weather of Ophelia's winds. Vince heard it banging out his culpability. If he had stayed on Luxus. If he had only stayed on Luxus. He would be there now developing some brilliant design for an Architectural masterpiece. He could crawl casually into her arms and hold her.

Leyla-

The metal banged in the wind. A surreal metal voice clanging his guilt, a metallic guardian at the gates of hell saying to each who enter, "You did this to yourself."

It wasn't the wind. The banging was in the boiler. It's pace and volume increased. A strange smell was filling the air around him and it pulled Vince out of his trance of regret, and back into the present where he was standing on a dirty I beam in a dark shaft inches away from seven stories of dangerously high-pressure units.

Someone was yelling. "Everybody down! She's gonna blow! Get down! Get down!"

Vince saw several workers scrambling for cover, tossing Cyborg units aside and running scared as men had always run from such dangers. They were making for the lower decks.

If I just stand here when it blows, it will all be over. He stared at the loud rumbling wall with a strange fascination, waiting for the explosion to annihilate him. From somewhere a sense of himself came back, a sense of self-worth, even if he had made grievous errors. A sense of a duty to live, even an imperfect life.

The giant unit was rumbling and banging. He jumped to a grated deck and found some stairwells. His work boot came apart on one side and he stumbled on the stairs. The air was smelling acrider with every moment.

There came a ripping, hissing sound and a wave of air and debris. He staggered to one side behind a huge pipe and watched a massive cloud of insulation, types of cement, and wire grating falls into the air and down toward maglevs below.

Steam filled the air and he covered his face until it cleared.

About a hundred meters away, where the other boilers began, he saw a figure lean from behind a duct to look at the damage wrought by the explosion. Even at that distance, Vince could make out an unusual horn projecting from the side of the man's head. Vince had seen such a cyborg attachment at Luxus, the ripjackle men from the red yacht. *So. They've come here to finish their destruction of my life. Well, horny little Man-I'll not go so easily as that.*

Vince moved back among the other workers. The foreman was shaking his head. "Guess who's going to rebuild this?" he said to the crew. Vince looked at the splintered wall. A small hole after all, but very nearly deadly just the same.

Shane Perry

The Freighter

I heard a joke once about an ancient Earth institution called the Department Of Motor Vehicles. The "DMV", as it was called, regulated ground cars in the twentieth and twenty-first centuries. The joke was that "here lies the origins of Cyborgian Central." The comparison was laughable, of course, but perhaps more true than the jester realized. For people living in that era, pleasing the various regulators of ground cars was crucial.

It was an ugly little labyrinth of excise taxes, forms, and nonsense that was always injudiciously applied. That early man-machine relationship was prophetic. By the beginning of the twenty-fifth century, Cyborg implants were necessary for nearly all types of work. Little by little CC wound its way into every aspect of human work, human relations deriving from work, and ominously, trade. It was fortunate for humanity that nation-states still existed on Earth at the time of the great diaspora, and had sent out ships with the seeds of independent civilizations. Very fortunate...

-Winteroud Sole, Caldris

He was being tailed.

Vince didn't know how much access the golden horned guy and his syndicate had to CC files. They might have complete satellite readout on his every movement. Or not. One thing was certain; they had a lot of pull, or bull, to be able to get on the world at all. This was still a penal colony. Working to Vince's advantage, however, would be CC's complete arrogance and indifference toward the prisoners in general. If a sharp, effective group of syndicate men wanted Vince's head on a platter (and there were any number of reasons why they might-he only knew they did) they'd have to sort through CC slugs to get to him, and that would slow anyone down.

235

"We got company from the syndicate. Meet me at the cascades." Vince kept the call short, he knew it was probably traced and bugged. Sag and Moss were there a few hours later. An old tourist attraction from the days of Ophelia's grandeur, the cascade was a three-kilometer drop where some rivers tumbled from one continental plate to another. A lot of ice had formed over time dragging several sections of old hotels into the ravine. Huge statues of lions were tumbled among the ruined structures so that to Vince it seemed as if the lions were battling amongst themselves and tearing the city down.

Sagamore saw several figures tailing Moss and himself as they came toward Vince's favorite grill. A convict who'd once owned an elegant restaurant now managed a greasy spoon for extra trade. "Vince was right about the syndicate boys. They sure do get around don't they?" Sag said to Moss as they went into Captain Mike's Clam bar.

Nobody asked twice where he got the clams. Mike would just smile.

"This isn't good Vinny. I haven't finished analyzing Leon's break yet." Moss said from a table near his. She was assuming the syndicate would be getting satellite traces either now or later. You got any ideas about these guys?"

"No. They set me up on Chrysler's world. I know they killed and tortured some people to get to me. Then they were content to let me rot here. Now it seems they've reconsidered."

"Lovely. Sounds personal." She ate her clams and looked slightly to her left, eyeing the entry.

"Sag was flying out space. They wanted the two of us together. Set up a reunion on a ruse through an old associate."

"Nice. What have you two done as a pair that would afford such trouble?"

Sagamore interrupted, "Lots of things. But it doesn't matter now. How long until you've analyzed Leon's plan?"

"A few more days," she responded coolly.

"They planted a bomb at my assignment yesterday. It didn't function right so I had time to get out.

"I suggest I take a run through all the unrestricted zones I can manage for the next several days. You continue your work.

Get Sag's chip out like Leon did-set it up in a simulator with a booby trap in case they try and rush him. When I get back from my diversion we do the same with me and you. Then we make our break and leave them hunting down chips in a loop."

Moss raised a glass. "Now I remember why I like you Leavel. You're as slippery as mamonth in a mud bath." She pulled out the muffle he'd used while getting the software. "Here, this will give you six or so hours to get a lead and shake on them. Enjoy your run. Don't let them take you down, Mr. Leavel."

Vince went out a back door.

There was a long empty promenade that went toward a large group of buildings with a glass atrium.

Once it had housed a collection of exotic plants. Vince made his way into the dusty garden. He was halfway across the atrium when he saw two figures enter behind him. So "Golden horn" acquired allies on a world-a couple of tawdry crooks no doubt.

Dangerous, none the less.

Vince was out of the garden, and making his way toward a maglev yard where several maglev trains were powered up and idling when the ground behind him steamed with disruptor fire. So, they were no longer seeking subtlety. He ducked among the maglevs. An engineer was pulling out.

"Hitch a ride?" Vince asked.

The man smiled and nodded affirmatively. Vince clambered in the cabin and felt the rush of speed as the maglev acquired more and more velocity. The Mohanga River rushed by beneath them, then a bulky Herculean mass of beige ornamented towers with the look of ziggurats stretched tall, now a long and seemingly endless stretch of abandoned warehouses and sculpted hundred story towers as they made along the edge of the inland sea.

Vince might have shaken his last two tails, but he'd no illusions of "Golden horn" giving up the chase.

They rode along the sea to another huge city center, and Vince hopped off. He made his way among the maglevs past a group of white ornate towers which he took to be ancient administrative offices for the local governments of the region. CC was still using some of the upper suites. He found a tunnel train still working by asking around and made it further away from the center. He barricaded himself into a service room hugging some heated pipes and went to sleep.

Moss knew the clock was ticking. Sagamore found her banged up on stim, working late, as he made his way into the giant robot head.

"Leon must have had a wet suit to stay alive in the water as long as he did. I've already got several being constructed," she said. "They'll include protections against scans. One would think the freighter would certainly have some standard observational scans, enough to protect them against stowaways. But not as dear Leon has shown."

Sagamore ran his hands through his locks of blonde hair and stared with an intensity Moss had come to recognize as his business end of life.

"The software Vince brought back from the station is fabulous-it's taken on the tasks I've requested on its own. It has figured the shutdown of drive fields and the subsequent rise of security fields isn't perfect. There's a pause-enough for one to get inside the perimeter if you're at the perimeter just as the drives shut down. But the break is only for a moment."

"And I think I know what happens if you miss it. Like you said before?" Sag offered grimly.

"Diced human on ice. You're either sliced in two or, depending on the intensity of the force field-blasted into a billion bits of fish food." Moss chuckled.

"You might be conscious for a few seconds if you're sliced in half eh?"

"Right. No fun. Make sure you get deep in the perimeter though and the fields will protect you from the weather and CC satellite scans. It's an all or nothing shot."

"Do or die." Sag agreed.

"With the syndicate sniffing around you won't be able to ride out quietly like I'm assuming Leon did. We'll have to disable the crew. Set new coordinates, and take get the darn thing off world pronto."

Disable the crew. Before they disable you.

"They might be armed and ready," Sagamore whispered.

They might point a disruptor at your face at any turn once you get on deck. Boil your brains inside your head till your head explodes all over the nice shiny new interior of the ship.

Moss smiled, gave a slow nod.

"In seconds you could run a trillion different coordinates into a swing and shuffle navigational. But we'll need to be getting fast out of the solar plane."

Straight up or down, then folded into a hyper stream. CC will probably still be relaying messages back and forth among drones. By the time they figure out we're gone, we'll be gone.

"In possession of a first-class late-model hyperdrive ship 'bout as fast as any, eh?"

"You got it. Fifty-thousand tons. Sliding sweetly through another pleasant black frigid night on this dirty snowball and out."

Her grin was hungry.

"Yeah, buddy!" Sagamore's hulking form was in, win or lose. He liked a good gamble, thrived on high stakes.

Moss turned and pointed to a pile of surgical equipment sitting on a console. "Now let's get these damnable chips out of our guts."

Mercurio slapped down the two whining pseudo thugs he'd managed to rummage up after snatching back the disruptors he'd lent them. Leavel's chip had been muffled the day before, and now CC was sending up red flags. Max had come downworld with false documents authorizing him as an observer from Chrysalis Isla's Royal Police and hadn't drawn nary a yawn. CC had given him the run of this relic of a world and he nearly managed to snuff out Leavel at his last try.

Again, the man had nine lives.

Harry would not be pleased. Max decided not to mention anything until he had a kill to report. Leavel could be anywhere on the planet hiding out now. His next duty assignment wasn't for several days. Max could wait there and snuff him when he showed up for work. Leavel would already be in a world of pain with CC about twice muffling his chip in as many weeks. He wouldn't risk more time on his sentence, yet he might identify Max and squeal for help.

That could be ugly as CC would be obligated to check his story-especially after the boiler exploded. With Ossa still pissed off about Max's adventures at Ocho's world, CC finding out more about Maximus Mercurio than he'd told them would be…problematic.

Weighing all the options, Max figured his best bet was to dust Sagamore Salvatore and hope Leavel showed up looking for Salvatore later, before his duty assignment. There was an ACD out on Leavel now with Planet Security. If Leavel didn't show up at Salvatore's place, Max would have to be quick to get to him. Before Security started questioning him when they found him. Hopefully, a report would come in from a street camera, and Max could beat everybody to the punch. CC had provided him with a sweet, fast air car.

"Thank you very much." Max had said at the air dock. "This will be very useful."

The aircar banked and turned, heading back toward Salvatore's signal.

The deeper levels of the underground trains had become a world unto themselves after Ophelia had become a penal colony. Unravaged by the weather over the long centuries, there remained an elegance and newness about them that was refreshing. A large population of the prisoners had made it their home. Vince knew CC would be sending out calls for his detention for muffling his chip again. He had to lay low, even from other prisoners. A stoolie would gather a nice reward-a lessening of sentence for sure.

There would be cameras in the train stations. Golden horn might have more thugs patrolling the stations now too. The muffle was secure but he needed a change of clothing and a cover for his face. In a locker, he found and donned a set of work coveralls and a Cyborg helmet that covered most of his face. Unless he ran into a foreman, he could have been anyone returning from or going to a duty assignment. Easy enough. That would give him a little breathing room from the auto scans of the cameras.

More likely to draw Golden horn and his boys out though. Big old disguise and all? Nah.

The underground didn't carry back to Moss's sector, so he made his way up to the surface when he reached the last station. He looked longingly at the dark tube that once ran a line to where he wanted to go. Oh well. He was most of the way there. A short hitch on a surface maglev and he could walk the rest of the way.

It was another dreary grey sky hanging over the maglev rails as he hoofed it.

Not a ride on site.

Mercurio looked at the impossible figure of the loading robot and scoffed. Its metallic Art Deco features were gargantuan, fantastic. They echoed the Lady Robot from Fritz Lang's Metropolis, a reference meant to entertain tourists who passed by the waterfront. It was a reference lost on Max. He was a soldier of fortune not given to distraction, only strategy.

Sagamore was reading as being in the giant robot head by CC chip tracking. There was another con with Sag-a woman. No matter, he'd take them both out. Sagamore wasn't at his domicile, but it hadn't been hard to track him with the CC chips.

Like dissing fish in a barrel.

Max took the stairs, cursing whoever chose such an odd place as a home. He couldn't risk alerting them with the lift. His scanners showed no booby traps and no cameras. Who would they worry about on this dump of a world? Burglars? Heh! He crept stealthily, slowly up stairwell after stairwell taking nothing for granted. On his visor, he could see their chip signals sitting quietly in the room above. They might have been sleeping they were so still.

Like a horned crab working his way silently along, he stepped sideways with one arm pointing up and ahead. His disruptor was gripped neatly at the end of that arm, ready willing and able to take a huge chunk of everything in front of him and make it molten gunk.

Harry had wanted this done cleaner. Max knew he didn't have that luxury now. Kill them and let CC scratch their heads and wonder.

"Vince should be getting back soon. If they haven't popped him." Sagamore was saying flatly. The meds were taking effect now and some of the pain was easing up from his belly. Moss had cauterized everything once she'd gotten the chip in a loop. He didn't ask where she got the meds. They were expensive healing compounds delivered by nanobots that also removed scar tissue. Top shelf stuff.

Someone was walking in the door.

"Vince-" Moss turned.

It wasn't Vince. The man before them was dressed in an expensive offworld cold suit with white trimmings of high tech Borg lacings. Protruding from a matching hat was a golden horn, easily recognizable also as Cyborg implants. A clear Eva field encased his head, glistening. He was holding a first-class disruptor.

"Sagamore Salvatore, the Butcher of Baal One. How nice to see you," he said.

Moss gave Sagamore a sidelong glance.

What is he talking about?

"Corporal Mercurio. Nice to see you too. Glad you made it through the war. But what is this business of 'the butcher'?"

Max stared dumbfounded. His mouth dropped open stupidly then he laughed. "You dumb son of a bitch, you don't even know do you?"

Sagamore looked like he'd have taken apart Mercurio slowly and for fun. "Know what?"

"Hmmm. All this time. Well, I guess it was never going to make the newscasts. That wouldn't have done. The King wouldn't have allowed that. The ground war on Baal One. When a certain deserter makes off with drop-ship thousands of infantrymen are left with no retreat."

Sag sat up straighter. "That was one ship-why it wasn't even a major troop transport, it was a little shuttle. There were other ships, huge ones. I didn't strand anyone!"

"All the other ships were grounded until release codes were sent out by the commanding officer.

He was killed and the codes were on the ship you absconded with. Enemy forces had acquired predecessor technology upgrading their weapons. It was a massacre. We would have all been cut down running but a young officer reorganized our forces." he explained. "Thousands died anyway when the dropships didn't have the release codes. At least they died facing the enemy. Then your friend Vince blasted the air corps out of the sky and made clean your escape. Meanwhile, much of Coral sky battalion died on the hot stones of Baal One."

Sag was a stone. His face was white. "The news reports told of a heroic charge? You took the enemy command center!"

"After we were damn near wiped out. Because you had the codes."

"Leavel didn't know what was happening. When the air corps came after me I flew towards his ship figuring they wouldn't fire on me if I was close to a noncombatant. They kept firing anyway. They must have wanted to disable me and board, get the codes back…

"We were all flying the same flag; Vince had no way of knowing what was happening. But the air corps was firing in his direction. So he defended his ship."

"And saved you."

"Yes. The ship I pirated away with was disabled at that point. I put her down and went EVA. Leavel picked me up. I crewed with him since then. But he had nothing to do with the drop ships-and neither did she." He indicated Moss with a nod. "Let her go, let him go. It will be the murder of innocent people if you don't"

"Vince should have turned you in. But he couldn't he-he'd have to explain how he got that Overlord frigate then wouldn't he? There'd be an inquiry and CC would demand access to his ship logs."

"Leavel wouldn't cooperate with any CC prosecution of anyone-not even you."

"Me? I'm not the staring down a disruptor barrel, Salvatore, you are."

"Who killed Roland Dansky?" Sag demanded suddenly.

Mercurio smiled. "Same guy that's going to kill you."

A woman's voice from behind Max froze him. "Don't move a muscle."

Mercurio stood still as the grave, waiting for the death shot. Underneath the EVA field, he'd been using to protect him from Ophelia's weather was a visor with chip indicators for Moss's loft. It only showed two cons. Was this some sort of CC patrol? "I'm not moving. Who are you?" He could see her reflection in his peripheral vision on the visor.

She was a slight blonde woman wearing a green sundress. She held a hand weapon he was unfamiliar with.

Moss watched her evenly. "Yeah, who are you?"

"I'm a friend of Vince's. I've been watching this whole mess. Give your weapon to Sagamore. Now."

"Can't do that. He's guilty. He caused the senseless death of thousands of brave men. He's going down." Mercurio held his ground. The lady in green would have to kill him before he'd give up.

From across the room, one of the surgical lasers came to life. It flashed a beam at Mercurio's gun arm and sliced his hand off at the wrist. Sagamore moved like steel wheels. The disser was in his hand, its handle flying up and slamming Max in the face. Max took the blow painfully and held his wrist. Blood splattered over the floor. Sag hit him again and again. Mercurio took blows that would have rendered another man unconscious and smiled.

"That the best you got, Butcher boy? Deserter?"

"Sagamore?" Moss didn't voice it, but the question what there; are you going to kill him?

Sagamore looked at his former battalion mate in horror. Whatever crimes Mercurio had done, he would always be an amateur compared to *the Butcher of Baal One*.

"Leave it be. Tie him up." Moss quipped. She turned to the lady in green but she was gone.

"Sag, who was the woman?"

"Never saw her before."

When Vince arrived he found Max tied and angry in the giant robot head. "Oh boy," he said. Moss and Sagamore were behind him working up equipment for the break.

"Freighters coming in tonight Leavel. Nice of you to show up." Sag chided.

"Who's the woman?" Moss demanded, arms akimbo.

"Woman?" Vince hadn't a clue.

"Well, not quite a woman." came a voice from behind Vince.

"That woman," said Moss.

"Hazel! How did you sneak into the software?!" Vince grinned.

"I am the software." She replied.

Moss and Sag awaited an explanation.

"I'm a program," Hazel said. "A sentient program Vince found when you sent him out for software. I'd been off for centuries in the transportation center. I knew I might not get another chance of getting off this planet and into a functioning system again. So I downloaded myself into the panel I told him to take. I've been watching, helping you all since then."

Max shook his head. Put out of commission by a hologram!

Moss pointed to Max, "When horny here arrived to bushwhack us" then to the holo, "Hazel spooked him from behind and activated my surgical laser. Ala' no gun hand." then back to Max.

"I want to go with you," Hazel said.

"She doesn't weigh much." Sagamore offered.

"Why not? She's pretty good with a laser." Vince grinned.

The ship was coming.

The meds hadn't had as long to heal up Vince as the others, but at least they'd gotten the chip out. From an abandoned building not from where Leon had watched, they observed the approach of the freighter. It was windy that night and the light of the ships was lost now and again with rushes of snow.

"Time," Sag said. The visors of their screen were counting down. In their homemade wet suits, they looked like lizard men from a low budget horror holo. They clambered and waddled through the snow. The ship was taking to the water. They broke into a sprint, moving silently over the ice.

Numbers estimated to field shutdown flashed in their eyes.

Only a moment to get through. Otherwise, you'd be sliced in two, or exploded in a billion bits of fish food.

There was no time to consider alternatives. Ice and snow flew beneath their desperate feet. They pushed onward toward the water. The ship seemed immense now-had it been so long since they'd been close to one? A big black demon in a wet lair. Come and get me, fools.

The ice gave way under their combined weight. A moment of utter horrid darkness as they struggled to right themselves in the deadly water. Ice banged their ribs and limbs. Vince oriented himself toward the light of the ship.

He saw Sagamore. Where was Moss?

He dares not call out.

"Where's Moss?" Sag hissed through his teeth.

For a long unbelieving moment, they watched the surface.

"No!" Vince dove to find her but the darkness was complete.

"Time Vinny. She's gone. We've got to go."

"We can't leave. She's got to be close."

"You've got a syndicate hit man tied up in her loft, and a missing Outpilot who could be on the bottom of this sea-we have to go now!" Sagamore grabbed him and tugged. They both went under for a moment.

"Thirty seconds, Vince. They got Leyla. Moss knew the risks."

Vince looked at the dark waters with an aching sadness not unfamiliar in his life.

If their estimates were wrong, they still could die too.

Vince turned to the freighter. Twenty-six seconds.

Both men moved then with savage determination. Their lungs strained with the unfamiliar effort. They slashed at the water, tried to keep their paths straight.

Come on, push!

Twenty!

The ship towered above them. It was alive in the night and fields. It seemed a wicked enemy. They were mad to think this would work. Moss was dead. Leon? Who could say? They sucked air noisily. CC and the syndicate wouldn't have to worry about killing them if they misjudged this. Vince remembered swimming the seas of Rip, the Nyulen Nyasa rift sea, dark and cold. Steady, stroke, pull.

The ship's fields were so close they could touch them. An iridescent wavering and sparkle. The wet suits would not protect them against that. Vince shivered. Water had invaded his suit. Adrenaline and fear kept him from focusing on it.

"Shit. That fields not stable." Sagamore grumbled. "Whose flying this tub?" he cursed.

Zero!

"Go." Vince barked. Both of them lunged forward-into the sparkling light and their deaths, trusting that the fields would be gone when their bodies reached the perimeter. But the fields were still glowing, malevolent.

"Stop! Don't touch it." Vince snapped at the last second.

"It's gotta go down," Sagamore said and lunged. Vince knew it was suicidal, but they were crewmates.

As they reached the perimeter, the barrier fell.

Only a moment yet they were through!

They clambered over the freighters hull like desperate starving rats. Vince felt elation at the touch of a ship again. There was any number of hatches. CC had never expected anyone to get this far. Who would be so foolish to dive at a gravity field? Ha! The hull was expansive and complex with equipment that powered the drives. Vince had never seen this particular make before, but the basic structures common to such ships were visible.

Fusion plant, Collider field manipulators, communications tower, armored access corridors...same shit, different decade.

Suddenly noise began rumbling from deep inside the freighter.

The ship was powering back up!

Sagamore's hands were swollen with the cold. He struggled frantically with his cyber plugs in the dim and reflected light. "I can't find an inlet! I can't find the damn inlet!" He growled, clambering around the portal. Vince cursed. Maybe there was none. This ship was delivering to a prison world.

Vince felt along the edge within the dark.

Time seemed to slow to a stop as the cold sea and the unknown ship conspired to destroy them.

Then he felt the tell-tale dip in the metal. Just like on Rip. "Here!"

Sagamore let out a long breath. He went in. "Piece of cake."

The portal opened with a rush of hot air from some distant corner of space.

Someplace warmer.

For the second time in his life, Vincent boarded a CC ship as a pirate. Sagamore followed. Now Vince was Cybering in, tumbling through a kaleidoscope of blocks and codes. The access numbers from the Taloned Sire cut through the matrixes like titanium through wet sand.

"Memorize the numbers," Elias had said so long ago, "you are the instrument of your survival."

"Ship's reading us as an anomaly," Vince said. "The crews in the forward cockpit-two borgs. Move!"

They broke through the second lock and sealed the outer hull. Running now, they made down the gangways with devilish purpose. The hall walls were clean, virginal. They flew by Vince and Sagamore's vision in a flashing blur. The sudden change from cold to the warmth of the ship pressed against their consciousness and their lungs.

Their presence was detected with a sudden burst of CCCE Empires and warning calls, "Unauthorized boarding on deck three."

Was prison security notified?

They came to a balcony.

"Jump!" Vince yelled. They sailed through the air slamming down to the base deck. CCCE claxons wailed.

The freighter wasn't truly prepared for duty on a prison world, or they'd have been unable to get this far. Vince had counted on that. Rushing the cockpit, they found the pilot and copilot staring dumbly and unarmed.

"Don't kill us!" The male pilot howled.

The female just glared. She was heavy, bullish.

Sagamore pulled a long shank. "Show me your throat and say your prayers." He said.

The woman scowled. "Prayers? You Wilds never change. Kill me now. I don't believe in fairy tales, and I am not afraid of death."

"Not afraid of death? Oh, shut up. That's just your programming talking. I wouldn't be afraid of death if I were as ugly as you either. Unplug now!" Vince pulled her plugs.

The other pilot pulled his. Offline they were disoriented. One could see the sudden stop of information leave them as if standing in a terrible void.

"Get up." Sagamore barked. "Time to go."

Prison security had been notified. They were being hailed on a hundred channels. Vince ignored them all-all but one. He sent a single message to Central. "Touch us and the borgs die." Sagamore rushed the power-up and ejected previous navigation documents. Ignoring all flight protocols, he went to the emergency manual. Vince escorted the CC pilots to an escape pod. He stood between them and the door.

"I don't want to kill you-I just want to leave. We break the atmosphere and you ride down in the pod. You get another freighter and I keep this one instead of a lot of unjust tariffs I've paid over the years. Tell your buddies in the big hard drive that they've pissed me off now. This is going to be a war of one, me against CC." Vince's smile was feral; he pointed his shank like a trained animal on a leash.

The freighter's engines wailed, outside the frigid air of Ophelia's World superheated over the hull.

"They'll find you, you wild outlander. Next time they catch you they'll lay you so deep in cyber you'll live out your natural life and never recall a moment of your prior days. Give this madness up now and they might let you keep your mind when your sentence is served," the fat Borg said coolly.

Vince started considering her for a moment.

Then he smiled, "Tell me, did you say that, or was it radioed into your head from some dusty files somewhere in an orbital relay? Think about that, when was the last time you had an original thought?

Truth is, you have no way of really knowing what's you, and what's them. Me, I like being unplugged. Lessens the chance they're messing with my mind. If I screw things up, at least I know it was my screw up. Get in the pod."

The engines strained.

Vince stared silently for a moment. She wouldn't have said that, but she had. They were transmitting her speech. Vince wondered if she even knew it. The man was silent, terrified and alone. So they weren't transmitting to him. If his disposition changed Vince would know he was on. Vince slammed the escape pod doors shut and the two cyborgs plummeted back to the prison world, sans freighter and cargo.

Vince pressed a ship com. "Saggy…how much longer?"

Sagamore's voice was steady, cool. "We're topping the atmosphere now. They've got a low orbit security bot array, low-density pulse fields. Soon."

The rushing of the atmosphere quieted. A wavy metallic rhythm splashed the hull.

Sag had slipped into the hyper stream.

Turn the big keg down boy!
Turn the big keg down!
Papa got a shipload of diamonds,
Kroug city she has gone far behind!
Turn that big keg around the crew,
Papa gonna drink till dawn!
-New Nyulen Nyasa drinking song.

Again Captain Leavel made the Galactic hypercasts. "Turn the big keg down, boy!" became a top forty hit across known space, Sagamore had cast it back at CCCE before they broke hyper in the new freighter. Harry Stark and Starky Barky Holo's was furious he didn't have the rights to the song, which turned out to be owned by an obscure musician by the name of Leon Percival Po Tsai, who had purchased it from Captain Leavel in a card game.

Leavel and Sagamore's recurring fame was to shine again soon, and Harry and the Dark Corps were to find that…

-Winteroud Sole, Caldris. "The Ophelia Prison Break."

Roy Rudder

Book Six: Silurian World

The Bounty hunter of Rigel Six

...like the Roman Empire in its long fall, the Cyborgians hired muscle from the barbarians. Called "Sheriffs", these mercenaries came from all walks of nasty life. Background checks were intentionally sketchy. Their presence among the Outer Republics chaffed at the populations. They were given wide berth as CC armed them well. When they committed crimes apprehending bounty, CC would throw its hands up, "So sue them". One seeking reparations for overzealous, often violent Sheriffs, would soon learn the expense and Byzantine confusion of legal systems centuries in the making. It was a no-lose proposition for CC. The sheriffs, desperate men with little fear, were more deadly than a score of Cyborgian police.
-Princess Clairissa Maggio, Caldris, "Deneb IV, Empire of Light and Darkness."

He was a strange, silent giant of a man. Even at the Sheriff Induction facilities, he turned heads. His whole body was encased in the grey animal hide of indeterminate origin. Only his deep-set blue eyes proved him human. His DNA scans showed no known previous arrests and his shaky identification papers passed him without too much trouble. The office workers were glad of his departure when they handed him his authorization discs and sent him packing for his CC hunter-ship. They stood staring when he made his way for the lift.

"That's one scary customer." One was saying.

245

"I thought I'd seen it all." another added. "I wouldn't want him snooping around after me. Sheriff 182-61, enjoy the ride."

"Yeah Buddy. Did you catch that outfit? What the heck was that stuff, human skin?"

"Petrified human skin?"

They chuckled and moved on to the next potential sheriff, a far less imposing character with mere tattoos and genetically altered teeth.

182-61 showed no emotion as the lift carried him down to the hunter-ship bay. They were single person crafts. Black and waspy, the hunter ships were deadly scouts. Nothing about them indicated grace; they looked like the innards of other ships without hulls. Endless antennae, weaponry and other devices slapped together with complete disregard for appearance, and so they were. State of the art hunter killing hardware that would never make it to a consumer market, and thus needed none of the styling of a hyper yacht, or even the voter appeal of military glamour. They looked like what they were-mechanistic predatory technology. Just the sight of one chilled nerves in hard men on dirty stations.

182-61 took a long glance, leaning back like an automaton psycho from a slasher sensorama. Without comment, it seemed to win his approval. The ship and the sheriff were of like natures. Single-minded purpose, frightening resolve. No negotiations. No compromise. The business end of an ugly business. He climbed aboard his new home with the ease of one raised on interstellar craft, ran through system checks smoothly.

His new role as sheriff gave him access to the hive mind although he was an unborged Outworlder. 182-61 didn't stay long, the hive mind and his didn't have a taste for each other. He registered for his quarry-two renegade out pilots recently escaped from Ophelia's World. Vincent Mariner Leavel and Sagamore Mad-dog Salvatore.

The information he was able to obtain from the hive mind relevant to his quarry sickened even this strange man. Leavel's lover had been transferred from Ophelia to the Silurian nebula for unknown reasons. Rumor was the place was a human chop shop. It was theorized Leavel might pursue her into that system. 182-61 ran course projections through several systems where CC control was less than ideal, surmising Leavel would keep a low profile.

The hunter-killer ship lifted, with the occupant, and ferried to an ejection port. Without ceremony, it was released from the side of the processing skyscraper and attained flight. It moved into the traffic of air cars buzzing among the towers, and then into higher traffic, again, and again until finally, breaking orbit, it made for the shipping lanes and system gateway.

It took the Gateway to New Galen system where dead worlds served as reminders to rebellious star men of Cyborgian dark resolve. From there, he made hyper toward a few choices, and ignoble worldlets of a bad reputation.

Stanis Station, Kaster's Moon, Sagittarius Arm

Mel "No Deal" DePaulo was making his way back to Mel's Monkey ugly haste. He'd left a perfectly fine dancer back at The Colony with an unfinished service fee. He wasn't happy about it. A friend behind the bar had warned him of a sheriff on station asking Mel's whereabouts.

Arriving at station bay he saw the hunter-killer scout ship parked three ships down from his. He uttered an expletive and boarded the Monkey. Storming into the piloting Cabin he came to a dead stop.

His crew was all in their seats, white as snow. A nightmare of a man dressed in grey hide sat in his captain's chair.

"Captain DePaulo, I presume," 182-61 said softly.

Mel gathered his courage. "I am. And I'm not wanted in any system on any charges. What business do you have with me?"

The sheriff snickered an awful laugh at that.

"You are wanted in several systems on tariff violations, Mr. DePaulo, but the bounty on those wouldn't buy me a night dancing The Colony.

"My business here involves a couple of pilots you've sold out in the past, so your conscience shouldn't be too troubled. I'll forgo those other bounties instead of some information concerning your involvement with Vincent Leavel and Sagamore Salvatore, who recently performed the outrageous task of escaping CC's most notorious penal world.

"That Leavel and Sagamore are on the loose with an ax to grind with you should be another motivation to tell me everything you know. Better for you if I apprehend them before they meet up with you again."

DePaulo fumed.

"I never sold them out. I was compelled to frame them. I never made a penny off it."

"So you say? Who compelled you?"

"Good sheriff, even you don't want to know that."

The sheriff raised a weapon. "This is a first-class heavy combat disruptor. After you're boiled into soup there will be a big fat glob of carbonized goo in your hull and navigation systems. Tell me again what I want, or don't want to know, and I'll find out from some other third rate smuggler who put you up to it, and I'll do it with salvage money from your ship."

Mel looked at his terrified crew. His squealing now would make them all financially motivated to tell tales.

"Harry Stark. Harry was in an honor guard in the Royal Pleiadian army in the ground wars at Baal One. Sagamore was in a unit guarding the escape ships. When the battle went sour, Sagamore panicked and deserted with the dropship codes in a cruiser. They were the only codes. Harry's whole battalion was nearly massacred."

"And Leavel?"

"Leavel was a kid at the time. He was doing a blockade run when he got caught up in a firefight with Pleiadian air corps fighters pursuing Sagamore in the cruiser. They all were flying the same flags, so he took a desperate gamble and lost-he took out the fighters. Sagamore crewed with him ever since. Harry blamed Leavel more than Sagamore. He wanted them humiliated and spending long miserable lives with their wings clipped.

"Harry traced Leavel to me, ambushed my people. He held the others as a ransom to insure me setting up Leavel.

"Harry's powerful. He'll be looking for Leavel and Sagamore too.

"That's all I know."

"I see." From behind the skinsuit, "So you were damned if you did, and damned if you didn't. Like today."

"What do you mean? I told you everything I know. You said you wouldn't bring me in."

Again, that awful laugh.

"I won't bring you to the authorities, Mr. DePaulo. Now, however, you're stuck with a crew of cutthroats that can sell you out to Harry for informing a Sheriff-who'll soon file murder and conspiracy charges against Harry with CCCE. Not that they'll follow through, but it certainly can annoy him.

"I'll be naming you as the informant; I've recorded this whole conversation. As for your crew, well, I don't know.

"Happy flying, Captain."

182-61 stood up, bowed, and left. Mel looked around nervously at his crew members, "What?" he bellowed.

247

Hyperspatial Transit, Orion Arm

Red tracers fired over the sandy hill, smacking fire in his memory.

Sagamore had withdrawn to himself after the break from Ophelia's World. The stolen CC freighter careened through the deep wells of the hyper streams with a series of tachs and maneuvers that would shake any would-be pursuers. The memory of the war that Mercurio brought to Sag, and the implications of all he said, wore heavy on the bulky engineer.

Deep in the bowels of the freighter, Sag shook at the memory of those days, the slaughter, and the pointlessness of it all. The carnage was one thing. He could have borne that. The lie that it mattered, that he couldn't have endured. The war still raged in his mind, a conflict between the real and the ideal. It had driven him mercilessly over the years to strive for a perfection that could not be obtained. Relentless in his pursuits, he had become, in many ways, like a CC drone.

His life was always that battlefield.

Of course, there too, now there was Moss's death to add to his tally.

Footsteps. Vince appeared in a gangway, he leaned into the chamber. "What? Is it my breath? You've been down there more than need be. What's the deal?"

Sagamore stretched and forced a smile. "Personal things 'Cappy, you don't want to know."

"Well, we're still in CC space. They snag our asses here, and it will get a lot more personal."

"Thought we were going to take this bucket to the rim?"

"I had a brainstorm. Langley Stay. Do a little shake and shuffle. I figure they'll be expecting us at the rim, right? Why not unload the freighter in their backyard?"

"We're dumping it?" Sag looked worried at the implications.

Vince gave him a hurt look. "Did you say dumping? Never. Perish the thought. We're traders again, Sag-pirates if you must.

"We'll sell this ship for salvage and head out-system in something with a little more style. An early model hyper yacht modified to stretch the limits of anomalous motion.

"We'll bend space-time till we're riding yesterday's noise over the galactic halo."

Sagamore grunted. An early model hyper yacht. Modified. He burst out in raucous laughter. If they were going to hell, at least they would do it in style.

The freighter heaved into normal space above the stellar plane. They went to the middle of the system, queuing on the second-largest gravitational object. It was a gas giant of ten Jupiter masses. Langley Stay had started as a Security base on a large planet orbiting next in from the gas giant. The planet had thrived as a glorified garage due to the number of mechanical service operations that had come in.

System traffic control scanned them for proper codes-Vince's code manipulations proved worthy. They got in the system unnoticed. Vince watched the yellow seas fill his view screen and the planet become a world. They put down among a vast spread of warehouse blocks serviced by canals the fjords shouldering the sea. Vince knew somebody here, someone not afraid of CC. The freighter touched the ground gently. They watched the roof of the hangar, make a slow landing.

Herb Lahman was an old warhorse who served behind enemy lines taking out supply depots. He fought in wars most people only knew from history holos. He was old, old in an era when age meant more than centuries, and skinny as a prisoner of war in a nasty camp.

He was stubborn as a glacier. Vince met him after a hurricane had blasted the city one year when Vince had ported there. The storm left a whole bunch of strangers getting to know one another and digging out. That was one night Vince shouldn't have been off ship drinking. There was this brunette, a dancer, and he'd been preoccupied. Modern dance. Fascinating subject.

"Where the hell have you been, Leavel?" Herb snorted, his ancient face drawn back in a huge smile.

"Jail. You remember Sagamore Salvatore?" Vince chirped.

"I know. I know. Everybody knows. You're all over the hyper casts. Big jailbreak. Big news. You're famous again. The whole galaxy wants a piece of your tail." Herbs' chin still jutted out like the dangerous soldier he once was. He weighed almost nothing anymore, but a lifetime of ornery piss and vinegar still clung to his persona.

"Well, we're here!" Sagamore smiled sarcastically. Vince had a feeling Sags patience was going to wear thin with Herb's 'tell it like it is' bluntness.

Herb scowled. "Nice freighter. New. Too bad I can't pay you what it's worth. "

Now Sag scowled. "You'll make three times what it's worth parting it out. And it had a full cargo!"

"Yeah, in a hundred years. Heh, heh! The cargo I can pay you what it's worth. You boys got big prices on your head, you know? The syndicate. Word has it you sliced a hand off a mobster?"

"Not me-this lady, well not really a lady but-"

"Since when you been courting with any ladies? Hah!" Herb was fondling a cigarette. He was always fondling a cigarette.

Vince scowled.

They took a lift up to the roof. As they went Vince could see rows and rows of ships being worked on in the hangar. Up top Herb surveyed the delta and the canals with pride. "Don't imagine CC will take you alive next time, eh boys? Those snooping, taxing, metal-brained, plastic-dicked, retrofitted, spunk vermin."

"Easy Herb." From Vince.

"Cost me a fortune for an accountant slippery enough to go rounds with them."

"I can imagine. Not to cut to the quick, my friend, but we need a fast ship with reasonable cargo capacity so I can get back to earning some money." Vince said.

"Get back to smuggling you mean."

Sag raised his eyebrows. Then he smiled. "Yeah."

Herb scratched the back of his head in a timeless gesture. One hand was in his pocket; his ciggy was tucked in his lips jutting up. He considered the horizon for a moment and said, "Tell you what; I got this yacht just came in out 'a Kappa Crucis. One owner. An old Mercury Monterey Star cruiser. But first, let's eat. "

They walked over to a roof pavilion where a couple of droids labored over a stove near a cabana. Sag eyed the sky full of ships drifting up and down, air cars buzzing between. The canals were even more overloaded with traffic, gondolas, water ships, and houseboats. Fugitives they were then, hiding in plain sight.

After the meal, they hopped into a small air car of old and very rare make. It alighted; they swung around and over several of the warehouses, herb filling them in on all the essentials of his operation. They moved through vast superstructures of water ships, past buildings whose crumbling limestone told of immense age, and finally into a smaller warehouse where rows of used yachts sat in dry-dock. Some were being reworked, the flash of welding arcs and lasers glittering. Men and women climbed like bugs over the sleek yachts.

Vince eyed them appreciatively. Most of the sportier models Herb could pass off on wanna-bees that clung to the fading glamour of their ancient youth with synthetics, surgery, or even vat-grown clones of themselves. Not Vince. He was a hard spacer. He would know the show from the go.

Of course, when Vince saw the Monterey it was all over. Sag whistled.

"How'd you like to run your hands over those manifolds eh?" Vince whispered.

Stanis station dropped from the sheriff's view screen to a shrunken point on the light in milliseconds as the rushing sweep of forces of the expanding Crab nebula's shock wave crossed his path. Easy at first, as he came up behind the shockwave, then tightening with a shattering of ions and waves of compressed radiation, his scout ship crossed the wave.

He basked in the glory of color and power, alone among the roaring spectacles of the Milky Way. He let the hunter-killer ship ease into automatic pilot moving further along an arc just short of light speed, bent and swinging higher on the galactic plane.

He was no closer to his quarry. Mel had provided him little insight that he hadn't already suspected about the nature of Leavel's dilemma.

If the syndicate got to Leavel first no one would ever see him again, CC included. The sheriff wouldn't be able to scrape a molecule of Leavel or Sagamore off a rock then. The chronometer was running. Leavel would need to unload the pirated freighter in an unregistered shop. Those were too numerous to run checks on, especially at the periphery of Governments.

Where could one hide when the entire galaxy was talking about you?

Leavel would have to trust the person implicitly. Trust that the person was beyond greed for syndicate money and beyond the fear of either CC or Harry. CC records on Leavel's life were sketchy. The smuggler had deliberately falsified almost every registered entry into CC space during his whole career. One never knew who was crewing for him, or what they were transporting. Most of his runs in Republic domains had been under false ship registry so weren't recorded at all. Beneath the hard Cyborg equipment, the human face of the sheriff smiled. *The weasel!*

A hologram map of the galaxy came up on his screen and continued to run course projections from Ophelia on it. He started at a maximum range of flight given straight flying time. The circle was huge. But there were no likely stations on its circumference. He began pulling it tighter, inward like a shrinking net. Stations eventually showed up. Details of ship traffic and port services flashed across his vision.

Too numerous to run checks on, he began running them anyway.

Herbs' favorite watering hole was a little dive called "The Bavarian". It rested on the edge of a small cliff overlooking one of the canals. Inside, snowy mountain scenes and quaint lodges adorned the walls above the bar. Herb suggested that Vince and Sagamore wear tech visors to disguise the upper parts of their faces and they readily obliged. Drinks flowed. Vince was standing at one end of the bar enjoying some synthetics with his rum trying to pretend he was following some bores conversation when Sag stood up and took the tech visor off.

Vince watched him turn around from the bar and walk steadily to a table full of toughs. They all looked up at once. Sag looked at them all, one at a time, until he figured who was the biggest. Then he slammed him hard on the head knocking him in one fell swoop to the floor. That one didn't get back up but there were five more at the table and they all stood up in unison.

Vince watched amazed as Herb sailed across the room in a flying leap and knocked another one down.

Vitamins.

Vince set his drink on the bar and joined the melee, pummeling one of them across the room and under a fixed bar stool.

The man kept trying to get up at which point Vince kicked him in the face until he lay still. Bouncers were managing the crowd at that point and the three men eased into the mass of people looking like bystanders. The bouncers threw the toughs out one at a time and shortly Vince turned to Sagamore.

"Guy was making fun of my visor," Sag said.

Herb shook his head. "Feisty one ain't yah?" He snickered.

"Nice leap," Vince said. "We better get rolling."

Later that night a call was placed with the local authorities alleging an assault. Six drunks all signed off that three men, one of them described as aged and feeble, had assaulted them. At first, the officer taking the report broke out laughing. But a captain working the shift raised eyebrows and asked for a more detailed description of the men.

He filed his report as suspicious-possible professional criminals-and it was logged onto a wider police reporting data network.

Before the morning it was on the satellite ring and then the hyper casts.

The sheriff 182-61 picked it up a few light-years off the Crab nebula the next day.

"Still in stasis over a thousand years," Herb said proudly. He ran his hands over the gleaming surface of the stasis hold, peering at the time-frozen CC war pilots beneath. There were four of them strapped into their MERGE chairs. Ready to continue a long-forgotten skirmish in a Star system ages now populated with the descendants of their combatants.

"Interesting conversation pieces Herb." Sagamore looked at the Cyborg pilots with distaste.

"And it's semi-stasis. If it was complete stasis the hold would be black." Vince said.

"You sure?" Herb turned up his chin. His soggy cig bounced on his lip.

"I'm sure," Vince remembered the eerie black sheen in the shale on Rip.

"Well, semi-stasis, stasis. There've been a goodly number of these finds from the war. Seems something set them off and the systems didn't fall back out of stasis like they were supposed to." Herb pronounced knowingly.

"Their man-machine interfaces were fried," Vince said.

"By what?" from Sagamore. He leaned closer to look at the frozen men.

Vince looked at him coldly, "I wasn't about to replay the ships complete log under MERGE. I had a feeling it was toxic.

"So I didn't."

"Toxic MERGE logs-poison for sure! Good thing your curiosity didn't get the better of you. You'd be crazy as a loon.

"Probably tanked up in a nuthouse." Herb nodded. "Good thing."

251

"Thanks. I thought I used good judgment. Yet I've always had an idea, a theory about it."

Sagamore grunted. "I don't if a theory is the right word, Captain. Sounds to me like you're sold on this idea of HyperBogies slipping around behind dimensions."

Herb listened solemnly. "Hyper Bogies huh? They're out there, it's true."

Sag feigned disinterest and failed.

"Think of some fish fighting in a pond-well that would be humanity and the Arcturian genocide. The fish stir up and an unusual amount of ripples on the water and attract a large nasty thing. I think the war attracted something ugly. Something wrong.

"I think that thing stuck its snout in our pond to see what all the commotion was. I think it was so awful, so completely hideous that it shocked the sanity right out of the CC pilots. Snapped their minds like twigs." Vince looked frightening then. He looked like a man who'd held a dirty secret for a long time.

"Well Vince, if every failed stasis incident from the Arcturian wars is proof of a spooky, then you got lots of them things just sliding around the edge of our reality. Where they been ever since then?" Sagamore loomed.

Herb cleared his throat. "Reinforcements. They're standing down till the Calvary can come over the galactic halo and then they snuff out us savages."

Vince and Sagamore both drew their eyes up to Herb.

Herb realized he had touched on something that pieced in a missing puzzle spot. The picture of everything changed now if such was the case. The long Cyborgian Peace since the Arcturian wars were just a lull before a real storm of devastation that kicked humanity off the top of the food chain.

"Well, that's some imagination you got there Vinny." He took a couple of steps away from the frozen CC pilots. No more running his hands over the gleaming surface of the stasis hold. "Let's hope you're wrong about that hyper Bogie army then eh? Don't do you much good to arm up against a force of hyper-dimensional super beings that can drive you insane with just by showing their faces does it? Kind of like fighting a navy full of Medusa's!"

Sag fixed a long stare on Vince. "You been smoking something without telling me?" then he looked at Herb, "Those are nice toys you got there old fella, but what we need is something to help ensure the Mercury gets past the security array at the Diablo nebula."

Good. Change the subject.

Stick your head in the sand.

Vince nodded, "Here, here!"

Herb was undaunted. He looked out over the vast floor where his workmen inched over ships and engines of all makes and models. There were air cars and water ships, star yachts and in-system shuttles, even a Maglev. "Just wait a minute!"

He grabbed his pack of cigs and pulled another one out as he broke into a determined stride. Vince and Sag followed.

They made their way down to a deeper level. There were several huge rocks in a corner together gathering dust.

"They're rocks," Sag said flatly. "It's not good to land on planets riding rocks."

Herb waved on a light and the walls in the corner let off a soft blue glow.

"No, they're military issue faux meteorites. Landers to sneak past satellite arrays. They're only good in systems with unusually high asteroid counts-like those in a nebula. They've got nano screens in the rock that shield against scans; send out false scan returns that show the rock is solid. Most times the satellites are programmed not to fire on natural phenomena such as asteroids or comets."

"Most times?" Sagamore folded his arms.

"Used to ride these bears down behind enemy lines myself when I was younger. Nothing like it."

"Okay. I'll bite. I ride the stone down to the planet.

"Now how do I get around without showing up on their orbiting surveillance scans?"

Herb smiled. He wasn't out of tricks yet. "You're going to love this." He snickered and waved them further along in his basement. In the morning, the deal was done and the two fugitives were gone. Herb had another visitor, however, soon enough.

182-61 looked at the skinny old man with amusement, but not disdain. Aged and frail, Herb still exuded a fighter's spirit.

The sheriff knew authenticity when he saw it, in any guise. He also knew only his status as a sheriff protected him in realms such as this planet-labyrinths of stone and machine where anything might happen.

"Bounty hunter," Herb said quietly. "I should have figured as much. They've come and gone. You're too late." Herb glared at the ugly grey skin-suit covering the giant and the black array of insectoid Cyborg attachments. He'd never run up against a CC sheriff before. The combined weight of criminal ruthlessness and official authority was fearsome indeed. Even the steely nerves of the old soldier began to crawl.

A strange laugh growled from beneath the skin-suit. The laughter continued. It turned Herb's stomach as the sheriff slowly removed his helmet revealing the face beneath.

Herbs eyes widened. "You!" he exclaimed.

Diablo Nebula, Siluria
4210

"We're being followed." Sagamore groaned from his piloting chair.

Around them, the hyper streams raged and fluxed. In its distance, Vince too could see a faint trace of a small ship. Ahead, the Silurian nebula was crouched black and spitting fields that conformed to no known theories.

"It could be a supply ship, maybe a merchant's vessel."

"Want to lay odds it's a bounty hunter?" Sagamore snickered.

"Money's too tight to mention." Vince declined. "But I'll hedge your bet is right with a little ruse of our own. Let's break hyper, and make a big show of it."

Through the blur of hyper, beneath the gleam of the merge helmet, Vince saw Sagamore smile a wicked grin.

"What do you have in mind, Cappy?"

For a moment, all of Space went null white, brighter than the edge of super-space. With it, every monitor and console on Bandor Base flashed wildly. Clerics and CC drones raged, suddenly macabre with pain, ripping off merge helmets, squealing like dying giant insects in slave pits of Opa-Locka's world. Before calming programs could respond they'd pulled relays from systems, shut down sensor arrays, and set off a thousand transmissions at once.

The gist of it was: "Huh?!"

Looking down on the chaos of his command rooms, Bandor scowled and filled with dread. This nebula was the bane of sanity. He switched to his private hyperlink with a CC station just off the nebula. "What's happening? This is Bandor Base, we've gone blind. What is this?" He used CC short-speak.

The reply was garbled. Momentarily he heard, "Unknown."

Everything around here, "Unknown..."

He cursed a few expletives Harry had taught him.

The response was clearer this time, "Mr. Bandor, your exhibiting wild human tendencies. Perhaps you are reverting? An immersion in the will of the people may be beneficial at this time."

"Negative!" Bandor slapped back. The thought revolted him. "Too many unknowns. That would cause delayed response time. I need this autonomy to function. That light blast is a perfect example of why I need to act independently. You couldn't determine its origin, could you?"

There came a long pause. "We confirm the rationale. Investigate the light source. It could be a Paramon ship. Sources indicate three hundred and twelve possible known solutions that could cause such a flare."

Bandor saw data holos coming over the hyper cast consoles. One: a micro wormhole ingested by a neutron star. Two: derelict antimatter streams engaging an Oort comet.

He turned away as the third data holo rose on screen.

"We will investigate, Bandor out." He cut them off knowing full well that that too would send them calculating immersion procedures. He regretted it almost immediately, but his only role model among autonomous humans was Harry. Harry would have cut their throats for "shit's and giggles".

Bandor thought (surprising himself): *Wormhole? My ass!* That's human activity out there and they're not coming to study the fauna.

When Bandor got this assignment he hadn't known full personal autonomy since he was four. He couldn't have imagined or prepared himself in any way. It was like walking into a nightmare and finding the real world was the dream. Yet he couldn't go back. Simple humanity, whatever the circumstances, was preferable to being part of that mass of information, mostly misinformation. The data streams were only so much meaningless compulsions; compulsions that were sent from distant worlds for unfathomable purposes filling his mind.

If you don't have a goal, Harry had told him, you'll be used by people who do. You gotta get out now, Bandor boy, but first, you've got to do me a little service. You gotta get out-and I got the keys to the places they'll never find you. Look at me-you said it yourself. Ossa's got the First Strike and all those big toys looking for Harry, and I'm sitting here.

What a world, what a world...

"Get me some Chemical ships up there and find out what that light was." Bandor ordered his first officer."

"I'm on it." The man spun on his heels and drove to the task like molten pistons. Bandor's gaze fell to the holo-screens which had ceased receiving data from the station off the nebula and reverted to holos of the nebula itself.

Various perspectives from remote satellites shown endless violet and cadmium-red clouds littered with black and yellow silicate moons, ringed roaster gas giants too close to proto-stars and endless dreary wisps of darkness curling in, trying to become something.

One of the screens showed a fire trail like a comet shot through a matter cannon. It was a bulbous orange light spreading in sudden clouds. This place refused to follow any known laws of physics, and this was just one more for the log.

I gotta get out; out of CC, out of this nebula. Just out.

They dropped out of hyper under stasis, re-attaining mass instantly and freezing time in a bubble that ignited the gaseous nebula around them for a 180,000-mile stretch, banging matter into antimatter and back again.

Momentarily the stasis shields dropped and only their gravity bubble and a massive shot of magnetic field protected the Monterey as it careened toward Siluria.

Vince and Sagamore watched the field indicators pass maximum capacity and slowly ease into an acceptable range.

"Now everybody knows we're here," Vince whispered.

Sagamore's eyes drilled into his readouts with perfect concentration.

"Ba-boom!" Sagamore snapped. "We're clear, five, five, five."

They were a wall of fusion dust sparkling.

Immense wisps of the nebula ignited a flared out.

"Any more dense and we'd have ignited the whole firkin cloud." Sagamore scowled.

They slid the ships vanes out and looked around.

"Kind of like Theta Orionis." Vince offered.

"Yeah, but it's not. Look at them readouts."

The laws of physics were just suggestions. Nothing was right.

"If you're counting on our field manipulators navigating us through this mess, you'd better not do any close pass byes. Plot a course steering wide of any gravity wells, Cappy, I don't want to relocate here permanently."

"Use the ramjets and you won't have to worry field manipulators at all."

"But of course." Sag lit the jets.

"I'm Scanning for probes." Vince knew the place's reputation left scanning equipment untrustworthy.

Their vision encompassed a wide sweep of the towering nebula.

"It's a very big place."

The Monterey streamed on deeper along the system plain. Siluria's main star had several rocky worlds on its periphery and a golden-ringed magenta gas giant in the habitable zone. Siluria was one of the gas giant's moons.

"Mostly there's lotta dust," Sagamore growled. "Lotta dust! It's overloading the sniffers. What a place. If they're experimenting on Out Pilots against Interstellar law, they've found the cover. They've got a war zone on one side, and a pilot's nightmare of a nebula on the other. "

Vince grimaced at the mention of experiments.

Siluria gleamed before them

"Rip orbits a gas giant in the same manner. I was born on a moon-like it."

Lab rats, ghost ships and demons.

"Let's get a look at her. Enlarge planet image eight hundred percent."

A holo of the planet appeared huge before them. It was beautiful. Turquoise seas covered the planet from pole to pole.

Swirling patterns of cloud cover traced paisley patterns in ordered gentle lines. Island chains could be seen in endless rings.

Class M textbook; chlorophyll producing vegetation producing an oxygen-rich atmosphere. Sitting in the middle of this nebula, it was an Eden.

"This nebula is still forming stars, Cappy. Life shouldn't have had a chance to evolve here yet. And those islands-they're circular chains. The tops of craters that should have been long eroded by the time it took to evolve life. Same patterns you'd see on a terra-formed world. It doesn't add up."

No major continental formations. Crater remnants on a world with seas and organic processes...

"Paramon's drone probes never mentioned any civilization here." Vince's mind reeled.

"Think it was terra-formed?"

"It might have been. Could have been, but CC hasn't operated in this sector before-and Paramon trumpets every time they build an outhouse. It could be some process of stellar evolution we're not aware of. Maybe the system wandered into the nebula from somewhere else."

From Space, the island chains and archipelagoes ringed each other in delightful patterns, some in, some over each other. The effect was of some geo-architect designing with circles. Trying to create interest but within the discipline of a particular shape. But for its size it might have been any of a billion cratered balls spinning through the void, suddenly dipped with seas and biome. No wonder Paramon had eyes for it. If they could master the field distortions of the nebula, the world would be a valuable addition to their territory.

CC hadn't counted on that; one more sign they've lost touch with their human roots. Any bartender or armchair politician in the galaxy could have seen that conflict coming. Unless the war was what they wanted-as cover.

"No sign of the ship that was behind us," Sagamore said grimly. "All the more indication it was following us. If it's using cloaking devices to hide from our scans, it's either a government ship or a bounty hunter."

"Right. Well, this is where my little ruse comes to play. The big light-show we put up coming out of hyper will set him on your trail. You drop me and keep moving, back out of the nebula and lose them. I make it downworld and enter the base. You circle back again and come in as a backup."

Sagamore replied unconvincingly, "Sounds like a plan." He eyed the holo globe, "Nice place for a death camp, eh?"

Lab rats...

"Hazel, indicate base."

"There is a large concentration of structures centered on the largest island in the northern hemisphere." She said. A sparkling light appeared on the island. "Warm and sunny."

"Indicate their scanning perimeter," Sag added.

"Local scans operate to a forty-kilometer radius. But they're backed by a satellite array giving them complete planetary observation."

"Naturally," Vince said dryly.

Hazel provided direction graphics, vectors, microwave transmission directions and the like. Vince drilled it into his brain.

"Native life forms?" Now a sidelong grin appeared.

"The place is crawling with them."

"That's my cover. I'll read as organic. I won't raise any alarms."

"Hope you're a good swimmer," Hazel said.

"No, I loaded a bamboo catamaran in the landing rock back at Langley Stay. Herb's last little surprise for us. Seems he had everything down in that basement. It will read as organic too. I sail to their scan perimeter. They've picked up our entry, but this system is littered with rubble. We set the rock drop-ship out now and I ride it in. I'll come down here," he pointed to a spot on the planet," ride these currents," his hand followed a path, "and I'll arrive in sight of the base when?"

"Thirty to forty days, roughly, probably looking like a ragamuffin when you get there too." Hazel replied.

"You ever run out of those colloquialisms?" Sagamore asked.

"'I don't exist. Just a program, remember?"

"Don't argue with the hologram, Sag." Vince laughed.

Siluria gleamed blue and green like the promise of an Eden.

Herb's rock proved its worth in medium orbit. CC had mined the sky with a small satellite array. Nothing manmade was coming through, and that was how it read when Vince drifted in. In Cyber he could feel satellites scanning the surface of the rock, then the deeper scans searching for regular manufactured components.

Embedded in the layers of stone were sheets of reflective cloth, nano relays that felt, interpreted, and sent the scan back with false information.

The scans stopped, satisfied. There were too many meteor storms to waste precious cyber time shooting them all down. Vince could fly a carnival through now and nobody would notice. He wished he could notify Sagamore but that would defeat their purpose. The rock broke the atmosphere with an audible groan. Temperature gains were higher than calculated for.

Trace elements unseen at a distance were burning in the entry plasma.

Which of their data was wrong?

Could it jeopardize his landing?

The rock skin was burning off as planned. Like shedding a chrysalis, he'd break from freefall near the sea, coast a couple of hundred miles closer to his objective then dip into the deep waters hiding the ship offshore. If nothing went wrong, it was as good as a plan as any for an unknown world where CC had sequestered a base.

Data flows slashed through his vision as the rock burned away, nano splashes forming images of flaring light. M class planet, 1.07 Gees, a nitrogen atmosphere, oxygen, carbon dioxide, flaring past-something, something else. Reentry was running out of time and something eluded him; things in the readout that didn't make sense.

Gravity fields didn't quite work in the Silurian nebula, yet in seconds he would be depending on them to break his fall. Just to work for a moment, that was all. One short burst in a low-frequency transverse wave would read simply as cobalt irradiating in the heat, losing mass in a steady burn. *Just for a moment, that was all.*

Bandor sat alone in his office pondering the situation. Solitude, sweet and sorrowful, unfamiliar, had become the central fact of his new existence as an autonomous being. In the hive mind, he'd never felt the personal pressures an unknown. They were a horrifying dread that dogged him and his new will to be now, however. Something he had to face as an ordinary man.

Harry sent him music the likes of which he'd never heard over the peoples' channels. Strange and beautiful, it had all been composed by hand in eras before cybernetic technologies. Handel's Water Music played low now in his office.

He opened a cabinet he'd brought to the base with his other equipment. Secreted away there was a hyper cast unit. It was coded for one frequency; one Harry had provided that somehow didn't register on CC equipment. It cast to a hyper yacht outside the Paramon blockade where Harry was amusing himself watching the wars. Bandor leaned forward and switched on the signals.

A holo appeared covering half his office. It was the interior of a yacht. Opulent, it was appointed with fine exotic woods and jewels inlaid in sharp geometric designs. Orchids flowed out of crystal vases embellished with gold and platinum. Harry's muscled body stared back like a panther at him from behind a rosewood desk.

"Hello Bandor," Harry said. He excused a big blonde and she scurried away, apparently subservient and delighted to be manhandled like a tool by a man of power. Harry smiled and made a show shrugging his shoulders. "What can I say? Men want to be me, and women love me! Never a dull moment." he said. "Now, what is it?"

"It's this nebula; phenomena uncounted and unaccountable. There was an enormous stream of lights that blasted away for a couple hundred thousand kilometers. It was a ship. It streamed into the system, dove into an asteroid belt, and then broke back into hyper and left."

"Hmmm, that is very uncomfortable for you but indeterminate. A lot of ships must turn tail when they stumble into that nightmare of a nebula you call home. So what's bothering you?"

"I was considering the Outpilot and his warrior friend. What you said about his loyalty to his woman."

Harry registered surprise. "That is very astute of you Bandor. Yes, we always want what we can't have. "Harry became irritated." Don't mess with my head now, Bandor. That cheap little smuggler-" he paused, realizing Bandor's limited experience with normal human relations would leave him incapable of messing with anyone's head. Managing the charade with CC was all Bandor could handle while still coping with the base research.

New and strange emotions would be racking Bandor's mind.

"Never mind. So you think our little smuggler boy has come after his princess to save the day? You think he's in the nebula, send out some chem-scouts. Keep them out there. What about the lights, tell me more."

"I'm only echoing your previous comments. The lights indicated a wild fluctuation of anti-matter formation and annihilation."

"That would be a bit of a Roman candle. Why would they have wanted to get your attention that way? You never know what these boneheads are capable of. He flew into a Marauder firefight once and rescued a guildsman you know. That ship I've been trying to acquire since I've heard of it. Was it an old CC frigate?"

"No. It wasn't CCCE. But it was an older model. It was a Mercury model of sorts from what my clerks have deduced. More I can't say for sure."

Harry shot him an evil grin. "Just might be our boy. He has a penchant for antique ships. You've done good Bandor."

Harry watched the significance of Vince's willingness to die for others sink into Bandor's awareness. Bandor was white with apprehension.

"This is irrational. He can't pit himself against CC and win. We'll squash him like an insect. I have a force garrisoned here." Bandor was shaking.

Harry laughed. "Now that's an ironic simile. Like an insect. You CC clones and your hardware. CC has adopted the strategies of the insect, not Leavel. Pathetic, puny, cheap, and inconsequential-he remains, still human. You're new at this human thing Bandor. He's old. Still a child by current lifespan standards, but old nonetheless.

"He's survived by his wits in hostile environments all his miserable life.

"If he's coming, you better have your men ready. I want that pawn back in my collection. If your men get him, don't destroy his corpse, I'll want to reanimate it and torture what's left. Nobody gets away from my machinations. Rip his genitals off and stuff them in his mouth, but I want the corpse for a party trophy.

"Have your men ready for anything. This weasel is slipperier than a greased whore in an oil bath. The syndicates are making bets all over the galaxy on whether I'll get him or not. Some are betting against me. I don't like to lose money, Bandor."

The hologram faded. Harry always got the last word.

Bandor listened to Handel's Water Music and knew fear.

Sagamore's senses plunged into energy and magnetic fields, cursing the nebula. A million spikes shot up along his rear warp fields as he drilled the Monterey to its limits, making time to exit the Silurian clouds. The spikes were white chromium cones prickling his eyeballs. Cursing again, more violently with the pain of it, he ran a data stream searching for an explanation, meanwhile, the cones stung harder.

Compressed radiation flares organized on a grid!

He'd never seen that one before.

He refracted the resonance of his sensory input. The distortion fields bent hard, slowed, bent again. Flailing like a cat tossed off a cliff; he dove out of MERGE and eased the Monterey back into normal space. His last glimpse of hyper was a sparkling barrier of chrome reaching up and down into infinity.

He pulled off his sweaty MERGE helmet and focused his swelling eyes on the cockpit. He set his jaw grimly and ran a manual diagnostic knowing there was nothing wrong with the ship's nervous system.

Denebian slime dogs and sewer fodder...

Onscreen the vast and twisting nebula's dusty swirls belied what he'd just observed on the ship's sensors. Nothing was there.

The weaving contrasts of light and dark looked sinister, but not unusual. No causes of radiation flares, chromium walls or organized unnatural phenomena whatsoever.

Then, like a nasty teasing ghost, a ripple of static swam across the screen holo. Faintly, transparent as smoked glass, a sheet of chroma sprinted through his vision and was gone. The configuration of gravity wells and stars changed abruptly, even the galactic plumage reoriented- but his position indicators did not.

There was a fleet of ships before him.

He grabbed for his piloting controls and then stopped with the shock of recognition. It could have been out of a staged virtreal drama. Squarish, prewar fighter-carriers massed in disciplined rows awaiting orders. He'd never seen the particular make, but the technology and construction methods were recognizable.

Arcturian. Before the fireballs...

"Hazel, give me a modification of one of those standards they're flying."

The screen showed a bulky hull detail; the Union Jack and ring of stars.

The lost Arcturian fleet.

They were grand, neat, and clear on his holo. They couldn't exist. Relics would have dispersed.

Formations should have broken and drifted apart.

But running lights were signaling, field aurora, exhaust trails, shuttlecraft, fighter escorts. Attack formations.

A near time-stasis!

Madly now he reversed the Monterey. He went into MERGE and blasted through the chromium spikes screaming pain. There was a buckling wave, and he was out. The fleet was gone and the previous star configurations resumed.

"Beacon!" he snapped to Hazel, and a beacon fell from the ship. He would come back to this place again. He wondered how much time had elapsed while he glimpsed the Arcturian fleet. Sagamore remembered Leon in a grimy bar on Ophelia's world, "There's a lost legion of Arcturian Air Corps haunting that space, old' boy, I have seen em once. If you ever find a way off this snowball, don't go to the Silurian Nebula-don't go!"

Vince let the lander cool in the tranquil seas for several hours until it drifted ashore. He pulled himself out of the Herbs rock craft and surveyed his current domain. There was a heat full of steamy fragrances that were pleasant to the nose. The bright sun was more to the white spectrum than yellow, and glimmers of the nebula and stars shone through here and there in the brilliant blue sky. Islands of blackish-green were scattered in every direction with picturesque, chimney stack peaks sculpted in endless variety. Shallow seas and islets stretched away and away, full of primitive, stalk-like marshy plants.

Somewhere in this dream of primeval perfection, CC had inserted its death laboratories.

Ethereal spirits, death camps, and now, from across the waters came to the honking of an enormous host of sauropods splashing through the shallows. "Great! Tuba-headed ten-meter lizards. The things we do for love." Vince moaned.

259

He pulled the scorched lander onto the sand best he could and set to making a camp for the night. He would start fresh in the morning and face them. In a few hours the planet's sun wound down and the night was aglow with the nebula and fat stars. A huge golden arc-the gas giant's rings-climbed on the horizon until the night was gleaming yellow. It cast purple shadows.

Lotus-like flowers, big as ground cars, bloomed with audible pops. They cast streams of scented clouds to the languid breeze. Fat insects glowed, swooping by, rumbling like clockwork aereoplanes and set busily to feeding on their nectar.

Reptilian wings with tufts of soft feathers glided in sweeps through the moist night air, cackling, cawing and then flutelike resonant calls. Suddenly then, like a red god come to survey the dawn of a new universe, the magenta and teal gas giant rose up to join its rings. It would come to fill half the sky. Vince thought of Tyhrin and Rip but the comparison could be made for countless inhabited moons that orbited a gas giant. Still, the splendor of such skies humbled the tiny, mortal man-as well it should.

Rip hadn't been this full of primordial power since its dawn, however. Siluria was a Surreal Carnival of Primordial power. Something eerie and intangible was in the air.

Something is watching me.

Sleep came, a dreamless needed rest, curled up in Herb's lander.

Bright morning sky was a dozen sheens of luminous rays bursting through cumulonimbus clouds stacked high into the dawn. He was immersed in scents of flowers and ferns and mushrooms; birds calling resonated and permeated the air. Tubas rumbling. Tubas? Not tubas, sauropods with sound chambers in their skulls-Siluria! Vince lifted his head and surveyed the bay and marshes. He oriented himself by the planets sun and a few daylight stars shimmering in the nebula.

He took a long hunting knife and a small hip pack of provisions from Herb's lander. It included a small plasma pistol-twenty shot.

He unfolded the bamboo catamaran Herb had included and christened her the Taloned Sire II. He dragged it to the marshes and drifted to deeper water beyond the reaches of the stalky plants. The water was turquoise clear and teeming with life.

Below him, he could see a reef of kaleidoscope colors and ceaseless movement. It stretched out into the bay seeming without end, broken only by bits of sandy blue of spaces between the reefs.

The whole planet's a reef!

His mind rebelled at trying to put order into the cacophony of color and movement below him. He concentrated on the catamaran. A soft wind tugged at his sail and he moved eastward. CCs sensor satellites could see him now, he was sure. But he had bet his life on knowing CCs incalculable gall and arrogance-they could see him but they wouldn't be looking. They would be scanning space for intrusive warships, mighty things worth noticing. Not one man with an audacious plan sailing toward their base on a bamboo catamaran.

He had sailed for several hours when he began to see signs of the planets dominant life forms. One by land and one by sea.

It was the sea creatures he was worried about first. Vince had seen a reconstruction of Earth's Silurian period at a science museum on a voyage to Earth once. The aptness of this world's name was staggering. There were eurypterid-like sea scorpions a little larger than a meter; nearly identical to the ones he'd seen in the reconstruction of Earth. Several of them ghosted his catamaran, darting along in the water.

They were brilliant orange, with large insect eyes of emerald that looked out with expressionless hunger. Besides the strange tail that doubled as an ugly threatening stinger and paddle, their mouthparts were fitted with huge flat claws.

The dominant land creatures didn't fit the Silurian period at all. They more resembled the infamous T-Rex. Smaller, a little less than twice the height of a man, they were crowned with a crest of feather-like antennae and wore a glorious coat of skin that could change color like a chameleon. Vince watched them too. They were observing him from the shoreline, occasionally foraying into the water as if stalking him, then turning away as if losing interest.

Like the Eurypterids, the giant water scorpions that inhabited the shallow seas of earth millions of years before the dinosaurs rose to prominence, the things scooting beside Vince's catamaran were gliding over the reef with supremacy of territory. Long, golden, and sinister, they eased alongside his craft with upward compound eyes staring with mechanical patience. Their long forward sweeping claws looked like something from a cheap thrill horror sensorama, almost comical if not for their obvious intent.

The curve of their tail came to a needlepoint sharpness that occasionally dribbled an ugly brown fluid into the turquoise waters like drool.

"I don't suppose you guys are ambassadors?" Vince asked grimly, easing his craft closer toward the shore. The scorpion tails lashed at the catamaran. They spattered its surface with brown. Vince had no doubt that would be perfectly toxic. His EVA field kept the stuff off him.

"I'm adrift on a Silurian world in a Silurian sea! Being hunted by giant waters scorpions and three-meter chameleons," he said aloud trying to hold his crossbar steady in the breeze. The sailing RNA programs Herb had given him were telling. Phrases came to mind, the air in motion, true wind, apparent wind. He knew them, but he had never heard them before.

The catamaran glided steadily closer to the shore. Perhaps he could fashion some long spears there and impale the creatures as they harassed his little craft. The catamaran slapped against the gentle breakers. Billowing cumulonimbus clouds stood high and proud on the bright sky. Vince had a sense then of something he had not sensed in some time. The magnificent wonder of creation.

The eurypterids oval compound eyes peered strangely up at him, sizing him up as a meal. Vince wondered too if they were edible. *King crab al la Siluria?*

He sailed all that day, stopping only once to make a spear. Having speared a large fish, he pulled the catamaran onto a small island and made camp, running the fish through a protein scanner to make sure it was edible. It was. Among the foliage on the island, he saw huge sculptures-dead ringers for the T-Rex things he'd seen earlier. He followed them along a path and found a temple. It could have been Angkor Watt. This was unexpected. Here was a discovery that should have been trumpeted across the galaxy. Yet CC had found a reason to hide it with its "research" base.

What was behind their actions?

Nothing struck at him that night. He'd set up a motion detector and it remained silent. He'd curled up in a niche in the temple and slept soundly. He found fruit on the island, did more scans, found it was good. Soon he would soon have a repertoire of a diet assembled. He sailed again eastward for several days, repeating a routine much the same. On the afternoon of the fourth day, he felt the catamaran being bumped by something from underneath the water. It was the eurypterids creatures. They had massed for a kill.

There were dozens of them in some kind of swarming frenzy. Claws were coming at him from every direction, snapping with mechanical clinking and speed. He kicked them away and reached for his knife. There were four of them clambering on to the catamaran, actually leaving the water now as if the swarming behavior had pressed them into some abnormal, desperate behavior.

"Shit," Vince yelped. Like they'd been waiting, sizing him up. Vince moved with lightning speed plunging the knife into midsections between their shells and kicking them back into the water oozing brown body fluids. He was cursing at them all the while, slashing and howling a war song of expletives. The catamaran slammed onto a rock outcropping and lodged there. Vince took the opportunity to leap for safer ground.

The eurypterids flung themselves about in the shallows; water scorpions from hell. He'd killed one of the things and the others were cannibalizing it, providing a distraction. Others were moving in, snapping at one another in a feeding frenzy. Vince considered jumping back on the catamaran and getting the plasma pistol a moment and thought better of it. A moment later he wished he had grabbed it. One of the T-Rex things was standing behind him.

Vince froze for a long moment calculating how long it would take him to leap back on to the catamaran and get his pack open. Barring any intrusive eurypterids, he might make it. The T-Rex was huge. Vince began to back away slowly.

"They'll ease up if you stay away from your craft for a while." The T-Rex said suddenly.

Vince froze completely.

He took a long moment and let what he'd just witnessed sink in. "Thanks." He rasped in a weird, disbelieving state.

"I mean you know harm. I seek to ally myself with your quest. Those of your kind who've built a settlement on this world mean you harm. I can help you in your struggle against them." The thing changed color as it spoke. Its feather-like tentacles moved in the air as if listening or feeling the wind.

Vince thought: *I'm going to wake up any minute now. This is a sensorama tape. CC captured me in my sleep. This absolutely can't be happening.*

He said: "I could use an ally. This world is unfamiliar to me. Why would you help me?" Vince found his own words sounding silly. What does one say to an unknown creature who suddenly speaks? There had been no sentient life forms of such intelligence ever encountered. Only the Predecessors-and no one ever knew what they had been. Perhaps this thing is a descendant of the Predecessors?

"The enemy of my enemy is my friend," it said. Then it assumed a sitting position.

Vince found himself the first ambassador of humanity to a new species. A species with a working knowledge of humanity. This was no accidental meeting. It could have strolled over to the CC base at any time. Yet it had waited for one of CC's adversaries. It had an intimate knowledge of human affairs.

"Your enemies being?" Vince asked.

"The metal heads in that settlement for one-Cyborgs, hive minds-horribly distasteful concepts. I'm sure you'll agree, eh, Mr. Leavel?"

I need a drink.

"You'll excuse me but, I uhh, don't get this." Vince was white from shock. Like the rest of mankind, he'd gotten used to being the only show in the galaxy.

"I've been monitoring hyper casts for, well, a long time, from day one in fact. They suspect you'll storm the planet. You're a bit of a celebrity. Master criminal. You keep getting on the casts. Though I understand that time at Chrysler city was a big set up."

The thing knew about the Chrysler city takedown!

"Shouldn't I be saying something about 'greetings from the Human race'?"

"Yesss. Greetings. Greetings. However, dispense with the formalities. I've been eavesdropping on your species long enough to write a history on you. You're not a bunch of buttercups, but that's okay because we're here looking for allies in a very dangerous war. Buttercups wouldn't do."

"I see. Well, wouldn't you want CC then? They're the dominant military force in this galaxy."

The T-Rex's head bobbed up and down and Vince took that it was amused.
"Yeah? Then why is one guy with a handgun storming a base full of them?"
Vince grinned wickedly.
"The element of surprise."
T-Rex's head bobbed some more. It was laughing.
Vince decided he liked the dinosaur.
They talked long-on into the night. It was a fortunate meeting of minds. Vince found himself laughing and spinning yarns with the creature. His name was Leph. He'd been listening to human casts for centuries and had a working knowledge of humanity's affairs. Vince sensed there were answers here to important questions. Yet he would have to wait until the creature was ready. Ready to forever change Vince's world, and with it, Humankind's.

Leph had a hologram of Siluria floating before him when Vince awoke. Vince looked for technical apparatus that projected the hologram and did see any. He didn't ask. "We are here." Leph pointed to a spot on the globe. "The CC settlement is here." he indicated another spot. "Along the way is a place I wish you to see. I can show you much there concerning things which concern my kind and yours."

Vince nodded solemnly, understanding that his role in the scheme of things had changed by several orders of magnitude. His importance was no longer simply a matter of his person or his friends, but one who would hold information crucial somehow to the future of the Human race.

He sailed all that day among the chimney stack islands and the endless reefs, staying close to the shorelines with Leph strolling along the shore, occasionally picking off something in a fierce rush and swallowing it in a joyous series of gulps. The evening was coming upon them, the golden rings looming in the sky. Vince's alien companion indicated an island with several temples-"There." he said. "We must go there."

Vince noted the eurypterids made way from the T-Rex. They dragged the catamaran high onto the shore among reeds and flowers.

They made their way into a rainforest grand and spectacular with massive trees. There was an endless noise of wildlife calling, singing, screeching. Waterfalls spilled along at every turn. They followed paths along the falls.

Vince could see carvings of beings such as Leph in the stone among the falls. Giant faces and figures appeared here and there between streams of clear cool water. At length there were towers and ornament among the waters. Then, rising before them a vast temple complex, the stone was violet and pink with bits of gold, of a type Vince had never seen. Leph led him along and they entered a huge portal to a corridor. On and on they walked until Vince was aware that they were in a circular room of vast circumference.

"Your people refer to us as the Predecessors," Leph said. Vince smiled in triumph-he had suspected as much. "Once, ages ago, the galaxy was ours. We gardened worlds as hunting grounds for sport, and our level of knowledge, confidence, and achievement was unparalleled."

As Leph spoke visions of that time filled the circular room. Vince saw others like Leph in crystal cities, flying in machines over terraformed worlds of their devising, going about the galaxy as if it were their private garden.

They hunted fabulous beasts, created Astro-architecture of phenomenal scope, and carried themselves with a demeanor of mastery over all.

"Then the horrors came," Leph said. Vince witnessed shadowy bits of half-formed animal parts dropping out of nowhere and tearing apart the Predecessor beings, their cities, and even the beasts in their gardens. Leph's people fought hopelessly against shadows from a nightmare.

"They appear to be a life form that crosses dimensions. We called them shapeshifters. Their hostility to any sentient being made of matter is total. Before they destroy, they torture at length. They devise gruesome scenarios pushing their victim to madness. They feed on fear. Perhaps organic chemistry hyped up by an organism's panic. We don't know."

Vince now understood what had ambushed the CC cyborged crews in the Arcturian wars.

Leph looked at Vince's recognition. "You suspected them?"

"Yes," Vince replied. "It was a pattern during the Arcturian wars. CC was plagued by something that downed their ships and has halted their advance with Gateways. They won't even communicate on the hyper casts outside their realm. There are tales of hyper Bogies. Most people don't give them real credit though."

"They will," Leph said with sadness. "When CC nuked the Arcturian colonies, a cry must have gone up from the victims. A cry of horror, unlike anything which Humanity had as yet produced. The shadow beings came rushing in to see what manner of creatures would do such a thing. They looked into our dimension again and saw CC. Of course, CC must have gotten a little taste of them too-and liked it not at all."

"Then why haven't they attacked humanity in force?"

"Reinforcements take time to get across the intergalactic spaces. They've been gone for a long time. They're coming back.

"They know we're here. This world is an ark of life forms they destroyed elsewhere. Part of our defenses has been a Time Wall-they don't like it when you mess with time. But our energy sources have been diminishing for eons.

"They've known our defenses are slipping. That's why they were foraging in this galaxy when your Arcturians were nuked. You probably surprised them. Not many species kill each other en masse as humans do."

Foraging the galaxies…

Leph stared into the big circular room where a giant holo of the galaxy had appeared further illustrating his thoughts. "Our galaxy is far from theirs. They have a long way to come. They will be arriving shortly. Once again to decimate this galaxy of sentient life. Like it or not, they are a higher life form than us in many ways. More multi-dimensional for one. But you know, they eat themselves into poverty with each sweep of a galactic realm. In many ways, they're like addicts. They can't resist the delight terror creates for them in the encounter with sentient beings"

Vince looked at Leph with a vacant, wasted stare. "How can we fight them?"

Leph waved a huge green arm. "Near the end, we discovered some defenses. Time walls for one-although that can be problematic. They just don't cross semi-stasis or stasis shields. This whole nebula has been laced with semi-stasis fields. In some places, one can enter and fly into singularities of space-time and not even know it. They also have a strong distaste for certain character traits. We found the most ruthless, the most desperate, and often the most courageous of beings can fend off their mental attacks. But you don't know until you're going rounds with them."

"CC has discovered many Outpilots do. They haven't been able to figure out why."

So…CC's reason for experimenting with Outpilots.

Vince looked hopeful. "Have you figured out why? I think they may be wrong about their pilots. They're making an assessment based on something that happened a long time ago, with a different set of pilots."

"Not for certain. But I have a few ideas...Outpilots continually face uncertainties in deep space. Perhaps facing uncertainties-without a net so to speak-does something to a human."

Vince swallowed. "CC pilots may be getting data streams, but they're not Hive mind since the Arcturian Wars." Through the ages mankind had waited and wondered at contact with intelligent life. All the years he'd carried the memory at what he'd seen in the CC ship on Rip-it had all come to this. A warning of doom and vague speculations for hope.

"Why haven't you made yourselves known before now?" he asked.

"No point until now. Why bring half the galaxy down on us touring and poking around?"

Leaving the temples and their strange recordings, Vince and Leph returned to the sunlight of Siluria. They stood in a courtyard among temples and statues. The warrior statues took on a new significance for him now; now that he understood their foe.

"So you seek an alliance of sorts against the shapeshifters? The 'death eaters'?"

Leph head bobbed. "Yesss."

"I'm a fugitive. Why me?"

"You're a famous master criminal, remember? Besides, I don't imagine there's anyone out there with the title, 'ambassador to ancient aliens' ".

"Who do you want me to bring this information to anyway?"

"Time will tell. But first-you have a pressing objective. You want to storm the CC settlement, yes?"

"Yes," Vince said and followed Leph to another of the temples. Inside was a cache of weaponry and vehicles as Vince had seen in the temple of records.

"Superior firepower," Leph said. "Won't matter against the shapeshifters but it will give a clear advantage over CC."

"We'll knock out their main generator," Vince said.

The sheriff had finally come to the Bandor base. Bandor realized he should be glad of the aid but it was just another Wild in his opinion. Another piece of the Chaos beyond the Hive mind. The man was obsessed with his quarry, the smugglers Sagamore Salvatore and Vincent Leavel. Bandor grimaced-such a life, existing on the margins of trading based on outlawry.

"He's here." the sheriff said bluntly.

Though separated from the hive mind for the sake of independent action, Bandor was able to utilize much of CCCE Cyborg faculties to his advantage. Information streams could be gotten when needed, although even that advantage was diminished by the sheer distance of the base and its strange fields.

He could see this sheriff had taken a determinedly long voyage pursuing his quarry. He also had a list of the man's fighting equipment. It appeared the sheriff had enhanced standard issue with some private upgrades. That was disconcerting.

This one's relishing this, Bandor thought uncomfortably. He ran data streams scanning the base perimeter.

"I sense nothing. What makes you so certain?"

"I can feel him. He's here." Beneath the grey skin-suit, the sheriff's head cocked to one side. "Have you read his files?"

"Some." Bandor lied.

"But I don't see what biographical information on a loser-con can matter. He'll be hydroponics fodder very shortly." Bandor said acidly.

"Perhaps." the sheriff adjusted his weapon.

Bandor grew more fretful by the minute with this sheriff's presence on his base. The man was obsessed with his desire for Leavel's throat.

Like he was hunting tigers on Rigel Four.

Harry's in on this! I know it! Bandor felt his control in the scheme of things slipping away. First Harry, now this monster.

"You should read your files, Mr. Bandor. That's what Cyborgian Central provides them for.

265

"Leavel was smuggling contraband when he was barely past legal age on one of the Outworlds. Shortly after that, we find him in possession of a frigate and a trading guild member.

"Don't underestimate your enemy, Bandor."

The main generators shut down with a sudden lurching, gasping whine.

Lights flickered as emergency systems went online.

"He's here!" Bandor yelled.

Then came the explosions, ripping through the base continually, steadily getting closer. Bandor lost contact with wing after wing, group after group of his men.

Information and databases shut down one after another. The sheriff stalked off into the melee of noise and confusion and was gone. Amazed, Bandor stood in his office overlooking the research area and watched the far wall collapse under disruptor fire.

He watched Leavel walk through the smoke and step in among the research subjects reading identification tags.

Equipment had been knocked over spilling fluids everywhere…

The smell of urine and acids assaulted Vince's mind. A bellow of insidious flames and plastics burned perilously close. His brain refused to move further along another moment. Anything further led to an abyss.

The tag on the corpse in front of him gutted and ruined with all his hopes of the life he had been making with her, said "Leyla Veronica".

Kneeling by the table where the ruins of his love lay dissected, Vincent pressed his lips against her forehead. Tears came steadily to him now as images of their short time together flooded his mind.

"What have I done?" he whispered.

Only the smoke and flames answered.

He saw her smiling, spinning with him on a dance floor at the club "Twenty-five Twenty-five". He felt her lips pressed against his and heard her bright laughter in his memory. Yet there were only the flames and the smoke.

Remorse and regret and mourning would have to wait.

Someone was watching him from a room above the research lab; the director of this insane operation. Vince suddenly found the will to move forward again. He strode savagely ahead and burst into the director's office facing the true banality of evil.

Bandor cowered with his hands on a handgun. Vince struck and the weapon went flying uselessly against a pile of equipment.

Incongruously there was a hologram of an elegant room on one side of the director's office. Vince turned and before him was a hologram of Harry Williams Stark sitting calmly in a seat carved from the ivory of sea beast tusks.

"You small-time smuggler," Harry said. Bandor huddled in a corner fascinated.

Vince realized who he was seeing. He was amazed at the man's reach. Even here.

"Space Engineer, hah! Why don't you get a job in a supermarket and leave the big boy world to real men, eh? How did you like repairing dirty old equipment on Ophelia? Carcinogens taste good? You cheap blockade runner.

"Ha! You dreamer.

"Me, I know what I am. I'm a garbage man and they pay me to move it around and take it away and when they're through with it, they're through."

Vince looked at the opulence that man sat in and wondered.

Harry leaned forward, "Yes, Vinny Boy, I could eat whole planets for dinner! You, you're nothing-nothing!" He flipped Vince a middle finger.

"What the hell do you want?" Vince asked.

"I want you to know this. That corpse down in the Lab isn't your Leyla. I got Leyla out of Ophelia. She came with me.

"Long black air cars, cruises. You were rotting on Ophelia; she was with me. Loving it. LOVING IT!!

"Live with that, sport. She was glad to be done with you. Live with that."

Vince's mind reeled. Of course. They set him up, then they take his lover. An ever more perfect violation of his life. *Run him through one hell, then another, then another. Drive him insane as reality seems to be baseless. Whom the Gods will destroy, they first make mad.*

Vince saw Harry's eyes move beyond him and knew there was someone else in the room besides he and Bandor.

Harry snickered. "Oh, Vinny, say hello to the Sheriff for me! Ehhhh-heheheheheh!"

Vince set his weapon down slowly and raised his arms. He turned to edge around slowly and glared at the figure that had come up behind him. A huge sheriff in an ugly grey skin suit. The man was removing a cyber-helmet.

First a collar of colorful patterns with a silver brim, then a blue tattooed face looked across the room.

"Hello Captain." Millin Quinoa said.

Vince dropped his arms and let a weary smile cross his face.

Harry stood up.

"Oh, come on! You've got to be kidding me! Bandor-do something, you idiot! That sheriff is one of his old crewmates!"

Bandor just stared.

Millin walked over to the hologram of Harry's office.

"Mr. Stark, let me be the first to inform you that General Ossa's fleet has surrounded Chrysalis Isla." Millin pulled out a long Pleiades cigar.

Vince looked over at Bandor. "This was your operation, wasn't it? Shut that transmission off, will you? I've heard about enough of him." He ran his tired hands through his long red hair, looked to Millin." And what of the Taloned Sire?"

Millin was lighting his cigar, he gave Vince a sidelong glance. "She's waiting for her Captain."

The Swarm

Consider an eyeball. Billions of years ago a few light-sensitive cells on a mere blob of primordial protoplasm. Fast forward and we have two hundred million cells in one of nature's great visualizing tools, hooked up to the brain, scanning the universe. Wonder, then, what other senses may have developed in the untold eons and the eleven dimensions. Wonder and worry. They might be watching us now.
-Winteroud Sole, Caldris.

Ocho's World
Provincial Space 4217

General Ossa glared at the holos from spy ships for weeks. He'd seen every seedy O'Neil station port and every two-bit ore hauler with fraudulent registries in three systems. He had a team on it working around the clock. Nothing that indicated private navies. Nothing that even indicated a stray Guildsman trading without tariffs. Yet that wasn't his true concern.

Yes, he would do his duty. Private armies were a bad thing. His real desire was another search, the search for the missing intergalactic matter signature signal that had been edited from the probe reports before it hit the hive mind.

The ensign he'd assigned that covert research was standing before him now. Tamara Fortunato had grown up on Earth's moon in industrial regions humankind had occupied since the conquest of the solar system with sub-light drives. It was a world with traditions of mastering a complex artificial environment old as any, and people conditioned to subterfuge techno bureaucracies as a way of life. She was perfect. Ossa admired her for decades, but he was a general. That was that. Little did he know she was in love with him.

"Ensign?" he queried.

"Sir." She hesitated a moment and Ossa realized she was about to throw him a curve. "I tried eight-hundred different ways of getting at the data but it's locked up with overlord only security codes on every channel. I came in under a different auspice each time, but sooner or later red flags going to go up if it hasn't already- and the Overlords are going to come after whoever is hacking the data."

"Are you requesting we surrender?" He chuckled.

"No Sir. I'm not. But on a hunch, I thought maybe the matter we found out there was something we sent. I searched historic migration records and there was a colony ship-a huge one. It was sent out centuries ago.

"About a hundred miles long, really an O'Neil station with mega drives strapped on the back. Religious fundamentalists-they wanted out of our galaxy completely because it was too darn sinful, Sir. So they left on a journey that will take an eon to finish."

"The trajectory? That matter was coming towards the Milky Way, not away." Ossa knew she'd have an answer for him, but they had to run through this inquiry by the numbers.

"That's correct, Sir. Its orientation was in the departure trajectory, only reversed. They turned around."

"Too much of an assumption. I don't buy it. They turned around an arc ship a hundred Kilometers long and started coming back?"

"I know it's a lot to buy. But I figured if they did turn around they might have had trouble, sent out a mayday. So I went through the files of spy guard satellites outside the Hercules cluster. One had a record of transmission but the codes were so old it hadn't translated them, simply filed. It was our mayday. I've managed to convert the file." She laid it on his desk.

"Have you seen it?"

"No Sir."

Ossa threw his hands up. "You never fail to amaze me, Ensign. Put it on."

Nervously, she loaded the file and adjusted a flat-screen projection.

It showed the hull of an O'Neil ship. Several people in Eva Suits were walking along the outer hull as if on routine maintenance work. They were followed by a couple of auto bots hauling equipment. Suddenly one of the humans turned and seemed to look up.

He stared for a moment and then began scrambling in a frenzy away from where he'd been. The others watched him for a few seconds and then began after him as if they were confused.

Suddenly the image changed to a suit camera and the perspective was now one of the workmen's. You could see the fleeing individual swinging his arms as if to ward something off, but there was nothing there.

"So we got a worker bee who goes off the deep end staring at the intergalactic black." Ossa chirped cynically. "What's the big tie in with the Overlords?"

As if in answer, something appeared over the frenzied man. Like a door suddenly opened that hadn't been there before, a thing was there. An indeterminate mass of horror that sent adrenaline shooting through Ossa's veins like ice water.

Fortunato muttered an expletive.

The thing gripped the worker and pulled him up like he was a mouse. He was spinning, changing. Exploding and bleeding, his arms and legs flailed in rapid ugly motions.

Then he was being dragged through the "doorway". For a second one could see into the doorway. There were rows and rows of ugly black smudges curled away in line; a swarm of them.

Ossa had seen men die in battle all his life. He'd never seen anyone in as much pure terror as was conveyed by the workman in that image.

The tape stopped.

Ossa and Fortunato looked at one another silently for a long moment.

"So the overlords finally found something nastier than them. Take that tape apart frame by frame and do an analysis. Find out as much about the bogey that snatched that workman as is possible. See if it even resembles any life forms we've encountered. I've got a month's salary says it won't."

Fortunato was cold. Suddenly she was no longer on the top of the food chain, and she didn't like it. "Yes, sir."

When she was gone General Ossa looked about his office as if its familiar accouterments could somehow allay the images he'd just witnessed. His polished metal surfaces, the glowing gems of lights, leather sofas floating in repeller fields, a thirty-fifth century engraved laser pistol mounted on a wall; command perks that were now all taking on the aspect of a Neanderthal's cave.

Whatever had captured and killed that man in the tape, it did it in intergalactic space. Where nothing save dark matter and primordial hydrogen atoms existed for untold billions of years.

It had preyed on a man riding the hull of a craft moving at super-light speeds like it was fishing in a mountain pond. Then it had disappeared from the known universe like it was walking across a street.

From the portal where it snatched the man there appeared to be more of the things, many more. Yet what disturbed Ossa most was the creature's familiarity. In some deep corner of his mind, he'd known such as it in nightmares and black dread. When an unsolicited report from a sheriff tailing The Leavel Case had come in concerning syndicate information, Ossa's mind was still fresh with the dread of this newly discovered "swarm".

His actions would forever be different in his relations with men.

The current King of the Pleiades ran protests at the mass of CC ships moving into his star cluster. The Overlords sent him a scathing dressing-down and Ossa continued massing his ships. Mr. Stark had been forewarned of the impending occupation of the Pleiades only hours before when he was finally contacted by General Ossa.

Harry glared into the view screen at the general. Ossa knew he'd never take the man alive, and certainly not without a great loss of life. His thoughts went back again to the swarm, and he wondered how a man such as this might meet them.

"Mr. Stark." the general addressed him calmly.

Harry smiled. "General."

Ossa was glad he had so many ships.

"I have arrest orders for you on a series of crimes against humanity. I also have, however, the power to pardon. I understand you have previous military experience."

That was an understatement. Harry's eyebrows raised, "Some."

"There is a certain threat to the galactic realm that must be addressed. All other concerns remain secondary."

Harry snickered. "You want to draft me?"

Now Ossa smiled.

"In a manner of speaking, yes. You and your whole private army."

Harry looked over to Maximus Mercurio. Max shrugged.

"So. Am I finally going to find out what's had those Overlords so up and jittery all this time?" Harry asked.

"Sure will," Ossa said flatly. "And it's not pretty."

Harry Chuckled.

"I figured." He leaned back and turned to his men. "Well, boys?"

There came a sound of affirmation from the men.

Harry winked at Ossa, "It ain't over."

Ossa had not revealed to CCCE the evidence Millin Quinoa had supplied him under the Guise of Sheriff 182-61 and thus was able to engage his whole under-the-table deal with Harry and the Dark Corps with the none the wiser. There was a strange turning symmetry to the whole matter, Harry once an honored warrior, then a syndicate pirate Lord, now a covert operative of Ossa's. Ossa, with his every move becoming more the rogue general himself...

-Winteroud Sole, Caldris

Amnesia

Uncharted Space, Far side of the Milky Way.
4217

Where the devil is the crew?

Maximus Mercurio wiped a mass of blood and grime from his face, orienting himself in the steaming gangway of the fighter-bomber. He found himself lying on a wall. The bomber's gravity bubble was off. There was, however, gravity-a rolling pull that pinned him hard to the gangway, a meter and a half off the floor.

A gravity well, he thought; his compact round face glaring around in sudden understanding of danger. A gravity well would mean a world-*or worse*. He gathered his senses.

There was a streaming sound against the hull-a decaying orbit.

Thick air, heavy gravity-a gas giant!

The ship was dropping into the atmosphere of a gas giant!

Springing to his feet, he steam-rolled toward the cockpit. His mind careened with the sudden rocking and shaking of the vessel. With each piston step, he assessed his situation. The gravity bubble was off, thus it was only a matter of time before the pressures outside burned the ship up, crushed them, and sank them in a stream of metallic hydrogen deep in the planet's innards.

Where the devil is the crew?! Something had knocked him on his petard and cut his face open, rendering him unconscious. He had no memory of the event. *Rat chewing worm worshiping refugees! But someone's going to pay with black and blue booty!* He balled his fists up and looked this way and that. The floor was now a wall to his left. He cursed in three languages and continued down the gangway avoiding swinging hatches. *Who unlocked all the hatch doors?*

Atmospherics were shot. Steam was blasting everywhere. Nobody was at the helm. Something had happened; *something bad.* There was a gutted corpse twisted on the floor in front of him. He made his way toward the piloting cabin.

Uh-oh. Won't be paying any booty.

Mercurio paused, put his back against plastisteel. He pulled out his disser, kept moving.

There came a groan of metal fatigue from the ship's hull.

Ship's sinking-fast.

The piloting cabin was empty.

He glared at the room suspiciously with a sharp challenge, but there were no takers. *All the rats have jumped ship, and I'm going to Davey Jones' locker like a watership made of cast iron.*

He slipped on the piloting helmet and merged into the ship's senses. The MERGE helmet replaced his sensations and perceptions with the neural net of the starcraft.

Lightning! Miles of it. A sea of lightning, shuddering in titanic waves and streams. Broken by radio storms in sheer walls, like mountains, twirling in the far distance flanked by cliffs of cumulonimbus thunderheads. A falls of super dense helium glimmered from horizon to horizon, sweeping down to lower layers of the gas giants atmosphere. His fighter was being swept through the torrent of atmospheric currents with increasing speed...

The control and power systems had been shut down. He reactivated them and watched as dozens of programs flashed to life. The fighter bomber's gravity bubble eased into being, breaking his descent. Atmospherics, hull nano repair programs, drive systems, then navigationals-all systems returning to normalcy.

The fighter made upwards, away from the maddening pressures. This deep in the planet's atmosphere he was blind. He could be anywhere.

271

Slowly, he gained ever more altitude. The ship's senses were starting to perceive things above the dense layers of hydrogen, helium, and lighting storms...quasars...the galactic plume! He was somewhere in uncharted space, on the far side of the galactic core.

The ship wouldn't have just powered down. There were protocols and sequences. Someone had turned it off. Turned it off and left him lying in it, dazed and bloodied. Falling to an ignoble and unknowable fate. *Why hadn't they just killed him?*

Seas of ball lightning coalesced below him as the planet shrunk away in maddening slowness. The fighter's programs continued to reboot. The seas were the swirling of a Jovian stratosphere now. Above him, the teeming stars and plasma of the atomic clouds roared their fury. The galactic plume showed high; it was giving him the finger.

You too, you wicked wench.

No sign of the crew. Abandoned ship? Somebody wanted him dead and this ship lost. No, not lost-eviscerated back into its primal elements like a thing returned to nature, so rarefied that nothing could ever be found of it. It was like a demon of undoing had carefully unraveled its elements and cast them into a six-dimensional drain.

Maximus frowned. *Where the devil had that thought come from?*

There would be booty to pay! But who? Who would dare betray him-not the gutted corpse in the gangway; that was a self-inflicted wound. Rather than comply with the betrayers, that one had gone down at his hand. No more Ray. Good man, have to be buried with honors when Max got back to-Max winced-back to where?

Who am I?

I'm Maximus Mercurio. Two hundred pounds of an unforgiving, death-dealing, payback-getting, golden-horned Hellcat. Loyal unto death to Harold Stark, warlord extraordinaire, Don of the dark corps, an avenger of the King.

Never forgive. Never forget.

Gangsters, thugs, and smugglers, privateers, if you will!

Not one to be stilettoed in the solar plexus. No. No wonder they had to get rid of the body. But why hadn't they offed him? Time? What would be their hurry out here in the big bad boonies? Or had they just gone yellow when the time for the dirty deed was done? Perhaps they wanted him to wake, dazed and amazed as the fighter imploded in the frozen metallic hydrogen. Having his last thoughts go: Drat, I've been boons waggled!

Maximus sneered. No one in the Dark Corps would do it. There was someone else. Someone they'd come gunning for.

Why was he out here anyway? His mind drew a blank. They'd been on a mission, yes. The mission...reconnaissance? Intelligence? Scouting? Way the hell out here beyond the settled worlds?

The mission.

Bits and pieces of his memory were flickering, fading into being. It felt as if someone had reached in his brain, using it for an amusement park simulation; dizzy, convoluted and about to rupture. Yet the mission parameters started to coalesce in small increments perceptibly. It was an unusual assignment-General Harry Stark only trusted Max, the bulldozer, the golden horned bulldog. A Cyborgian general had gone rad, slipped the Overlords' command chain. Was assembling his alliances to fight some kind of new life form. The Dark Corps of the Pleiades had been given a choice.

A smuggler they'd been stalking threw them a twist, dragged half the Cyborgian Air Corps after them-then unexpectedly the general had pivoted- *join the fight or deal with the authorities.*

Stark had damn near died laughing, "Sign us up!

We'll fight your damn boogie man." Max had laughed right along.

He wasn't laughing now.

He scanned the far horizons of his flight path for any evidence of other ships. Fleeing betrayers. Scooting back to whatever hovel betraying rat chewers go to.

He wasn't surprised to find nothing, not even an irregular wake in the zero wave cycle. Zip.

He sneered at the magnificent galaxy spread out before him. The billions of stars, the galactic plume. The aurora plasma streaming into the huge void.

He slipped out of the MERGE helmet. The interior of the attack ship hummed back at him telling nothing.

"Okay, you little bone heads. Let's see what old Maximus can discover today," he said and set about looking for clues at the scene of the crime.

Deneb IV
4217

It was a particularly foggy patch of Capitol world. General Ossa's air limo darted along with towers a mere hundred stories in the air. Once the heights of power, perhaps, but over the centuries just another bunch of tower levels left behind in the race toward ever more impressive heights.

Ossa had seen it many times, many times before with dread. The tower and halls of his Overlord Transhuman direct superior. Ossa was Air Corps-traditionally removed from the Hive mind for the sake of autonomy-raised from birth in a special warrior caste. His Overlord contact, Omm 6X, was an ancient post-human entity.

Omm, like all the Transhumans, had whatever remained of their most recent clone incarnation tanked somewhere safe while their sentience romped in virtual worlds of their whim and will.

The Transhumans were the most ancient of mankind. In direct control of its largest and most powerful ancient empire, Omm and his ilk sickened Ossa. Their bizarre indulgences, obtuse and useless intellectual pursuits. These seemed ever, and ever more at odds with managing the society they ruled. Instead of practical or even possible objectives, an endless sequence of disastrous fiats, programs, and reconfigurations of social engineering which made him want to puke. That these lunatics and refugees from reason were in charge of civil society was bad enough, that they were the ultimate authority over the use of force was a pure theater of the absurd. At every meeting with Omm, baroque and surreal symbolism laced his every word with games and multiple meanings.

Enough with the games Omm. Enough theatrics. Give me my orders and let me be on my way...

The Halls of OMM 6X glistened about General Vega Ossa in a ghostly manner, losing opacity. Ossa grimaced; Omm was going to put on a virtual show for his amusement, and the penalty of a wrong move would be an un-virtual death. Omm's large head full of snakes smiled hugely and a tuberous baritone laugher croaked out like a death throe. Ossa wondered what happened to the Transhuman-Cyborgian Overlords in their long centuries of rule. What was it in the Hive mind that predicated all their bizarre elaborate behaviors? Surely nothing good.

Ossa smiled back and steeled his fear. Omm could conceivably torture him here for years upon years. How long before the overlord would break his spirit? At least in real space, in the real universe, death could only take him once.

"Ready to ride, star man?" Omm asked.

"Gallantly Sir." The general said coolly. If he was to be broken, tortured, and racked, better to do it with style.

They were suddenly riding in a herd of giant tarantulas. The thundering of the thousands of spider legs was deafening. Omm was wearing a cowboy hat, like the ones of the pampas. The herd was stampeding. Ossa looked down at the creature he found himself on and froze with disgust. On a thousand worlds, he'd never seen such an awful thing.

"Shopping with the Decorators!" Omm bellowed.

The thunder spiders rode on, across a broad purple plain. They pursued fleeing impala-like creatures. Ossa recognized the impala beasts as a variation of something he'd seen once in a nature hologram program, but couldn't recall their name.

Omm gave him a sidelong glance, "I understand you haven't found the sixty-five hundred assassins and mercenaries I sent you out to Ocho's world for?" Omm waved his big cowboy hat. "Hooyah!"

Tell me the truth now, General, and perhaps I'll let you walk out of here without taking your head off and feeding it to my spider pets.

Ossa patted the big spiders back. "No, Sir!"

The spiders and the plains disappeared and the two of them were suddenly back in Omm's favorite Halls, the baths of Caracalla, circa the second century. Omm's big cowboy hat was still on his head, though. A little snake peered out.

"You sure of that?" Omm demanded.

"Sir. I'm an officer. I have my duty to defend." *Now, I live or die.*

"Yes, I'm sure. The question is, 'Who defines your duty?'"

They looked at each other, and Ossa knew he suspected everything.

No, not suspected-he knew. But God was in the details, and Ossa hadn't given him that.

"General, I believe you will do what needs to be done. I'm a pencil pusher. We Overlords, well, we administer civilization to the civilized. You, and the military, however, administer its opposite to the uncivilized. Be careful of riding tarantulas out there. In the real universe, where you play, they can't be made to run and stop with a programming signal."

Whatever game you're playing with the felonious rouges in the star lanes better come up aces or I'll feed your burnt fanny up for din-din.

Ossa raised an eyebrow. Omm's way of warning caution? How nice, he cared.

"I'll be careful."

"I know you will, Vega me soldier boy. My spider pets here, they're a children's holo program to what you'll be facing soon. I know someone was sniffing around in the Imperial archives. Whatever you found there remains in tight military circles. However, you're defining military these days; I suspect that is taking a pretty wide orbit, but again, it's your call.

"The public finds out about exterior and undetermined nonhuman threats to our hegemony, and civilization will collapse in... six weeks, three days and thirty-seven hours."

Ossa looked at him sharply.

"Oh yes, and that's an optimistic estimation. I spent a decade once just running over scenarios. Of course, life would go on. Just what manner of life will it be? Well, humanity has tolerated all manner of strange arrangements in its long and twisted story, aye, General?"

Ossa knew better than to ask permission to speak freely. Omm was already showing signs of distress. If the conversation kept going the giant, ancient Overlord could slip into madness. Fear edged his words.

Not fear, no-panic. *Holy terror.*

"But of course," Ossa replied calmly, implying a soothing manner.

"Good, then! Do your thing. Find a way. Win, Starman. I'll be watching your back, here at Deneb. Any of the other Overlords tap my data banks, I've set up an ugly relay to the deep Merge recording of the original contact with the things for them. Leaves a nasty taste in their mouths, and I can vouch for you. As long as you win.

"Now, go do your job. Break things and kill people. Or better yet, break people and kill things."

Things. The things that keep me awake.

Ossa turned to answer but he stood alone suddenly in the antechamber. A golden woman with butterfly wings was waiting to take him to his air limo.

"Have a lovely day," she said glowingly.

The air limo bolted into the crowded stream of traffic and Ossa sighed.

"Call from Harry Stark on the line, sir." The driver said in reassuring military crispness

"Right. Computer, make a gin and tonic. And make it a double." Ossa said.

"Yes, General Grant." The computer said.

"Don't be a smart ass."

Harry floated in the holomap of the Milky Way and ran his hands through the stars. On the other side of space, there was a limo interior with a man drinking gin. About fifty thousand light-years high, Harry mused.

"What have you got?" Ossa asked.

"We analyzed the data you sent and figured out the hyper signature from the tapes. When the thing came out of hyper and grabbed the workman, there were distinct patterns and spatial distortion; ripples in time. I sent out several ships on an arc trajectory above the galactic plane, dropping drones into space set to look for that particular hyper signature. Low and behold, a number of them indicated activity that matched it." Harry replied.

He paused a long dreary moment and Ossa thought: Now the bad news.

"One of my crews hasn't reported back. They're out there deep. Past the frontiers, past the core."

"Marauders?" Ossa offered.

A sad cackle erupted from Harry. He shook his head, "No such luck. My people eat Marauders for lunch. I've caught these guys hunting Marauders on vacation. The call that 'surfing safaris'. No. I'd venture good money they ran into your spookies. I should have prepped them better."

"This is war. You can't anticipate everything, Mr. Stark. We're dealing with an unknown enemy." Ossa offered consolation. Only another commander who had lost men could do so.

Harry remembered the carnage of the ground wars at Baal One. He was young; the enemy had acquired a new weapon. The death toll had been brutal.

"These men were all survivors of 'unknown factors,'" he countered.

"They're all veterans-fearless, ruthless, and motivated. If none of them could survive an attack of one of your spookies, we might be looking at the extinction of our species."

"Give me his coordinates. I'll send an attack ship out there for recon."

"Any new toys?" Harry queried.

"I'm working on a hyper-fritzer."

"Which is?"

"Sort of like a dimensional grenade. They stick their heads into our dimensional space; we drop a nice wall of multi-dimensional sheer into the opening. Part of them slides into the fifth dimension, part into the sixth, another part into the seventh, etc."

"I like it." Harry's smile was feral. Once he'd been awed by a Titian painting to the point of tears. With time and experience, he'd learned to appreciate the beauty of a well-honed gravity bomb, or even a simple stiletto…

Mercurio found three more corpses in the fighter. There wasn't much left of them. There were traces of fights all over the ship. Blood, broken things. But there was nothing in the ship's log. The black box was gone. That was a new one. There was blood there, too. His hyper caster had a human head bashed into it. He could recognize who it had been. A good soldier, a close friend. The body was on the other side of the room. More indications of conflict.

Indications that their opponents embraced brute savagery.

Maximus steeled his rage. He silently tabulated each record of a firefight and each lost comrade for a payback date and multiplied them by ten.

He checked the body and found some cash and a fake ID. That had been Achilles Bell. Of course, the ID didn't say that, but Max knew. He knew all the aliases.

Made sense too. Bell would have defended communications. He was the first mate. But why bash in the caster with his head? They could have used a hammer. This was hatred here beyond mere war. The crew had fought back. It looked like they pissed off their adversary. You've got to be one sick degenerate to get so angry as to rip the man's head off and use it as a tool. Max remembered Baal One. They hadn't taken prisoners.

As you've done unto my men, thus will be done unto you, sewer slime. Max felt his eyes grow dark. Why couldn't he remember? There was something special about this op, something important that he needed to remember. The targets were-it skirted the edge of his consciousness. Just out of reach.

Like someone had tweaked his brain.

Could they do that? Out here, deep space? No labs, onboard a small fighter, close quarters, hand to hand combat-and then drag in medical equipment to mess with his grey matter? He growled, "rat chewing, worm worshipping, cowards!"

How had they gotten on board? Last port of call? No.

Max dropped back into MERGE and set the fighter on a heavy rush into hyper heading back for civilization. He might encounter Marauders when he set over the galactic core. Alone that would be no surfing safari. But he'd get through. A good story for next when he hit the taverns.

The small fighter streamed into zero space and Max felt the gleaming winds of the hyper-gamma spaces brush his cheeks. He watched for hyper trails like a starving hawk. Somebody was going to give him some sweet red payback tail.

He only wished he could remember who.

The last of the pig-monkeys was howling as Babayaga ate its face. She dropped its ugly little body back into the flat dimensions, felt the thrill of its fear and then stretched in delight at her superiority. She could see, far into the intergalactic black, the horde coming. A hunt! A feast would be! A whole galaxy of fearful beings. Ohhh! (she hears in the resonance of high dimension her roar of ecstasy, the kill! The kill!) The fears she had explored in the corners of their flatworld minds. Yummy, so good, the electricity running through its mind, coursing through the organic patterns of flatworld flesh. Pathetic creatures.

Except for the one pig-monkey. Aghh! Her anger raged around the dimensional curls and she rolled on, over the flows of radiance seething, hating. No matter what corner of its brain she searched, she found no fears to taste. The others, they were strong, and she had to work to find the drug of fear, flashing through the dimensions of their memories, deep into their lives, their past-the things pushed away, the shadow things repressed. That one, he was the strongest.

Defeat haunted her. He'd looked at her squarely and kept coming! She remembered the bitter taste of his mind. It had repelled her. She couldn't kill him, nor could she let him live to tell his tale. If the other pig-monkeys figured how he'd eluded death it would be a disaster for the horde.

With his primitive scooter craft (so weak these preposterous flatworld affronts to the universe, they need a device for everything) scuttled into the belly of a gravity well, she'd watched him sink to his doom. She shook a million black tentacles. She felt the curling fronds of her proboscis. She needed rest after the feast. She felt the electricity and ionic vibrations flow through her senses and lingered in the magnetosphere of a star for long lazy moments. She made a face like one of the pig-monkeys, ha! What fun. The good plasmas and forces of a crowded galaxy soothed her hate and hunger after the long voyage across intergalactic space. Such life forms to feast on...!

Ring around the rosy

New Galen, Arcturian Space
4217

An empathic mind, that sixth sense so finely tuned
ASHES! ASHES!
Feeling the tenuous strings of four-dimensional runes
ASHES! ASHES!
I hear their death throes resounding in the well of time
ASHES! ASHES!
A pocket full of posies, they all fell down
-Winteroud Sole, from "Two centuries among the ruins".

It occurred to Gibbon, when Winteroud's convulsions started again, that stretching one's mind along four-dimensional string echoes may not be an adaptive mutation. The Chromium droid was merged with Winteroud and could see the visions which the historian was enduring. Above the ruins, a transparent and sinister starport (that was no longer) appeared to live out its last horrible moments like echoes on a holoscreen speaking unfinished phrases over and over. Ghost hologram graphics glittered over the phantom terminal: *New Galen StarPort, Gateway to the Galaxy!*

Winteroud's convulsions were always worse here, at this StarPort. As soon as he entered the ruins, convulsions would grab him violently, and this time was no exception.

"Hold tight good friend." Gibbon offered. "You'll snap out of it momentarily." Gibbon hoped. The reality was, more often than not, the historian slipped into a coma. His chromium droid grabbed at Winteroud's shaking form then and injected him with a sedative. The convulsions eased to mere tremors, and Winteroud eyed his surroundings with a strange resignation and sedated fascination.

"So many" he rasped, "So many dead, look at them, Gibbon."

"I see them Sir-I'm merged with you." The droid offered calmly, "Truly a calamity."

Winteroud steadied himself and considered his course of action. For two centuries they had been coming back here trying to solve the mystery of the green echoes; starliner ghosts, that had a green tint rather than the ordinary tan. "Something new among the ashes?" Winteroud could see the ghosts of crowds moving through the empty terminal. In the piles of skeletons, he could see individuals in their last days, waiting for rescue and aid that never came. The visions flashed and flickered. He saw glass walls imploding, fireballs scorching the confused crowds.

"Something new- "

277

Winteroud's eyes raced to the landing strips chasing the edge of an idea. He saw the wreckage of star liners caught moments before liftoff; tan ghosts. But there were other ghost liners, forever lifting off, some of which were not tan, but a turquoise greenish hue.

"Yes, Sir." Gibbon had long understood that Winteroud's "thinking out loud" needed merely the affirmation of recognition. Then the historian would move along in his deductions. "Something new, Sir...we will find it."

Winteroud's eyes scanned the strips, again and again, something new, something we haven't seen a thousand times before. Something new-the turquoise trails. Gibbon looked out at the airstrip and saw the giant caskets the starliners had become, dissolving derelicts that had once been the stuff of star dreams.

Even their burnished alloy wonders had crept toward ugly decay.

"See something new," Gibbon said as if he could speak the revelation into being. Both sensed it was there, staring them in the face, of course. It was looking back at them, like the faces in the porthole window from the green ghost liners. Smiling and waving as they set off to their destinations which were never reached.

Never reached because most of the liners would make emergency landings deep in the Sagittarius frontier upon finding that Cyborgian central had nuked their home-worlds. The ones that made it off world before the fireballs were already in the hyper gamma spaces.

"You have a hypothesis, Sir?"

"Yes, Gibbon!" The mystery of the turquoise liners, he smiled. "What if the turquoise ghosts are the ships that endured? The ones that made it to the Sagittarius arm? What if their distinct and different light is a function of their relationship to their progeny? They may have proceeded outward and onward to people living now. Perhaps in that sense, unlike everything else we see here, they are still alive among the Outworlds."

Progeny conferring a form of immortality.

"But of course Sir! What other explanation could there be?"

"Actually, Gibbon, most probably an infinite number, but let's run with this for a moment. If we follow the ghost trails to the Outworlds, which we know the survivors settled, we could see those very ships. Most are enshrined on their various worlds as venerated objects."

"Perhaps the veneration explains the green lights?" Gibbon wondered.

Is the universe so convoluted that among the celestial and immense tides of the cosmos, that the veneration of infinitesimal beings such as humans would be noticed, or reflected in the quanta? Perhaps the sheer complexity of human sentience is its own form of immensity?

"If so, we could trace the green strings out across space, to the various worlds, and look into the faces of their descendants!"

"And so, we are voyaging on?" Gibbon asked, grateful to be departing this ashen world of the dead.

"In time, Gibbon, in Time." Winteroud was scanning the airstrips. Choose. Why does this place call me back? This starport, this terminal, looking out on this airstrip-beckoning?

"You see Gibbon, something new was the key. The tan starliners are dead; all the passengers were lost. They are end trails of death. But the green ones, nay! They survived, and the life forces of their passengers are passed on, even now, ever into the future-*something new*. That brightest and oscillating one; that is the one! That is the one!"

Winteroud had neither kith, nor kin, in the Sagittarius Arm, and was therefore not as free as air–but he was as free as the income of a wealthy scion would permit a man to be. Under the circumstances, as he and Gibbon had already noted, the green trails all pointed to the Sagittarius Arm, they would naturally gravitate there. That great menagerie into which all refugees of the Arcturian war had irresistibly drained.

Thus emboldened, they began to make haste to their starcraft, when suddenly a ghost of a thought came to Winteroud.

Moments like this and he felt the ghosts knew he was there.

Winteroud knew it was a ghost thought connected to the liner trail whey were to follow. He saw a vision man standing at the rain-soaked window watching the liner take off-*Fly on lovely one, take the stars and make them your own-I'll remember holding you tenderly while you slept. Fly on free, free and bright as ever and always you were. Looking out from here I'll stand eternity on guard, watching you take to the heavens and wishing angels stand about you. Fly on lovely one, ever and always, bright.*

Then come the fireballs, vicious and unrelenting heat which swept away worlds and civilizations. Yet somehow it is unable to erase a moment's tender love, safe in the time continuum, standing at a window in the rain; time and the hosts of Hades fear to tread.

In a sense the man at the window stood as he promised, on guard for all eternity, wishing her well, whoever she was. Winteroud hoped she had been aboard the liner. He felt the thought again, the word echoing in the continuum, but there were no more. Perhaps at the far end of the journey, he could look into the eyes of one of her descendants. Carry the man's love to rest in the living of her progeny.

Would he know? The big old starliner had carried her so far away.

He turned to the droid, "Onward then."

Gibbon provided not with mammalian analogous hardware in his positronic nano brain, could not feel, but understood his fellow's pain. He was always glad when they left these places and returned to the sanctuary of their ship, the Lord Kesey. The star yacht sat on the landing strip like a bright glimmering bird of light, a phosphorescence of violet and pink shifting sheen, sparkling in the dusty wind. Among the dead hulks of the other starliners, some shot black with macabre scars; she was phoenix-like among the gravely dead.

The historian and his android stepped aboard her.

The Lord Kesey was airborne in moments, trailing the turquoise echoes Winteroud plotted into the flight plans. Those centuries ago, the fleeing ships had not returned to the Gateway but had flight plans heading deeper Outspace, the Sagittarius Spiral Arm. Away from the Gateways and the older realms of mankind. Such circumstances surely ensured their survival from the nuclear first strike which had been poured out upon the colonial worlds. The Lord Kesey flashed in the pink and dusty sky and was gone.

New Galen was once again the land of the dead-with one exception. High, where it had orbited in the sky for centuries quietly, the massive gateway reflected now the constellations from Deneb. Suddenly Deneb's massive white orb gleamed dully in the circular gateway, and then, like worlds colliding, Deneb 4 swept slowly into view. Once again the great Gateway linked two points in the universe as it was meant to do.

The Transhumans had been watching Winteroud all along.

From the Gateways main operations chambers, Cicero had been sent as a hologram. He detested when Omm 6X sent him into the physical world, it reminded him of his ultimate lack of substance, even while he disdained matter completely. At least the physical human had a real being-the droid-with him. (Omm 6X granted him reprieve from various tortures he delighted upon Cicero when it served him) and at that Moment Cicero's chin lifted a bit prideful of his masterful spying.

The historian had run about the ruins of the starport like a cockroach, immersed in his visions of the past. Omm and Lourdes had watched the transmissions silently except for once, when Lourdes quipped, "Empaths-ugh, disgusting creatures," and Cicero had been given a quick window into the mind of an Overlord.

Now Cicero, almost comfortable suddenly in the physical world, being the only sentient thing on a gateway the size of a large moon, watched as the Overlord's grand visages appeared as the faces of Greek demigods in the Gateway operations hall. Omm's snakes writhed. Lourdes diadem was encrusted with jewels from the age of bronze. They were, if anything, authentic.

279

"So what is it?" Lourdes demanded impatiently. "I hate Empaths, I despise Gateways, and I tire of the land of the physical. WHAT is this pathetic madman wandering around in the radioactive deserts looking for?!!"

Omm was bemused. A thousand years before he had walked the streets of New Haven City promising peace and trade agreements while Lourdes had planned an unprovoked genocide of their people behind his back; he had never forgiven her this duplicity, and any small discomfort she felt brought him a quiet delight.

"Please, Lourdes. I have my reasons. Remember, it was the shocked horror of these planets' millions, crying out to the ether as we opened Hell before their undeserving eyes, which brought those Things to our universe." Omm said, and for a moment he thought he had gone at last too far, and that Lourdes would erase him from the hive mind in one savage and vicious rage of delete.

But his gambit was true; he knew her fear, for he shared it. She dared not delete him now, when those Things crawled at the edge of reality, dropping in at will. She needed him, and any possibility that his work was bringing defense, or power, against the black gaping maw that threatened to ingest her.

"He writes histories and has come back again, and again. Such a break in his patterns of behavior raised flags with the sentries we have monitoring mankind, and since it was one of the worlds where I got to be the last man standing, I was notified; which, naturally, was enormously annoying, as you can imagine, since murdering all those people has always bothered me a tad.

"However, it beckoned my attention because it was, indeed, tied to the appearance of the Bogies. One of the ships that had made for refuge Outspace that day, to the Sagittarius arm of the galaxy-alas the very one he's following now-had been trailed by the air corps," his Bronze Age Godlike visage peered at hers boyishly in a sly mocking glance which she did not miss, "The air corps' ship disappeared. Seems the Bogies had popped in to see what was happening, and of course, their mere presence drove an entire flight crew of hardened, welded airmen mad in moments. We still have a recording of the airmen's' screams, and they are quite disturbing.

'The refugees, however, survived; it appears the Bogies retreated for some undetermined reason." Omm finished and waited for Lourdes to consider the implications. She did. *The Bogies had retreated from the refugees.* Why? The Empathic Historian had singled THAT particular ship's flight path out of a couple of dozen invisible flight trails after a thousand years...

"Good work...David." Lourdes said and then was gone.

Cicero froze, she had used Omm's ancient human name. He dared not look, but he knew Omm's eyes would be as cold and hopeless as a billion graves. If Cicero had looked then he would have not seen the face of a Greek demigod, but the blank and shocked sadness of an ordinary man looking out across the years at a grim and terrible sin. In the ravaged eyes, he would have also seen a frighteningly icy determination for redemption.

Cicero began the power down sequence of the gate and prepared his sentience to be transferred back to Deneb IV. Curious about the empath, he accessed the man's writings that were recorded in the Hive mind libraries. He preferred to work in ruins, as an ordinary living company constantly assailed to poor soul with every thought of anyone within a hundred feet. He closed out of the library impressed with the man's depth of work, including his poetry-one phrase lodged in his mind as particularly fitting of the evening he spied on his at the ruins of the New Galen starport:

An Empath? It's a thing that rolls in ashes
Dreams in shadowlands
Drinks a toast with the dead
Hears their shocked tears with each turning
of derelict worlds spinning celestial threads

Crying "Gone, gone, all... is...gone"
-Winteroud Sole, Caldris

Making his way back through the Gateway to Deneb IV, he turned and took a last look at New Galen through the hyper portal. There, a different starscape and a different world filled the ring. The sudden change in reference shocked him; from a dead world to a live one, like a new target in the lens. Whatever could make the Overlords cringe in terror? World destroyers, they were. World destroyers in fear of something that destroyed not worlds, but galaxies full of minds.

It was with some surprise arriving back at the virtual baths of Caracalla that Cicero found Omm 6X had let Cicero's hands and head remain attached. It seemed Omm's first steps toward redemption would be that small pardon. Yet it would not be without cost.

"I'm preparing a body for you Cicero. You're going to be my agent in the physical realm for a season. Consider it an adventure of great import. We must determine the nature of that which decides which men are driven to madness, while others are left standing on new worlds, founding nations on planets of barely charted stars."

Curiously, Cicero felt none of his usual loathing at the thought of the physical world. It had suddenly taken on a new intrigue for him. Alas, even with the pale horse, and Hell following after, Omm was not without a sense of humor. "Cicero," he chuckled "Your new body...you're going to be one VERY attractive woman. Beauty, after all, is far more powerful than any number of other lethal weapons we might grant you."

There was a vacantness in Omm's eyes then.

Cicero felt a sudden shock-he would be a woman? There was more to that than Omm was letting on. Cicero often wondered what he had been before he was morphed into a sentient program. His original personality had been subverted-a sort of spite, something he never really understood, but one of a great number of Overlord oddities he took without great concern. A woman, he thought; where angels fear to tread. A woman seeking to find out, "the nature of that which decides which men are driven to madness, while others are left standing on new worlds founding nations on planets of barely charted stars".

281

Out of the Solar wind and into a rad box
Uncharted Space, Far side of the Milky Way
En route to the Pleiades. 4217

Return to base. To Chrysalis Isla.
*That was all for now, a simple clear objective. That was the way Maximus Mercurio liked
things. Merged with the ship's nervous system, he felt the nucleonic cloud of the galaxy brush
his face like cool sea air, he saddled the currents of the interstellar winds, and heard the roar of
the galactic plume as a steady song of bells. Flying alone, over the top of the galaxy, higher
then, among the isolated globular clusters, he took in the grandeur of the greater galactic cloud.*

He willed the ship to form a tight gravity bubble of normal space about the fighter, and
bending normal space away, he fell hard into the hyperstreams of the fifth dimension. He
pressed on through the hyperstreams for months.

His body rested tanked in an autodoc, cleaning, healing, being restored at the molecular
level by billions of nanobots. His mind remained merged with the ship, which was also working
its repairs through the long months of flight. Nanobots healed and repaired it too as if it were a
living thing. Only the firefight damage in the interior remained as it was-such would be scoured
over by forensic crews for clues, and superficial structural damage from the drop through the gas
giant's atmosphere.

When finally, the fighter moved into the mighty blue star cluster of the Pleiades, Maximus
let a small swell of joy pass through him momentarily, then checked it with stoic resolve. Things
were what they were, never too much joy or pain, should one feel.

I am home again, alive. Never forget the lost. Never forgive the enemy.

Now his real trials would begin. Even Harry would not stand by him if it was determined he
had failed to protect his men, and there had been such a possibility. He cleared system ID
without pause, of course; it was Harry's world now. A new King had gone to the throne, but
even the King knew it had been Harry that had paid in blood taking up the sword against the
enemies of the Pleiades without, and within.

Max's fighter-bomber, the Baal Baby, cleared the chromium bubble field of Harry's estate
and made for the shipyards. A dozen yachts were at the estate, all of them rigged for speed and
armed discreetly to the teeth; a pirate fleet. Sitting among them like a Queen bee was the candy-
apple red Riptide, Harry's war-yacht. When Max stepped out of the ship there was a grim silence
among Harry's officers.

"Welcome home soldier," Harry said. He stood gallantly there in his white uniform with the
silver rose of the king and a long sword.

Ahura-Mazda birds glistened in the gardens of the estate. They were life demigods of
another era lingering as witnesses to humanity's follies and dramas. The Ahura Mazda estate,
once known and famous on the planet, sat now hidden behind huge security domes. The Ahura-
Mazda bird emblem had emblazoned all of the businesses for centuries. Harry had taken
possession of the estate through a bold series of business moves, and an arranged marriage with
a former lover that had jilted him. His reflective force domes provided security, privacy-and they
removed his "wife's" proud heritage (too proud for a struggling ex-soldier at the time) from the
view of Chrysalis Isla's public. The sequestering of his wife's snotty heritage was a juicy bonus.

Never forgive, never forget, and never surrender.

A salute went up among the officers and Max saluted back. Techs and droids then scrambled to the fighter, and the group of officers moved more informally towards Harry's mansion. Formality, however, returned when Max saw the officers of the dark corps seat themselves along with a board of inquiry table in the briefing room. Harry took his seat of carved sea creatures of ivory with leaping dolphins. Harry looked at Max evenly and without emotion. The Dark Corps had come together after the war. Harry had been in command of a battalion assigned ground armor defense of a continent-sized mass of craters along with thousands of others on a backwater planet-Baal One-whose value to the King of the Pleiades was questionable. Their retreat was a heavily guarded group of jump ships dug into escarpments at the far south of their front lines. No one could use the ships without jump codes, and a special "Mad Dog" platoon held those.

Enemy forces came in for days butchering the King's men; an alien predecessor technology had been discovered that allowed them to breach the individual soldier's force-field shields. The merciless double sun of Baal One cooked the corpses they couldn't reach. Busted EVA suits spattered men in bloody fireworks. The retreat threatened to become chaotic as discipline broke down. For months Harry fought bravely and watched his friends die. If he hadn't driven his tank headlong into a disorganized retreat broadcasting a giant hologram, calling the men to courage, many more would have perished that day. Their survival had begun with Harry's courage, and it had continued under a ruthlessness the man had acquired later when his more noble qualities had failed to win the respect and attention of a corrupt government and business elite.

"Where is your crew, Captain Mercurio?"

What happened to our men?!

"Some of their bodies are on the fighter, Sir. Three are missing. I am the sole surviving member of the mission."

"Did you encounter the Extradimensionals then?"

Max looked unknowingly back, and the realization that he was unaware of the mission's original objective sent a freezing electric shock through the room.

"Extradimensionals Sir?" He paused, looked for words and the officers saw a rare expression for Max-uncertainty. "Sir, I woke bloodied after the attack unable to recall the events. We had been in some matter of trouble; the fighter was doing a slow spiral a gas giant. We were plunging toward the core, an uncharted Jovian on the far side of the galaxy, that I was able to determine when I pulled the ship out of her dive.

"I was the only one alive. The crew's bodies had been…butchered and mutilated. The ones I could find. I had been injured and was suffering amnesia of the whole attack. It appeared they had managed to board us and bum rush the crew. That much I was able to ascertain.

"I was lucky to bring the fighter home, as she had suffered much damage. Since I have no recollection of the attack, an investigative unit will have to mine the ship's data core and my memory, and pull out whatever answers we can, Sir."

Max saw Harry take it all in. Max had always carried a certain strong favor with Harry, but even Harry had a code for his men. They were ex-military, and though considered privateers, or mobsters, or any number of evils by others, amongst themselves they were soldiers first and foremost.

Harry felt a grimy sense of being bettered by the Things. But Max had managed to survive, and so their victory hadn't been complete. Max would have to face a grueling unmerciful investigation to determine if lives had been lost needlessly due to negligence.

Harry's face was like an automaton with a dead lead toxic nano feed, inscrutable. Mercurio showed neither fear, nor concern, nor challenge. Faithful unto death. His combat record was nonpareil. If they faulted him, he would face his punishment silently, with a manly stoicism, but certain of their error.

Finally, Harry spoke. "Alright then. You have my confidence Captain that your tactical record speaks for itself, as knows everyone in this board of inquiry. The adversary we are facing in this conflict is highly unknown-perhaps truly unknowable. That one of our most decorated combat veterans returns with such losses, in my opinion, will play out as a consequence of encountering a vicious unknown.

"Sanfillipo will head up the investigation immediately. Dismissed."

Men saluted and dispersed.

Sanfillipo was a good foot taller than Mercurio and there was an aspect of the "bad boy" answering to big brother when Mercurio set off with him. Few in that room would have ever wanted to tangle with that "bad boy", however. "Mad Dog Mercurio" (Mad Dog tagged to each member of the Mad Dog unit in the Baal war) had never flinched at a fight, and everyone in the room had seen his stalwart figure holding ground stubbornly, as flames and violence burst all around, and many had seen him do it more than once.

Max was confident whoever-or whatever-had taken out his crew could have been bested by no force of men of comparable size similarly equipped. He was as eager as the rest of the corps now to get the investigation underway.

Rat chewing, boneheaded, bug meat!

Payback was forming in the dark and merciless corners of Max's tar pit of a soul, like an angry arachnid peering from a sandy, dank, primordial burrow. Back in a suite with his name on it, that he more often than not was absent from, there came the time to face the dark; the echoes and the names of them that were lost.

The suite and all its pretense of collected art and mementos from across the globes, beyond the stars, time, wars and battles, were pathetic relics to vanity. Now there was only the sense of his men obliterated, their voices and smiles and personas now existing only in his memory and the data core. He would feel a pang of sadness at their loss, a sadness whose gray and overwhelming nihilism would have obliterated most people. Like a radioactive tank streaming vicious toxins, and the burning corpses of its crew, as it careened over the rocks at Baal One.

It was then, staring at the dark that had taken his men, that he would stare back with his memory of them. Knowing full well the dark could eat him too, he would laugh at it. In all its final monstrosity of blackness, he asked only one more screaming charge with a raised weapon, one more swipe at the dark. That was all he asked; not victory, not triumph, not even another day for his precious hide-but one more blood-soaked dance of battle-preferably, to music.

Goodbye, good men and women, I salute you; faithful unto death. I salute your smiles, your warmth, and your courage. The silly masses of chattering analysts were not there. The herds of sheeple in their safe little hovels were not there. They did not stand on the hot steel and peer into the well of night. They did not see the mighty forces of an invincible enemy looming under the merciless heat of a double sun, and hold firm, side by side in the bloody mud.

What, this time, has culled for the dark? These "Extradimensionals" making harvest of my crew?

Preliminary evaluation of the fighter's exterior damage revealed only damage concurrent with the fall into the Jovian gas giant. There was no residue of particle beams, gravity bombs, or matter cannon. Harry expected that. The damned things can move through hulls. His mind raced trying to configure a plasma field that might hinder fifth-dimensional transition. He wished he paid more attention back to the military academy when they were studying quantum theory.

Then there were the tapes. On a hunch, Harry had cameras installed beside the normal black box equipment. A black box backup. His reasoning prevailed. If the things can get inside our heads, he thought, they are limited to what we know. No one in the crew knew he had the backup cameras installed, and thus neither would the Bogies. The cameras would prove telling indeed.

He approached the Baal Baby with the apprehension of a funeral, but he knew it would be worse than that. A couple of young guardsmen posted saluted. He saluted back. "No one is granted entry while I'm in here. No one."

The young guards would have walked through fire had he asked. They knew he would do it for them. "Sir" they snapped to attention.

He walked the gangway quietly and made his way. A lift and a corridor. Past the uncompromising and nearly silent power arrays. He sat down in the piloting cabin and called up the protocols, holograms flashing to life; predecessor technology he recalled as the various icons flashed in front of him. Expensive and secret. He began to watch the last hours of the fighter crew.

The Reckoning

Rip orbit, Sagittarius Arm
4217

Starlight ladies, Herkiestown's calling.
Lighthouse or Canal Row-City air is free air.
Captain Vincent Level of the Sagittarian Trade Guild hadn't seen his mentors face in many years, though they occasionally hologramed each other at guild meetings with a wave, and sent each other coded tips across the void to where good trading might be. So it had been with some surprise that Vince met Tristan Elias's gaze on the big screen of the Taloned Sire. The holoscreen became a room with the large bearded man on a golden chair regarding him with piercing eyes. Sea creatures leaped from aquatic carvings on the golden chair. Elias was still slightly obese, with an air of great mental and physical powers held in check. His persona remained, after all these years, as Vince had first been impressed by it; an authority honed and practiced in realms where intelligent assessment continually meant life or death.

"There are a lot of traders reporting Bogies now Vince", Elias seemed like he was wrestling with an unwillingness to believe the reports himself, "strange things. Some have even come back with some very bizarre recordings. Ships have gone missing. Reports have come in from the Omega Centauri, and some of the other clusters, of a series of horrible unexplained murders and mutilations. The clusters are far out, but a simple charting of the reports shows an increasing number and an inward movement toward the Milky Way." Elias's huge frame and blue eyes seemed to be ready to jump through the screen he was so intense. Vince had never seen him this spot on about anything but money.

In the streamlined salmon and chrome piloting cabin of the Taloned Sire, three figures stood in black and silver guildsman uniforms, Vincent Leavel, Sagamore Salvatore, and Millin Quinoa. Each of them had heard rumors in the trading bars of a dozen ports.

"And?" Sagamore asked grimly.

"Well, we have a client. Big family business, old money. One of the family is, well, he's an empath."

Captain Leavel looked tired. "Elias, I don't really go for all that psychic mumbo jumbo. Is this going anywhere? I pay my crew rate plus, and-"

"Hear me out. You got what-two guys crewing? You haven't properly staffed that monster since you stole it. This empath, he's been researching events on New Galen for a couple of centuries now."

Sagamore raised his eyebrows: "And?"

Vince filled him in. "New Galen was the port of origin for Rip's original ship, downed in the great refugee flight from the Arcturian wars."

Sagamore grumbled. *Outworlders.*

"He's traced your home world's original ship from empathic echoes he says are still glowing-quantum visions he sees on New Galen. Traced the ship all the way to Rip. Says it's special. Important."

"Well, Hell yeah! Pretty important to us Rippers. But why is it important relative to your Bogies and…" Vince stopped, knowing the answer.

The Sire, under a different name and command then of course, had been the Cyborgian pursuit frigate hunting Rip's original refugees. Inexplicably, the Sire had gone down under time stasis. Vince had found it, and brought it out of time stasis.

It had been many years since Vince first took the Taloned Sire. The original crew had all been in a bizarre state of shock. Some were crying, some were shaking-a few just stared like scared rabbits. He slashed away, again and again. In the midst of it, one of them stared coldly into his eyes. "Kill me! Please." The Cyborgian Air Corpsman had pleaded. Vincent's answer was a grunt and a lunge with his lasers. The Cyborgians head spun away from his body.

"The Bogies," Vince said quietly. "They had brought the ship down in the first place. Drove the crew mad. By the time I boarded her, it was like fishing in a barrel."

"That's all she wrote. Look, the empath guy wants to meet with you and 'feel" your ship, heh, heh. Humor the guy. Whatever the mutant gene is packing these visions for him, they're verifiable-he records them with his droid. They're authentic. Maybe he can get some insight into the damned Bogies. Something we can use. A lot of Guildsmen have gone missing, and some nasty looking corpses are turning up in The Globular Clusters. He's waiting for you at a place called Herkiestown, says you know it."

"Been a couple of hundred years but yeah, I know Herkiestown."

"Look, Vince, I need you to take this guy seriously. That mumbo jumbo, as you call it, just traced a thousand-year-old flight path across a hundred and fifty light-years. When he found the muddy hole you dragged that ship out of, he saw the ship's original registry numbers in his mind. Is that real enough for you? I owe you, you saved my life, man, my cargo, and my crew when you came barreling out of nowhere that day, but-and I mean this with all due respect-you got a real knack for trouble. I mean, that thing with the mob tailing you, and then Millin dragging the CC air corps behind him."

Millin smiled "Hey, it worked. The mob hasn't bothered us since."

Elias groaned. "Well, you're not out of the woods there either, my big blue friend-word has it one of the generals has them working covert ops, so, you run into that little collection of battle-hardened pirates again, don't count on CC Air Corps to save you. No offense Sagamore, I know you fought as their comrade in the Baal Wars."

"You also know I took an early leave." Sagamore bit back, "How was I to know evacuation codes were on the ship?"

"Alright, alright already. Elias, you rank me anyway. But I'll take it seriously-*for you.*"

Elias looked at some point on his ceiling and took a long breath. "Vince. You're a Guildsman. Do you think we're asking you to do this for free? How many stolen air corps frigates you think the Guild has? You lunatics are the closest thing the guild has toward a military component. You're getting top mercenary pay on this run."

The three men visibly brightened. "That's what I'm talking about," Millin said.

"Why didn't you just say so in the first place? I'll babysit your astrologer boy." Sagamore added.

"And?" Vince's gaze didn't move a muscle from Elias.

"The empath and his yacht convoy with you. If there's any trouble anywhere, anyhow, kill everyone you have to, except our empath of course, and we'll sort it out for you later. We want to find out how to stop our people from disappearing or turning up carved into meat sculptures and babbling like drug fried-well, no prisoners, got it?"

"Prisoners?" Sagamore smiled. "What's that?"

"Done," Vince said.

"Trade well." Elias Tristan gave a little salute with his thumb and finger-like he was rolling coins, and then he was gone.

"Trade well," Vince said to a blank screen and mimicked the gesture with his hands.

"This is worse than he's letting on," Millin said flatly.

"Of course it is." Vince agreed. "And it's fitting together like a Greek tragedy. No prisoners. We're going to need that astrologer."

"Psychic." Sagamore corrected. "Psychic. And you still haven't told them about the talking Dinosaur."

"And we aren't going to. We gave our word. Nobody finds out about the Dinosaurs." Vince said quietly.

"Tees, Sag. Tees. Not Dinosaurs. Tees." Millin smacked him on the shoulder, "What's the matter with you, eh?"

So it had been that a long series of events had circled around again to an even longer series of events. Vince thought of Hindu cosmology, then Mayan. He was in a pattern that no amount of hyper gamma-space-leaping interstellar ships put on random courses seemed to be able to break. Back to Rip. Back to the city of First Fall. The Sire's past drew it back into the pattern.

Tyhrin's Golden rings filled the piloting cabin's big screen. Rip was a blue and green orb speckled with white-the standard M-class Earthlike world humans had been either exploring for, terraforming for, or mimicking conditions thereof on countless settlements for two millennia plus.

"Nice planet Cappy'" Sagamore boomed, "Is there going to be a friendly welcome or a bunch of cops waiting for you at Herkiestown? They know you killed the whole crew to take this ship?"

Sagamore was kidding, but Vince's face remained grim. "I don't know if it will be cops or old friends there to greet me. Nobody knows I killed the Cyborgian crew-if they did there would probably be a statue of me in the town center and an honor guard to meet us. But nobody knows. They may know now, however, since this Empath guy figured out about the ship."

Millin Quinoa suddenly said, "I think we should go see the Dinosaur when all this is done."

Vince smiled. "Leph, Millin, he has a name. Leph."

Sagamore chuckled, "He's a sixteen-foot friccing Iguana with purple dreadlocks, who talks in bits and pieces of Lyrics and advertising jingo he's been picking up off the Hyper casts since the dawn of the space age."

Millin countered; "He's a Predecessor, Millin. He warned us this was coming. I think we should keep our meeting with the psycho, I mean psychic, as short as possible, and make a b-line straight to Siluria when this is over."

"Herkiestown has a way of getting complicated gents; let's talk about the Dinosaur when we come to that bridge. Come on, we got a landing to execute."

The men went to the respective piloting seats and put their MERGE helmets on. Millin called out, "Hey Captain, I think that bit about knifing an entire crew of Cyborgian air corps is something you might have mentioned over the years."

Sagamore laughed, "Ya' think? He told me back on Ophelia's World, but is there anything else we should know Captain?"

The ship began a roll, and for the second time in a thousand years began a descent to Rip.

"All kinds of things guys, but you've always managed to ace the game without knowing them," Vince replied.

Outside the gravity bubble, (where a thousand years before the ship had frozen into a black time stasis plunging straight down) purple phosphorescence began a shift to blue heat. The inland seas, shale hills, and fern forests of Rip went from a huge ball to a wall of color, to a world, as the Taloned Sire made a decidedly more leisurely and controlled entry this time.

"Great." Millin quipped.

"Five, five, five, and the Sire's alive, HELLO 'Rippy, whatcha' got for papa now, eh?" Sagamore laughed.

Winter.

Rip had Winter waiting for them-a a five-year-long season of deep cold where their entire planet fell below freezing. It was morning as the Taloned Sire drifted down to the Harbor at Herkiestown. The Sire came down painfully slow as the Captain dragged Millin and Sagamore through a series of background information as to where all the illicit tunnels were in the city.

"Avenue L looks like a simple promenade but underneath there are dozens of smuggling tunnels and gambling dens and houses of ill repute. If you get in trouble and I'm not there, head for the Yellow Jaguar. It's a dung hole full of Levi-Boca but you can access the tunnels there. Ask for Jane."

This went on for some time as the captain outlined various aspects of Herkiestown. Eventually, he switched the main screen to landing, and the three MERGED men set her down on the Ice. She was a wasp, a Cadillac Fleetwood, a raptor; built at the height of the Cyborgian Air Corp's Imperial zenith, she was an Art Deco Samurai sword with quantum computers and lethal firepower.

A young fool with big dreams had rescued her from an ignoble fate, but it had cost him his first love and unlived life. Now, a weary man of many years, Vince looked out over the port of Herkiestown, amazed that the more things change, the more they stayed the same.

"So this was home aye, Cappy" Millin snickered. "Outpilots. We've all got some dreary little town on some forlorn forested world as our point of origin. Someplace to be FROM."

A thousand water ships were birthed for the winter. A couple of guild ships could be seen; spacers. Beyond that Millin saw what appeared not unlike Potters Falls on his homeworld of ObscuroFrio-hundreds of massive ornamental stone buildings, none more than a dozen stories high, all crowding the harbor in the densely packed urban schema of a preindustrial refugee settlement which had fought and beat its way back from oblivion after the Arcturian wars through long hard centuries.

Captain Leavel remembered his speedboat plying through the oily blackness of those chilly waters, past the warehouses, when he had last been here. *It had been summers end and the waters hadn't yet frozen. Flotsam and litter from a dozen continents had floated in the inky blackness. Corpses had been hauled out of the harbor in the bright light of early mornings on past visits to Herkiestown. He had wondered what unfortunates might lay frozen under the ice waiting for winter to end.*

But that distant night and long ago youth were a dim memory. This morning, groups of men were ice fishing around fires and camps far out on the frozen sea. The Sire had queued in on Winteroud Sole's yacht the Lord Kesey.

"Juicy little piece of hardware there, aye Captain?" Sagamore observed as the Lord Kesey appeared on the ship's main screen.

"That's a Skylark 4000. It should be equipped with three drive systems and backups. Wide reach gravitational antipolar repulsor field-a helicon magnetic plasma sail system for movement in and out of heliopauses-a hyper string enabling system to negate mass through five-dimensional wormhole hyper streams-strange matter.

"Buzzard ramjet array for normal space bursts through complex field distortion areas.

"He's got some additional field hardware modifications on aft and stern; I have no bloomin' clue what for. But the whole rig is as good as it gets."

288

"I wonder if he knows he's got it sitting in the most dangerous harbor on the planet." Vince chuckled in disbelief.

"Well Captain, he is an empath. I guess they'd have a hard time sneaking up on him." Millin replied.

"Still, he just got a lot better guarded with our arrival," Vince said quietly and positioned a number of the Sire's big guns in a menacing array. The pretzel trails of ironies in that move did not elude him. Had this ship succeeded the first time its guns had been presented to his ancestors, he would have had none.

Millin was still MERGED. "He's calling us now, on the main screen?"

"Yeah." Vince folded his arms and leaned back a little in his piloting seat.

Winteroud Sole's face appeared on the screen. He could have been any age; wealth had kept his features young. But there was weariness in his deep-set eyes that belied time. He had a goatee, immaculately barbered. He had shaved his head. He smiled, and one was reminded of graveyards and days of future past.

"Captain Leavel?"

The three men of the Sire looked at each other surprised. "Yes, Winteroud Sole? I would have thought from your reputation you'd recognize me."

"You've aged, my good man, from the visions I saw at your salvage site. You were very young then-just a boy, aye? But yes, I see now. The eyes; always ready for another horizon to conquer."

Sagamore laughed. "He's got you, Captain."

Vince laughed. "Guilty as charged. Word has it we're your new bodyguards. You'll need us, especially at Herkiestown. Quite frankly, Mr. Sole, I'm amazed you're still in one piece."

"I've been able to avoid several traps with my uh, "gift." But yes, I'm glad you've arrived. I have my ship rigged with some…special field manipulators that can ease back some of the visions and impressions that assail me, and I will be more comfortable availing myself of it now that you are here. A lot of bad things have happened in this port-the echoes of those events even now creep upon my consciousness."

Millin pulled his MERGE helmet off and Sag automatically scanned the gun port screens. Consternation scowled across Millin's face and Vince knew he was eager to cut to the chase and begin addressing the issue of the Bogies.

Vince wondered how much Winteroud had seen in his visions at the crash trail. The place where Charon had died.

She yelled out at him, "Border patrol! You've got to be-"

He turned wildly then, delirious, lifting the cutting lasers around.

The lasers cut through the support pillars he had carefully left, the stone slipped, moved with the inevitability of physics, down upon her, hard, fast.

She folded like a rag doll.

He screamed, "Cherri!" and his howl reached from the bottom of time and all human regret followed after, rolling upon him in a wave of shock and horror. He clambered to her, tripping, once, twice, finally reaching her supine form laying among the stone, bleeding and broken. He arrived in time to witness the last shudders of her life shaking out of her, and then she was no more, forever.

There was a silence, then only his breathing.

From over her, he stared at all his dreams remembered and wept.

She was dead in an instant, gone forever.

There was blood everywhere.

He stood over her, now monstrous, shaking. Too late he snapped the lasers off. He fell to his knees, and hands still in the diggers, stroked her bloodied corpse in agony, longing, and confusion.

289

Then he saw it.

Just below her twisted flesh where the lasers had cut away a few more centimeters of stone. The perfect jet black of a stasis shield, barely discernable and glimmering beneath, the hull of a starship.

He had been right all along.

"Charon..." he said tenderly.

"Yes, Captain Leavel, very glad you've come back. Sorry to drag you out here. But sometimes it helps me see things better when the object and the site of the events are closer. I don't know why, quantum echoes and higher dimensions, well, who understands these things?"

There was a pause and only the sound of the Sire's systems humming.

"Have there been any reports of Bogies or bizarre mutilations on Rip Mr. Sole?" Millin asked suddenly.

Bizarre mutilations.

"I have…well, we'll talk in person. The natives haven't exactly opened up a welcome wagon. Most of what I read from people is an immediate deep distrust of outsiders and a strong desire to avoid me. Clouds anything else I might gather, even with ESP," Sole replied." And call me Winteroud. You would be?"

Millin smiled, noting the distance Winteroud's sixth sense was limited to. "Millin Quinoa, Systems Coordinator."

"ObsucroFrioian?" A rhetorical question from Sole.

"Unless people in the more fashionable corners of the Empire are dying themselves blue, but of course." Millin's swirling tattoos danced on his face with his big bear smile.

Sag snapped, "Blue and everything else, they are, but he's the real item. He could walk out on that ice naked and sun himself. Ha! Sagamore Salvatore here, Winteroud. Chief Engineer. Born and bred in the Sunny Pleiades, thank the fates. I'll also be your main hammer man should the shit get ugly. Just call me Sag."

"Or Mad-dog. Good thing we're on a short cast." Vince smirked. "Meet us down on the ice, Mr. Sole. Let's take a walk into Herkiestown. Perhaps I can help inspire a little less fear since I am one of them."

Even across the screen, Winteroud's raised eyebrows expressed doubt at that. The scarred and more heavily muscled Captain he saw in the shiny black and chrome guild uniform bore a faint resemblance to the young smuggler he'd seen in his visions at the crash site. The lean boy in hand-tooled leather boots with the raking sweep of red hair; yes, it was the same face beneath the scars and hard lines, but it was not the same man.

Yet strangely, impossibly, when the three Guildsmen met him on the ice dressed in black and silver, it was the same hand-tooled mamonth boots. All those years, all those worlds-he had kept the boots Charon had tapped the intricate patterns of her clan on to and given him. They were like a symphony of love, a symphony of pain, and Leavel had carried that weight such a very, very long time. The boots crossed the ice with a strange and powerful homecoming. Rip in the daylight welcomed them back.

The glorious arc of Tyrin's rings tinted the crystal blue sky with an enormous curve, the color of a giant lemon rainbow from one end of the eastern horizon above the frozen sea, as the men met face to face for the first time and shook hands. The berthed water ships were a forest of masts stretching as far as the eyes could see throughout Herkiestown harbor. The air was tinged with the scents of fern's smoke, fried grease, and wood oils. A hundred bits and pieces of city sounds carried across the ice with a faded roll.

Sole wasn't very tall. Still, he had a quality of intelligence that commanded respect-one sensed he was not unused to giving orders. Perhaps not from the authority of a Captain to a large crew, then to one born of position to those who weren't. However, like all men born to such (that were not petty), one also sensed such authority was something that would interest him little. The crew of the Sire felt themselves suddenly more at ease with him, and he was welcomed into their circle more or less on face value, in spite of his empathic senses. He had a chromium android of Thirtieth-century styling with him which he introduced as "E. Gibbon." It was a slender androgynous being that seemed to glimmer of brass and chromium. Vince remarked, "You match my ship E Gibbon-amazing era."

"Indeed I do Sir. And yes, it was an amazing era. "Interesting times" as they say; a time we still recover from yes?"

Vince smiled. He looked at the stone hulks of Herkiestown and compared them in his mind to holos he'd seen of New Haven city. "Recover? Probably never quite E Gibbon. The fine, shining flower of youth's brilliance, once scuttled by misfortune only limps ever after."

Millin guffawed. "Or not, Captain-could be all a matter of what one defines as valuable. That shining youth of the Arcturian Democracies was bested; these limping Outworlds, well, here they are still alive."

Sag wondered what Gibbon would go for on the black market, how much of it was period, and how much was retrofitting. Only Millin caught the historical reference in the name; Gibbon had written "The Decline and Fall of the Roman Empire" back in the Eighteenth Century.

Yet standing there, shaking hands, making small talk and walking toward the Central Wharf, it was not so easy on Sole. Bits and pieces of the crews' memories and emotions, their essences and motivations, impinged on him even as they walked. The Captain had had accidentally killed his first love here, and it was a memory he had spent a lifetime both suppressing and conversely refusing to forget. Winteroud could feel her in his heart, even now.

Charon covered the glow tubes." Never mind now. Come here." she said softly then. Come love me....

Vince stood in the doorway staring at the star-filled night.

There had been a conversation; Winteroud could feel Vince's iron will crushing its memory over the long years. But unlike the fragile body of the woman, his love for her would not die.

Then he said no more, only then he came to her silently, falling into the white softness of her arms.

He imagined he could see the gold specs that sparkled in the blue of her eyes, but it was too dark. He pulled their goose down quilt over them and she cooed in delight. They touched each other tenderly, pressing in the elation of first love, rolling luxuriantly in its oblivions and ecstasies until yesterday and tomorrow were no more and there was only that moment and each other.

Winteroud pursed his lips at the Captain's memory of that long-ago night. It had been a beautiful and triumphant love. He had fought hard to win her, broken laws to keep her, managed miracles with slim resources, scrambling to convince her to move on with him, only to have it all come to its horrible and violent conclusion. All these years, Winteroud thought, all these years his every step shadowed by the memory of her loss-

Winteroud caught his breath-and more.

Winteroud understood why the captain had become so feared in the dark stations of distant interstellar trading posts-one can't frighten a dead man.

Leavel stepped with the courage of the damned. "So Winteroud, how have you liked your little visit to my homeworld so far?" he smiled his feral dashing grin, an enigmatic smile one could trace back to an Etruscan funerary statue, and legend had it the streets of Troy before that

"I find all the Outworlds particularly refreshing, actually, from the slick metallic worlds of the Empire." Sole replied.

291

"Yes, out here on stone and in unterraformed climates, eh?" Millin chuckled. He was looking at the white stone shaft of Khitaman's lantern-the oldest lighthouse on the planet, Vince had informed him from the air. Herkiestown, which included the famous district known as "Firstfall", had been the site where the original refugees had ditched.

"Yes, lots of stone." Sole observed and felt a rush of impressions-Millin's home kith on Obscuro Frio: *his father coming through the door late one night from a long ride on the ice crawler, bringing candies. Then on a mountainside, later that same fortnight, black stoneflies, long and waspish, flew in a maddening frenzy when the boy appeared. Hovering over a corpse, they were a cloud of sudden, surprising motion. The boy recognized the corpse immediately, it was his father.*

Just like that, a glance, a moment, his life irretrievably diminished.

Swallowing hard, young Millin Quinoa pulled out his Kith blade from his long white boot and swung a full circle scanning for the murderers. They had gone, leaving the body exposed to the wildlife for food-an ultimate sign of contempt.

He stood among the flies, approached the body. The flies came at him to sting and lay larva but Millin swung his blades wide side and the crack of hard fly bodies smashing sent the whole buzzing mass away.

He took his father's tools and small belongings as mementos, but it would be the flies that he would remember. Their buzzing calls like words from the dead.

ZZZZZZZ-Remember this!

Winteroud swallowed hard. He sensed something more, turning and unclear in the back of Millin's mind. The man knew who his father's killers were-he too had walked with shadows all these long years. The shadow of his father betrayed and defiled. The shadow of the future too, when his imminent revenge must be taken in blood upon the killers-members of his own Kith.

Yet all these years-Millin had not gone back. A duality then, the act of vengeance he felt he must take being rejected instead for strange mercy. Though a certain code of honor defined it justice, another part of him refused the act as it would further allow the killers to define him. He would take life only at his determination, and not be compelled by them. Yet the boy in him still raged for justice.

They came to the winter steps where they left the ice and walked up to the city proper. Central Wharf was where the great canal met the sea. Canal boats were also frozen for the interim by the hundreds; one could see up the long canal that centered Herkiestown. The buildings of central wharf also fronted a river, originally a delta, dredged by the inhabitants centuries before. There were two levels of covered walkways running the front of the building of the wharf which strung along in a collection of five and six stories; offices, shops, hotels, and of course, bars. "Raygun's" backstreet bar was tucked in an alley among the conglomeration.

Central Warf was its separate city of a sort.

As they entered, Winteroud was hit with another impression from Vince-this had been his meeting place with another smuggler in his youth. *"Well, it's old Vinny-always a tale or two, eh? Nothing like a low profile," Andrew said and pushed him a drink of fern mead. "Any trouble?"*

"No. No one. We're good. It's in my boots."

The door opened and four Coast guards came in. One of them looked right at Andrew. He walked over, "Nice boat Deck," he said smiling. He let a silence weigh down with implications.

"Thanks, I try." Andrew smiled back, staring innocently, perfectly believable. The guardsman looked at Vince.

But there were no Guardsmen as Winteroud and the crew of the Sire took a booth along the long narrow wall behind a pointed arched alcove. Neither was Andrew there; Vince's long-ago partner in crime had been killed in a run on the sea with the coast guards, slamming into the dock at high speed in an amazing fireball that had made the papers. Winteroud felt for quantum echoes of Andrew but there was nothing. He lived only in Vince's memory now.

"Thanks, I try."

Raygun's had the quiet strangeness all usually crowded bars do when empty in the day time. Winteroud adjusted a link on a chain that contained a small field manipulator around his neck. It would drive out some of the echoes for him and allow him to focus more on the present company.

"This your old stomping grounds Captain?" Sagamore said with a mocking flourish. "The humble roots of our fearless leader."

"Don't laugh. There was a time I had to work my way up to get in here." Vince replied with a self-effacing grin. A waiter came and Vince ordered fern mead all around and deep-fried "smelt". It wasn't smelt of course, but the generic name had managed to cross a dozen worlds and land again on another species.

Winteroud looked at the three Guildsmen and knew it was time he explained more. "Of course we'll get working an empathic study of your ship here soon. I need to see what manner of echoes she carries from the original attack. Not the records of the attack on the Rip Van Winkle, flight 1079 as it were. That is well recorded-and I've been to that ship in the Firstfall Museum-which the authorities conveniently alerted your Trade guild to by the way.

"No, I refer to the attack on the ship's original crew of Cyborgian Air Corps. The beings that are now returning to swarm our galaxy had many scouts here a thousand years ago. A couple of them followed your refugees and the pursuing Cyborgians after New Galen was nuked. In my studies there, I've documented quantum echoes of the war for many years. But there was always a certain echo that didn't fit with the ordinary horrors of war. Another horror so to speak, faint; alien. Like snail trails from Hell; smudged, dark, animal thoughts. Hunger and hate, bloodlust.

"I believe they had been roaming about the universe, the dimensions. The shock of the psychic echoes of millions of dying humans-it attracted them like hyenas to a ripjackle kill."

"You've got your worlds mixed up there Winteroud, hyenas are from Earth and ripjackles... well, they're not. But we get your point, Sagamore quipped."

Vince gave him a look.

Sag chuckled as the mead and smelt arrived. "So the Bogies were sniffing around looking for a wounded animal-and we provided plenty in the form of a dozen planets nuked back to the Stone Age in the Arcturian wars."

Winteroud eased his block up more and the chatter of impressions from the Sire's crew quieted a bit. Gibbon registered the change in the block in his sensors.

Winteroud turned, looked square at the others each in turn. "There are stories, Captain Leavel, that the screaming ghosts have returned to the granite fjords of the Ten Thousand Lakes."

Vince almost spit out his drink. He put the glass down and Millin registered a surprise on the Captain's face he had never seen in all his years. The Captain never bothered to have his scars fixed or his genes rebooted since his arrest at Chrysler City and the years had suddenly aged him then. Uncertainty and culpability swept his face like a confession.

"Yeah, well, that happens now and again, stories." The Captain whispered and put his drink to his lips again slowly.

The bartender wound up a device and a strange metallic cord of music twanged alive suddenly: *"Starlight ladies don't you mess with no backwoods dreamer- "*

"Not stories-there have been bodies and witnesses."

The Ten Thousand Lakes. Vince used to smuggle illegal mushroom hallucinogens through the lakes; people avoided the area because of the screaming-ghost stories. Vince had never believed in the stories. He found the Sire buried in a hillside along the slopes of one of the Lakes, impacted deep into the shale but protected by its time stasis field which had gone up automatically at a shot from one of the Arcturian dogfighters.

293

The dogfighters engaged, plunging into the line of fire and sweeping above and below it on three vectors. One fell back and around, swinging a deep spline path beneath the frigate and hammering it with gravity bombs. The frigate shields took the beating with a purple sparkling flashing of light but held. Kroug could see they had stasis shield defenses blackening around their hull. He'd never seen stasis shields flash up and off so quickly. There must have been upgrades.

They had to lure the frigate away from the gas giant. The gravity bombs continued to harass the ship's vectors yet it returned fire with an even, mechanical discipline that only staid Cyborgs could manage. Kroug and the other dogfighters rode their shields' purple frenzy with a screaming, biting pain of overstretched neuron connections. Each second was their last, yet they remained, amazingly, fighting on.

Something edged into Kroug's mind like a hairy fat spider ready to snap his spine. It crept over his soul and he was keenly aware that its curiosity sought something else-something that would nuke whole systems of innocent civilians.

Then, there came screaming over the cast channels, a god-awful screaming he would remember until his dying day. Suddenly, not believing even as he witnessed, he watched the Cyborgian frigate go into a deep stasis; black and gleaming, reflecting all the light of the universe around it, the frigate plunged to the planet below.

The other Dog-fighter Pilots laughed with a sudden burst of triumph.

"Did you see that?!" One was saying over and over again.

"Did you see that?!"

"Straight down!" from another.

They hadn't felt the spider-like Kroug had. Something had forced the Cyborgians down, something dark and ugly. But it hadn't done it to save the day for the Arcturians. It was simply assessing another evil.

The Frigate-Vince had renamed it the Taloned Sire because the mining lasers had been like talons on his hand. He had named his ship and no one, not the guild, not the thousands that had come to hear of his legends across the galaxy over these many years knew why. But Vince was certain this strange empath, Winteroud Sole, knew why had seen the event with his mysterious sixth sense.

Vince looked him in the eye. Winteroud, a man who lived among the dead as if they were living people, looked back. "No Captain," he said, "there is more I must tell of what I saw at that hole where you mined and salvaged your "Taloned Sire".

Sag sensed his Captain's discomfort with the direction of Winteroud's speech, and that was enough for him. He placed his disser hard on the table. "Do tell, Mr. Sole." He challenged and his eyes showed none of the warmth from the suns bleached worlds of the Pleiades. If the man so much as embarrassed his Captain, Sagamore would boil his brains in his empathic head with the disser.

Winteroud, sorting out the man's emotions among the three hammering at his empathic senses only smiled. "Yes, yes. Captain Leavel-you will be surprised. Your ship, when it had gone down originally, in stasis, in a wild firefight."

"Straight down" Vince offered a phrase that had become part of the lexicon of Rip speech since that very fall.

"Yes, well-straight down it had fallen. The black stasis shield had gone up. The ship was time frozen." Sole smiled.

This guy is one strange ranger. Millin thought, and Sole, hearing his thought, chuckled a bit-*strange ranger*-ha! "Can you cut to the Chase Mr. Sole?" Millin asked.

"By all means, yes, well-I arrived here at Rip following an energy echo that seemed somehow different from numbers of other Echoes at New Galen."

"Rip's original refugee population's origin", Vince said flatly.

"So far, and so long ago. So strange coming upon the world and seeing the cities alive, Rip-alive with the teeming people whose ancestors' graves I had studied for two centuries."

"Like the dead had come back to life, only now they weren't echoes, but living people again. Well, they weren't of course, they were their descendants, which solved the mystery as to why some of the trails I see as turquoise and some not-the turquoise echo indicates an extant and living lineage. How wonderful it was."

"Well, I made my way through the city in a sort of glorious elation. But I sensed something, something else. More to the story. I spoke with the Coast Guard and founds there were recent murders in the Ten Thousand Lakes area-horrible mutilations. They had put it down to some copycat serial killer playing up from old stories of historical murders in the area and legends of a screaming ghost." His eyes were animated as if with a dreadful secret.

Sagamore toyed with his disser. "Don't tell me; you went out to the Ten Thousand Lakes, alone."

Sole Smiled-Vince saw the young aristocrat through the years the historian had marked-a gallant, confident, entitled nobility sure of himself as a Renaissance prince. "Well, I wasn't alone. E Gibbon was with me. He's a battle droid-he's marked your disser even now-should you reach for it you'd get a hand full of molten goop and an expensive bill replacing the hand, I imagine." His smile was elegant.

But Sagamore's was feral. "Mr. Sole. The disser is fielded. Amateurs we are not." And Sole sensed suddenly Sag's thoughts and it was indeed so.

"Well, then it appears I am better protected than even I imagined. But back to my travels in the Ten Thousand Lakes.

"Along the shores of jutting peaks of quartz-like igneous rock cradled inlets and fjords where occasional settlements could be seen. Up from the shores into the lowland plains the settlements grew into hamlets and towns with vineyards and orchards.

"The settlements faded off as the plains rose to highlands and hills full of hollows. I had the coast guards' coordinates to where the murders took place and I went there.

"Strangest thing, the first one-a blood-red brick road had been paved through the hollows at some distant point in time. I came to a residence-a single tower of residence-three stories high. One window facing away from the Lakes-like an eye peaking open from a bad dream, on the second floor. A single window on the same side on the first floor."

Millin took a long pull on his fern mead. "You see any echoes of killer screaming ghosts?" He asked coolly.

"I saw the echoes. Travelers walking up and down the road. Uncomfortable, fleeting people wishing they were far away. Then the echoes of the first victim. A woman of course, somehow I knew it would be a woman. She was running as fast as her bare feet would take her.

There was something dark-a spider, a face, like-wolves, no, scorpions-Levi Boca and the ripjackles-a cloud of predatory things like they had been impressed into one another, no like their souls had been jammed together-and they were after the woman. But they were wounded. They had been ripped in two."

Charon? Vince sipped his drink, his gaze thick, leaden, aching.

Sole looked at him as if he had spoken aloud and answered him so, "No, Captain Leavel, something else. Something that had been trapped on your ship when the ship had gone down."

Vince looked up sharply. *Of course.*

Winteroud paused and let the implications fill the space between the men.

The music from the bar droned on, *"Starlight la-dies!"*

"There was a Bogie on the ship then, and I freed it when I disengaged the stasis field," Vince whispered. "That would explain why the area had been reputed to be haunted."

Sole's eyes widened. Here came the punch line. "It had been sticking half out of your ship and half-frozen in the stasis for a thousand years; feeding on the minds on insects and vermin, reaching out, screaming mentally through the hills, horrifying and driving men mad. Freed it? In a sense, no matter, it was ripped in half, mad itself. It had tried to work its madness on you while you mined the ship, you know. But either its wounded aspect or something in your character drove it back from approaching closer."

Vince remembered.

Two days had come and gone of cutting and hauling. Inside, the mine was growing rooms and shafts. The central room seemed as big as a house. Vince began taking stimulants. He hadn't slept in twenty-six hours when Charon came next upon him.

He was covered with scratches and welts. His face was drawn back, pale, a skeleton's head. His hair was matted and filthy. His arms were moving frantically, digging, pounding at the stone with a savage flail of lasers and elbows.

He was breathing hard and talking to himself.

He didn't see her watching him.

She bit her fist and quietly began to cry, pushing herself to try and remember why she had ever loved him. How could she have loved this idiot who was digging in the middle of a forest for a starship?

His ranting carried around the walls of stone to her.

"Gotta be here!" he was saying, "Where is it? Gotta be here! Stone! Stone! The compact layer- here- gotta be right here. The trail, only a ship makes a trail like that. Andrew putting some kind of jinx on me. I swear. I couldn't bear to put her in the stasis house this winter, oh God, not that. Oh please."

He stopped. He seemed to come to some realization.

"Or worse, the border patrol will find the rest of the mushrooms."

The last was too much. The irony of the border patrol coming upon this fool digging was outrageous. Disgusted, a fury rose up in her.

She yelled out at him, "Border patrol! You've got to be-"

Vince looked at Sole. How could this man be smiling, knowing what he knew?

"This thing, Mr. Leavel…it had driven an entire crew of airmen mad merely by touching their minds, but you were able to live alone in the dark woods in a hole in the ground with it and remain sane."

"Barely sane," Vince added.

"Yes but here you are. Well, it has driven others mad since-and killed and mutilated. I went to the sites of seven killings and indeed, this thing had been able to reach out to people's minds, even chained to the starship as it were, and drive them mad with horrible visions-visions of itself, of its dimensional reality-I merely see shadows and echoes. I have no idea what mental damage I should sustain if I were exposed to the actual thing."

Millin lifted a muscled blue arm, "So we have a Bogie on world."

It was Sagamore who spoke next. His engineer's mind had been moving like clockwork. "No Millin, we have our first information about forming a weapon against them. We know whatever they are, and whatever dimension they herald from, we know that can be held in a stasis field."

"Bravo Mr. Salvatore, bravo. And a wounded one, at least, wasn't able to mess with your Captain's mind."

"Not completely," Vince said, letting the implications sink in. There had been something else operating in the mine that awful day- something evil.

"Now," Sole said suddenly, "When are you going to tell me about the talking Dinosaur?"

Walking After Midnight

Deneb IV
4217

Be sure that it is not you that is mortal, but only your body. For that man whom your outward form reveals is not yourself; the spirit is the true self, not that physical figure which can be pointed out by your finger.
Cicero-Roman author, orator, & politician (106 BC - 43 BC)

"The spirit is the true self, not that physical figure which can be pointed out by your finger," David Omm said. He sat quietly by the window and looked to Cicero as if a simple push might take him over the edge. The medusa snakes were gone, and for a fleeting moment, Cicero was bewildered with recognition and disbelief. Then an aircar passed and Cicero could see it through David. He was merely a hologram. However, a hologram of how he had appeared centuries before when he was fully human.

Cicero held up his hands. They were attached, and as Omm had said, they were a woman's hands. They were beautiful. "What manner of system is this?" The sunlight glitters in the room across the translucent glimmering floor and the machine undertones of the Forty-third Century whine and cackle and moan from the mighty towers of Deneb IV. Memories; memories spin and rage and flow just outside one's reach, yes-this is the world you knew once, once when you were human, before. This is what they took from you when they crammed you into that nightmare which is Omm's world. Remember, try-remember-were you a woman or a man then? Were you a soldier or a statesman? Why had they made you a reconstruction of a Roman Patrician?

"Semi-human. Ha! Whatever-you're flesh again on the outside. Flesh enough to command any man you'll meet to do your bidding, I imagine. But of course, you're Cyborgian, Cicero. Throughout your skeleton various nanosystems are incorporated that will allow you some...well, limited powers shall we say. You'll have access to the hive mind, but that, my pretty, will have its limits once you go deep Outspace. A full rundown of your systems will be presented to you later."

"Thank you," Cicero said, eager for a mirror, and wondering if this was all a cruel joke, and he would blink and find himself back a tortured construct of a sentient program in Omm's virtual world.

David was staring. "You're a masterpiece, Sissy-a real work of art. Beauty and the beast all rolled into one...our very own femme fatale?

"You have two things to remember lest you go AWOL on us. One-your body is real. You're a genetically engineered superwoman. Your lifespan, without enhancement, is five centuries. So you have something to live for. I've pressed the Overlord council to waive entirely the charges for treason that had been pressed against you from your previous incarnation. Secondly, well, there's this."

He tossed a small purple cube over on the bed.

"I suggest you don't look at it until you've given yourself a few days to acclimate yourself to the real universe again. It's rather disturbing.

"We've commandeered you a small ship, nicely appointed I might add. Aspects of your former self will start to begin to come back into your awareness over time. Yes...you're sensing it now. Yes, Dear, you were a woman."

Suddenly they were not alone. Lourdes was standing in the middle of the room. "Well David, can't tear yourself away from her now that we've restored her can you? Tsk tsk, love never dies, after all this time. She betrayed you once, and now here she lays in full glory. Only you would have given her another chance. Off with her then! The transfer is complete, she's in the flesh now, go on and kiss her goodbye."

Cicero looked over and saw a flash of annoyance in David's eye, but the sardonic and cold heart that never melted remained on the lips. "Kiss, kiss," he said. He formed an "O" with his mouth as if to blow her a kiss and he faded away.

Now Lourdes was staring. "Devil woman, ha! Look at you. He's given you it all back and more. The irony. Well, Lisa- "

Lisa!

"You're Lisa Lynne Sulla. You're an art dealer officially; black market unofficially. I want to know what the empath is doing, which is problematic for you...but if anyone can wrap a lie around a promise and slip it between his ribs with a kiss-well...never mind. Since your personality is subdued under layers of memory blocks he'll have a...devil of a time sorting you out.

"One more thing- I'm not as much as a lovesick puppy as Omm was-you'll not get centuries in virtreal as a tortured construct if you cross me. You'll get a virtual hell, and I'll make sure you're the last living thing on the planet before that hell goes offline. Got it?"

Lisa said softly: "Got it."

Lourdes looked at the purple cube on the bed. She frowned.

"Then there's that." A dark shadow swept across her face like the grave, and she was gone.

Lisa looked at the cube. Then she got up and walked over to a wall-length mirror by a sink.

She was tall, strawberry blonde (her hair could change color at will she realized suddenly, one of her powers), She was elegant and athletic.

Back in the saddle, it seemed, and ready for blood.

Outside the window, the towers of Deneb 4 gleamed in the sunshine.

"Miss Sulla." A soft voice called.

Lisa turned and there was nurse android standing at the doorway to the room. She was a pale grey model with lines and patterns where flexible panels formed its body. It had a female aspect. There were some garments and bags in its hands.

"A handsome young airman brought you these. He was from the high command." A knowing smile formed on the android's face-courtesy protocols.

"Thank you." Lisa took them and laid them out on the bed. High-end jumpsuit-she smiled. Retro 3000's look. Omm's idea of a joke? Yet when she ran a scan in the Hive mind under fashion, there they were-all the modeling agencies out of Chrysalis Isla were showing them, and they were considered very "it". There was a red sequined purse shaped like a jet. She brushed her hand across it and it unfolded. She ran her hand back and it closed.

"Miss", she called the nurse who had made her way to a station, back. "Can you open this?"

The android ran her hand over the purse and nothing happened. "It's keyed, miss Sulla. I believe it will only open for you."

"Just checking," Lisa said. "Thank you."

Lisa opened it again and emptied its contents on the bed. A weapon she was unfamiliar with. There was a model name engraved in a sandalwood pistol grip "Rohr 92". She ran it through the hive mind and saw it was a collectible disruptor. There were nano field generators in the body of the thing that projected high energy beams when fired. It would silently fry someone's brain from a hundred yards, or boil their organic molecules down to constituent elements in seconds at close range. She examined it, light gleamed on the disser. Whoever she used it on would be graced with an elegant, beautiful sight before their demise. Nice.

She brushed her hair back; played with changing colors for a moment. With another thought, her complexion could take on a variety of tones and values. She was human, fully human, but shot through with nanoparticles and genetic enhancements. She might be discovering sweet little tricks she was capable of for some time before she was aware of all the powers they had invested her with.

Whatever they were fighting, they weren't going down without a fight.

She had now gone from being their prisoner to their tool. Cicero. She had been Cicero. Why had Omm chosen that construct to impress her into? From Lourdes's conversation it was apparent Lisa had betrayed Omm's trust, no, his love. What point in torturing her consciousness that way?

Her sentience-the literal electrical field must have first been expanded with access into a complete quantum computer model of her brain, a simulation so exact the ephemeral essence of her consciousness could have flown along an electrical channel from the brain to the simulation without any disruption of her sentience.

They had stolen her soul. Once in the Overlord's network of quantum supercomputers, she had been their prisoner. A sentient toy. David Omm, moving through the centuries in various clones and upgrades, Omm Six X, had never been able to either pull the plug on her sentience nor allow her the power of her true self. He knew her very presence, his first love; she would have eventually either sparked his rage or his unfolding demise from grief. As Cicero, he had the comfort of knowing she still lived and avoided the torture she might have inflicted on him with a glance or an expression bringing back memories of his loss and his love.

"I'm not as much as a lovesick puppy as Omm was" Lourdes had said.

He must have loved her very dearly indeed. Who had she been? Had she too been an Overlord or merely high Aristocracy?

Lisa looked out into the hospital nurses' station. No one appeared to pay her much attention. She was an art dealer who had reported in sick for a day of observation. A handsome airman had brought her things. She was a very ordinary scenario-but she had been Cicero.

Cicero, the great orator of Rome. He had called for the return of the Republic at the dawn of Rome's Imperial age-and paid for it with his life. She shuddered. Nightmare-a nightmare.

She rifled through the rest of the objects from the purse. Identification discs, some snacks. An antique ship phone-she was sure it would work. Predecessor jewelry. She paused, something about this century she remembered through the fog of her internment in Omm's Baths of Caracalla.

Predecessor jewelry is never what it seems. Omm would have surely meant for her to examine the jewelry later. She put on the jumpsuit, put her things back into the purse-along with the purple cube, and searched the Hive mind for the floor plans out of the hospital.

Who had she been?

"Have a pleasant day, Miss Sulla." The nurse offered as she made her way to the lift. From the clear plexisteel walls of the lift, Lisa waved and smiled. She was on the three-hundredth floor and the nearest aircar dock was on the hundred and fiftieth. She made her way down in a flash of floors and plexisteel. It was a large hospital and serviced a good number of the Air Corps, it seemed. Of course, Omm had a limo waiting for her at the aircar dock. The driver was a full combat unit robot-no pretense of a droid here.

A slip? Tsk, tsk. Her cover was already blown, and she hadn't left the hospital. She ran the Hive mind and found out-no, no error. It was a popular Limo service and they advertised on casts across the system their combat unit drivers, "When you're important enough to warrant real protection," went the jingo. The ad ended with the driver blowing some riff-raff out of the sky and a smug customer lighting a cigar with a couple of buxom droids shaking themselves in a vulgar dance.

As the Limo alighted into the streams of air cars and the glittering towers of Deneb IV, Lisa looked out and watched the mighty city that ruled an empire pass around her. Imperial space. Forty-third century. There were giant hologram advertisements-indecent really, she realized with a sudden snap of context from her mental construct as the Roman Patrician. The scantily-clad human body was used to sell everything and anything.

Yet, it was all for show. The empire was a command economy, and the vast horde of the population semi-permanently buried in the hive mind-they would buy what the subconscious compulsions of the hive dictated. The advertisements were just part of the show, a necessary pretense of economic freedom. Only the upper echelons truly rose above the hive mind-who had she been?

Someone powerful and important? An overlord herself? She might be ancient then. The retro 3000's jumpsuit might have been more than a joke from Omm. It might have been a message-remember who you are! Her torturer for all these many years now reverting to the underlying love he had known for her? Perhaps his personality was coming apart? She had done something terrible in his eyes.

She considered the purple cube-answers, of course, were forthcoming. *The things.* Although she had assisted Omm in his intrigues now for some time regarding the menace, she had never been privy to the recording. It was the last moment of terror experienced by the crew of a frigate during the Arcturian war before the ship fell to a world, later to become known as Rip. The same world, Overlord spy bots had told them, that Sole had departed to.

She would play it in due time. She had to know, to truly know, what humanity was up against. But rolling the cube in her hands she realized there were two recordings-she held it up to the light and a second title glimmered above the cube in holo-Azure Thule Diary 4186.

Omm had been holding out. Did Lourdes know this was on here? Who could say? She laid the cube on a service panel and the limos internal system sensed the software.

The combat unit driver said an unlikely, "Two recordings, Mam. Sunrider event Outspace 3197, and Azure Thule Diary. Would you like to MERGE or have them played acoustically?"

At the word "3197" she felt a wellspring of emotion-repressed memories she realized suddenly. It was chilling, uncomfortable anguish. She composed herself. "Play the diary, merge." She whispered.

There was a merge unit above her head. Welcome back to the forty-third century, she thought. Deneb IV, Capital of the Cyborgian Central Command. Always ready to merge with you-and then the diary was playing. A man's voice. Unfamiliar accent.

Nothing pretentious or self-important-a working man's voice...

"You get to be the butt of a lot of bad jokes when you build a city on a world orbiting a dead star," the man was saying, *"Bethlehem Ice mines knocked out the H2O, clear and fine. Like a distilled crystal powder. And that's what everybody in this cluster wants, isn't it? H2O. I'd heard the jokes a million times, from an endless array of spacers. Ham-fisted freighter pilots, seedy Cyborgs running second rate game on third rate loaders.*

'Dark enough for you? Cold enough?'

'Hee-fraccin haaa! I just smiled. I love the dark, the ice. I could see a dozen shades of indigo in reflected starlight on the rippled ice sheet. I could see the red or yellow of a star as clear as a neon sign in a hologram add.

"'What the halo is in Bethlehem?' One of the dung-birds asked me, stone-cold and mean one time. I looked him straight in the eyes, and said, 'Freedom!' Calm as a Hindu cow.

"Freedom; his eyes laugh. Then his dung-bird mouth opened and a burp of a laugh chortled out. 'Freedom!', he kept saying as he loaded the ship. 'More like God-forsaken dark is what it is. Bringing my bird down on this puppy was just plain creepy, man, creepy.'

"I heard it all before. I mined the icy night. Then the dung-birds came and hauled it away. Off-hours I was down at the cruise. A game of billiards, some beer, some laughs. Teams off the deep casts; a soccer game from Alpha Centauri, someone even linked to a holo model show out of Chrysalis Isla! Whoa! Holograms of the bikini-clad lovelies strutted through the bar, and the miners went wild with cheers.

"Mine was a quiet, predictable life. The money was good, the dirt wiped off, and the money spent. The honky-tonk astercrete and plexisteel of the drop-city streets, dimly lit as they always were, well, they were a carnival of sorts to me. I knew every bar, tavern, stim parlor and lizard lounge in the whole sprawling town.

"Maybe that's why they asked me to guide the guy when he came.

"THE GUY. Everyone in town was talking about him. Antique Thirty-Something-Century star yacht. Antique android to match-and an attitude as wrong for Bethlehem as right for anywhere else. The irony of ironies, he was ecstatic to be here and he had a name to match Bethlehem's eternal cold-'Winteroud,' Winteroud Sole. Psychic, Empath. Historian. Brilliant, rich, strangely handsome even-the moneyed spawn of old imperialists from who knows how far back. The little bone head shows up here; a drop-city mining camp on a dead world orbiting a dead star in Palomar 12, the cluster with the muster...and he likes it. Go figure.

"'Walker, let me introduce you to Winteroud, Winteroud Sole. Mr. Sole is here from Caldris and will be touring Bethlehem. You will be off regular mining duty until further notice, and getting time and a half. I want you to take Mr. Sole anywhere he wants to go.' Jadusign Lomer smiled as he introduced me to Sole.

"Strangely, although he was smiling, what came across was a big fat lump of anxiety. Jadusign was just as clueless as the rest of us why Sole was here, down in the cold and dark with the nobodies scraping ice. The only place people like us would generally see people like him was in fantasy holo shows and virtreal sensoramas. So I knew orders had come from above. Higher up than Jad. A lot higher up. Maybe even the Mayor's office. Jad owned a franchise of scrapers and water packaging facilities-18 of them spread out on the big ice sheet. He was no small player, but seeing that look on his face as he presented Mr. Sole was classic. 'Sure Boss' I said, 'I know the big sheet like my Cabin.'

"What had happened when Kunger had blown up had never really been properly modeled on any computer simulations, far as I knew. No one was going to spend a lot of research money to find out either. Some of the techno-geeks in and around The waterworks had a sort of a running game of it, trying to create computer model simulations that would play out and leave the results one found across the ruined star system. Thing was, the models never worked.

"Yeah, I know the Big Ice Sheet like my cabin, no bragging; everybody knows I'm the best on the ice. Everybody knows me. We go out on the ice, everybody comes home alive, and Walker is buying rounds for the whole crew. Big Walker, they call me, and it ain't just my height, mind you-six four, no; big is in your mind. Big is who you are when you're standing on an ice sheet so cold an EVA failure will freeze you solid, faster than your neurons can register the pain, and the dark and cold and death is all around, and calm as a Hindu cow, you're doing what you gotta do. That's big. It isn't about ego or wrongheaded self-importance. It's about understanding the dangers out there, facing them square up and careful like, and bringing your crew home alive.

"Azure Thule 4186 orbits a neutron star smack in the middle of Palomar 12 a globular cluster in the constellation Capricornus that belongs to the halo of the galaxy. The neutron star may be dead, but anyone that's walked a night in a star-filled cluster can see just fine-a million stars works just as good as a big fat sun, sort of. Once you get the hang of it. N4186, also known as

Kunger 4184, or just Kunger, the neutron derelict, sends out less energy than an aged dancing girl in a convent.

301

"They kept the game going, and the big mystery. Most rudimentary simulations, although not expensive, could at least produce a working model: the various worlds and moons and asteroids were plugged in, their orbits and periods calculated, everything run backward to the proposed date of stellar collapse and explosion, the estimated mass and energy thrown out into the system, and the resultant damage found on the remaining worlds as the confirmation the model was correct.

"Kunger. You old dancing girl. All this time no one even has a clue what happened. Thusly, of course, I knew the background data Sole had been provided with by Jad was a crock of ripjackle dung and I told him so later-but Sole, he was a psychic-a real one too, not some candles and holo phony baloney. Sole knew. He could read Jad like a dead-tree book on an astercrete table. Sole knew.

"'So…Mr. Psychic, I said to Sole jovially as we rode the trolley out of the waterworks. 'Any thoughts on what caused that star to go whacko-off-the-chain way back when?' I sensed right away I didn't have to premise a lot with Sole. He just knew. So you went with it.

"He smiled. Calm as a Hindu cow. 'Well, I haven't any answers in my crystal ball if that's what you mean.'

"We both laughed. Me and the adventurer millionaire, riding the trolley. 'It's a double star, still is-both ruined shells orbiting each other in the dark. The potentials of all their planets snuffed out'-I snapped my fingers for effect- snap, 'just like that'.

"'Maybe a rogue planetoid slammed into the mix ruining the equilibrium the star system had,' Sole offered.

"'Whatever, whatever.' I waved my hand in control of mysteries and ages, 'Whatever it was that set off the chain of events, Kunger popped like a hormone hyped terraforming seeding pod.'

"Sole raised an eyebrow. 'You know a lot about that kind of thing eh, seeding pods? I love your analogies, Mr. Walker. Very colorful. I never heard a binary neutron star's collapse and semi-nova described in the terms of a cheap terraforming pod before.'

"I winked. I call 'em as I see 'em. 'Well, the old girl did. Popped like a weasel, she did and messed up the whole get-go for this star system, I tell you. You got more burned out ruined worlds in this system than you can count. Anything in orbit was either blasted into smithereens or had star side seared to a glassy crisp.

"'For Bethlehem, a planet that was seventy-five percent ocean, they figure, the heatwave instantly boiled the entire oceans. On the side of the planet unlucky enough to facing the daylight, we're talking sha-zayum! The entire mass of those oceans filled the atmosphere with one huge mass of super-heated steam. This, and I've seen some very good reconstructions in the office by the techno-geeks, they're very good at this stuff, well, it sends a compressed shockwave- BA BOOMA-right round night side with hot, violent, super-heated storms.'

"'I can see it now,' Sole said, and I wondered if he actually could see the geek reconstruction I had seen in the office, but I went on.

"Kunger, the unimpressive even in a nova, well, she only had one hot blast in her repertoire before she collapsed cold and stupid, virtually nothing, where there had been a living breathing star so to speak moments before. Well, now on Bethlehem the billions of tons of distilled water-the superheated steam-all that is suddenly now careening along around a planet orbiting a star that is now throwing out NO ENERGY.

"So the steam is rapidly condensing-raining back to the planet in the dark. It rains and it rains and it rains. Then, with the oceans filled back up and cooling faster than Kunger is spinning in the void, it begins to snow. Thousands of square miles of hail, snow, and ice piled conveniently-for us-on the surface. One giant snowstorm that rages and fades with every last bit of moisture-like a lifetime of tears till there ain't no more-every last bit of moisture is frozen hard and laying in the snow with a permanent night hanging above, and the Palomar 12 cluster, in all its sparkling glory, glitters like diamond angels in the perfect black, eternal night."

"All this ice and snow? No aggregate rock and mineral mixed in, no organics, no complex minerals-nada piquet, know what I mean? It's the cleanest, simplest H2O in the star cluster. And brother is it in demand."

"I'd always wanted to give one of these tours. I don't think my crude analogies would fly, hehehehe, oh well. He was welded. Couldn't take his eyes off me. Time and a half? I should be getting stage awards I was so good.

"Now the great ice sheet-that was the ocean on the night side of the planet when Kunger popped?" Sole snickered.

"Yesiree brother. That it was. She didn't steam the whole planet.

Bethlehem was a decent sized world-M-class, big as Earth they say, and in the habitable zone before the nova."

"'I gathered,' he said with an amused grin.

"'Yeah. Figures. It still has a magnetic field.' I said.

"'Just flew through it. I can attest to that.'

"'Surprising there have never been any signs of previous life forms on the planet?' He said. I smiled back at him. I knew where he was going with this and I'm not even psychic.

"'Yeah-surprising. Like surprising they suddenly call up a first-class archeologist out of the blue. What did they find, Mr. Sole? Why are you here?'

"He knew I knew. Because he was psychic, you see. And I knew he knew I knew he knew. Ha!

"The trolley rolled on and the drop city flashed by, buildings and tanks, domes and ice haulers. Home sweet home. 'There's a reason we can process water cheaper than anyone else in the cluster. No rocks and dirt in the ice. No organics. Should any evidence of organic come into the mix, well, even ancient ones, that introduces a whole other set of processing restrictions. With costs-big costs.'

"I let him consider the implications.

"'You think my mission here is to psych out any evidence of potential life so they can bury it, send out a false report to whatever regulatory bodies there are in this cluster, give it all a tidy stamp of approval and maintain the status quo?'

"I showed my hands and pleaded innocent. I laughed, "No, Mr. Sole. I would never suggest such a thing. But the non-disclosure clause in your contract? Is that standard for an archaeological expedition?"

"Again the eyebrow rose. He looked at me. 'Yes, Mr. Walker. Very good. There was, in fact, such a clause. Assuming they didn't tell you- and I need not assume-what are you driving at?'

"'What I'm driving at is there's a lot of money at stake and you're out of your league on this dark little world. You need an ally, Mr. Sole because even your sixth senses aren't going to help you navigate through this one. I suggest you tell me why they brought you here-what they found. I won't betray you, and you don't betray me-and this assignment becomes a lot safer for the both of us if I know what's going on.'

"The trolley was coming to the spaceport and the last vestiges of the drop city; the domes and warehouses. The drop-city structures were breaking up in line of the wide, spreading landing fields on the ice. Space service buildings stood silent and quiet in a strange distance.

303

"'So it goes.' Sole said simply. I was to learn Sole never said anything simply-the man talked onion speak, with layers and layers of meanings to be found if one began peeling. We walked silently to the docks. We climbed onto his yacht. Once onboard the ship's bridge, he opened a satchel and placed an object on a light table in the middle of the room. 'What they found,' he said, 'was this.'

"It was a blue bottle. There was some strange writing printed on the side. Some sort of animal in a pictograph design as well.

"'Predecessor?' I asked, referring of course to mysterious objects found occasionally from our dear departed sentient life forms who had previously occupied our Milky-Way Galaxy.

"'No, if it were predecessor they'd had simply fielded it in the black market and been done with it. This is something else. The technology isn't theirs.'

"'Well what do you sense about it- visions, insights?'

I could see in his face he was stumped.

"'It's very old. Older than our history. The quantum strings-they go too far back for my senses to get any strong feelings; something subtle, to be sure, but nothing specific like a name or a vision. The matter of the bottle has moved through space for many millennia but the strings, the echoes-too far for me to read all that well.'

"But there was something. 'Well, what do you sense?'

"'I sense a bottle. A day at the beach. A message in a bottle.'

"'A day at the beach?' I asked him, thinking that sounded one, all too human, and two-too ancient. We're talking before-the-Nova ancient, right, and here it comes, he looks at me with them Aristocratic stone-cold eyes, troubled a bit and says, 'Yes Mr. Walker. A day at the beach, and a human child tossing the bottle in the ocean.'

"Now I'm all ready to guffaw and hee-haw and say 'nice one' but he ain't smiling."

Book Seven:
The Magnificent Raiders of Dimension War One

The Yellow Jaguar

Rip orbit, Sagittarius Arm
4217

Blowfish brains and dancing dolphins!
Why the Captain had decided to go off on his own, on some trip down memory lane, when the entire galaxy was poised on the edge of horrific invasion from extra-dimensional soul-sucking things that could rip you from normal space, drag you into their bizarre folded and curled dimensions like Hermit crabs from hell snatching a slug, and digest your soul in a series of primordial, acidic nightmares that could last for centuries, well, Sagamore Salvatore couldn't fathom.

Mingya!
His mind raced for various curses of various worlds but little came to mind. But there it was. Inexplicable; an enigma wrapped in a mystery with a couple of holes drilled in it so it was an extra pain in the petard.

The Captain's com was being shielded-someone was blocking communication, and the Captain probably wasn't even aware of it.

A trap.
Sag moved down the dark brick and stone alley of the red light district like he owned it. He sneered with disdain; Outworlds. Lame preindustrial Architecture, bad organic booze-if you're going to sin, why there?

He saw the neon and second rate hologram:

"The Yellow Jaguar"

He knocked once; a blue face appeared in a peephole. "What?"

What?? You gotta be kidding me. Sag swung one back kick and the door collapsed. His motion never ceased. The Blue face was hit once, twice, three times. The man had grabbed a rifle but it was too late.

Sag had his disser out, the man's arms twisted around his back, and the disser pressed against the back of his head before he could engage his rifle.

"Tell me where my Captain is. Tell me where my Captain is NOW!" Sag bellowed. The whole nightclub became silent.

Winteroud Sole stepped through the door after Sagamore and adjusted his collar. "Well! I see we've made our entrance, and a grand one at that."

E Gibbon followed in behind and the whole club was doubly shocked. Androids, even chromium thirty-second-century androids were a rarity this far from Cyborgian Central and the Republics.

Gibbon looked over at Sagamore who still held the bouncer with his disser at his head. Then he looked at the club full of gawking patrons. He raised his chin, "What?"

"Where is my Captain?!" Sagamore bellowed again.

It was Sole who answered, looking up at the ceiling, "He's upstairs talking to Jane."

At the sound of the name "Jane", every face in the club turned away and the bouncer added, "Now you know. If you let go of me, I'll take you to see Jane."

Even through the ceiling, through the decades, Sole could feel Vincent's memories of this place and Jane hammering like an iron and nickel asteroid hitting the dark, icy atmosphere of some ammonia seas and ice crust moonlet in a mining camp nightmare: *Vince and Andrew clambered up a winding stair of fern wood, worn with smooth indentations. They went up, and then through a series of locked chambers. Jane was waiting. An ancient prune of humble origins, she'd amassed some wealth through patience and stealth, but hungered always for something more. She looked at Vince as if he brought fond memories of her younger days...*

Sole recognized the winding fern wood stairwell from Vincent's memories. The coral table-the room had changed not at all.

Vince was standing alone with Jane. She was not, however, the gnomish creature of Vincent's memory. She was young and fabulous. Somehow Jane had changed. She'd had a complete body replacement-either her brain or her consciousness implanted directly into a new body.

Then, suddenly, Sole knew-yes, the brain had been transplanted. And the body; she was a clone of herself. She had been fabulous-now she was fabulous again.

Sole's mind spun in the shock and disbelief Vince was feeling-for here, in Jane's Yellow Jaguar club-the truth of what she had done was like a sudden reckoning of having conversed with the dead.

Jane had become Leyla Veronica. Vincent's memories again flayed Sole's consciousness with incongruity:

Leyla Veronica lived with Vincent in a terraced apartment that hung, with thousands of others afforded shelter and shade, among sequoia-like arboriforms whose roots were twisted down and down into the soil since before the dawn of human flight. The towers and their hanging apartments had been magnificently commingled with the ancient trees with a minimum of environmental intrusion. One of the tenets of the NeoWrightians who'd settled the University world.

They had been on Lux University world-she had followed him from Rip, had brought herself back from an aged crone-just to love him. And Vince had never known all that time-Leyla was Jane.

Jane/Leyla was sneering at the Captain with contempt.

"Yes, Vincent. I sold you out to the Cartel."

Sagamore looked at the Captain. Sole stepped back-the rush of tension filling the room was feral. The woman's guards were waiting for a signal to strike. Sole could feel her double identity like a confusing overlay of self-images. She was at once the aged vicious crone, and at the same time the vivacious beauty. It was Sagamore who finally spoke.

"Let me get this straight. I spent all that time on Ophelia's World-hard time in a toxic prison because you wanted to run game with some sleaze-ball racketeer from Chrysalis Isla?"

There was only one Sag.

Sole could feel what was coming next like a series of snapping springs on an elaborate clockwork art sculpture going wrong. There came a sound bamboo wind chimes clanging in the breeze. Lines of black folded like doors opening upon spaces at intervals in the room; the world was unfolding into a shattering of fractals, rushing like a wave of sound.

Sole realized, then, his impressions were cascading at him rapidly from everyone in the room, a sudden wave of strange fears and discomforts coming from each person, only Jane immune; her thoughts were a gleeful delight of triumph.

The ObscuroFrioian with him felt a sudden dread of the floor as if it had become an ice sheet crawling with super dense worms.

Sag, Sole could feel, was suddenly hit with a particularly grim sense of nihilism; in his mind memories of a windstorm of fire shattering a group of his comrades on Baal One.

Sole felt the sheer horror of it with him, the deep loss, the meaninglessness of the sacrifice. Sole felt Sag's confusion as he searched the room with his eyes, rejecting the vision and seeking the sanity of place and time as if pulling himself awake from a nightmare.

For Vince there was a cavern that seemed to stretch on for eternity, Charon tumbling under rocks which continued to fall and fall.

And for Sole, there came the sudden and indescribable presence of an entity orchestrating these visions of personal terror. Something dark, wounded, and hungry.

Sole realized then that behind Jane there loomed one of the beings who he had seen in the visions.

As each of the men in the room struggled with the horrors the thing was pulling from their psyches, a lifetime of shielding himself from such assaults of others' thoughts now came to serve him as a defense.

He felt it reach out for his mind with tendrils, like looping, fractal insectoid proboscis. Wet, needy.

The noise of Sag's war memories, the crawling worms bursting through the floor which had suddenly turned to a rocky ice sheet, and the tumble and cracking of stone in Vince's vision were accompanied by a rising crescendo of noise from the dark walls of space and time that had been opened.

"Look at me Empath!" came a shriek from the dark being, and in its midst, Jane gurgled a sickening chuckle. She was reveling in the Bogie's power; she had been in league with the thing since her return to Rip, Sole suddenly realized, as a confused sketch of impressions came at him from her.

He retched at the vision, took a step back, aware then that Gibbon had thrown up protective shielding a sudden notch. Whatever manipulations the Bogie used to reach into a man's mind, it had not figured a way around these unfamiliar obstacles Gibbon was now presenting.

It turned its attention to the android and Winteroud became aware of its "face" in a flash of vision; a cloud filled with a multitude of strange life forms struggling as if to escape a gut-as if everything it ever ate was still alive, crawling in agony within. Like squirming maggots in an animated corpse of an entity comprised of fears and loss, shadows and dark rejections.

"Metal toy!" It hissed at Gibbon who appeared to be running various field manipulations in test patterns.

"PIG MONKEYS!" came a foul shriek, and Winteroud felt the room spin and go darker; then suddenly, like turning off a hologram, the room was quiet and normal again.

Jane was laughing. "Don't play with me, I am God here."

Vince and Sag took a hard breath and the blue doorman gave each of them a thick look as if to ask, "Ready to go?"

For a long stupid moment, no one said anything. Then Vince, as if remembering he was Captain and a crew member was present, snorted: "Dayung, Leyla, we can just call you Pandora now, aye?"

The look on her face was not human when she replied, "Time to go, it may come back, you know, and you might not fare so well next time."

Sag raised his disser, "Say when Cappy and she's fried monster meat."

Sole saw a faint light of expectation on the doorman's face. He felt a range of emotions turning in Leavel's mind; revulsion, loss, longing, anger. "Later. Let's regroup. I don't have a game plan for this horror show in the guild manual."

Slowly then, the three men and the android backed away from Jane and her blue slave.

Out on the street, Sole patted the Captain on the shoulder. "I'd ask you how you feel, but I already know," he said.

Sag looked back at the Yellow Jaguar expectantly. "And that was a wounded one. We are seriously in the ka-ka now."

It was Gibbon who replied.

"Indubitably".

And you will know us by the trail of our dead
Chrysalis Isla, Orion Arm
4217

The hearing on Maximus Mercurio had convened.

Colonel Mustafa Sanfillipo stood not as if they were about to address the question of Mercurio's culpability in the loss of the crew, but if he were addressing the question of the culpability of humanity itself. His face was ashen after reviewing the tapes.

The board of combat veterans looked uneasily to one another at the sight of him, and a cool discomfort shot through the room which had suddenly taken on a grave aspect.

He didn't appear as one prosecuting a question of culpability, he appeared as one on trial. Uneasily he began, "Gentlemen what we are about to see…"

He looked at Harry. For a long moment, he reached for words.

"Get on with it Colonel Sanfillipo, we've all seen death before" snapped Cosimo Mazak.

Mercurio, quiet in his seat, eyed him raggedly.

Sanfillipo shot him a pained look. "What you are about to see is a compilation of the events on General Mercurio's mission, as recorded by a series of devices implanted in the fighter bomber without the crew's knowledge."

The hearing board erupted in a sudden flurry of voices and surprise. After a few moments of confusion Mazak spoke, "Is it the practice of the Dark Corps now to spy on its member soldiers as they dutifully place themselves in harm's way?"

Sanfillipo had been ready for that. He stood like a piling against the tides. "It had been suspected that the extradimensionals might exhibit a level of empathic ability that would allow them to access the information humans possess about their circumstances. Since that information would, in the case of the crew, include their knowledge of black box recording devices, we felt it was prudent to secure additional data acquisition such knowledge could not betray."

He paused and let the implications sink in.

"We were right. The black box was destroyed, as you shall see, in an attempt by the Extra-dimensional beings, as we anticipated. They can acquire the knowledge of their victims. They can, as you shall see, read us like a billboard hologram.

"That appears to be their essential evolutionary weapon; hovering over their prey they cling like psychic vampires.

"Intentionally, no one on the fighter was able to provide them the information on the data acquisition because no one was privy." He raised his chin in a defensive quiet challenge waiting for further objections.

None came. The members of the hearing board sat darkly grim. Death had taken their fellows, and now impropriety followed in its wake. Their judgments of this scenario were misty already; with every unfolding of events, standards of alien hostility appeared to be rising against them.

"As you say," Mazak barked.

Sanfillipo drilled him a defiant glare. "You will see it was not only a prudent safeguard, but it has also provided the first detailed record of our enemy engaging an attack on our species."

Mazak erupted, "I thought we had one of those with the attack on the spaceman in the intergalactic black?"

Finally, Harry stepped in, "Gentlemen, please. It was my decision. Your right to censor, of even myself, is noted. However, this is no ordinary human enemy. There is no precedent for what we are facing. Watch the recordings. If you wish to mutiny later, so be it. I'll surrender all my authority and face a firing squad with Max. This recording is the only contribution those comrades taken in this fight will be able to share with us. It was an ugly safeguard, one I made uneasily. "

"But it was a safeguard, and their deaths will now testify, with their blood, to further our defenses Let not their loss be wasted on a question of protocols established under different circumstances. "He pleaded their sacrifice.

The board became silent but solemn. An air of understanding was starting to appear on their faces. Sanfillipo deflated from the raw edge tension that had been building; he'd been up on stim all night reviewing the data. Grimly, he began, "Play the first set".

Immediately, the center of the room came to life with a hologram of a fighter bomber. Technical information of the ship's status, drive system, weapons capabilities, and other ancillary documentation appeared around and alongside. Seasoned star men, most of them could have given a rundown from memory. What they were interested in, however, were the dates, and the location of the crewmembers represented by figures as the visualization became transparent.

"The Ripjackle long-range fighter-bomber Baal Baby was ordered to the far side of the galactic core for reconnaissance," Sanfillipo began, "investigating what appeared to be similar ripples in the space-time continuum that were observed from the tape provided by General Ossa Vega who has," he paused and looked acidly at the board, "enlisted us to help save humanity, as it were."

There came muttered grunts from the board at that. The irony of humanity now depending on the Dark Corps and the Cyborgian Air Corps as their saviors against the extra-dimensional beings was not lost on anyone.

He continued, "The tape Ossa provided, which gave us the understanding of the ripples, had been squelched by the High Overlords of the Imperial Command. There had been a religious ark ship that had sent it back as a warning. Ossa had gone to some subterfuge to acquire it."

Mazak turned roughly to Harry and interrupted, "Is all this back-story necessary?"

Harry smiled. You're pushing it, Mazak, "Let the man speak. I'm not about to be micromanaging every soldier involved in this hearing, eh?"

Mazak relented, but his displeasure with everything concerning the Corps involvement in aiding and abetting a CC Imperial General gone rogue was lining his every breath.

"The board needs to know how, and why, they were there in the first place," Sanfillipo chided. "Anyway, our analysis proved correct again. Whenever these things decide they want to drop down in our dimension for a little brain-frying and soul-sucking, they disturb whatever physics normally keep there from here, and we can detect it."

"Now that's a rather important premise in the whole affair. Why we were there. Ripjackle fighter bomber Baal Baby had crewed with ten seasoned veterans from the Baal wars.

Included were General Mercurio in command, First officer Lyon Avistar, Ensign Bormel Latour, and petty officers Beatrice Allfire, Zaslow Saddler, Chloe Venegas, Achilles Bell, Apola Svoboda, and Enos Nautica."

At the sight of the lost comrades, holos in full dress, the board members' eyes darkened perceptibly. Mustafa Sanfillipo paused then, taken aback with the real and present representation of those lost.

Mercurio ached visibly at the sight of each one of the hologram figures. His jaw muscles tightened and his face became a study in contradiction. He still didn't know what was contained in the data sets. Word around the base was that he had been in love with Beatrice Allfire. What would it take out of a man to love someone and be responsible for her death? That question hung over him now like a polished guillotine.

"The Baal Baby had arrived circling past the galactic plume. They hadn't encountered any of the Marauder cultists known to be inhabiting the galactic core-not even heard any chatter of them on the hyper casts," Sanfillipo continued.

A holomap of the galaxy swung into view and zoomed in through a series of increasing close-ups; the core and swirling arm nearest, through several large cluster formations and nebula, and finally, the holo of the ship were seen with a diagram of a single star system-a binary with numerous planets, mostly gas giants.

"After retrieving the probe we had sent out which indicated the space-time ripples, the fighter bomber began a series of "mowing the lawn" movements doing a standard recon of the system. We begin the data observations from that morning"

The holo appeared of the interior of the bridge.

Achilles Bell was at navigation. "General Mercurio we have ripple sign," he said.

Holograms of the soldiers appeared as he listed them, in full dress uniform, and brightened in the hologram ship as well to show their locations at the time of the recording. The hologram Max and the real Max both raised their heads in a strange twin echo of concern.

The holo Max said, "Red alert."

Claxons sounded through the ship and various crew members were seen to rush to duty positions.

"We have a Bogie," Allfire could be heard saying as she activated weapons systems and shields. The hologram Max leaned forward in his command seat, "I want every crew member battened down and in combat gear-now. This thing pops us open and your EVA fields better be five, five, five."

Most had already done so, a few stragglers hustled their gear on.

"It's circling the ship. Twelve kilometers and closing," Bell said calmly, his deep tone thrummed with precision and calmness. His black face glistened from behind the MERGE helmet.

Max didn't hesitate, "Fire at will. Hit it with everything-everything!" he ordered.

There came a metallic rattling, and a whine of fields and generators rattling.

"Like shooting at a ghost General. Right through it." From Svoboda, sharp and fierce. "Disruptor volleys, matter cannon, arming gravity bombs now!"

Bell's chin came up.

"Four kilometers."

"Bell, dogfighter mode, spline us away, make for hyper".

"Done."

Systems lit up across the cabin like a carnival, holograms dials and system data flooding the room in a light show. There came a long moment of silence from the members of the crew as it seemed the ship itself was in a hysterical frenzy.

Max was like a bronze statue, timeless, solid.

"Steady..."

"No good general, it's on us." Allfire switched her EVA field on.

There came a strange moan of metal fatigue from the hull.

"What the devil? Tell me something, Svoboda," the hologram Max stood up in his seat and fingered his disser.

"It's in the ship, Sir," she looked up.

Then she screamed.

Inexplicably, in a wild frenzy, Svoboda howled and leaped from her seat and came up hard against his battening belts.

"Get it off, get it off!" she was yelling, her MERGE helmet spinning away and her arms flailing at his flight suit.

"Sedate her." The hologram Max shot order to Zaslow Saddler who moved with a quickness that sent a moment of awe through the hearing board. Zaslow flowed with athletic perfection; Svoboda paused in her wailing for a moment then turned a strange hysterical look at the crew.

"NO! Run, get out, get out-open the airlocks don't let it take you-DIE!"

There was nothing in the cabin.

Svoboda, you're a member of the corps, soldier. REPORT! What do you see?"

"Eternity's hole-and it's dark-No, she's here-she has a face-that face-no. Kill everyone, General, kill everyone!"

"Saddler, more!" From the hologram Max.

But even Saddler's lithe speed couldn't prevent Svobodas' weapon; it fired, and Svoboda's' head sprayed in a bloody mess of goo on the ceiling.

The hearing board moved visibly.

"Latour, take her position," Max ordered his gaze grave but steady.

Latour moved doggedly past his fallen comrade whom Zaslow was lying to the side. Before Svoboda hit the deck, however, a strange cloud had appeared over Saddler's face, his head began shaking with a mechanical ferocity.

His shriek filled the cabin, then the hearing room, and suddenly tendrils could be seen appearing from the cloud, and clinging to his face; blood spurted in every direction.

Max's disruptor fire sizzled the tendrils cleanly missing Zaslows' face. A strange reply emanated from the cloud and then a voice-"Heiyaagh! So the party starts pig-monkey!"

The cloud appeared like a hole in space from which something indefinable squirmed. Zaslow was still bleeding and screaming- "Don't let it take me, General. It never ends on the other side, please-kill me, kill me now!"

"Buck up soldier!" Max ordered and rushed toward his subordinate to meet the creature which was tormenting Zaslow's body and soul.

Amazingly, strangely, Max took a swing at it, his arm in the hole. "Come and get ME you wormy piece of slime!"

The hole and the shadow, the tendrils and the cloud darted away, across the room to Beatrice engulfing her head like a hand, she howled, "Maximus!"

But he was already there, screaming, cursing, firing with hair-fine accuracy not to hurt Allfire.

"Freeze," Sanfillipo said suddenly and there was the image of Max hard at hand to hand combat struggling to pull his crew member away from the creature.

"I analyzed this section in detail last night," he said. "General Mercurio fired seventy shots into the creature while wrestling with it and Allfire at the same time. Not a single shot went wild. It's the single most amazing use of a firearm I've witnessed in over two centuries of service, and he did it with his cyborged replacement hand-albeit that may have helped. But I want it going on record. His tenacity and accuracy, duty and willingness to place himself immediately into the thick of the fight for his comrade.

"Off," Sanfillipo said, and the holograms were gone.

"Board members, you may review the rest of the tape on your own, I believe General Mercurio has had enough for the day, and I am requesting an adjournment at this time.

"You will find the rest of the tape to be the same-the creature moves through the crew, one at a time, with various members-always including General Mercurio-struggling to rescue their fellows. They appear to be driven mad instantly from the contact with the thing, which seems to possess a Medusa-like power over the human psyche. The creature appears to have the ability to master our language, and an eerie familiarity with us, our weapons systems-everything. It can access our memories.

311

"At the end of the tape, there is only Max struggling with it. It does not, however, appear to be able to drive him to madness, or overcome him physically-apparently it needs one to achieve the other-to drive us to madness, then control our actions. A close review shows each of the crew, besides Mercurio, were driven to self-destruct." He turned to Harry with a cold, numb look.

The implications filled the room like a sudden ice age forming.

"Motion to adjourn until the morning" Harry repeated Mustafa's request.

"No," Maximus said suddenly. "I want to see what it did to my crew. I want to see it now."

You could almost hear a hurrah leap from the board then, which stood unanimously, and clapping came up from them, then a salute. Finally, Cosimo Mazak spoke,

"Admiral Stark, unless there is any objection from the board, I move that this hearing immediately remove the question of General Mercurio's culpability and that we view the rest of the tape to honor the fallen, and take what we may use against the enemy."

Harry looked at his old friend Max with the fierce vindication of his judgment.

"Done. And let it be noted, before the mission their personalities were downloaded into the supercomputers here at the base. They will be reloaded into clones of themselves. The crew of the Baal Baby is lost to us, with honor. But their essence shall fight again."

Sanfillipo ordered the recording to continue and the horrific events from the far side of the galaxy played out to finish. Mercurio never flinched through the whole awful recording.

Something was going to pay.

Afterward, as they moved into the night, Harry pulled him aside. "You understand, Max, the reason why that thing diverted your fighter to the gas giant?"

Max returned, "Well, yeah, it was trying to kill me."

"But it couldn't kill you like it killed the others. You were able to resist it."

"Sir, I have no recollection of these events-watching them was like watching a caricature of myself-a dream".

"Yet that is the moot point we need to discover. Why were you able to resist it? The fate of humanity may ride on that question, Max. The fate of our species."

Maximus Mercurio, hard-headed and brutal, sneered. "Me?"

Harry raised his eyebrows. "It is what it is."

A low chortle growled up from Max. "If that wasn't so friccin sad, it would almost be funny."

"Come on Max. Let's grab an aircar and go down to The Trap for a little R & R. Tomorrow we need to review those tapes and see if we can't jog that thick skull of yours. Tonight, we'll get it lubricated."

Deneb IV
4217

The air Limo buzzed on through the tower and cloud reality of Deneb IV with a sheer ferocity of speed. "Lisa Lynne Sulla" was quickly adjusting to the new century, yet she was still dogged by a strange feeling of discomfort as the personality imprint of Cicero slowly faded from her consciousness. More and more of her real self and pre-submersion mentality was returning, and the Roman patrician fading.

The soaring, glistening, heroic towers of Deneb, which the Empire shows to the galaxy as its official image, were not, of course, its only aspect. Every city had red-light districts, industrial districts, manufacturing centers-and Deneb IV was, at the end of the day, one big planetary city. The shining spires reflecting light and enlightenment were also accompanied by the back districts, the dumpsters, the dark alleys, the parking ramps and juke-joints where the hustlers of hard labor and heavy metal plied marginal trades and grimy necessities.

It was one such industrial district the air limo brought Lisa to, she found with surprising distaste. An ugly slab of a squat thirty-story storage building that was nothing more than a shell covering a rack of star yachts in dry dock. She exited the limo and looked around the dusty floor for an office. The place was packed with all manner of star yachts; one would have expected a minimum of security.

The Hive-mind. She smiled cynically, not much of a chance any of these sheeple be able to resist compulsions if the Transhumans felt this particular collection of yachts was sacrosanct.

She wondered if any humans even knew these yachts existed; it was entirely being serviced by androids, she realized, after a few moments when no one greeted her. A government stash of star yachts for whatever, whenever. An android was coming.

"Miss Sulla, welcome, we're bringing your yacht down now. A fine purchase I might add." The android was an androgynous, husky unit doing double duty as a human interface with some lift capacities as well. Useful one would imagine in a building full of star yachts with their gravity repulsion off.

She smiled and returned a level gaze. So the fiction continues, Lisa Lynne Sulla Art dealer just purchased a yacht. Delightful.

"Thank you, but I really can't take credit for it. It was a…corporate decision."

The android didn't miss a beat, "I see. Well then, let me make sure you're fully informed about your new vessel. "The Ipanema 3600 was the racing yacht that took the Feynman Cup for eight decades straight. She comes equipped with three android crew members and a full complement of sentient navigational programs. Her nanosystems repair the hull skin and neural net with a complete restoration of molecular integrity each twenty-four-hour cycle."

"Just the disk, Dear" Lisa interrupted, "I'll run through the rest at MERGE."

He made a face: *Impressive*. His eyes growing perceptibly larger at the thought of her all strapped in, pulling hard at the wheel so to speak, and absorbing all the specs in flight.

She smiled wider seeing his reaction, knowing the reality would be less dramatic-she'd go over the detailed specs during boring hours of flight-time when the yacht was deep out-space. He handed her the spec disc and she made no effort to disavow his illusions. Dashing reputations are made of such little discretions, and the universe is always and ever entirely short of the dashing.

Pretend, surely the Overlords are seeing through him even now, watching her. She also knew they would not venture with her past the Gateways, so her time to "leave an impression" as it were would soon be over. She didn't want Lourdes' last vision of her to be the confused and star-crossed recently resurrected at the hospital.

She couldn't remember why, yet. But she knew it was important she begin to reestablish a reputation that-yes, a reputation that once had been quite daring.

They were bringing her yacht. Its huge curving hull was polished and gleaming in the lights of the building. She raised her chin a bit. Very nice.

"Madam Sulla, may I present, "David's Reprise".

For a moment she was Lisa again. David Omm was smiling and below the aircar, a thousand square miles of artificial reef teemed with sea life like a kaleidoscope carnival of joy dancing in the languid turquoise waters of Electra in the Pleiades.

"Poser!" she laughed.

"Como no?" he replied.

"Como no?" she said and stepped forward running her hands along the side of the hull. She turned and looked at the droid square in the eyes with cold intent. Okay, Lourdes, the fates have conspired for one more play, perhaps, in this very old game? I shall not go out this time without élan. She swung her hips ever so slightly then, "And my bags?" and stepped onto the floating in suspension fields making her way up to her yacht. Of course, they hadn't prepared her bags yet. David had selected this particular yacht after seeing her in the hospital. It was probably much nicer than the one he originally picked out.

"Right away, Madam, they are on their way now".

"I know," she said and was beginning to realize why David had kept her subverted into the personality of an ancient patrician for so long. *She was dangerous.*

As she stepped into her starcraft, music came alive with the halogen brilliance of the sparkling lights and sheen; Dean Martin singing, just in time. Looking around the teak and mother of pearl interior, lined with pure gold trim, she realized what a statement David had made. If she failed him now, the Overlords would show no mercy-to him or to her. They both would go down with this ship.

Her bags came. She donned the MEGE helmet with an almost tender affection; Life's what you make it. A moments' hesitation over the drive command, then a thought: UPWARD, then another: ONWARD and she was airborne over the city, glistening in the city lights of Deneb IV. Dean Martin ended his song and she thought: *one more time.*

Finally, the towers faded to a point below her, then a pattern, then a world. Above her the circle of the Gateway.

Up to the Gateway where the Overlords had diverted several hundred starships that she might break for open space and the zero wave cycle, the mesons stirring, breaking through the barriers of time and space to be-suddenly and inexplicably at the orbit of New Galen which lay broken, dust, and past-but not forgotten.

David-

Then, easing, she sank into hyper, the yacht breaking the dimensional barrier in a slow soft push-then all the stars like jewels in her hands. She felt the rush of the hyper-gamma spaces and thought: No surrender, no retreat. David's Reprise made easy work of the dark and the cold distance; autopilot to Rip. Of course, then, she must return to the tape of the ice miner and the archaeologist, her quarry. She felt the heave of the yacht on autopilot in a long stream and switched her MERGE program with a thought.

Momentarily, her senses returned as those of the yacht withdrew. She felt herself sitting in the cabin. Through the clear glass of the MERGE helmet, she saw the purse David gave her resting on the console. She opened it and took out the purple cube. She placed it in a player built into the console and felt herself immersed in the diary of the ice miner once more...

The Kunger Diary

"Message in a bottle he says. Day at the beach, what? Half a million years ago? Now I know what you're thinking- this guy has been smoking some funny cigarettes, and I'm getting a whiff or two of second-hand stupidity.

"But this isn't some android in a penny arcade pitching bad horoscopes to old ladies here, this is a genuine authentic psychic empath, and when he says he felt the mind of a child playing at the beach when he touched that bottle, well, you can bet your fat fanny it was a child that had been playing with that bottle at some point, and on a beach to boot. But I'm not without my reservations on the matter either.

"In the morning, dark and early, as it is ever dark on Bethlehem as she careens along in her eternal night in the Palomar 12 cluster, we got ourselves an air-truck (and you can bet I got the best-danged ride out of Jad's collection, hehe) and made out to the ice sheet. They wouldn't give me the coordinates to the dig, but they did program them into the truck so there wasn't anything for me to do at that point but shoot the bull with Sole.

"Which wasn't going to happen-Sole is a no-bull kind of guy. Somewhere his brainy self had acquired more geology data and he had it up on a screen he'd brought with him, happily munching through the information while he slugged down a mug of coffee.

I decided it was time to see where this bad-boy was going with all this.

"'What are you looking at?' I asked.

"He put down his mug which vibrated little ripples in the cup as the air truck zoomed along in the dark. His expression was inscrutable, unpredictable, always coming as it were from trains of thought that were only tangentially related to the man's current environment, in other words Sole was always off in his own little world.

"So you never really knew how he was going to react when you spoke to him. This time his reply was mechanical.

"'Core sample compilations for different locations on the planet. There is a distinct difference- all over the planet- between the deep core material and the mantle. The distinction is so strong it's unlikely the material is from the same planetary formations. At some point in this world's past, it was comet showered- heavily. That shower resulted in an entire second skin for the planet. Its atmosphere, oceans, and continents arrived late in the formation of the planet.'

"I'm like, so zoomin' what? You know?

"But I nod my head like I know what he's driving at. Of course, he knows I don't. Cause he's psychic, and that's what he does-read people's minds and all.

"'Well, what this means is that your ice sheet was originally a whole lot of comets deep in the system's Oort clouds. Somehow they all managed to move from there, to here, and that's another curiosity in an already curious scenario.' He said coolly with a slightly self-satisfied air.

Thinks he's Sherlock Holmes, but of course, Holmes never had any ESP, so I guess maybe he's even a better sleuth than Holmes ever could have been.

"'A mystery wrapped in an enigma.' I replied.

"'It's quite rare. Planets are formed in accretion discs. The material generally has a similar distribution of characteristics over wide parsecs of space before accretion, or relatively so I might add as a qualifier. But certainly not the dichotomy we see here. The material that was deposited by the cometary bombardment all had-well, water and tillable soil material. Either a very fortunate accident or'-he paused unable to say what comes next because the timeline was all wrong.

"'Terraforming' I said. 'What you're talking about is terraforming. But the Predecessors were extinct half a million years ago and humanity was still throwing spears at antelope on the plains of Africa.'

"'All true' he said quietly. 'So we must look elsewhere for our cause. A freak passing of a dark star that would have shaken the Oort clouds-perhaps the same thing that eventually destabilized the star. Yet there is something else. No underground lakes.'

"That was a new one. 'Underground lakes?'

'Yes.' He ran his hand through one of the hologram diagrams, 'The planet still has a magnetic field. Which means its core is molten metal spinning. The heat from the molten core should create underground lakes at some point. There are none-the ice reaches down and down into cold rock as far as the cores have drilled, which was quite far. All the evidence here suggests the core is not molten but is solid material-as such it wouldn't produce a magnetic field. But there it is. A perfectly stable, almost model perfect field.'

"Outside, the icy night moved by the air truck with crystalline indifference and darkness, rolling hills of ice broken by the occasional jutting peak of stone. We moved on. I took a nap. A couple of naps-it was far to the dig site. No use tiring one's self out. I told Sole to get some rest, it was a long haul, but he was excited about his data. Kept talking about the whole thing pointing to something, but he couldn't assess what.

"By the time we arrived at the site, he was sleeping and I was on a MERGE link with the air truck. Now I don't know why they had set up a dig out here, to begin with. The company does it once in a while. Sets up far out and there is an added expense of setting up facilities far from the main center. I think it has something to do with the way claim laws are filed- you get so much ice claimed at a perimeter distance from each particular claim, so it is probably something along those lines, but here we were-in bum-run Egypt as they say. To make the whole thing even more preposterous, they had shut down the dig once the little blue bottle was found.

"We donned a couple of EVA suits and backed them up with EVA fields. We were standing in the airlock of the truck. Sole wasn't looking too good all of a sudden. 'You okay champ?' I asked.

"'There is more to this than we've imagined.' He said and sealed his helmet. I adjusted my communication frequency and indicated to him as well, so the two suits would be able to talk to one another.

"'Testing, testing.' I said, adding a little levity to the situation.

"'You're good, "he confirmed and I coded the door open. There came the sound of vacuum seals and then the darkness. We adjusted our helmet visors to enhance the view. The dig spread out before us, a reverse stepped pyramid going DOWN. It was a couple of kilometers to the other side of the digging edge. We could have taken the air truck straight to the bottom but we didn't.

"We began a walk, and with each step, it was apparent something creepy was happening to my new found archeologist friend. Something he didn't understand either. His android trailed us quietly, but it too seemed to be involved with what he was feeling-it recorded the impressions it seems.

"'Where am I?' he yelled at one point and bent over.

"I thought he was going to vomit all over the inside of his EVA suit. I looked back and considered that it might be better to get the truck.

"He grabbed me. 'Where are the people? Where are the people? WHERE ARE THE PEOPLE!!?'

"I looked to his droid, 'Go get the truck. I'll stay here with him. Hurry.'

"It was a very fast droid. Watching it buzz back to the truck was impressive, but I was afraid it wouldn't get back in time before Sole had a stroke or something. It did, however, and the three of us made our way to the main cabin and I got him some coffee.

"I was afraid to ask him what he saw, but it didn't matter at that point because he was going to tell me anyway.

"'They won't be doing any more digging here, I think' he said. At least none they'll be advertising about or selling ice from.'

"A small trickle of blood ran from his nose, and he wiped it. I was suddenly struck with the reality of his pain, the awareness that he lived with what others must have joked about would have been a living constant ache.

"He fixed a leaden stare at me and I knew, here it comes. 'People were here.' He said. Half a million years ago people, human people the same as us, the very same-don't ask me how. I haven't figured that out yet but as we moved down in the ice dig I could see it as if we were in a low flying aircar. There is a suburb below us.

"*'It had been an ordinary night. A sprawling suburb and families are in their beds. Their homes are still there- under the ice, you will find them. The heat came fast- from the other side of the world, they were all dead in moments, merciful that, and then the sea was airborne and soon freezing them over, burying them in the snow which fell, and fell and fell.'*

"*Then he stopped. I didn't question what he said but the implications, well, you do the math. You'll come up with a 'half-a-million-year-WRONG' answer. There was no way human beings were out in this corner of the galaxy way back when, washing their ground cars and playing ping pong in suburban sprawl, listening to big-band music and going to sock-hops.*

"*He felt my thoughts. Then he did something I'll never forget. 'Gibbon' he said. 'Play your recording of my impressions for him.'*

"*The room came alive suddenly then with a vision. We were suspended above a world of people, ghosts I realized, living their lives in a world beneath the ice of half a million years. Homes along streets, streets forming towns, towns across a countryside-a world there was, a world of people, stopped and frozen in mid-motion one horrible day and night, there, beneath the ice which I had spent most of my life working above, unbeknownst to me. My world was an ice sheet above a graveyard of cities.*

"*I too was feeling sick now. Who were these people, and how had they come to be in this place, at that time?*"

Lisa pulled the MERGE helmet off her head with a speed of one suddenly surprised at something bitterly unpleasant. The recording David had given her-what a horrible how-do-you-do welcome back into the Forty-second century. What was he putting her in the middle of? Where did it end? Another mystery, another unanswered question into the unknown she had suddenly been resurrected to face.

So there had been a human civilization on some distant world half a million years ago. How? Species didn't evolve the same line on different worlds. But Sole's visions had been clear-these were humans.

They could not have evolved there separately from the mainline of human beings on Earth. Additionally, there was no evidence of a space-faring civilization on Earth at that time.

Someone or something had placed them there. That much was certain. Humanity couldn't have evolved the ability to populate a distant world and kept it hidden from future generations as such at that distant era? No, the advent of such a civilization would have left traces across the globe. This smacked of alien involvement.

Then there was the evidence of terraforming. A distant world terraformed...like someone was creating a human zoo-or a farm? Were the humans there some sort of food source for the Bogies? Had they created a world full of prey to swoop down on at leisure for a psychic thrill of the hunt and kill? Her mind reeled with the implications. Farming humans, the Devil's orchard so to speak, on a global scale? One vast supermarket to pluck victims from?

She shuddered.

SILURIAN NEBULA
4217

Who knows what strange realities lie unseen and teeming in the various corners of the multiverse? Perhaps an Earth where Columbus never landed, or one where he made it to China? Who can say? When I see the echoes of what was gleaming in the stream, are they somehow compounded through the multiverse into other Earths of a multiplicity of realms? The echoes and the uncertainties and the quanta shimmer.
    -Winteroud Sole, Caldris.

General Vega Ossa glared at the nebula filling the holo-screen of the bridge with a vicious disdain. The government had exacted illegal experimentation on people convicted of transportation infringements, petty smugglers skimming the fat by avoiding tariffs. This was what he and his men were defending-butchery? He wiped his face in a gesture of unconscious disgust. His anger was palpable across the bridge. He looked at each of his bridge crew in turn, searching their faces for their reactions. He was pleased, at least, that his disgust seemed a universal reaction.

How far the Overlords had fallen from even any pretense of humane values.

"Take us in, ahead slow. I want data on everything that makes this nebula tick."

Science officer Demaio Klaver nodded, "Yes Sir." And indicated to his data team to act but they were already in motion, the instrumentation already at work gathering information.

When Cyborgian Central had originally placed the research base on Siluria it was a calculated move to avoid prying eyes. Even the military was essentially clueless. The research base would violate every norm of human law for several millennia, as they experimented ruthlessly on live human test subjects in a desperate attempt to gather data on Outpilots, who seemed to move through space unhindered and unhampered by the Bogies which CC knew to exist.

Which CC knew they were coming in greater number, a swarm in fact.

They had taken some poor tech, Bandor 1225, a bright fellow to be sure, but someone who had spent his entire life under the hive-mind influence on Deneb IV. In the world of the trans-human Cyborgians, all men were created equal, but some were more equal than others. Bandor had been pretty much less equal his entire life-and the less equal one was in CC, the deeper one was under the influence of hive mind impulses, suggestion, and motivation.

Bandor, like most of the great well-washed-and-manicured masses of the CC hive, had lived his entire life moving through a carefully constructed series of mental and physical paradigms that defined his every thought and action as sure as the proverbial clockwork orange. Then, they had moved him, like a babe in the woods, to run the experiments on the base they had built in the Silurian Nebula.

The essential disconnect between the Overlords, who were presumably running things, and the great machine bureaucracy that was, could never have had a more perfect illustration as Bandor trying to run a research facility illegally in the middle of a nebula that was immune to the normal laws of physics.

Harry Stark had been watching the activity as the transport vehicles had moved out of Imperial Space and had been ready to manipulate Bandor with rather gleeful delight.

Unfortunately for Harry, Bandor was no more informed as to the real nature of the experiments than anyone else outside the circle of the Overlords, who were romping through their bizarre virtual universes. Moreover, Harry's action of framing the crew of the Taloned Sire had ensured that Bandor was going to have at members of the crew.

Veterans of the Baal Wars, Harry had never forgiven Sagamore Salvatore for his role in accidentally ensuring the death of many soldiers when he stole a jump ship that held the command codes for a retreat. Trapped in the Hellish combat of Baal, without access to the jump ships, Harry's men had fought on a bitterly pointless sacrifice. Sagamore had no idea, until decades later when Harry had finally caught up with him.

What Harry hadn't counted on was Vince Leavel, and Sagamore Salvatore arranging a meeting with Bandor on their own.

Ossa, looking at the nebula, thinking of the research base and Harry's inscrutable viciousness, wondered with a breath at the sheer horror of man's inhumanity to man. Harry had created a perfect frame-up that would eventually land Sagamore and his associates not only in a life of ignominious shame on the prison planet Ophelia's World, but an eventual fate under Bandor the Butcher's finely tooled lasers.

The sweet piece of fruit on top of that cold revenge desert had been framing Captain Leavel's fiancé as well. But after a few rides in Harry's air limo, that fruit ended up on a side plate-Harry had gathered a taste for her, himself. Thus it was that Harry inadvertently pressed Leavel and Sagamore to new heights of piracy-they escaped prison planet by commandeering a supply freighter.

Amazingly, CC had been running deliveries of supplies to the prison planet on a regular schedule. The bureaucratic ineptitude knew no limitations. Thus the game of cat and mouse that Harry had pursued with Sagamore Salvatore began to backfire. Sagamore and Vince once again turned absurd defeat into a form of victory as their escape from Ophelia's World became legendary. Of course, Harry had ensured their fame when he had hyper cast their arrest in the first place, and an obscure fading folk-hero Vince was once again thrust into the galactic spotlight.

Harry switched out Vince's fiancé Leyla from the mix on her way to Siluria for his enjoyment-something he neglected to tell Vince of course, assuming the poor man's mental anguish would be ever more despicably painful with the knowledge that he had consigned his love to Bandor the Butcher. So Vince arrived at Siluria with a vengeance of his own and single-handedly demolished an entire CC facility.

Of course, Ossa mused, there were some odd occurrences in that little attack. Firstly, it was far and away more destructive than a single individual should have been able to effect.

Secondly, there appeared to be Predecessor technology assisting him. A lot of Predecessor technology. Where had the smuggler acquired it and how had he mastered it to such a level of expertise? Why wasn't it showing up on the black market or reverse-engineering labs as usually is the case when such Predecessor technology was discovered?

Clenching with tension, and feeling the strain of the past months in a racking series of aches throughout the tired muscles of his overworked and under-slept body, Ossa considered the Silurian Nebula in all its diabolical glory. Some called it the "Diablo", the Devils' hole. It moved counter the turn of the galaxy-speculation immediately came to mind at that as to its origin. Was it a mini-cluster that had been pulled into the Milky Way's gravitational orbit from somewhere else? Then there were its field distortions.

Every supply and service vehicle sent into the nebula had been dependent at some point on ramjets-essentially primitive rocket technology. The gravitational and magnetic field manipulators that allowed starcraft to bend space, breakthrough to the fifth dimension, and otherwise get from A to B were plagued with problems in this nebula as nowhere else. That, of course, had been the very reason Cyborgian Central had originally chosen the place to locate its illegal research base. The nebula was anathema to pilots-avoided like a disease.

In typical bureaucratic fashion, however, the Transhuman Overlords of Cyborgian Central Command economies had never seen fit to figure out why this was so, which seemed a rather important piece of information, Ossa mused. He went to his command seat and drilled a dark stare at the holo-screen with all the intention of the primordial thrust of a spear.

"Contact recon and intelligence back at the fleet. I want them out here running observations on this thing twenty-four-seven until we know the what, why, and how of every field dynamic, every planetoid, and every star system in this mixed-up ball of gas and star-forming region like we know the plumbing in one of our tugs."

"Sir" from Klaver. He looked to several of his officers, each with a glance in turn and each knew what to do. They were encrypting messages across hyper relays within seconds. In distant corners of the galaxy, elements of the fleet looked across their boards to see red holos flashing "Urgent, message from First Strike".

Skirting the shoulders of the nebula, their attack ship gleamed in the light of its thousand suns and phosphorescent burnished orange and violet.

Klaver watched the general with a wince; he knew the man longed for action. But the long months had given them only and endless run around chasing ghosts, digging into the petty dramas of smugglers and syndicate riff-raff, bureaucrats and now-revolting medical research in this nasty corner of the galaxy. The general's granite visage was a study in angles and disciplined lines-a man meant for the death song of swords and fury, not the mundane and deliberate sleuthing of a second rate private detective outside a cheap motel.

Ossa saw his look of apprehension. "Relax Klaver, I'm not coming apart at the seams."

"Sir?" Klaver responded defensively.

"Sir nothing, Klaver. You look like a mother dog who just lost a pup. Look, we received a new Intel of a sheriff. He was tracking an escaped prisoner off Ophelia's World that the syndicate in Chrysalis Isla was mixed up with the research director on this base, here in this nebula. Turns out he was-that was seven years ago.

"Well the director was a useless tool of a bot, but the syndicate warlord was a veteran of the Baal Wars-as were his whole little private army that has taken to running the Pleiades. He was someone we could talk to. A good soldier, a man who gets things done.

"So I enlisted them. The whole psycho, a rag-tag group of world-beating, mad-dog maniacs."

Klaver looked at him darkly, "If I may speak sir, the King of the Pleiades didn't exactly run a good game out there."

Ossa showed his palms. "It's a dirty business. They won. Baal One is even now being terraformed."

Klaver was unmoved.

Ossa gave him a sidelong glance and snickered. "It is what it is. Nothing more, nothing less. But anyway, back to this nasty ball of bad gas." He indicated the nebula on the holoscreen with disdain. "This is the answer to everything-I'm certain of it. Central has been sitting on it the whole time, playing in it even, and not seeing the blunt truth staring them in the face, well, with big old lizard eyes."

"Well if that's the case, Sir, I think we're going to be struggling with the lizard for a while there are more questions here than answers as far as I can tell." Klaver offered stolidly.

"Siluria." The general said flatly. "What do you know about Siluria?"

His first officer looked back questioningly. "I'm updated on all the briefs. M-class planet, tropical, abundant and thriving primitive life forms. Series of oceanic seas circling the planet in the remains of super craters-probably formed from cometary impacts.

Various stone temples in a state of ruin indicate the planet's higher life form-a large reptilian creature resembling Tyrannosaurs-once achieved a rudimentary civilization but has reverted to barbarism."

Harsh relief tinged General Vega Ossa's' face. "The standard take that everyone has seen." He waited for Klaver to digest his implication.

"So there is more to it?" Klaver finally said.

Ossa nodded. "Oh yes. Look again. The whole thing unravels as an illusion once examined a second time. "Navigation, call up a holo of Siluria please" he requested.

His navigational officer bent over his dials and holos a moment and a world appeared floating in the room. The size of a small aircar, Ossa rose and walked through it. "A Good general scouts the field well. Central is no longer being run by good generals. They gave the most important field of contest in the galaxy a cursory review by a robot probe, and filed it under "curious but unimportant". Then they used it for useless-dangerous actually, should the public ever get wind of it-radical garbage research of a kind that disgraces our whole civilization."

Klaver looked at him uncomfortably; this is all on record, Sir.

Ossa understood his look but dismissed it. Central was in the dung too deep now to throw him out of the aircar, so to speak, over badmouthing their call on the research base.

"Klaver," the general said, "What's wrong with this picture?" He motioned at the hologram globe of Siluria turning slowly in the control room.

Weather systems spun across a globe of concentric seas. Emerald-green and turquoise island chains, archipelagoes and tiny continents sprinkled the sphere.

His first officer considered the planet for a moment. "Well, those craters have held up well for a natural world. You never see that in an unterraformed…" He stepped forward and looked closer now with urgency.

"Did Central terraform this planet?" he asked suddenly.

Ossa was smiling. "No, good officer, I can assure you, they did not. Central didn't even actually discover it, that honor goes to others. Yes, however, it was terraformed."

"Predecessors, Sir? If that were the case the craters would have been worn down via weather systems. You'd either have a muddy swamp across the whole globe by now or evidence of some tectonic activity. Those assumptions are why it probably has slipped through everyone's recognition."

"Yet a natural world developing higher life forms would not possess primordial crater rings beneath a biome. Biomes take too long to develop. Craters get worn down." Klaver insisted.

"Yet there they are. So no other answer fit-the biome had to be planted there after the seas."

"The seas which were placed directly onto a cratered newly minted planet. Comet seeding, a pretty standard reality of terraforming. You wrap a comet in a protective field, drag it into the planet from an Oort cloud. This whole thing is a construct, Mr. Klaver. A construct created by a non-human species. There have been only one non-human species in this galaxy capable of that kind of planetary engineering that we know of.

"This is a Predecessor job. Not a relic, not a ruin, an active, live, still in the game Predecessor masterpiece."

He drilled Klaver a look as if he'd just dropped some ordinance on a target.

Klaver forced a smile.

"The reptiles? The ones who built the temples-Sir, certainly those Tyrannosauruses down there chomping on vermin and sloths-they can't be the same beings that once possessed a galactic civilization." His smile was indignant.

"Check your premise. Why not? Because they're carnivores? Because they're crude? Think about it. Predatory species, more often than not, evolve an edge of intelligence.

"They enjoy hunting. Humans still do it for recreation, even now. That world down there isn't a primeval collection of seas and islands, it's a theme park for bloodthirsty adventurers that got turned into a hideout when even more brutal bloodthirsty adventurers-the Bogies-strolled into the galaxy."

"Theme Park sir?"

321

"Sure. THEME PARK. Happy hunting grounds, State preserve, amusement world-live action vs. virtual gaming. That, Mr. Klaver, is a dinosaur playground."

Klaver's head bent sideways as if to look at the holo from a different perspective. "Everything I've seen on the Predecessors indicates they haven't shown their snouts in this galaxy for over tens of millions of years. Couldn't this be a third sentient life form?"

Ossa brightened. "Indeed it could, indeed it could." He walked back through the globe and out again, "But if they were a third sentient species, why the stealth? If they are capable of planetary engineering, why hide in this nebula?"

Klaver snorted, "Who can say? But millions of years, General? You're suggesting they've been kicking back here millions of years? You pointed out the crater formations aren't showing that much erosion."

The General said nothing then but waved his hand over his command chair and the holo-model of the planet faded and the nebula replaced it again. "Navigation," he said then, "Field model."

'Which fields sir?"

"Electro-magnetic, gravity, meson-dimensional, and tachyon."

Pattern after pattern illuminated the hologram then; tracing, interlacing, dancing patterns like a kaleidoscoping musical rubric of fractals. They steadied into a series of pleasant vibrations and then-shattered and reformed along slightly different lines. The bridge crew watched for a few minutes but no pattern repeated itself.

"Non-repeating encryption; dimensional disruption. Time, ladies and gentlemen, is relative. Space-time manipulated, is more than relative-it's a defensive weapon-a fortress as it were."

As the pieces fell into place, the bridge crew once again understood why he was a general, and they were his staff. Mouth agape, one of the junior crew members muttered, "That's brilliant, Sir. But a fortress against what?"

Ossa was too pleased with himself to point out a minor breach of protocol on his bridge at that point, however. He merely replied, "That nebula is a time fortress against fifth-dimensional intrusion into our space-time, of course." The shadows nipping at his heals these past months cleared a bit. If he was right, the Predecessors had found, if not a victory over the trans-dimensional Bogies, at least a sanctuary and solace. Survival. Before all else, one must survive.

Nothing short of the survival of humanity was at stake.

"Alright then," Ossa said. "We go down there and find out what is taking place on that world. If there are Predecessors alive and well, I want us breaching some form of communication with them. If not, I want to know if there are functioning machinery still throwing up defensive fields. Form exploratory teams, and start getting me the hard science that Central declined to acquire. I want to know the what, where, and when about the history of this planet-this whole nebula. I want scout ships scouring every corner of this gas cloud, every star charted, right down to the planetoids orbiting. Get the Hammerheads ready, we're going on a field trip."

One could feel the excitement across the bridge as the General stepped out. There wasn't a single person not engaged in some sort of motion, programming, or otherwise "looking busy". For Ossa, another step into the unknown had been taken, and Cyborgian Central Command Economies had been neither asked permission nor notified. Of course, it was always better to ask forgiveness than permission, as the old saw went. However, one didn't ask CC for forgiveness. If that day came, it would be a one-way trip to Omm's' wonderland of horrors, with no ticket back.

When First Strike finally arrived at Siluria, Vega Ossa stood along in the docking bay looking out at the planet and its gas giant like the first man on a new continent. This "Silurian world" as it had been named so many years ago, had answers. He was going to get them, come what may. Here, he suspected, was the last stand of the Predecessors. The last efforts of a great race of beings to stem a tide of horror the likes of which our dimension had not produced.

He couldn't return to Deneb IV now and ask permission for the mission. His disconnect from the hive mind precluded that; it was defined as such for just such situations. Technically, there wasn't a pressing attack, so in fact, he could be brought up on charges. Reports from across the galaxy told another reality however, murders and mutilations were increasing, missing persons, cases of madness and incoherence-small things really, among the trillions of mankind, small enough incidents so that they could remain under the cover of anomaly, petty crimes, ordinary atrocity-a sad commentary on mans' inhumanity to man that atrocity could ever become mundane. They were not mundane, and Ossa knew it.

The things were already here, and their number increasing by the day.

The Ensign he'd assigned the covert research that broke open the case of the HyperBogies was standing before him now. Tamara Fortunato had grown up on Earth's moon in an industrial district humankind had occupied since the conquest of the solar system with sub-light drives. It was a world with traditions of mastering a complex artificial environment old as any, and people conditioned to subterfuge techno bureaucracies as a way of life. She was perfect. Ossa adored her for decades, but he was a General. That was that.

"Ensign?" he queried.

"Sir?" She replied.

"You're going back to the Empire to meet with my superior. It will be an ugly, strange business at best, but he has given us some…latitude and he deserves to know what we are doing. I'm not putting it over the casts. I would dearly, err," he paused then and for a split second an emotion shot across his features only to be wrestled to control by his iron will, "hate to lose an officer of your abilities. I expect you to use every bit of your talent for dealing with Byzantine Bureaucracies to make it back here in one piece."

She took the instruction with a salute. "I'll await my orders" and stepped away, wondering at what she had seen on his face. For a flickering second she felt a pang of wonder at the thought that, then, no, he couldn't-not that nickel and platinum planetoid. Any man could lust for her, she knew, but she thought she saw something else. Something tender and artful, a gracious longing.

Striding down the corridor she laughed, what was she thinking? The commander of the First Strike was sending her into the clutches of Deneb IV, hardly the act of someone in love.

Hammerheads were not specifically attack vehicles though they had that capability. They were reconnaissance vehicles, used to bring in troops and secure areas already attacked. Mini-bases. Ideal for this mission, there were twenty of them onboard the First Strike, and Ossa sent ten down to various locales on the planet.

Making through the atmosphere he marveled at the beauty of the planet. If he was right, and it was a piece of planetary engineering, once again the Predecessors mastery of "form follows function" was married to an unerring sense of forms' inherent beauty. The long curving island chains, the circular seas, the mountain ranges formed from the underlying craters, spun with the pinwheel formations of storm systems, all set against the backdrop of a gas giant and the spectacular rings-it was a study in curves, motion, the music of the spheres made visible.

"No need for the ramjets yet, Sir. Whatever talk there was of field distortions making this place a hell-ride, ain't happening now."

The rush of heavy atmosphere against the hull of the hammerhead pulled his thoughts away from the sublime. Of course, the pilot had acquired some goofy music to accompany the ride down, as was traditional.

He looked back to the General from his flight helmet. "It's the Chowder-head booboos, General, they're HUGE now across the galaxy." He said with a boyish grin.

"Yes, they are pilot. Now watch your dials" Ossa came back with a smirk.

"Five, five, five and alive, Sir." He said.

They're turning down the disruption. They know we're here, and they're letting us in. A welcome? Or a trap?

The Hammerhead broke below a cloud bank, and the landscape spread out before them like an Eden, pristine and primordial. A dinosaur playground. They continued lower, and lower until the geography became a landscape one could imagine inhabiting.

"We've got unidentified twelve o'clock!" The navigator called out.

Shapes moved in the sky ahead of them, pterosaurs. With the appearance of the pterosaurs, Ossa knew his suspicions were confirmed. Life had been brought here, and from the looks of it, a variety of life that was lost in other places in the galaxy. So the planet was more than a refuge and a fortress, it was also an Ark. Come the deluge, a species of Noahs.

"Pull up" Ossa ordered coolly. "Make Sure it gets cast to Fortunato. I want her to have all the evidence when she hits Deneb IV. She's going to need it."

The landscape was like a modern art sculpture. Whatever molten forms had arisen in the planet's terraforming, remained without the half a billion years of wear and tear that weather systems would have wrought, had life arisen here naturally. Islands of blackish-green were scattered in every direction, with picturesque, chimney stack peaks sculpted in endless variety.

Shallow seas and islets stretched away and away, full of primitive, stalk-like, marshy plants. Somewhere in this dream of primeval perfection, CC had inserted its death laboratories.

They put their Hammerhead down on a ridge above the jungle. From across the waters came the honking of an enormous host of sauropods splashing through the shallows, tuba-headed behemoths. Lotus-like flowers, huge and sultry, bloomed with audible pops. They cast streams of scented clouds to the languid breeze. Fat insects glowed, swooping by, rumbling like clockwork aereoplanes.

 Two men remained with the ship, and eight made their way down into the foliage. "You keep your EVA fields on as if this place is deep-space regardless of how Honky-Dorey comfortable you may get. I want no contamination. Stat. Is that clear?" Ossa barked, as they began their first venture into the Silurian terrain.

A series of affirmatives snapped back from the men and women. Klaver took point. The environment was immediately disarming, and at the same time disconcerting. Anything seductive and lovely could as easily be poisonous. Several of their small group set about recording data streams.

The data would be poured over for years to come-if they survived. It had become apparent from the species they encountered that a great number of extinct higher life forms, known only from fossils, were moving about here like a schoolboys fantasy come to life. Schoolboys from a hundred worlds as well; the menagerie seemed to include as broad a stretch of fossil life as had been encountered on many worlds-worlds, Ossa noted, where Predecessor ruins had all been found.

Every step seemed to writhe and slither with another living fossil come to witness the beings from the distant future. But they were here, alive, and real. This was no jaunt to the past. Something-some Predecessor thing-had preserved them. The exploratory team found themselves wondering when they would come to the fence of the cage bars or the display case window with the signs. This place was a living fossil zoo.

Several times they were rushed upon by one thing or another. Standard issue force fields held the animals back until they tired of slamming themselves against the invisible walls and drifted off.

But there was no sign of their Predecessor keeper or Predecessor equipment.

They determined a southerly direction, and a broad sweeping arc search pattern that would wind around the escarpment, and bring them back to the Hammerheads by nightfall. Down through the jungle, they moved, recording, mostly silent, but for the occasional pause to awe-it was a magnificence that no human had ever encountered in world after world where mankind had tread, the ruins and remains of past vibrancy could be found, but nowhere a world as alive and teeming such as this.

Earth had been once close to such vitality, then slightly less vibrant as mankind had arisen and conquered the wilds. Then, as mankind had removed his civilization to the cosmos and made more of a preserve of his planet of origin, with only the city centers remaining. Such came to mind. "Any of you guys ever been to the forests of Earth?" Klaver asked suddenly at one turn in the exploring. A few nods of affirmative from the older troopers. "This is richer than that. The carrying capacity of this world is off the charts."

Earth's restored forests had been managed for nearly two millennia now since the bulk of human industrial production and expansion had long since moved spaceward.

Ossa took it in with a sense of awe. If they finally did find Predecessors, it was going to be a humbling experience. Restoring Earth's forests had been largely a process of healing- this world had been created from a proto-planet, and the plethora of ecologies here gathered from across a hundred thousand light-years of the galaxy.

As nightfall came they circled back around to the Hammerhead as planned. They had acquired an enormous library of data, yet not a single sign of the "zookeepers". They passed through sterilization fields, showered and bunked down, doing rotating guard duty. It was a tropical night of splendor and phantasmagoria. The gas giant and its brilliant rings arced a sky lit with the nebula.

Ossa and Klaver ran through some of the tapes they had made, identifying various species and cataloging them to databases from the First Strike that included fossil records from various worlds. It seemed that as they had moved through the hillside, they had crossed through replications of different biomes.

How the Predecessors had managed to pull this off and create self-sustaining ecologies was another question to add to their growing list.

Human experience had shown that introducing various non-native species into one another's ecosystems was generally a disaster. Somehow they were keeping these ecologies tangential to one another in the same space.

That would be some doing; how it was being done appeared to be incomprehensible-but it would have to have been affected.

"They say an advanced technology is indistinguishable from magic" Klaver offered after a while.

"Well, there's a lot of "magic" here pal, and we need to find its source.

It isn't Merlin out there with a wand, I'll tell you that for nothing. We have to assume they're aware of our presence. That folk hero smuggler from the guild was here-alone. He survived long enough to take down Bandor base."

Klaver snickered, "Ah yes, the immortal Vincent Mariner Leavel."

Ossa chuckled, "Don't laugh, he's still OUT THERE. That rogue has more lives than the proverbial cat. He took down the base, and bested Harry Stark." Ossa winked. "But he had help. One of his crew had infiltrated CC mercenary units." He added, slightly annoyed that such an independent shoot-from-the-hip character had acquired a reputation throughout the years as being indestructible. The reality, he knew, was dumb luck, or angels.

"Help?" Ossa mused. "He had inspired such fierce loyalty that his crewmembers would risk life and limb, infiltrate the most vicious mercenary organization known to man, track down his superior officer across known space, fly into a haunted nebula, and walk into the director's office of a lab engaged in torture experiments? That kind of help?"

Klaver's head lifted in a sardonic laugh. "Point taken. But then again, Sir, you've got a whole division doing damn near the same thing for you now aye?"

Ossa beamed, "I know."

Klaver pointed to one of the giant beetles in a holo tape from their afternoon in the jungle. "That's extinct."

"Not anymore." Ossa countered.

"Not any more…" Klaver repeated.

"Brave New World, eh, number One?"

Klaver darkened, "Let's hope time isn't running backward here. I've heard some very strange things over the years."

Eventually, Ossa knew, they would have to discuss the greatest ghost story of the "Diablo Nebula". Being a good reader of faces, he saw the darkness across Klaver's face for what it was- an an unresolved question of culpability.

It had been the CC Air Corps that had ravaged the Arcturians. Only, as time went by, accusations arose that the war was trumped on false and misleading intelligence. If the fleet, ever discovered, showed, in fact, there had been no plans at raiding Imperial space, they would be proven to have been duped. Worse, they would have been proven to have been duped into being the most horrific mass murderers in human history.

"Which brings us to the missing Arcturian Fleet, the flying Dutchmen of the galaxy," he said at last.

"What if we find them and discover they weren't engaged in plans to attack us but were merely defensive, Sir?"

Ossa looked grimly back. "You honestly believe they're still flying around this nebula in some sort of time flux from a thousand years ago?"

Klaver pointed at the beetle. "That Sir is gone now these sixty-three million years, and it was crawling on my boot today."

Ossa nodded. "Touché."

"What would you have done Sir, given those orders?" Klaver seemed suspended in space before the holo tape of their afternoon research as if he could call up the war as easy as the afternoon.

"They were under the influence of the Hive Mind-the last time the military was so compelled. I imagine under the compulsions of the Hive Mind I would have acted as directed. Otherwise, I would have refused.

"A warrior doesn't butcher unarmed civilians," he said in a stone face packed with ruin.

So many of the ships went missing-the Bogies he realized now- that afterward the military was disconnected from the hive. Yet Ossa had begun to suspect more-that the horrors of the Bogie encounters had crossed the hyper cast relays had impinged directly into the Overlords consciousness. Omm would not be the only mad one then. Omm had been away on his faux diplomatic mission.

He might be the least insane among the Overlords.

Outside, the night rumbled and groaned, a world of strange life forms turning in a dance they had managed for-how long? Time was less a certainty here than even the rest of the strange relativistic pull and sweep of the galaxy. Here, it seemed the Predecessor ark careened in its orbit under the invisible guidance of its Noah race. Ossa was determined to unlock the secrets, things he suspected were only known to a vagabond Trade Guildsman named Leavel.

The next watch came alert, and out of their bunks, to relive their superior officers. Ossa was glad for a reprieve of rescuing the galaxy and picking the locks of ancient mysteries. The simple bunk in the Hammerhead was like an oasis of oblivion from the weight of a thousand worlds. Morning found the Hammerhead alive with activity as Ossa woke and made for the Hammerhead's canteen. He slugged back a quart-size drink of nutrients and stim; caffeine, carnitine, lipoic acid, and some vitamin mix rich in proteins. His special blend programmed into the canteen before leaving the First Strike. That and the autodoc knew every aspect of the teams' metabolisms. He had barely made it through half his drink when he realized something unusual was heady on the holograms. Chattering voices drew him to the forward cabin.

"What's all the commotion?" he cocked an eyebrow and looked at the jumble of soldiers standing around the hologram.

They stood to attention.

"At ease, please. Anyone care to inform me what's on the show? We watching a soap opera, or a nature program? That's the million credit question."

Embarrassed looks passed between them. Finally, one of the PFC's anteed up.

"I lost my disser, Sir," Yates confessed.

Several of his comrades looked like they were about to burst into laughter. A couple of others held back in sheer dread.

Ossa held his stim and stared. "Did you lose it in this compartment?"

The eyes of the soldiers searched each other from poker faces.

"No Sir. It slipped from my holster while I was operating scans yesterday in the jungle. On the hologram, strange lizard creatures were moving in a small group around an object. Ossa realized it was a disser. "Looks like they found it."

"Yes, Sir! When I called up the video link on the disser GPS, with the First Strike, to retrieve it…we discovered it has already been found-by the dinosaurs."

"No chance they're Predecessors?" Ossa asked with a straight face.

The hologram lizards jumped and darted about in a clambering comical pantomime of birdlike gestures sniffing at the disser and hissing back and forth to one another.

The entire platoon now was struggling to maintain their composure as the holograms leaped and bobbed their heads. The PFC watched them for a few seconds more.

"I don't think that's them, Sir"

Several of his comrades' faces were beat red now as they held their breath. Ossa afforded them the pleasure of a sideways smile.

"I need more coffee. Carry on."

He turned and retreated to the canteen, and the forward cabin erupted with the mocking laughter of the PFCs' comrades. PFC Yates answer, "I don't think that's them, Sir," would become a new catchphrase among the troops in the coming days.

"Pulling a Yates," became mankind's first cultural contribution to the language from its experience on Siluria.

Yates and a couple of his comrades retrieved the disser without any trouble, and a conference call was scheduled to collate the experiences of the Hammerheads. In the forward cabins of all the away ships, the soldiers and their commanding officers discussed and reviewed the previous day's intelligence. They had amassed a wealth of zoological data. An Astro-paleontologist's dream for sure, but nothing that brought them any closer to discovering the creators of this world or their relationship to the present invasion of dimensional invaders.

After a great deal of listening to reports, platoons in forwarding cabins of Hammerheads around the planet, and officers on the command bridge of the First Strike looked to the General for the next orders. He had another quart of coffee.

"Well if the Natural Science Society were heading up the military we'd be getting fleet honors right now." He smiled. "Keep the data on the planet's ecology coming in, it's important. But we need a new strategy, now, to fast forward this whole process, and get us in front of the actual builders of this Ark, if they still exist.

"We know several things from previous probes and the previous…installation Central had established here before it was overrun by Outpilots."

Most of that story had been squelched by the government-controlled media. Yet rumors filtered in from Outspace and the Trade Guild. It ranked among tabloid holo-journals at best in the minds of the population, somewhere among the tales of the mysterious beings of complete romantic delight, and whether aliens had built the pyramids of Egypt.

"We know that architectural temples of relative sophistication-resembling Cambodian pagodas-exist at various places on the planet. We know that the dominant life form appears to be a six-meter animal resembling Earth's long-extinct Tyrannosaur family, after a fashion."

The sounds of soldiers taking action came across the conference call from the Hammerheads and the First Strike, and Ossa felt an empty pang of dread. Years before he had visited an archaeological site in Central America that had long before unearthed some Mayan ruins.

The archaeologists had discovered makeshift walls along with the temple steps, where they realized one of the Mayan Royal families had made its last stand against an opposing clan. There, stone per stone, as they had been laid, a Royal lineage of centuries had fought its last, bitter fight to the death.

Ossa, long a student of military history, remembered standing there, where that desperate struggle of blood and defeat had played out, and a proud line of warriors met their end as warriors often do. He couldn't help but feel a sense of recognition, looking out on the jungles of Siluria. Had once here, also, a proud group of beings made a final stand against the incomprehensible?

Surely, to Royal Mayans who had known century upon century of rule, the concept of utter defeat had been incomprehensible. Even to a rival clan. But how could the Predecessors, known to have had the galaxy as their domain for untold eons, have reacted when faced with the Bogies?

"On the double," one of the NCOs was saying.

All these eons; now the stage set again for a Bogie feast of souls?

Ossa eyed the holograms, screens, and data streams filling the room. With scars and a detached rugged disdain, he thought: Bring it. But there was only the clamoring of his troops.

"Now, you know that ain't natural," Yates said as the platoon approached the temples which Ossa had selected from orbital data beamed down from the First Strike. Ahead of them, in perfectly stacked blocks, as they made their way up the rise of amount, there stood a group of pylons. In ancient human sculpture, there were typically symbolic kouros figures; their vertical stature was sometimes little more than a fattened oblong, but they represented the figure as surely as if someone was standing guard. Ossa recognized the implications across species. Whoever had placed these here meant them to represent guardians.

"Get a man on those, I want molecular analysis right through the core-now!"

One of the men stepped forward, scanning. "Got no rads, Sir."

Ossa looked down at the rocky ground. No indication of pavement or a path. Vegetation twined and burst in the eternal slow-motion struggle for light and water that vegetation everywhere makes.

"Passive nano-technologies? Could the thing be reading the fields around it and sending data along with predetermined links via passive pathways?" he rumbled.

The soldier's bottom lip raised and his head nodded. "That's a distinct possibility. I would venture passive systems without moving parts-conduits for energy transfer-that would conceivably eradicate concerns of parts wearing out. No moving parts, very little wear. But these surfaces are worn pretty well.

Data transfer would have to be linear to the surface, and then be able to wear down without affecting its function."

"Keep looking, soldier. I think you'll find the nano links." Ossa smiled. Very quickly he was beginning to think on the scale, and in the manner in which a Predecessor might have operated. Nebula sized fortresses, eons for functional life spans of hardware; cosmic scale, geologic time. They may have been beaten back to a single nebula, but in their retreat, their minds had adjusted to a different form of controlling the dictates of the conflict.

In the intervening time, humanity had arisen in the galaxy.

So the remaining Predecessors had purchased time for themselves-now they had a new ally; Humanity. But would an alliance ever be formed? Ossa looked at Yates, Klaver, his troops moving up the hill toward more of the stone temples. They were an odd diplomatic crew, half of them brandishing dissers the other half science equipment.

At the top of the hill, their surprise was complete-beyond a tumble of stone, they moved into an area of temple far less worn. There were functioning fountains, patterns on tile walkways, colonnades and intact roofed palisades and pavilions; a palace. Several creatures of an amphibious quality lounged in and around the fountains. They looked at but generally seemed unmoved by the soldiers.

"I've seen these patterns at Predecessor ruins elsewhere in the galaxy, Sir." Klaver offered, running his hand along the pavement. They were indeed packed with nano circuitry. If this section of the temple still has functioning nano repair"-he broke off.

"That would explain the apparent lack of wear." Ossa finished.

No sign of the creators of this menagerie, just more clues as to the certainty of their origin.

"Take five. If you want to refresh yourselves, there are the fountains- keep your EVA fields on-even if you bathe. And don't drink the water!" he said.

Klaver looked concerned. "A little early to get comfortable, Sir?"

Ossa chuckled. "Look around officer. All our lives we've heard about what a deep dark devil's hole this nebula is-but in all reality it's the safest place in the galaxy. Everywhere else these life forms are extinct. Get comfortable? This place is looking more and more like it's destined to be our new command center with every passing moment. Unless we get an eviction notice from the previous occupants-and yes there is a good chance it is unoccupied-you're looking at headquarters, my man. Headquarters."

Klaver looked out over the island and sea afforded from the temple view. "Roger that".

Days passed, and the exploration team became at ease in the new paradise. Some of them took to making pets of a form of tame amphibian the size of a large dog and were occasionally out of uniform sunning themselves and relaxing in the gardens of the temples. There had to be more to the temples than met the eye-they were the only indication in an otherwise pristine and primordial paradise of an intelligent origin. Ossa had been right about the passive nano technologies-the stones were riddled with them. Alas, more data for study. But no sign of the creators acting in any way anything but large predators.

The First Strike identified packs of them from space and a couple of the teams observed them from a distance-the only species that appeared across the entire planet. Ossa's granite visage took on the dark shadow of concern as the species made no attempt to communicate. At least they had not attacked or otherwise interfered with the humans.

That, at least, was a good sign. The first time in his life being ignored could be construed as something positive, but Ossa's instincts told him there would be an encounter at some point in the near future, and he needed to gather as much knowledge as possible, or it would end up like Cortez encountering the indigenous peoples of the Western hemisphere-and this time he would be at the disadvantage of technology.

"Sir?" Klaver asked one evening as Ossa sat brooding by the fountains. Ossa shot him a reassuring smile. "Taking my temperature again Mr. Klaver?"

Klaver lifted his right hand in a gesture with two fingers pointing, darting this way and that. "Always watching," he replied.

"Good man." Ossa sighed. "What are they waiting for? They know we're here in force, and they certainly are in the same boat as us, pertaining to the extradimensionals."

Klaver nodded. "The Art of War, sir. They're controlling the time and place of events.

Reconnaissance is being done on us, too, we can assume. If they are indeed the last of the Predecessors, they've been holding out here for millions of our years. Apparently, they are masters of Time."

The two men looked out over the mounts of the islands and seas. Ever and always, seas on this world, and waves against shores unnumbered. Unnumbered at least by Mankind-but Ossa felt everything on Siluria was watched, however. Every animal, every tree-every insect, and microbial system.

This ark of a world, sheltering as it were an archival living memory of what had once been the teeming ecologies of the galaxy-it was more important than anything he had ever encountered across a thousand star systems.

The fact that the Overlords at Deneb had deemed it a mere curiosity shamed him.

"Masters of time and practicing The Art of War. What chance do you think humanity has in this scenario when such beings were reduced to a single nebula, from a previous pedestal as masters of the galaxy?" Ossa mused.

Klaver was scanning the horizon and jungle. Always watching. "Well," he said, "Mercurio fought one of the extradimensionals and lived. I suggest we begin broadcasting that encounter. Probably a good bet it will be received and spark their interest."

Electricity gleamed in Ossa's' grim smile. "That's brilliant. Get her done. Also, get us the tapes from that Leavel character's attack on Bandor Base.

If he was using Predecessor technology I'll venture he's already made First Contact, and has some alliance with these creatures running. Perhaps CCs' stupidity and atrocious behavior with those experiments ruled us out in the minds of these beings as a worthy ally."

"Morality? Leavel was storming a base to save his love. Perhaps they saw something nobler in his actions than CCs'. Honor, loyalty-love. Maybe he earned their respect." Klaver ventured into conjecture-but it was a line of thinking he knew Ossa was already following.

"You think?" Ossa eyed him sardonically. "I agree. That would mean if Leavel has revealed the alliance to the Trade Guild we're way behind the eight-ball on this one. If he hasn't, the question would be, why not?"

A couple of pterodactyl creatures kited the sky. "We've been following the trail of fossils across the galaxy since humanity first ventured into space. No, before that. The Extradimensionals appear to have hit even Earth at some point in the distant past-sixty-five million years ago I might suggest-the end of the Cretaceous. The higher the life form, the more likely they are to attack it, it would seem."

The question of the "morality" of the Predecessors came to a grim concern the next day with the discovery of what the team named the "people mushrooms." Recordings from the First Strikes' orbital reconnaissance showed the "People Mushrooms" had risen out of the swamps over a period of eight standard hours. How long they had gestated below was anyone's guess. It was Yates that had discovered them riding an air bike in a scouting run. In typical Yates fashion his recording, of the event was loaded with "Yatesisms".

The recording showed the landscape of Siluria flashing by as the soldier made a too quick survey, banging the air bike out to the max, when he should have had it running at half capacity.

Klaver gave him a stern look and shook his head. "What's with the speed, Yates? You burn that bike out, and it's coming out of your pay."

Then the air bike turned toward some pillar-like objects in the swamp. There were glowing oblong shapes all along their sides. As the Bike approached, the glowing oblongs revealed more detail. Inside were gestating creatures. Humanoid in form-too humanoid to be an accident of evolution. Their appearance smacked of Chimera genetic engineering.

The recording of Yates' voice came back over the replay. "Chowder-head-BOO-BOO! Dayung!"

There came the sound of his fumbling with his communications unit. "Hammerhead, this is Yates!

"Get ready for a playback of this scouting run. I just found something and it looks, well, wrong. Just wrong!"

Klaver looked to Ossa. "Still think our friendly neighborhood Predecessor remnant has morality issues?"

Ossa said nothing, but let the hologram "people mushrooms" speak for their morbid horrific selves.

"There's human genome in those things- I'd bet my rank on it," Klaver said icily.

Ossa sighed. Then he shrugged. We've been manipulating the genome for two thousand years. We were doing it here. This ain't going to be pretty, but let's get a Hammerhead out there ASAP.

"And Yates," Ossa snapped. Yates stood to attention. "If I see you spanking the dials on MY equipment again, you're going to be doing KP for a century, got it?"

Book Eight: Havoc Storm

Enter... Pandora
Rip, Sagittarius Galactic Spiral Arm

Winteroud Sole eyed the crew of the Taloned Sire with the cold grey reserve of someone who could reach in and take the answers, but whose iron discipline and principles were trained by a lifetime of pattern.

"I think now I need a rundown on the dinosaurs," he said coolly.

The memory of their recent encounter with the extra-dimensional hung in the piloting cabin of the Sire like the fifth persona.

"Siluria." Vince finally said, deflated and detached. "I had gone there determined to rescue Leyla."

Winteroud felt the memories rush at him then. He felt Vince's overwhelming regret of having mixed Leyla up in a smuggling venture that had turned out to be a set up; of having once again held everything that was dear, and having it slip through his fingers as his pride and lust for money had driven him off his chosen path at the University world of Luxus.

"Yes," Winteroud said involuntarily. "But it was never really Leyla at all."

There was no Leyla.

Yet there she was.

"We used an old military trick of shielding a landing vehicle in a faux asteroid skin with nano shields. It worked," a brief smile flashed across his face at the memory in spite of himself. "I sailed then toward the base where she was a prisoner."

Sagamore's chest rose as he held back a comment. He hadn't trusted Leyla from the first, and he'd only been in the room with her as a hologram. Sagamore's instincts for treachery were better than Vince's. He watched his Captain's back many, many times. Winteroud felt Sagamore's anger at himself for not having followed through on that hunch. But it had been Sagamore and Millin who had been taken by the smuggling ruse to begin with. His culpability smothered any wisecrack.

"The dinosaurs, well...they're not dinosaurs at all. They're sentient life forms. They constructed Siluria in a nebula, much as we created the worlds of the Pleiades-terraforming freshly formed planets and then importing and establishing the ecologies."

Vince couldn't know that even as he spoke his narrative his memories were flooding Winteroud's mind. With each sentence background, images and sounds-everything he had experienced and all he had associated with it were following after, like waves along a shore.

"The last of the Predecessors," Winteroud said suddenly.

Millin involuntarily closed his eyes. Born fighting, he more than anyone in the room sensed in his genetically engineered self the raw contest of species that was upon them; and their disadvantage. "If the Predecessors were stamped to a remnant, hiding and near-forgotten, what chance have we?"

Vince ignored the interruption. "One of them approached me; an ordinary Trade Guildsman, outlaw and trying a jail break-suddenly I was the emissary for the whole fraccin Human race. He took me into their underground-it's how they maintain the illusion of primordial wilderness and scattered temples. They have everything under the surface. Cities, factories, computer networks. Everything that runs the planet. It's like a theme park. All the mechanicals are concealed."

"They preserved what they could from the onslaught of the Bogies." Winteroud, again, finishing his thoughts.

Vince cocked an eyebrow. "Well, why don't you just 'read' me?"

Winteroud gave him a Devil-may-care smirk. "Don't worry, I am. But it works better if you tell the events as you experienced them."

Finally, Sagamore could avoid wisecracking no more; "Yeah Captain, it works better if you tell the events as you experienced them. Don't you know that?"

A moment of levity broke the weight of civilization's destiny from the small cadre of companions, and laughter filled the cabin. The men let the hum and flash of technology fill the silence for a moment. The Sire laughed with them.

It was Gibbon that next spoke: "It's a testament to their brilliance that such an endeavor has persisted across all these millennia." The levity that had delivered them from the reality of their present condition evaporated like a ghost.

Vince's scarred face darkened. "Yes, well, the one that approached me played me recordings of the era when they were decimated by the Bogies. It wasn't a pretty picture. They call themselves 'Tees', and the one I interacted with was 'Leph'."

"That would be 'Leph-Tee'. "Sagamore interjected. "You traveled across the galaxy, and discovered a lost race, and the guy's name was 'Lefty'. You realize that's funny."

Millin shook his head, "Can we get on with saving the Universe now, please?"

Gibbon raised his chromium head. "Or you could call him 'Mr. T'" he said.

The four humans looked at him uncomprehendingly. The android had just made a joke, but they had no historical database frame of reference to Twentieth-Century Earth Television Media for that particular character.

"Mr. T. He was in a television show." The android explained uncomfortably.

"What Millennia?" Sagamore said dryly.

Vince put up his hands.

"Sag, now you got the robot making jokes. Can we continue?"

Everyone nodded their consent.

Vince looked to each in turn. "No more comments until I'm finished. That thing we just had a run-in with at the Yellow Jaguar could pop its pretty face back in our dimension any time, and go for a second round with us, aye?"

He allowed the seriousness of the situation to let its dark reality fill the cabin like death. When the cabin was once again filled properly with dread, he smiled his inscrutable grin. Happy to be skirting the edge of black oblivion again, he continued. "So Leph told me he had encountered primates on a world that fended off the Bogies-just like we did this evening. He feels humanity may have the stuff it takes to give these...devils a run for their money."

"We're primates too. Conceivably something in our genetic makeup is different from theirs-the Tees are, well, like you said, kind of reptilian lizard things. The Bogies take them down every time."

"So we're, like, going to save the Predecessors?" Sag asked with a tinge of outrage.

"That's the spirit!" Gibbon said.

Vince nodded. He didn't know how to answer, it seemed an impossible contradiction. Every human born since interstellar travel had been raised in awe of the relics the Predecessors had left across the galaxy. The concept of Humanity saving them seemed like a lead dirigible.

Winteroud straightened his back and squared his shoulders like a man about to pass an unpleasant judgment. The three Guildsmen tensed in anticipation as Winteroud's face went strange with emotion. "There's more," he said. "I don't believe the Tees showed you everything. For some reason, they've held back something. I felt it in the being we experienced at the Yellow Jaguar. There's another part to this-the Bogie, it wants to cross over."

Bitterly Millin leaned forward and shot him a look of challenge, "Isn't that what it just did? Cross over?" he asked sharply. "You mean it didn't get all the way over? Sure makes an impression from across dimensions."

Winteroud shut his eyes and breathed deeply. "It's a horrid being-unlike anything I have ever felt, in all the life forms I've ever encountered. The Bogies-they're literally addicted to the horror and fear they create in their victims-like a shabby drug addict, they crave it. They've consumed whole regions of the universe. They're not even good farmers, so to speak, they don't even leave seed stock for future consumption."

"You got all that from the encounter?" Vince asked.

Winteroud drilled him an affirmative stare. "And more. It wants to cross over into our dimension completely."

"Leave wherever it came from?" Sagamore queried.

"Yes," Winteroud said icily.

Vince looked expectantly. "So…what will they be like when they're fully crossed over?"

Winteroud's eyes glazed, they were two dark open graves.

Somewhere in a deep, dark broken corner of Vincent's soul, his younger self wailed with horror, sadness, and longing for Leyla.

Leyla-Jane moved through the upper rooms of the Yellow Jaguar with a cataclysmic awareness of the shadow that now hovered behind her every thought and action. The thing from…elsewhere. She had relished the power it had offered her, coming to her thoughts when she had gone out to the haunted lakes upon her return to Rip. Having purchased a clone of herself she'd paid dearly-a fortune-to be young again. To have Vincent. Every treasure and every wonder they'd shared he risked in a foolish gambit of pride and stupidity when "No-deal DePaulo" showed up with black market goods and the promise of easy money.

It had been a warm afternoon as Vince had made his way to the water-ported Taloned Sire, his precious ship of rogues. Yet for her, it had been as if a Rip winter had fallen. There could be no more evidence than that departure, in her mind, that her love for him, that everything she had accomplished and ventured-turning back the hands of time itself-had been for a fool, and a cad. She had peered at the Sire breaking skyward that day with a depth of disdain she had rarely felt for any man; and days before she had relished his every gesture.

When she had turned from that sight, Harry had been there. Smiling, tall, confident.

"Pretty athletic," he said calmly.

She had looked at him aghast. "What did you just say?" she asked in disbelief.

That grin. The white uniform. The silver rose.

"You know what I said, and you know…what you want now is a glass of apple wine, and someone to share it with. Let's go." He held out his white sleeved arm for her to take.

She laughed so hard for a moment she thought she might break even his glassy confidence. Yet she took his arm, and it was strong, hard, and amazingly warm. She thought she was playing them both when Harry took her to Chrysler city, and she had gone out to surprise Vince with a lie about shopping-only after Harry showed up to deliver her from a CC sentence on Ophelia, did she finally suspect in fact that she was being played in a game of Harry's creation.

That grin. The white uniform. The silver rose. You know what I said, and you know…what you want now…

She returned to Rip with a credit jack he gave her and parted with a look of shared betrayals. Harry smiled, even then. They were too much alike. She resumed her operations at the Yellow Jaguar with a vicious vengeance. Her reputation only expanded in her absence and mysterious return. Harry had broadcast the arrest over all of the known space in real-time. Bang a gong-the she-devil queen of darkness walked back into Herkiestown without a scratch and Empire be damned.

Every scoundrel on the planet must have been blabbing about her. Perhaps that was how the thing had found her. She knew it could read minds, after a fashion. It must have trolled through her narrative and found just the steel it would take worlds afar with.

334

Her grim little tale of struggle and determination.

Everything she had done over so many years-every calculated move to power-had led on, and on, to that moment when she had been selected to be its companion. Or perhaps it was her affiliation with Vince; the one who had crawled into the trap it was held in? Half of the thing was time stasised to the Taloned Sire-and Vince unlocked it. Had it read his mind even then, and seen her?

No matter.

So many years before, all this fear and uncertainty had stalked her childhood. Her father had returned from the war with Khita, and had taken to drink. The family was ever and always on the edge of confusion and uncertainty. She knew what she wanted-power, security, and comfort. Love was for losers. Then Vince had come into her life, she an aged crone, and he as dashing and bold a man as she had ever known. She'd worked her plan only to have him scuttle it.

Returning to Rip she found that none of her triumphs consoled her. Even her new youth. Her fears welled up within her like she was a schoolgirl again. Uncertainty even her gold could not assuage. Mottled fears with shabby mouths and desperate whispers that haunted her every waking hour and careened through her sleepless nights like the event horizon of a black hole. An emptiness so profound, that the entire galaxy seemed to her a ship of smelly fools gibbering through the dark, cold ocean of night into a looming field of icebergs.

"Own them all!" A voice said to her one grimy night as the fools caroused and drank themselves silly in the nightclub below her.

There was no one else in the room.

"Who's there?" she snapped, but even then she knew. She could feel it moving through the air, through the walls, through the music.

"Humanity is such a pathetic sweep of grunting pig-monkeys. I will make you a goddess; I will show you the dimensions, and all the gleaming heavens of the multi-verse and you shall surely never die."

She was not afraid. Her chin had lifted. "Tell me more…".

It had done all it had promised. Several attempts on her life by rivals were squashed with delightful scenes of them fed to it, the sight of the rats jabbering into madness. Every enemy, every contender-every murderous leach on the planet smacked down to jelly. Rip was her world now, and she enjoyed the company of every V.I.P. in every port with a sheen. She was thinking of expanding onto the other Outworlds when Vince had come back.

Looking for Jane.

Why? Had some part of him known, always known, who and what she was, though the evidence denied it? Of course. Not consciously, but somewhere in his mind, he knew, and he had loved her anyway. Thus his gamble with the last smuggling ring-somehow he had almost expected her to understand?

Too many questions; all she knew was that even now, as he had stood with the extra-dimensional devil conjuring up visions of madness, in a pit of ruin on a world he had staked everything to escape, he had stood there with love in his eyes. She had given him ruin and madness, loneliness, regret and betrayal and still, that inscrutable smile showed loyalty. Once a friend, once a lover-ever loyal after his strange fashion. She could hate him in a thousand ways, but for that. He would go down with his ship, no surrender, no white flag.

She felt a strange disturbance in the air then.

The thing was reading her. Something in her thoughts had shaken it; she could feel its dread. It dreaded Vince. Why? Because he would die for her.

The quality of self-sacrifice disgusted it, horrified it.

How curious.

"You must deny him." It said.

She chuckled, an ugly chortle of a hiss. "I've denied him a thousand times."

335

"Bring me a meal." It said.

"I'll have one of the rouges reveling downstairs sent up" she replied coldly.

"NO!"

She stepped back and frowned. "What then?"

"A Law man. Someone tall and strong. Someone who has never known defeat, or doubt, or reversal," its voice was hilarious with glee and anticipation.

She laughed. "Where would I find such a man?"

"I have one in mind."

"I see. Why this particular man?"

"Because he thinks he is a good man. He thinks he is a strong man. He believes his work has a purpose. I want to show him doubt. I want to show him meaninglessness, and chaos, and the mocking shadows of his days like leaves from brittle fern-wood in the ice, blowing across a dark lake where everyone he knows is dust, and all disorder reigns.

"And then, I wish to become him, a man of authority and reputation no longer with a diamond soul, but with my heart and mind."

She cast on a shawl. "Where?"

"Come."

When the fire wagons arrived, all brass and bells, Officer Nicholas Nash was standing among the burning buildings, his cloak waving in the firestorm.

His hat was missing and a vague, lost stare seemed to possess him. Several of the firemen pulled him away from the flames at last, shocked themselves at the speed which had consumed the building. Nash was obviously in shock, so his strange detached and confused manner was not noted with any import.

"I couldn't save them," he said, "I couldn't save any of them".

Behind him, in the rubble of the flames and ruins, corpses could be made out with an ugly pop and hissing whine, as they burst in the fires.

Suddenly then, through the smoke, along the icy cobbles, came a gilded sled-carriage pulled by four imported white mamonths. Jane Veronica. The carriage door opened with the well-oiled and finely tooled hinges (surely imported by the Star Trading Guild). Inside she was lit with a glittering array of glow tubes and jewels.

Nash looked at her with an odd familiarity. Everyone knew who she was, but surely Nash had never consorted with her sort. The firemen watched in disbelief as she held out her hand, and he stepped forward and into the gilded cage of a carriage. She saw their confused faces, turning from the rancid holocaust, and then back to the strange unlikely pair-the Law man with a reputation for hardheaded resoluteness, and slithering seductress of softness and repose.

They thought they heard her say, "A tidy night of juicy delights?" but surely that was a trick of the wind.

At last, she leaned out, 'I'll take care of him now, thank you gentlemen" and the mamonths were off, and the sled rushing forward through the smoke.

No one noticed the driver never signaled the mamonths.

At that very moment, across the city and past the harbor, out on the ice and the darkness, Vince Leavel was repeating his question to Winteroud Sole. "What will they be like when they're fully crossed over?"

Sole pulled his eyes out from the grave, "Like us" his voice cold steel, "like whomever it is they possess".

David's Reprise had registered in the Rip system out of Earth, but the Trade Guild suspected there was more to the story than official registries were offering. Either way, independent Traders were more or less uncommon in the Sagittarius Arm of the Galaxy, and high-end Art dealers, well; they were generally a little farther up the food chain than to be sporting about the Outworlds looking for curios. Sole was the ace in the hole in this little surprise scenario, working with the Guild now, he could do a little voodoo for them and pull out some answers.

David's Reprise complied, oddly enough, by planting its happy hull not a hundred yards from the Lord Kesey. Then, without a care or a fear in the world, its Captain, Lisa Lynne Sulla, strode off on the ice with a couple of androids at her side. She was walking with a swagger carrying a little purse in her hand; retro deco of course. Watching her on the big holoscreen of the Sire, each man took a different assessment of her to comment.

"Nice petard," Sag said and stuck his chin out in approval.

"Good on the ice," Millin commented.

Vince just gave a knowing smile.

Winteroud frowned. "There's more here than meets the eye. I can't get a sense of it at this distance, but I'm feeling-layers."

Gibbon chimed in, "Those are antique droids like myself. She has a great deal of wealth and taste".

The humans all looked at each other.

Sagamore burst out laughing.

Gibbon looked at him with surprise.

Then at each of the other humans; "What?"

"I never programmed him for humility." Winteroud offered quietly.

"Gentlemen," Vince said flatly, I think we should go welcome Captain Sulla to Rip, personally."

Sag lit up. "She might need a little more back-up than those two droids in this town," he said.

Winteroud smiled knowingly. "Probably not, I think. But the Captain is right on one account. We should go meet her."

"Suit up boys. We're going on the offensive" Vince said.

The men moved into action heading off to various parts of the frigate to gather various weapons and jackets. Making their way down a gangway Sag said to Millin, "Want to lay odds she makes straight for the Yellow Jaguar?"

"You're on. Ten to one she doesn't."

"One Hundred credits?"

"You'll be paying me a grand" Millin countered.

"My psychic powers tell me she's on a mission."

"Psychic powers, my blue fanny. We know she's up to something more than scoping for relics."

"I'm getting vibes." Sag cocked an eyebrow.

"I'm getting a grand. Keep your vibes." Millin stepped into his cabin and checked the charge on his disser.

Sag hung in the doorway for a moment. "Maybe the Guild isn't the only organization that knows there's a Bogie on this planet."

"From what Sole was saying the Bogie is going to look like a person in short order."

Sag snorted, "Well it sure as the super-massive black hole in the center of the galaxy ain't her. She just got here."

"Want to lay odds she goes for me before you?"

"Ten to one?"

"You'll be paying me a grand." Millin snickered. Sag just stood there.

Millin looked at him questioningly, "We going to your cabin to get your piece or what?"

Sag pointed to his boot. "Never leave your bunk without it" and winked.

Of course, the Art Dealer bypassed the wharf bars and warehouses along the port side and made a b-line straight for the retail districts. With winter in full strangling freeze, there were not cart vendors. All the activity was in the great Market Arcade, whose giant stone arches were full of carved mamonths and various stone ornaments.

She paused outside the entrance and made a fuss of having her droids record and document the architecture. Sole tried to get a reading at that point but found the street roaring with too many quantum echoes. Gibbon stepped up and steadied Winteroud as he stumbled with the shock and at that point, Sulla turned and observed the little group.

"Where did you find that droid!" She exclaimed and moved toward them.

Winteroud straightened, and discreetly adjusted his muffles so the echoes would no longer beat at his brain. He faced her now with no empathic abilities, just a man meeting a strikingly lovely and mysterious woman. He felt his disadvantage as if one of the sculptures above had come slamming down on him. He determined to move ahead with her on his own simple human presence. He smiled through the racking pain in his head.

"That, my dear lady, would be in the Tarantula Nebula. There was an old mining colony that had been all but abandoned. I restored him with loving care-and I dare say a few upgrades-a purist one cannot be with an active service droid." Winteroud replied.

"E. Gibbon, Mam." The droid curtsied.

Sagamore snorted.

"Winteroud Sole." He bowed.

"She offered her hand, "Lisa Sulla. I've read your work Mr. Sole-quite an unexpected honor to meet you out here. Doing research?"

"Yes, yes. I'm working on a survey encyclopedia of the Outworlds and their histories. But I forget myself. May I introduce you to my companions from the Trade Guild."

Introductions went around. She made no note of the Sire's crew having also its own bit of fame-a wise discretion, as "infamy" would be more accurate, and of course, they were wanted men in the Empire. She did, however, give a slight expression of surprise, which indicated acknowledgment of the situation's strangeness-a crew of Trade Guild protected outlaws accompanying a famous historian.

"Shall we?" Winteroud gestured toward the arcade.

"Of course-dreadfully cold this season on this world!"

They stepped inside, and the warmth noise and skylights of the arcade engulfed the little group. Everyone in the arcade immediately paused to note them, and then politely resumed indifference. Nearly all the shops were full of foodstuffs, but there were the occasionally manufactured goods, and that was where they all pretended attention-she and they both continuing the fiction they were merely seeking exotic handmade trade goods to sell in the empire at outrageous prices.

Thus the afternoon passed into evening, and Vince suggested they all take an expensive dinner at "The Cloister". They rented an ostentatious Mamonth sled-carriage and it clomped and slid through the icy Fernwood Avenue mansion row, higher and higher, until it came upon the restaurant. There was an enormous mural of Rip wildlife in a primitive, but colorful, style along one of the walls of an ancient converted mansion. They stepped out to gaslight and uniformed greeters.

Into the foyer-and instantly Vince's rationale for selecting the place became evident. It was decorated, from ceiling to floor, with antique Rip curios. Lisa beamed with delight, and Winteroud shot Vince a wink as if to say "Good call". Signed photographs of various famous performers were included in the mix, a fascinating array of faces smiling back from centuries past when the planet was even more isolated from the mainstream of human affairs than it was presently.

The *maître d'* intentionally took them through each room of the sprawling establishment, in a grand show of pomp. Each room had massive fireplaces, and was decorated with a different aspect of Rip's cultural legacies; first was the Mamonth hide tapestries decorated with ornate fish dyes, then Fernwood sculptures, ceramics, glassware, metallurgical objects, and lastly the crystal and mirror room where the most recent imports from the stars were each finished with local handcrafts-a strange glimmering of phosphorescent high-tech lighting and vernacular trappings.

"You've been holding out on me, Captain Leavel. This place is amazing." Winteroud chimed as they each took a high-backed hand-carved and gilded seat at the table. The androids stood like butlers at the corners.

The enigmatic grin. "I stand corrected, Mr. Sole. For my defense, however, I present the Lady's beauty as having pressed us, where angels fear to tread."

Lisa blushed a bit. Then she laughed, "Blaming it on the ladies? For shame Captain, for shame. A strange twist of chivalry there, somehow."

Huge loaves of nut-bread appeared, and fern mead in hefty pewter vessels sweating with ice. Then complimentary broiled smelt-like fish. Then menus on engraved mamonth hide were offered. Vince made recommendations to each. They ordered and thus began a long night of conversation-and more fern mead.

Lisa's conversation flowered with her knowledge of the arts until she realized with a solid certainty that David Omm had not contrived her role as an Art dealer. She had been, indeed, exactly that. This became apparent whenever conversations drifted into art movements after Thirty-one Ninety-seven. She knew none of them, but she could speak with eloquence and knowledge on every aspect of Art before that date.

Winteroud noted the strange ambiguity and the inexplicable absence of quantum streams that pegged her as being very young as if only recently born. The contrast between her apparent physical age and her mental frames of reference was disconcerting, but he was a man and one look at her dispelled common sense and prudence. She was celestially beautiful, elementally sensuous, and intellectually exciting. He found himself wishing he had chosen better finery for the expedition.

In all the hours of fascinating anecdotes, curious insights, and Star-set galactic conversation, however, it would be the overheard talk of the wait staff that would galvanize Vincent's attention. A waiter and a busboy were chatting during a lull in their activities about a recent fire in Herkiestown, and how a relatively well known and respected Police Captain had strangely disappeared at the event with the Notorious Jane from the Yellow Jaguar.

Vincent's dread was palpable.

As the revelers made their way back to their respective ships and the lovely art dealer and her androids seen safely aboard their yacht, Sagamore asked him about what he heard. Vince explained-and his foreboding was shared by Sole.

"We go back to the Jaguar tomorrow," Vince told his crew as they entered the Sire. "And we're bringing a gravity bomb."

Millin stepped back, "Captain, a gravity bomb will take out three city blocks-even with these deep stone walls."

Vince looked at him with desperate culpability.

339

"Better three city blocks of casualties than a whole planet of corpses. We have to find that thing and we have to kill it."

In the morning not even Sag was making jokes as they armed the gravity bomb. The thought that a lot of innocent people were going to spend their last moments in the clutches of a small singularity was particularly grim. As the bomb imploded, sucking three city blocks of buildings and people suddenly into its black vortex, they would find themselves lunging toward a miniature black hole, with time slowing down for them as they approached its event horizon.

For them, an eternity would pass, suspended in a fury of chaos and confusion. No one knew exactly how victims of such a weapon perceived their death. There never could be any survivors to describe the effect.

In all reality the fact that the Sire could even get such a weapon on the world was disturbing. But when they launched their small air car from the Sire and flew a broad quick arc over the city, Vince's dismay and shame hung heavy in the cockpit once again.

Sag didn't have to kick the door in this time. The place was wide open and full of Cops. Millin stayed in the aircar with the bomb, his disser grimly hidden under a jacket and pointed in the direction of the swarming police.

Vince and Sag approached the door and the police looked over in recognition of their Trade Guild uniforms.

"No entertainment today gents, this place is closed pending an investigation," one of the higher ranking detectives said, palms first.

Vince and Sag could smell death and blood oozing from the nightclub.

"Guild prerogative-we need to know what happened here." Vince snapped back in a challenge. Sag shot a look to Millin who gave a slight nod.

Kill them all if you have to.

The detective paused for a moment, unused to challenges to his authority, but realized after a fashion the Trade Guild was a quasi-official agency-a vital one, in all reality, and they were going to find out sooner or later. He sighed, shrugged his shoulders.

"That's the thing, Guildsman. None of this makes sense. One of our officers was at the scene of a fire a couple of days back and for no apparent reason, happily walked off with a known racketeer. He didn't report for work the next day so we sent one of his buddies from the force over here to get his fanny back to work, and out of, well-bad company.

"When he arrived here, he found this mess. Over a hundred mutilated corpses in various states of mutilation. You don't want to go in there."

Over a hundred mutilated corpses.

You don't want to go in there.

"Was the officer among the dead?" Vince asked pointedly, quietly.

The detective gave him an ashamed and confused glance. "No. And neither was the racketeer. A star yacht departed the port last night-her registry. Her accounts have been cleaned out. If they're innocent of this mess, well, they're making a bad go of it. It doesn't look like they've much fear of being caught-they're leaving a trail of dead and clues like billboards that say "Come get me.""

"What do you mean?" Sagamore barked.

"What I mean is the yacht registered its destination before it left. Even their destination makes them suspect; Phlegra Station in the Hercules Cluster. Outlaw Heaven, Pirate Colony," he wheezed with a detached sadness-apparently he had known and respected the officer in question.

At least they're off Rip, Vince thought with an ironic relief.

"Can you have your Department send me a data file on the suspects, so I can run it through Guild channels? I'm from the Taloned Sire, we're out on the ice in the harbor.

340

The detective looked at him almost sheepishly, "I know who you are, Captain Leavel. It will be sent over before you get back. Our guy's name is Nash, Nicholas Nash. You know Jane, I presume. She recently had a skin job done and implanted her brain in a clone of herself, in case you didn't know, so don't expect to be looking for the old Jane, this is Jane 2X."

Vince turned to walk away, made a few steps toward the aircar when the detective called out, "Phalen!"

Vince paused but didn't look back. No one had called him by that name in a very, very long time.

The detective called out again, "He's one of ours. Try and bring him back alive-if it's at all possible".

Try? Detective, he's already gone.

Compelled by some strange inexplicable urgency, Winteroud brought Lisa Sulla into his confidence. He teleconferenced to her star yacht and told her his theories and insights regarding the murders at the Yellow Jaguar, played a recording of the event with Jane and the Bogie, and waited for her to politely tell him she would be leaving Rip immediately, and wanted nothing to do with any of them. She did not. She was riveted the entire time, and threw her support behind him-financially if he needed, which he didn't, and otherwise. He ran up an image of Nash as well for her-at least in the scheme of things she now knew what their enemies looked like.

"We're making History, Mr. Sole, rather than writing about it, or selling it off a gallery wall on Mulberry street. This is the stuff heroism is made of." She waxed poetic. She sounded like a kid off to her first summer camp excursion rather than a woman who had just been told they were at the advent of an age of dread and horror.

"Nightmares, my dear. Nightmares," he replied abruptly and with a tone of deep seriousness, "Keep a hypo of sedative in your purse-the things gain strength from your fear. If you should have an encounter, sedate yourself immediately, and call us.

"I believe now that it has taken up residence in Nash; it's 'grounded' in our dimension now, and can't merely flit about space and appear at will. There may be others. One can't be too careful," he warned his voice choking with uncertainty and concern.

For the sake of her professional pride, she refused to reveal the depth of her fears. One of the tapes Omm had given her had already yanked her hard out of the paradigm that she was at the top of the food chain. The tapes from the CC air corps encountering the Bogies were worse than what Sole had recorded with his droid at the Yellow Jaguar. Omm's recordings were Hive mind perceptions.

She had experienced the mind-bending approach of the things through that tape long before Sole's encounter. The fear, as such, did not fade-it seemed to curl, and linger, and reappear in one's memory like an ugly revelation, in bits and pieces, like recollections from a drunken evening the next morn.

The tape she had of Winteroud at the ice mines at Bethlehem, discovering a lost civilization of ancient humans on a distant world, remained a piece of the puzzle that nagged her.

There had to be a connection.

Who were those humans and how did they get there? Mankind's evolutionary record on Earth sealed any question of Human origins millennia ago on Earth, full stop, so the humans under the ice had to have been brought there.

Only the Predecessors possessed such an ability. Yet even that certainty was suspect-it had been assumed that the Predecessors had long been extinct at that point in time. Why would the Predecessors do such a thing? Were they farming humans? Did they show up in the night, and haul them off to canning factories, or throw them into jungles to hunt for sport?

She thought not. Meat vats where a highly efficient way of creating protein food-stuffs. Sport then? A hunting preserve? That was more likely.

341

Somehow it didn't fit. A zoo? A gene pool? Certainly, an endeavor of that magnitude implied a serious purpose. Why Kunger?

Azure Thule 4186 orbits a neutron star in the middle of Palomar 12, a globular cluster in the constellation Capricornus that belongs to the halo of the galaxy. Kunger would have been as far out of the mix as one could have gotten without breaching the great void.

Deneb IV:
Fortunato and Omm 6X

Tamara Fortunato had long seen General Ossa approach his meetings with Omm 6X with an uncharacteristic dread. She knew the Overlord himself was contained somewhere in the vast building perhaps, encased in a vat of sustaining nutrients in a form of animated suspension, and his mind was expanded, trans-humanized into additional databanks such that the being she would encounter was virtual construct. Once inside the building, she would pass through arrays of MERGE technology that would translate her nervous system directly into Omm's world.

Ossa had only warned her that it would be surreal-and dangerous. He had trusted her Lunar background to deal with the exigencies of the moment as she would read them. Bureaucratic minds ever after a fashion, life on Luna had long been one of dealing with their irrational entrenchments. The trick was to follow the game, learn the rules, then learn how to break them with impunity.

Fortunato was a striking figure of a woman. In her combat boots, decked out in her flight suit, she was downright intimidating. "Freezer Queen" her underlings called her-behind her back. Yet even the Freezer Queen was awed by the towers of Deneb IV. From space, she had gone to the bridge and looked at the planet from orbit-a mottled orb of endless interwoven intricate patterns whose image everyone knew from virtreal tapes from a child. The actual globe itself conveyed a sense of power and import, of human mastery that humbled the individual.

Since wiping out the Arcturian Colonies, the Air Corps had raised itself as a separate caste of warriors. Engagement with the Hive Mind proved inoperable in combat. Like the Spartans millennia before, she was bred, raised, trained, and selected for service from birth. Lunarians of the caste, however, rarely remained within the system of Sol-they had come to be an elite even among the Corps. As Earth had retained its sole and unique place in human experience being Mankind's homeworld, so Luna had taken a unique place among all the worlds of Humanity as the first world beyond home to be mastered.

The first piece of the Celestial realm mankind had fought to make its own, there the protective womb of Earth was but a vision in a dark and irredeemably hostile sky-the reality of the universe. Low gravity, airless arid wastelands, rabid radiation; the list of hostility was perfect, and still humanity had come, clever, patient determined. By the time of Tamara's birth, it was, in fact not unlike Deneb. A globe enveloped with the architecture of man's will. She had read of and experienced in virtreel, the wastelands of the frontier-but her Luna was a place of urban design; hundreds of stories deep and high, thousands upon thousands of square kilometers sprawl.

-Princess Clairissa Maggio, Caldris, "Deneb IV, Empire of Light and Darkness."

Stepping from the air limo and taking a glance at the similar construction of Deneb's endless cityscape, she realized Ossa had chosen the perfect person to meet his superior, the ignoble and bizarre Omm 6X. Sighing, she tightened her shoulders and lifted her chin in unconscious defiance and strode into the antechamber.

It was filled with butterflies. A dozen of them flitting about in the air-*human butterflies*. She almost broke out laughing; the banality of evil, she realized. One descended toward her.

"Welcome, Officer Fortunato. I trust your voyage was safe and secure. The Hive Mind welcomes our noble warriors from the stars," the android said.

"Thank you," Tamara offered, in as courteous a tone as she could muster. Her underlying contempt for the corruption she saw in most of civilian life was thick-and ironically, she realized, so too as strong her will to defend the same civilian reality. The military servant, she thought briefly, superior in every way to those served. The essential corruption, stupidity, and sheer folly of civilian life was not for her "to question why". Such absurdities seemed the price of free will. She was grateful for the disciplines of space and the air corps.

She followed the arty droid down the Halls of Omm 6X and watched as the walls shifted, morphing with each step. Ossa had once told her the Overlord had a penchant for late Imperial Rome and Twenty-first Century America-two great Republics that had decayed into bizarre tyrannical parodies of themselves, before collapsing in horrific chaos. Did Omm seek to keep in front of himself then an ever-present reminder of the potential fate of such empires?

Not this time. As Tamara stepped forward the walls melted away, indeed, but not into distant America or Rome. Omm had created something special for her; New Haven City before the fireballs. She was standing suddenly in a forward viewing room in a winged craft. The two viewing windows were tinted and curved- like giant eyes, and all about her the carefully sculpted and planned hanging gardens of New Haven City and its skyscrapers and stacked buildings by the edge of the Atlas sea. She recognized it instantly from Military History classes. Of course, everything she was witnessing now was presently in ruins.

For a moment, seeing the Colony alive and majestic, her breath rushed in sudden awe and held there. That wild and unpredictable people-*the Galaxy had never been the same without them.*

"Hello Officer Fortunato," a voice came from behind her and she turned away from the spectacle of New Haven for a moment to observe a youngish beautiful man.

He was tall, perfectly sculpted in a tailored suit with dashing locks of wavy blonde hair and piercing, ice-blue eyes. His smile spoke of joy and laughter; life as it was meant to be in perfect innocence and beauty-mankind before the fall of Adam. His warmth seemed boundless, a force of nature that could run on and on, until the stars burned out and then, with a whim, light them all again, for fun.

She was sure Omm had never shown this aspect of himself to General Vega Ossa.

"David Omm." He said and held out his hand like long lost family.

She shook his hand, stepped back, and saluted properly.

"Please, at ease. Fly with me a while. You recognize of course New Haven City before the war? Spectacular, yes?"

The winged vehicle arced and rolled; perfect in their gravity bubble, a stemmed glass of wine wouldn't have felt a ripple-it was the world and the city which appeared to move. They were the center of reality, and all the universe moved about them. A common enough effect in bubbled vehicles, yet somehow now a luxurious novelty of human ingenuity.

"Yes," she replied awkwardly. David Omm had been the ambassador on a faux peace mission, even as the Air Corps had stolen across the gateways in a massive first strike. *The First Strike her command ship had been named for.* She stood in the presence of history. He smiled back at her with a boyish charm and warmth.

I am the deceiver of billions, and unto the fire, I have led them. I smile at you now.

She straightened involuntarily. "Sir."

A white-coated steward came and set a tray of food before her, bowed and stepped back and away to the interior of the ship. Omm glanced at the steward as he left, "Sentient program. He thinks he's real. After the flight tonight he will go down into the city and meet up with other members of the airline at a dance hall.

"He's in love with one of the other programs, and she too does not know that they are ghosts in a world no longer. It's a dream I have. My little New Haven city as it was. I come here sometimes and-" he stopped, looked at her from lowered eyes with a naughty boy look, "but I digress".

She looked at the food.

"Go ahead. …no calories" he said and shrugged.

No calories.

She held back a laugh, gave him a grateful smile instead, and stepped forward selecting a piece of meat wrapped artfully in a sautéed vegetable. The Bureaucrat had named his game then- *let's remember what I have murdered, over a fine dinner and in a delightful winged aeroplane-* and so she would play the game, and play with élan.

The food was delightful beyond anything she had ever eaten of course, and for many minutes there was only his smile, the delicious fare, and the towers of New Haven City gliding past in the baby-blue sky all beneath the incomparable star of Arcturus.

"And now, good officer, your report. How goes Ossa's' game?"

In spite of herself, she found he'd disarmed her to a degree. Touring the scene of his crimes over dinner shouldn't have put her at ease, she knew, and she wondered whether she was being influenced by the Hive Mind. No, Omm 6X was a bit of a rebel himself, she realized.

He had his agenda-separate and distinct from his fellow Overlords. He, like Earth and Luna, was unique even among that caste of ancient Trans-humans. The Hive Mind would not intrude here. Certainly not for this report.

"General Ossa sent me to inform you that he has moved an attack group into the Silurian Nebula, and they are establishing Command posts on Siluria. He believes the Nebula is filled with a construct of a time field that shifts and prevents the Extradimensionals from penetrating it. Siluria appears to be an ark of sorts, a terraformed world created by the remnant of the Predecessor race, who he believes was nearly brought to extinction by the Extradimensionals in the very distant past" she said curtly, and then gave a crisp professional silence to observe his reaction.

He raised his eyebrows. "Well, that's a mouthful. I imagine he's right on all counts. We've suspected as much, though we didn't have the sense to follow through on it beyond using their construct as a convenient place to commit further crimes against Humanity-the infamous Bandor Base of which I'm sure you're well versed" and then he folded his arms and considered the city.

He grinned wearily, "The standard thinking on encountering races more advanced than ourselves has long been that it will be a disaster for us. Such is modeled in history. Such is the impending disaster with the Extradimensionals.

"We felt that if there was anything good that could have come from such an approach, the Predecessor race would have initiated it themselves.

"Certainly their encounter with the Extradimensionals proved their undoing."

There was a frustrated urgency to his tone that sparked alarms in Tamara's mind. Ossa believed the man thoroughly insane. Would he now begin to exhibit bizarre behaviors?

"Ossa believes a synergy and gestalt might be possible-by combining technologies and efforts, we might be able to achieve together what neither could achieve alone." She said quickly, hoping to assuage his anxiety.

344

He looked at her dryly, aware of what she was doing. "Never fear, my dear, lady warrior. I'll not go ballistic on you. Of course, yes, I sense your concern and my chivalry runs only so deep. There is no time for tantrums. As I have said to Ossa, we administer civilization to the civilized. You, and the military, however, administer its opposite to the uncivilized. There is a reason you are kept separate from the Hive Mind, and these are decisions you must make independent of our perspective. The fact that he is, indeed, taking a different approach-well, that proves the veracity of the separation"

She choked back her uncertainties, "Thank you, Sir."

He stared pointedly at her then, "But remember this-every time a Predecessor technology has been reverse engineered there has been a wave of economic and military reconfiguration, which most often includes markedly unpleasant consequences. Most Recently the Baal Wars almost tore apart the balance of power in the Pleiades after so many centuries of felicity among those Republics. Humanity is not in a place where we can afford any more internal strife."

They passed amazingly close to one of the towers, and Fortunato could see people through the windows working in their offices. One of them waved. She let her fingers raise and dance a little reply and smiled, wondering if they too were sentient programs like the steward or merely animated scenery. Nothing Omm presented, she realized, was without meaning, allegory, or metaphor.

As if reading her thoughts, and perhaps he was, David cleared his throat (gracefully!) "Our calculations and thoughts before the Arcturian war were such that we ran various scenarios out on super computers-economic and military models as it were-which showed that Humanity was branching into two separate civilizations; the Trans-human Cyborgian Central Command Economies and the Arcturian Colonies. Eventually, it appeared they would almost function as two species. The Hive Mind becoming...as an ant hill-a single organism with ambulatory parts, and the Colonies, remaining as the original Human species-a collection of individuals with independent self-will.

"In every test, we eventually collapsed, and they thrived."

She took in his words solemnly.

"I was not a party to the scenarios. I was the scion of a wealthy family that traced its roots back to pre-space industrialists. They used me without my knowledge to deceive the Arcturians that we were seeking peace terms to prevent an impending conflict. That we were seeking to divert, rather than escalate the conflict.

"Later, we used their creation of a new fleet as justification for our First Strike-but their fleet had never been intended to attack us.

"They were noble people, only seeking to defend their independence. The last thing on their mind was moving backward into our space. No, they were the great explorers in the heart of our species-and yes, I still consider myself a member of our species, even though I have become Trans-human.

"We Trans-humans must understand our place, and reinvent the dignity of true service that once was at the heart of leadership. Perhaps if we survive the onslaught of the Extradimensional horde, I shall make that my next endeavor."

His icy blue eyes were rueful. He smiled.

She realized he had told her things and revealed parts of his experience that he had not with General Ossa. Vega Ossa had chosen his messenger well. The comradely collusion between men indeed had a flip side-with each other they were harder as well. Omm would be no foolish gawking male, however, to spill his guts or wear his heart on his sleeve for a woman. No, Ossa's' choice was a clear statement to Omm-I need to know more. I need to understand. You can say to her things you would never say to me.

345

Tell her what I need to know. What are your motivations? Where is the loci of your heart, man? We are fighting for our lives, and the walls men erect between each other can only weaken us now.

David Omm had complied with Ossa's' unspoken request.

"After the war," Omm continued, "we realized the dread folly of our actions. It had been the Arcturian Colonies, and not the Trans-Human Command economies, that had been the driving genius of Mankind. These long centuries have seen nothing but a nearly dark age.

"On Deneb IV I often see the same model star liners drifting off to space as we fielded back before the war. The economies-limping along even as they are-would die without the underground economy of the Trade Guild and that too was a product of the Arcturians.

"Even in their death throes, robbed of their birthright, devastated and diminished, they had produced something we could not.

"The Trade Guild sustains the galactic economy by smuggling the resources we would tariff and tax out of existence so we could…have butterfly droids in our office lobbies and half our population on the dole and dancing while sedated.

"Tell our Dear hero General he has my blessing, and Godspeed his actions. The time of the division of our species is at an end. The time of wallowing in our weakness and regrets is finished."

He glared at her now, and she saw a sign of courage and beauty in him that mirrored Ossa himself in battle-and she realized-yes-David Omm-Omm 6X-had been learning from his visits with General Ossa. Learning once again what it meant to be human.

"Go now, Officer Fortunato. Tell General Ossa that I said 'this will be our finest hour, or it will be our last. If it be our last, then let's give the Extradimensionals a wound that shall linger through eternity'."

And so it was that for the first time since Omm 6X had been in Command of the CC Air Corps, an Airman strode from the Halls of Omm with the spirit of a warrior gleaming in her heart.

When she was gone David Omm stood alone in the winged plane still flying over the virtual recreation of New Haven City. He had forced himself to watch its destruction under the fireballs innumerable times, reflecting on his sin. That evening, however, the fireballs did not destroy the city again, and the sentient programs living there went about their virtual lives. Omm would not watch the fireballs ever after, would torture himself no longer. He was determined, in an embrace of the strange duality of man, to reserve that torture and those fireballs for the Extradimensionals.

The reports from the distant outposts of Humanity of strange disappearances and horrific murders were increasing. The Swarm was upon them and even now blood and death chewed at the edges of things.

It ain't over
Chrysalis Isla, Pleiades

Somewhere in Sagittarius
On an industrial moon
There lies a tepid salt flat
Orange against a shot black night
You done left me in a stasis field
But Darlin', it's incomplete
Cause everybody knows
You can't feel a thing deep in stasis
And I feel the drag
And the slow pull of time.
-Star Peace "Meat machines"
Starky Barky Holos

Maximus Mercurio looked at the faces of the dead. They looked back with an earnest determination not become so again. The clones of his crew, lost in the last engagement with the Extra-dimensional demon things, had been recreated with the memories of up to the moment when they last left Harry's Ahura Mazda Estate and set out for the far side of the Milky Way. That moment when they had set out for duty past the galactic core, into uncharted space, seeking the anomalies that indicated Bogie activity. They could not remember the deaths of their former selves-but they had been played the tapes.

Of course, that had been a disturbing enough experience. The Dark Corps had a motto, one among many, but one unofficially taken from their fearless leader Harry Stark; "It ain't over." Their very existence was a rebellion against man's fate-an assertion of that unofficial motto growled back after their defeat in a particularly inglorious battle in the Baal Wars. They had come back like proverbial Hellcats then, retaking the field, and then the planet, and then the Baal system.

Upon their return to the Pleiades, they found after winning the war they had lost the peace. The Noble families took by a series of judicial fiats the freedoms that commoners had long enjoyed. It hadn't been over then either. The Nobles were soon to disappear in number mysteriously; the freedoms were eventually restored. The remaining nobles would never again seek to take more by fiat and subterfuge that which was given with defined limits of the constitutional contract, and lawful consent. They had broken faith with honor and reason and met the inevitable response to such tyranny-their scions blood watering the tree of Liberty.

Harry, regardless, had no intention of ever disbanding the Dark Corps. If ever the Nobles sought to act with malfeasance, the Dark Corps would be there to slit their throats as they slept, and ensure their last moments, bloody and awakened in the night, would be regret of such action. Now the corps had been offered service in an unlikely alliance with the Imperials in a contest for the very survival of the Human species. Like the battle on Baal One, the Dark Corps' first contest with the Bogies had been a horrific route. Like the battle on Baal One, they would fight another day.

Each of the clones knew their previous selves had died horribly-they had watched it, again and again. This time they would be armed at least with a better knowledge of what their opponent was-the tactics and manipulation of their minds that the Bogies used to disorient, confuse, terrorize, and then dismember their prey as they fed like junkies off the wavelengths of fear. This time the crew knew.

347

"And this time you're going to have hyper-fritzers." Mercurio was saying, holding up a grenade-like object in his hand. "This little bad boy is a dimensional grenade. When the Bogies slime their way into our dimension, they have to open a portal-neat trick, that. Then they can stick their demented heads into our reality and start to mess with our minds. The hyper-fritzer creates a wall of multi-dimensional sheer, slicing the enemies into various dimensions where they will drop into those space-times like, well, the slimy loads of crap they are. In pieces."

Laughter from the assembled clones.

Bell chimed in, "Mini-singularities popping off like a distributor in sequence with different frequencies?"

Max grunted, "Geek points for you, Mr. Bell."

More laughter. Max wondered if the clone's laughter was a little too forced. Witnessing the images of what appeared to be themselves dying horribly, the lurking question in the back of each of their minds had to be the same-would I fail again? Somewhere in that question lay the answer to this riddle of how Max had endured. He couldn't know with certainty, but there was an essential aspect of knowing thyself that rested in the heart of the matter.

Warriors all, each had mastered their fear of combat. But unlike most men and women, Max had brooded on his other fears more than might be considered normal and healthy-thus he knew them intimately. The Bogies had no surprises to shock him with.

He looked grimly at them, "I'm no psychologist and you're all-or your originals all were-veterans of combat. Proven, tested, and scarred. But facing one set of fears-violence at arms-does not mean you've faced them all down. Perhaps none of us ever do, repressing them, denying them, avoiding them, content that we have mastered the boom of a claymore or the pop of an Eva field.

"It's not enough! Before we take to the sky again, I'll need to take an inventory of your souls. Find time alone. Write them down if you have to. We don't know what those lost were seeing, as the Bogies dragged them into insanity-but I suspect it was the deepest fears they weren't even consciously aware of."

Sanfillipo interjected then; "We have a theory about them. Predators stalk their prey in every ecology known to Man. Often, when the contest is engaged, the predatory species will seek to make itself as fearsome as possible, causing panic and disorientation in its target. These things seem to get a rush off their victims' fear. That too would follow an evolutionary chain of development in a reward-punishment scenario, where the devils that enjoy the fear they create would be rewarded for the kill. The pleasure principle-these things are enjoying your dismay-your holy terror. Your descent into madness.

"Being creatures of other dimensions, their perceptions of us and our thoughts seem to border on the prescient. They can feel the fears you've repressed and denied, and the mirror them back to you in a dung-show of surprise that hammers you senseless-then suicidal." Sanfillipo's dark visage was the grim reaper discussing technique.

"At that moment, at that time, you're not going to be able to distinguish reality from illusion, we suspect. Know your fears. Know them, well-like lovers. You are about to go meet them intimately and dramatically. Embrace them, then crush them-and we suspect you will survive."

Max held up the hyper-fritzer. "Then you can give them a little present."

At that, the clones of the crew of the Baal Baby chuckled. Later that night, alone in their cabins, there was no levity. Each clone searched the memories they had been created with, searching hard in the depths of themselves for that which they had repressed or denied.

The fighter had been retooled to perfection. Additional field manipulation equipment added in the nanoarray of the hull. Ossa had sent word that his work on Siluria indicated the defensive nature of time fields. Humans didn't have the know-how, or hardware to create such manipulations on a nebular scale-yet-but space bending was old hat, and a hard bend and unbend in a gravity field was known to slow time and then return it to normal. The theory was that when the Bogies appeared to be breaking into normal space the fighter could set up a staccato fire of bending and unbending the space around the ship.

Use the same strategy of disorientation they sought to unhinge the humans with on them. It would be particularly effective if they hadn't seen it before. If they managed to kill one of the things with a hyper-fritzer perhaps it wouldn't be able to "tell all its friends," and the element of surprise could be effective with each new confrontation.

Like the originally hidden recorders, this wasn't given as common knowledge to the crew. Only Max would know of it, and once activated, sentient programs in the fighter could repeat the process randomly when the fighter was under attack. So the crew hopefully had two new weapons and the additional benefit of more knowledge as to the nature of their opponent.

Combat droids were also added as a retreat back up. Should the humans become chaotic and self-destructive, the combat droids were programmed to sedate the crew, and pull the ship into hyperspace, retreat to the base with the time manipulators rattling off intermittently.

One of the crew had painted "Eat this" in red decorative letters across the front of the hull. The mood of the Ahura Mazda Estate was still one of anxiousness as the fighter prepared to launch, however. Harry watched, leaning forward at a parapet above the rose gardens, as the fighter lifted off. His lips slightly parted it appeared to the launch team he said something to himself, and for a shocking moment, the thought that he was saying a prayer for his team seemed to run through the minds of all the observers at once. No one was going to be the first to suggest that the vicious and ruthless realist had found a moment of religion.

Then he gave a crisp salute as the team of clones and Mercurio made for the far side of the galactic core once more.

There had indeed been anomalies in the area, and moreover, several Marauder ships had been reported drifting in the Trade lanes. That news had given Harry some ideas as well. No civilized Humans had attempted to interact with Marauder society since that chaotic and bizarre collection of punk rockers on steroids had formed their cult worshipping the great black hole at the center of the galaxy, some centuries before. Maybe it was time Harry collect a few of them and find out what made them tick.

The enemy of my enemy is my friend, was the old Arab adage.

"Get me a line to Sanfillipo." He called to his com. A moment later Sanfillipo's voice came back. "Sir?"

"Mustafa, fire up the Riptide and a couple of ripjackle long-range backups for a surfing safari. We're tailing the Baal Baby, I just decided. We'll go as far as the core and then we're going to add some new flyers to my collection."

"Sir?"

"We're going to get some Marauder meat and bring it home to study. If the Bogies have spanked a few Marauder ships already, the Marauders are probably aware they're in a brand new sweet little mystery, and they might not like the tune."

"You want to capture them and propose they join our covert alliance with CC? All due respect Sir-the Marauders are psycho puppies."

Harry burst out laughing for a moment then regained his composure.

"Mustafa, so are we."

There was a long moment of silence. Then Mustafa Sanfillipo said, "Hughahh!"

The Riptide was powering up in under a standard hour, and Harry Stark was at the Helm with a crew of ten-same rundown as the Baal Baby for the armory. His crew would fit in the time manipulator upgrades in flight. Slipping his MERGE helmet on, he stretched deep into the sensory array and felt the hyperdrives at his fingertips.

"Been too long, soldiers. Let's get some booty," he said as his convoy went airborne with a wail.

Nearly all of the Dark Corps stepped out to watch the launch, and a cheer went up "No surrender, no retreat!"

Harry Stark was back in the saddle. *There would be blood. There would be fire. There would be glory.*

There would also be long weeks in the hyper gamma spaces. Such too was the reality of war. Hurry up and wait. Harry coded over to Max what he had decided to do. Max replied with a laugh," Cool-the more the merrier," as they roared through the hyperstreams and the Pleiades sang their blue diamond song of beauty. The galactic plume never looked more like a raised finger than it did that day. Then it was duty rosters, system checks, data recon, repeat, and repeat. That would come later. The first flight-shifts were always simply speed, beauty, power, and joy.

Beatrice Allfire's clone came to Max's quarters that first night. She stood in the doorway for a long moment and Max simply stared, breathless and humble. His stocky, scarred, bald visage took her beauty in with all the wonder and depth of admiration any man could feel.

Still, Max said nothing. His lips tightened and his chin jutted forward as if to challenge her to hit him. Metaphorically, she did; lowering her gaze with a smile that would have melted the stone-cold heart of a nine-pound hammer, she said: "You loved me."

He stared. Her smile widened.

"Yeah," he said, and for him that was the same as a thick volume of confessions.

She walked over to the wall and touched his music collection. "Oh my, who would have thought?" she said, browsing the titles. She selected "All night long", then she turned and took his hands-and taught him to dance. The song repeated as the title said, all night long.

Sometime in that long and beautiful night, Max determined if she did not come back from this fight, he wouldn't either. Max had been born on the most beautiful world, in the most beautiful star cluster in the galaxy.

There were no flowers draped over tropical gardens in the starlight, no kaleidoscopes of lights, and rum-filled nightclubs, no artful skyscrapers challenging the heavens-and no sweep of charging combat and victory, that he had ever known that compared to that long dance, and her lips pressed against his face, her scent filling his head with a perfect completion.

The next duty shift the stars had never looked so full of promise to Max. They were riding upward in an ascending arc above the galactic clouds, tangential then, parallel to the arched filaments, mirroring the curve of the galactic disc, the bright UV sources and the OB stars. Radiation hammered the nanoarrays, providing an independent power source; not needed but giving the nanoarray a strange life of their own. Should the whole ship shut down, the nanoarray could run independently. Submillimeter emissions from the cooler dust provided interesting data as well-disturbances in their normal patterns told of trade routes like footprints.

Max set up the nanoarrays to move to automatic, and tap the UV sources upon any shut down-they couldn't power the time manipulations with that energy, but other aspects of fielding could still function-especially interior emergency magnetic fields to protect a disabled crew from the super rads of the core.

With each moment, the spiral arms and the realms of humanity's vast collection of civilizations receded, and the giant black hole at the core was closer. The core was its own reality. The vast number of stars, their dense proximity, and the plume. In many ways like a grand and glorious metropolis in the center of a larger region of small towns. Of course, Humanity had its last outposts there-the Marauder societies.

Max had been galvanized like an electroplated bayonet when Harry told him he was heading out on a separate surfing safari. They were taking the initiative-and that was always a good sign in the realms of war.

They had never taken prisoners before with the Marauders. They weren't called Marauders for nothing. Like the ancient Vikings, the Marauders harassed the fringes of civilization, raiding, and pillaging. There wasn't a government in the spiral arms that didn't offer privateering to anyone who would take them on.

Looking out from his Merge with Beatrice merged as well, Max rode the hyperstreams and thought, today is a good day to die.

Hell rides
Phlegra Station. Echo
Hercules Cluster

Rage destructions' fury above the glittering rings epochal
Rage, flying fierce, riding high-high
Riding the hyperstreams-rage
Speed and blood, fire and fury
No retreat, we go to meet Valhalla-ride!
We will go down with these ships
Rage into the breach with me, our guns singing their deaths songs
Rage, the music of the spheres our chorus of angels
Rage and speed, fire and ice
Fire and fury
No terms no surrender
We will go down with these ships
And going down raise our horns full of mead
In the halls of Valhalla!
"Cutting the Dimensional Barrier"
-Chowder Head Boo-Boos, Starky Barky Holos Unlimited

The Hercules cluster is a long, really nasty haul. Pilots making that run through the void are generally running some sort of game-black market dodges and they don't want to be followed. Jane and Nash had taken a CC Gateway after trolling into the Republics. Sulla provided the Intel; helping the quest so to speak but raising flags with Sagamore-how an Art dealer was getting access to CC gateways registrations creeped him out in a big way. CC would have liked to see him and Vince finishing their sentence on Ophelia's' World for sure.

"I think she's a CC spy, and they're going to nail us at the Gateway," Sagamore said flatly.

"How many fake registries does the Guild give us any time we want to use a Gateway? Like a gazillion?" Vince rejected his concerns on the matter coldly.

"Hang on, hang on, hang on!" Sag placed his arm against the gangway wall so Vince couldn't escape and brush him off.

351

"Sag, we have enough guns on this bad bear to rip CC a new one if they pull anything. Even the last time they took us down the only thing that prevented our escaping Chrysler City in a bloody holocaust was Millin's respect for innocent civilians. If he had opened up, half that city could have been fried faster than you can say 'Nova shockwave'".

"So if it's a trap, we fight? Come on-read your Art of War. Are you going to deal with the Guild after you take out a Gateway? They'll drop a load of dung so big on us, we'll be selling ice cream from an air-truck."

Vince raised his hands in the air, "It's not a trap. Sole hasn't been able to get jack-diddley-doo on this woman and he's been closer to her than any of us."

Millin Chimed in from the bridge, "Hey Sag how does that affect our bet? She didn't go for either of us, she went for Sole, so-bet's off."

Sagamore's face broke its grimace of concern for a moment and his features relaxed, "Uhhh…okay", then resumed his frown as if changing back channels, "Winteroud says she's new. This is becoming a clone convention. Jane, Lisa-do we even know a woman who didn't pick up her body from the lab a few years ago now?"

Vince smiled. "Hey, they want to look good. They do what they do. She's got bucks-that's what women with bucks do. They visit the cloner and skip down the street after that looking like yesterday.

"That's like housecats and holograms-everywhere. Am I supposed to throw her into a singularity or drag this crate through the void to get to Phlegra station because she's not 1X? Ain't happening."

Sagamore ran his fingers through his long golden hair. "She's new because they needed new-because they wanted to get to Sole and needed a body whose history Sole couldn't read because there is none. She's suspect goods. I'm not talking red flags here-I'm talking red dress made from red flags. She has "Agent Sulla" printed in a dancing neon hologram circling her like orbiting dancing bears, and you won't see it. What's your motivation here? Are you still trying to rescue Leyla?"

Vince swallowed. "Not. She's a killer."

"Oh come on," Sagamore scowled and his face went red with absurdity, "Do we know anyone that isn't?"

Vince went white with an honest offense, "Look Sag, there's a big difference between killing for self-defense in the line of…work than offing a whole nightclub full of losers for shits and giggles."

"We're MERCENARIES on half our jobs! This is going nowhere. Captain, what have you done to ensure we don't come under Imperial fire at that Gateway to the Hercules cluster?"

"He's got a point, Cappy." Millin came across the com. His voice was edged with an uncharacteristic tension. Perhaps he was reliving the Chrysler City run in his mind. He'd crewed the Sire long and hard while Vince and Sagamore had been incarcerated on Ophelia's World for illegal transportation of goods in Imperial Space. That had been a hard, guilty time.

Vince sighed and the weight of ages issued forth in that sigh. He stepped to a panel and coded up a hyper cast. After a moment a grainy holo of Elias Tristan appeared in the corridor. He was bent over a large pot, stirring something.

"What!? Can't you see I'm working on a sauce?"

Millin's voice came across the com., "What are you making?"

"That information will cost you. Otherwise, I would have to kill you. Ancient Chinese family secret."

"How much is it going to cost us to run a check on this Art dealer schmoosing Sole?" Sag broke in abruptly. Elias' hologram looked up from the sauce.

"Your Captain already did that, Mr. Salvatore. Doesn't he tell you anything?" Elias broke into a gruff, deep, baritone laugh.

"Beauty, Elias, feed the fire." Vince shook his head.

"Well, you did, Sire boy. Cost you plenty too, didn't it? Why haven't you told your men?" Elias was enjoying himself.

"You just did for me. I'm trying to get this battlewagon from point a to point b in a hurry and don't have time to report every dead end to my crew regarding Sulla." Vince retorted.

"It wasn't that dead of an end," Elias said firmly. "Our girl was famous prior to 3197-like she says, an Art dealer. Big time. Then she went off the grid. For like a millennium. Now, like a phoenix, she's running antiques again-in the Sagittarius Arm? The Outworlds didn't even exist as civilization last time her pretty face graced an Art opening. That's a really big hole in her story. Whoever sent her was not counting on the Trade Guild being in the mix. They figured Sole would be out here alone. She's an agent."

"BINGO! I knew it." Sag looked darkly accusing at Vince.

"Finish the story, Mr. Tristan. We don't know that she's an agent, we suspect. Finish the story, before you undermine my trust with my crew any further, please."

Tristan's bearded face was gleeful. He was an ancient Mesopotamian despot toying with a victim and liking it. Vince was banking payback points in his mind, and wondering what mischief he could work up to get back at him.

"Your Captain's right. We don't know anything. She was AWOL for a very long time for all we know there could be a dozen ordinary stories to explain-her ship could have gone stasis and she might have just been found. She might have gone under because of some psycho-drama and terms in a trust fund called for pulling her back out-who knows? But either way, your Captain has laid out a very large chunk of change, and we purchased every bureaucrat on that Gateway.

"Dang, the Sire can run that chute any time it wants-open up a private berth for retooling if she pleases. CC isn't going to find out you're there-ever, even if you tried to tell them, those Gateway officials are in so deep now they'll have layers of protection to make sure that bit of felony trivia remains undiscovered.

"You're good. Go through the Gateway already and catch or kill this thing before it eats more people's heads, okay?" He sipped his sauce, then smiled delighted at his work, "I am the king!" he announced.

Sagamore raised a finger, "Hold up, you haven't paid off her. If she has CC entanglements, what's to stop her from picking up her hyper caster holo and telling them herself?"

It was Millin whose comment settled the matter. "Blow her cover? No way. That yacht isn't casting a pebble we won't know about. No, Sag, if she's an agent she's under deep cover now, and on her own.

"Which means we'll have time to resurrect our bet and see who gets her all hot and bothered first, me the great Blue hope, or you, the little blonde girlie man?"

"Little? I'm six-two." Sag snapped back.

"No, I mean your other thing. She will be mine, and you will pay me a grand." Millin's voice prodded.

Elias chuckled, and his grainy hologram, still stirring the sauce, then vanished.

Vince looked Sag straight in the eye. "So we go to the Gateway, okay? Work on your bet with Millin. You don't need that "little" comment gaining any credence in the Guild, or things will be very difficult for you at Guild nightclubs on shore leave." Vince smiled.

Sag stared for a moment. "Okay Millin, two-k on the bet and we add the caveat that whoever snags her has to do it in front of lover boy Sole, walk her right out of his ship or wherever."

"That's a deal killer, you throw in that caveat and she's not going to play. Are you intentionally trying to make this not happen, Salvatore, because that will only dig the implications in deeper about your little friend?"

353

"It's no deal killer, I just want Sole there so he can read her mind and let me know if she's going to kill me in my sleep. I mean if she is a master spy as I'm certain she is, it will probably be my last love affair. If Sole senses bad intent on her part, well, I can dodge the bullet."

"Three-k."

"You're on. She will be mine."

Vince rapped against the gangway wall, "I'm going to shoot her myself if you guys don't get this ship powered up and pointed at that Gateway."

"Easy Cappy, we've been naved and running this whole conversation. I said he had a point, I didn't say I was going to let this nervous Nellie cause us to miss an opportunity to shoot a few CC patrols out of the sky. Heh, heh, heh!"

Sag pointed at the speaker from which Millin's voice laughed, "Now you're grandstanding, you were as worried about it as me."

Bending space, the mighty Taloned Sire broke through to the hyper streams for Clipper Gateway, blithely unaware of chick bets, spies, and Trade Guild bantering. David's Reprise and the Lord Kesey were given convoy permissions and the three ships arrived almost simultaneously the next day.

Of course, none of that would show up on any Gateway manifests. According to official Clipper Gateway records, the three ships were Wrinkle Kitty, Akhenaton Three-k, and the Astrud Gilberto. But trying to access the manifests at Phlegra Station, on the other hand, would get you tortured to death unless you were working for certain corporations there, and even then, you better have a very good reason.

The Gateway dropped ships at the far side of the cluster-thus maximizing its utility.

Phlegra Station was not right at the Gateway, that honor belonged to a small cadre of corporations with CC contracts. But you don't deal with them leaving the Gateway, you pay them entering it to return to the Milky Way. Phlegra station hugged the system, looking out to the final void of intergalactic space just past the Echo City mines and the alloy camps littering an asteroid field of immense size and wealth.

There were a couple of billion people in the cluster, and a third of them camped mining and smelting in the Phlegra system. Then there were the Marauder wanna-bees. Not the genuine psychotic cult at the core of the Milky way, copy-cat groups formed in the Hercules cluster as such people inevitably repeat history. They didn't have the numbers or the complete insanity of their inspiration, but when they're pointing a matter cannon or a high powered disser at one's freighter, the fact that they're wanna-bees is a relative perception. Yet even then, the line between legitimate and outlaw in the cluster wasn't just blurred, it was a downright sliding scale with more gradations than a molecular engineer's quantum instruments.

No one was going to notice Jane and Nash, even after the bodies started piling up.

The little convoy ported, purchased some berth space and registered under the false names: Wrinkle Kitty, Akhenaton three-k, and the Astrud Gilberto.

"Astrud Gilberto?" One of the techs sneered to Millin as he stared at the bold TALONED SIRE on the side of the frigate. These guys knew Millin by his first name.

"What's that all about, brother?" one asked Millin with a knowing grin. "We got your back out here-you don't need any aliases."

"Incognito, on vacation, my man. Got this psycho girlfriend stalking the great blue hope and I just need some space."

The tech laughed. "Good story. For a few pennies extra, I'll keep you posted if any… 'stalker girlfriends' come sniffing around.

Vince walked up. "Captain Leavel. How you doing?" one of them said.

"Good, good. Was just telling your mate here, who I've serviced his vessel before, I might add, I can run a little extra security."

354

Sagamore glided over like a bulldozer with an anti-gravity repulsion field, floating like a butterfly, but able to sting like a cast-iron bee. The tech raised an eyebrow. Everybody knew the story of the famous Ophelia's World jailbreak. He was in the company of legends. Sagamore farted, then smiled.

"Gang's all here aye?" The tech said, and Millin showed him a number on a com.

"That'll work" The tech brightened.

They met up with Winteroud and Lisa at their yachts. The Art dealer and the Historian were just sealing up and giving instructions to their droids. Winteroud was adjusting his muffle, or he'd be talking with the quantum echoes of murder victims lingering in the space docks for sure, Millin mused. Lisa looked at her nails with an air of superiority. "Rip was fascinating. This place is just dangerous." She said.

Millin moved a little closer, "Hey Lisa, never fear. I've been here a lot. They know me here. Stay close to me. You'll be safe." He put his huge tattooed hand on her shoulder. "I'm always watching".

"Thank you." She opened a retro-style purse and showed him her antique disser. "So am I. Always watching" there was a warmth in her grin.

"I feel safer already" Sagamore grumbled.

"So what do we do now, wait for an additional trail of their dead to follow?" Winteroud wondered aloud.

"No, that would be sloppy," Millin replied. "We go to Bongo Joe's down the hatch and order up a couple of rounds of the Hercules Cluster's finest."

Vince pointed a toe of his Mamonth boot at the floor checking for grease. "Lead on," he said.

Millin strode toward the exits from the docking bay leading to the station proper. "Last time I was here I came across an old Spacer who was rambling on and on About the Bogies. If I only knew then what I know now" he said, his gaze always moving, as he said-always watching.

"What did he say?" Sag asked.

"Said he saw something crawling around on his gravity bubble like it was glass. That it was talking to him. Called him a Pig-Monkey."

At the words Pig-Monkey, Vince remembered the encounter at the Yellow Jaguar. He looked at Millin darkly, "So your buddy did see a Bogie?"

"I wouldn't call him my buddy, although he might have been, at one time. He saw a Bogie alright. Drove him half-mad. He blew his brains out in the bar that night." Millin reported.

Winteroud looked at Millin with a stark grin. "The last time you were here someone shot themselves at the bar? I'm sure we'll get a warm welcome."

"Sometimes, you just gotta shoot yourself," Sag said laughing.

"Depends on the food" Lisa added, giving him a drilling gaze held a tad too long and tap on the arm.

Winteroud discreetly adjusted his muffle to catch the last of Millin's thoughts and memories concerning the spacer's suicide: *He was sledgehammer drunk and hotwired to the neurons. He stared straight ahead as if his merge helmet had malfunctioned and left him permanently trained on a quasar beacon.*

"They'll be back," he said flatly, taking a long oblivious sip of his gin. "They'll be back."

Winteroud moved with his companions through the eight-story high cruise of the station, teeming with people with Millin's memory pressed over his vision like a fading hologram.

"The hyper stream is easier up there, fainter. Better for the old boats. Must have made that plunge, shee-it, fifty times if I made it once. It's quiet up there. If you've a mind to, you can look out over the arc of the stream and out to the fade between. That's the run I was making, ten years ago now.

"The Silurian Nebula was right in my flight path, but me, hey I'm a rational man. I don't buy-in for old myths of ghost ships and lost star systems. I'm not about to recalibrate a half a million hyper stream calculations to avoid a grim spot on my galactic travels now, eh?"

Millin's thoughts were drifting away from that day, and Winteroud's mind was suddenly full of the curves of Lisa walking next to Millin. Those he could see himself, so he readjusted the muffle to quiet the intruding thoughts impinging on his mind from all around the cruise. But in his mind, he played a little galactic geography. The Hercules cluster. The Silurian Nebula.

The vector of the Bogie swarm. The bulk of the Bogies would hit the Hercules cluster before the Milky Way. Here, then, humanity would make its first real stand against the things. Assessing the rouges and pirates all about him, it would probably be a better fight than much of the rest of civilization will provide.

They arrived at Bongo Joe's Down the Hatch. A hologram figure playing an elaborately ornamented set of bongo drums smiled at them as they entered. A tall Afro-Caribbean looking man, the holo was an interactive program, responding to people entering along a variety of predetermined gestures to give the impression it was a more expensive sentient program. A pair of female dancers-one on each side writhed to the rhythms with inviting smiles.

Port Royal Jamaica could be seen behind them.

The interior designer had recreated a portion of the actual street plan of lost Port Royal; the sprawling nightclub's rooms too followed to old port's plan such that the bars were open to the street. Above, a faux hologram sky even had the giant cumulonimbus clouds of the tropics rising in muscular brilliant white billows.

"What is this?" Sag asked as he walked up to an open storefront with stools and a bar.

"Seventeenth-Century Port Royal!" Sole returned with delight. He picked up a dish from the bar and examined it, "Accurate too."

"The wickedest city in Christendom," Sulla offered. "lost to the sea like Atlantis, in a matter of seconds in an Earthquake."

Sole looked back and cocked an eyebrow, "Prescience?" he asked.

Vince gave him a dark glance, "Let's hope not".

"One of the greatest Pirate havens of the era. Let's get a table." Sulla intuitively knew Millin would have contacts here. They moved into the front room of one of the facades, and Winteroud marveled at the wrought iron fittings of the sturdy ebony tables.

They ordered food and drink. Music drifted in from different eras. The crowds hustled and reveled and conspired and traded. Millin signaled a bartender over, a well-muscled black man. Winteroud turned his muffle slightly down to catch the man's essence and intent.

"'Ello Millin. Welcome back to Bongo's. Been too long mon, far too long."

"You changed the decor." He replied. They shook hands. Introductions were made. The bartender's name was Ari. He and Millin had some sort of history together.

"Was a bad situation with the old Spacer you know. A ting like that, mon."

Millin nodded and gave an appropriate moment of silence. His eyes narrowed a bit. "He wasn't wrong, Ari. Insane, driven, broken-but he was right. The Bogies are real. We've encountered them-they're crossing over, possessing humans. We're after one now."

Ari looked across the faces at the table waiting for the punch line. None came, the faces all masks of doom.

"Alright then," he said, "would you like some chips with those rum drinks, me brother from another mother?"

"I'm not kidding." Millin asserted. "I've witnessed it. We have evidence-holographic recordings of a trans-dimensional breach. I need to talk to the Board of Directors."

Ari showed his palms, "That ain't happening my friend. I know you probably carried some guilt over the Spacer offing himself, but it wasn't your fault, Millin. It sounds like you're taking this too far."

Winteroud shot him a bitter glance. "He's telling you the truth, Ari. I was there. I'm an empath. I not only saw the Bogie, but I also read its mind. There are untold numbers of them ready to swarm into the star cluster on the way to the Milky Way even now. There is going to be a conflict on the scale of which Milton never dreamed-a genuine 'war in the heavens'" he said.

Ari began scrutinizing the group more intensely now. "An empath? Like a psychic? Like a fortune-teller? Astrologer? Is this part of a new shop you are planning on opening?"

"Fine" Winteroud put his head down and closed his eyes. He adjusted the muffle and reached with his mind for the quantum strings of Ari's life. It hit him with a jolt, the electricity of the string, Ari moving backward and backward in a four-dimensional rewind with his thoughts, body, atoms, streaming back, and Sole reaching for moments, insights, background information like pulling rocks from rapids while tumbling down them. Unlike Lisa, whose recent cloning prevented a genuine plunge into the quanta, Ari was older than he looked, much older, and the quantum strings were rich with detail and branches.

Sole raised his head. He looked at Ari; everyone at the table was looking at him. "Your name is Aristotle Rolle, but only your closest family members call you Aristotle, everyone else calls you Ari. You were late to your shift today but no one mentioned it because you've been negotiating for a share of ownership in the club.

"You chastised one of the cooks today because the sautéed vegetables from the hydroponics level were overdone, and one of your investors was coming to lunch later. You sent up a droid to the hydroponics to get replacement vegetables so they would be right. Everything you do, you do your best; which is why at every turn of business or venture you've endeavored you quickly master the skills-but tire of them and move on.

"With the one exception: Bongo Joe's down the Hatch. You never tire of looking out over the floor and seeing the parade of life pass through. Where another man might consider service-even fine dining-a second-tier living, for you it's an art, a moment, a performance.

"A gift.

"Most of the rabble and posers never realize just how well this place is run. Need I go on?"

Ari smiled. "Very entertaining Mr. Sole, but nothing there that a sharpie or a confidence man couldn't have gathered any number of ways. The answer is still no. I cannot contact the corporation for you."

Sulla leaned forward. "How did it go with the investors over lunch? Did the fresh vegetables cook to perfection-just right-close the deal?"

Ari's face drooped.

Sole answered for him, "No, they declined-but wished him luck. Two years with that particular group, eh Mr. Rolle-reports, executive summaries, income statements, expensive flights to meetings, endless conference holo-meetings, then, nada."

Ari took a defensive tone, "I have this in front of a lot of people. I'll get the financing." He forced a smile, "Enjoy your food and drink." He began to turn to leave.

"Of course you will, Mr. Rolle." Lisa piped in. He drilled her a hard look and you could see he was struggling with his anger. When she went on, however, his expression softened. "I'm sure you'll close the deal sooner or later." She was opening up her purse and pulling out a credit Jack.

"What were the terms you offered them?" She asked. He pulled out a com, manipulated the screen and handed it to her.

"May I?" She asked. He nodded his consent and she loaded the data into her jeweled com, "I accept." She said coolly. She showed him the screen of her com. Now you own it, and I with you. The funds are in your account; so, tell one of the managers you're taking the afternoon off with your new co-owners. Then please, review Mr. Sole's recordings of the encounter.

"We need to speak to the people who run this Station. We need to find that Bogie and we need to get this cluster ready in some form to deal with what is coming."

357

Ari sat down as if in a fog. Emotions pounded him one after the other-the shock of seeing four years of work and struggle just come to fruition from this woman's whim, and then the contrary shock that he now owned an expensive sprawling facility in a Star cluster that was on the verge of some bizarre war.

He pulled out another com. A holo of a man appeared. An attorney. "Rich, verify that these transactions have closed and that proof of funds are secure. Thank you."

His attorney began to speak but Ari cut the link. "This is wonderful Miss Sulla; I appreciate this more than you can imagine but I still need to review Sole's recordings. The Corporation wouldn't appreciate me bringing people to them after I just received a large sum of money. It would look like a bribe to set up a hit." He dropped the Caribbean accent somewhere in the discussion. It would reappear later, Sag noted, along with several others, depending whom Ari was speaking with.

Ari was unconvinced after reviewing Sole's holo-tapes. Better special effects, he said, are pumped out of Chrysler city every day. But the funds cleared, and Sulla's credibility combined with the strangeness of the whole affair convinced him it was indeed, not a ruse for a hit on the Board of Directors. Still, he was nervous as he called up the holoscreen in his office. First, however, he sent over the data. To his surprise, the response was swift and unequivocally not skeptical.

The corporation had an aircar on the cruise in minutes. Millin and Sag dropped out and headed back to the Sire, but Lisa, Vince, and Winteroud got into the aircar and were soon finding themselves off the station and headed downworld to the Echo City mining center. It was a bit of a stretch for an aircar, but Vince had no doubt, and Winteroud confirmed with a small quantum feel, that the whole thing had been through a rebuild from the frame up, and was, in fact, a great deal more than your father's aircar.

It did not, however, have a gravity bubble, so when they broke off from Phlegra station they were flying with real G's. First came the acceleration then a wide spiral arc toward the planet. Echo city was stretched over the night side in a six-hundred-kilometer radial pattern. Built over a massive crater, the city "echoed" the forty-million-year-old blast pattern from the collision that has almost ruptured the planet when the crater formed.

Massive amounts of heavy metals had brought up from the core of the planet with that collision. It was sand-box simple there to acquire all manner of highly prized minerals and gems. There had even been discoveries onworld of Predecessor relics. It was that thought running through Sole's mind-the Predecessor relics-which combined with his loosening of the muffle (to get a better feel of the aircar) that brought on a fit of quantum sensitivity as the aircar arced over echo city.

The space between Phlegra station and Echo city was rank with strings, of course-thousands upon thousands of vectors and forth dimensional ghost trails. Behind it all, however, were other things. Distant in time, their etching into the fabric of the universe had been too powerful to erase. The human activity was in fact like new actors staging a play at the ruins of an ancient amphitheater. The Predecessors had made a stand here too, he realized. The crater had been part of that battle. One of the contestants had thrown an enormous asteroid at the planet.

Sole couldn't sense which one had done it, and the exigencies of the moment were a Hercules cluster syndicate air car making Mach ten for the board of directors. He tightened the muffle, and the strings and voices quieted.

There was only the heavy buffering then of the planets relatively dense (by human standards) atmosphere. Their course turned away from the night side as the arc continued and the aircar sprouted wings giving it a decidedly insect-like appearance.

They rode past the dark, into the twilight, through a series of metal processing towers fitted with offices and suites. Hardly the lap of luxury one would expect for the Board of Directors of the Hercules cluster corporation- until one realized that there was no permanent locale for said directors. To remain stationary would make them a target. They would remain at these offices and suites for a time, and then they would be at other facilities. It was the nature of such places to prefer to be a moving target over a stationary one.

Still, when the aircar settled on top of one of the towers and they were escorted into the interiors, the quality of the decor was spectacularly ostentatious. "You know," Lisa said with a sidelong glance to Winteroud and Vince as they made their way through the luxurious interiors, "there's always room at the top" and she winked.

"I've heard that," Vince replied, "if I ever get there I'll let you know."

Winteroud snickered. "I believe, Captain Leavel, that she is suggesting that we are about to arrive at once such place now."

"They haven't asked us for our weapons, Mr. Sole." Vince countered. "So we may be arriving at the top of the Hercules cluster's society-but we will be meeting with their holograms, and not themselves."

They entered the board room and one's first impression was that the exterior wall was missing. Floor to ceiling, running a good ten meters the plastisteel glass had been formed in one single piece and the landscape beyond, in all its twilight burnished glory, stretched from horizon to horizon. There was one large round table with twenty men and women seated in tailored suits and designer dresses. A couple were wearing EVA suits of colorful and expensive makes. All, of course, were holograms. Where the original board members were at this time, well, Vince had better sense than to ask.

"Welcome to Echo." An aristocratic-looking woman greeted them. "I am Director Roshan. Please be seated. The board has been informed of who you are, and what you are suggesting." Her long fingers caressed the back of her chair-unlike the other members, she remained standing. "You realize your reputations precede you, Captain Leavel and Mr. Sole. You, Miss Sulla, we haven't heard of, yet-but your little purchase of Bongo's on a whim is already starting to garner you a bit of celebrity at Phlegra station."

"It's a pleasure to be here," Sulla replied out of protocol. "However I wish it was under better circumstances."

"Indeed." added Sole.

Vince made for the seat as requested, "Thank you Director, but in all honesty-it is distinctly not a pleasure to be here under these circumstances." He gave Sulla a sheepish look of apology then went on,

"That thing inside of Nash is a drop in the bucket. There will be more-more than we can imagine- and if we don't learn how to kill them, humans are quickly going to find themselves on an endangered species list or a menu."

Winteroud and Lisa also sat down. Now only Director Roshan remained standing. She smiled, unmoved and unfazed. "In most circumstances, Captain Leavel, we would have laughed at your stories of Bogies and put it down to Marauders.

"The last several days have seen many unexplained murders and mutilations. That too would have been put down to Marauders; they have a penchant for torture, and we are not so squeamish as to be unable to return the favor, tit for tat."

She looked toward the conference table and several holos appeared. Scenes of carnage.

"These individuals possessed no particular…positions within any gangs, syndicates, or black market affiliates where anyone would want them dead. These are all ordinary men and women with banal and unassuming lives. The meek that usually inherit the Earth, as they say. These murders, again, would have thus been chalked up to bad luck with the Marauders. There is one thing that sets them all apart-and that one thing is what has forced us to take your story seriously. Look at holos a moment-look at the sheer viciousness and brutality of the murders."

Sulla swallowed and her eyes took on a defiant look.

"See anything in common?" Roshan asked, her voice lowering.

"They're all suicides," Sole said irrevocably.

Roshan's face darkened with vindication. Sole had confirmed her suspicions on the killings to the board-obviously there had been some disagreement. "Yes, Sir Sole-my assessment precisely. Now you claim it is a Bogie-possessed Outworlder policeman.

"We will bring our considerable resources to the fore in tracking down the pair you described. The Trade Guild has informed us as well that you are operating under their authority and have informed numerous Guildsmen trading in the cluster on the manner of the fugitives." Roshan's face was riddled with doubt.

Vince made an ironic smile. *Great; the Guild is informing the Hercules Corp before the Taloned Sire now.*

"Take a couple of armored aircars," Roshan offered, "We'll forward the intel. Bodies are turning up all over the place."

Sole broke in with urgency. "It will help me get a read if we are allowed to survey the crime scenes before too many police and other authorities run through there, clouding it up with their emotions, impressions, and actions."

The members of the Board didn't look too pleased with the suggestion.

"That's rather unorthodox." Roshan looked at him dimly. "I'll get you as much time as I can, once a cursory recon is sent out-but we have a responsibility to any survivors to try and get them medical attention etcetera. If our subcontractors get word that the Hercules Mining Corporation Police are delaying response time for the sake of a psychic, there will be a lot of, well-unhappy people. Especially where serial killers are involved and on the loose."

The holo from the Yellow Jaguar played silently in the center of the table. Indeed, it looked to most of the people arranged around the conference table like something beyond credulity, yet there it was with the witnesses asserting its authenticity.

One of the men in an EVA suit at the table bore a silver shield on his chest-HMCP. He didn't say anything, but his displeasure at Sole's suggestion was palpable. After a moment he finally said, "If we get the Empath-Mr. Sole-and his associates out to a reported disturbance before we arrive that wouldn't be a problem, Director Roshan. If anyone asks- they're working for us."

She nodded in agreement.

"I have recording equipment. My droid's back at Phlegra station. I'll tight beam the recordings of my impressions to the droid and have him process the data and send it over to you in a similar format to this", he waved at the hologram in the center of the table.

The HMCP officer looked to Vince-one uniformed man to another. "Captain Leavel I'll need your com info. I'll send you directions to the next site to investigate. One of the mining camps in Smoke Canyon hasn't been reachable. I'm assuming you're going to find more victims there."

When they made their way down to the offered air cars, in a section of the tower packed full of such, Vince had directed Lisa to take the more heavy-duty model, while he had taken a more stylish but less well-armored vehicle in a bit of chivalry.

In the less a standard hour from arriving at the Hercules corporation they were airborne again. In the board room, Roshan let out a sigh that sounded like a slow leak in a water ship.

Another of the hologram conference members spoke up, "Sole's credibility is impeccable, Director Roshan. We've run checks every which way but loose, and they all come up aces. He's the genuine article-one of the most respected Historians in academia, and a well-documented empath of the first rate-arguably the best Humanity has ever produced."

Her face took on a matronly and ominous aspect, "That's what I'm afraid of." She said quietly. "If he is correct, and there are more of these entities swarming at the edge of the galactic halo even now, we're the first star cluster in their path before they hit the Milky Way proper."

The landscape of Echo spread below Vince and Sulla's air cars like a mottled porridge of sculpted ruin. Sole rode shotgun with Lisa, focusing his mind as best he could on the quanta. Maglev trains crisscrossed the geography of sudden towns and strip mines that appeared with the irregularity and inexplicability of lode strikes. Here would be a series of small camps and then suddenly a series of massive towers. Ground vehicles of various sorts crawled about with the trudging persistence and rugged indifference of automatons. At this height, one couldn't tell if they were bots or piloted by humans, so their ubiquitous busy work brought no sense of the comforting presence of human numbers.

From the aircars, they could have been looking at a world already devoid of human life, a clockwork of animated relics going about their business after the demise of mankind. When the occasional figure appeared, Lisa felt a pang of relief. Then, with a second look, she saw it was an android and her dread returned.

Vince tight beamed Millin and Sagamore. He filled them in on his meeting with the Hercules Corporation's Board of Directors. "Keep the Taloned Sire powered up. I don't have any model for this conflict, gents."

Sagamore growled. "Say the word Captain and I'll rain Hell down."

Vince cast a worried glance at the aircars' holoscreen, "It's already here, apparently" he said in a rumpled voice. "But yeah, fight fire with fire when the time comes."

Vince had read once of various angels, close to God, who were, at the end of the day, quite terrible in their aspect.

He longed for one now.

In a matter of an hour, the aircars arrived over the coordinates of the mining camp. It was nearly invisible under the fog. Vince ran an infrared scan and the only thing warm were bugs. Big bugs, the size of ripjackles, and lots of them. They put down the aircars through the fog into a camp of corpses. Vince could hear Sole making an ugly moaning sound across the com they kept open.

The mining camp was silent but for a limp wind that rose and died.

Their first site of the Echo City massacres was bathed in an eerie, putrid fog and a spattering of blood. The mining slag was piled in weird towers. The smell was so bad Sole covered his face. Around him, the quantum strings sang their vicious death songs. Vince saw him pull out a disser at one point; Nash had eaten the flesh off the heads of the victims and set them in a display on mining drill tips. The effect was of a series of primitive head-hunter totems; *these are mine; I now own their souls.*

Several of the large bugs, crab dogs he knew suddenly from the echoes of the miner's minds, scampered feeding among the dead, Sole's disser exploded their clambering shells one after the other in a series of well-placed shots.

Nash knew the crew of the Sire and Winteroud would be in pursuit. He had practically sent them directions. Come join the party.

Sole bent his head as his visions flashed before him. With a jagged gasp, his body clenched. The visions were fresh, strong, imminent.

"They came into the camp from the North," he said, "They set their yacht down and a number of the miners approached, curious." His eyes narrowed behind his sun goggles, "The miners had been anticipating an offer to buy the strike when they saw the quality of Jane's vessel," Winteroud said after they had pulled back to the air cars, away from the carnage. He vomited several times until all that was left was a retching dry heave. "Nash had the first group in a psychotic frenzy before most of the others in the camp even had stepped away from their work.

"He set them upon one another-they were tearing each other apart with their bare hands and teeth when more from the camp came pouring out." The fog and the smell overwhelmed him then and he broke off. Vince signaled Lisa to put him in the aircar.

"Come on, we don't have to discuss it here. Let's find higher ground, some light, and air." Vince offered and they clambered into their vehicles. Vince led the way toward a rise above the fog. The normalcy of the light of day and distance from the quantum echoes stilled Sole's shattered and racked body.

In a brighter, warmer place he and Sulla put their aircars down. Vince brought him a bottle of synthopiates and nutrients to calm his nerves and he drank it down clearing the vomit from his throat. He looked up gratefully. The aircars were well stocked with food and drink.

"The Bogie has completely taken over Nash's will-reduced him to a human puppet. I can feel the officer's rage and horror with each act the Bogie takes in his body-he's still in there, a prisoner in his flesh-but unable to overcome the beast."

Sole's tone sharpened, "After the first of the miners set upon one another, their fellows came out to see what was happening. Jane was standing to the side, watching. She's annoyed that there is more killing than power, and is waiting for the thing to effect some sort of Dominion over humankind, with her as some quasi queen of air and darkness."

Vince remembered her on Lux watching a live Holo of a fashion show out of Chrysalis Isla. Her longing for status and glamour-unearned-had set him back in ways he wasn't aware of. The depth of her avarice was like a dark, cavernous underbelly of ice-like the labyrinth of pits Vince had glanced at on Galapagos Not, the sad little moonlet where he had met with "No deal DePaulo" and sealed both their fates. His memories of his life with her-this Harpy, this she demon-kept intruding in his mind with an unwelcome pull at his resolution to take her and the Bogie out.

"Nash was on them like a ripjackle-first a storm of confusion in their minds and then-then-he's moving faster than a human should-he's burning the officer's body out-changing it morphing it slightly"-Sole bent about to retch again.

Lisa grabbed at Sole's shoulders, pulled her to him, "Easy, easy. Take a breather." She said.

"Then he's on them, his teeth-biting, slashing, ripping." Winteroud finished in spite of her appeal to rest.

Vince thought of the sculls placed on the drill points and wondered why they weren't simply using lasers. They could have used the lasers to slice Nash into a million razor-thin wafers. He knew it wouldn't have mattered. Laser, drill point, disser; all useless if your will to use them has been shoved into a surreal nightmare of confusion, lost in an illusion of vertigo and shimmering waves of disorientation.

He realized then that the higher the life form, the more effective the weapon of the Bogies mental tortures. Like spiders, they paralyzed their prey before they fed. With a creeping dread, a part of him was also beginning to realize they could paralyze with the promise of false pleasure as well as horror.

Leaning against the armored air car hovering off the ground, Lisa moaned, "So these entities cross over into our dimension, possess things and then become cannibals? This is mind-boggling. If they are such advanced beings, what is the point of all this mad destruction?"

Vince gave her a wry, sardonic grin, "What's the point of ours?"

Sole sneered through his pain, "Just because they're intelligent and capable of trans-dimensional behaviors, is no reason to assume they're going to adhere to any sort of morality that we contrive" he said firmly, "My sense of them is they're a reality gone wrong. Whatever ordinary biological-if you can call it that-needs they were fulfilling by hunting life forms in our dimension...well, that's out of balance. They're a race of hyper-addicted lunatics now, scouring, warring, feeding-annihilating."

"Out of balance?" She asked.

Sole nodded. "At the end of the day, any species which breaks out of its primordial place in ecology is out of balance. Humanity itself is a species of primates that evolved in small hunter-gatherer tribes. It broke out of balance as soon as it discovered agriculture. Civilization soon followed, and we were no longer subject to the ecosystem, but gradually its pinnacle."

Vince chuckled, "Now we're being hunted. We're not even being farmed-these things simply sweep through a region of the universe wiping everything out, and then make a second go-round afterlife evolves again.

"We're lower now than farm animals-we are merely wild prey again. We've just been set back to Australopithecus."

"Australopithecus?" Lisa asked.

"Proto-human hominid. He means before the cavemen picked up a spear. Way back. Just a walking ape-thing looking for a nut while filling the eyes of a Saber-tooth with glee." Sole answered.

"Munchies on two feet," Lisa quipped.

"So they're not farming us." She said grimly. "Why aren't they farming us? Wouldn't that be a better scenario for them? Create a situation where their food and drugs-whatever-don't get completely wiped out?" Her train of thought appeared spontaneous, but she was leading.

It worked. Sole's mind, whether sensing her lead at some level or merely responding to a series of premises, returned to the ice mines at Bethlehem. "There is evidence they might have been farming us in the distant past. I've discovered proof of a human civilization off Earth about half a million years ago."

The nano shielding Omm 6X had placed in Lisa's body went into activation as her excitement rose in what might have been a betrayal of her thoughts. She had achieved one of the original points of her assignment-get him talking about the ice mine discovery. Mildly, imperceptibly, the nano shielding covered for her.

Sole continued, "Under the ice, on a dead world in a cluster off the galactic Halo, there was evidence of a human community. A global civilization on a technological level of say, twentieth-century Earth.

They didn't appear to have space travel. I wasn't asked to continue any research there. But it may be important. They might have been farming us-perhaps it was a test community.

"They might have discovered us on our homeworld and decided to set up human farming elsewhere-maybe at that point in their addiction they still had some control. I couldn't sense how the humans had gotten themselves there-my impression was they didn't know it wasn't their home ecology. The star, however, exploded. One of the oceans on the dayside was instantly boiled to a plume of steam, went through the entire atmosphere killing everything, then fell as a perfect icy cover over the entire sphere as the collapsed star wasn't providing any more heat."

"Maybe the Bogies were attempting to rectify their mistake with the Lephs? After all, when they ravaged Predecessor civilization in the galaxy they might have rediscovered hunger in a big way." Vince offered off hand. He was signaling HMCP that they were through with the crime scene.

Winteroud joined Lisa at the side of the aircar, running his hands over the warm plastisteel of its surface and feeling comfort from the heat. Lisa had reduced her clothing down to a minimum of a sheer and revealing outfit and he found himself distracted by thoughts of warming himself in her arms. She didn't need empathic power to read that-such awareness of a man's intent, women learn early. She gave him an inviting, assuring smile but it was out of pity for his current wracked and strained state, and not any cat and mouse game of male and female.

Vince saw the wordless rapid exchange of glances and thought: Even on the road to Hell's fury, flirting. "You got the data on this discovery, Winteroud? Why haven't you let us in on this little factoid-which might be kind of important in the scheme of things?" he asked looking away, back toward the Smoke Canyon's edge where, down and down in the mists and miles, a village of the dead lay waiting as HMCP had already begun to arrive after Vince's signal.

Sole snorted. "I signed a non-disclosure. The ice mining company is scared witless they're going to lose their cash cow if the rest of the galaxy discovers they're sitting on one of the Galaxy's greatest mysteries concerning human origins. Technically, I just violated my contract and am liable for some serious financial consequences."

Vince, scanning the horizon for signs of the HMCP team moving toward the ruined mining camp, raised his disser a bit, "There won't be a mining company on that ice-world if we don't figure out a way to conduct this war to our satisfaction, my dear historian-there will be another massacre like we just witnessed. They're going to have a hard time pressing the terms of their non-disclosure contract while their laying in frozen bloody messes as decorative corpses for the entertainment of psycho Bogies."

Even in his pain from the quantum read, Sole managed a laugh. "True, that," he said with an evil grin. "And yes, I have data. When we get back to Phlegra station I'll get you the whole data set. Run it through the whole Guild if you like but make sure the Guild is ready to lean on these rats hard if they press me."

"That can be arranged," Vince replied, "with pleasure."

Lisa's face screwed up in concern, "So if their little farming experiment failed, why did they wait so long before deciding to feed again?"

"I'm not convinced it was them. Remember, Vince here has discovered a remnant of the Predecessors of Siluria still alive. So in all reality, it could have been the Predecessors that had set up the human farms."

Lisa's mouth dropped open and she gaped at Winteroud with an unattractive glare. David Omm hadn't told her that one.

"WHAT?" Her voice rose, "This is unbelievable-you two are both squatting on scientific knowledge the human race desperately needs right now like it's your country club gossip."

"Country club gossip. Nice." Vince responded sharply. "What do you think would happen across the galaxy if all this got out? You think it would make the coming stand easier if the whole of the teeming billions suddenly realized the elaborate construct of every institution, technology, and social order mankind had created in the galaxy over the last two thousand years was suddenly going to have its structural columns taken out at leisure by insane psycho cannibals from Dimension-X?"

Sole nodded. What he said.

Lisa knew he was right. Humanity wasn't ready for the truth it would have to be spoon-fed them among reports of horror and murder from the galactic clusters while every tech lab in human space ran a super-geek race to come up with some defense against the onslaught. Otherwise, the bedlam loosed upon society itself would destroy billions without the Bogies having to rip anyone's sanity apart. Omm realized this too, she suddenly knew. They were orchestra conductors at a riot; raising their hands hoping for order even as the first rocks of chaos took flight.

"So the predecessors hauled humanity over to some distant cluster, set them up on a planet with a level of technology where they could enjoy the benefits of civilization, but not the ability to star hop." She offered, not revealing that, in fact, that too was one of the implications she had considered.

She wasn't supposed to have known about this. "What's the payoff of farming higher life forms? Why eat a human, when you can eat a cow or a fish? Mere delicacies?

"The joy of knowing that before your dinner died, it experienced the full self-awareness of impending death, and all that such a foreknowledge entails? Is the universe truly that vicious?" Her voice carried out over the sun-bleached flats.

One of the big bugs clambered out of a hole and hobbled toward another where it disappeared.

Winteroud looked to her bright eyes, "You betcha" he said with a rakish grin.

Vince interjected, "Maybe everything the Lephs-and that's their real name-has told us about the origins of humanity and the Bogies is a lie. Maybe they brought us too that planet from humans found on Earth. Maybe the Bogies too are one of their experiments gone awry?"

"We could sit here and debate forever, and it won't mean a pig in a poke. We need more evidence for answers. Meanwhile, our Bonnie and Clyde from Hell are still on the loose." Sole gave them a weary look

Vince looked at Lisa, "Bonnie and Clyde?"

She rolled her eyes, "You Outworlders! They're Twentieth-Century American bank robbers, a particularly notorious pair who went on a Hell ride across that nation-state before they were finally gunned down by the authorities in a shower of hand-held matter cannon. What do they teach you in those schools, aye Captain Leavel?" Her beautiful smile belied any frustration.

"Our history begins with the day you nuked us all back to the stone age setting up a millennium of ceaseless labor armed only with any sticks and stones we could gather on worlds we had little knowledge, of etcetera, etcetera, etcetera. American police trivia, well…just ain't on the curriculum." He returned the warmth of her gaze.

"Should be though. The Americans were one of the largest group contributing to the Arcturian Colonies." She countered.

Sole wiped his face with a look of a wounded man, "Bonnie and Clyde, Samson and Delilah, Romeo and Juliet-Hansel and Gretel-they turned to the West-sunrise on this planet. I suspect a bit of a military gambit in that. Historically the hour before sunrise is when a sleeping army is most vulnerable. Since they are in fact at war with the worlds and everything in them-everyone is in the enemy camp. They'll be hitting settlements before dawn when most are asleep and any guards have just spent long uneventful hours having their tenacity eroded by boredom."

"I'll get with HMCP. They'll have another set of offices and suites in that geographic direction I'm sure." Vince said and began manipulating his com.

They were given coordinates to another mining outpost to the West. The highlands of the Echo crater's rim.

It was colder there, and an ugly frost scoured the ground around the sculpted towers of the installation, whose angular architecture bore a subtle element of anthropomorphized nonobjective art. They were grey, machine-like pylons that, however mechanical and streamlined their construction, their effect, Winteroud mused, was that of a group of Easter Island sentinels. Easter Island's civilization had fallen in an orgy of cannibalism and chaos, he thought morosely.

"Easter Island," Lisa said as the towers came into view.

Sole laughed, "I was just thinking the same thing. It's like you can read my mind." he gave her a sly look.

"More riddles.' Vince snapped across the comm. I'm going to have to tap a historical reference library to keep up with you two." He said.

"This is the Pinnacle station, HMCP. Come in, aircars." A bored voice came in over the open channel. Obviously, the intensity and import of their mission hadn't filtered down to the lower ranks of HMCP. "You have clearance to docking platform and space for your vehicles in the VIP garage. Accommodations have been assigned-and paid for by the Trade Guild. Personal messages have filed and will be delivered upon your arrival."

"Thank you Pinnacle, this is Captain Leavel." He circled high and wide in an informal reconnaissance of the area. Sulla made straight for the parking garage via holo nav-diagrams that suddenly appeared on her screen. Then he too followed the diagram. The VIP Parking garage was heavily fortified and located at the base of the outpost's towers. Everything on Echo was readied for Marauder raids-or just plain opportunistic terror, mayhem, and piracy.

Convenient, Vince thought, now that Dimensional war was upon them. Now, if they only knew how to create fortresses immune to extra-dimensional surprise attacks, they would be on the way to a real defense. At least Nash probably couldn't appear in the middle of the air any longer.

Could he? Probably not-once inhabiting the matter from this dimension, and invading Officer Nash's form, surely the Bogie would be confined to a certain degree by the physics of our space-time.

The Board of Directors made their private suites available to Captain Leavel and his companions, and of course, the facilities were astounding. Vince disrobed almost immediately, and made for an all-round shower, micro lifts, nutrient bath, and detox. His clothes were cleaned and presented by a service droid before he could even finish the luxury of his bath. The suites were adjoining, and in a few minutes, Lisa and Winteroud were with him again, leaning back in floating chairs.

A holo-call from the Sire came in, and Sagamore appeared in the room. "Sweet suite," he observed, "toughing it out for the team?"

Vince showed him his palms, "It is what it is-one day you're walking thin ice on dung world, the next it's a roast rooster in London. What can I say?"

Millin popped his head into the hologram. You have floating sofas and signed holo-art from sleazy art dealers from the Empire-no offense, Lisa-we have big cannons ready to rip apart continents and stuff. Enjoy your sofas."

Lisa looked at Vince. He shrugged his shoulders, "Sleazy art dealers from the Empire? Really Millin, a nice way to win friends and influence people. I'm sure she's never sold a piece for more than it's worth."

Millin pointed at an ugly holo across the room, "I was referring to that. I mean, what goes through these bonehead's minds before they make that crap?"

Lisa leaned back and hooted a decidedly unfeminine roar. "I agree, Millin. Pure drivel from narcissistic pseudo chumps since the dawn of modern art. And you" she smacked Vince in the shoulder, "shouldn't insult me."

Vince looked at her uncomprehendingly, "What? I was defending you."

"Defending me? You implied I never sold a piece for more than it was worth. Au-contraire, the Bulldog of Newberry Street never sold a piece for less than it was worth. And what goes through the bonehead's minds before they make that crap, Mr. Quinoa, is angst, self-absorption, and ideologies rank with contradictions."

"It shows." He chuckled.

"You know we're probably being recorded," Winteroud grumbled. 'If that turns out to be a piece made by the director's niece, you may find interior decorating to be a poor choice of topics when the danged sky is falling so to speak."

Sagamore looked around the room again. "Uhhh, yeah, okay. Anyway, we just wanted to give you an update from the Guild. You got additional unsolved murders in that cluster popping up in the News Casts.

"Maybe not for too long, since HMCP will probably quell that data stream faster than you can say shut the flock up. But Nash isn't the only Bogie gone possessing humans in Hercules. He's building a club. We have three new suspected psycho killers."

He waved his hands several times and holo IDs came into view with additional personal info chiming in on Vince's comm. "Have fun." He winked and was gone.

367

Berg Chanticleer had heard through the grapevine there are some pretty horrific killings of late, so when he came to guard duty at the Precipice station he was a little more apprehensive than his ordinary sense of things that evening. Four suspect males and a female were on the main holoscreen as he sat down at his desk and sent the previous shift home. His partner, Phoebe Lokhawandala was the type of girl who had all the martial arts and attitude but systematically let the men do any heavy lifting or approach delivery inspections first. Great, the bug heads were loose and spilling blood and he was stuck with Prima Donna Lokhawandala working the back door.

"Any deliveries tonight?" She asked as if she would be the one stepping outside on the platform to do any work.

"Three." He replied. All drops from Phlegra station. Standard regs', milk and cookie runs" he replied coolly.

She ran the zip of her collar down a bit, "Hot in here tonight. They got the heat up?" She asked. Pure manipulation, he thought. The more work he did, the sexier she would act to make his evening more pleasant. Knowing he was being manipulated, twelve hours was a long haul, and it went a lot more pleasantly if she poured on the charms, he would pick up more of her duties anyway. Twelve hours with a charming female co-worker flew by like six. Twelve hours with an obstinate and contrary female co-worker was like an eternity where you wished your mother and father never met.

"Creepy suspects," she offered, looking over the bios. "Weird though, aside from the nightclub owner from the Sagittarius Arm, they all were pretty squeaky clean before going rad."

He took a closer look at the bios. "Yeah, that is weird. One was even a cop."

"Oh, and a bad cop is out of the ordinary? Not." She countered.

"He wasn't a bad cop. Look again. They managed to pull his file out of the Outworlds-that ought to tell you something right there. There's more to this than a few creeps coming undone. Something ain't right with this."

"Iww." She snorted. "Your right. Hey, look at this. His face before he went AWOL with the club Madame." She pulled up an image of Nash. Handsome, self-righteous, solid. "Now look at the clip made from the fire wagon."

Berg snickered, "They're equipping the fire wagons in the Outworlds with cameras now?" he laughed.

"Apparently so," she replied, "but look, look." She waved her hand and the holo from the night of the fire came up. Nash's face looked totally different. It was the same man, but there was a wildness, an amused look; hardly appropriate for an officer who had just witnessed a tragedy.

"He was already whacked out." She said triumphantly. "The next day he and the owner of the club decided to kill all the customers and chop them up."

A feeling of coldness ran through the room and they both looked at each other uncomfortably. She tightened her collar. He glanced at the temperature indicator and it remained unmoved. He glanced at the door; readout-seals were tight.

There came a sound from the walls; a banging.

"Sounds like we got a crab dog crawling in the ventilation ducts." He raised his hands. "What a way to start the shift."

"I'll get some bots" She replied and began calling up bot programs. On another level of the facility six service bots the size and shape of bread boxes came online and dropped down from storage and began making their way to the back service entrance.

The banging came again.

Berg called up a sweep of the cameras in the vicinity of the service doors. He saw nothing. He ran a back-check; the same. He went as far as the other shift clambering in vehicles and making away. Nothing out of the ordinary. He decided to log a report. "Nightshift, Berg Chanticleer, we've got something in the air ducts. It sounds like a crab dog trying to get in out of the cold. No indications from a camera check, however. Running bots into the ducts now for a spot check."

No matter how circumspect he was, it would drop in his lap of course that the crab dog got in, and his supervisor would run him over the coals. Best to follow protocols tightly-if it came up for review the record would show him doing his job. That would make it harder for his chump boss to throw him into the singularity.

"What was that?" Phoebe asked as she came over to his playback of the security tape.

"Just running a back-check but I didn't see anything," he replied.

"Didn't see anything? I'm sure I saw a figure standing just outside the lights. Run it again." She said.

He ran it again and neither of them saw anything. There was, however, a disorienting point in the playback when each of them rubbed their heads together and there seemed a blurring of vision. There was only the night, the sweep of the crater side going down and down into the darkness, and the stars of the cluster, numerous and cold.

The bots had begun to run a pre-programmed sweep of the air ducts and their attention moved to other screens. There came long boring minutes looking at the interior of air ducts.

"*Berg*" came a whisper.

He looked over at Phoebe. "What? Why are you whispering?"

"What are you talking about, I didn't say anything." She snapped. "Pay attention-if there's anything I hate, it's crab dogs. You deal with this one and I'll work my shift in a bikini." She laughed.

He cocked an eyebrow. "Really?"

She punched him lightly on the arm, "No. But hang on to that when the bots find the Crab."

A few moments passed. "*Berg*" came the whisper again.

He looked at her with annoyance. She must have wanted him to get the bug. He would play it for what it was worth he decided. Maybe she would go out with him for a day-cap after shift.

Bang, from the walls again, harder.

In another part of the facility, data streams had been running back to Roshan's office. She had asked that double blinds be put in place anywhere Leavel, Sole and Sulla went and the security team had called her out of her quarters for what they deemed an emergency.

"What is it?" She demanded with the uncompromising tone of an event horizon.

"Your double-blind. Something's going on at Precipice station. One of the guards at the back service door ordered up some bots to look for a crab dog in the air ducts. Ordinary enough stuff. Then he ran a back check on the security cameras-spot on doing his job. Yet here" he called up a spy camera of Berg at his screens, "he looks right at a figure on the security playback like it isn't there. His coworker sees it and asks him for a replay. When he replays it, she then looks at it like it isn't there. Look at their hands go up to their heads as the figure appears on the screen."

"*Sole was right*. These things can mess with your perceptions," She barked. "Get on the guns from here. They're going to be attacked and probably not know what the heck is happening before it's too late. Whatever is messing with their minds doesn't know about the double-blind because they don't know. Don't notify the main security office at Precipice or the things will know then too. Just run the guns from here. Any delay won't be significant."

"Roger that. Stat," he replied and four police MERGED into the Precipice facility's guns.

"There!" One of them called out. "The figure is making to the door, calm as a stasis chamber, too."

On the screens, they could see the dark figure move like an automaton, closer and closer toward the service doors.

From the double-blind, they could hear Berg and Phoebe chatting as if nothing was happening, focused on finding the crab dog.

"Stop doing that" Berg was saying to her.

"Hello! You're delusional." Phoebe replied.

"It isn't funny, Phoebe-it's darned creepy."

"You're the one whose creepy, Berg. I'm not saying anything. If you're hearing voices, I suggest we call the Med lab right away and get someone out here to finish your shift because, there is just way too much weirdness going on lately for me to be working with a schizoid, okay?"

He glared at her. "It will all be on the playback."

Unaware of the figure moving calmly across their security screens, toward the door, they continued their inane bantering.

Sternly, Roshan called up a satellite scan of the area around the base. "One figure only, Director. Moving toward the door."

"Blow its legs off and sear the arteries. Let's see if we can't get him alive."

"Back door guns firing...now" One of the officers called out, and there came a flash of laser fire. The figure doubled over. One of the other officers operated a close up of the camera and they saw the figure turn as if in pain- he was cut off at the knees. Expertly he fired again cauterizing the arteries and stopping the bleeding.

At the firing of the guns, Berg could be heard calling out an expletive and turning to the screens. This time he could see someone was there.

"Holy smokes, there's somebody out there!" Phoebe snapped, hitting a red alert.

"Command this is Lokhawandala at the back door. We have guns shooting people down here. Are you operating the guns?"

Command came back, "Negative on that Lokhawandala. Keep the doors sealed until you have more information. Do not let anyone in. I'm checking now-yeah I see him."

Roshan sent a priority holo silently to the Command at that point. Confused, Precipice Station command suddenly saw the words "Do not engage, do not inform the rear service door that you are being overridden from HMCP command."

The holo repeated until he replied with "Acknowledged, will not engage, will not inform the service door team you are aware of the condition."

Berg's voice came across the coms, "Command, request permission to engage. Going outside to see who the devil we just shot."

"Negative, Berg. Sit tight." Command shot back. "Repeat, do not open the service door, do not engage a person of unknown origin." Berg couldn't know that Command had just locked his whole system down tight.

The figure began crawling toward the door with his arms.

Back at HMCP, Roshan whistled, "Will you look at that?" she blurted out.

Suddenly Berg began yelling, "Phoebe, settle down."

His partner was moving about the room in hysterics, "Kill them, kill them, Berg, damn it!"

"Kill what?" he bellowed, "Put the gun away Phoebe, stand down! There is nothing there!"

She began firing into the wall. "Son of a pup!"

Berg tackled her from behind, and attempting to disarm her received a savage kick to the groin.

Roshan understood what was happening. "Kill the intruder, headshot."

The officer on the gun complied with deadly accuracy and the intruder's head burst in a sudden pop. The corpse collapsed.

Phoebe immediately stopped screaming, breathing heavily and swinging her pistol around, again and again, looking for the crab dogs that moments before had filled the entire room. She was panting rapidly, and Berg was bowled over in pain.

"Precipice Command," Roshan barked, "Get those two in an infirmary now and double the guard on the back entrance. I want them sedated, under observation and tied down. Double-blind the infirmary as well."

She looked to her team, "Good work. Get a satellite record from the last twelve hours. Find out where the figure came from-match him up as well with the suspects in the recent murders, I'm sure you'll find it was one of them."

She looked over the security screens with an icy gloom. Winteroud's warning had given them some insight into the nature of the Bogie's method of attack, and allowing for the double-blind has saved the facility from becoming a complete loss. Eventually, she knew, the nature of their double-blind defenses would get out-if the things could read minds they would eventually get a hold of someone aware of the blinds. Then the humans' defenses would be compromised.

They had held their ground today and taken one of the enemies down. They were going to need rotating encryption programs and lots of bots. She wondered darkly if the Bogies could manipulate sentient androids and programs, as well as they seemed to be able to create illusions in the minds of organic creatures.

When she got back to her suite, she doubled the guard. They were unaware of the blind. She made sure her HMCP staff NCO also rotated the blind and went off duty. She didn't know who her blind would be, and that NCO was off shift. A game of cat and mouse had begun. She didn't like being the mouse.

Two days ago she didn't know who Winteroud Sole or the crew of the Sire were, today they had just provided her with the insight to save a great deal of life at one of the company's most important facilities. Humanity was in its first interspecies war with something the likes of which she had never imagined. She would need all of her wiles now. She went to the window and looked out at the stars of the Hercules cluster, her home. She had spent her life watching the corporation grow-building, settling, creating. She had no intention of going down without a fight.

The Cat's Paw Nebula, Scorpius.

Harry Stark could smell the Cat's Paw Nebula long before he glided the Riptide out of hyper, easing back into normal space, and it was like a field of flowers. Of course, since everything one experiences in MERGE is a virtual construct, the gasses of the nebula could have been made to smell like anything. But the Riptide was a luxury yacht before it was refitted as Harry's private battlewagon, so the Cat's Paw smelled good- yacht owners don't take well to programmers who make the flight experience unpleasant.

"If you can't be Goulet, don't play" the yacht salesman had explained. Harry had shrugged and bought the whole shipyard.

NGC 6334, the Cat's Paw Nebula. Fifty light-years of some of the biggest star nurseries in the galaxy, toward the center, toward the core. He surveyed the broad sweep of gas and dust clouds with a run of different infrared and x-rays. He consulted the charts. He became familiar in more detail with the territory-as he had been doing in the long weeks of hyperspace. He looked at the big young stars-some ten times standard solar mass. He cataloged the accretion discs, proto-planets, heaving billows of the nebula. Asteroid belts raw and red with impacts.

The hunting ground.

At the edges; shaken into coalescing by ancient interstellar shock waves, there were remnant Oort clouds of icy comets, dropping into the maelstrom of the star-forming region from the distant blackness of the void again, following the complex vectors and apogees of a gravitational beehive.

The boredom of hyper had been grueling-ever and always the same. The rush and bang of the early legs of the space journey eventually giving way to the uncompromising responsibilities of keeping the crate airworthy, staying alert, staying alive. Then the joy of arrival, the sense of accomplishment. Harry's head, deep in his MERGE helmet, bent forward unconsciously- arrival at the Cat's Paw wasn't the accomplishment of this mission. This was going to be a waste of mesons if he didn't take some prisoners.

"Surfin' Safari!" Mustafa Sanfillipo smacked Harry a high five as he came out of MERGE.

"Cat's Paw is ours. Throw out a beacon with the Ahura Mazda flag. We're taking this nebula." Harry said casually.

Snickers and guffaws from the crew.

They think I'm kidding.

"Go ahead, drop the beacon." He said. "The Pleiades too was a region like this once-not long ago in cosmic time. Today, the Marauders raid the burnished celestial wastelands. Today, the Bogies are creeping at our heels like emissaries of death-but this day will pass." He gave them a rakish glare of challenge, "We will take by storm, we will grind our enemies at our heels, and we will plant orchards of cherry blossoms on uncharted worlds-worlds which we will name."

The bridge crew stared silently back.

He returned the stare, "Hey man, we're making history here, write that down."

The Riptide hit the nebula with a plasma shockwave slamming the gasses, a light show, a beacon, and a song broadcasting high and wide: *My Maria*. They had to look like a drunkard's dream to the Marauders, busting in noisy and oblivious like a twisted wealthy tourist too long removed and sheltered from the nature of reality.

Just what Harry wanted them to look like; a fat huckleberry for easy picking on a sunny day.

So they laid themselves noisily and brightly into the Cat's Paw nebula as bait for the Marauders. The question, Harry mused, was what exactly did the Marauders use the nebula for? To catch a thing, you had to know a thing. Any planets formed in this nebula were still molten spheres of Hellish landscapes. The Stars themselves had barely beat away the raw hot gasses of the halos of their formation. Yet reports of Marauders here were so common as to become synonymous with the place. Fifty light-years of spanking hot new stars most everyone avoided- because of the Marauders.

In his Cabin, Harry spun a hologram of the Cat's Paw and wondered, "Mustafa, my man, there has to be an economy to this that we're missing. There isn't enough traffic here for the Marauders to profitably sit and wait for booty. No, they come here for something. But what does this place have which they can't get at the galactic core?"

Mustafa had a bottle of rum out and poured a couple of glasses.

"Less other Marauders?" Mustafa mused. "Maybe these are like second-tier Marauders. Outcast psychos? Maybe there's nothing special here at all- just that it's not the core, where the Marauder hierarchy may lay a special claim-holy space or something as such."

"What is Jerusalem worth?" Harry replied.

"Boiled down to the essence, that's a good analogy. There hasn't been a whole lot of documentation of Marauder culture-if you want to call it that- but we do know they worship the giant black hole at the galactic core as a god of sorts. We know they've acquired some Predecessor technologies and may have somehow been influenced by a Predecessor religion." Mustafa lifted his glass, "Cheers".

Harry did the same and the two officers belted their shots and breathed in the rum taste to their nostrils.

Harry waved away the holo of the Cat's Paw and waved another into view. "I found this when I was tracking down the Taloned Sire. The chowder head captain had solo piloted his first flight-right through the void and into a firefight answering a Trade Guild distress call. Dumb luck of virgins. Anyway, between him and the Guildsman they busted up that raid and the Marauders fled. The ones they hadn't killed.

"A university from the Pleiades sent out an Anthropology team later to scour the Marauder ship derelicts drifting after the firefight. Seems the Marauders discovered a cache of Predecessor recordings. Of course, the Predecessor technology wasn't designed for the human organism, so there are all kinds of side effects-like insanity-when the Marauders suck on that nipple like piglets.

Mustafa winked, "I got the memo, Sir, reviewed the briefs, where are you going with this?"

"Don't give me that wink, yes I have a relative point. But bear with me, genius; Generals must have our stage. If we can capture any of these demented freaks, we'll need to present them with motivation. In their mind, Ninety percent of the universe is Dark Matter, and our whole reality a simple test of worth before one goes 'into the black hole' and on to the "real existence". They actually won't see the Bogies raping and pillaging the rest of humanity as a problem. They'll see it more like the retribution of their black hole god, for us not paying homage."

"Until the Bogies come in force to the core." Mustafa laughed.

"Yeah…well, if it gets that far we'll already be roach dung, so that scenario isn't going to work. Maybe they've had a few Bogies nipping at their heels. But not the horde. Neither can we count on the Marauder's love of humankind. We'll need to impress upon them the very real possibility that the Bogies will exterminate them, and their black hole god will go un-worshipped."

"That might work." Harry agreed.

Mustafa ran his eyes idly over the rosewood panels of the cabin's interior. Various trim and wainscoting were detailed with hand-carved sea nymphs and creatures and mother of pearl trimmed touch-panels which opened to various cabinets and systems. He was sure there probably wasn't a millimeter of the room Harry hadn't brooded over and refit with unnumbered contraptions, upgrades, and delicious mystery.

"Anyone ever catch one of these Marauders before?" he asked with a full knowledge that no one had. It was part of his job to prod his superior, however.

"Of course not, because never was there a Pirate clan like the Dark Corps, heheheh! We are the mighty hunters before the great black hole god."

"Like Nimrod before the Lord?" Mustafa chuckled.

"Something like that. I don't know, spin it for me when the smoke clears."

Something here, some reason, some wonder, something-something-something.

His mind methodically ran through fifty light-years of the charted Cat's Paw nebula.

Something uncharted, something the survey teams failed to note or evaded as they skedaddled for the university quads and their mommies rather than standing and fighting like they had a pair, returning with a proper survey.

Mustafa drilled him a hard stare, "Spin masters we will be. Of a hard necessity. You realize the plan you've contrived is 'we're trespassing on their turf, blasting them silly, kidnapping a few', and that is our diplomatic effort. Not exactly one for your political science master's thesis."

"Hey, they're Marauders. They'll understand." Harry smiled. "I still say there's something else-some reason why they're here. Find that and we'll find their whole raunchy lair."

Something-something-something.

It turned out to be rain.

In a Goldilocks region where the heat of the Nebula met the cold of the teeming Oort clouds, there was rain. Rain in gaseous space, rain on the comets, and rain on the forming planetoids. A region of rain that ran for a good twenty light-years along an arc. There was so much water in so many places Harry understood then, too, why the Marauders had made such a point of eviscerating any ship that wandered into the region-leaving just enough alive to limp home and report the nebula a flight risk.

"You know," Harry announced to the bridge crew when the reports of the rain came in, "these Marauders aren't known for backup systems. I'd bet this yacht these freakazoids are tapping this region for their entire water supply and don't have an alternative."

"A water Empire, Sir." One of the men offered. "One band of barbarians and the whole set of dominoes tumbles."

Harry gleamed, then chuckled. "Hey, who you calling a barbarian?" His attempt at light humor as they sped further, alone, into a what was a Marauder super-nest failed to ease the bridge crew's nerves which were steadily hardening as they readied for combat mode. Good. Harry thought.

"We got traffic." Mazak said coolly, "Lots of traffic. Twenty-three, fanning out and wide, headed toward us."

"Trace their vectors, find out where they originated." Harry came back.

"Done, Sir. System-here." Mazak called up a holo and a system came up floating in the bridge room.

"Recon bots- I want to know everything we can about that system."

"Standard ten?" Mazak asked.

"No, send all thirty. Hyper cast to Electra base if we don't make it out of here alive, as an alternate Intel destination. Until then, we receive encrypted code. Now…what are they throwing at us?"

"Twenty-three attack ships. Fanning, as I said." Mazak put all twenty-three ships up as holos in an array. At this distance, the holos were little more than fists of wrinkled grey with tails of fire shimmering.

Mustafa looked them over each with a quick disdain. "Typical Marauder junk. Magnetized and cemented panels or raw ore propelled from giant blast shields, and antenna that manipulated anti-mass rip shots."

Harry smiled. "Effective for surprise attacks on civilian shipping. Let's see how they like the Riptide. "Wormhole behind them now." The rest of the convoy remained back.

Mustafa fired a short stream of a wormhole and the Riptide leaped through the space-time and was suddenly behind the Marauder front. Mazak didn't need to know the next call but dutifully waited. It came: "Distortion wave."

The Riptide bent space in a savage, rippling shockwave. They hadn't fired a shot and all twenty-three of the Marauder ships had just been given a smackdown from Hell.

They responded with a volley of anti-matter orbs that came in from all directions.

Mazak did a little dance in his seat as he guided the Riptide between and around the volley. "Standard anti-mass shots." He drawled.

"Okay." Harry began. "We're on a diplomatic mission here, so…let's send them a message. Cut their blast shields from their main engines. Then, engrave 'Hello, kitty-cat' with laser blasts on the side of each vessel."

Mazak was splining his flight plan hard and wild, while a second gunner popped the blast shield of the first ship. Anti-matter fire was coming in, but Sanfillipo edged their bent space wave such that by the time it rounded the curve it went past harmlessly. The first blast shield went spinning off taking a piece of the Marauders magnetized panel in a grinding splash of metal, rock, and light.

In a blinding flash, the lasers of the Riptide engraved.

Hello, Kitty-cat.

Sanfillipo shook and bent the space around the ship in an artful series of warps. "Too many antimatter shots coming in, suggest we back off a bit Sir on the next run."

The volleys of antimatter balls streamed in, and Mustafa fielded them away with a steady focus.

Harry raised his eyebrows, "Oh come on there's only twenty-two left." But nodded to navigation to do as Mustafa instructed.

The first Marauder vessel was dead in the water, so to speak. Mazak imagined them yelping at one another helplessly inside. One of the Riptide's gunners seared their antimatter gunports closed.

The Cat's Paw Nebula gleamed about the Riptide like the light of glory. The Riptide raged, rippled, and waved the space-time, spun the mesons, and lasered "Hello, Kitty-cat" through the attack group of Marauders. One after another, she popped them silly until they lay like so many dumb asteroids in a field. Quite an insult actually, for a mission that was attempting diplomatic contact. But Harry wanted to establish his outfit's superiority in their minds. Diplomacy always worked better when your adversary is completely convinced you can wipe the street with their shorts and bloody face.

"You figure a command targ?" Harry asked, looking at Mazak.

"Encrypted codes, but most were to this one" he called up a holo of one of the drifting Marauder attack vessels. "And from it as well, so we can pretty much call him a team leader."

"Okay, then, start peeling away her shielding. Slowly, so they'll have time to think about the radiation they're eating in their chromosomes. Time to get into their EVA suits. When you peel the hull open keep an eye out for disser fire. They come spilling out into space in their spacesuits they might still be armed. I would. Let them float out there for a couple of hours. Then we'll pull them in."

As expected the Marauders didn't send another wave of attack ships. Apparently, they left themselves no reserves and would be busy converting other vessels for combat as Harry played with his quarry at leisure. Mazak did the dirty work of peeling the Marauder ship open like kicking an anthill.

By then the recon drones were sending back data from the marauder settlements and the rest of humanity got its first ugly introduction to the Marauder religion.

The recon drones were specifically designed to be small and unobtrusive-at the level of actual data gathering, they dispersed cameras and sensors as small as insects. The Marauders never knew they were there. They flew in high over the Marauder city. A series of stepped pyramids and plazas surrounded a larger collection of ramshackle hovels. Fields of agriculture spread out from there.

"A lot more of them here than one would have gathered," Harry said with uncharacteristic surprise.

The drones flew closer and figures could be made out in the plaza. Figures on the temples. Lower then, and slowing, the images flashed in on an array of thirty holos. Everyone was tattooed. But not the thoughtful, artful tattoos common to mankind-rather a vicious erratic happenstance of runes and symbols like ground car tire marks scrabbled over a dirty alley.

Dehumanizing marks. Assertions of worthlessness.

Numbers of people were tied to poles. They had been tortured-some were wrapped in skin suits cut off other victims. The skin suits were squeezing the life out of them in the grimy heat of a bloated new sun that shot a ragged light through the Cat's Paw Nebula in intermittent sunbeams of hate. Others were dancing. On the temples, human entrails spilled in a cascade of gore.

Mazak barked an expletive.

Harry smiled. "Hello Kitty." He said. "Witness the heart of your brethren."

Sanfillipo sneered, "Hey, I don't mean to state the obvious but anyone else here get the feeling someone resurrected the religion of the Aztecs?"

Mazak nodded. "I've seen a lot of degenerate, retrograde-horse-balls concocted as 'new' in this galaxy, but this dung show takes the cake."

Harry said: "There is nothing new under the suns."

The drone holos continued to flash atrocity after atrocity, and even the battle-hardened crew of the Riptide was moved to disgust.

"Looks like the Bogies have already established their devil's orchard," Sanfillipo said quietly.

"That's a good question. Is Marauder society manipulations, or merely the dark side of human nature?" Harry said with the cold estimation of a statistician, oblivious to the irony of him raising the question. The dark Lord of the Dark Corps.

The answers would be forthcoming. Mazak announced they were tractor beaming in the survivors from the Marauder ship they had just opened like a tin can. Mazak was having fun with the other gunners punching laser holes in the handguns the survivors brought out in their EVA suits. They were taking bets on who could disable the lasers without punching holes in the Marauder EVA suits. Nobody missed so nobody won. Targ technologies on the Riptide where always state of the art.

They pulled six of them into the airlock, filled it with a sedative gas and then punched discrete holes in their EVA suits. Fish in a barrel; the terror of the spaceways, the mighty Marauders, were tied, disrobed, tied down and on a slab in the med lab, waking up in compromising positions.

Its business is done, with "Hello Kitty" engraved on a small flotilla of disabled Marauder attack ships, the Riptide turned and broke into hyper with its new cargo, and was gone before the refitted ships of the Cat's Paw nebula could mount a counteroffensive. Diplomacy at its finest.

Harry stood in the med lab leaning over the first of them as they came to. "Son," he said with his face close to the rune-covered Marauder, "are you ashamed of what you are?"

The Marauder tried to head butt him, but Harry was too quick, backed away and then head-butted him instead.

"Don't even." He screamed. "Or I'll slap your skank self in a pain simulator and you'll rot there for a century before I come in, defecate on your head and tell you I'll see you in another century. I am not the law."

Then he slapped him a couple of times for good measure.

The Marauders' nose was broken.

"Watch the blood Sir," one of the Med techs said idly, almost amused. "We don't know what this turd is carrying."

"You will be fed to the dark god." The Marauder shot back. "We will watch you scream at the event horizon as time slows and spaghetti is your essence."

"Put a pain simulator on him," Harry said casually, and the med-tech plunged the Marauder's head into a MERGE device.

The man's face could be seen beneath the clear plexisteel of the MERGE device. It wasn't pretty. His screams filled the small med lab as Harry moved to the next captive. "I have more of those simulators if you want to be as rude as your comrade," he said coolly.

The man considered the anguish of his crewmember. "What do you infidels want?" he asked as defiantly as possible.

Good, Harry thought. They aren't as completely schizoid as they pretended.

Harry stood up tall and showed his palms, "We're just here to make friends."

The rune-covered maniac glared at him unmoved. "The one who walks behind the event horizon is our only friend. We, its food. You are unworthy. Your tortures of us, no matter how long you contrive to extend them-they are finite. This universe is finite. It is drying up like the rain on a hot day-its neutrinos fading into nothing, like Hawking radiation. We are the servants of the event horizons. We will shine in the next universe when you, and all your subatomic particles, have faded into non-reality."

Harry glanced at the med-tech who read his intention and injected the marauder with a truth serum-sedative.

"That all may be true," Harry said with a soothing tone. "But there is a war in heaven. The one who walks behind the event horizon has a new enemy-the evil ones who would steal his food, and though we, as you say, do not serve the one who walks behind the event horizon, we too are targeted by the evil ones who wish to make us their food."

The injected Marauder looked at him with a wild consternation.

Harry signaled and the pain simulator was removed from the other Marauder. There was a detachment to the Marauders that belied a difference between them, and what might be considered a normal human.

"Although we could have taken much life today, we killed no one. We have disabled your flotilla and destroyed one ship. But we have taken none of the lives of those who serve the one who walks behind the event horizon," Harry said enticingly. "We are not here to do you harm, but propose a strange, and unlikely alliance.

"There have been ships of your people killed by an unknown enemy?" he drilled the runed face with an uncompromising stare.

The truth serum was taking effect, and slowly, against the Marauder's better judgment, he admitted; "Yes. There have been strange deaths. We are aware…of evil ones."

There you go, little psycho, tell me more. "And these evil ones, they kill how?"

"They are the ones the great voice of the oracle spoke of. The war in heaven, the great evil. Surely you nations of the disc-away from the great black hole and the one who walks behind the event horizon-surely you will find your place in neither light nor darkness, and be cast from the outer galactic disc to oblivion."

"Your oracle. What happened to its "nation?" Harry asked-knowing full well the "oracle" of the Marauders was a Predecessor MERGE style recording.

"They were cast down. Smitten by the evil ones, their souls have journeyed on into the great black hole. They are with the one who walks behind the event horizon. We have been gathered to stand against the evil ones."

Back in Harry's cabin of the Riptide, Mazak joined Harry and Sanfillipo for a glass of rum. "Work with me gents. Ideas are turning in the back of my head in regards to what the Marauder said. The first thing-the origins of Marauder culture. Probably outcasts, rejects, misfits, and petty criminals settling the core. At some point, one of them discovers the Predecessor relic; an ancient MERGE facility with a message pertaining to the Bogie swarm."

"There was also a group of researchers at a Predecessor Base as well. That might have went sideways too. Maybe it was a warning to other races and they had them planted around the core assuming if higher life forms were to evolve on the periphery of the galaxy, exploring the core is something all of them would inevitably be drawn to?" Mazak interjected.

Sanfillipo nodded. "Sounds reasonable. Except at that time, there were no other races. The Predecessors were alone in the galaxy when the Bogies slammed them."

Harry frowned. "Presumption, assumption, whatever-we don't know that. We know they were the dominant, most advanced species at that time. But there must have been a plethora of other species-other higher life forms-that had also been moving toward sentience."

"MERGE technologies are pretty species-specific I would imagine. Neural nets, their particular organic construction and a critical mass of cell features needed to effect self-awareness-I just can't see a MERGE system ever created that can function across species."

Mazak mumbled negatively and sipped his rum with a relish.

"Yet we have an example of a species-the Bogies themselves-that have evolved just such a capacity without resorting to technology. They can sense and read the electrical fields produced by the organisms' neural net. So if it can evolve in nature it can be mimicked with technologies." Harry countered.

"Maybe the Predecessors realized it had happened in nature and had begun research and development along those lines. This could have been some project of theirs, abandoned after a Bogie attack wiped out their facility, and then discovered by humans many millennia later."

Harry nodded, "Yes...we'll need at some point to see this oracle ourselves. We can't just go in there guns blazing, odds are we'd damage it. We'll either need a spy-disguised as one of these Marauders or to achieve enough diplomatic status that we'll be granted rights to examine it."

Sanfillipo looked at him grimly. "Their brain scans have shown consistent abnormalities. This follows logically. The Predecessor Merge oracle would have been designed to function with a Predecessor modeled brain. Finding analogous structures in the human brain it would have then interacted-and affected them. We find the more primitive cores of the brain's stem, and immediate structures around them, hyper stimulated-extra thick cell growth, density, etc. in the Marauders we captured."

Harry smiled. "Which would explain their fondness for a direct attack. Since they're operating from the primitive lizard-brain, part of the human mind inherited from our most distant ancestors. This also fits in with what CC has been suggesting about the Predecessors-that they were reptilian. Their super advanced-but reptilian-brains create the MERGE oracle, and when humans step up to the plate eons later, the thing only communicates with our remnant lizard hind brains-and with an intensity that super-stimulates them creating these altered personalities."

Mazak growled, "Effectively another form of Transhuman. So now we have the Imperial Overlords taking their humanity down the road of the quantum computer, and these characters of the other end morphing their brains into lizard mirrors."

Harry cocked an eyebrow, "There is only one thing to do." Mazak eyed him expectantly. Sanfillipo made a half-smile. "Give me another shot of that rum, brother, another shot of that rum." Harry finally said.

Mazak did, snickering. "To Chrysalis Isla."

"Saluda!"

Behind the Riptide, the Cat's Paw nebula shrank slowly in the rear window of the cabin. Of course, the window was a facsimile of what one would see if light could keep up with the ship, which it could not, as they were deep in the hyperstreams now, deep in the rush and celestial power of heavy-metal, gravity squeezing, space bending, field shielded, cannon-laden oversize-hyper-driven yacht at its best.

Back in the Cat's Paw Nebula, the Marauders were rescuing their stranded fellows left by the Riptide with their blast shields separated from their ramjets. Over and over again they came across Harry's message, furious with one question-Who engraved "Hello Kitty-cat?" all over their blast shields?

Pleiades Cluster, Honey-Pie
Long black air cars
Silver spires shrouded in suns-lit cloudscapes
Motion, relentless motion
Sees me to the other side of the world
Home in time for dinner

And your rosy red lips
"Virtual Tinsel"
-Chowder head boo-boos, Starky Barky Holos

Roshan recounted the attempt on Precipice station to Vince, Winteroud, and Lisa the morning after via the holo conference. Sole was still sick from the stresses of reading quanta and hung on her words with a desperate effort. His head felt like someone had poured a liquid gel into his brain which had hardened, setting all his thoughts in slow motion. The muscles of his back ached in a way that disturbed him because it seemed the flesh itself was somehow wrong in ways that portended worse things to come. Yet he took an earnest satisfaction in knowing his insights had proved useful in combating the horrors of the Bogies.

Lisa insisted on getting to the satellite tracking of the intruders' origins, following the lead back to where the man had come from. Even Vince noted for allowing himself neither comfort nor safety, was concerned that her driving pursuit was going to damage Sole permanently. He said as much, and she seemed to realize only then, the strains Sole's quantum readings had been taking. "I'll go alone," she said, determined.

Sag would have seen in her fearless determination another flag-such fearlessness wasn't born of Sophisticated Art dealing, it was born of the knowledge that she was capable of more than they were fully aware. Vince, however, had already begun to take her and Sole under his protective wing and made no such gestalt leap of intuition-his mind was on protecting his people rather than examining them for potential subterfuge.

In the aircar, the sunlight was beaming down on them and the landscape like a canvas spread far and wide, over an unfamiliar world, Vince sensed a bright joy-a lovely woman, a new adventure-and realized he was in all reality feeling a sense of life that was passed irrevocably into another era. Long ago, when he had been much younger and had taken his first crewmember-Roland Danski-onto the Sire, Roland had warned of dark days to come, that they were in a new era-an Age of Pandora. Roland was still missing, presumed dead after Harry took down his ship the Serpentine. Harry was a strange ranger, however, Vince thought-vicious without remorse if one was his enemy, but not without a code of honor. Vince was beging to think he wouldn't butcher innocents and had merely been messing with No-Deal's mind.

Here then, he thought, were the first scattered skirmished of the Pandoran War? No...that Age had begun with the bombing of New Galen.

Eras of long wars invariably redefine societies.

The question here was not the redefinition, which would come as sure as the galaxy turns, but whether Humanity could survive at all. Somewhere, inside himself, he would have to find a way to keep some joy alive inside his soul regardless of the Hell-rides and smoking disasters. Without it, he would surely fail.

Whether a form of magic or madness, he would cling to joy. He knew at one level from certain experiences that the song of joy could sing from a sword as well as a harp.

For that morning, he chose to hear it in the sunlight on his face, the company of a beautiful woman, and flight. It would be fleeting, but he would find it and hold it wherever it might be in the storms of fury and confusion common to war.

"Penny for your thoughts?" Lisa asked with a smile.

Vince returned the smile, "Guitars, Cadillacs, and Hillbilly music."

Sulla had a handy-dandy scanner she used to examine Fine Artworks to test for forgeries and the eye-piece had an amazing range of uses. When they arrived at the next mining camp-the origin of the previous night's intruder-she had it out, performing a variety of examinations of the area and recording on a wide range of spectra. Vince watched her with a certain admiration-but his joy had slipped unnoticed to a combat mode of expectation and hyper-awareness. There were several more corpses-Vince called HMCP and made them aware they would have more bodies to rack up. Lisa recorded the scenes with a detached coolness and professionalism.

HMCP arrived a little while later. It was a stone's throw away to a larger settlement. They all headed over there and began questioning various people. Nothing out of the ordinary came up and Vince pointed out if it were mere numbers they had wanted, the closer settlement would have functioned as an easier target than Precipice station, which was looking increasingly like a coordinated action with the intent of getting at Sole, Sulla, and himself. Jane or Nash had sent the other victim in after them. Was there a hierarchy then in the Bogie universe? Possibly.

Everything was looking pretty copasetic at the settlement-no strange murders, no reports of missing people-when one of the HMCP cops pointed over toward one of the buildings. Several people were standing there. They didn't move. Vince followed the officers' observation. "What's wrong with this picture?" he asked rhetorically and pulled out his disser. Yet they seemed oblivious to the threat, staring blankly out into the bleak landscape.

Suddenly a seething blot twisted up out of the sand, an inky serpent-like maw of disruptive power rattling stones and sand into fury and bursts of flak. It was moving rapidly toward them.

"Split up!" One of the HMCP officers snapped, and they fanned out each looking for shelter, firing their dissers toward the automatons who were generating the disturbance. It rolled and expanded its black seething turmoil like an oil spill across the sand. The projected rubble battered the side of a mining unit which Vince and Lisa had taken shelter behind. Vince managed to pop off another shot-taking out one of them with an explosion of blood. Winds and sounds continued to rage-this was no illusion or manipulation. The Bogies had begun to cross over in numbers, and pooling their mental powers were able to affect matter in ways that could be used as tools of destruction.

One of the HMCP took another of the automatons out with a shot center mass.

The strange black disturbance diminished some, but not before it reached Lisa. Vince looked over to see her twisting and firing wildly into the clouds of sand and black strangeness that was enveloping her. It was with a great power that lifted her off her feet while rushing around and around her in a whirlwind.

Vince strode in the middle of it and was immediately buffeted back with a savage force that sent him sprawling, landing on his left side.

He dropped his weapon, and the HMCP officers could see his muscles struggling against the blackness. On a hunch that the origin of the strange black force was the weird figures by the buildings, the HMCP NCO barked, "Center mass!"

Their firing was a rapid staccato smacking-one of them had pulled a larger gun from their air truck. With the bloody shattering of the figures, the black force dissolved. Vince and Lisa, picking themselves up from the dusty ground and examining themselves for cuts and bruises, struggled to gather their breath.

"Thank you." Vince managed to the HMCP gunner, a huge grizzly old veteran with, "Hammerstein" emblazoned on his uniform. The gunner patted his weapon and smiled. "No problem, Buck."

Back at Precipice station, Vince informed Sole as to the morning's events and Sole, racked with pain and exhaustion already, soldiered on, reading what he could. Sole didn't look good. His face was white, his eyes sunken, his muscular body taking on a soft, sagging aspect as if his flesh was turning to mush.

Vince was uncomfortable with Sole reading while he recounted the attack. Winteroud insisted, however, assuring him that he was able to handle the pain.

"They channel energies together," Winteroud said at length. "They, the manipulations they manage, can be more than deadly illusions-they can be deadly realities. They're not omnipotent, however. The illusions are almost without any limitations, but actual forces over matter-they're defined by the physics of this universe and remain so."

He stumbled over to a window and took in the day like a man taking in his last meal. *Breathe. Focus.*

Try and stay in the land of the living.

"The one we met at the Yellow Jaguar-she's been here for centuries, and no, I don't mean Jane. The main horde of them has been elsewhere in the universe. They're not as adept at dealing with humans-that will be an advantage. But there is another group, stragglers that have been lingering around human civilization like psychic vampires for eons, causing havoc in people's lives-feeding like junkies off the misery and confusion they can inspire."

He wheezed collapsing into one of the floating chairs then.

"Enough! You rest now. You aren't going to save the universe if you push yourself to an early grave, Winteroud." Vince demanded.

Sulla waited without expression. Then she made a drink at the kitchen and brought it over to Winteroud. "Relax. Heal up."

He smiled up at her and sipped the drink, "Thank you."

A hologram of Director Roshan appeared in the room, glowing and fading, glowing and fading to signal her call.

"You going to answer that?" Sole asked.

Vince touched a panel on the wall and Roshan solidified visibly. She looked around the room and it was apparent she was linked in. "HMCP gave me the update on your fight with the Bogies today. Good work." She looked toward Sole and realized he was under duress.

"Rest up as need be. We've been contacted by an operator out of the Hercules company, another mining syndicate. They've managed to kill several 'psychotic individuals' in one of the smelter facilities who went wild. They're convinced it's some kind of virus. I haven't told them everything. When you're ready, we'll send you out there with HMCP back up." she took a long look at Sole. "Take the time you need, Mr. Sole looks like his health is at issue. Contact me in a day or two."

Vince looked to Sulla, then to Sole. "Fair enough", he said.

There would be no time for rest. Back at the Sire, Milin was at the helm of the Taloned Sire snoring. Sagamore is surfing a dating site. "Yeah baby, we're Guildsmen. One of the top ships in the organization-"

Suddenly the dash came alive with warning lights. Millin jumped up and leans toward a screen with a metallic sheen in his eyes.

"Gotta go, sweetie, " Sagamore switched off the screen and turned to Millin. Millin looks over cooly.

"Coded message from HCP. Massive spatial disturbances moving toward the cluster. A swarm."

Siluria

Ossa Vega and his men were busy examining the temples when suddenly one of the dinosaur creatures walked out of the shallows and moves directly toward them. It is wearing jewelry.

Several of the soldiers draw weapons and Vega waves for them to put the weapons down. "Hold! Stand down, everyone, standdown!" *At last.*

The dinosaur walked directly to Vega.

"Hello General Ossa." It said in deep, disturbing tones.

Vega straightened, suddenly faced with his scheming and intuition alive and breathing. "Hello."

In the sky suddenly a giant ring of light formed among the daylight stars. The Dinosaur looked toward it. "I've created a temporary hyper-gateway to the Hercules cluster and the planet you call Echo. It is where my race made its last stand, and where the things you call Bogies are returning.

"You need to take your ships and get there as fast as possible. The Bogies are back, in force."

"You expect me to drive my fleet through an alien gateway without Reconnaissance, and into a firefight? Just like that?"

The dinosaur made a groaning laughing sound. "Do your thing. Find a way. Win, Starman. Break things and kill people. Or better yet, break people and kill things."

Vega glared back, "Those are Omm's words-how did you-"

The Dinosaur leveled his frightening gaze, "Omm, yeah, pretty strange ranger, aye? Time to go Starman. Win. Or we're all finished. It's what you came here for, isn't it? An alliance? Okay, we're allies. Now go kick some Bogie-booty. He turned and headed back into the shallows.

Vega, dumbfounded looked at the hyper gateway and then at his men.

"Alright then. You heard the dinosaur, on your feet. Time to break people and kill things!"

There was a long moment of silence, finally broken by Yates, "Hoo-aghh!"

The soldiers spring into action.

Chrysalis Isla

Harry had the Marauder captives under guard and medical observation at one of his hospitals used singularly for Dark Corps requirements. There would be no leaks. His questioning of them was proving enlightening, but raised as many questions as answered, and was providing as yet no insights as to how they might be approached, as a society, for an alliance against the Bogies. He dug in for a long process, and read the encrypted reports from Max and the clone crew of the Baal Baby. They had reached the galactic core and were scanning with the drones in areas where anomalies had continued to be reported.

"I've got a pool of anomalies not far from the gas giant system where the first expedition was routed. Going in. No surrender, no retreat, Mercurio out." came the last report, and there was nothing to do then but wait.

Harry looked to Sanfillipo with a hard, worn stare. "It ain't over," He said.

Galactic Core

The Baal Baby passed the Gas giant where Max had woke up in a dive. Maximus is at the helm of the Baal Baby now fully staffed with his crew of clones. They are in combat gear.

"We have a ripple sign." Achilles Bell said in a quiet but feral tone.

Mercurio blasted back, " Red Alert. Steady as she goes. Hyper-fritzers on deck!"

"It sees us, it's moving toward us," Beatrice Allfire chimed, "The same pattern as before. Circling the ship. Some hesitation, however.'

"Here it comes!" Achilles added.

Suddenly the cabin is alive with smoldering clouds. An awful monstrous head popped through the smoke and looked at Max. Its eyes widen in horror.

It gleamed, "You! Maximus Mercurio! No! No! It can't be!"

The Bogie's face morphed rapidly in strange incoherent animal forms of hysterical rage and then the cloud dispersed and it fled back into space.

Everyone on the bridge looks at each other in disbelief.

Looking to Max Beatrice said with a vicious smile, "It's fleeing!"

Max returned a wicked grin and leans forward. "Follow it. It's payback time."

The Baal Baby swooped after the fleeing Bogie which showed as a ghostlike dark presence on the screen. The Bogie moved quickly and planets swept by. It dashed careening toward a wormhole.

"It's headed toward a wormhole, Captain." Achilles said.

"Follow it in. No retreat!"

Beatrice looked at Achilles nervously, then back at her navigationals. "Entering the wormhole in five, four, three, two-"

The Baal Baby dove into the wormhole, sweeping through a blinding series of forces. The Bogie can be seen ahead.

Apola Svobada warned, "Hull pressures at critical, permission to activate the gravity bubble."

Maximus scowled. "Do it. Do it now."

The wormhole stormed in a deadly spin and the Baal Baby continued its foolhardy plunge through the strange abyss. The Bogie fled out of the wormhole into a distinctly different part of the galaxy. The Baal baby was careening after rolling and spinning within its gravity bubble then righting itself. It fired off a volley of shots.

Maximus's face was metal, "Where the flock are we?" he snarled.

Beatrice's face showed shocked from behind the MERGE helmet, "Twelve AU above the galactic plane, roughly one-third of the way out of the galaxy, Sir.

Maximus whispered, "Steady."

"There's another wormhole in its path, Sir." Achilles said.

Maximus looked darkly amused, "Yes, of course-it's an ancient being. Probably knows a network of them. Keep it in sight. Get ready with the gravity bombs."

Echo

Vince and Winteroud and Lisa stood astounded as the sky filled with dark clouds of Bogies transferring into out dimension.

Back in the Sire Millin is following Sagamore to engineering. Sagamore has an idea.

'So...what is it? What's the big idea?" Millin asked impatiently. Neither knew yet the swarm was breaking Dimension.

Sagamore swept his hair back with a rakish move, "Oh, yea of little faith! Who is the most brilliant engineer you know?"

"I'm from the Outworlds. We fell back into barbarism. I carry a sword."

"Okay then, so that would be me. I'm the most brilliant engineer you know."

Millin rolled his eyes, "So what is it?"

Then Hazel's appeared in the gangway. "They're here." She said.

Sagamore's demeanor suddenly darkened, "Come on, I'll have to show you quickly!"

Siluria

Vega Ossa watched patiently as the crews of the Hammerheads gathered up gear and returned to the fleet. The giant Leph had returned to the jungle as unceremoniously as he had appeared. Its stellar gateway gleamed huge in the sky. He made his way into his cabin in the Hammerhead and ordered a secure channel on the hypercaster.

Harry looked grim, but also feral, "So you think we have a chance?"

Vega returned the feral look, "Like a snowball in Hell."

"And you're going in anyway?" Harry brightened.

Vega winked, "Yeah, Buddy."

"Beauty."

The Hammerhead lifted off and in moments approached the First Strike. It had barely whined down antigravity server's and the last of Ossa's fleet entered Leph's gateway.

Unknown Wormhole String

The inertial dampers were straining as the Baal Baby banked to enter yet another wormhole pursuing the Bogie.

Maximus barked. "Where is it going?"

"These wormholes are all uncharted, Sir. We're running blind." Achilles Bell returned.

Maximus beamed madly, "Chasing a devil, blind down the rabbit holes...

ECHO

The Bogies begin dropping out of the sky and attaching to people's heads in amorphous clouds, the victims reacting in nightmarish fury from which anyone near them retreated in stunned panic. Across hundreds of kilometers of Echo City mining camps and stations the black, shadowy visions dropped like manure from flying beasts. At the head of the fetid swarm were Leyla and Nash like a duo of carnival barkers from Hell.

E. Gibbon lowered her gaze and felt for Winteroud's response to the sight, "Mr. Sole, it appears to be the end of the worlds as we know them."

Winteroud, not without a grim dash paused for effect, "Yes, yes, I see that. Are you getting this on tape?"

E. Gibbon smiled, "But of course."

"Very good. Wouldn't want to be thoughtless, some future species archaeologist will want to know!"

"Hi-Def sir, with surround sound." She showed a holo of the status.

"Nice!" Winteroud nodded, and they stepped forward into the swarm of demons.

Director Roshan watched in horror as Bogies dropped on to the city by the hundreds of thousands. An underling approached and handed her a tablet with a message. She looked at the message. "The Pleiades Syndicate at the Gateway? Well, let them through for Heaven's sake! Alles auf!"

Almost simultaneously an enormous stargate of pure energy appear tangential to the planet and the Imperial CCCE Fleet ships began moving through. Roshan looked out over the technicians and screens who had all looked back to her with dumbfounded disbelief and wonder. One could see strange nebula and planets through that energy gateway. One of her eyebrows rose as an ironic comment. If it was the end of the worlds, it was at least full of surprises.

Hundreds of Hammerhead attack ships burst forth from the fleet dropping toward the planet.

Crewman Yates watched his screens from a MERGE helmet as the strange swarm twisted and writhed across the expanse of the skies, and the fireballs of Hammerheads made their fiery replies. "Dang," he whispered.

There came a strange reverberating sound. His hammerhead suddenly penetrated by a Bogie, Yates ripped off his MERGE helmet and clambered savagely around the cockpit. Wildly swinging at the Bogie as it clung to his face, Yate's struggled with the abrupt barrage of horrific imagery violating his mind.

The hammerhead spun ferociously out of control and his co-pilot struggled with the controls. The dropship had several near collisions with other hammerheads in the drop. Yates, stepping out of his seat grav pins, went in free fall, and was bashed like a rag doll against the interior walls of the hammerhead. Bumping into his sound system, he activated it and the CHOWDERHEAD BOO-BOOS blast the cabin interior on full volume.

The Bogie is confused and disgusted at the sudden noise; this gave Yates enough time to remember his hyper-fritzer and he pulled one out of his pocket and shoves it in the creature's proboscis.

"Come on! Come on! Come on!" He bellowed violently, activating the hyper-fritzer. The Bogie is sliced into a million sheered parts.

Yates looked at his sound system, "Thank goodness for the Boo-boos!" he said.

The copilot leveled the ship's dive.

Smoke and strange lights rose from Echo City in a Halloween phantasm of Death rising, the smoke and dim lights framed two figures walking over a rise. It was Jane and Nash. Vince glanced at Lisa furtively, then checked the charge on his pulse weapon.

"Captain Leavel! Did you miss me?" Leyla-Jane's voice rang like a brass gong as if from some deep torture chamber in a surreal hell in the dimension of the Bogies, "How do you like me now?"

She stepped out of the smoke, bloody and filthy and half-naked. She raised her arms and spun macabrely dancing, waving dissers.

Lisa's jaw hung open for a long moment then she turned to Vince, "That was your girlfriend?"

Vince shrugged and booted the charge on his disser to max. "A rather difficult relationship," he said and shrugged. "Let's Party!"

Vince fired off a shot and dove through a massive steel wheel of a still-operating mega-mining mega machinery.

Nash responded with a long volley from a minigun matter canon at the direct of Vince and Lisa. Suddenly Lisa's Rohr 92 seems entirely inadequate. She pulled it out and began showering fire in Jane and Nash's direction. The fire, however, seems inordinately more powerful than it should be for such a small disser and she realizes David had modified it. This was no ordinary Rohr 92.

Lisa's eyes darkened, "A thousand years in a virtual prison and they bring me back for this!"

Winteroud and E. Gibbon had caught up.

"What?" Winteroud asked.

E. Gibbon added, "She said a thousand years

Winteroud cut the droid off, "I heard her, I heard her," and fired into the smoky distance.

The two groups of adversaries kept firing at each other and the sky full of Bogies kept dropping like black snow. Explosions and destruction could be heard from Echo City.

Lisa looked back at the historian now with a feral grin, "Yes, Winteroud. I'm a clone. From 3197. But I think you suspected that already."

Shots. Explosions.

Winteroud feigned casual interest, still firing, "So, you're like an ancient artifact? From a distant past? A living fossil?" he said.

She looked at him angrily, "With an expensive and loaded gun in my hand!"

Winteroud straightened. "I think I love you. Since we're about to be cast into a terrible fate with the Bogies, I just wanted you to know that."

E Gibbon fired off a few shots from her arms. She had slightly morphed into a combat mode and was close to shifting to a masculine form.

Lisa smiled condescendingly, "That's very nice, Winteroud. But I'm in a relationship with a transhuman, from my own century."

E. Gibbon made a half-smile.

A dozen pirate Vessels-headed by Harry Stark's ship the Riptide swept in vicious fury over the expanse of Echo's landscape, lashing wormholes into the swarm of Bogies, ripping them to shreds. Harry cast to his ships, "No surrender corps! Death before dishonor!"

The pirate fleet was a hurricane crushing and mashing whole flocks of the demon Bogies. As if in some strange symphony of death and chaos, another huge wormhole appeared and a single Bogie leaped through. Then suddenly there too, gleaming and red from the titanic forces it had traversed, the Baal Baby, alnico sheen and guns blazing. The single Bogie plunges on, darting this way and that like a fly.

Maximus glared out at the thousands of Bogies. "So..." he whispered, and a slow, hungry smile of hate formed on his granite face.

The Bogie, furious and confused, sent out a field wave to the swarm.

Maximus glared, "Okay, enough toying with that devil thing. I want one shot, center mass, hyper-fritzer now. Beatrice, take the shot."

"Honored Sir," she said. She leaned forward into the targeting hologram, aims and fired.

The hyper-fritzer shot made a long tracer line to the Bogie, igniting and slicing the monster into various dimensions.

Then Baal Baby banked and made for the swarm.

Mercurio growled, and it was like a pianist in a crescendo, "Fire at will!"

A pitch-black mass of Bogies surrounded Harry Stark's vessel and Harry saw them slip through the hull of his Riptide with a sudden memory of overwhelming charges at the Baal Wars. "Fuckers," he said, spitting at them. Facing them down as they continue to pour into his cabin., He is forced down from the controls as he and his crewmen wrestle with the beasts around their heads.

The Riptide plummets to Echo. There came long raging moments as the men, away from their controls of the ship, swung their hyper-fritzers into the deluge of demons. There was the whine of the Riptide, a flaming surge of air around the ship and harry and his crew steeled their hearts for death with honor.

Then there was the Taloned Sire. Two savage magnetic shots with a stasis field between them and the swarm massed on the hull of the Riptide was blown away in a comical explosion of batwings and horror and the candy-apple red sheen of the Riptide gleamed free.

Sagamore leaned over to Millin, "Stasis me boy. The Bogie on Rip was held by a stasis field. It's all in the wrist action!"

Millin gave a knowing look as he pausing for a moment to acknowledge Sagamore's wisdom. "Stasis. Wrist action." He said, and they continued firing.

The Riptide careened to a rough landing and Harry and his flight crew stumbled out. Above them, the skies are ablaze with battle. The Taloned Sire did a fly-by and roll.

The Bogies are in massive retreat. As the Bogies flee, Nash and Jane collapsed. Vince, Winteroud, E Gibbon and Lisa approach them.

Lisa, who had hardly broke a sweat Vince noted, frowned. Finally, she said, "So what are we going to do with these two now?"

Vince shook his head in bewilderment.

E. Gibbon was morphing back to a more female aspect. "Call the cops...?" She suggested dryly.

Winteroud beamed, "Ahhh, now this is the stuff of legends..."

Vega Ossa tiredly dragged himself to the hypercaster and coded in Omm. Omm's madness was absent. No snakeheads. No cowboy hat. No Romans. No Giant spiders. Vega looked at the calm and somewhat distracted face of a Diplomat, albeit dressed in clothing a thousand years out of style. Omm sighed, "So, Starman, morning has come and the demons are no longer at the door. You have done well.

"I noted the pirates I sent you after have made a strange appearance as your allies, however, that won't go in the official report.

Vega feigned surprise, but it was a game between them now. Surely by everyone knew. "Pirates? There were pirates in this battle?"

Omm tried to look insulted but played along, "Perhaps not. However, you made quite an entrance-last I heard you were on an exploratory campaign at the Silurian nebula. Did you make contact with the Predecessor race?"

"The dinosaurs?"

Omm's eyebrows rose, "They're dinosaurs?"

"Not a thing, Sir."

"Are you sure about that?"

Vega paused, and with a half-smile said, "Sir, I'm an officer. I have my duty to defend."

Omm's chin lifted slightly, "Yes, well, thank you for saving the galaxy with your assorted pirates and dinosaurs that don't exist. I must be off now, to cover for you, I mean file a report with the Overlords."

Omm disappeared from the screen and Vega gives a rueful smile.

The Baal Baby eased down from the sky to the Riptide where Harry and his flight crew are examining the damage to the vessel. Maximus and the clones disembarked the Baal Baby and approached Harry. Harry looked up and smiled as Max approached.

"Only you, Max, only you."

Maximus replied solemnly, "I came as soon as I could."

"You get your payback?" Harry asked.

Max glared, "Always. That and more. Looks like the galaxy is saved from the extra-dimensional demon horde, aye Sir?"

Harry paused and scanned the skies over the Echo city mines "Max, you know how it goes. They'll be back. They always come back.

Harry and Max looked challengingly to the sky.

Harry snarled, "It ain't over."

Deneb 4

Omm 6x had been called to a meeting of his immediate superiors on short notice and had made his appearance in an unusual fashion-as David Omm, his original self. The message was clear-*I have come full circle, and if now I must face my doom I will do it as myself, the self I was before the Arcturian genocide you called a war.*

Facing off with them arrayed in a tower of the winds from some mythical epic which he was unfamiliar with, he glanced out the window in a detached fashion as they sat at a large stone table.

Their clothing styles were an eclectic ensemble from half a dozen worlds and ages. He had no idea if they were congruent with the myth being played out. He thought idly that he might arm himself with information by accessing the Hive mind, and decided to face them with his wits alone.

Lourdes spoke as the others sat like executioners waiting for the order. "Omm we've become aware the First Strike and an attached attack group is in the Silurian Nebula-at Siluria itself. We assume you've authorized this." She said accusingly.

"I have." He responded.

"Yes, of course. You are aware that there is, in fact, a Predecessor remnant present on the planet?"

"I am." He offered them nothing. Amazingly, he realized with pride, his only concern at this juncture was for Ossa and the fleet. He was willing to sacrifice himself to whatever horrible fate they would concoct for him. This fact brought him courage, and joy, he had not known in many centuries. Courage. Self-sacrifice. It filled him like a host of angels, and he returned their gazes with it.

Two of them faded away from the room. There had been discomfort on their faces before they had opted to leave the conference. He felt a sense of vindication-and awe. He had driven them away with the mere thought of his concern for others. *That was telling.*

Lourdes betrayed discomfort as well. She looked to the remaining Overlords with her at the impromptu hearing, and he knew she was deep in the Hive mind with them, collating. Her face brightened, whether from the anticipation of his head on a platter, or possibly the sheer delight of an unexpected turn of events-he could not say. "Well, then…you realize you're making a gamble we've never been willing to engage in-direct contact with a technically more advanced, and arguably higher life form. One whose record in confronting the Bogies was an abject failure. Our assessment has long been that there was nothing to gain, and everything to lose in regards to the established order."

She looked at him then with her steady, beautiful gaze, dressed as a queen from some Outworlder castle, in a tower of winds. He realized she was looking at him with anticipation. *Hope.*

Say something. *Something wonderful.* Rage against this present darkness with your new-found courage, David. Is this another of your mad ravings? Prove it not so!

For Ossa, for Fortunato, For Sulla and her menagerie of Guildsmen and the Empath, and even for the rouges Ossa had enlisted from Chrysalis Isla, he, at last, brought his sanity into focus. He thought of Ossa riding his steel contraptions through the vicious indifferent universe of forces which would annihilate him and his crew in a moment should a system fail.

He thought of the Rouges from Chrysalis Isla carrying their bloodied comrades back from the edge of madness the Bogies inflicted, places he knew all too well himself-those dark corners of the mind most will not recognize, much less confront.

"Sulla and the Empath have engaged the Bogies in combat and survived- more than once" he made no mention of the Guildsmen crew of the Taloned Sire-leave that ace in the hole. "As have other…mercenaries we have engaged."

Now the shock was on their faces to read like a child's awe. The two who had faded returned, and theirs was neither hope nor fear-but sheer confusion. David realized he had completely trumped their purpose. He had to move now before they had time to reconsider.

"So who is the higher life form now, us or the Predecessors? I make no mistake-leaving information we could acquire from the Predecessors on the premise that they are our superiors, is folly. Brains isn't everything. In this contest, we come to the table with other weapons. Courage. Duty. Honor. Self-sacrifice-Love. Those aspects of humanity which the wild organic societies whom we belittle, whom we marginalize, and whom we ignore-well, they still treasure them. Live by them. Die by them.

"Our wealth, the Predecessors science, and the long train of unworkable premises we have engineered society by now for a long millennia-you know as well as I, they're all a house of cards blown by" he looked to the window and realized their metaphor now and why they chose it, "blown by a fierce wind into the darkness of futility."

"Our hope now lies in the hands and hearts of those willing to fight and die for something...something we have been laughing at for far too long."

She looked back, collating, he realized.

"The human factor, how quaint." She said with a cold, forced, snide look. "Fine, run your gambit-Overlord. But don't forget who, and what, you are. Their victories you are clinging to now are hardly some masterful triumph. At each turn reports of mayhem still filter back to us-even from the Out World Rip and the Hercules cluster. A level of destruction that if continued will mean little even if we possess a trophy here and a trophy there. Civilization in this galaxy is like a rainforest ecology, Omm. The more complex the system the more easily it is pulled down. We await your next report."

Then she was gone, and he stood alone in the tower of the winds, staring at the empty table.

Don't forget who and what you are-Overlord.

He closed his eyes and the tower of the winds faded. He was flying over New Haven City before the fireballs. Her noble skyscrapers shone in the virtual light of his memory, complex and simple patterns both-form following function, sculpted and organized, for the service of life, of mankind, the Arcturian colonists of that long-ago age of pure reason; the materialists of the abstract.

Some things he could never forget, his part in their destruction. Some things he would be forced to do anyway, whether he was worthy or not-make his stand in this war in the heavens. Some things...they simply had to be done.

He remembered his words to Ossa, *Find a way, star man. Win.*

ABOUT THE AUTHOR

Dante D'Anthony was born in South-Buffalo New York and grew up there and in the Chautauqua New York wine region. After graduating from SUNY College at Buffalo where he studied Design, he moved to Miami Florida where he worked in Architecture, Art Education, and Commercial Finance. He was in the US Army Reserves and was a Union High-Temperature Insulator on power plants.

Made in the USA
Columbia, SC
05 July 2020